How was Josh dead?

"Natalie," Cadence asked, knowing the guardian couldn't answer. "What's happened?"

"Shhh," Amber's voice crept as gently as the command of Death's own. "We're being hunted."

Books by D.L. Fairchild

CIRCLE OF DOGS

The New Paladin
Wolf
Eulogies

OTHER TITLES
The Exodus
Where's the Blood?

Eulogies

BOOK THREE OF

CIRCLE OF DOGS

D. L. FAIRCHILD

ISBN 978-0-9826355-7-5

Cover art by Brittany McConnell

Four Doors Publishing LLC
Spanish Fork, UT 84660

Printed in the United States of America.

A Word from our Author

(An Otherwise Preface)

I am of the circle. Mine is the role of historian. I did not choose this responsibility, rather it was given me for the survival of my elders. When the others pass, I shall be the last. All stories of ancient blood are in me.

I am the observer.

My place is not involvement; not to make choices; not to repair nor steer; simply to observe, memorize and pass on when my time as observer is done. I speak many languages. An accurate count, I could not say. I kept track once, when I had nothing better to do, but I stopped at one million. It was a nice, round number. I find a few dialects of horse and cockroach confusing, and I tend to struggle with the fallow deer. They are a brilliant bunch, as well are the primates, whose language I have tried to master, but they just don't understand anything. They are those who get linguists excited because they appear to be communicating, but they are only playing. Believe me, I know. Don't believe me? Just look at the time two primates that were placed together and they kept signing "tickle me" back and forth. Since neither knew what the other was saying, they just started sitting around and ignoring everybody. Oh yes, primates just like screwing with scientists. That's their true intelligence. However, my job is not to opine, but to observe; and when you listen as long as I, you hear and learn much.

I must admit, it sometimes makes me miss killing.

All that my circle knows, I know. All that our line experiences, I witness. Many others have come before me, but their vision was not as mine. They were incomplete, incapable and blind of just enough to remove them from their posts.

I am the record of my race. Although I wasn't the first, all thoughts and images since the first are in me. I answer whom I choose and ignore the slothful. I have too much to attend to, and listening is such consumption of energy, to attempt speaking as well. So I hope you appreciate the toll this effort thus far has taken on me—for even as I say this to you now, I still hear all I am called to hear. For, while you speak and hear nothing, I speak and hear all voices that can get to my ears and psyche.

My role is to record the liars and remember the heroes who have kept my circle. It is not to make them public, nor to warn; that's what prophets are for. My role is to simply watch.

I see all that has ever been in the lives of our blood, for I am of the circle, and no other knows all. I am the constant. I have the knowledge to broach, but not to be broached. Not all historians had the skill. I learned that on my own, which is why I was given this responsibility in the first place. I see all thoughts of my own, whether they want me to or not. Through such, am I capable of seeing all truths of the story. That is what makes me unique—for unlike my predecessor, I am too humble to be blind.

This story that I have uttered until now has been out of respect for the fallen, and it is my own voice that you have been so patient to hear. I admit that it has been filled with confusion and lack of humanity, but again, I am an observer, not an artist. All humanity has become the same to me, silly.

Though it is confusing for you, it makes perfect sense to me. Should you continue to find it unbelievable, might I suggest becoming an observer to see how well you tell the stories when you're not allowed to separate your thoughts from all those of others that scream constantly into your brain.

Now, let us be clear on the topic of stories. I am not a storyteller, just an observer, but as our storyteller has been dead many years before my time, someone must attempt to fill the role until we find a suitable candidate. So forgive me. I'm new, and, unfortunately, our numbers dwindle. Mind you, I'm sure our old storyteller was much greater. I, or—I should say—historians before me granted her the history, and she gave it energy. She breathed life into our history. Unlike her, I simply say it as I see it, and, as I see it, is not always grammatically correct, but it is only the stubborn and pompous who need to learn more care about that. Although I know the storyteller only from memories of those before me, it is through those memories that I claim personal kinship to her. Therefore, since she is not here to share her talent, it is up to my boring self.

Thus, I present a shopping cart.

The shopping cart held his shoes. Its driver put them there. He liked shoes, loved shoes, appreciated the stories of shoes. Shoes for every occasion filled the cart, new and old, mostly old. Boots were not allowed. Boots took up the space of two, sometimes three pairs of regular shoes. Boots were bulky, expensive. Boots needed too much maintenance. So, he stuck with filling his cart with shoes.

Plastic shopping bags hung from the sides of the cart. He put other treasures and trinkets in these. Some of the items were doubled-bagged. Some were quadrupled. Some were octupled. The jumble of bags hung heavy, more so on one side of the cart than the other. The vehicle should have toppled under the unbalanced weight, but the shoes held it down. They had all been good shoes. They were a lot of shoes, and they held many miles of malice.

The cart itself was old, older than the footwear it carried. It was flimsy compared to most of the carts shoppers used today, which were molded in plastic. This one was completely metal, and every corner nut and bolt were loose so that, as he pushed it through the streets, the cart leaned side-a-side as though it should flap apart at any moment. Yet, it continued to stand—swaying, yes—firm enough though. Crusty, brown mold, crowned almost every inch of the rough metal cage, save where his palms gripped the handle. These patches were dull, silver and green. The plastic hand-grip that once coated this bar had long disappeared. The orange flap that, upon-a-time, folded down to support a screaming child, or keep a purse from falling to the ground, had fully chipped away to a small sleeve that the cart's driver flipped around for fun with his left thumb.

A black Scottish terrier slept on the pile of shoes. Her permanently poised ears had become used to the sound of the rattling of that one wheel that wouldn't completely touch the ground and, when it did, would either catch and spin horizontally or sometimes halt the cart altogether. She was accustomed to the bounce and wobble from cracks in the sidewalk; the gravel beads of paved roads; the jolts of climbing and descending curbs; and the unfriendly terrain of dirt and grass. To her, this open cage was home.

Three boxes of binders and ledgers slid around beneath the basket. Weathered electric cords kept the containers from falling away.

The vehicle screamed a chorus of worn bearings, loose nuts and battered, hard rubber wheels. People cleared the way when they heard it coming. They had to; the cart bumped anyone who wouldn't move. Pedestrians gawked at the lanky man who hunkered over his mobile trove of outlived treasures. He was a frozen, twisted image who may very well have inspired the essence of Mother Goose villainy.

Then, just now, he stopped. He shouldn't have. He had places to be. His Scottie jostled awake at the sudden stillness in her comfortable calm. Both the animal that was now widely alert in the cart and the animal pushing it looked over the man who caused the sudden halt.

"Get something to eat my friend," the clean-cut liberal yuppy said as he closed his wallet and wore the pre-tears of an idiot. "There's a homeless shelter three blocks in that direction."

The cart man said nothing. He chewed his wad of gum and stared at the unjust Samaritan. A large, green bubble hedged from the cart man's lips. It grew to about half the size of his face before it popped and plastered into his long, grisly beard, leaving behind the resemblance of a flat, dead and gangrenous tongue. He wiped his beard against the torn sleeve of his yellow-stained jacket to collect the gum from his facial monstrosity. Then he rolled his hand over the rotting fabric until he gathered all the spent gum into a ball. He shoved his deflated bubble back into his mouth. Next, he plucked at his beard and licked down the smaller pieces from the tips of his fingers, all while he stared at the five-dollar bill carelessly tossed into his cart. Without a thank you, he began his journey once more past his hasty benefactor. Presently, he continued past storefronts and miserable people of Plattsville, his pet falling quickly to sleep again.

Every town had one. He just had to find it. After five blocks in one direction and two in another, he stumbled upon the quiet building. Fewer people walked here. Delivery vans and trucks filled a nearby parking lot. A one-story, strip mall with five small stores waited for the cart man. He didn't care for what the other businesses were, he was interested in the one establishment that was second from the right. This one had blue, peeling letters in the window that read: *Dale's Shoe Repair.*

The cart driver stared through the window for a bit, and he waited for the only customer inside to buy his bag of goodies and leave. The cashier followed him to the glass door.

"Get off," scolded the bald, round owner with square, silver glasses and unkind eyes. He waddled to the cart man and glared up into his haggard face. "No panhandling."

The cart man tugged at his long, tarnished coat so he could get at the deep pocket of his blotchy and thick corduroy pants, where he pulled out a couple of grayed and crumpled dollar bills. In the process, he found a piece of gum he'd missed and nonchalantly ate it up.

"That's not enough," replied the disgusted cashier at the paltry offering.

The hobo moved to the side of his rolling luggage and opened one of his thick bags where he began to rummage through a collection of wallets. He unsnapped a red, leather one, looked inside and pulled out a couple more bucks. He dropped the empty wallet on the ground and proceeded to withdraw a grey, Velcro envelope.

"Where did you get those," the cashier asked.

The cart man stepped between his trove and the cashier. He brandished a small pocket-knife with a black, tarnished blade towards the cashier, a man several inches shorter than the hobo's own height.

"Okay," the cashier said. "I don't want your money. God knows you need it more than I do."

The cart man withdrew four fifty-dollar bills from the lining of the Velcro wallet. Then he sealed the fabric bank once more and dropped it back into his plastic bag with other types of purses and money clips. He tied the sack off again and turned to the store owner.

The little man nodded for the unsightly stranger to follow him. "No dogs. No cart neither," he said, opening the door to his store. "And no knife," he added.

The cart man folded his weapon and tossed it into the trolley with his dog, who gave no impression that she was willing to wake from her nap atop her nest of shoes. Then he followed the cashier into the rustic, narrow store. Most of his product filled the shelves on one wall; the bottom two belonged to used and repaired inventory. The other wall was filled with soft customer benches.

"What do you want," the cashier asked, leading the homeless person past displays and towards a counter that definitely looked handmade of cheap wood: stained with polish and shoe oil, and scarred from all sorts of sharp tools. It reeked of carnauba, mink and spirits.

The cart man reached into his coat pocket and pulled out a battered strip of paper and handed it to the cashier.

"Madrigal wingtips," the cashier read aloud. "Ten-and-a-half long, ten-wide and—Really? Those start at three hundred dollars."

The customer stared at the bills in his hand, then made some gestures to his cart before turning for the door leading out of the store.

"Forget it," the cashier called after him. "Let's get you out of here before a customer sees you." He turned to the farther depths of his store. "I think I have some repaired Mads in the back, but they're like new. They might work." The cashier opened his counter to the cart man and led him to the back of his small shop. "This way."

They ducked into a small cove behind a wall of shelves that hid the back room. It may have appeared that the store owner was trying to be polite, but, in truth, he wanted the customer where he could watch him better while he dug through his stock room. Here, a workbench, tools, a sewing machine and all sorts of leather and rubber parts filled organizer bins and pegs. Where shoe-making equipment was not, unopened boxes of new footwear sat. Hardly an extra inch of space appeared. The owner ducked into a small hallway, leaving his client alone for a moment.

Upon entering the small alcove, the cart man almost instantly located the pair he wanted: oxblood wingtips with a hint of black accent and laces. He found a box with his measurements and took it down from the shelf

"No, those are new," the cashier said as he returned from an adjoining alcove. He held a similar, but brown pair. They weren't as shiny, and the laces were fatter. A slight gouge, cleaned and polished so it wouldn't show, sat nearly on its tip. "I told you, more expensive."

The cart man pulled a shoe from the box and began to inspect it.

"Five hundred," the cashier said, tore the shoe away from the ragged customer and set it on a small worktable next to him. "Before tax!" He held the brown pair out to the stranger.

The cart man rejected the brown shoes; took up the red pair once more; and held out his handful of money.

"Not enough," the cashier said, grasping at the one new Madrigal within the box clenched within the filthy visitor's fingerless-gloved hands. "Not practical for you."

Before the cashier's blackened, callused fingers could tear away the shoe from the cart man's equally filthy grasp, the silent hobo drew the blood-red Madrigal from the counter-top and, with inhuman strength, pounded the blunt heel against the side of the cobbler's head.

After the store owner dropped lifeless to the black, tile floor, the dirty man collected the matching shoe.

He slipped on his new wingtips and made his way to the cashier's counter where he tucked his wad of bills into the register drawer. Then he returned to the dead cobbler and took his eroded leather wallet from his shirt pocket. Then he gathered up a polish kit; turned out the shop lights; set the *closed* sign in the window and, upon exiting the small store, jammed the lock with his pocket knife.

The cart man returned to his tank of rust, dangling plastic and footwear. He set a fairly decent pair of tennis shoes, with many miles left in them, onto the pile and dropped the cashier's wallet into one of his supermarket saddle bags. The cart began rattling and swaying down the sidewalk once more.

A few blocks in another direction brought the traveler to a second store front. This one was larger, nicer too. Mannequins lined the windows with suits and pricey dress-wear. Again, he opened a bag of wallets and began rifling money from their bellies. The Scottish Terrier still napped, hardly acknowledging her master's actions.

"This isn't Goodwill," a young man announced as he approached the cart man, barely inside the front doors. His female co-workers didn't attempt to hide their contempt and mockery of the situation. The young man had lost the lot and he was appointed to get rid of the hobo.

The cart driver held up his wad of bills and pointed to a tan, Ozepki, double-breasted suit with a shawl lapel.

The young salesman smiled. His female counterparts frowned. After all, dirty money was still money.

Within the hour, the customer decided on a new suit, paid the young man and left his old clothes for the women to clean up. He returned to his gondola of shoes and continued his journey, which soon brought him to an old-fashioned barber pole. He hadn't planned on stopping here. He'd wanted something more uptown, more him, but he found nostalgia and comfort within the spinning white, blue and red pole—at least, he wished it spun. Plus, there was something painful and potentially dark in one of the women's eyes inside that intrigued him. He went inside to meet her.

"He's all yours," the manager said, pawning her duties down to her employee. The manager retreated to the back of the salon and became quite interested in hiding in her office.

The employee, however, had no choice. She was fresh out of beauty school, but older than most graduates. She didn't have the luxury of choosing her walk-ins as her boss did. While her supervisor had freedom, Loraine had three children, all who lived with her ex, Scott. She didn't want this job, but money was money to a parent strapped in redemption.

What she needed was an edge, one that would tell that fat hispanic judge, who took her children, who was the better parent. What she needed was income: a high-paying job—no, to own this salon and franchise it. That would give her the demonstration she needed to take her husband back before that disgusting magistrate. Piles of money, that's what would show that judge how wrong he was. Piles of money, that was power. That's what she needed. She needed power!

Alas, she currently had a salon station.

"How can I help you today," Loraine asked and, as an afterthought, began clearing her chair for her mangy customer.

The cart man brushed his fingers through his long-matted hair and tugged out a piece of something he wasn't sure what its purpose once was. He flicked it on the floor. Oh! Another piece of gum.

"Would you like a wash," Loraine asked.

The cart man smiled and held up a handful of bills.

"It won't cost that much," Loraine said. The cart man smiled even more.

"Don't be so sure," the manager mumbled to herself. Loraine didn't hear it, but her customer did.

Loraine helped the well-dressed stranger's ragged head and jungled face to the wash basin, where she tied back her blonde hair and went to work on his appearance. For a moment, she wondered, *what if I just held his head under? what if I just let him drown. "Oh no, officer! He just died in my sink. I tried pulling him out but the faucet got stuck in his beard."*

"Too hot," she asked.

He shook his head.

She used every technique she had been taught to pick out gnarls, even invented a few new approaches just now that didn't hurt the customer so much (always good for better tips). The gnarls disappeared one by one as Loraine's fingers, comb and steel shears tore the knots asunder.

I could just stab him right here. "I don't know what happened, your fat honor. He jumped in my seat and my shears stabbed into his brain. Here! Let me show you too, you Mexican monster."

Obviously, the stranger didn't take care of himself, Loraine could tell that from the ropes of neck hair erupting from beneath his new, white and tan collars. When the time came, she peeled back his new apparel from his neckline and trimmed his nasty lack of hygiene away. He was polite. If she'd done anything to upset him, he didn't let on. So she didn't let on how entirely gross she found her work to be just now.

She soon had the man in a chair that faced a mirror surrounded by Loraine's stash of hair styling tools and gadgets. His once wavy and wretched hair now resembled dark strands of satin rope draping down his face and over his shoulders.

Loraine gathered the strands and combed them straight back. She began to cut.

I wonder what it's like to scalp a person? I have his hair. What's he going to do? Turn on me? Stab! Stab! Stab! "He just turned on me, detective."

"How's that," Loraine asked after she spent several minutes bringing the hair length up to the cart man's shoulders.

Her customer nodded.

"Shorter?" She raised her steel shears to gauge his reaction. "That short," She finally asked, then grimaced at all the gnarl-depleting work she had done previously for no reason.

The cart man agreed.

"Top too?"

He frowned.

"Longer on top? OK. Parted?"

Again, he frowned.

Loraine began snatching away long stretches of growth from the cart man's head.

I really want to snip that ear off.

She tried to be gentle. Once she thought she cut his ear and she couldn't apologize enough, but had she meant it? Cutting the ear? Yes. Apologizing? No. The cart man pat her hand and turned slightly to pet her face, which reminded Loraine to ask if he'd like to add on a manicure.

Disgusting burden on society—what homeless man has eyes like this?

As she finished, the cart man gave silent, jovial approval of her work so far.

She might have let him go right there because her shift ended over thirty minutes ago, but business was slow lately. People didn't come out like they used to, not many of them anyway. Many spoke about something strange happening in the town, but Loraine didn't give heed to any of it; conspiracy theorists loomed around every corner. She had no concern for silly rumors. All she wanted was for something good to come out of her life: her children back, maybe their father, and that bronze chip was just a week away.

"Would you like your eyebrows trimmed," Loraine asked.

The stranger appeared puzzled and rubbed his beard.

"A shave," Loraine asked.

"We don't do that," the manager called from her office.

The stranger glared towards the manager's den.

"Oh, go swim with your hair dryer," Loraine said softly and was soon holding a set of electric shears. The smile in the mirror before her suggested the homeless customer appreciated her joke.

With each stroke of her shears, she freed more of a most friendly and attractive face. She shaved the cart man down to his stubble before she applied a bit of foam and, using a simple chrome-handled straight-edge, carved a fleshy, smooth sideburn out of his creamy, white mask. Surprisingly, his flesh seemed soft, healthy too, maybe more than her own. She held the blade for another stroke. She could do it, right here. One clean slice across his throat. She would. She needed to. Why not?

She met his eyes.

He knows! Don't do it. He knows!

Trying not to shake, she finished slicing through the foam and whiskers, leaving his face unblemished. The mid-fortyish-looking man finally examined his new appearance in Loraine's hand-held mirror. He removed his thick fingerless gloves and felt through his black hair.

"What do you think now," Loraine said. "Eyebrows?"

He considered for a moment and touched his bushy unibrow.

She held up her trimmer. He gently reached up and guided her hand to return the trimmer and take up her scissors once more.

You did know. Why are you taunting me? Don't you know I could destroy you. I want to destroy. I need to destroy something just once, just to try it.

She held the tips of the scissors and snipped each hair above the bridge of his nose that connected his eyebrows. She finished without snipping flesh. Then she escorted him to the manicure station, where she spent perhaps forty minutes cleaning, softening and smoothing his hands. Yeah, she asked if he wanted it after all.

"Look at you," the young manager said, suddenly at the side of the cart man's chair. "You look like a millionaire now."

The customer stood and held out a wad of large bills to Loraine. He bowed slightly and smiled to his hairstylist as she tried to refuse the outrageously large tip. Loraine found him placing the money in her hand and gently curling her fingers down over it. Gently? No. He was crushing her fingers. He did know. She wanted to scream to beg his forgiveness, but she held it. He released.

"You're a generous tipper," the manager said. "Please feel free to stop by any time."

Loraine cringed at her boss's insult.

Without acknowledging the manager's comments, the cart man returned to the glass door leading out of the front of the store. As soon as he opened it, the black Scottish terrier raced past his legs and crashed through the cashier's island, which set between a blue, carpeted waiting area and the tiled work-hovel. Chunks of counter strewed the twelve-seat salon after the abrupt explosion. The cash drawer clanked to the floor and might have smashed open were it not built so well. The computer monitor didn't fare as well. It cracked the moment it struck the floor of yellow tile and its chunks of embedded sapphire.

Amidst the chaotic rain of destruction, the black, rug-like dog leapt for the manager's throat. The manager toppled backwards, grasping with reddening fingers at her draining neck. Loraine finally screamed, but, just as suddenly, fell silent as the black terrier then dragged the manager to the back of the store. The salon fell silent except for Loraine's choppy, frightened breaths. The cart man's dog returned and set her attention upon Loraine.

"Please don't," Loraine begged.

The cart man returned a smile and threw her a friendly wink. The Scottie strode besides Loraine and sat before her. Loraine's customer gestured to the dog as if awarding Loraine a gift.

The dog yipped a sound that should have been much younger in a dog this large.

She understood, she thought.

"I don't want your dog," Loraine said. "You've tipped me too much already."

The cart man's face drew sullen, and the terrier growled.

Loraine changed her mind, and the cart man welcomed her decision. He ushered the friendly hairstylist and her new gift from the salon. Outside, the terrier jumped as a new pup wanting to play. It ran off a few feet, barked and returned to Loraine's feet where it tugged at the toe of her shoe.

The cart man pulled a bag of wallets from the side of his cart and handed it to Loraine, bowing once more to her for her kindness.

Then the cart man tossed his demeaning, fingerless gloves into his shopping cart and led Loraine away from his basket of untold stories.

* * *

The check-in process went smoothly, but not friendly. Mr. Michaels hadn't met the new curator, didn't hire him, wouldn't even get to see his application, but had to run him through the orientation and tour nonetheless.

"Who am I to argue with the powers that be," Mr. Michaels complained, but held out a set of keys to the new curator. The curator recoiled from the offer and nodded to his assistant, the ex-beautician.

Loraine cautiously took the keys from Mr. Michaels.

"I ask for budget to hire another secretary, and I get the run-around," Michaels continued and didn't care who heard. He'd earned his reward. He hated to see himself so close to finally getting it. "But my new curator gets his own assistant. Don't count on that job sticking, ma'am."

"I appreciate your concern," Loraine replied.

Michaels continued complaining as he walked away.

The curator pulled open one of the tall doors leading into the empty gallery and gestured for Loraine to enter first. Beyond the gallery was the back storage area and the loading dock. It was mostly cold and concrete with a few unlabeled doors leading into closets or other rooms. A large, wooden crate, taller than Loraine, sat deep within the room.

Here, the curator opened a heavy, steel exterior door. Instant, rays of sunlight nearly blinded him and Loraine, as they peered through clear windows and across the glazed concrete floor. Two tall, one-armed beasts and a black Scottie dog rushed in. The sunlight shrank to a sliver as the door closed and was eventually shut out by a steel *clunk!*

The Scottish terrier dropped on its rump to Loraine's right. She paid respect with a scratch to the head.

No sooner had she done so, than the curator approached Loraine and gestured towards the crate. One of the single-armed monsters approached the crate and broke off its front panel.

Everything was so new and dangerous to her. The curator reached for her, and he led her towards the crate. A fat Hispanic man sat bound and gagged on the floor. He tried to retreat, but a chain held his neck to the floor of the crate.

"I know you," Loraine realized. "You gave my children away."

The judge cried in fear. He smelled from being confined so long in his cell.

As he had done so many times before, her new employer smiled at her and pat her hand as a sign of gratitude.

She heard a rattle of metal against the concrete. Her black dog had dropped her pair of styling shears at her feet. She took up the pointed shears and stared coldly at the prisoner.

Her master had not bitten her, but he had given her power.

An Encounter From the Past

(A Previously Omitted Scene)

Headlights peeked around the corner, slowly turning onto the rural street with its conformed, middle-class houses and well-lit intersections. They gazed forward and pressed past locked garages, their gas guzzling SUVs and commuter sedans loaded with lithium nonsense.

The lights stopped at the largest house, squealing its tires due to hasty instruction to suddenly halt.

The black door cracked open, and a fat boot with a metal brace smacked against the pavement. Its owner began to climb out, cussing the driver for being a moron.

The passenger stood fully, rifled through his fur-lined pockets and drew out a wad of bills, He uncoiled a few, threw them at the driver and tossed an extra large bill as a bonus.

"Watch the ditch turnin' 'round," Speatsh suggested, then kicked his door shut. "Don't make me have to pull you out and knock the genius outch'ya."

He approached the dark house. Security lights flared over black grass. His furry shoulders growled and winced.

"Oh, someone deserves a fat bag of burning toilet splat in his cereal bowl, Richard," Speatsh complained before kicking the tall wooden gate open. He mocked the cheap securing mechanism that fell to the ground, then picked up the broken latch and chucked it at the most annoying security light. The beam snuffed out with a crunch.

The gate slammed behind him, and Speatsh clanked his way to the front door. He rang the bell: once, twice, then pulled the screen door open and knocked before finally punching the solid wood slab out of its frame.

An alarm screamed. Speatsh grunted, reached into his bundle of furs and cursed some more. He found a small piece of paper and, in the dark, read the code scribbled onto it. His fingers then repeated the digits into the rubbery keypad.

The infernal chime died, and Speatsh punched the wall. He kicked the end table that sat beneath the panel into pieces as he did so. He then proceeded to do the same with the oval coffee table nearby. Then he tore up a couch cushion, broke the flat screen television over his knee and began beating the wall straight through to the bedroom on the other side. He yelled, bit his lip and kicked the entertainment cabinet into large chunks.

"Are you done," a voice asked from the dark.

Speatsh turned, he allowed a metal disc to fall into his grasp.

The gold eyes stared back. Speatsh could see the outline well, but not as much detail as he would have liked. The figure was large in stature, perhaps even a good rival to Speatsh's. Cheatham said nothing, waited for the man sitting on the end of the couch before the broken coffee table to make his move.

The phone rang. The silhouette picked up the receiver and handed it to Speatsh. Speatsh held a short conversation with the alarm company and put the agent at ease.

"The great Speatsh Cheatham," the silhouette said once the phone had returned to its cradle.

"And," Speatsh spat. "If you got a problem, just say and I'll fix you right quick."

"Not at all. I'm a huge fan," the silhouette replied. He laughed a little. "I'm all about freedom of Speatsh."

"What do you want, wolf," Speatsh asked.

"I always thought it would be fun to match wits with you," the stranger said. "And now that I have the chance, it's very anti-climatic."

"I'll match wits with you," Speatsh encouraged. "Bring your brain over here."

The silhouette laughed. "Figures," he said.

Speatsh wanted to attack, but the shadowed figure made no move, gave Speatsh no excuse.

"Have you completed the task you desire," the shadow asked.

"What are you talking about," Speatsh asked, realizing his foe was more dangerous than he had anticipated.

"Is your mind at ease," the shadowy figure asked. "And believe me when I say it is in both of our best interests for the truth on this one. Is the procedure done?"

Speatsh grunted after him. The silhouette seemed to understand the statement hidden beneath the snort.

"You understand I know things then," the figure stated. "Usually, I encourage an open mind, but, in your case, I'll make an exception."

"It's time for you to leave," Speatsh replied.

"Shame," the figure said. "I thought we were finally defining our friendship."

"You ever had your upper lip ripped off your eyeballs," Speatsh asked.

"Such eloquence," the shadowy figure said as he reached the door, but stopping. "There are three scouts and Stan locked in the basement."

"So, the wimp survived," Speatsh said.

"Strangely, I understand that comment too," the stranger added. "There's one more, I'm sure she'll show up later."

Before Speatsh could grunt or complain, or do what an unhappy Speatsh does, the shadow turned back. "Consider the Dobermans orphaned."

"You brought me orphans," Speatsh asked, and began petting the scruff of his bear pelt around his shoulders. He contemplated throwing it at the intruder.

"I said consider them orphaned," the stranger said. "In fact, it's best if they were."

"You have any idea how long it's gonna to take me to break them," Speatsh blasted.

"Help them before you reveal yourself," the figure said. "They'll serve a better purpose."

"Who made them?"

"Not important," the stranger said. "The orphans must not be made conduits to their master's mind. Do you understand?"

"Coward, general!" Speatsh threw something big at the silhouette. It missed.

"Be glad I didn't give you the fiancée too," the silhouette said.

Speatsh threw a silver disc. The gold-eyed shadow was suddenly standing before Speatsh, cautious, calm, unsettling. Speatsh could see him now, a burly man dressed in motorcycle garb from head to foot.

Speatsh could feel his breath in his face.

"You're fasting," Speatsh observed.

"See, you're not so dumb," the shadow said.

"How did you make them if you're fasted," Speatsh asked.

"I never said I made them," the stranger replied. "But they might think I did."

Speatsh invented a new curse, something to do with the cross pollination of rabid gophers and Republicans somewhere in man-o-war breeding waters.

"They may not have a connection to who made them," the burly stranger argued. "But that won't keep the rogue from their minds; they'll be the perfect spies."

Speatsh grunted his displeasure.

"Well," the silhouette replied. "Do your best."

The stranger brandished a dark envelope and a book.

"If you feel your wits are getting in the way, read this," the stranger said, but suddenly retracted the gift. "You know, some personal reading. You know, personal. Burn it, if you feel you can't wrap your mind around it just yet."

"What is this," Speatsh asked after snatching the fat envelope from the shadow's hand.

"It's a dirty haiku. The Japanese kind, not that English insult," the biker said, laughed and then chided Speatsh for his lack of humor. "One is a letter with some information you'll need. One is a book. You know the book. You've seen the book. This one has notes in it. Burn it when you're done with it. We don't need two of them out there. And we don't need anyone else reading it. Understand?"

Speatsh sniffed.

"Information," the stranger finally relented. "Sufficient for your needs."

The stranger withdrew to the door once more, allowing Speatsh to contemplate the slow insult that would never come.

"Break the dogs," the shadow said. "Disconnect them all."

"Don't make me pull the bear," Speatsh replied. "I'm not in the mood to fry my brain."

"Don't take this request lightly." The stranger opened the front door to leave. "Oh," he said quickly pulling back in once more, mostly to needle at Speatsh's patience.

"You don't hold my leash." Speatsh threw the envelope, but not the book at the stranger.

The stranger instantly threw it back. "You will read that and do exactly what it says. The rogue's success depends upon it. If you don't, you will become who we hunt, and we have the means to find you in ways vampires can't protect you from."

"You will leave that and bloom exactly what it fits," Speatsh repeated the tones, but not the correct words. "The rogue's eagerness ripens within it. If shoes want, you will condone what is junk, and he is so mean to bind your days damn near Cat Stevens and his mom."

The stranger appeared baffled, opened his mouth and made a sound before suddenly chuckling. He gripped the envelope as Speatsh threw it once more at him. "Ah, so that's how you keep him out," he said. "Didn't realize you were so genius."

The stranger was out the front door. He allowed the envelope to fall to the floor.

Speatsh fumbled through the dark for a light switch, while gathering the dropped envelope under his foot. Once he found the switch, he took time to search Richard's house for Stan and the three scouts, two Doberman pinschers and a golden lab. He looked them over and assessed that they would be resting a while.

Next, he searched for a piece of complicated literature. He settled on the Bible. Several chapters into Isaiah, he tore the stranger's ivory envelope open and began to devour its contents while simultaneously reading from Isaiah.

And the inhabitant shall not say, I am sick: the people that dwell therein shall be forgiven their iniquity, Speatsh read to himself. *Come near, ye nations to hear, Speatsh Cheatham; and hearken, ye people: pay particular attention and let not this letter let the earth hear and all that is therein fall into any hands other than your own, the world and all the things that come forth from it.*

You will prepare a small group of friends for war. For the indignation of the Lord is upon all nations and his fury against the armies of the rogue. He hath utterly destroyed them and knows the mind of the heir's son. He hath delivered them to the slaughter.

In this manner did Speatsh take time, every so often, to read more of Isaiah along with the stranger's message. He read every detail about Cracey's abduction; Josh's idiocy to attack a general; and a few other gory details that he regretted not being present to stop. He read the ambiguous language and cursed the stranger's tactlessness. The letter was ended, signed with a single name: Bean.

Aha, Speatsh thought to himself and even cheered himself out of his seat. "What kind of a stupid name is Bean?"

Alas, this stranger named Bean was not around to take offense.

The Book of Rogue

1 ~ The Master's Plan

The man in the side-view mirror hated the one staring back at him. His brow was too sharp, angry and afraid, had lost, yet gained perception. Only an idiot would have agreed to such absurdity. It wasn't the first time he had to either. He loved his home, loved Plattsville, loved the streets that were never too busy for his childhood basketball net. He may have outgrown his youthful stomping lands, but, no matter how many houses sprang up, he remembered them. So, when the paladin requested him to return to work, Sergeant Chandler made no hesitation to preserve his city. He had done enough to destroy his own home before the paladin had saved him. Now, he needed to help recover it.

From his hospital bed, he had seen his children only a moment, his wife even less. His instinct was to tell them to run. But they deserved to know the truth about the danger even less. He'd figure something out that would protect them.

In truth, he was a coward. He didn't used to be. There was a time that he was willing to stand up to any bully, the larger the better. That was before he joined the force, prior to having children. Somewhere along the line, his thoughts turned to earning his pension, wearing Kevlar and praying his shifts were uneventful.

Then he was assigned a dog, and it watched him. It betrayed him, held him hostage, forced him to ensure similar dogs shipped in, while others were turned away or destroyed. It threatened to kill his children and wife, not in words, but actions. It trained Chandler to know when he was to follow the dog's lead. When Chandler obeyed, he was rewarded with a happy family pet, but when he didn't, injuries happened. He tried telling his wife and awoke to find his K-9 partner threatening to tear her throat out while she slept. He never disobeyed or raised issue again.

He turned from fighting bullies to helping them frame any potential threats that might keep them from getting a foothold. He tried it with Josh, and was rescued. Now was his time to fight back, to undo his evil. Knowing the world he had encountered, he couldn't bring himself to tell anyone about it. He wasn't sure who was watching, or who was helpful.

Presently, Chandler held a piece of candy. The jelly bean that his youngest son, Zender, had given him grew sticky and wet between his palm and the inside of his splint. In a month, Zender would be nine, and Chandler began wondering if he would see ten; if his oldest daughter, Tina, would see 21; or if his teenage girl would live to be in her first fender bender. He knew one was inevitable. He'd ridden with her before. He couldn't put voice to his frustration about that either. His family was unlikely to forgive him when they finally learned. He smothered that awful jelly bean into his flesh and hoped his son would live so he could at least hate his father for it. He had forgotten what color the bean was.

Twenty minutes ago, Chandler had been in his hospital bed when he was ordered to meet his captain. His nurses and doctors objected, but didn't seem to be around as he was forced to walk out of the hospital on his own under a police escort. The least they could have done was let him get fully dressed. Now, as he sat in the patrol car, he directed his anger, fear and annoyance at his own reflection—well, that and the jelly bean.

He tried to rub his shoulder, and twenty stitches pulled at the back of his hand. If he returned to the hospital, he'd ask the staff to loosen the wrap. He'd also ask if he should expect any news concerning the patch over his eye. Perhaps he wouldn't be going back though.

He barely noticed his captain approaching the side of the car right before yanking the door open.

"Let's go, Sergeant," the captain said.

Before Chandler could plant or steady his crutch against the curb, the captain repeated the order. Chandler took his time even more after that. The man shouting the orders wasn't even a real captain anyway, and Chandler knew it. The whole force knew it, the whole *real* force that is. This rookie would never have passed the fitness exam. Chandler imagined he was an overused security officer who wished he could be a cop, but never had the capacity. He'd just appeared out of nowhere, it seemed, which was ironic to Chandler, considering how difficult it was to miss seeing him on account of how rotund he was. Speaking, in itself, seemed like a demanding task for the obese captain as his lungs sounded like they were trying to catch their breath between each sentence.

Chandler, on any other day, might have rapped the impersonator with the rubber end of his metal crutch, but he had a purpose: sell the injury; sell that he was the only officer who was able to keep up with the fugitives that were Josh Revlon and his deadly friends; sell that all other officers engaged in the pursuit had failed; and convince that he wouldn't rest until he had captured those fugitives himself. So, instead of offering retaliation, Chandler stood; took the insults from the man who thought he was Chandler's superior; and nearly dropped his son's jelly bean in the process. He realized that it bothered him, more than he wanted to admit, that he truly couldn't remember the bean's color. As he took his first step on his crutch towards what might possibly be his end, he concluded he didn't care what color it was.

The captain inspected Chandler, who still wore his hospital gown over a pair of bloody boxers. Somehow, Chandler felt as though this entire situation should be his fault. He pretended embarrassment and attempted to fix what he knew he couldn't. The captain straightened out Chandler's hospital robe and tried to pull the edges down to cover the red stains in Chandler's underwear, but nothing seemed to please him. He withdrew and looked out across the campus garden towards its silent weekend city.

"I hate this town," the captain replied.

Right here, Chandler decided that, if he could, he would humiliate the captain within the course of the paladin's orders.

"Give it time," Chandler said, hoping the pain running up his back wouldn't black him out. All he needed to do was finish his task for the paladin, "This town's got a lot of life in her yet," he added.

"I doubt it," the captain replied and began leading, or rather prodding, Chandler towards the white visual arts building and the doors under the word *Museum*. As Chandler pressed inside, past the glass doors and their aluminum frames, he began wishing he'd have thought to observe the sky in case this was his last time to see it. He knew his role, but the moment of failure or success was quickly upon him. Either outcome frightened him. He pressed Zender's jelly bean and felt his own sweat carry its sugary nectar farther up his arm and into his cast.

As they entered the commons with its black metal chairs and yellow tile, two more officers, a detective and a lieutenant joined Chandler and the captain.

The detective, Chandler had known since fourth grade. His name was Harvey Bruce. They were friends who had been drawn apart by office walls and the seatbelts of other vehicles, but they were friends, or had been before. Although, no one would have known that unless they had gone to school with them too.

The lieutenant, on the other hand, was new to the force in just the past six months. He was some rookie, just like the captain. He too managed to appear out of nowhere and climbed the ranks rather quickly. He looked upon Chandler as if the injured sergeant should have been intimidated by him. Chandler wondered if he should be.

Last night, Chandler thought he had died after being thrown around inside his truck. Today, he wanted to warn his family to leave town and never look back, but no one left town anymore. They were always herded back or disappeared. Reports of missing people were always on the rise these days. Maybe Chandler should feel intimidated. The lieutenant seemed to be more informed about monstrous plots against humankind than Chandler, so this might be a good clue that the lieutenant actually should be feared.

Chandler was suddenly horrified for his family. They could be hurt. He didn't have the strength to stop this man, let alone a super-powered dog. Maybe he could keep them safe through his own submission. Maybe he'd end up being food, maybe his loved ones would too. Maybe he'd be turned. He'd ask for his loved ones to be turned too if that was the case. At least they'd be together and alive still. If he was loyal, or appeared to be, maybe Chandler and his family stood a chance to be numbered among the rogue's. How to make that transition without betraying the paladin who had rescued him not so long ago though?

As the captain and the lieutenant began once more to lead the way before him, the detective took up the rear, possibly to keep Chandler in line. Chandler wondered, if he should decide to take on the younger lieutenant, would the detective remember their friendship and take the captain. No one else seemed to be around as the footsteps of Chandler's escort echoed through the spacious commons area. They approached the abnormally tall, cedar doors leading into the Lowe Memorial Gallery, where large signs announced the museum was closed for lunch.

The captain stopped short of knocking, as one of the doors abruptly popped open, and a soldier dressed in full, black military garb greeted them without saying a word. An M-16 crossed his chest, while pomp filled his eyes. He quickly assessed the group, finalizing his immediate hatred upon Chandler, before allowing the officers access through the gallery doors.

This room, white in every direction except for the blue marble floor, might have normally been more blinding under the eight-foot spans of track-lighting overhead. However, today, it was mostly frightening.

Along the walls, stood tall, thin creatures. They appeared aged from dust, decayed to bone in many places around their faces and torsos. Their eyes appeared to be sewn shut, and the metal frames holding their bodies in place made their dog-like features more terrifying. Such a horrible exhibit! What kind of monsters were these? These white figures looked like nothing he'd seen so far.

A rectangular, folding table stood in the center of the room where a middle-aged, and light-blonde woman sat studying a pile of papers. She looked up only after she had seemed finished with the page she had been scrutinizing.

She gazed straightly to Chandler, and her face turned cold before she dropped her reading back to the tabletop. She stood; turned away from the group; and walked to the far wall. Here, another man, middle-aged, maybe younger, stood still atop a folding ladder and before a large metallic mural of a violent forest scene of impalings. The woman approached the ladder and stood at the bottom quietly for several minutes. The man was too invested in his mural to notice her. A black bundle of fur beneath the ladder sneezed away and into the center of the room. The man at the top finally acknowledged the woman's presence and smiled upon her. He closed up a clear, plastic box before sliding it into his pocket. Then he climbed down the ladder and welcomed the black dog with a scratch to the head.

The woman gestured towards Chandler's group and, as the man observed Chandler, his smile quickly disappeared. He allowed the woman to lead the way back, both of them appearing upset and focused on the paladin's spy.

So, this is how death approaches, Chandler thought to himself.

The black dog glided across the floor as though someone were blowing it towards Chandler and his group. She appeared to smile.

"Officer Chandler," the woman announced, her hand stretching towards him. "Thank you for joining us, I'm Loraine. I am the assistant curator. And allow me to introduce our curator—,"

"Love your work," Chandler's nerves blurted and he took Loraine's fingers in his mobile hand. He greeted her as pleasantly as he could. Afterwards, the curator reached forward with an open palm as well. Mid-shake he tussled the shoulder of Chandler's hospital gown.

"I'm sorry we couldn't seem to let you get dressed," Loraine asked rather than stated, and the curator's eyes darted from Chandler to the captain.

The Scottie snorted and sat himself beside Loraine.

"I felt given the circumstances," the captain replied.

The silent curator grinned at the fat officer and pulled the small plastic box out of his pocket. He opened it, revealing a small handful of metal-head stickpins, and withdrew a single, steel sliver. He returned the box to his shirt. Without warning, he drove its point into the captain's shoulder, then held it in place, gripping the captain so he couldn't flinch away. The curator slid the pin in until even the head disappeared through the captain's uniform. He continued to press as though insisting the head go beneath the skin as well. The curator's smile never faded until the captain finally composed himself as if not in pain. The curator patted the captain's shoulder and urged him towards Chandler.

"My deepest apologies, Officer Chandler," the captain said and, at the command of the curator's forceful gesture, he reached to Chandler with a rueful handshake despite the smallest of rapiers cutting through his muscle movement.

Chandler ignored the handshake, but cupped his hand down on the fat man's shoulder and said, "Don't mention it, Cap. I know you meant well." He patted the shoulder a few times to genuflect the comradery he truly felt with his superior. He could tell the captain was too fearful of the curator to respond.

Only then did the curator's smile disappear, and he moved towards the table in the center of the room.

"Have a seat, Mr. Chandler," Loraine invited as she followed her boss.

Loraine moved to a chair beside the curator; pulled his seat out; and waited for him to sit before moving to the one she had occupied previously. The Scottie leapt onto the table and stood at attention between Loraine and the curator.

At the far corner of the gallery, a section of wall opened. In walked the two monsters that had attacked Chandler and killed Speatsh Cheatham the night before, each black beast missing an opposing arm. Genre approached the table and stood at either end, peering only at Chandler. Chandler knew who Genre was. If Chandler hadn't been attacked by the monster, he wouldn't have believed the story of the conjoined-twin-turned-werewolf, a truly destructive power of one mind.

Chandler wanted to faint, to run, but he seated himself in the only other chair at the table, facing the curator who now rifled through the box of pins like a child examines a candy bowl. He studied Chandler in his measly hospital gown.

"My employer is curious how three fugitives ended up in a police vehicle, with you driving it away from town," Loraine said.

Chandler tried to remember the script he had memorized under the paladin's scrutiny, but for some reason couldn't. He wasn't sure if it was the injury; the meds managing the injury; or straight-up fear.

"Is the question difficult," Loraine asked.

Chandler nodded. "I caught them," he finally said. "When no one else could find them, I brought them into my vehicle voluntarily."

"You disobeyed orders," the captain replied.

"I followed orders," Chandler snapped back and risked a haughty lean-around to his captain. "I don't know where you were, but I know I took those people right where Jasper told us to. Perhaps if you weren't running wild through the streets with the rest of your chicken-run outfit—what am I saying? Perhaps if you could run—"

"I assume you're finished now, Sergeant," the captain interrupted.

"Not at all! Way to keep the havoc down there, Cap," Chandler shot back. He didn't know what kind of leniency he had over the captain after the curator, assuming he was the rogue, didn't seem too pleased about Chandler's rude handling of attire earlier.

Genre yelled at Chandler. "And you two were worse than Dudly Do-nothing here," Chandler fired back, jumping from his chair to his crutch and giving his all to make his anger appear confident. "I put them right in your hands, and you nearly kill me, your one ally out there, then you let the paladin and the girl escape." Chandler went for it. He turned to rogue. "Maybe if your hairy goon here hadn't spent his time trying to kill one hairy hillbilly, we could have caught the one traitor who actually betrayed us."

The Left Arm poised to backhand the insubordinate Chandler.

"Truth hurt," Chandler cried into The Right Arm's stance. *Please don't let him kill me,* he prayed.

The master struck the table. The Scottie now stood, growling.

"I'm sorry," Chandler replied, trying to calm down. "But considering I was perfectly fine doing my job until the Black Yeller's got involved, I think I'm entitled to a little gratitude, and a lot of butt-kissing."

Chandler glared back at the curator only a moment before starting in again. Something told Chandler to stop, but all he could think about was if he was going to die now, he was going to go out fighting. He looked back and forth between The Right Arm and The Left Arm. "You two make me sick."

So much for the paladin's plan, Chandler thought. Finally the suicidal sergeant flounced back into his seat, an action which hurt more than he was willing to let on. "I swear, I'm surrounded by idiots."

"Let me take him outside for five minutes, Boss. I'll teach him respect," the captain replied.

"Believe me, it would be my pleasure," Chandler retorted. Geez! He hurt. To take his mind off the pain, he continued his rant. "The Cujo twins may have dropped the ball, but at least they showed up, you pathetic slug." He wasn't sure if it was extra measure towards conviction or something he thought was a joke, but he decided to look up to Genre and add, "Why don't you two take him outside and tear two-hundred pounds off of him already so he can keep up next time."

The master's eyebrow raised, and he might have smirked. Genre lunged for the captain and dragged him out of the far corner of the room. The captain's voice pleaded for his life, shriek upon shriek, until one final scream reached an octave that only death could sing.

Loraine shook and stuttered a moment. The curator took her hand and gently kissed it. He smiled at her and pointed at Chandler, who suddenly realized he had just killed a man and couldn't react.

"I believe we've found our new sheriff," Loraine said, trying to sound confident.

Chandler couldn't speak. The sound of the captain's cries had carved their scars too deep into his memory. He heard dying pleas from the back of the museum, but couldn't make them out. He might have attempted to run out of the room if he wasn't too busy keeping himself from soiling his hospital gown and bloody boxers.

"I'm hardly the man for the job," Chandler finally replied, realizing the way this curator treats his leaders. "As you've noted, I don't exactly dress the part."

"The mayor's abandoned his post as far as this town knows, and the people need leadership. That means law enforcement," Loraine explained. "Besides, I don't think the master is asking."

The curator sat and tapped one of his straight pins against the table, his eyes locked onto Chandler's, the curator's face bearing no emotion.

Chandler realized his jelly bean was completely flat, practically dissolved in his palm. He no longer had anything to press his stress into anymore. "What do you want me to do?"

The master pointed to a white pedestal with a black drape hanging over it and buried under a clear, plastic box. Loraine moved towards it and called Chandler to her side. She carefully removed the cover and set it on the marble floor. Then she folded back the black fabric, revealing a set of grey, flat stones, each about the size of a serving tray.

On another podium a few feet away, a leather book of ancient sort sat sprawled open.

Loraine focused on a stone with an engraving of an old carriage, hearse-like, pulled by four horses over mounds of bodies and broken bones. A post of some sort, Chandler guessed it was trying to depict a form of heavenly light, falling down upon the center of the carriage, and the figure of a man seemed to emerge from the front seat.

"What is it," Chandler asked, approaching.

"This is life, if I understand correctly," Loraine replied. "The book is much clearer on the topic, but this should do for now." She touched the carriage in the center of the frame with the bristles of a small brush. "This can restore life to these ancient creatures you see here today."

Chandler couldn't help but steal another look at the decayed monsters surrounding the museum walls. Ancients? Okay, Josh told him about ancients.

"Why would we want to bring life back to these scum," the brown-nosing lieutenant asked. "They're traitors, aren't they?"

A commotion broke. Chandler turned to see the lieutenant grabbing at his throat, where the black Scottie dangled, shaking angrily, at his neck. The lieutenant crumpled to the floor, and Chandler turned back to the book before he had to watch what he believed would certainly be a gruesome outcome for the officer. He'd seen what a dog companion could do before. He didn't need to see it again.

"So what do you want to do," Chandler asked.

"You're not as ignorant as the other people in this town," Loraine explained. "For the most part, we've managed to keep them so. Except for a few dogs and a power outages disrupting communication, not many people know our intentions. We need to keep up appearances. Our followers are keeping the outskirts under control. You've probably noticed the construction vehicles maintaining access to the roads. We have no problem taking care of any careless adventurers. Although, if anyone discovers the truth and starts communicating it, things will become chaotic rather quickly, and the master hates chaos. Chaos wastes lives."

"Why does it matter," Chandler asked. "We humans are no match for your kind. Why hide?"

"When we humans fight," Loraine explained, ensuring that Chandler understood she was not a wolf. "We die. We have a strange devotion in life for freedom. We are prepared to round them all up, but we need live humans until we can retrieve what we need."

"And what's that?"

"This carriage," Loraine said, nodding to the image of the old hearse. "We must have it to revive the ancients."

"And what's to keep them from turning on you," Chandler asked. He suddenly felt another person standing next to him. He knew who it was without looking. The master leaned towards the display of stones and pointed to a set of images beside the hearse.

"This is power born," Loraine explained. "And a new ruler will emerge. That is my employer's purpose."

"And my part," Chandler asked, afraid to hear the answer.

"First, we need to prevent the paladin from wasting the valuable lives we need, wolves and humans alike," Loraine said. "We need to wake him up, so he can hear the master and silence the hunters. They're the only real threat and the only ones that need to die. He wishes to bring the paladin here so we can wake him ourselves."

"That won't be easy," Chandler said.

"The paladin is using a wolf to search for the master through the psychic connections he holds with his minions," Loraine continued.

"We have prepared a general who has proven to be a disappointment. You will make sure he falls into the hands of the paladin. We will use him to lead the paladin directly here."

"The paladin protects the people," Chandler said. "He won't leave them."

"He'll be encouraged," the soldier announced, sliding to the other side of the detective. "I'll see to that."

"If you're wrong," Chandler asked. What did the soldier mean?

"Then we'll destroy the compound," Loraine explained.

"How do you plan on doing that," Chandler asked.

"That's our business," the bald soldier replied.

"Well, now it's my business," Chandler replied. He wondered how thick to lay it on.

The soldier laughed.

"Listen." Chandler forced his way against the soldier's body-armored chest. "You may be the big bang in your backyard, but this is my home. I get to know everything at my disposal or I'll do the job myself."

The soldier sneered and drove two fingers back at Chandler's ribs. Chandler cracked the soldier's shin with his crutch.

"That's enough, Dee," Loraine interrupted politely.

The soldier nodded and withdrew.

"We are guests in his town after all," Loraine added.

"Now, answer my question, Dee," Chandler abruptly demanded.

"Colonel," Dee corrected.

"Not mine, mercenary."

"My crew and I will be there," Dee replied with much chagrin. "If anything goes wrong for any reason, we will level that compound."

"No explosives," Chandler cried. "No explosives in my town. We've stayed stealth all this time, we will not lose that by blowing the city up."

"I don't take orders from you," Dee replied.

"Yes you do," Chandler replied. "Jarhead!" For added conviction, he dropped his crutch and drew himself face to face with the soldier. "You start blowing things up, and who knows how his crew might react. They have some pretty good toys of their own, you know. Or did you miss that slaughter of wolves in the field and the forest last night?"

The curator was suddenly standing extremely close to Chandler now. He reached to Dee and restrained him from retaliation.

"We are perfectly capable of destroying the compound without explosives," Loraine said. "Now, can you do your part?"

"Let's see how far your loose cannon here gets retrieving the hearse after he blows up the paladin," Chandler replied, and he began marching towards the doors leading out of the museum. His old friend stood frightened at Chandler's sudden rebellion. "You clearly don't need my expertise."

The curator applauded, which was enough to stop Chandler in his footsteps. Thank heavens! Had Chandler somehow bolstered authority?

"You will give this officer the respect he deserves, Dee," Loraine replied. "That includes obeying his orders. Understood."

The curator leered him over.

"Understood," Dee replied in a tone that Chandler himself had used with his own superiors when he disagreed.

"You will ensure our general is delivered to the paladin," Loraine added, turning her attention now upon Chandler. "You will also take a squad of men, your men, to the local cemetery where you will find a backdoor to the paladin's underground warehouse. We need you to use that backdoor and retrieve a carriage that is in there."

"Sounds simple enough," Chandler said regrouping with his new and ignorant cohorts.

"The backdoor currently has some intriguing protection, namely a giant grounds keeper who is the son of a vampire. We have also been unsuccessful in getting to the bunker as of yet, and only the backdoor provides a large enough exit for what we need," Loraine explained. "You will draw the giant out and kill him. Then you will use the backdoor, which is protected by an extremely high-end security system. This shouldn't pose a problem. We can break the code. Once you are through the security doors, we will help you recover the carriage."

"Why not just send wolves," Chandler asked. "Surely, a general or two could handle this task."

"Are you still suggesting you are not needed," Loraine asked.

The curator, smiled just a little.

"Because where there are wolves, there are hunters," Loraine explained. "And where there are these enemies, there is no secrecy to us nor our plans. Humans are less likely to question a police presence than a monster's. We will hold you responsible should our plans be advertised in any way. Do you understand, Captain?"

The curator tapped his foot once.

"It would be a shame," Loraine continued, "If we had to extend an invitation to those you care most about."

Chandler knew he'd reached the limits he could push now. Time to pull back.

"So we're not certain that it's there," Chandler asked.

"Mostly certain," Loraine replied. "But no, we're not certain."

"Makes sense," Chandler said. "And what about Jasper?"

"Jasper and his companion don't worry us," Loraine replied. "They're where we want them to be."

Then Chandler knew he had to ask the dangerous and selfish question or it wouldn't seem real, "And what do I get out of this?"

"You and your family will never be bothered by wolves again," Loraine said, but it might as well have been the curator with the way he seemed amused at Chandler's self-interest. "You'll be free to go where you please."

"And him," Chandler asked looking to the detective.

"What of him," Loraine asked.

"When I leave, I'd like to know I have a place to go. Give him a companion dog, just like you did with me, and let him start finding me someplace new to live. Someplace away from here where my family can have space to buffer us from whatever else you plan in the future."

Loraine laughed. "You want the master to spare this man to find you a new house?"

"You think you haven't just scared loyalty into him," Chandler said, making sure not to blink. "He'll have a scout."

"Anything else," Loraine asked amused.

"I think a bit of money isn't unreasonable, something compensatory for committing treason on the human race. I suspect you have no problem with gaining the resources."

Loraine kept laughing.

"I hate hotels," Chandler replied coolly. "And you hate publicity. I think my request is quite reasonable. And if the detective's going to do the footwork, he should get the same payment for him and his family as well."

Loraine looked to the master. The master looked only at Chandler: no emotion, no blinking, no tell-tale signs of any. He turned an emotionless face back to Loraine.

"The master agrees," Loraine replied after reading just his feature. "A more than reasonable sum of money and a scout will be delivered to the detective within the hour."

"In that case," Chandler said turning to his old friend. "I'll need a ride back to the hospital, detective. I would like to get dressed. The dog and money can be delivered there."

The detective acknowledged, but said nothing.

"If you don't mind then," Chandler said as he began to make his exit. "I have a bit of work to do." He suddenly stopped. "With your permission, of course."

The curator smiled.

Chandler didn't believe him. The newly-appointed captain, albeit illegally, quickly eyed down the soldier named Dee. "Have your team assembled at dusk, soldier boy. Your situation will be more convincing with wolves involved." He turned back to the curator. "If we may have use of some of your best actors?"

The curator bowed his head in agreement.

"You'll have your paladin and carriage before the next full moon," Chandler said before allowing the detective to open the tall door to exit.

"You know how to find us." Chandler said back to the curator. "That is, if that's satisfactory with you, sir."

The curator nodded.

As the museum doors shut behind him, Chandler discovered himself in a commons room and still alive. He would be sure to enjoy the sky as soon as he left the building, but soon realized he couldn't admire it long, for time was not on their side.

He led the way out the front doors and to his previous captain's vehicle.

"You sure about this," the detective asked after both men were secure in the front seats. Chandler waited after several blocks away from the university to respond.

"Harv, we may not have much time," Chandler quickly explained, driven by nerves. "They're going to give you a dog."

The detective's hands clenched to the wheel.

"You understand then what that means," Chandler asked.

The detective nodded.

"When we get back to the hospital, I want you to get in my closet and take one of my ammo clips," Chandler explained. "Don't show it to anyone. Don't try it out. This ammo will kill your dog. Don't try your standard issue, it won't work. Do you understand?"

"I think so," Harvey replied. He looked hurt.

"One more thing," Chandler said. "We have friends in Cherry Heights, the Nomads."

"The biker gang? Under investigation by just about everyone," the detective said unnerved. "Those aren't friends."

"I have a feeling they'll come in handy," Chandler said. "Drop the money you get from that museum psychopath and hire them to come back here and lend a hand."

"They'll shoot me the second I make that offer," the detective said.

"You'll give them proof to trust you," Chandler said. "Walk in there and shoot your dog. Don't let him see it coming, or else what your dog knows, a stronger monster will know and we'll both be exposed. You'll only get one opportunity, so make sure you have a surefire shot. Don't guess you have the opening to take it out. Know. Know it, or don't do it. They'll listen to you after that. They love a good fight, but won't want those monsters in their own homes. If they don't listen, offer them immunity, deputize them. Do whatever it takes to get them here. We need all the help we can get. If that still doesn't work, there's always Cylinder. He owes us."

"Cylinder," the detective asked, but was overcome by realization. "If he's still alive!"

"Yeah," Chandler said. "It's an old favor, I know, but we need it."

"What do I tell them if they agree?"

"Tell them to find a band of rebels led by someone called the paladin up at the old junkyard," Chandler explained. "He'll have weapons and ammo. Tell them he calls the shots, and they do not want to push that no matter what their first impression of him is."

"Who is this paladin," the detective asked.

"One bad kid," Chandler said. "And I reiterate, they do not want to be stupid with him. Tell them that they do not want to be stupid with him."

The detective laughed. "I think you're getting that backwards."

Chandler wasn't amused, and he glared his old friend into silence. "No, and don't you press that matter either. You do what he says, when he says."

"All right," the detective relented.

A few more miles, and Chandler and the detective were walking towards a set of hospital doors.

Chandler shook now. He worried that his old friend might be more tempted to turn sides rather than to sway the Nomads. Chandler felt his grip and decided it was probably okay to relax his hand. The top knuckles of his fingers whitely peeled away from his cast, and he peered inside.

So, the jelly bean was blue.

Book of the Protector

2 ~ Wet

Cherry Heights—home to one horse track, fourteen stop signs, two traffic lights (one that never turns green after midnight—for either direction), and six bars, all of which were closed at this time of morning—except one because no one dared tell anyone inside it was time to go home.

Her body had succumbed to numbness quite a while ago. She might have known how long she had been down in the dark cavern could she see the sky, but, for now, she saw nothing.

Occasionally, Jasper's eyes would give light just right, and she thought she could see the outlines of his or even her own flesh within the abyss. Otherwise, she saw nothing. She was soaked through, not just her clothes—but her skin, deep and cold to the bone.

She shivered, and her flesh ran raw. Her fingers felt puckered. Clenching and re-clenching didn't warm them any. She couldn't tell which lines and pits ran deeper, those in her fingers or those in her palms. Her hands felt larger, swollen, and she wondered if they might pop if she accidentally poked them with her boot knife if she tried to grab its handle. Her body cringed at the horrid thought.

Her feet felt worse, decaying and perhaps growing lethal. Sometimes the old man massaged them through her boots and tried to convince her that she was fine, but Cadence knew better. She knew she was broken. Jasper even had to help reset her leg, although he tried to claim it was just a sprain. The pain was enough that it was numb now and she wondered if the cold and the water, which logged her system, was causing harm to the flow of blood needed to begin the healing process within her bones.

Yesterday, she'd been all too happy to kill this old man. Yesterday she was strong, but today she was cold. Today, she clung onto him trying to bleed him of every ounce of warmth that he had to spare. Sometimes he shivered himself, but he kept her alive.

Jasper carried her and waded waist deep through the water's current. Usually, like now, it was calm, but he had given the impression a few times that he might stumble under its bearing current.

Cadence wasn't sure, but she thought she had lost a gun or two, even some clips and their diamond glycerin cartridges. She was too cold to care or feel. Occasionally, she ran her frigid hands over her person to make sure she could still reach her closest of weapons. She was constantly relieved that enough were still attached to her magnetic suit. Still, she checked. Her rifle rattled over the old man's back; her sawed-off shotguns were now tied into its strap after nearly taking off the general's arm the first time he tried to carry her. He lugged all he could comfortably manage of her weapons. Even his deadly walking stick, he clenched tightly as he cradled Cadence into his chest and carved a path farther against the cold, river flow. He walked and she had to give Jasper his due. She would surely die without his aid.

She supposed she was grateful, but her mind was more concerned for her friends. The memory of what had happened, prior to being thrown down a hole in the ground, was still vile in her mind.

Jasper had offered to help her. He could have repaired all of her broken parts, but it would have involved infecting her, turning her into one of his own monsters. His servants could have done it without infecting her were they here, but they weren't. Of course, who knew how sick even that would make her this time?

"No, no." Jasper shook her awake. "Not here. Too deep."

Cadence wasn't sure if her eyes were even open, but her head felt heavy.

"No sleeping," Jasper said. He pinched her awake.

"I need to," Cadence replied.

"Tell me how I got it wrong," Jasper asked.

She had to think a moment about what Jasper was referring to. "I told you this already."

"You must have been dreaming," Jasper replied. He hid a shiver in his breath.

"How could I have," Cadence asked. "You won't let me sleep."

"You've slept four times already," Jasper replied, then took a moment to regain his grasp on Cadence's beaten body. "You're not wolf. How are you the protector?"

Cadence was tired of this game.

Jasper shook her. "Just a little longer. Try clenching your muscles again."

"My mother was the protector," Cadence struggled to get out. She tried her best to sit up straight against the old man. She was too tired to clench every muscle in her body to build heat; release adrenaline; or to do anything else. "I'm adopted. I didn't get it when she used to tell me her nonsense stories, but I think I do now."

"Get what?"

"I don't have her scent," Cadence said. "I couldn't be tracked."

"So, she raised a mortal child to protect an ageless god," Jasper said.

Cadence wanted to laugh, but the sound that came out of her was more frightening than entertaining. "He's hardly a god."

She let loose a shiver that caused Jasper to heave her body, just a little, to get a firmer hold. Finally, her body drained of its last ounce of power, and she let the color of dreams fill her head. Granted, they were bad dreams, but at least she could see things again.

* * *

It was the cough that woke her, and, at the moment, she thought she might puke, had she anything for her body to purge. She had already lost what little she did have amid her shaking. That was well before she found herself laying on soft ground.

"There's not much of it," Jasper said. "I found some roots, tried to squeeze out the water. They're still smoky."

Whatever heat her body had drained from Jasper, the earth had now leeched from her.

"Don't get up," Jasper said as he gripped her by her shoulders. "Shiver and sleep. It'll be better for you. Contrary to belief, shivering keeps you from freezing to death in your sleep." He dragged her body across a dry surface—not sand and not dirt, something spongy. "Sorry about the smoke. This place should be warmer in a bit."

Had she been more awake, she might have noticed the small flame sooner. It was a trying flame, bullied by dampness, but she could see it wanted to grow. A few feet away, water garbled. She tried to sit. "I can help find wood."

"I'm capable of finding wood," Jasper replied, kneeling to her. "Look at me."

She looked. His eyes reflected the struggling flames, if the flames had been gold.

"Sleep," he said and suddenly disappeared from before her.

The dreams suddenly came rushing back.

They weren't as bad as before. For a moment, she remembered some of the more enjoyable parts of her life before all the monsters appeared. She was back in school. She dreamed about her boring American Civilizations professor, not boring because he was monotone like all the other history teachers who loved to drone on in lifeless merit, but boring because he really was boring. He always seemed to know the one way to present history as limp, empty and stationary.

"You realize he's never going to let the pilgrims land," Natalie whispered as she leaned in close across her folding, lecture-hall desk. "They get tired of waiting on him and head to South America to find cocaine instead."

Cadence could almost remember smelling the spearmint on her breath.

The sizzle woke her. Cadence shot straight up and screamed upon suddenly remembering her injured leg. It was definitely broken; she knew that now.

The fire was larger. She felt warmer—dry, for the most part. Jasper turned abruptly from the fire with what appeared to be a long stick and a large blob wriggling on its end. "Feeling better?"

"How long was I out," Cadence asked, but the pain was still too fresh for her to really care for an answer.

Jasper pulled up a gray sleeve and looked at a flickering band around his wrist. "Don't know," he said. "I can't remember when

I wound it last. Or did this one take batteries?" He returned the wriggling blob and the end of his skewer back to the fire and asked if she was hungry.

She was.

As she tried to find a more comfortable sitting position, she noticed the pain more now. She was still numb, but not from cold, from injury. Still she seated herself better.

"Give me a minute," Jasper said. He reached into the flame and squished the blob at the end of what Cadence could now see was the sword from his cane. The blob suddenly flapped a time or two, despite being speared to Jasper's sword.

"What am I forgetting," Jasper asked.

"I beg your pardon," Cadence replied.

"I remember it dying faster than this," Jasper replied.

Cadence slid up to the frail-looking man until she could see the blob was some sort of trout.

"Whack it," she said.

Jasper took pause before finally withdrawing his blade from the fire. He punched the fish. The trout stopped moving. "I don't remember doing that before."

"I imagine you smacked it against a rock before."

Jasper cracked the creature against the ground. He smiled. "Yeah, that seems familiar. Amazing the things you forget with time." He smacked it again to reinvigorate his memory, then stabbed the small, lifeless trout back onto the tip of his sword.

"Did you remember to clean it," Cadence asked.

Jasper looked at her. "Ah, that too."

Again, the fish came off the point of his weapon, and the old man appeared lost as he stared at the dead animal.

"Here," Cadence said and pulled her small knife with its smooth back from the sheath in her boot. She held out her hand for the fish, and Jasper handed it to her.

"I like to start here," she pressed the tip of the blade beneath the jawline of the dead trout. "Some people like to cut from the belly and tear, but it's just a mess; and some people like to tear back from the gills but it's a harder pull. I just cut here and create a second mouth." She cut the slit beneath the jaw, then pierced the fish's anus and sliced straight up towards the new mouth, all the while explaining to be careful not to cut the false mouth or cut so deep that you make a mess. She gripped the new mouth and tore out the innards in one stroke.

She flung the insides of the fish into the flames.

"That it," Jasper asked.

"It's hard to see, but I like to dig my thumbnail in here and scrape this blood vessel out of the spine." She drove her thumb into the belly of the fish and pressed it up along the length of the back of the trout's ribcage. "Then you take your knife and scrape it this way to get the scales off." After a moment of guessing whether or not she had completed the job in the shadows of the flickering light, she handed the fish to Jasper to rinse off in the water, which he did and then in two short strokes cut off his tail and severed its head.

"I think I remember doing that," he said before returning the gutted fish back to his sword.

Cadence couldn't help but to chuckle.

"It's really not that funny," Jasper said. "You swear you'll never forget who you were; where you came from; or that shred of humanity that kept you moral, but then you learn that hunger trumps morals. Stomachs are so small, and blood digests quickly. It works its way through your system so fast and the taste," something in the way his eyes flashed over Cadence and then quickly darted away frightened her. "Still, there's nothing sweeter," he continued. "And you forget, grow old, hate who you've become. You hate who you were so much that you change yourself to forget all you knew and change your name to something uncommon only to have it made popular by a series of teen vampire porn novels. You know, if I were Thomas, I'd be offended at all of it, more than I am as a wolf."

"You've read them," Cadence asked.

"Worse than the movies." Jasper snapped.

Cadence began laughing then bit it back.

"When this is over, I might hafta eat some writers."

Cadence laughed and wiped her nose.

"I don't get it," Jasper continued. "All these years we've been here, and no one ever gets the story right. I imagine someday someone will write the real story, and everyone will be too tired to hear it." He shifted to his other knee. "Geez! Teen-wolf porn. That's all anyone writes anymore. When this is over, I'ma eat that entire cast too."

"Why don't you just write something and correct all the ignorance," Cadence asked.

"Nah," Jasper said. "I'm smarter than most, practically everyone, but I'm no grammarian."

He pulled the sizzling fish from the flames and pressed it towards Cadence, who nearly skewered her hand on Jasper's sword as her body clenched in pain upon reaching to feel the fresh meal.

She pinched the fish. "Not done."

"The offer still stands," Jasper said.

She shook her head. "We've lost enough humanity as it is."

"You'll be stronger."

"You just said I'll become someone else."

Jasper said nothing and extended his skewered fish once more into the flame.

"How did you lose yours," she asked.

"My what?"

"Your humanity?"

Jasper stared into the fire.

Cadence was about to remind Jasper of the question, but decided to change it instead.

"Who bit you," Cadence asked. "Was it the priest?"

"Hardly," Jasper retorted.

"The inquisitor?"

The old man laughed.

Cadence chose not to speak for a moment before, "Not so close to the flame."

Jasper adjusted his handheld spit. "The master made me."

"You mean the rogue," Cadence asked.

"That's why I'm able to do what I do," Jasper explained

"What's that?"

"You wouldn't believe me if I told you," he said turning the fish perhaps faster than he should have.

"You did try to kill me," Cadence said. "You do kind of owe me."

"I saved your life," he replied. "We're even."

Cadence gestured for the old man to turn the swelling fish a little more slowly. "Then do it to pass the time."

Jasper laughed. "My perception of time would frighten you."

"All right," she said. "Then do it to pass my time."

"I can't tell you," he said. "You don't realize it, but the most subliminal of thought could tear down my block against the rogue."

"I think that's done."

Jasper withdrew his sword and offered the fish to Cadence.

She tested the temperature before ripping off a chunk, but leaving the fish on the bladed spit.

"Take all of it," Jasper urged.

"What about you?"

"I can't," Jasper replied. "I've started my fast."

Cadence removed the trout, burned her fingers and dropped it. Jasper caught it and dipped it in the cool water running past the narrow bank where they both currently perched. He handed it back to Cadence, who graciously thanked him and then ate her meal in silence.

Soon after, she fell asleep once more. When she awoke, she was no longer numb. It was not longer light. She screamed as Jasper heaved her into his arms again. The rattle of her shotguns and rifle told her that her journey along the underground river was about to begin again.

Jasper re-entered the cold water.

"You're sure it's upstream," Jasper asked after the long walk finally seemed to get to him too. He'd only asked a thousand times before, but he asked again.

"I'm not sure of anything," Cadence replied. "I never actually saw it myself, but everyone seems to think it's there. Haven't you seen it?"

"Only once," Jasper said. "Through someone else's eyes."

Cadence clenched Jasper's shoulder as the water's current hit her ankle just wrong. The echo of the cave screamed back at her.

"Maybe you're right," Cadence said after catching her breath again. "Maybe you should bite me."

"Her name was Annalina," Jasper said ignoring her request. "She was when I lost my humanity."

Once again, the cold water was up to Jasper's chest, which meant Cadence now sat almost fully emerged herself. Her body began to set into freezing again. She was sure they had plenty of room to walk along the somewhat dry bed, but she couldn't bring herself to complain because she remembered that a freezing, broken ankle felt better than simply a broken one. Perhaps Jasper understood this himself. It took a while. She thought the shivering would kill her before she fell numb, but eventually she did lose feeling in her feet and legs once more.

"Who was she," Cadence asked after some time through hypothermic breaths.

"Huh," Jasper asked. "I think I've kept you in the water too long" Jasper replied. "I'll find us a place to warm up."

"It was your family," Cadence asked. "Wasn't it? Who was he? She?"

"She," Jasper replied. "My Ruthelle died giving birth to Annalina's mother. I'd always wanted a boy," Jasper replied, and suddenly his tone sharpened. "Hold your breath."

The water rushed over Cadence's head, and she jerked only a moment before she realized that such reaction didn't serve Jasper who fought to swim against the current. Her head suddenly erupted clear of the water.

"Breathe," Jasper ordered once before the water rushed back into her face; up her nose and down her throat. She coughed, even started to while under the surface and emerged once more spitting water away from Jasper.

"This time breathe," Jasper demanded again.

Cadence continued to cough out water and would have coughed out more had Jasper not buried her face into crook of his neck as she plunged under the river's skin once more. She waited for the roar of the cavern above the surface to fill her ears again before she tried to resume her cough and finally draw in much needed air. The sound was almost all she had to let her know that she was completely breached. It was better at announcing than Jasper who had to catch his own breath and yell at nearly the same time.

"Breathe!"

She barely heard him, over the scream of the water but she breathed—albeit barely—and once again fell into a muffled pool of white noise.

The next time down, Cadence cracked her foot against something hard and sharp. She screamed under water, and, when she emerged, filled the cavern with a sound that seemed to frighten even Jasper. He lost his grip upon her.

She plunged alone into the black nowhere that had no end and no beginning. Could she see, she might know which was the direction to the surface, but a kick in any way could have sent her farther into danger. She tossed to the current's will and she dared not kick.

The more dangerous matter now too was that she had screamed her air out. She was heavy. Her lungs began to lurch within her body, demanding she open her mouth and fill her lungs. She felt herself lunge and placed her hands over her face, covering her mouth and pinching her nose.

She shook and pressed her face harder, nearly feeling her grip go a time or two. Her body lunged one more time and so powerfully that her hands fell away from her face. She found herself drawing all that surrounded her into her lungs.

"Breathe," Jasper ordered, cuffing Cadence at her collar.

She sucked in all she could. Water hadn't filled her lungs. Crisp air rushed in, and she continued to refresh her lungs with oxygen while coughing out any residual liquid.

"Hold this rock," Jasper instructed. No sooner had she luckily discovered a slimy, but secure, hold on a cold sharp ledge, than Jasper left her once more alone and in the dark.

Behind her, screams, splashes and nasty, deafening squeals filled the cavern.

These sounds she didn't know. Several wet thuds slapped walls near and far, while more splashed back into the river.

Jasper said nothing, but the splashing and squealing continued. Had this been Speatsh fighting—well, she could imagine the colorful language he'd be muttering.

One time, she thought she felt what might have been breath at the back of her head, but a splash buried it. Then something heavy floated past her, pawing at her flesh to catch hold. She startled and swatted away what felt like small, clawed hands. In doing so, her grip slipped, but she somehow regained it.

The sound of fight grew gradually louder as Cadence's ears finally agreed to drain of the water that had deafened them. As if it hadn't been loud before, she now heard sounds of a most vicious fight between Jasper and many foes, but she still didn't know the sounds of these creatures.

BLAM!

A dull light flashed only a moment, and Cadence recognized the sound of her own rifle, which was still strapped over Jasper's back.

Jasper laughed. "Of course."

Cadence's ears rang. She wanted to help, but how?

Jasper let out an odd kind of sound. He was unclear, but it definitely meant a turn for the good. Something flew past Cadence's head and splashed far down stream of her.

The commotion lulled until only Jasper's breath betrayed his actions.

"I hate rats," Jasper wheezed. Cadence could hear him bob back towards her side, where he immediately took the burden of her weight upon himself again. He carried her, all the time complaining about the nasty features of rats until Cadence could no longer bear the topic and complained.

"Are you even listening," Jasper replied. "These weren't normal rats. They were bit."

"You mean like a were-rat," Cadence cried.

"That's very disturbing," Jasper said, and then he found a small patch of mud to set Cadence upon.

Cadence rolled to her back and cried for a moment at the dull numb in her ankle. It was worse, more exerted.

Jasper let her cry and started off to searching the walls and ground for anything to build another fire. Eventually, he connived some wet roots into hissing and filling the cavern with unclean air, for which Jasper couldn't seem to apologize enough about.

"So Annalina," Cadence decided to ask after the fire had some time to grow and the air could clear a bit. "Your granddaughter then?"

"Really," Jasper scoffed. His dark shadow appeared as if set in stone, etched darkly and enamored with the dancing firelight of the bowl of flames set between them.

"He broke you. Didn't he?"

Jasper laughed.

"But your ambush on the inquisitor," Cadence inquired. "I thought—

"Leave it alone!"

She did. After she had regained her warmth, Jasper kicked the fire into the river and cradled Cadence once more as he began a slow trudge along whatever narrow riverbank allowed them travel outside of the water. Jasper's feet splashed a time or two, and, when they did, she shivered. She didn't get wet. It wasn't the same as being wet, but the memory was all too fresh.

"The inquisitor broke all the master's new-turns," Jasper said as he carefully marched along. "The master turned you, but the inquisitor made sure your monster within was complete."

Cadence wanted to ask more, but decided she liked hearing a voice in the dark rather than feeling ignored out of offense. She chose not to upset him.

After several minutes of her silence, he started again.

"Hunger is a powerful tool to rally the troops," Jasper explained. "It doesn't matter how high up the food chain you belong—hunger is the alpha predator, and it always conquers. Rich or poor; weak or righteous—hunger possesses absolutely. Once you've realized what you're willing to feed upon, and you find yourself wallowing in clotted blood from the previous night's feeding, the inquisitor leaves you alone, tamed by that all-powerful predator."

"I'm sorry," was all Cadence could say. "I should have left it alone."

"Surprisingly, it's very therapeutic," Jasper repudiated. "Freud said so himself."

"Okay, I get it," Cadence replied. "Funny joke. Forget I asked."

"Very entertaining human being actually," Jasper said. "He wasn't as smart as you might think, definitely loved his—well, let's just say he wasn't always clear-headed."

"Everyone knows that," Cadence politely chided.

"Ah," Jasper replied. "But not everyone knows he got that way because of me."

"You can't be serious."

"I was on a sabbatical from this town. Pretend you're a psychology student, and your roommate turns out to be a werewolf," Jasper said. "And I was very convincing. So, yes I'm serious."

Again silence came, but not from being ignored. Jasper and Cadence had inevitably returned to the water taking stance upon stance against the loud current.

"A good man actually," Jasper started again once he was able to find another sedimentary sidebar. "Helped me learn to control more of my mind. He was very good at it, helped me plan my revenge."

"Now I know you're joking," Cadence replied.

"No," Jasper replied, "He thought it would be good therapy to plan it."

"For turning you."

"For cheating his way into my home under the guise of being my apprentice," Jasper spat.

"Apprentice," Cadence asked, baffled. "Him? An apprentice?"

"We may be old, but we still educate ourselves, and I was a pretty good woodworker in my mortality."

"A woodworker?"

"You don't believe me," Jasper asked.

"I remember what your house looked like," Cadence chuckled. "Some handyman!"

"How did you get *handyman* out of the word *wood*," Jasper scoffed. "I made toys."

"You're a liar," Cadence laughed. When she finished, she realized Jasper wasn't amused, and that she was back to being ignored again.

That is, until Jasper suddenly stopped, and a different type of chill froze Cadence's flesh.

3 ~ The Circle of Dogs

If you thought it looked like an outhouse for about two hundred sitters, you would be correct. It was unpainted and appeared out of place for its time, like two angry gunslingers might topple through the front doors at any moment and show each other who had the larger caliber of ego.

Had she not been drenched, she might not have noticed it, but she did notice—or, she thought she noticed. Before she could say anything, Jasper had already stopped.

"So it wasn't just me," Cadence said. "What is it?"

"Roots," Jasper replied. "A wall of them."

"There's a breeze here," she observed.

"Where there's a breeze, there's an opening," Jasper replied.

"A way out?"

"Or more," Jasper said. "Possibly. Could it?"

"What are you talking about," Cadence asked.

"They did throw you in here to find it, right," Jasper asked.

Cadence let what Jasper was suggesting settle in. "You don't think we actually stumbled upon it do you?"

"Truthfully," Jasper said, his voice a little shocky. "I think I'm getting a little giddy here. This is holy grail even for me."

"I assume we've decided not to escape through the school basement, then" Cadence said.

"Basements are boring," Jasper said. "I should know. I have two basements. They're both boring."

Cadence tugged at what turned out to be a small root.

"Wait," Jasper said grabbing at Cadence's arm, frightening her. "Let's not leave any clues for anything else that might be hunting us." Then he set Cadence down once more.

The sound of him rustling in the darkness was a welcome one. Footprints and water had worn out its allure long ago. Had she been anywhere else, she was certain she would have mistaken Jasper's rustling for what might have been a burrow of small critters with sharp teeth.

"It's tight, but I think we can do it," Jasper said. The rustling continued, this time centralized towards the ground, and something sounded like scraping across soft dirt. "This definitely goes somewhere. You'll have to crawl. Hold my hand."

Cadence got down, cursing Jasper.

"I'm sorry," Jasper added. "Follow my voice."

She followed the golden glint of his eyes.

"This way, keep coming," Jasper continued to coax. "That's it. You're doing fine, just—It's me! Stop screaming and give me your hand already!" His eyes now faced Cadence, looking away every so often. Clearly he must have been crawling his way backwards deeper into the tunnel of roots.

"I know it's you," she cried. "My leg's caught."

Jasper apologized then began his rustling ahead of Cadence once more.

Jasper's hand guided Cadence into what she discovered was a twisted path through the roots. While Jasper somehow crawled backwards, pulling Cadence with him, she was turning onto her belly, her back or sides as she slithered after Jasper's lead—all the while, her leg cursing her for every direction she bent.

"Maybe I was wrong," Jasper said. He then left Cadence for several moments to grunt, rustle some more, half-curse and then grab her hand again. "Lay on your right side and bend forward."

Something tore at her pant leg: maybe a root, maybe a rock. Who knew? She panicked only a moment before Jasper helped her break free.

"Don't panic on me now. We have air, and I can see." Jasper encouraged. "I'm not leaving you here." He suddenly stopped and spent a few moments silent, but rustling. "Listen to me," Jasper soothed once more as Cadence found her own breathing betraying her confidence within what she was beginning to believe would be her tomb.

It wasn't paranoia, the walls really were growing around her. With each fattening root, the space shrank. To make matters worse, if Jasper decided to betray her, she'd have no direction. She realized that, despite the fresh odor permeating the roots living all around her now, she could smell the suffocating grip of dirt encapsulating her surroundings. She wished for a moment for her night-scope, but that had disappeared in the fall from Taichomée village. Then she realized she couldn't have used it anyway. She could barely extend her hand straight in front of her, let alone bend an eyepiece back to look through.

So this was what it was to be buried alive.

"We're okay," Jasper said. "The roots go on for a ways. That means stronger walls. The ground isn't going to fall on us."

"That's not as encouraging as you think," Cadence said.

"We're safer in here than we were out there," Jasper encouraged.

"Do the were-rats know that?"

"You're kind of a negative person, aren't you," Jasper shot back.

"By the way," she added. "While I'm thinking about it, which way is my rifle facing."

"Don't worry," Jasper said. "I emptied it some time ago."

"You sure," she asked.

Jasper let go of Cadence for a moment and proceeded to rustle in the dark.

"Yeah," he said. "I'm sure."

He pulled at Cadence once more, and several small beans of dirt fell into her face from above.

Cadence froze.

"It's okay," Jasper said. Something about his voice was different, friendly. "I didn't carry you all this way to lose you here."

"And what if any wolves track us," Cadence replied. "And I'm serious about the rats."

Jasper suddenly stopped his progression. "You're right," he said. "Let's speed things up a bit." Again, he let go of Cadence to return to the familiar rustling of flesh, clothing, earth and old roots. Cadence soon found his hard-heel, wingtip, sopping and muddy, in her hand. "Ah! Facing forward is always better."

Still, they pressed forward, dodging and weaving through the openings that Jasper saw fit to wind his way through. Occasionally, he announced troublesome areas well enough for Cadence to manage herself alone, which allowed Jasper to adjust his own posture to discover the next turn in the maze ahead of them both.

The roots grew even thicker. Still, the two spelunkers maneuvered through them.

"How are you holding up back there," Jasper asked.

"I think I lost the rest of my ammo clips," Cadence replied.

"You're bleeding," Jasper said. "I can smell it."

"I think I got cut."

"Can you stop it?"

"Maybe. If I can find it."

"I lost your rifle," Jasper added.

"That's okay," Cadence replied. "I found it."

"Make sure the safety's on, please," Jasper said as he paused and twisted forward once more.

"You said it wasn't loaded," Cadence replied, doing her best not to scream through her anger.

"I didn't want to scare you," he replied.

Cadence took a little bit of extra time maneuvering her rifle so she could inspect it.

It was empty after all. She started following Jasper once more.

He came to a standstill, and Cadence could move no farther. "We might be in trouble here," Jasper added. "If I can smell the blood, others might also."

"Will the scent carry back that far," Cadence asked. "We've been at this for hours I'm sure."

"Then maybe we're almost done," Jasper suggested.

But they weren't almost done. They continued. The roots grew denser. Jasper complained more and kept demanding that Cadence be careful, but she could do no more than she already was. She was cut, in several places perhaps. She knew one laceration had crossed her shoulder after she wrestled with one particularly spindly and enormous earthly talon. One barb, or stone—or something else sharp—cut her waist, and a most-disagreeable pebble had subtly embedded itself in her shoe right beside her sprain. The rock seemed intent on sawing through her flesh.

"At least the mud should help it clot," Jasper said. "Better to bleed a little and keep moving than get sick and slow down."

But now Jasper appeared to be getting angry. Rather, it occurred to Cadence that he might be getting hungry.

"It's not your fault," Cadence said.

Jasper said nothing, but kept rustling his way deeper into the roots, or out of the roots. Who knew?

"Oh!" He finally blurted. "You're trying to help."

"What was she like," Cadence asked.

Jasper grunted.

"Well, what else would you like to talk about then? The weather? It's black out."

"At least you remember what black is."

"You don't see black?"

"Honestly, I can't remember," Jasper replied. "Sometimes I think I remember black skies and white stars, but I haven't seen dark skies in a long time. I don't even remember them enough to know if I miss them."

"That's okay, I guess it's just a color," Cadence said. "If you haven't missed it yet, it must not be too important."

"On the contrary, I'm awfully fond of colors," Jasper said. "Freud and I were students together, did I tell you that?"

"Roommates," she replied.

"Ah," Jasper said and even appeared a little less agitated. "I have a very fond interest in the mind. I used to be a psychologist."

"You were serious about that?"

"I'm always serious," Jasper said. "Unlike some generals, I don't lie."

"All right," Cadence said. "So you were a psychologist."

"A doctor can only take so much of others' narcissism in a single lifetime," Jasper explained. "Not to mention psychology is always changing, and you have to keep getting new degrees if you don't want to raise eyebrows to your mortality."

"Do you ever miss it?"

"No, I started painting, which began about the time I was ordered to return to Plattsville," Jasper answered. "Now painting, there's a way to see how twisted your own mind truly is."

Cadence didn't know where to go with that. Psychology wasn't her favorite field of study.

"Consider the color blue," Jasper suggested.

"Blue?"

"You know what it looks like?"

"Of course," Cadence replied. She wasn't stupid.

"There's a sharp rock here, be careful," Jasper informed.

Cadence held up the conversation while she pulled herself safely past the sharp object sticking straight out of the ground.

"So what does it look like," Jasper asked as soon as Cadence was past the tricky part.

"I couldn't see it," Cadence retorted. "I can't see anything in here."

"Not the rock," Jasper laughed. "Blue?"

"It's blue," Cadence said.

"But what's it look like?"

"It's calmer than black."

"I hate poetry," Jasper replied.

"I'm confused," Cadence said.

"How do you know what blue is," Jasper continued to prod.

"I just do."

"Yeah but how?"

"I've seen it before," Cadence retorted.

"So, how do you know it's blue?"

"I guess because grownups told me what blue was when I was little," She explained.

"Ah," Jasper erupted. "And how do you know that they knew what blue was?"

"Maybe someone told them."

"That's just it," Jasper said. "We only know colors by name because other people have said that's what they were, and we believed them."

"So? What's wrong with that?"

"How do we know that the human minds all see colors the same way?"

"Well, there is color blindness."

"I'm talking color ignorance," Jasper blurted.

Cadence said nothing.

"Look, you know what blue is because someone told you what blue is."

"Yeah, so."

"And you continued to know what blue was because its appearance became imprinted in your mind," Jasper continued to babble. Cadence was beginning to wish she hadn't tried to help, but now Jasper wouldn't shut up. "How do we know that the person who showed you blue wasn't really seeing red? Maybe the person who told them it was blue really saw yellow. How do we know that the blue you see is the same as the blue everyone else sees? What if blue to you is really green to me? So how can we be sure that we know what blue really is?"

"My brain's hurting," was all Cadence could think to reply. "Why would someone even think about these things? Are there really people who care about this stuff?"

"I'm just saying. You said the weather is black. I don't remember what black is so how do we know that black is even really a color? How do we know, you're just not choosing to see."

"Not choosing to see," Cadence asked. "There's nothing to see here."

"Are you sure," Jasper replied.

"What?"

"Exactly."

"Are you suggesting I'm seeing black because I choose to be blind," Cadence asked.

"Interesting question," Jasper replied. "Why do we assume blind people see black? Why can't it be white? Or blue?"

"Just leave me here and let me bleed to death," Cadence pleaded.

Jasper sighed. "What I'm saying is that the more you understand how a brain can work, the more you can understand how others might use it. You're fighting wolves that lose their humanity every day, wolves who forget their mortality and the philosophies associated with those understandings of that mortality. Those wolves are hunting prey that have minds that don't understand the arrogance that comes with such vicious power." Jasper fell silent, then sighed when he realized Cadence wasn't going to respond. "The wolf doesn't see black. They see you. You try to hide in the black because, to you, black conceals, but you are really in the open to them. You're an easy target."

"Speatsh never mentioned this."

"That's because his sense of color's been rejuvenated," Jasper explained. "He's been human too long. That's a lot of conflicting perception for just one brain."

"This is a weird conversation," Cadence relented. "It's over my head."

Jasper sighed once more. "Thank you!"

"What is it?"

Jasper helped Cadence pull herself free of the vine path, and she couldn't help but to let out a cheer herself.

"Sometimes, the way to win a fight is to think about how others might see a situation and how that might affect the way they approach you," Jasper explained.

"You see colors brighter, don't you," Cadence asked after a moment of thinking.

"Perhaps," Jasper replied.

"That's why the spotlights blinded you that night you chased us."

"Don't trust that."

"I can't believe we just spent two hours talking about the color blue."

"It wasn't that bad, was it."

"I swear, if this were a book, I'd burn the last few pages of this conversation."

"Oh, I hate books that do that!" Jasper helped Cadence to her feet.

Cadence stood on her own now. The ground was solid enough to favor her sprained ankle.

"There's nothing here," Jasper complained. His feet crunched in the dirt nearby.

"What do you mean," Cadence asked.

"There's nothing here," Jasper repeated. "It's a dead end."

"You mean we have to go back," Cadence screeched. "But the breeze. I felt a breeze coming from the tunnel."

"How could I be so stupid," Jasper scowled. "Trees make oxygen. There were so many roots, it would have felt like a breeze—wait! What's this?"

"Find something?"

"A rope," Jasper replied. "I think I can reach it."

Suddenly Cadence was gasping for breath, again. The room filled with deafening water as thousands upon thousands of gallons fell from above, throwing Cadence against the wall, flooding her nostrils and throat with something less fresh than she had previously been drowning in. This water was treated; she could taste the chlorine.

The cavern fell silent as her ear canals suddenly drowned. Attempts to search the wall behind her for any means to help pull her head above the surface were met with a stronger current pinning her hands as well. So strong was the current that it forced her foot into a hole in the wall behind her. An instant later, the wall suddenly collapsed beneath her. It washed away, and she surfed into a blinding pool of light.

She regurgitated that which annoyed her lungs. Here, she realized she was on her back in a pond of mud. She winced at the sea of light drowning her brain and waited for the fluid deafness to drain from her ears. An image of a man, coughing and arching, came into view.

"Jasper," Cadence called to him, but could hardly make a sound as she instead choked and began coughing out still more water. She yelled again and clenched her eyes shut against the painful light, which continued blinding her after so much darkness.

She waited for her eyes to fully adjust to the red backing of her own eyelids. When she was finally able to open them, she saw Jasper face down, convulsing and swallowing mud. She crawled towards him and rolled him onto his back. He spit up the mud and continued to shake. He instantly fell limp, but continued to breathe.

Somewhere in the distance the sound of white water trailed off into a diminishing chorus. Yet, no more rushed around Cadence and Jasper.

Upon first impression, she saw a large and earthy room. Light seemed to come not from above, as she originally thought, but from the walls of what was slowly becoming a strange cathedral of purple and melting red-blue. Then she realized an all-too-familiar light source flooded from tubes, complemented by long strands of fluorescent bulbs.

After deciding Jasper was unconscious but well, she finally began to understand her surroundings more accurately.

The room was circular and, except for the mud that had washed in with her and Jasper, was wax-like. Here, ancient fluids molded into stalactites and stalagmites. Tall, skinny crevices lined the walls and reached from ceiling to floor. They were at least twenty-feet high and arched towards the center of the domed roof where long mineral-spears lunged down from the ceiling. Cadence would have preferred not to be standing beneath this cluster of javelins.

Within each wall crevice, a podium of some sort—flat, yet round—stood. What were upon the podiums gripped Cadence's breath more than anything else in this room. From their mummy-like perches, they stared down, watching Cadence. They were trapped behind cages of calcium spires and columns. Their feet melded into each podium, cemented in from the many years of drip-drip-drip. Their silver eyes seemed intent upon Cadence, and their narrow heads with sharp snouts cocked with her movements. She brought her balance to her good leg and hopped towards one of the walls.

They watched, but only watched. They were tall, lanky and emaciated. Their thin coats of decaying white hair barely hid their gray scars of hunger and purple freckles. Their limbs were stretched, abnormally long and seemed brittle. Their bony arms crossed up their chests, and their hands gripped their shoulders in bat-like poses. No. Cadence saw wrong. They weren't holding their shoulders. Their hands were tied up and around their necks with some sort of material that she couldn't quite make out. One of the creatures yawned, his snout pulling back and his white teeth jutting forward like a shark's. Then his mouth suddenly snapped shut; his head perched itself against the side of the cavity that held him; and he closed his eyes.

However, the others watched.

Cadence's instincts wanted a gun. She gripped her mask still tucked inside her clothing. Didn't lose it? Good. But something was different. Against all common sense, she approached one of the creatures. She, like the rest of her imprisoned others, only watched. Cadence expected an objection, but she wasn't sure what that might look like. This creature didn't put on a ferocious show like her roommate. She simply watched Cadence.

This one was different. She was more alert, poised like a soldier as though she might miss some crucial opening act. Her hands, unlike the others, were not tied. Although one did grip its opposing shoulder, it was not tied to it as the other creatures' hands had been. Her other gangly paw held one of the stalactites, the calcium drip had covered her hand like frozen rubber, trapped, like her feet in the podium. Cadence wondered how many years she had held this stance that it should be cemented within the slow-growing liquid stone.

The closer she drew to the creature, the taller it became and the higher Cadence realized the ceilings really were. How long had it taken the spikes to grow from the ceiling and floors?

Cadence didn't know why, but she reached out to the mummified creature. It broke its grip on its own shoulder to reach slowly down to her. An excited chorus of cracking joints and knuckles sang praises to the transaction. The other lanky and tall wolves, watched, even tried to shift on their podiums to get a better view of the entertainment at hand. Even the sleeping creature woke from nap, much more interested now in Cadence's presence.

The strange wolf before Cadence reached through her cell with a hand that was decrepit and translucent behind thinned hair. Beneath its smooth and unscarred skin, bones appeared dark white, the veins blue—that is, as well as she understood what blue was. The nails were more human than animal, shrouded in hair that streamed from beneath the monster's cuticles. Its hand turned out to be soft, however cold, and yet comforting. Here, she noticed that this creature didn't seem as emaciated as the others of her kind, trapped behind their prison walls.

"So now what," Cadence asked it.

"Now, you should probably eat."

Cadence jumped at the sound and turned to it.

"Didn't you forget to bring someone," Bogi asked. He was wrapped in what appeared to be a small judogi to cover his recently shaved body. He scratched at his bald neck.

Cadence might have laughed as she realized that he no longer looked like a Persian cat so much as a hairless pug. Instead, "Are you kidding me," Cadence blared.

Bogi approached Jasper and looked upon the silent general.

"Are you kidding me," Cadence screamed again.

"Is this some kind of a joke," Bogi replied with a face that twisted into fierce loathing.

"He brought me here," Cadence replied. "He saved us."

At these words, Jasper screeched, and his body arced and strained as if his soul were trying to break free through his navel and slingshot straight into the bladed, cavernous ceiling.

"He's hurt!" Cadence wanted to run to his side, but she moved much more slowly than her body wanted to allow her.

"No," Jasper cried in agony.

Cadence now hovered over him. His eyes were white from staring at his brain.

"He's fighting," Bogi said, or rather asked perhaps. "Why, you square." At that, he turned and ordered Cadence to follow, which finally seemed to catch Jasper's attention. Jasper appeared calmer now, his eyes still white.

"I'll be all right," Jasper said.

"Thank you for your permission," Bogi said, clearly uncomfortable with Jasper's presence. He seemed much more high-strung than his normal self.

Cadence hopped as she followed after Bogi. She cursed Bogi's cruelty for the hike. He left her far behind and disappeared into a tunnel hiding in the far corner of the room. It grew dark, though not as black as the journey she had previously taken. She followed, and an all too familiar odor and the unreasonable sound of white noise overcame her. A new light appeared, and she then followed it to the end of the tunnel—where she found herself behind a curtain of water that she had only ever known from the other side, falling and deceitful. A small green path led out from behind the waterfall. Had Bogi ever allowed anyone to venture into the area, she might have found this a good spot to relax, meditate and forget that she had ever been locked up in that horrible dungeon.

But this was that horrible dungeon!

She barely set foot back into the trophy room of the underground bunker, that Josh's uncle Richard had built, when Bogi immediately began chiding her.

He dropped a small collapsible TV tray beside the dominant trophy that was the large white wolf. By the time Cadence had finally made her way out of the diorama, Bogi had a small step ladder set up and was scaling it to the wolf's back.

"Don't flip your wig, ma'am," Bogi pleaded. "But things didn't go to plan. Your family never seems to do what you're supposed to. Hand me the blade." Bogi held out his small clawed hand to Cadence.

"A what," but before Bogi could grunt and point, she found the tray held five items: a clear bottle stopped with a cork, a large key, a scalpel, an empty syringe and a blue dress folded over a hanger, dangling from the side of the tray.

"Watch the blade," Bogi urged as Cadence reached for it. He snatched it out of her hand almost as quickly as it was in range. He kneaded the back of the wolf's head and suddenly drew the scalpel across the back of her thick neck. Here, he peeled back a large roll of fur and skin. "Bottle."

Cadence handed up the stopped bottle with clear liquid.

"Hold the blade."

She did.

"Now, what's gonna jive here," Bogi said, popping the plastic stopper. "Is I don't know." He flipped the stopper towards Cadence and then rolled his eyes as she missed it. "We're talking a very fast metabolism. I'm going to reconnect her brain stem and nervous system, here. It might take a minute. It might take five, but she might be a little hostile, and she's a bit angry with you right now."

"How do you know that?"

"My link may be severed with her in this condition," Bogi said. "But I know her well enough to know she'll be angry."

"Hold on, I thought you guys did this to her to break that psychic connection so the rogue couldn't find her. Do you guys even know how to tell the truth?"

"We don't have to tell you everything," Bogi scowled and returned his attention to whatever he was doing behind the white wolf's back. "We should have never let Speatsh talk us into this."

"That makes no sense," Cadence cried. "First you don't want to wake Josh because he'll restore the psychic connection unwittingly then—oh no, the rogue's going to kill us all—and now you want to make him aware. And why are we waking Speatsh's mother up at all if she's only going to get hostile? It's not like she's been a big help so far."

"What are you rapping about," Bogi asked.

"Why are you waking this monster?"

Bogi answered by taking a fat swig from the bottle, swishing it in his mouth and then spitting out something pink, or maybe it was blue, into the wound on the wolf's neck.

"She's probably going to lunge for one of us," Bogi explained. "Take that key and lock yourself in the holding cage if you need to. When she comes to her senses, she'll let you know when it's safe to come out."

"She might eat me, and you want me—"

"You will uphold your oath to her."

"My oath ends with the—are you kidding me," Cadence snapped and watched as Bogi snatched up the blade again while dropping the bottle at the same time into Cadence's hands. "That's the queen?"

"Don't act so surprised."

"Speatsh's mother is the queen," Cadence screamed.

"Yes!"

"Speatsh is the heir all this time," Cadence realized.

"Yes," Bogi said casually. "One of them."

"Speatsh said Josh was the heir."

"Is that what he said."

"Are you kidding me," her rampage continued.

"That's right, I'm kidding you with my hands buried in her brain. Ha! Ha! Funny, huh?"

"You could have saved a lot of trouble if you'd have told us."

"I tell no one!"

"You should have told us," Cadence screamed. "After all we've been through, we're practically family."

"Wrong," Bogi replied. "You should have never been brought into this. You have—what—maybe ten good hunting years left in you if you're really lucky. The abuse you take, you'll be beaten down with arthritis before you're thirty. I however am immortal. I am the keeper of this secret. No one, not Speatsh, not Thomas, not even her own past husbands nor children know about what you've seen beyond that waterfall. There could be no chances."

"That's a load of garbage," Cadence replied. "Richard had to have known. This is his bunker."

"Who do you think found the land to build it in the first place? Me. Who do you think designed it? I even made a nice weak wall behind the waterfall and dug the tunnel to the cavern myself after it was built," Bogi explained. "He knew nothing because I protect the circle."

"And I protect the queen," Cadence was suddenly yelling.

"You can't even protect yourself," His mouth curled as he glared down on her. He resumed his posture to cut once more. "You might want that key now."

Once again, he cut and, with a quick flick of his wrist, he threw the scalpel to the side. It flew past Cadence, barely missing her, due mostly because of her own reflexes, and stuck in the heavy, wooden door leading out to the swimming pool. Next, he flung his paw into the back of the wolf's neck. Cadence was glad she couldn't see what Bogi was doing. Bogi's handiwork made a squishing sound. Something cracked, then popped then squelched again and, "There we go," Bogi announced.

The white wolf turned quickly and bit the step ladder from beneath her surgeon. Then she threw the platform and snatched up Bogi before he could fall or react. Instead, Bogi flew headfirst into a glass cabinet and tumbled to the floor, landing on all fours and shaking the disorientation out of his head.

"I told you to run," he bellowed as he dodged a shower of raining glass.

However, Cadence froze. She was now clinging for the grip of any sort of firearm that was no longer at her side. Instead, she found Bogi's key cutting into her palm. As the creature turned on her, Cadence didn't know what to do. Mostly, because, as Bogi still failed to understand, Cadence couldn't run.

The wolf directed its attention at Cadence, cocked its head and bit at her.

"I made a promise," Cadence screamed, stumbling backwards under the pressing bullishness of the monster. Her balance gave with the sharp pang in her ankle. "Please, stop."

Then, just in this moment, Cadence made a disturbing realization. It was the kind of realization that might have frozen any other person to the core, but Cadence wasn't one to freeze easily. They were all liars, weren't they? Speatsh, it seems, most of all. Maybe this wolf wasn't his mother, but maybe it was the queen. If it was, and if Speatsh was lying, it may have been to protect someone in the group from the truth. That could still mean Josh was the heir, and if that was the case, then— "Mrs. Revlon," she asked.

The wolf suddenly stopped. As if something had just now called to her, the magnificent beast's head jerked to the side, and the monster ran into the diorama, smashing through the curtain of water and disappearing into the tunnel.

"Looks like we didn't all forget who you were," Bogi said appearing at Cadence's side and holding his chest. He snatched up the blue dress and chased after the reawoken beast.

Cadence drew to her feet, ignoring the light-headedness that followed. Her first instinct was to get back to Jasper as quickly as possible, but took to rummaging through broken glass and cabinets for familiar weapons and ammunition instead. Armed once more, she attached the sawed-off shotguns to the sides of her thighs after making sure they were loaded. She checked the scope on a new rifle for night vision. She felt her magnetic suit grip its long barrel along her spine and wondered how quickly her ankle would drop her the moment she pulled the weapon. A few more preparations, and she again knew where every gun-grip waited. She couldn't help to pay a small homage to the metal cage set within a cabinet near Bogi's work area. It was just as clunky as she remembered, but it did appear somewhat sturdier now that it was fixed since the last time she wore it. She shuddered at the thought of putting it back on, especially with her injury.

"My design's better," she said after looking Speatsh's bulky invention up and down a time or two. Lastly, she set off to search for the one weapon she hated even more than the cage, the mouthpiece to her mask that she swore she'd never wear.

She hated it, feared she'd take out an ally with its devastating spread. However, she was alone now, scared. Although, she felt she had gained a bit of control over the possessed mask enough to work with it under the circumstances. She'd warn Jasper to stay out of her line of sight once they started their journey back to Josh or their next fight, whichever came first. The last thing she needed was the accusatory mask lashing out at Jasper, who had done so much to rescue her.

What a waste!

Why did Speatsh send her here if he knew the truth of this place? Why the deception?

The mouthpiece was in a small drawer. Part of her hoped it wouldn't be there, but it was, along with a few dozen metal cylinders the size of an old 35mm film cannister, each filled with thousands of small, horrible needles. She shook one to make sure it was packed so full that it didn't make any kind of loose sound. She stuffed it into one of her pockets down the side of her calf. She dropped six more cylinders in with it. She might have added more, but the thought of any one of those cylinders breaking under pressure and during a run worried her. The last thing she needed were metal slivers digging into her leg and shredding her muscles. Then she wondered what it would matter whether one cylinder or a thousand broke within her clothing. She concealed six more into her pockets. Once Cadence felt confident she was armed enough to get to the junkyard to inform Josh, she made her way back to the cavern.

Jasper was still crumpled on the floor, his body now twisting. In front of him was the frame of Barbara Revlon draped in the blue dress. She heaved Jasper into her arms and proceeded to carry him up round, stone steps to a mossy ledge beside a well that was trimmed in black stone. A spring of clear water poured from the wall above it where calcium had formed itself into a sort of spout and spit it down to the small pond. Another small stream of water leaked over the lip of the pond and trickled to the stones that encircled the well. The water then meandered down a barely noticeable path to the wall of the cavern where it disappeared as though it were being swallowed away. Barbara set the convulsing, old man into the moss before the pond.

"My brother has a strong mind," Barbara explained without any hint that she had seen Cadence re-enter the cavern. "Either Jasper will keep my brother from following your path or he will die trying." She stepped to the well, its water only inches from the top, and reached inside its rim. A moment later, she withdrew a black leech. It dangled from her palm, curling disdainfully to its shocking new environment.

"This man saved my son," she knelt beside Jasper; tore his matted and muddy dress shirt open; and dropped the leech onto the center of his chest. "If we bleed him enough, it might act like a sedative, though it won't cure him." She returned to the well and thrust her hand in once more to withdraw another of the blood-thirsty slugs.

"Why didn't you say something," Cadence asked.

"Like what," Barbara asked turning back to Jasper.

"Do you know how much time I put into hating what my parents told me," she asked. "I could have been ready."

"To do what," Barbara asked, reaching for yet another leech.

"I devoted my life to you and your family," Cadence said.

"You failed." Barbara retorted calmly. The leech between her fingers popped. Barbara shook off its guts and returned to the water. "My son is dead because he was protecting you when you should have been protecting him. Don't talk to me about your role to my family."

Cadence almost drowned on her own breath as she struggled to find the words to ask, "Josh is dead?"

"Not Josh," Barbara replied. "Speatsh."

"Speatsh is—wait, he's your son?" Then she realized. "That was true?" She realized again what Babara just said. Speatsh was dead.

"Was," Barbara corrected with scathing rebuke. "And now my other son is out there while you're in here. You failed. I'd put you to death myself right now if I wasn't trying to help the one good person in this room, it seems. He protected my son. This is what a protector looks like."

Cadence watched as Barbara stretched two more leeches across Jasper's chest and belly. As the queen of the wolves made her way back to the water once more, Cadence threw one of her Glocks at the side of the woman's head. Barbara turned suddenly, her brow focused and pointed at Cadence. Bogi dropped to all fours and prepared to leap, but Cadence already had him in her sights.

"Put me to death," Cadence cried. "You're not my judge and executioner."

"I am your queen," Barbara scolded.

"You're not my queen," Cadence laughed. "You're a nobody, a coward in hiding. Even my own parents, your blood, couldn't protect you so they had to steal a human baby to do it for them. I'm not one of your dogs."

"My, you sure think highly of yourself, don't you," Barbara asked.

"You should be kissing every inch of my mortal, human butt for all I've done for you, both of you."

"How dare you," Bogi shrieked.

"How dare you," Cadence returned and seemed rather impressed that Bogi seemed startled at her own stare-down. "I don't know much, but I know you're not her family any more than I am. Don't think you rank higher on the pecking order than I do. What are you? Someone she bit. You're no ancient. You're no family. You're bit, that's all you are. At least I had a choice to be here. "

"I would watch your words wisely, mortal," Bogi snapped.

"Am I supposed to be offended at that," Cadence asked. She almost pulled the trigger just to see how fast Bogi could really be. "This is my home, you feline shut-in. You're just the doorman, the senior citizen greeter. You two are the most ungrateful cowards I have ever known—the most powerful creatures walking no doubt—and you hide in a cave while expecting us mere mortals to serve you." Cadence popped back two hammers as Bogi appeared to shift his weight. "You didn't bring us here to stop a war against humanity. You brought us here to grow fat and serve you. I thought the whole reason we were fighting was to keep humanity from serving wolves. Is that how you repay humans for giving you solace?"

Cadence expected a response, but none came.

"Accept responsibility and show some respect," Cadence braved. "You should have told us."

"We," Barbara started and then stopped. "I was afraid he'd bring my brother here and destroy us."

"You don't have to explain yourself," Bogi interjected.

"That's enough out of you," Barbara replied.

"But, she's wrong."

"She's right," Barbara conceded. "We made this war. We built our armies and security on humans. I have my own husband roaming the world to rally hunters to our aid. None of my other husbands would have done that."

"That was his choice."

"It was a husband's and father's choice," Barbara said.

"I disagree."

"Of course you would," Barbara said. "You've never been human."

"You're not even human," Cadence asked. She realized she shouldn't have probably said it. "All this time, I thought you were just a strange breed of wolf gone wrong or something, and you really did turn out to be—what—some house cat?"

"Don't compare me to house cats," Bogi replied. His teeth flashed, and a fire in his eye suggested that Cadence was done with this line of insult. "I am the only one of my kind. I am the only of her bitten who has learned to master the spirits and stay in control of both forms. You show some respect."

"How many did she bite?"

Cadence had another wonderful retort to throw at the beast that had acted as mentor and bully for the past couple of years, but, just now, something refreshing occurred to her.

"I just realized you guys are idiots," she said while mentally thanking Jasper for his boring discussions earlier. "A cat locked in a cellar for so long that he doesn't know the real world, and a wolf who's been human too long, she's not smart enough to be a wolf anymore. You guys are so conflicted that no one really knows what you want."

Barbara returned to the pond and pulled another leech. "This wasn't the plan."

"You mean you had one," Cadence asked. "We mistook everything you said for experience because we were too stupid to think you should actually know more."

Barbara hesitated a moment. She didn't give any clues, but Cadence was certain she wasn't happy with the remark. She asked, "So what would you suggest?"

"Why does Josh need to wake up if you believed he'd connect with the rogue and start some mass war," Cadence asked.

"Because he's the heir of an ancient," Barbara replied, striping Jasper with yet one more leech, this one at his wrist. "He'd be a stronger ally awake than he is now."

"He's doing just fine without waking up," Cadence replied. "We're doing just fine."

"Unfortunately, Josh's allies are too weak," Barbara said.

"And Stan recruiting hunters," Cadence asked, understanding a little more than perhaps she should have. "And you lobotomizing yourself?"

"Recruiting hunters was my husband's idea," Barbara explained. "Speatsh suggested we sever my brain stem to protect Josh until the appropriate time to wake him and repel the rogue, but since Josh isn't waking up, that doesn't seem to be a concern anymore," She trailed off as she appeared to be asking more than explaining.

"My thoughts exactly," Bogi replied.

"Speatsh got to the bunker before we arrived? How did he get here so soon," Cadence asked.

"That was Josh's uncle," Barbara corrected. "He called Speatsh the night Cracey was taken. The one we didn't plan on getting involved was Thomas, despite Amber's irresponsible letter to him. We assumed he had washed his hands of this place. But I suppose he thinks he can keep Josh in check if he turns."

Cadence thought on the matter a moment. "Will Josh remain an ally or become a new enemy?"

"That depends on how he wakes up," Barbara said. "We had hoped you'd bring him so we could wake him here."

"Why not wake him the day we locked ourselves in here then," Cadence asked. She knew her tone was facetious. She didn't care.

"You guys are too dangerous," Bogi added.

"Would you have been able to keep from killing him if he turned? Or would you have been capable of killing him if he was too dangerous," Barbara replied. "We couldn't take that chance."

"And until he turns, he's a walking time-bomb who could turn on us at any time," Cadence replied as if to herself. "And with Speatsh gone, there's no other wolf to keep him in check if he detonates."

Cadence seated herself on a stone near an alcove holding a creature that still watched her. Why was this monster so interested in Josh's adopted protector? Cadence sat because she chose to, not because of the pain, not because of a lack of hope neither. She now stared at the dirt and listened to Barbara and Bogi talk about possible outcomes, and who knew what else. However, she chose not to listen to them just now. Although, when Barbara questioned whether Cadence still needed to hold her and Bogi at gunpoint, Cadence reluctantly holstered her weapons, slipping them back about her person. When she was done choosing not to listen, she stood—again, ignoring that her ankle was friendlier when she sat rather than stood. She had a feeling she'd have to ignore the pain soon enough anyway. In two years, she felt she'd never once been able to catch her breath. Without the twins nor Natalie to heal her, she feared she'd be on her own for any fight about to come her way. It was time to return to Josh, and she was certain neither Bogi nor Barbara would be leaving the bunker with her.

Yet, a question stuck in her mind, aching to be lanced.

"We've spent all this time trying to keep the rogue out," Cadence said to herself. "Why would he care?"

Barbara started to answer, but Cadence didn't hear her over her own her one-sided conversation.

"Speatsh said it was to get vengeance, but why would the rogue need that," Cadence asked herself. "He roams the world, while you hide in a cave. You're no threat to him."

She looked up to the creature nearest her and wished she could read the mind behind her white eyes.

"Why is this one different," Cadence asked. "The other's hands are bound, but this one's is not."

"She is the historian," Barbara replied.

Now, that *was* interesting.

"Historian of what," Cadence asked.

"She observes," Barbara explained. "All that there is to know about our existence is retained by her. The others requested to be bound to keep from being tempted to leave the sanctuary and feed, but she, our historian, is incapable of such behavior. She must observe."

"And the rogue can't connect with her mind," Cadence asked.

"The rogue's mind could not handle the abundance of knowledge in our historian's head," Barbara explained. "We're smart, but she knows intelligence beyond the comprehension of intelligence itself, and all she knows has been handed down to her by those who knew everything before her. She wouldn't help the rogue in any way. She's useless trivia to him, boring and empty."

"But he's already won," Cadence replied. "Hasn't he?" And now Cadence was thinking. "What in this decaying pit could he possibly want?"

Cadence looked about the room to find anything that appeared of interest. "Is it the water?"

"Water," Barbara asked. Now she was watching Cadence, trying to measure her thoughts. "Why would you wonder that?"

"Because there's nothing else here besides dying family," Cadence replied. The wolf before her scratched her encased forearm and sneezed a sweet, unnatural aroma into Cadence's face. Her free hand gripped her shoulder once more, the other still trapped in the calcium seemed to flex to no avail.

Cadence moved to the next alcove and stared up to another tall creature. This one surely hadn't aged as gracefully as the historian. Its hair was thinner, its skin a little more wax-like.

"There are plenty of places to get well water," Barbara explained incredulously.

"Nothing else makes sense," Cadence observed.

"Yes it does," Barbara said. "If you are to protect us from the rogue, you have to understand the rogue. What is the rogue?"

"A wolf," Cadence replied. She almost didn't notice the little marks at first on the sickly creature she examined. Two rows of purple dots stippled his neck: freckles, not freckles, not scars, but not healed.

"Think more," Barbara said. "What's more than a wolf?"

"I don't know," Cadence replied. "Just tell me."

"Why," Barbara replied.

"Josh is the thinker, not me," Cadence explained.

Bogi laughed.

Barbara chided him.

Cadence was annoyed.

"You're the protector," Barbara finally said. "You have to think ahead of Josh and the rogue."

"I can't even think about what's going to happen tomorrow," Cadence replied. Now she stepped to the next alcove, where another beast stood lightly snoring.

"Try," Barbara snapped. "When you know the goal, you anticipate. What's Josh's goal?"

"Stop the rogue," Cadence replied.

"I can't think for you," Barbara said. "You see the step, not the goal. What's Josh's goal?"

"Save the world," Cadence shot back

"Don't be snide," Barbara replied, bemused.

"To get out of here. To end this madness," Cadence said.

"Why?"

Cadence thought for a moment, more out of caution this time as she searched this other creature for similar purple marks, which she found. "Because the rogue destroyed his family," she finally answered.

"That's the cause of my son's goal, not the goal," Barbara said. "What's the goal?"

"He wants his life back," Cadence yelled out of frustration. "We all do. The whole thing stinks—and I don't know what Josh wants, I'm not his conscience."

"Are you sure?"

"He wants his life back," Cadence repeated. She found yet another set of marks on a third creature's wrist in the same system of purple pin marks. "He wants his house, his friends, his sister, his mom's cooking, his studies."

"And?"

"He wants to go home," The next creature practically brandished his little marks for her as he lightly turned his outer thigh towards her. When Cadence's eyes met the monster's, its eyes seemed to sharpen.

"Why," Barbara asked.

"Because that's his haven."

Barbara smiled, which made Cadence uncomfortable because she wasn't familiar with this appearance, especially since she usually only knew Josh's mother in the presence of Natalie. She remembered how much Barbara hated Natalie.

"So, what's the rogue's goal," Barbara asked.

"He wants to come home," Cadence replied.

"What's the difference?"

"Difference?"

"Him and Josh, what's the difference? They both want to come home."

"Josh wants this to end," Cadence replied quickly and, without thinking, added, "The rogue doesn't want it to end." The realization hit her. "It's not revenge."

"Why not?"

"Because he wants a fight," Cadence explained. "And his brothers and sisters are all too weak to fight him. There's no vengeance in defeating cowardice." Was *cowardice* the right word? For the rogue maybe. "But what he calls cowardice, you call respect, don't you? You hold life sacred. Blood is the drink of murder, it makes you unclean. This place is clean, but you're here, Barbara. And I do believe you've taken of the drink of murder, haven't you?"

Barbara opened her mouth to reply, but Cadence didn't see it because she was too invested in the neck line of yet another creature.

"Which means either you're a hypocrite or you've repented," Cadence continued. "But you haven't repented because you've eaten something. Generals can't turn into wolves without blood. Is it different for ancients? Speatsh doesn't turn, he's fasted. He's your son you said. That makes him an ancient, right? How ironic! To stay a true wolf, you can't murder, but fast after you murder and you can't become the wolf. Some natural defense your species has."

Barbara may have started to rebuke Cadence's lack of respect.

"The evidence was all over the walls in your home," Cadence asked. "What was it, deer?"

"Yes." Barbara asked, caught off guard.

"Really," Cadence asked.

"It's tasty to one who's been dormant for so long," Barbara replied. "But I have been forgiven."

Cadence honked out a laugh and decided that Barbara's unpleasant appearance warranted an explanation, but decided she wasn't finished questioning the queen of the most ancient of werewolves.

"One flaw to that logic," Barbara said. "These ancients have not eaten, and you can clearly see they are not in human form."

"You have a point," Cadence said. "Let's put a pin in that for now."

"It's confusing, I know."

"What do immortals eat," Cadence finally asked. "What is your ambrosia? Something keeps you alive. The moss! No. A race devoted to the respect of life, to the verge of their own extinction would respect the life of the moss. The dead moss?" Cadence glanced quickly to one of the creatures and remembered it yawning. Yep, the marks were here too. "But you're not herbivores, so that leaves," and then she thought she might have understood. "The leeches? You eat the leeches."

"But they're alive," Barbara replied.

"Yet, you sustain yourselves somehow. What do they do for you," Cadence asked, and this time she allowed herself to hear Barbara.

"They cure disease," Barbara explained, and a strange smile drew across her lips. "We may be immortal, but we are still lycanthropic. Like our far-reaching, canine descendants, we are prone to many diseases. Leeches, such as these, keep diseases at bay."

"So the rogue wants the leeches," Cadence asked as she scratched the small of her back and cautiously felt the nearest Glock to her left hand. Barbara didn't seem to notice. "Why doesn't he just go find his own? Leeches aren't uncommon."

"These are," Barbara explained. "Leeches have always been used for medicinal purposes, most for their anti-coagulation chemistry, but some, such as these, filter disease. Although, they're not easy to find. If it weren't for Bogi's diligence, we wouldn't have this spawning pool. Something funny?"

"But Bogi doesn't leave this place," Cadence observed. "He guards the front door. How could he find them?"

"Speatsh helped," Barbara replied.

"But Speatsh doesn't know this place is here," Cadence deflected once more. "Bogi said as much himself and we needed a map to find it."

"He doesn't need to know it's here to hunt the leeches we need."

"I'm sorry," Cadence tried to cover. She couldn't believe she'd laughed just now actually. Speatsh Cheatham, the mighty leech hunter. Wait until the others heard this. She stifled her laugh into a chuckle. She shouldn't have chuckled. The truth was, at this moment, she was frightened more than she'd ever been. "I couldn't help myself."

"The rogue is an immortal breeding ground of the most vile diseases known and unknown to your humankind," Barbara explained. "If he bites you, I'd worry more about getting flesh-eating bacteria than turning into a wolf. That's why he wants this place."

"How do his generals live then, if he's so diseased?"

"That's the human factor," Barbara replied. "Humans fight diseases with white blood cells. Dogs fight with bacteria. The joining of these two create an intense immune system that we ancients don't have. It's why our followers can heal—speaking of which, you should really let Bogi fix your ankle."

Cadence politely declined the offer and reached into her pocket for her mask.

"Something wrong," Barbara asked. Clearly, this time she noticed Cadence's weapon check. Bogi must have noticed then too.

"I just wonder if any of you creatures can tell the truth," Cadence replied. "He's coming for leeches. That's the best you could do?"

She quickly drew the leather mask over her face.

Death to the traitors, the mask screamed into her brain.

4 ~ Wrath of a Queen

The sign over the door was simple, hand-carved and wooden with one spotlight shining directly on it. A yellow bulb, made the wood look the color of crap and the orange letters the color of foul urine. The right colors to keep away family-friendly strangers.

"Hackmanyatoya," Cadence's voice cried. She found her arms both extended towards Barbara and Bogi. Her fingers squeezed carefully against the triggers of the two Uzis that, a moment ago, had been tucked into holsters against the back of her waist. She squeezed, but not so much to spray their bullets yet.

Kill them, the mask ordered.

Not yet, Cadence replied. *Let's see how they answer.*

Barbara calmly kept Bogi's clear rage from allowing him to leap for Cadence.

"Diseases," Cadence asked.

"Cadence," Barbara urged. "I know this is confusing."

"You're the queen," Cadence said. "You're more powerful than the rogue."

"I wish that were true."

Cadence squared her stance, and Barbara stopped inching forward. In this, did Cadence realize that Barbara understood the ancient language that the mask translated its wearer's words into.

"I think I get it now," Cadence said. "This was never about keeping the rogue away."

Barbara's face suddenly turned stern—and Cadence didn't care, she was certain hers was equally as stern as her realization began to cement.

"The ancients didn't go into hiding," Cadence observed. "They're your prisoners, aren't they?"

Barbara laughed. "And you said you weren't the smart one."

"You're the rogue."

"Hardly," Barbara guffawed.

Bogi leapt for Cadence, but Barbara quickly restrained him by his worm-like tail.

"Not yet," Barbara said. "I'm curious how smart she is."

"You've waited this long," Cadence said.

"What gave it away," Barbara asked, finally assuming that Bogi was safe to release from her grasp.

"You just don't know anything," Cadence said. "I don't know how you didn't know. Maybe the information didn't make it back to you or maybe your brain is so old with information that you forgot."

"We're only human," Barbara replied. "But that's not all, is it?"

"Bogi's teeth marks," Cadence said. "He's not protecting the entrance, he's blocking their escape, isn't he? He feeds on them to keep them weak, but not dead. At first, I thought it was the leeches, but the marks are all identical. I'm guessing they match Bogi's teeth. And when there' not enough blood to drain, Bogi eats the leeches. That's why he can lock himself in here. He has all the food and water he'll ever need."

Barbara's glance to an increasingly-infuriated Bogi told Cadence she was right.

"Whatever your reason for lying," Cadence said. "I imagine if you wanted these crearures dead, they would be. That's some job you have, Bogi."

Suddenly, Jasper rose to his knees, screaming with pain. He rolled out of the moss, stumbled to his feet and hobbled to the fountain where he threw up in the water.

"That's just gross," Bogi said. "Can I please have him now?"

Before Barbara could answer, Jasper keeled forward and slipped headfirst into the well.

"So much for draining him slow," Barbara replied. "But whatever works on that old fool."

"You underestimate Jasper," Cadence said.

"You underestimate the breeding ground of leeches," Barbara replied. "Well, you were supposed to die anyway, that idiot just complicated things."

Cadence was alone now. She'd never been alone in this war. She always had Nick somewhere nearby; held Speatsh or Josh in her sight someplace; or had someone's voice in her ear shouting commands or requests. What comfort, she suddenly realized, that the sounds of Amber's deadly whistles would bring right now. It took her entire team to bring down a single general, and usually she had some sort of supernatural ally in doing so, but she had none of that here.

"Perhaps," Cadence said. She and the spirit in her mask quickly calculated where to prepare an aim that would catch at least one of the fast monsters. She'd never fought either of them before, so she really had no idea. "But I'll bet I take one of you to hell with me," Cadence added.

"Doubtful." Barbara shook her head while shooting a disappointed glance to Bogi who had decided to creep a step towards Cadence. He stopped and stepped away instead.

Cadence realized that Bogi's step was more strategic than cowardly.

I can't take both, Cadence thought.

Do you see what he's doing, the voice of the mask's spirit replied. *The queen's letting Bogi have the kill. Aha! Try to antagonize him and trust my aim.*

'You're a coward, Bogi," was all Cadence could think to say. "You think I don't recognize the old duck-behind-the-queen-and—

Bogi turned back for Cadence and looked to Barbara for approval, but Barbara appeared more amused than angry, shocked to some degree even that Cadence might be more prepared to fight than either of them had given her credit. He stayed his ground.

"Should have brought Josh," Bogi said.

The reality came together in her mind as a million mental pieces of jigsaw puzzle suddenly snapped together in unison. She saw a plan to awaken Josh, but he needed to do more than awaken. He needed to have his humanity stripped, just as happened to Jasper. He needed to destroy one of his own as well. Not just destroy, he needed to devour them and then live with his consequences, new power fueled by Cadence's blood. Bogi was to be Josh's inquisitor. Josh's friends were to be his last self of being stolen from him.

Cadence imagined Bogi sneaking around the underground bunker when they had first gone into hiding, perhaps wondering which one was Josh. A plan, a simple plan, bite Josh; let him destroy his helpless friends and then raise him as only a motherly monster could do. Bite Josh? Did he need to be bitten? He's the son of an ancient. Perhaps he just needed a secret word uttered in his ear.

So, why didn't any of these options happen?

Was it because Cadence and the others learned how to fight? But Speatsh was the one who trained them? He wanted them to fight. Did Speatsh stop Josh's destruction? Why send Cadence to the ancients without Josh if he knew Bogi and Barbara were traitors?

Because of me, the spirit of the mask entered Cadence's head.

That made sense. If Josh had come with Cadence, he would have fought against Bogi and his mother. He'd already made the mistake of trying to kill Cadence once, and the betrayal of his own mother would have broken him. His humanity was still too riddled with guilt to have allowed it to happen a second time—and her mask would have sensed who was loyal, identifying the traitors to Cadence. The mask would have seen it. Cadence was a lie detector. Yet, if the mask was able to detect such deceit, why hadn't it noticed Bogi or the queen before? Or had it?

It's not what I see, the mask spoke to Cadence.

Of course! It's not what the mask sees. It's what Cadence sees. Speatsh tried to tell her. She controlled the mask. She was the brains. The mask simply reacted in an amplified way.

You knew all this.

Yes. Cadence did know all of this. Even now, the mask was amplifying her subconscious. Perhaps a spirit had possessed the mask, but it hadn't been speaking to her, it had been acting as a loudspeaker for her most unknown thoughts, giving her more control over her own motor-control accuracy and allowing her to hear her own suppressed ideas. Yet, when she spoke, she spoke in another tongue. The others heard it.

That is the spirit in the mask.

Now, Cadence understood. She was in control of her thoughts. They told the mask what to amplify and how to act because Cadence could not. Even now, she barely realized that she was not actually awake, but in some sort of mental hibernation. She was drawn so deeply into her thoughts that the spirit in the mask possessed her motor functions. It wasn't a weapon of accuracy. This was a weapon of the mind: the host spent so much energy exploring buried thought and skills, and the mask possessed the body to do the rest. It acted for her. It spoke for her, all because she could not, and it knew her thoughts. That's why she didn't hear the strange tongue the others claimed to have heard, Cadence wasn't speaking at all. It was the spirit.

Barbara and Bogi understood her possessor's tongue. Speatsh had understood her. What was the tongue? They knew it. They'd probably been around it. She realized she couldn't get trapped in that thought right now. She had to get back to her previous reflections. Now that she understood, could she get lost in her own consciousness? Where was she before she got here? Oh yes, Speatsh.

She thought she could see Speatsh's plan as to why he sent Cadence to find this cavern. With the mask on, Cadence would have revealed her doubt to all the surrounding clues, just as she was doing now. Josh would have been angry and would have certainly sided with the human over his own wolf kind. He would have trusted her attacks, her accusations that Barbara and Bogi were traitors because he knew he was the traitor to Cadence once. Even if he were to awaken during this, his anger would have fueled his own denial. At least that's what she imagined.

Still, why did *they* want Josh there with her now? She believed she understood Speatsh's reason, but what was Bogi and Barbara's? This answer didn't take so long to formulate. Josh's allies had become strong enough to fight back. They could have destroyed Josh had he simply turned on them. Cadence believed it came back to the mask. Were they uncertain that the mask would expose them? They probably thought it controlled Cadence just as she had thought. She knew better now though. Speatsh had known how it worked, didn't he? He didn't tell them. If he had, Bogi at least would have never let it fall into a human's hands. Speatsh kept secrets from them. That said something about Speatsh's role. He must have known Barbara and Bogi planned on Josh destroying his friends.

Was that how they planned to rob his humanity? So Speatsh had planned to use the mask to expose Barbara and Bogi? Or was Cadence over-thinking this?

Why would Speatsh think she and Josh could survive exposing an ancient and a general?

Speatsh! He planned on being here right now. He planned on Josh being here too. Bogi and Barbara would have lowered their guard thinking Speatsh was their ally. They would have been wrong.

Why?

Somehow they didn't see his agenda. He stopped their plan. Speatsh fought it. Speatsh and Josh were both supposed to be with her—but only Speatsh knew the plan, which explains why Josh fought it as much as he did. The only thing Speatsh didn't know was how to get here. Bogi truly was deceptive if he could keep this place secret even from Speatsh. Or was it a secret? Was Cadence giving Speatsh too much credit in being an ally to Josh's friends?

He had to be an ally. For someone pretending not to know the entrance within his own sanctuary, he put too much energy into finding it. Maybe it was an act? No. She believed Speatsh, as loathsome as he was, genuine. He prepared them to fight, after all.

Just how far did Speatsh's distrust of Bogi and his own mother run? Or was Cadence only making all of this up in her mind?

Still, Cadence was only evading the fact that she was now alone. She hadn't known before how dangerous getting into her thoughts could be.

Very well, she supposed she had best put up some kind of fight before Bogi or Barbara sent her down Styx. Surely, she wouldn't make much of an escape on her disagreeable ankle, and her closest exit was back into the cavern of roots. Then it occurred; her ankle was no longer hurting. Was that part of her possession? Did that mean she could fight at her peak once more? Had she even noticed pain before while wearing the mask?

Supposing she could handle the fight, she was now alone in this confrontation against Bogi and Barbara. She needed a more comfortable environment if she was going to survive. She had to get out of this cavern. This meant she needed to get to the trophy room. She'd have to get past Barbara and Bogi. If she could get back into the underground bunker, she'd at least be on familiar ground. Of course, it was familiar ground to them too, but she also knew it.

She needed an opening to get there. They'd have to come out of the tunnel to attack her. If she could get ahead of them, she could subconsciously calculate how to shoot them through the waterfall as they exited the hidden tunnel. Now that she understood the mask, she believed she could do it, but Cadence needed them to make a mistake big enough to give her the lead she needed.

She needed to rile them.

"Only a coward hides in a hole and feeds on the weak," she said drawing close to the historian's hovel and its thick columns of calcium. "I guess we can't all be a warrior like Speatsh, Bogi."

"You think you can face my general," Barbara replied, seeing Cadence's words for the taunt they were. "Even when I found him near death, he had strength to face a dozen hunters. Those hunters, they were real cowards."

"I guess they'd have to have been," Cadence shot back, her mask translating to her new opponents.

Bogi's face froze, revealing his anguish over the horrible memory.

"And after I turned him," Barbara continued, a little colder now. "I let him have the village that hunted him."

"The Taichomée," Cadence replied.

Barbara smirked agreement.

Bogi Scowled. "Speatsh talks about their unknown general. I am their unknown general, and I've been under their noses all this time. You humans and your short lives remember nothing."

"I guess, good thing for Speatsh and Thomas then."

Bogi sniffed in amusement. "Hardly! Speatsh was blinded by pride and Thomas forgets who his enemies are. I am quite safe from his discovery."

"I think you underestimate Thomas," Cadence said.

"Do I," Bogi asked sternly. He began removing his judogi. His hairless, naked cat-like form, shaved from Thomas's practical joke, almost made him appear fragile and weak, especially with a long scar that had run from his navel to his neck. Cadence wasn't so foolish to believe that illusion.

"Do you see this scar," Bogi asked. "This is evidence that vampire bufoon has fought so many enemies that he's forgotten who they are. This is Thomas's handiwork. He gave this to me centuries ago when he nearly hunted down my queen. He comes around now, strutting his godly airs and adopting us as friends, yet he doesn't remember nearly killing me and leaving this scar. Do you know how deep you have to cut to scar a general? And he doesn't even remember who I am. He doesn't realize who he tried hunting. My Taichomée even left him for dead, and he survived and still forgot. He'll wish he hadn't, when I'm done with him."

"I get it," Cadence said. "Two entrances into here. You watch from here, the real dogs have the backdoor."

"Real dogs," Bogi screeched.

"Followers?"

"They are my slaves!"

Cadence chose not to state the bad shaved-cat pun and cliche that had suddenly swollen to the tip of her tongue. She wanted Bogi to make a mistake, not find too much angry focus.

Bogi leaned back and continued to shout towards the ceiling, his voice growing in volume until no more sound came out. At once, his body cracked and limbs readjusted for a completely new balance and stature. Cadence's temptation was to shoot. The mask tried several times to make her, but the change was mesmerizing. It wasn't that she wanted to see it. She hadn't killed anything in transformation, however. She wasn't even sure if the heart was where it should be. If she fired and missed, would Bogi give her time for a second chance? As much as this might appear to be the opening she needed, she desired something more certain. Barbara, after all, was still in control of her physical form.

Bogi, on the other hand, sweat rust-colored scruff from every follicle on his skin. It continued to grow and fall into long strands of thick, coarse hair. Two arm-length tusks burst from his upper gums. This time, Cadence let the mask act. Bogi's heart better be where she assumed it should be by this point.

She unloaded an entire Uzi clip at Barbara. That was her opening. Put Barbara on the offensive while Bogi was out of the fight. Kill her and Bogi dies from the shock. At least, she hoped generals died when their ancient maker did.

Barbara dodged Cadence's bullets, managing to stay one step ahead of the diamond chorus, which was powered by Speatsh's strange nitroglycerin melody. Barbara maintained a relaxed stance, her face beaming with entertainment.

Cadence reloaded her weapons.

Put it on, the mask ordered.

Cadence dropped one Uzi back into a holster, without dropping Bogi from the sight of her second. She slid the hated mouthpiece onto the mask; bit down on the inner ring to hold it in place and quickly shoved a cylinder inside. It lightly locked into place.

Bogi's transformation ended. He stood on all fours and now held perhaps the size and muscle of a jaguar, but with more of the forward tilt of a bear. On all fours, he stood half as tall as Cadence, which might have brought some comfort to her, except that he wasted no time deciding to leap for her.

She dropped. It was a simple tactic really, she just pretended to let her body succumb to the pain of her ankle. It was a stupid gamble. He'd attack straight past her. Cadence would then run, perhaps accomplish a few effective dodges and sprays of bullets to help her make it to the tunnel that led to the trophy room. With such tight quarters in the tunnel, no creature could dodge her magnificent aim. It was a solid plan, but as she regained her footing, the flood of pain shot up her entire leg and into her waist.

She was wrong. It wasn't that she hadn't felt the pain with the mask on, it was that her pain had been amplified so much that it magnified numbness as well, but a new pain lit within her. This one was fresh, something new that only comes from ignoring one injury to create another. She didn't know what it was. All she knew was that it was too much. She doubted she could muster the presence to dodge another attack.

The cat's mouth drew wide as if trying to roar, but no sound came out. He snapped his mouth shut. A pointy beard drew tight within the crevice between his fat canines. These canine roots crawled far up his brow and out the back of his head, where they curled like the anorexic horns of an outcast ram.

Bogi, leapt, but not for Cadence, for one of the underground walls. He scaled a set of cavernous spikes and dropped from the ceiling at his opponent Cadence let herself fall sideways. Four gashes appeared in her arm, and she struggled to decide whether to scream or to somehow find a way to create another opening to escape. Bogi leapt to another wall and rebounded straight for her.

Cadence blew as hard as she could into her cylinder and stumbled to the side. When she regained her footing this time, she found that Bogi now danced in his own agony, slamming the ram-like roots of his tusks into a calcified pillar until it toppled, cracking into a couple of large chunks against the floor around him. They unfortunately blocked her escape route in that moment.

Time to trust me, the spirit of the mask said somewhere deep inside Cadence's brain. *Let me lead, just for once listen to me.*

Yet, Cadence had already thought she wasn't leading.

You'll only confuse yourself, The spirit argued. *I can possess more than the body.*

Before Cadence could think a reply, Bogi kicked a chunk of the broken pillar at her and, this time, she didn't dodge. Her chest crackled. She knew broken ribs and would never forget that injury. Although the pillar had fallen away, it still pressed the last of her air out of her lungs. She reached for a gun, but crumpled instead completely to the floor. She tried to stand, but found herself on her back.

This was a bad time to realize we were symbiotic. The spirit spoke into Cadence's brain.

Bogi now appeared over her. He gripped a section of the broken pillar in his smallish palm with long, crescent claws and slammed it down on her chest once more.

More cracking. Something stabbed her insides. She couldn't make a sound, though she sure tried. All she was able to cough up was a bitter, warm taste.

One of her weapons discharged, amusing Bogi, and giving Cadence a second try to cough up some of the warm bloody syrup that now blocked her breathing, but the mouth piece and the empty cylinder held it in. Her other alternative was to drink it down as quickly as it filled her mouth.

Bogi threw the chunk of pillar to one side of the room, then kicked Cadence to the other. Something sharp sank into her back and kept her from sliding down the wall, which was now behind her. Strange how she realized that she would have taken more comfort in being able to fall for once. Good, however, was that her empty cylinder had fallen from her mask.

Cadence coughed a river of blood, doing her best to spray as much of it as she could into Bogi's face as he drew near once again.

The saber-toothed monster looked her over one last time as if to relish his goodbye. He opened his mouth, turning his head sideways so his jaws could find a large enough angle to fit Cadence's head in to gnaw upon until his teeth could crack open her skull for an easier feast.

Just then, a ball of brown and black interrupted the attack. Bogi stumbled away from her, surprised and trying to recover from the ambush set upon him from the Doberman pinscher whose ferocity Cadence knew could only belong to Nick.

Nick railed into the saber-toothed monster, as only he would have. His bites, maneuvers and clawing were more maniacal than Cadence had ever known. He bit Bogi on this side of his shoulder, rolled to the other side and bit again, feeble bites, but annoying enough to keep Bogi off of Cadence. The Doberman, filled the air with canine obscenity as he dodged and fought the prehistoric feline. Nick bit at Bogi's throat, wormed around his back and chomped at his shoulder blades before working his way down to Bogi's hind quarters for similar attacks.

Bogi attempted many times to counter, but may as well have been swatting at an elusive fly who knew how to predict a swatter—worse yet, could withstand the blows.

Now, don't think Nick had planned such maneuverability. He was hardly graceful. He seemed to bite at whatever was in front of him, all the while taking the brute force of Bogi's swipes, sometimes dodging, and other times appearing unfazed at the stripes of blood that appeared in his silky sheen.

Cadence expected no less out of Nick. She was grateful now, but would be more so later if she survived and when he might be human.

A second Doberman appeared, this one more reserved, less chaotic. He circled Bogi and Nick's battle, assessing. Dustin was careful that way. He dodged when he needed, and his attacks seemed more methodical: biting at Bogi's joints when they were loose and bent to keep his attacks contracted; chomping at the line of ligament in an extended armpit to retract the strength and power of one of Bogi's swipes.

Bogi screamed at one bite made to his hind knee, one revealing a torn chunk of flesh. He made a dry growl. At this, the thoughtful Dustin locked his jaws over the left side of Bogi's face and ruptured the sabertooth's eye with his tongue. He made sure to drain and swallow its pieces and juices so that there was nothing left to repair.

Before Dustin could launch his next attack between Bogi's anger and Nick's anxious uprising, Barbara grabbed the Doberman Dustin by the scruff of his back.

She hurled his body against the ground. Nick leapt from Bogi, who was now shaking his head in confusion, and charged Barbara. She side-stepped and kicked Nick into a pillar headfirst, where Nick then stumbled and struggled with a daze.

Barbara returned her attention to what appeared to be the smarter of the twin Dobermans.

"I'm disappointed in you, Dustin," Barbara said.

Dustin retreated from Barbara's reach, never turning his back to her. He eyed both of his foes, one dangerous, the other cursing his half-blinded pain. This time Dustin growled. Cadence hadn't heard him create such intimidation. Even Barbara appeared surprised, but not shaken.

Bogi lunged for Dustin. Dustin retaliated in like, and before either could land a blow, Barbara had Dustin once more by the scruff. She kicked Bogi onto his side.

"A little respect," Barbara yelled down at the saber-toothed cat as she pinned his chest with her foot. "He's like a son."

Dustin flailed and snapped helplessly at Barbara.

"You know me better than to lash out for no good reason," Barbara said. "Jasper led her here."

Dustin stopped struggling.

"If you're ready to listen, then," and Barbara set him back down. "Think about it," she said and released him from her grasp. "She was working with Jasper to help the rogue. We killed him. His body is at the bottom of that well now."

Dustin took in a set of long deep breaths and followed the direction of where Barbara's finger now pointed. He perched himself so that he could make a quick escape or an appropriate attack if he needed to.

At Dustin's compliance, Barbara allowed the defiant Bogi back to his feet. Bogi took stance, his eye socket draining new trails of blood that flicked about like rat tails down his face.

Dustin looked to Cadence and soon found Nick standing guard of her. At this, Dustin coughed. Who knew what was going through his head.

"Go home, Dustin," Cadence said, but not in any language that Dustin would understand. She would have removed the mask to repeat the order, but she couldn't seem to lift her hand away from the top of Nick's head as he continued to dangle on the wall.

"She's trying to convince you to kill me," Barbara said, realizing that Dustin didn't know the language. "Does that sound like the Cadence you know?"

Yes, it did.

Barbara had given herself away. If Cadence had been a traitor, she wouldn't have been wasting what appeared to be her last moments feeling Nick's head one last time. That was the behavior of a friend. Knowing Cadence as he did, he believed that if she had been beaten as she was now, she would have been begging them to flee, to warn Josh, to go home.

No. They were all going home.

Dustin moved. He dove to Barbara's side and leapt up her back to her shoulder, but never finished his attack.

This time Barbara took him by his throat and held him before her.

"You could have hat my power," she said plainly. Then she threw Dustin straight up to the ceiling, skewering him into the sharp, young and unforgiving stalactites.

Cadence watched him as his body set into the long, cavernous teeth, wishing him to have some super-ability to survive the encounter, but he made no movement nor sound. He began to make his transformation back into his human self, that transformation that only came with a full moon or with death.

"Do you think you can handle these two on your own," Barbara asked. Her voice might have quivered in an emotion other than anger—but Cadence didn't have time to decide this moment, she was too busy dying.

Bogi said nothing but prepared to pounce. While Nick prepared his own defense, Cadence prepared to die with her friends, soon to greet Nick into heaven herself.

Then, finally, Jasper decided to come up for air, startling the entire room as he spit up water and took in a deep breath.

He pulled himself out of the well, laughing, coughing and breathing, mostly for dramatics, hopefully to appear weak so that someone might make the mistake of assuming advantage.

"Why do they always rebel," Barbara asked. "You of all people should have known to stay down there."

"And you should have known better than to let me feed," Jasper replied.

Barbara started to speak, but Jasper was faster.

"Why wouldn't you choose to hide out in a penthouse in Brazil? Security is so wonderful there these days," Jasper said. He took on the cold demeanor Cadence was more familiar in seeing in him. Jasper walked to a small patch of mud where he had first fallen in the cave. Then he kicked at it, and his walking stick leapt up to his hand. He poised himself upon the cane like some magnificent circus ringmaster about to welcome the crowd with a lively song and dance. "Nothing says royalty like a hole in the ground," Jasper said. "I expect that behavior from cats, but not from a dog." With a quick glance to Bogi, "Oh, sorry."

Barbara leapt for Jasper. It wasn't the leap that appeared to startle anyone. It wasn't the stride she took that could have easily been a quarter the size of the cavern that frightened Cadence. Yet, the fact that she left the ground from her human form and changed into her white ancient self before she even landed down in front of Jasper, surprised everyone—except Jasper, it seemed.

Jasper back flipped in that moment, with what appeared to be minimal effort, then landed on the stone rim of the well and perched himself once again against his cane. His face suddenly drained of blood, white and all emotion. "I'll bet you didn't see this one coming," he said.

They leapt from the well like long, black throwing knives, and lunged for Barbara and Bogi. Hundreds upon hundreds of the leeches, thousands perhaps, rained out upon both foes.

Barbara coiled into a frenzy of fast, simple attacks, slaps and throws as she tried her best to cleanse her flesh of the blood suckers.

"I'd never thought of trying to turn an animal before," Jasper said. "It just seemed so undignified. I have to wonder what kind of inept wolf would resort to turning animals, but then we did run into your rats, and then there's also your stone age Hello Kitty there. I suppose if one doesn't understand the business and was prone to a taste for barn vermin." Jasper's careful direction of his final comment didn't seem to be received well by the saber-tooth, as he too laid into his onslaught of vicious worms.

"You have a leech just there in your ear Puddy Tat. Might want to get that," Jasper added.

Cadence's firearms spit several diamond rimfires from the sides of her Glocks, which Bogi and Barbara had little difficulty maneuvering around, especially since her aim was barely strong. Still, she felt she had to try.

The entrance leading from the river and tunnel of roots filled with crackling explosions.

"I see you've called for help," Jasper said. "Isn't this exciting. You have friends, and I have friends." He laughed. "It's like Yulin, but who brought the cat." Then Jasper moved. He'd built up the illusion enough of a taunting bystander with no interest of getting into a fight he couldn't win. In fact, Barbara was now ignoring him, and so he moved for her first.

His blade skillfully caught Barbara. She seemed surprised that Jasper had invaded her so suddenly. She screamed in anger, annoyance and hatred.

Jasper screamed back. Both fell silent and stared each other down, neither willing to make a move that would open themselves to a deadly attack.

"Ah, to hell with it," Jasper finally said, breaking the silence, and quickly snapped his middle finger into Barbara's nose.

Barbara reeled back, most likely in surprise of such a feeble insult, and kicked Jasper away from her, or he let her think she'd caught him. He was fast. He rebounded quickly, dove to a wall and ricocheted towards Bogi—who was again after Cadence, despite the continual onslaught of leeches swarming him like bees. It would have been a smart tactic to make Jasper react, the worms growled and hissed their warnings to Jasper who suddenly understood the language of leech. He commanded them to continue their best efforts to sap the fight from both Bogi and his queen.

Jasper landed beside Cadence, where he held Nick back from executing a poorly-timed attack on his part. He smashed his palms against the outsides of the roots of Bogi's canines. Bogi rebounded quickly, well out of Jasper's reach and shook his head.

"They have implants to help with that pain now," Jasper mocked.

Barbara had yet to give chase to Jasper, probably waiting for the right calculation. She turned an instant and snapped up a leech that had found a particularly annoying spot to feed on her back.

Exactly the type of move as Jasper had hoped. He threw his sword, and it stuck in Barbara's inner thigh before she could even think of launching her next attack for Jasper.

"A lot different when you're not fighting snail-like reflexes, isn't it," Jasper asked. "Shall we see how well your reinforcements can keep up?"

The tunnels now rumbled and shook the holy ground before the circle of dogs.

Barbara tore Jasper's sword from her leg and threw it back at the old man. Jasper, mostly for show, caught it in his sheath; quickly drew it again and sliced Bogi's shoulder open during a simultaneous attack.

Barbara charged Jasper, and even Cadence could see that the old man couldn't duck it, but the attack never landed.

Reinforcement had arrived.

She charged into the room, a filthy mummy of sorts, the steel post from her left arm retracted while a second pole on her right arm expelled several yards, narrowly missing Barbara's throat. But the next telescopic attack, re-emerged from the left arm and popped Barbara in the side of the head. Bogi suddenly darted out of the room towards the tunnel of roots.

This was all Jasper needed. He gave chase to Bogi. "What'sa matter," Jasper cried. "You no like this game?"

Nick took advantage of the opportunity and began searching Cadence for an open gash to start healing. Cadence wanted to tell him about the opening in her back; she wanted to lean forward to help him see it. Nick made his own opening at her collar bone and began to heal her from an entirely different angle. When he discovered the spike of calcium hanging her up through her lungs, he began to remove her, allowing her to fall where he could work on her injuries more attentively.

With greater effort than she imagined it would take, Cadence fired off a few more shots, each drastically missing Barbara, but, more importantly, missing the ancients.

Acotactac's wrists popped with deafening explosions, each either discharging a pole to launch her away from Barbara or pushing Barbara away from her. A few times, Barbara appeared to have outsmarted Acotactac, but Acotactac was uncanny. Cadence could barely see Barbara's attacks, but Acotactac seemed to be holding her own. The Taichomée had taught this lost little girl well.

Suddenly, Jasper was back at Cadence's side and glancing over Nick's work on her injuries. "Good idea," he said. "But imagine that you're rolling a joint with your tongue when you slide the ribs together," he instructed Nick. "You have rolled a joint before, right? Of course you have. You're a jock." He turned to Cadence. "Lovely party, can't wait to see what it's like when we start passing a real one around."

Jasper flew once more at Barbara, and her throat spurt with black as his sword plunged deep into the side of her neck. She refocused on Jasper for just a moment, and that was the moment that betrayed her.

Suddenly, Barbara's body crashed into a set of stalagmite prison bars before a now very alert ancient, trapped within its cell. Acotactac's telescoping poles drilled into her opponent over and over. The poles tossed Barbara into the air, caught her, whirled and flopped her then slammed her into the ground again and again, until the fight had left her. Her body began changing back quickly, her violent responses finally pummeled out of her.

The stream of black blood continued to shoot from her neck. It regrouped and shot out once more. With each spurt it became a little redder in color. She tried to speak but found no words. She looked in Cadence's direction, Cadence was now finding it easier to breathe with less blood filling in her own mouth. Barbara's face twisted, and she appeared to try to break Acotactac's clamps over her. She lunged for Josh's sniper.

As she did, Dustin's body finally broke free of the overhead spikes, falling in Barbara's path, surprising her a second long enough for Jasper to make another pass at the queen. His sword punched into her back and through her chest once, withdrew and then poised itself in offensive guard as Jasper planted himself between the deceitful ancient queen and Cadence.

At the sight of Dustin's body, Acotactac's rage erupted. She released another barrage of attacks upon Barbara's body before finally breaking it for good.

"She's dead," Jasper yelled.

Acotactac punched Barbara with a pole again anyway. Her lips curled as if to cry and turned away.

Nick was now at Dustin's side. He nudged his friend's body, licked one of his smaller wounds and pressed him again.

Dustin made no change. Jasper pushed Nick out of the way and bit into his bicep. He jostled with Dustin's body for a few moments before finally withdrawing a strange twisted tongue from the open wound he had just created.

Just then, it was silent. The fountain dripped. The leeches crawled back to their well. No one made a sound until Jasper placed his ratted and dirty sports coat over Barbara's shoulders.

"She still deserves some respect," Jasper said. He was about to help Nick return and tend to the rest of Cadence's wounds when Bogi bounded back into the room. It almost caught Jasper off guard, which seemed to frighten the old man, but Acotactac unleashed a frenzy of attacks preventing whatever the sabretooth's next intended feat was. It gave Jasper the time he needed to regroup and lay his own tactic into the cowardly monster.

Bogi retreated back into the tunnel of roots, Jasper followed once again. Acotactac pursued behind them both.

Sounds of battle erupted. Cadence would have followed to help, but was too busy enjoying her health returning to her body, all while realizing the flu-like symptoms of healing dog saliva were already beginning to take their hold on her own physical and mental stability.

Moments later, the sounds of battle stopped, and Jasper returned to the cavern cursing Bogi's escape.

"You're bleeding," Cadence announced at the sight of the large gash down the side of Jasper's neck which turned his muddy, white button-up shirt not so muddy or white anymore.

"So I am," Jasper replied.

"He bit you good," Cadence added.

"No," Jasper replied, thought about it and then relented. "The queen did." Jasper walked over to Barbara. Her body maintained her ancient form. Jasper took his jacket up and slid it back on. "I was wrong," he said. "You don't deserve my chivalry, your majesty." Clear hatred seethed from his every syllable, and, with a sleight of his sword, separated her head from her neck.

"Well," Cadence said looking around the room of entrapped ancients. "This changes things a bit doesn't it?"

5 ~ Ring Around the Rosie

The sign read: "Thirsty Sasquatch (keep driving)." A sea of motorcycles between his unmarked police vehicle explained specifically why that was.

This time she stood under her own strength, and Nick, once again, returned to her side, but not before her knees buckled beneath her. Cadence wiped her head of sweat and begged whoever would listen to just let her die. In a few moments Jasper appeared with a bowl of something red, which Cadence would discover was a cold, open can of oil-clumped chicken soup. She laughed, but then realized that Jasper probably didn't remember any better.

She sat a moment longer and ate the mess anyway. Cadence needed something to replace all that she had thrown up. She was certain she'd need something to replace this meal soon too.

Her head pounded and welcomed the cool cloth that Jasper set above her brow to help keep the fever down.

She hated this part. The traces of Nick's healing saliva left in her system from setting her ribs and ankle bones were almost as bad as the breaks themselves had been. She ate quickly, but little, before setting the can down and standing again. This time, it was Jasper who got to her side first. She waved off the two companions.

Meanwhile, Acotactac stood before one of the enslaved creatures. She pounded at the columns of calcium with her poles, chipping them apart. The ancients were all awake now and stood watching the group. The historian was particularly alert. Her eyes flashed quickly about the room and over each creature, paying close attention to those who acted the most. The pillars that once entrapped it were now broken and on the floor.

"What are you doing," Cadence asked.

"Looks like she's freeing them," Jasper replied.

"Why," Cadence asked. "We don't even know what they'll do."

Cadence thought she had pieced everything together. Were they innocent? Really trapped? Were they involved? Regardless, she doubted the rogue had actually been exiled as she had been previously told, but she couldn't explain why he had waited so long to return home. How much more contemptuous history was hidden from her?

Or was Cadence off the mark here? Was it really revenge after all? Had she thought too hard upon it? Had she played her hand incorrectly against the queen? Were the ancients prisoners here, or were they truly hiding?

She believed the rogue knew they were here, yet chose to wander the world.

Why?

Perhaps to wreak havoc; perhaps to live a carefree existence; perhaps to hunt human for the game of it?

Her parents flashed through her mind once more. They hadn't hidden their purpose from Cadence. They were always upfront. She took their teachings as the fairy tale stories of good parents with children who thought magic was real. When her parents died, Cadence had assumed her entire life that her memory of their stories of monsters and great warriors were simply pleasant grasps to remember her happy family. Had they told her everything? Had she forgotten it since her youth?

So what hadn't they told her? She really wanted to speak to Speatsh right now.

Whatever the reason for the rogue's purpose in leaving the circle, Barbara and Bogi had taken great pains to act as wardens over these trapped ancients within this cave. Why would the queen give such power to the rogue as to do his bidding? Clearly, she held him in some esteem to warrant his wishes.

Nearby, Jasper finished tying up a round bundle of bed sheets from the upper floors of the bunker. Despite his fine wrapping technique, red splotches seeped through Dustin's leprous bandaging.

Cadence wanted to be angry—and she was, but for more reason than the lifeless corpse that Jasper tended to. The real blessing for her right now would have been to simply let her pass out and sleep away the flu-like symptoms, but even she knew she couldn't allow that to happen. Unfortunately, she didn't have the time to keep these new developments from Josh and her other friends.

"If I were better at the habit, I would say something to comfort you," Jasper said.

"It's okay," Cadence replied.

"I was sad when my monkey died."

Cadence laughed a moment, but only because she didn't find the comment humorous. From the silence that followed, it was clear that Jasper didn't appear to find her response humorous either.

"We need to move them," Cadence said, and she began her walk towards the tunnel to the trophy room. She limped, not from pain but from muscle memory. She was glad to be healed, but still cringed as though she weren't. She bent over only once to pick up her rifle and check its well-being. "Who knows if Bogi might recruit a few friends and come back."

"Where you going," Jasper asked.

"Change my suit," Cadence replied. "And throw up."

"Wait," Jasper said. "There's something you should know."

Cadence waited for Jasper to continue. "Well," she asked when nothing came.

Jasper winced and checked his shoulder. It appeared almost healed from the recent journey and battle, even through his torn shirt. "It's nothing, we can discuss it later."

*　　*　　*

The cage looked heavier than she remembered. It only made sense that, despite Cadence's objections, Speatsh's pride would have been hurt if he couldn't breathe life into the deathtrap of a contraption again. The fool had repaired it. She tucked her long-sleeved, pull-over shirt into her jeans as an extra precaution to make sure nothing could catch. She found a blade and cut her sleeves short. Then she took up her magnetically-upgraded suit and wondered if it could be salvaged. Even if it could, she didn't know how. She tossed the magnetic clothing into the garbage can. The magnetic suit was so much better that the tank of a cage, but it was too damaged.

Cadence fought the urge to vomit once more, knowing she wouldn't be likely to eat for some time now. Realizing time was short and that she could put it off no longer, she called Acotactac to come help her. Jasper, however, showed instead. When he saw Cadence standing with the leather straps about nearly every part of her body, he frowned. Cadence, like Jasper, suddenly didn't want to revisit the past memory they once held over this piece of armor.

"Her bite isn't healing," Cadence asked, noticing the blood still seeping through his shirt and over his left shoulder. "Shouldn't you be healed by now?"

Jasper took a moment to understand the question. "I should think so."

"You okay?"

"I don't know," Jasper replied. "Her blood is stronger than the rogue's. It's different, cleansing."

"But she's dead," Cadence said.

Jasper pondered the logic. "Isn't that something," Jasper asked. "I feel fine though."

"So what does that mean?"

"Are you under the impression that I would know," Jasper asked.

A set of brass hooks rattled in Cadence's hands as she held them out to her surprising new ally.

"Lend me a hand," she asked.

Once Jasper understood what Cadence was asking of him, and he took the hooks, she turned her back to him. After a brief moment of inspection, and only one failed attempt, Jasper understood how the hooks attached down her spine. He ignored the sound she tried to silence, pretending it didn't happen, but after he attached the final hook, he let her cry a moment more before asking what else he should do. After muffling her tears, she turned back and heaved the strange cage from the floor. She managed it open it and dropped it over her shoulders. Jasper reached once to help her, and Cadence nearly lost her grip when she flinched at the sight of his outstretched hand and flared fingers. He recoiled, clearly ashamed.

After they were both more prepared, Jasper helped attach the smaller cages to her forearms, re-attached the tubes to her thighs and pouches along her belt. She locked two sawed-offs into the tubes; dropped the two familiar pistols into her ankle holsters; and began her search for the flat silver guns that locked into the cages around her arms. She made sure they were loaded.

She could still hear Acotactac's attacks continue against calcified stone from beyond the waterfall. They sounded angrier. What was she thinking letting these creatures loose?

All the more reason that Cadence should be prepared to arm herself in case any of them decided to exercise any further attack upon her.

Cadence pulled open the cabinet of Glocks and began loading the weapons as quickly as she could. When one was full, she asked Jasper to load it into her contraption. Then when she heard the track of chain, hooks and steel ratchet around her body, she screamed at the fact that she had once more put the contraption on.

Jasper inquired if she was OK, to which she responded unkindly.

After loading three weapons to fill one side of the machine, Cadence reached up and felt for the grip of the first weapon. Jasper loaded three more on the other side.

"Have your sword," she asked.

"Always," Jasper answered. He reached for his walking stick and winced. He appeared to stumble a moment before catching himself from spearing Cadence's arm.

"What is it," Cadence asked.

"I thought I heard something," Jasper said holding his head. "Just a headache. Nothing to fret over."

"Can't be her," Cadence said. "Is Barbara alive?"

"It's not her."

"Is it him," Cadence suddenly shivered in creeping fear.

"Seems different," Jasper said. "I'll block it."

Cadence gripped the back of her hair and drew out what she had been able to grow since saying goodbye to her awful prison. "I need you to cut it."

As soon as he did, she gave up any restraint that remained, allowing her tears, fear and hatred for the machine to scream completely now.

"Get out," Cadence lashed out at Nick when his soft footsteps announced his appearance. He quickly retreated behind the waterfall.

A few moments later and she attached the holsters about her diaphragm and secured two .45 revolvers within them. Then she set her rifle into the center of the back of her cage and, after finding what ammo she could to fill her pouches and arsenal, she turned back to Jasper who had rummaged the magnetic suit from the garbage can.

"That thing's going to kill you," Jasper said. He tugged at the edges of Cadence's polarized uniform. "I think I can fix this. Tools?"

Cadence pointed towards Bogi's workstation with the steel desk set in the corner near the entrance by the large double doors.

Jasper went straight to the desk and started rummaging through drawers and cabinets. He withdrew a rivet gun, some wire and some thread.

"I really hate you," Cadence said staring at her wasted clump of red hair littered upon the floor near her feet.

"That's right, you focus that sexist hate," Jasper said. He began mending a tear in Cadence's magnetic shirt. He repaired a few other spots and popped more rivets into the rigid material.

"You sleeping, or turning into a pillar of salt," Jasper asked as he continued repairing Cadence's discarded, black pants.

"Just thinking," Cadence said.

"You have to be careful there," Jasper said. "Many a person's gone crazy doing that."

"Josh's uncle made his fortune trading antiques," Cadence said, after ignoring him long enough. "Did you know that?"

"I'm aware," Jasper replied.

"His specialty was tracking down weapons," Cadence explained. "He found the weapons and brought them back here thinking he was building an arsenal for hunters, but I'm starting to think he was really hiding them from hunters so they couldn't be used against the true monsters."

Jasper hadn't realized this, but he wasn't going to admit it.

"But he built this suit," Cadence continued. "All these weapons at his fingertips and he helped Speatsh build this suit."

Jasper suggested the steel suit she now wore was making her crazy and that she should take it off. She suggested waiting to disarm herself until Jasper had finished his tinkering.

"They designed bullets that could pierce a wolf's skin," Cadence continued. "Why do you think he'd build weapons for hunters when those closest to him would have probably preferred they were disarmed?"

"Maybe they thought they had control since they were here and not out there in hunters' hands," Jasper said, hardly meditating on the question at all.

"Why not destroy them, then?"

"I don't know," Jasper said. "They were idiots maybe. Or maybe it might blow their cover if Josh's uncle thought he was finding weapons, and they kept getting destroyed."

"Do you think it's possible Speatsh didn't know the truth about Bogi and Barbara," Cadence said. "Did you know Speatsh?"

"Every wolf knows Speatsh."

"Did you know he was more than a general," Cadence asked.

"It explains a lot," Jasper said. "I'm good, but I wouldn't have lasted against him when he was pure. Even as a gimp, he was a nasty piece of work."

Cadence laughed. Jasper didn't ask as to why, he was too busy cursing himself for stabbing his thumb with a piece of wire.

"Imagine the look on Josh's face when he hears he has a brother with a huge age gap," Cadence replied and suddenly stopped laughing. "Had a brother."

"We have to move," Jasper instructed.

"Did you sense something," Cadence asked.

"I don't sense him at all anymore," Jasper replied. "That's bad."

"How? If Barbara bit you, and overpowered the rogue's blood, and now she's dead," Cadence asked.

Jasper's work at the desk seemed to freeze at what was coming next.

"Are you still wolf," Cadence asked.

"I'm still wolf," Jasper replied and returned to his task.

"I mean, are you still you," Cadence asked. "Do you know if he's sending anyone after us?"

"I'm sure he is," Jasper replied. "It's all gone quiet. Kind of nice actually, but I can't anticipate him now."

"Is it her? Did she push him out of your head," Cadence asked.

"I've been trying to keep him out of my head for so long, I don't know," Jasper said.

"All the more reason not to sit around here," Cadence replied. Suddenly, she turned and made her way to the side of Bogi's work space. She drew open a bin filled with wire, diodes and a bunch of other small, sharp odds and ends. She rummaged a little more through drawers and retrieved some black earpieces. She sounded hesitant about their operational capacity as she pulled them out but then cheered somewhat after a moment of inspection. She handed off two to Jasper and dropped the rest of the bunch into her own pocket. When she realized that Jasper didn't know what to do with them, she slid one into her ear and tested if anyone could hear her.

"You knew your friends wouldn't hear that," Jasper said.

"I'm willing to try anything right now." Cadence explained. "Bogi helped create the security system here. The rogue will know how to override it, and we can't stay."

"Could try a phone," Jasper said. "Or Instagram."

"I think you overestimate the connectivity of our social circle. If we needed to contact each other here, we yelled down the hall."

Jasper laughed. "I don't think he does know," Jasper said.

"Huh?"

"Speatsh," Jasper said. "I don't think he knew, not everything at least."

"Why wouldn't he," Cadence asked.

"Just pretend I might know what I'm talking about on this one and leave it at that," Jasper said. "I assume you want to take the ancients."

"I hope I don't regret saying 'yes,'" Cadence replied. "If they were his prisoners, we should hide them."

"And if they're not?"

"Let's pretend they're prisoners."

"Guess it's a good thing the mute girl decided to beat up the walls, then," Jasper replied. He held up Cadence's magnetic suit and inspected it. "It's not my best work, but it's safer than that death trap you're wearing." Jasper dropped the rest of Cadence's mended magnetic clothing back onto the table. "Don't ever put that cage on again."

"I don't plan on it," Cadence replied and gladly began to strip the contraption from herself. Jasper helped with what she couldn't reach. The two of them heaped the mess into a pile on the steel desk.

"We could destroy it," Jasper suggested.

Cadence was tempted. "No," she said. "Speatsh made it."

"Back to the river then," Jasper asked

"No," Cadence replied as she began gathering her preferred magnetic armor once more and made her way to the largest set of doors in the room. "Bring them all in here."

"What's in there," Jasper asked.

"A backdoor," Cadence replied before opening the heavy wooden entrance to the blackness of the warehouse of weapons and parking spot for the Silver Bullet.

While Jasper wasted little time dashing off, Cadence spent a little more changing back into her rightful clothes and reattaching her firearms. Then she entered the warehouse and began looking for a light switch. Once she found it, she waited for the flickering fluorescent tubes to all sync to the same steady burn. Two bulbs couldn't seem to find the same beat, and a half dozen of them refused to operate at all, shading the giant room more than she liked.

Where did she start? This place was so huge; she wondered how Speatsh understood where anything was here. What she wouldn't give right now to have Aggon around. He lived in this room, she imagined he would know every inch of the place.

She looked over the empty spot where the Silver Bullet usually parked. That would have been the perfect way to transport the ancients. She glanced over the tall stacks of shelves, dark corners and dusty, brown tarps that covered everything large.

Several shelves held books, most of them old, and Cadence quickly discounted their defensive merit. She doubted throwing any of them at her canine targets would have any necessary effect. Near them, she found four columns taller than she of empty, stacked five-gallon buckets. She found it unlikely as well that they'd be useful in a fight and moved on with her search.

Throughout several alleys of high shelves, she found sets of strange armor. The next three aisles, revealed vases, lamps and jewelry. Five more rows held farm tools. She was tempted a moment by a pitchfork, but when she tried take it up, it gave her chase and stabbed for her heels. She warily dodged the blows until she found a dusty and folded blanket at the end of the row, which she threw down behind her, hoping the pitchfork would trip over it. Instead the blanket immediately wrapped itself around the fork and wrestled it to the ground. The two struggled with each other even as Cadence disappeared into a more open area of warehouse.

Beneath one tarp, she discovered a slatted barrel filled to the brim with black ash. For a moment, she was tempted to touch it, even reached for it to see what a handful felt like—but something inside of it moved, and she thought better of trying her luck. She left the barrel alone.

Under another tarp was a porch swing. Black plastic concealed a red, custom-built, two-seater sports car on tank treads. Another tarp hid a giant, steel ball with a harness for a human being inside of it. Nearby, she found a flat wagon with no wheels, propped on saw horses. Several yards from this, was a large Conestoga: pitched in red; trimmed in turquoise stone and coverings made of skin with long fur. However, as she inspected it more closely, she discovered it wasn't fur, but human scalps. Upon even closer inspection, she was happy to learn that all four of its wheels were where they should have been and in condition to move. It had escape potential. A large barrel sat in the back of the wagon with some piled up coverings overflowing from its brim. She made note of the vehicle's existence.

Farther into the dark quarter of the warehouse, she eventually flipped a switch that added a little more light, revealing another carriage: this one, black from top to bottom. It was finely painted with decorative lines within hand-chiseled canyons. The carriage was mostly square with tinted windows, double doors on each side and a wide back. A crown of jagged pinnacles sat atop it. A small seat that could hold one person, barely two, perched at the front of the vehicle.

Unlike the Conestoga, this cart appeared new. Cadence might have believed it was had she not discovered a golden date of 1680 etched into the side of the driver's seat. The wood, unfettered by time, had only been insulted by dust. Mostly, Cadence appreciated that it had all of its wheels. This one could move too.

"That's also a possibility," she said aloud. Although, she didn't quite know how to pull either of the wagons she had found. Maybe the sports car? But she needed the sports car for something else.

Something rattled in the distance. Naturally, she absolutely had to follow an ambiguous sound, such as this, deeper into the dark warehouse. Who knew what wonder she might miss out on. She sought out the noise. What if it could be helpful?

Back into another maze of steel shelving, she found a mirror that refused to show Cadence's reflection, while the other side of it refused to reflect anything except Cadence. Next to it, she found an unmarked book. It was leather, hard, perhaps a hundred years old. Sitting atop it was some sort of cube draped in black satin. She removed the drape.

"Yes, food," a head screamed within the rusted iron head-cage. "Human! Meaty tastes like moo, kicks like goat." It reviled in its own delight. Its leathery brown face pressed towards the front wall of the cage and contorted as it strained to push its mouth between two bars. He snapped his filed down teeth at Cadence, his jaw bending and forcing its way beyond the cage. Suddenly, it stopped, pulled back, and tried another time or two.

"Not fair," he screamed from behind black eyes. "Hungry, not fair. Not fair!" He smashed his face against the bars and mauve blood began to run from his brow but absorbed into the corners of his mouth. It took Cadence a moment to realize that his long, white hair was tied to the bars from nearly every side of the cage except the front. "Curse hair," the wretched head screamed.

Cadence thought it best to cover the cage and reached to set the fabric once more over it.

Only the head started laughing, which frightened Cadence, and then it started smashing itself in all directions that its tie-downs of white would allow. Suddenly he stopped, grinned through its horrid teeth and watched Cadence.

"Perfume," the head said. "Never forget scent." And then it laughed again, sounding like a slow jack-hammer designed to tear apart confidence. "You give me, I give you. We make deal, yes?" He ended his question by yelling until his face turned white.

"Who are you," Cadence asked.

"What," the head replied.

"Who are you," Cadence asked again.

"I am What," the head shrieked. "Name is What. People ask what is that." At this his voice grew to an unsettling falsetto that was even higher tone than what his voice had already been. "And I say," and his voice trailed into a low mumble.

"I didn't catch that," Cadence replied.

The head muttered again, and Cadence unwittingly began leaning forward to hear, but suddenly stopped and wondered why she would do such a thing.

"Smart girl," the head cooed and laughed. "Smart girl, but give me flesh!"

"No," Cadence replied, and was afraid to cover the cage.

"Then I come to you," and the head began to swing back and forth in its self-grown harness, and here the cage appeared to walk on its own, tipping from side to side, hobbling towards Cadence. "Come to you," he shrilled. "Come to you. Ha, ha! Come to you."

The cage toppled off the ledge of the book, and What went into a flurry of trying to maintain his balance and keep his box from falling over. After a rather clumsy dance that nearly dropped him off the shelf, he squared himself once more.

"My book," he cried. "You find, I gift." He danced some more, occasionally drawing carefully towards Cadence. "You find, I gift." Suddenly he stopped his dance. "Your perfume. Aha! You are fish, need raspberry."

Cadence reacted as she naturally knew best: she drew one of her six-shooters and held it to What's head.

What laughed before suddenly biting the gun from Cadence's finger and quickly eating it. Chewed up filings rained from What's neck.

"Not flesh," What said sadly through a mouth of metal and diamond cartridges.

"I'm sorry I woke you," Cadence said and attempted to carefully toss the black fabric over the cage.

"But I give you treasure," What said.

She should have ignored him, but she couldn't help it. She was far too fascinated.

"Give life, and I give treasure."

"Give life," Cadence asked.

"Give finger," What cried and propelled his cage for Cadence. She tried to avoid the attack, but he was fast enough to tear a chunk from her bicep. He landed on another shelf across the aisle, nearly toppling onto his side, but then did topple. Cadence screamed, trying to cover the sudden eruption of red running from her flesh where What had bitten her.

What swallowed Cadence's flesh, savoring the very last taste of its single bite. Nothing fell from his neck.

"Give life," he announced. "Now you get treasure."

Her first instinct was to kick What in the face, but wondered what might happen to her foot if she did. Instead, she bagged the cage in the cloth and rattled it against the concrete floor, all the while screaming, until suddenly she dropped the cage and felt herself being pulled back.

Jasper asked something; Cadence didn't know what, but she figured it out once she realized Jasper was stunned by the blood left on his hand after letting her go.

Moments after calling for him, Nick appeared at Cadence's side and, once again, began to fill her body with healing saliva and more flu.

"Give the life, now get treasure," the fabric with What's cage repeated until Jasper finally took the initiative to discover the clamor. He took up the concealed cage by its edges and removed the fabric.

What screamed at the sight of Jasper. The head's mouth contorted to bite through the space between the bars. Each snap of his teeth was fierce and hangry. Jasper dropped the cage and quickly covered it again.

"I like him," Jasper said. He took up the cage, this time carefully gripping the bottom side, which seemed to be out of reach of the maniacal head's teeth.

"I know what you are," What cried. "I know what you are. Foul! Bad! Evil! Worse than me."

"I'm sorry, what did you say?" Jasper asked, and he twirled the cage by the length strands of What's hair. What tried to answer, and Jasper bumped the cage against the metal shelf several times. "I just can't understand you when you're like this." Jasper harassed What a little longer before finding an empty slot on a different shelf, than Cadence had found him. He set the cage on the shelf and then assumed correctly to cover the cage with the black cloth. What objected, and Jasper rattled the cage with his cane.

What continued his tirade against Jasper. Jasper appeared amused, but not so much as when he quickly flipped the cage upside down.

"Evil," What cried. "Not funny."

Jasper covered the head and cage once more before returning to Cadence. "Now, I'm going into the other room to start bringing in the old geezers. Stop making enemies with the exhibits."

"Remember treasure," What demanded from beneath his cowl. "We made deal. You take treasure."

"What treasure," Jasper asked.

"I think he means this book," Cadence said taking up the leather book. "It was under his cage."

Jasper lifted the book from Cadence and rifled its pages, they were filled with nonsense scribbles. "We'd need a rooster to translate these scratches."

"Not chicken scratches," What replied.

"I'm sorry, I have to know," Jasper said. He removed the black fabric once more from the cage.

"Not tell you anything," What huffed. He rocked his cage once more until it fell on its side. Then he threw a tantrum when he couldn't rock his cage upright.

"All right," Jasper said and he turned the head right-side up. "Now, I helped you. You tell me now."

"I write," What explained as the fluorescent light settled on his face once again. "Old language. See? Have pen." What rattled around in his cage until an oxidized tip of a fountain pen appeared from within one of his vines of hair. Through his maniacal rattling, the pen began to slide down the side of his face. A little more shaking and What caught the silver tip in his mouth, then he manipulated the pen along his lips until the opposite end was between his teeth. "Write more, but have no ink."

"What did you write," Jasper asked.

"Never tell anyone," What replied. "Why trapped in this room."

"For your treasure," Cadence said.

"They ask," What said. "Like him, dogs too, ask. I read them book."

"You bite me, and I get a book," Cadence asked.

"Book not treasure," What replied. "What not written in book what is treasure. I not read dogs all because no more ink, plus not like dogs, so shh, not tell them what in head. I not tell anyone what in head. I give what in head for eat. I give you farmer's son."

"Farmer's son," Jasper asked. "Who cares about a farm boy?" Then his face suddenly changed into something confused, frightened and pale all at once, and his face fell deeper into this state with each passing moment until What suddenly laughed.

"See, you know my treasure, What not so nutty-nut! Ha-ha, huh?"

"The farm boy? You know where he is," Jasper asked.

"No," What said as he smiled back through dark chiseled teeth and shook his head. "Know who does though."

"Who else have you told," Jasper asked.

"No one," What replied.

"Bogi?"

What hissed. "Monster! Poke with stick! Disgust! Disgust! Drown in litter, may he! Not tell him anything. Not tell filthy Speatsh or anyone who cover me in black blanket!"

"If I free you, you'll tell me," Jasper said.

"You're not letting him out of that cage," Cadence said.

"I think that would be a bad idea," Jasper replied. "But he's still hungry for flesh. So treasure for flesh then?"

"Not your treasure. Not your deal," What replied. "Not tell you anything."

"We'll catch you at the storytelling festival, then," Jasper said and covered the cage once more. "We don't have time for this."

"I wait this long," What shouted after Cadence and Jasper as they left him and his book behind on the shelf. "What could always tell someone else who finds me though."

Cadence continued her investigation for anything helpful. As Jasper left the room, Acotactac was entering with an ancient on each side of her, each one using her as a short crutch and ducking through the doorway from the trophy room. They all moved slowly. For now, Cadence directed Acotactac to the empty spot where the Silver Bullet would have been parked.

Again, Cadence returned to her chore of browsing the armory for some transportation.

Jasper returned with another ancient, this one unable to walk on its own. Nick dragged another in, while Acotactac returned several minutes later with two more. Nine ancients now stood against the wall of the confines of what had been the place designated for the Silver Bullet when it was parked in the bunker. The equipment Cadence could find, she didn't seem to understand how to use.

Finally, she stopped to dig through a metal armoire she had come across and started screaming into it when she found nothing but garden tools. She calmed herself and finally tried the obvious.

"My kingdom for walls that could talk!" Cadence threw whatever was in the closet out into the aisle and pressed on in her hunt. "How am I supposed to find anything in here."

Then he answered deep from where he had been left behind, "You ask What. What find anything for smart girl."

Against her better judgment, Cadence found What once more and removed his covering. He smiled at her through his sharp, black teeth. "What give you. What you give What," he said.

"What do you want," Cadence asked.

"Hungry," What seemed to growl rather than say.

"And what do you eat?"

"Bone," What replied. "Best is inside of Bone."

"Marrow," Cadence asked.

"Marrow," What shrilled and followed with a moan of elation.

"What kind of marrow," Cadence asked already wishing she hadn't.

"The darker the better," What replied. "That my promise. I give you. You give me."

"All right," Cadence replied. "When you sprout arms and can pull a wagon, we'll talk."

"Finger first," What replied coolly.

"You still owe me for the flesh you took. Pay up."

"That was different deal," What replied. "Flesh for treasure. Finger for pulling wagon."

"No," Cadence replied. "Help first or I'll pull it myself."

"You cheat!" What's cage shook under his frustration. "First you no take treasure. Now you cheat."

Cadence grabbed the black drape and began to cover What's cage once more.

"A plow," What cried. "It's slow though, so slow, but strong, plow is strong."

"Give me a break," Cadence said and resumed covering the cage.

"Plow breaks barrier. Plow is pulling plow, points to wolf and goes there. Can be steered, Nothing stops plow." What replied. "Slow and steady. Always get there though."

"You mean it follows a wolf," Cadence asked.

"Follows, yes," What replied. "Look for mountain of rope. Plow hangs on the wall over it. Hates the wall, needs the ground. Finds wolves in the ground, but can't move fast. Easy to track too. Now finger."

"What if I give you an entire body?"

"You have," What's face couldn't hide the excitement.

"It's possible."

"For body, forget plow," What said. "I pull cart myself."

Cadence laughed and realized she'd been suckered into a realm of nonsense.

"Much faster than plow," he said. "Oh yes, much faster than old plow."

"And smaller, and impossible," Cadence cried.

"Not with body," What said. "I pull with body."

"Why didn't you mention that before," Cadence bellowed.

"Not like you," What said. "Not like you at all."

"Fine," Cadence said. "Where's your body."

"Albania," What replied and laughed.

"Give me a break," She started to cover the cage.

"But What use any body, you give it him," What said. "Then What pull."

Cadence would have slapped the cage if she didn't think she'd lose a hand.

"You're certain you can do this," She asked.

"Yes, and then give you treasure to complete other deal."

"All right," Cadence said. "I'll get you a body, but you bite me again and the deal's off."

What cooed. "What wait here."

Cadence started to cover the cage again.

"What said he would wait," He yelled.

"I'm sorry," Cadence replied. "I thought you preferred the blanket. You seem capable of moving on your own."

"Not with blanket on," What said. "Blanket too heavy for cage."

Cadence set the blanket on the next shelf down and wondered if she should have while she walked away.

"What waiting," What yelled after her. "Don't make him go postal."

By now, Jasper had returned to the room and set down another two bodies: one, Cadence remembered yawning earlier. The other was Dustin wrapped in bed sheets.

Acotactac entered the warehouse accompanying one last ancient—the historian, this one still quite different from the rest of her weakened and lethargic family. The ancient remained alert, her eyes glancing over the bodies, among the living and then scanning her surroundings. She made no sound as she observed that which lived around her. She was cleaner than the others too and didn't need to use Acotactac like a crutch.

"I know I'm still new to your little club here," Jasper said. "But Bogi should have been back by now."

Acotactac shrugged.

"As much as I'm raring for a fight," Jasper said. "I have a more important debt to settle."

And that's when Cadence noticed, Jasper was smiling.

"What's changed," Cadence asked.

"Clarity," Jasper replied. "Ah, that'll do." Jasper sprinted to a 55-gallon, steel drum and cheered that it had its lid. He tore it out from under the broken wagon and barely seemed to care as the wooden bed fell over and cracked. He found a bucket a moment later.

"What's that for," Cadence asked.

"It's empty," Jasper replied. "I intend to correct that flaw."

"There's a wagon over there," Cadence pointed out the Conestoga, assuming the black carriage was too small to carry all of the ancients and cargo in one load. "I might have a plan, just make sure your bucket isn't taking up any seats."

"Sure you want to leave this place," Jasper asked. "It's not poorly defended."

"We got in and took it over," Cadence replied. "And we didn't know the cavern was here."

"True," Jasper said. He hopped up on the side of his steel drum and rode it out of the warehouse as though he had been a master log roller at some time in his abnormally long life. Cadence thought perhaps he probably had been.

Cadence, herself, returned one last time to the trophy room to replace the gun and ammo that What had eaten. This time, she also looked for a flare. She found one. Although, she had already failed once before, she tried contacting anyone who could hear her earpiece.

"I know this is a dumb question," she yelled after failing to get a response a second time she asked it. "Do you think these ancients could walk it on their own?"

Her question was answered with a sound of Jasper picking a fight with growls and snarls from the cavern behind the waterfall. Cadence pulled the mask over her face and immediately put two bullets through the skull of a bull mastiff just as it burst through the wall of water.

No one else, the voice said.

"You sure," Cadence asked.

"You okay in there," Jasper's voice called from behind sounds of white water in the diorama.

"We're fine," Cadence replied.

"Sorry," Jasper called back. "One of 'em got by me."

Cadence pulled the mask away. "What," she cried. "I found you a body. Come and get it."

"What coming and getting," the maniacal head announced over the rattling of steel as his cage wobbled side to side, bouncing into the room. What laughed at the sight of the changing creature. His face smashed against the front of the cage in anticipation, much as it had done when she had first encountered the strange villain. His head swung on its tied down tufts, and suddenly the iron box leapt into the diorama and then onto the fallen scout within the pond. He began to devour the monster's scalp, laughing, choking, coughing and vocalizing the satisfaction of his dinner.

Cadence tried not to watch, but was too mesmerized at the strange sight to turn away. That is, until the crunching and cracking of skull and the sound of slurping. She turned away and found it upsetting to have been desensitized to such a gruesome scene, yet the sound of What eating turned her stomach.

What called her attention back.

"You see," What asked, his face and front of cage masked in red. "You see what What can do. Don't you forget."

"Don't you forget we have a deal," Cadence replied.

"And when deal is over?"

"I told you. You bite me again and the deal is off, which means you'll owe me a refund."

"Maybe What bite someone else then." What broke into laughter again and disappeared into the sounds of his meal.

Cadence returned quickly to the warehouse and found most of the ancients loaded into the back of the red Conestoga made of human scalps. She clenched her hands to hide their shaking from what she had just witnessed of the head in the cage, only to find herself facing similar gore in the wagon itself.

Acotactac helped the final, remaining and weak ancient into the back of the flat carriage while the historian climbed her own way in, taking time to feel and observe the texture of the wagon's walls.

"That would be a good clue we don't have long then," Jasper replied upon reentering the warehouse. He log-rolled the now-sealed 55-gallon drum. Sounds of water sloshed beneath his feet. He hopped off the barrel at the back of the wagon and decided it might be wiser to care for the barrel himself rather than push the capacity of the old wagon too much. "So what are we doing," he asked.

Cadence tried to think through the too-much-noise in her head. "If Josh wakes up, how dangerous will he be to us?"

Acotactac's face suggested concern. Jasper, himself, appeared to inquire of Cadence and then of Acotactac.

"Got me. I'm just the company," Jasper explained. "But if he wakes up out there, he may be a danger. He might need someone strong to break him otherwise."

"Thomas can stand up to him," Cadence said.

"Hope you're right," Jasper said. "In a confrontation between Josh and Thomas, I'd probably put my money on Thomas too."

Cadence suddenly screamed, turned and shot off a revolver into the concrete wall.

"The rogue knew everything," Cadence shouted and holstered her weapon. "All this time, Josh's heritage was on the other side of that waterfall, and they hid it so Josh could kill us when he turned. I don't buy it. I thought I could, but I don't know why. Tell me why!"

Jasper didn't attempt to answer. He recognized a one-sided conversation when he heard one.

"Tell, me toymaker," Cadence said. Jasper glared. "Why would Speatsh Cheatham spend time looking for an entrance to the ancients' hiding ground if he already knew where it was?"

"Logic would suggest it was because he didn't know," he stopped almost smiling. "He didn't know where it was, just like Bogi said."

"Why wouldn't Speatsh know where it was if this was all just a con to turn Josh on us," Cadence replied and then quickly answered herself and fell deep into thought again. "Because they didn't trust him. Why? Because he gave up being a wolf? No, Barbara gave up being a wolf too. He discovered something didn't he? That's why Josh's oracle uncle had to tell Speatsh where to start looking. Did Richard know some of it? What did he say? 'Convince them all to hide.' That's it!"

Jasper clearly didn't get it, so Cadence explained.

"We misunderstood him," Cadence nearly shouted herself out of her skin. "He said to find them and convince them all to hide. 'If they're in hiding, maybe the rogue will withdraw,' that's what Richard said. They weren't in hiding. The rogue wasn't worried about finding them. He knew where they were. If Josh and Speatsh found the ancients together, they could free them and hide them somewhere new."

"And weed out the truth about their captors," Jasper added.

In one final breath, Cadence added, "So, I was right. Speatsh wasn't helping them." At that last thought of Speatsh, she would have cried if she didn't understand what she needed to do. "We do, indeed, move these ancients out of here completely. If the rogue doesn't know where they are, maybe that will delay whatever he has planned." Then the realization of the futility of this idea struck her. "Doesn't matter where we hide them, he's connected to them, isn't he?"

"You know," Jasper said almost hemming over the thought. "As dumb as this might sound, maybe we could blindfold them, keep them from seeing where we move them."

"Yeah," Cadence said. "And maybe—and I'm just thinking out loud here—maybe, we could give them earplugs and freeze them in carbonite while we're at it."

"Don't know unless we try," Jasper said. "And don't think I don't get your sarcasm."

"We need to move this wagon," Cadence said. "What said that there's a plow in here that can do it."

"No," What denounced. "The deal for the body is I pull the cart, young lady. You kept your end, now I keep mine. Always pay on your deals."

Cadence had nearly attacked the creature that walked into the room. She saw What still in his cage, but it set now sat atop the headless corpse of the human that had been a bull mastiff. She wondered if What realized his new body was naked. She wondered if What knew what naked was.

"I help and you pay," What said. "I honor deals, as long as there is a deal to honor." His cage wobbled, and his body skipped towards one of the barrels with black ash. He breathed deeply, savoring the moment of a memory long visited. Then he reached into the barrel. The ash drew away from What's hand, as if repulsed by his presence. He withdrew a bone—a femur of some creature perhaps, maybe even a human. He inspected it for a moment. A row of small holes lined its entire length. He twirled the bone in his palm, drew one end to his mouth and lightly blew into it.

A soft tone filled the warehouse. What smiled, relieved.

"Ah. Sanity! Sanity! All is Sanity." What said, then as if remembering he wasn't alone, returned his jovial attention upon Cadence. "Oh, how music heals the mind and soul." He pegged out a few more notes on his foul instrument. He quickly ran a scale and began laughing. "A new body doesn't hurt either."

He continued to play a few more scales before stopping and appearing lost in the silence that followed.

"Been so long," he said and seemed pleased with himself.

"You still remember how to put clothes on, right," Cadence asked.

Suddenly What fell serious. He may have even been blushing.

He gave life to more notes from his flute, and several handfuls of black ash leapt from the barrel, painting his body in what appeared to be an old frilly tuxedo with a high collar, drawstring shirt and knee-lenth pantaloons. All of his instant clothing, including his smooth stockings and buckled shoes, with their high heels were black. Another note sang, and a black cap and feather grew atop his head, impaled throughout his cage, the feather bobbing out the back bars. His restraining bolts of hair pierced through the skin of his haberdashery as though tailored to fit each knot and strand, which still held his head in place within the bars.

"Many years ago, I rescued a village from the plague," What explained and began playing again.

"You were a doctor," Cadence asked.

What laughed and blew a few more measures of music. "I lulled the rats right out of the town, and let them to the sea to drown. But when the villagers refused to pay their debt, I took what they owed me with interest."

"What exactly would that have been," Jasper asked. His tone, rather his seriousness, frightened Cadence. She would have asked him what his thoughts were if it wouldn't have given away her own fear.

What stopped playing and appeared almost offended at the question. "Their future," What replied.

"I don't understand," Cadence said.

"I took their children," What explained. He seemed to relish Cadence's ignorance, or maybe it was her buried fear. He broke out laughing.

"I know this man," Jasper said in realization. "We've passed ways."

"Monster's remember monsters," What replied.

"Monster," Jasper asked. "Is that what you demon's call yourselves now?"

Cadence was about to demonstrate her further ignorance of the topic of conversation.

"Every child knows this man," Jasper said, as though anticipating Cadence's lack of understanding. "He is the pied piper."

"You aren't seriously suggesting he's that fairy tale, are you," Cadence asked.

What dug his hand into the barrel of black soot. "The ashes of my payments owed," What replied and blew out a few morose note combinations. "The villagers thought they had gotten their revenge when they beheaded me, but everyone knows you burn a witch, you don't behead them." He rattled off a few measures of whatever tune he was playing, but suddenly stopped. "And you definitely don't take the head, when you realize you made that mistake, and craft it into an unbreakable cage without a lock, or he'll take the debt out on the village—adults as well, even though he is just a head."

He played something more joyful and, in the middle of a crescendo, stopped. "I'll move your friends to a new hiding place, because I honor my contracts."

"And then you're free to run off, aren't you," Cadence acknowledged.

"Our contract will be fulfilled," What replied.

"No," Cadence replied. "I won't help a child murderer."

"A new deal then," What suggested.

"Don't," Jasper urged.

"Deal is you stay here," Cadence said. "Guard this vault and never leave."

"Indentured servitude," What replied. "Not very appealing. What do I get?"

Cadence didn't have an answer.

"Bad bargain," What replied. "I will go my way when our deal is done."

"I'm thinking—."

"Help us fight then," Jasper interrupted.

"No bloodshed," What replied. "My children are innocent."

"Then help us how you can," Jasper said. "As long as you can."

"As long as I can," What asked. "And what do I get?"

"Corpses," Cadence said. "All the fresh corpses you could want."

"Not your contract anymore," What retorted. "Someone else started the deal you could not finish."

"Corpses," Jasper returned just as quickly. "All that comes from our war. You can join any battle and have first rights to any body, just as you got that one, dead."

"Not hunters," Cadence retorted.

"Not your deal," What said, then turned back to Jasper. "Deal."

"Wait," Jasper said. "She's right, no hunters' lives."

"The deal is cast," What said. "You offered. I accepted."

"Then no deal," Jasper said. "And I haven't accepted yet."

"You break a deal with me," What asked. "Because I take who I want when you break a deal with me."

Jasper thought a moment, then sullenly replied. "No, we are clarifying the current, potential deal. You don't touch the hunters, and I'll give you the son of an ancient."

"Not Josh," Cadence protested.

"And gold," What added.

"No one uses gold anymore," Jasper lied.

"You have it in this room," What demanded. "When you are able to return, you will fill me two sacks of gold and pay me, and if you don't," What's eyes settled upon Cadence. "I've always preferred a bigger family."

"Yeah, he has nothing to lose on that bargain," Cadence yelled.

"When you can promise no more corpses, I get my gold," What explained. "Don't bring me my gold, I take my interest. Break our deal, and I'll be a worse enemy than those wretched wolves. For that, I'll help—as you said, for as long as I can."

Cadence objected. She didn't know where to begin finding gold in this place, but she did know the carriage needed to be moved. She believed Jasper could pull it, but she hadn't asked simply because she'd had her fill of his omnipotent attitude. She should have asked. She certainly didn't need this demon's help, and yet she palmed her Glocks and prepared to shoot the cage off the headless body.

"Deal," Jasper conceded.

Cadence objected.

"Don't worry," What said. "Having a body does a great deal to help with my sanity. I promise, I won't bite."

"Break your word," Cadence said. "And I'll find your Mordor and drop your cage in it myself."

What suddenly appeared confused. "I believe time is short," he said.

He fingered a lively tune into his flute and jigged away from the barrel of charcoal sand. A moment later, a black hand reached up from the barrel and then pulled out the frame of a small boy. More children followed, all ashen from head to toe: boys and girls all in pretty black bows, dresses or trousers. The barrels emptied of contents and laughed, dancing with What as he entertained and jigged them towards the front of the Conestoga, where each child took hold of straps, harnesses, tongue and any grip they could get to pull or push the wagon.

Cadence moved quickly to the large steel door that opened into the tunnel, which led out towards the graveyard. She dragged Jasper behind her out of earshot of What and his immediate attention on the red wagon.

"Have you ever seen someone make a stupid mistake before and you just knew they were going to die," Jasper asked. "Not that I haven't found humor in such mistakes myself."

"Me," Cadence asked incredulously. "You made the deal."

"We need the help," Jasper replied. "We'll worry about his payment later."

"That's bad business," Cadence condemned.

"Yeah," Jasper conceded. "There is that."

"Then you have to at least protect the ancients until we can come back with Josh."

Jasper would have asked why, but Cadence answered too quickly.

"We can hide the ancients in the mausoleums. I wish Oliver was here. He'd know the best ones to throw their scent. Acotactac and I will go for Josh."

"Insane," Jasper yelled.

"We can't risk dragging them in the open across town to the junkyard," Cadence explained. "We have no choice."

"It's still insane," Jasper conceded.

"I have a fear that we've played right into the rogue's hands," Cadence said. "The rogue got us to focus our attention on the outskirts. By now, I'll bet Josh has built himself a nice little fort to fight the wolves. Why would the rogue hold Josh's attention on the other side of town? What's his plan?"

"I don't know," Jasper replied.

"I wish, with that little psychic link of yours to the rogue, that you could," Cadence said realizing Acotactac had been following the conversation and keeping pace the entire time.

"Let me get Josh," Jasper said.

"Josh isn't going to expose himself on the testimony of the arch nemesis who turned his sister into a werewolf," Cadence replied. "Besides, I'm sworn to protect the heir. You can protect the ancients better anyway."

The arrival of the red and turquoise Conestoga, which was powered by happy, dancing, ash-children, interrupted the conversation.

Cadence punched in the correct code, grateful that she only needed to know the code to get out, not the complicated combination that required the Silver Bullet to get in. Getting in these particular doors was much more complex. The steel doors slid open, wide enough to allow an enormous vehicle to enter and exit.

"Think Bogi knew everything about this place," Cadence asked.

"Why wouldn't he," Jasper asked.

"Think he knew the security codes," she asked. "He could have opened them to anyone any time he wanted."

"You're thinking he didn't," Jasper said.

"It's a thought."

"Perhaps, because Speatsh or Richard put in the security system and didn't include him in the process," Jasper added. "Ahh! That makes sense now."

"How does that make sense?"

"It's nothing," Jasper replied. "But you're right. You need to get back to Josh quickly."

"Once we get to the graveyard, we'll leave you to do what you need," Cadence whispered. "If the pied piper is truly a thing of his word, use him." Her volume then grew. "Oliver is probably with Josh by now, but just in case you run into him before we do, tell him that you are Man's friend and talking kitty is trying to hurt his friends. Hopefully, he'll help you, if he doesn't rip your arms off first."

At that, the children of ash hurried the wagon through the door. What danced atop the driver's seat.

"Get in," What invited. "We can pull."

Acotactac leapt in. Jasper retrieved his barrel and chose to ride it as a log instead. Cadence, however, ran back into the warehouse and climbed into the sports car with the tank treads.

Would it start?

It did. It felt rough, the entire frame shook just idling and grew worse as it began to move. She clenched her jaw to keep her teeth from breaking against each other.

She steered the vehicle into the tunnel, its metal tread clanking deafening complaints against the concrete. Once she had driven completely out of the warehouse and onto earth, she took a moment to exit the vehicle and close the steel doors. She climbed back into the driver's seat and reversed the car up tightly against them. She turned off the engine and imagined she could hear sounds coming from the warehouse—or maybe it was her brain rattling, she just wasn't sure anymore.

She stared down the long, earthy tunnel ahead of her, tall enough for the Silver Bullet. Halogen lamps dug into both sides of the shaft, showing the wagon of human skins in the distance and Jasper yelling for What to hold his horses. The bunker must be powering these tunnels too, she assumed and then wondered if electricity had simply returned to the outside world.

She doubted it. She wondered where her strange journey would take her this time. Then she set her footsteps into motion to find out.

She left the car behind her, stopping only a moment to chirp off a diamond bullet into the gas tank. The tank began to spill its contents. Cadence struck the flare she'd taken from the trophy room and threw it under the car. Before she could turn and run, Jasper had pulled her off her feet and steered his barrel back towards the wagon. He dropped her into the Conestoga bed and was ordering What to pick up the pace.

The wagon sped off at remarkable speed, and the tunnel exploded with deafness. Acotactac covered Cadence's ears because Cadence forgot to. The children applauded and hooted and hollered at the spectacular explosion. As the carriage sped down the hall, and its now flickering round bulbs, a wall of smoke plumed past them.

"And the rogue thinks Josh is the dangerous one," Jasper's voice complained somewhere from Cadence's right, hidden by the cloud of dark dirt.

6~ Dark Hymn of Escape

He had purposely not eaten all day so he'd be more believable about why he needed to stop. After several minutes of evaluating the unwelcoming bar, the grey and pepper Miniature Schnauzer yipped an approval, but quickly growled a warning for Detective Harvey Bruce to behave.

From the moment they entered into the well-lighted stone carver's studio, the group fell silent to the sound of battle beyond the exterior doors, which led into Oliver's graveyard. The children's play turned into shushes with each other.

Cadence flew. She turned off the lights in the room then carefully pressed the stone door open, hoping no one would notice the mausoleum disguise giving way. It took some time for her eyes to adjust to the bright of the day and discover the situation.

Outside, police swarmed with weapons drawn, firing upon the hulking giant.

"Guns not fair," Oliver leapt into a small group of officers. He hewed them down with a stone gargoyle, which donned a broken wing and was skewered at one end of Oliver's monstrous staff. A family headstone in the shape of a tall pillar held to the other end. Oliver spun the staff and the stones in front of him, somehow blocking the barrage of bullets firing upon him. He yelled one more time at his trespassers before smashing the chest of one officer with the unforgiving pillar. As the man fell, Oliver's staff made its loud click, and this headstone flew off of his weapon and bowled through a large group of officers.

Another click later, and Oliver hefted a cylindrical-shaped piece of slate with a flat, granite base off a graveside and returned to his defensive reproach.

"There's the man in charge," Jasper said, appearing at Cadence's side. He motioned to a brawny officer taller than most cops.

Cadence quickly spotted the man who shouted orders to the army of officers and SWAT agents.

"That's the cop who helped us escape, Chandler, I think," Cadence said. She drew her rifle into her hands. "Something's wrong. Why would he be here?" She drew her aim upon him.

"Good thinking, boy," Jasper said, gently drawing Cadence's aim away from the Captain. "He's Josh's doing."

"Talk to me," Cadence urged. "Oliver can't keep this up."

"That man went through a lot of abuse the other night to suddenly appear back with the police," Jasper said. "I have a feeling he's Josh's eyes and ears right now. Any defeat Josh's spy suffers will be his death if he fails. Whatever we plan here, the failure to beat Oliver can't be this Chandler's fault. We need a scapegoat."

Cadence watched a cop attempt to sneak upon the giant, grave keeper only to be greeted with the flash of teeth from the Pomeranian strapped to Oliver's back. A female officer quickly withdrew her tactic, cursing whatever was alive in the backpack.

"You stay here," Jasper said and stood his barrel up on end. Before Cadence could ask what he was doing, he ordered her once more not to move and began to push the door open. "If I get their attention, can you get out of here unseen?"

"I'm coming with you."

"Understand how delicate this is," Jasper said. "That man, Chandler, has to succeed or Josh will lose his spy. But he also can't succeed or the rogue may get something he wants, which, for some reason, appears to be Oliver right now. If that's the case, Chandler has to capture Oliver, but he can't capture Oliver. Understand the problem?"

"What's the plan then," Cadence asked.

"If I interfere, one of the rogue's generals will show up and take charge. General to fight a general," Jasper said.

"You want them to catch Oliver," Cadence said. "Why?"

"The only thing I can think of is that the rogue's a trophy hunter," Jasper explained. "Oliver will make a magnificent servant for the rogue, possibly more dangerous than Genre. If I know the rogue, and I do, he knows the cops' bullets won't necessarily kill him."

"I've seen him cry over pain," Cadence said.

"Pain isn't death," Jasper replied. "The general that comes to deal with me will assume he's stepping in to protect what the human cops can't do. The police could never stand up to me. The general and his slaves will step in to face me and take over responsibility to take the rogue's trophy back to him. SWAT will probably focus on me to keep me from attacking the kidnappers. I will retreat and draw the cops' attention. That's why you need to find a sniper's nest. Locate the general, probably isn't too far beyond the gates already. Shoot the general, a belly shot. Two or three if you can. Don't kill him."

"Whose side are you on here," Cadence asked.

"Shooting him in the head could kill him too quickly and the shock will kill his slaves," Jasper explained. "Remember the inquisitor. A belly wound can't be healed by his scouts nor guardians, the stomach acid will eat their tongues before they can act medicinally. Our metabolism is fast, but with enough belly shots, he could corrode from the inside-out before it can save him. The general will die slowly releasing his pack. A good number of them may be willing to bolster your own numbers once they turn human again. If not, they're a danger and we can take care of them later."

"You're assuming a lot here," Cadence said. "You don't know that's what's going to happen."

"Yes," Jasper snapped softly. "I do. It's exactly what I do. I see how things will play out. When this is done, the general, not Chandler, will be the one who failed the master by interfering with Chandler's work. If the general survives long enough, the master will punish him. If the general dies, however, the master will punish the henchman that's still alive, and that looks like it's Chandler." Jasper shifted his weight to move and suddenly stopped. "The general needs to live long enough to take the rogue's punishment. Can you do this?"

Cadence nodded.

"Good," Jasper pressed the door to the mausoleum open and quickly restrained Nick who was under the impression that he was joining the fight. "No," Jasper said, directing the Doberman back of the mausoleum doors. "Not this time." Jasper then sauntered out into the daylight cemetery. "You're not ready to fight humans."

Daylight! Cadence worked better at night. She could hide at night. She wasn't sure how Jasper would distract the entire force to keep their attention off of her. Cadence watched Jasper stroll towards the battle and listened to him greet the officers and demonstrate some of his impressive oral dodges, the likes she'd received herself. As much as she found herself enjoying being on his side when he delivered them, she couldn't get caught watching Jasper, she needed to locate a sniper nest where no one could spot her easily.

Jasper taunted the police and strode up next to Oliver, who nearly took his head off before Jasper was able to say what Cadence had instructed him to, which calmed the cemetery caretaker. Oliver flashed a quick glance over to Cadence who continued to hide behind the doors leading into his art studio. She wondered if anyone noticed his glimpse. Oliver raised his hand, probably to wave to Cadence. Jasper stopped it.

Verbal abuse broke out between the police and Jasper. Jasper appeared to deflect it. Cadence couldn't hear it, but she recognized the insult on the faces of Jasper's new opponents. Gun fire broke out again, which Jasper then dodged and Oliver deflected.

Three police fled. Chandler called after them. Jasper confronted Chandler, and somehow Josh's spy fended off the general, while Jasper dodged his bullets. Jasper grabbed his shoulder, and Chandler managed a miraculous escape. Two more bodies lay still on the ground now. Jasper taunted the police again, and one more officer fell while another fled.

Then something about Jasper's posture changed, he was no longer entertaining himself. This was something she hadn't seen him do, even with Josh.

Several dogs emerged from the street and confidently approached the fight.

A young bald man drove into the graveyard on a pink motor scooter. He seemed to chide Chandler and gestured for his men to leave. Chandler argued. The man on the scooter shoved, and Chandler fell back about ten feet. Cadence had no doubts that this man was the general Jasper had predicted would appear. Her time to move was running out.

Chandler stood, yelling that he wouldn't abandon his mission, and, if the general didn't like it, he could take it up with the rogue himself.

The police who had started to clear out of the area, now returned under Chandler's order. Jasper mocked them further and tossed a glance Cadence's way to share his amusement and to ensure her position.

More dogs filed into the cemetery. Jasper laughed at them too. The general cried an order and launched himself at Jasper, who feigned a stumble and fell backwards, but continued to throw scouts off of him. Oliver too had given way to a mountain of snarling teeth that forced him to the ground. The general gave another order, and the scouts began dragging Oliver towards the gates.

"Oh, no," Oliver cried. "Not to take me away from my home. Foul! Foul!"

Cadence wondered how the general didn't see through his monotone, bad acting. Cracey, still strapped to his back and in her pomeranian form, appeared to put up more of a fight than Oliver did. As the crowd drew Oliver away, Jasper threw the remaining scouts off of him in time to square off against the general.

The bald man engaged Jasper. However, it was Jasper who quickly took lead of the deadly dance, taking his routine into the officers who had been waiting their moment to reenter the fight. In an instant, Cadence found the general's back to her and every police officer on the field. She realized that by staying exactly where she was, she had ended up being right where she needed. Accident? Or Jasper's design? She drew her rifle; the high-pitched glycerin belted its shot straight from its chamber; down the sure barrel and between a maze of headstones.

The general's back arched, and Jasper drove his sword straight into his opponent's belly. Oliver then stood, kicking off mongrels and quickly demonstrating his ability with his staff once more.

The general hobbled towards his scooter, and Jasper made one last superficial slice at the back of his neck. Oliver shattered the scooter with one smash of his cudgel.

Again, Cadence found enough of an opening to fire another shot. The general, mystified, looked to his wounds and began scanning the graveyard for where the injuries had come from. He lurched again as a third slug dimpled his stomach.

Jasper stepped into Cadence's line of fire to suggest she stop now. He called Oliver to his side, and the two regrouped for another bout.

Chandler called his officers off, cursing the imbecile general.

Cadence squeezed off two more shots to the general's lower appendages, mostly just to make him mad. The general fell. His slaves dragged him off without putting up a fight.

"Unbelievable," Cadence said to herself. "That old coot called it."

* * *

Oliver chose the mausoleum to hide the ancients. It was one of the smaller ones, but it could hold the ailing monsters. Oliver provided a little bit of ventilation, after he bashed a hole through the top of each of the four walls. Surely, no one would expect a dozen old wolves to be hidden in something so small. Jasper and Cadence suggested what they thought were more suitable spots, but it was Oliver's graveyard—he buried the people here, even if they weren't dead. He locked the metal doors into the family sarcophagus.

Cadence stood before the entrance to a different mausoleum, hoping to misdirect prying eyes away from Oliver's work. Nick stood at attention beside her, his eyes never wavering from the handful of police officers outside the gate.

Acotactac seemed annoyed, like she needed something to do. She paced, angrily.

Cadence could understand. Even as day drifted away, she felt naked. Sure, guardians patrolled the night, but she could hide in the shadows as well as any wolf, or she thought she could. The presence of birds singing was as no war. The sky was clear and blue; clouds were bright; and sun was starting to hide in the west. She wasn't accustomed to getting her vitamin D this way anymore. How she longed for the night to come quickly.

Acotactac kicked a headstone over and glared at Cadence.

Jasper wrung his hands as he crept up. Cadence turned on him, but quickly withdrew from discharging any harm. Acotactac hardly seemed startled.

"I've always found graveyards a little morbid," Jasper said. "All those dead people make my skin crawl."

"And how many have you sent here," Cadence asked.

Nick huffed.

"It is pretty here though," Jasper replied even though that wasn't the answer Cadence had been looking for. "Oliver has a peaceful eye. He's quite the artist." His gaze wandered off somewhere more interesting, and he took a genuinely long, lost joy in a deep breath. "Tell you what," he abruptly said, startling Cadence. "If I die, bury me here and make my headstone a working toilet. We need more humor in the graveyard. Oh! And put a weight sensor on it so that, when someone sits on it, a hairy paw comes up and tickles their butt."

Cadence rolled her eyes.

"During my little chat with Chandler before he shot me, he requested that we get his family to safety," Jasper said. "Can you do that on your way?"

"Absolutely not," Cadence replied.

"Chandler's a dangerous person to not give what he asks for," Jasper said. "I'd do it, myself, but—you know—I got shot."

"We both know you didn't get shot," Cadence replied. "I've seen you move too many times. You're a good actor."

"I could have died out there," Jasper said.

"You a liah," Cadence replied.

Jasper seemed pleased with himself.

Oliver meandered up and whispered that the old, teddy dogs were all locked up.

Jasper complained that the mausoleum didn't have enough bugs.

"Not run filthy cemetery," Oliver scowled.

"Bugs camouflage the heartbeats," Jasper explained. "Maybe the leeches will be enough noise, but bugs couldn't hurt."

"Why can't we just stay in the workroom," Cadence asked.

"They want something from in there," Jasper replied. "I got it from Chandler. Better not put too many treasures behind one set of doors."

"So you did talk to him."

"Of course I did," Jasper returned. He seemed disappointed that Cadence should think otherwise of his abilities. "I told him to give whatever general showed up room to take command of the situation, but to stand his own in the rogue's name."

"I shouldn't have doubted you."

"Now it's your turn," Jasper replied. "You and the mummy need to retrieve Josh now."

Acotactac grimaced offense over her bandage clothing.

"You're too sober," Jasper cried at her. "There's something wrong with society when it can't even take a knock-knock joke anymore. Knock! knock! Who's there? Me. I'm offended! ."

Acotactac, glared more.

"Fine," Jasper said. "Next time I'll ring the doorbell."

"I'd feel more comfortable going at night," Cadence said ignoring Jasper's antagonizing behavior. "It's easier to go unseen."

"Your call," Jasper said. "And you should take your friend's body as proof."

Cadence complained that she didn't have something to drive.

"There's a nice supply outside the gate," Jasper said gesturing to the numerous officers and their patrol vehicles that stood guard over the entrance.

Chandler had remained with his officers up until an hour ago. His attention was suddenly drawn somewhere else and was compelled to leave. Since then, the remaining officers maintained their distance.

Oliver laughed. At least that's what Cadence thought it was. She imagined it was the sound that a constipated mule might make.

"I sorry," Oliver cried out and then laughed even harder. "Her tickles. Stop that."

Cadence had almost forgotten about her. "Can't you free her? She doesn't deserve this."

"And what," Jasper asked. "Babysit her? She's safer this way."

"And if you die with all the risks you take?"

"I have a feeling, we don't need to worry too much about that." Jasper couldn't seem to contain his cocky smirk.

Cadence watched the giant crypt keeper spin in circles laughing and grabbing at the small Pomeranian who squirmed in her backpack. Unlike the last time that Cadence had seen Cracey, she was less teeth and more wag. She yipped at Cadence when she saw her. Cadence hadn't forgotten that the whole world going to hell had started with her.

"She's stronger than she looks," Jasper added. "Besides, her fast little heart helps mask the sound of the mausoleum."

"Speatsh taught me how to control my breathing to hide," Cadence replied. "Don't they know how?"

Jasper laughed. "I admire Speatsh," Jasper replied. "No, I don't. He was a great hunter, but a bad wolf, nothing worthy of Klingon poetry. Intelligence was not among his strong suits."

"I'll remember that when I reincarnate and plug up your flushing headstone doing crossword puzzles, you jackaninnied bonesnatch," an all too familiar voice snarled. "So," Speatsh sneered. "I was right!"

"It's about time," Jasper howled. "What exactly were you waiting for?"

"Night time, doofus," Speatsh snapped back. "Moron."

She had hardly noticed. The day had gone. Dusk was entering its birth beneath a conquering moon, nearly full. More importantly, Speatsh, or rather an apparition of Speatsh had joined the party and sat on a squared tombstone.

"You knew," Cadence erupted.

"I thought I did," Speatsh replied. "But now I'm confused." He turned on Acotactac. "You look familiar to me."

"You let us all think we were safe in there."

"Weren't you," the ghost of Richard asked. Josh's dead uncle appeared against the side of the mausoleum door closest to Cadence. She greeted Richard with more courtesy than she had allowed Speatsh.

"How long have you known about Bogi," Cadence asked.

"Richard figured out most of it," Speatsh replied and began petting his shoulder. He frowned and abruptly stopped petting himself. "But I wasn't sure about my maternal birther until I was called to come help find my little sister."

Jasper guffawed and nearly inhaled his tongue. Upon the disconcerted looks he received, "Please, can we wait to tell Josh until I can see his face. That's the funniest thing I've heard since Edison said he invented everything, and Gore said he invented everything else. And you have to say it just like that when you tell him. Speatsh." Jasper walked a small distance off, laughing and wiping tears. "Maternal birther. Ha!"

"This isn't the way I thought things would go," Speatsh said. "You have to man up now. Go get Josh."

"However," Jasper said returning red eyed to the group. "If I may make a sugges—," and he started laughing again. "I'm sorry. I'm sorry." He turned away once more.

Speatsh swore at Jasper and punched him in the gut, or would have, except his contact had no effect and passed right into Jasper's lower bowels.

Jasper slumped against a tombstone and blared out a siren of laughter. "I think I'm having an aneurysm."

"Good idea," Speatsh cried and started swiping at Jasper's head, each time his spectral being passing through Jasper's body.

"Come on," Jasper said, unable to contain his laughter at all. "You're embarrassing yourself now."

Speatsh kept slapping, even diversified his moves to punch and kick at other places throughout Jasper's being.

Jasper's laughter slowly eroded. "Okay, now you're getting annoying."

"Really," Speatsh asked while keeping up his barrage. "Because I can keep this up all night, ya pig vomit."

"Pig vomit," Jasper bust up laughing again.

"Let it flow, slop refund," Speatsh scowled.

"Will you stop," Cadence complained.

"You won't be laughing if this gives you diarrhea," Speatsh said, now boxing with Jasper's stomach.

"Enough already," Cadence shrilled.

Nick screamed a long, howl that ended in an abrupt and intimidating bark.

The fighting stopped.

"I'm getting Josh," Cadence said. "Can you manage to keep things safe here until we get back?"

"Don't forget to take your friend's body with you," Jasper said.

"Body," Speatsh asked. "Don't tell me that brick-faced doodleberry finally offed himself."

"No," Cadence replied. "Your mom—"

"Ah-ah! Maternal birther," Jasper corrected.

"She killed Dustin." Cadence turned on Jasper to distract him from Speatsh's attempt to hide his insult. "And I really don't think parading Dustin's body is a good idea. It would kill Josh."

"Maybe that's what he needs," Jasper replied.

"He's already angry enough as it is," Cadence shouted, but found control in her volume.

"Anger is action," Jasper replied. "Know the person, and you know what he'll do when he's angry. But revenge comes from chaos. Death is the ultimate chaos, spiritually and psychologically. The psychologically dead plan more successfully."

"You don't know Josh very well," Cadence replied.

"I caught him didn't I," Jasper added, and, what appeared to be fat pale worms, but were really Speatsh's long fingers, pooped down from Jasper's nose and wriggled. Cadence tried not to react to the idiocy as Speatsh's fingers suddenly pulled back up into Jaspers face. Speatsh laughed silently behind the old enemy.

"As a hunter, Josh is the most barbaric I've ever seen," Jasper continued, oblivious of Speatsh's puppet show, which now consisted of what looked like worms wriggling out the side of Jasper's head. Speatsh stood behind Jasper, amused with himself.

"I've seen a lot of idiots in my time." Jasper said and caught a glimpse of Speatsh who suddenly recoiled his mischief and seemed confused as to the level of offense he should take. "Josh is driven by action, not plan," Jasper resumed, and Speatsh's eye now peered out from Jasper's mouth. "The rogue—I have to get used to calling him that—is a planner driven by revenge and thousands upon thousands of years of experience and preparation. He knows how humans behave. He knows the outcome of this war already. Someone needs to think, and I can't be the only one who does it, here."

"So what am I supposed to do," Cadence asked. "Tell Josh to get smarter."

Jasper tapped the tip of his cane against the side of his shoe. "Everyone has a monster in them, and they don't need a full moon to turn into it. Josh is a killer. One of the best, but he hasn't lost enough. Remind him of what he's lost until he breaks. Every little thing, show him how he could have stopped it. Show him the body of your friend and don't hold anything back."

"You can tell him yourself," Cadence said turning away.

"Can't," Speatsh said. "He's right. You have to tell him. He won't believe Jasper."

"Why me," Cadence replied. "You're back. You tell him."

"Who do you think I am? Aggon," Speatsh replied sharply.

"Well, then Richard."

"You don't know anything about ghosts," Speatsh said.

Oliver burst with laughter again and reached back for Craccy to tease her.

"Can we please put her somewhere safer than on his back," Cadence screamed. "Can we at least try to think about preserving at least some of Josh's family?"

"Her my job," Oliver growled.

"Could put her in Lucy's garden," Richard said.

"Lucy," Cadence asked.

Speatsh and even Jasper looked stunned.

"Lucy was Oliver's wife," Richard said. "Everyone knows that story."

"It wasn't his wife," Speatsh said.

"Her was so," Oliver said resentfully.

"That story's real," Cadence asked.

This time all three of the wise men fell silent and just looked at Cadence as if trying to understand how this brainless art had made it into the exhibit.

"She's buried in the restricted gardens," Speatsh erupted. "Everyone knows about the restricted gardens."

"It's legend," Richard added.

"It's where teenage trespassers go to die," Jasper added.

"No one trespassers in my garden," Oliver blurted.

"She might have been the first oracle in this graveyard if—," Richard blurted.

"She hadn't been a raving lunatic," Speatsh asked.

"Her was not," Oliver barked.

"She never liked me," Speatsh said grudginly.

"No one likes you," Richard laughed.

"I like doggy," Oliver said trying to pet Speatsh's head.

"Wait a minute! Oracles are real," Jasper asked.

"That better be a joke," Speatsh replied. He started petting his shoulder again before realizing his embarrassment once more to the absence of Bear.

Acotactac suddenly turned towards the dark beyond the graveyard. The sound had even alerted Oliver to stop playing with Cracey.

"Ooh," What's voice called from his perch atop the mausoleum. Even with his caged head, he blended in with the angels atop each corner. "Such pretty torches."

"That might be our signal," Jasper said.

Oliver's staff chose two headstones, and he took a guarding stance.

The Pomeranian backpack suddenly yawned and closed its eyes.

"By order of Plattsville City Police Department," Chandler's voice cried through a loud speaker hidden within the lights of flashing red and blue police lights with their quick strobes of white. "These premises are hereby being served with a search warrant. We're coming in legally, Oliver. You and your friends throw down your weapons and come out."

"Guess your friend survived his task," Jasper said and then explained the comment to Speatsh.

"Good one," Speatsh complimented.

Jasper turned quickly to Cadence. "Time for you to go. Don't be seen. If Chandler kept his word, he'll have transportation arranged. Use it."

"They'll spot her before she leaves the property," Speatsh objected.

"If they haven't spotted her already," Richard agreed.

"Give me strength," Jasper groaned. "How did you ever get your reputations."

Speatsh and Richard took umbrage, but Jasper laughed it off and called to What to do his thing.

What withdrew his flute and gave life to a solemn hymn. The shapes of children flew from the cracks of the mausoleum where ancients took refuge. This time, the children appeared to don the shape of medieval, plate armor. What Cadence had first perceived as tall and thin knights, were actually three children stacked on each other's shoulders. Then they all toppled, giggled and began choosing teams and teammates as to who got Cadence; who got the girl who couldn't talk; and who got Dustin's corpse.

"There's four of us," Cadence said.

Nick didn't need to speak, his poise expressed his discontent.

"We'll need him more than you will," Jasper said.

Nick growled.

"The ancients are the priority now," Jasper said. "Not you. We need muscle."

The ash children finally all chose their teams and cheered as they skipped towards either Cadence, Acotactac or the corpose of Dustin.

"I like that caged head," Jasper guffawed. "Why didn't you use him against me?"

"Even I don't make deals with the devil," Speatsh replied. "Whatever deal you think you've made with that, you won't be able to pay it."

"Is someone keeping time," Richard asked.

"I wasn't paying attention. I assume they won't give a second warning," Speatsh replied, and then he suddenly frowned. "I just realized I don't have a brace and I still can't kick anybody. Where's the justice?"

Suddenly, What's army of ash figures fell to the earth.

"Go with the children, Miss," What called from his perch. "They will protect you." As soon as he started playing a tune reminiscent of a funeral march again, the children's forms rose and encouraged Cadence and Acotactac to follow.

"Cue the tear gas," Jasper said.

A moment later, wisps of white smoke streamed through the air before blocking off the view of the gates.

"This is just too easy," Speatsh said. "The guardians will hate that."

"I'm beginning to like this Chandler," Jasper said. When he realized that Cadence and Acotactac were still standing with the rest of the group, he dropped his friendly demeanor and demanded they leave.

Cadence drew her rifle and felt herself whisked off of her feet and rushing towards the funeral chapel near another locked gate farther down the fence line. Acotactac and Dustin raced alongside her on their own clouds of ash. The children giggled beneath them as though they were playing a game of capture the flag, and they were all winning because they all had their flags.

In the distance, she heard the familiar sounds of Nick's snarls and Oliver's yelling. When the first gunshot screamed, Cadence was drawn to return to the fight. Wolves were one thing, but bullets were different. Jasper and Oliver had shown they could fight them, but could Nick. Then, just like that, Cadence remembered her own priority, retrieving Josh and getting back here as soon as possible before Nick could do something stupid that would get him killed. Jasper was right, priority would give her focus.

The dark children suddenly shouted a strange war cry as a small band of guardians stumbled upon their escape route. The wolves attacked quickly, but then fell to the earth in convulsions as the children exploded into a cloud of dust, which flew into the faces of the seven attacking predators. The dust funneled into the beasts' nostrils and mouths. What's tune had also changed to something sharper. After what appeared to be a vicious struggle for air, the creatures coughed out the ash and ran off. The dust then flew towards Cadence and Acotactac, encasing them completely in a black-ash mausoleum.

"Sssshhh," a few of the children's voices hushed each other until complete silence fell upon Cadence and her two friends.

"It's just men," a girl's voice whispered into Cadence's ear. "They won't find us."

"I don't see anything," a male voice announced from beyond the black barrier. The voice sounded close, too close.

"Check that mausoleum," a woman's voice ordered.

Some of the children giggled while others hushed.

"There's no door," another man replied, sounding close enough that Cadence could have simply cold-clocked him then and there. "No one's hiding in this thing if they can't get in."

"They couldn't have gotten far," the woman said. "Keep your eyes open."

Cadence and Acotactac sat in darkness for several minutes while they listened to Oliver and Jasper's opponents cry out orders in attempts to defeat them. The voices that had once been near, had trailed off.

The snarling of wolves grew among the cemetery, then fell silent, then grew again and continued to grow in numbers until falling silent for a moment.

"Run," the children's voices whispered and opened the graveyard back to their three-person cargo. As the children ran, once again in the appearance of armor to match What's tune, Cadence and Acotactac kept pace until they reached the tall fence. They both began to scale it, but were soon hefted once more into the air under the strength of the living black ash. The children continued to lift them up and over the fence before setting them down safely and silently to the other side.

"What's over there," a voice called.

The beam of a flashlight nearly fell upon the small party.

What's tune sharply changed, and the children of ash instantly flared into the single shape of a mausoleum, blocking the light of the flashlights from settling on Cadence, Acotactac and Dustin's body.

"It's that same mausoleum again," the voice said. "We've gone in a circle. They could be anywhere now."

Cadence began scanning the street for her getaway vehicle, but too many cars with their lights shining on the gates impaired, rather than aided, her sight.

"Which one," Cadence whispered.

Acotactac pointed down the sidewalk and towards the open entry way made of lawn. A figure stood stabbing his finger towards a particular vehicle and then looked around to see if anyone had noticed his behavior.

One vehicle quickly stood out from the rest. An empty SWAT truck with its backdoors completely open.

"That would be the empty one," Cadence said.

The children dropped their mausoleum disguise and swept the three friends towards the truck. They set Dustin in the back and then ran back into the graveyard where the sounds of battle screamed.

Cadence climbed into the back of the truck and sealed the doors behind them. As screams of agony sang from the cemetery, Cadence and Acotactac past the lockers towards the front seats. Cadence slid her rifle and several firearms between the driver's and passenger's seats. Before either could settle completely into the spongy chairs of the vehicle, Chandler was at the passenger's window where Acotactac nearly expelled one of her telescopic poles through his face except that Cadence stopped her.

"We have a deal, yes," Chandler asked.

Cadence nodded, and Chandler held out his hand with a slip of paper and some writing on it.

"Good," Chandler said. "Now listen. The rogue is looking for some kind of carriage that brings monsters back to life. He has spies, and he's setting traps for Josh. He's sending a guardian that will tell Josh to go the university which is where the rogue is. He's also sending a crew of mercenaries led by a man named Dee. They work for the rogue. What was that?"

He suddenly ducked.

"Don't blow this," he said reappearing once more. "You owe me." When Chandler immediately disappeared from the window, Cadence realized it was time for her and Acotactac to escape as well.

7 ~ It was Heads

The inside was the stench of a hundred drunken bodies that laughed, drank, argued, accused one man of being a snitch and then mocked him more when they said they were just playing with him.

The SWAT truck pulled to the four-way stop. Cadence read the piece of paper once more. Acotactac smacked the paper out of her hand.

Cadence ignored her, she'd been ignoring her for the past five minutes as the truck weaved its way closer to Chandler's address, using as many back roads as possible. Acotactac punched the dashboard.

"You think I don't know," Cadence screamed.

Acotactac screamed back, catching Cadence off guard. It was the only sound she'd made since Cadence knew her, and it was horrifyingly loud. Cadence understood her. Acotactac was disagreeing.

"Josh would do it," Cadence replied. "And so would Bricktain."

Acotactac was unmoved.

"Chandler is one of us." Cadence stared down the paved street she needed to drive and then down its opposite direction. "We wouldn't leave you."

Cadence was about to pull away from the stop sign and suddenly slammed on the brakes. A familiar horse ran out in front of the truck and raced past, its hooves stamped as if driven by the fates of hell, as though they were easily smashing through the pavement. Their hollow sounds muffled only lightly through the truck windows.

"Was that Thomas," Cadence asked.

A black, lanky figure ran past the front of the SWAT vehicle, driven by a madness more vile than any creature Cadence had come across yet. Her blood reversed flow in her veins, afraid, trying to retreat.

Acotactac pointed after the horse and black creature.

"Yeah," Cadence agreed and sped from behind the stop sign. She hardly flinched at the set of headlights that suddenly appeared at her left shoulder.

The lights veered sharply as Cadence abruptly stopped the SWAT truck. The headlights jerked sideways. Cadence nearly smashed through her own driver's side window with her head. She watched her front bumper flip through the air as a dark pick-up raced past and disappeared down the street flailing to regain its own control.

Cadence pressed down on the gas, but the vehicle didn't react.

Acotactac glared at Cadence and pointed off towards the direction of the junkyard where Josh would be.

"I know, but we're stalled," Cadence replied as the truck regurgitated angry clicks out of its steering column.

Acotactac kicked her door open and began to climb out, clearly set on following the chase.

Cadence grabbed her. "Don't you dare leave me alone out here."

Acotactac seemed to struggle with the decision and finally stomped her way back into the passenger side of the vehicle.

After a few more tries at the ignition, the truck finally came to life again. Both Cadence and Acotactac sighed in relief.

"Let's do this right," Cadence said.

Acotactac's face twisted and she pointed to her head.

"I am using my head," Cadence said. "No one gets left behind."

Acotactac smacked the dashboard.

"Thomas can handle himself," Cadence said.

Acotactac gestured rather rudely and this time, when she punched the dashboard, left a hole where her telescoping pole struck.

"Hey," Cadence screamed. "I just got it going again."

Acotactac put her pole through her side-door window, the long post pointing off towards the junkyard.

"All right," Cadence said. She fumbled through her pockets and then small and various compartments around the driver's seat and console. "Ha!" She said stumbling upon a quarter. "We'll flip: heads we help Thomas, tails we help Chandler's fam and get out of here."

Acotactac clearly hated the idea.

The coin spun through the air, and Acotactac quickly snatched it. She held it out in an open hand and frowned. She chucked the quarter past Cadence's head, and this time the driver-side-door window burst into a spider web pattern.

"What is wrong with you," Cadence asked, then hit the accelerator. "Bricktain will still be there when we get back."

The truck lunged forward and picked up speed. Cadence was angry, but reluctantly realized that she needed to invest her energy into being more alert and less on fighting with her passenger. The goal was to rally the team.

"We don't leave people behind," Cadence murmured. "We're better than that, and you know it."

Acotactac glared.

"Yeah," Cadence said. "I know you're mad," and then after nearly a block of driving away, "After you grow up, we can talk about that outburst of yours."

As she pulled onto her destined street, it finally occurred to Cadence just how dark her city had become—the streetlights all black, the power outage still in full force. Still, with the aid of the SWAT spotlights, she found a house with a number that matched one on the note that Chandler had written down for her, even though the silver numerals on the house were partially hidden beneath the overgrowth of holly-hocks.

Acotactac leapt from the truck before Cadence had a chance to apply the parking brake. The angry Taichomée disappeared into the dark of the front porch. The crackling sound of splinters and metal erupted from the house, along with the reverberation of her exploding telescoping wrist-posts. Cadence quickly made her way out of the vehicle, remembering to retrieve her rifle that she had slid between the seats.

She drew her night-vision scope to her face and peered down one end of the street and then panned to the other. She saw a couple of guardians watching her, their manes revealing their alerted state, but none charged. She could have probably taken both out from where she stood now, but that would only invite a larger fight at a faster rate than she was eager to at the moment.

Screaming erupted from the house and flooded into the road. The guardians kept their attention upon Cadence, but didn't appear to be approaching yet. She hoped they would maintain their reservation rather than take interest in her partner's activities. A few more moments and she'd be on her way back to her friends at the compound. Acotactac approached the truck, dragging a woman by the arm and a teenager by the hair. A young boy followed, kicking at Acotactac's heels and screaming to let his mother go.

"Let 'em go," Cadence ordered, but Acotactac dragged them anyway. She released the teenage daughter a moment to quickly open the truck doors, then she tossed the mother into the back of the vehicle. She helped shove the daughter in as well with the same lack of respect. The boy climbed in on his own and posted himself to contend with his kidnappers. Acotactac ignored him and locked the family in.

Even as Acotactac shut the doors, Cadence was in her path voicing her detestation for the bad attitude. Acotactac didn't seem to care, she pulled Cadence to the driver's door and pushed her up into the seat.

"Believe it or not, we're friends with your husband," Cadence announced to her oldest passenger as Acotactac made her way across the front of the van. "You're in danger and need to come with us."

The mother said nothing, but Cadence could tell she clearly didn't believe a word. Then, just as Acotactac took her seat and slammed her door behind her, the street filled with the giant guardians and a small number of scouts.

"I was so looking forward to a relaxing drive for once," Cadence said. She dropped her rifle between the seats again. She quickly checked her gear and made sure it was where it needed to be. "Diamonds don't grow on trees."

The teenager screamed at the sight of the beasts out the front window.

"What are those," the mother, Constance Chandler, asked.

"Not the time," Cadence replied.

Cadence pulled the mask over her face and withdrew the mouthpiece she loathed so much. "You better hope I don't kill you," she said to Acotactac who suddenly began climbing through her own door. Cadence locked the strange blowgun into her mouth and loaded the second, clear cylinder packed with deadly needles since discovering the ancients. She hated this.

She hadn't even finished opening the door and stepping back down from the driver's seat before she dropped a guardian with one of her Glocks. She tossed her weapons back towards herself; they magically snapped to her shoulders; and she barely struggled to yank her Uzis from her lower back. She sprayed everything else that was still stupid enough to charge at her door.

A crowd of monsters enshrouded the van. Cadence blew into her mouthpiece, blasting a rain of needles into the faces of every creature she could span in a single powerful breath and twist of her head. The creatures screamed, lashed out and hit nothing. She believed she had blinded every wolf that dared get in range. With this, she dispatched two more guardians and a scout with another spray of automatic diamond tips, while simultaneously replacing the emptied cartridge in her mouth with a full one. She breathed another blinding attack. She wasn't even sure where the needles went. All she knew was that when her enemies stumbled or screamed, she had hit them. She hardly noticed that her silent partner was meanwhile dispatching her own set of foes with her violent outbursts of poles.

Once or twice, Cadence turned when she thought she saw something immediately to her right or left, but realized it was just the glimmer of a beast getting hammered by the ends of Acotactac's long, collapsible banisters.

A moment finally came, a lull in the fight, when both Cadence and Acotactac knew it was time to flee and quickly made use of their stolen getaway vehicle.

"Those things are after us," Constance asked.

"You're safe with us," Cadence lied after removing her mouthpiece and mask.

"And what about our other daughter?"

Cadence slammed on the brakes and prepared for another shooting spree. "Let's go back and get her," she said glancing ruefully at Acotactac, who glared straight past the windshield and huffed in anger.

"She's not at home," Constance replied.

"Where is she," Cadence asked, instantly afraid she was going to regret it.

"Probably at the dorms," Constance replied.

"On campus?"

"At Berkley."

"Berkley," Cadence cried.

Acotactac rolled out of her seat with an open hand to smack Constance in the back of the truck. Cadence stopped her and pushed her back into her seat. Then she forced the vehicle to speed away despite the green reflective eyes gathering around the streets.

"We're being hunted trying to save her," Cadence complained to Acotactac, "And she wants us to drive around the world to get her daughter who's probably snug and happy in her bed." She killed all the vehicle lights except for the headlamps, in hopes of making her vehicle more difficult to track. She thought it probably wouldn't work, but she'd try it anyway.

Cadence bore down on the accelerator, and she sped through neighborhoods, taking corners at speeds that should have toppled the vehicle. Chandler's family screamed, cried and found anchor throughout the ordeal.

Dustin's uncooperative body seemed more of an annoyance to the family than the actual driving, as he rolled back and forth in his wrappings. Cadence thought a moment of telling the mother what it really was just to shut their screaming up. Cadence had reached a point that she didn't care. Dustin was the important cargo as far as she was concerned. She just wanted the family to stop complaining, she'd been through worse trips and chases. She felt better once she reached a road most familiar to her, the one she lived on, or used to. She still owned it anyway. She hardly recognized her farm as she sped past with its completely black back drop.

When the rear door suddenly tore open, and a guardian stood in its entry, Cadence leaned back in her seat and shot a single bullet through its brain before resuming her driving. She didn't need to see the beast die to know it had fallen.

"Geez, lady," Constance screamed. "Do you think you could take it a little easy on us back here."

For an instant, Cadence remembered the face and arm of a guardian clawing its way through a car roof and into her chest.

"No," Cadence snapped back and left it at that until she found the road leading to the junkyard. She had been a bit surprised that the generals in the new residential trailer park on Jasper's property hadn't prepared an ambush. She planned on forcing her vehicle through all those monsters she could when that obstacle appeared. Hopefully, by that time, she'd be in earpiece range with the junkyard and could fend off any conniving generals until her allies could show.

However, no attack came: no wall of wolves, no ambush—that is, none with generals.

When she came upon the sea of monsters between her and the front gates of the junkyard, she wasn't sure if she felt better or worse about her situation because she knew she had to get through. She slammed on the brakes.

"There are so many of them," Cadence said. She gripped the steering wheel to stop their shaking. She looked back. Nothing seemed to be chasing the truck anymore.

"Use these," Cadence said dropping three of her firearms into the back. "I imagine a cop's family must know something about firearm safety."

Constance took up the guns, snatching one out of her young son's hands and reprimanding him.

"Everyone shoots," Cadence ordered just as she forced the SWAT truck towards the epic gang of silvery-black bodies. She fumbled to find switches that would turn on any light the vehicle had. It might not be much of a tactic, but it could annoy the guardians enough to give her some kind of advantage. For some reason, she seemed incapable of locating any switches just now, and she stopped searching when she realized the wolves had a tactic of their own.

"What are they up to," Cadence asked as she watched the monsters allow a path to open among themselves, a path which led straight up to the compound's gates. As she drove, the creatures closed the path behind the truck. Then the realization struck her. "They're herding us! They want us in the junkyard."

She fumbled into her pocket, realizing she'd forgotten to put her earpiece on.

"Better idea," she said.

She spun the truck around and started to drive away from the compound. The path of wolves suddenly reappeared in her headlights and, no matter which way she turned, they steered her back towards the compound. For several miles worth of futile turns, the guardians continued to herd the SWAT truck back to an open path leading to the front gates. Again, she turned; ran over a few creatures; plowed through what she could, but they did no more than redirect her path—and with their numbers as great as they were, she watched her speed dwindle. Finally, she screamed and put the truck back on the path to the compound.

"What is that," Constance asked pointing past the front seats beyond the windshield.

Acotactac might have gasped at the strange sight brewing above the compound and filling its spotlights. An object, some kind of serpent, it appeared, leapt up from the compound and swam above its walls.

"Is that a tornado," Cadence started to ask but then inserted the earpiece so it could actually work. "Open the gates," she screamed.

"We're a little busy right now," an unfamiliar voice ordered.

"Wrong answer," Cadence scathed back.

"Cadence," a familiar voice replied.

"Amber, I'm shooting whoever that was when I—."

"Get out of here," Amber cried.

"It's not safe out here," Cadence replied.

The sounds of battle cried over the walls and truck engine.

"I need gates," Cadence demanded as she squeezed even more speed out of the square truck. Without wolves blocking the path, Cadence was able to pick up velocity again. She ordered the gates open once more, or what she thought were the gates; the compound appeared much differently than what she had seen last time. Its walls were larger, filled with rusted components of—well, she wasn't exactly sure of what.

"We don't have any way to open them," another new voice cried.

"Don't tell me what you don't have and make it happen," Cadence yelled as she watched the gates coming upon her rather fast.

"Get off, lady," the man's voice shot back.

"You're a dead man," Cadence replied.

Just then, the compound gates opened. Explosion followed, or at least something that sounded like explosion.

Cadence felt the ground move beneath her: uneven, soft, yet rigid, not right. Her head hit something, and all went black around her. She still heard the sound of breaking glass even though the noise eventually had disappeared.

And what was that smell?

Cadence coughed herself awake into complete darkness.

"Turn to the side if you have to chunder," A man's voice said that she didn't recognize.

"She awake," Amber's voice asked, echoing softly in the distance.

"Looks like it," the masculine voice called. A little closer.

Something large seemed to be dragging her. Something with green eyes right above Cadence. Cadence realized she was laying on a tarp or sheet of some sort.

"Natalie," she asked.

The body that was one with the blackness surrounding her huffed.

The male voice said. "Just need one more now."

"Acotactac," Cadence called out and attempted to sit up, but felt herself forced back down by Natalie's heavy paw.

"She's somewhere around here," Amber replied. "With that family you brought."

"Wait, stop," Cadence demanded.

"Lay down," the male's voice urged. "You haven't been looked over yet."

"Now's not the time," Amber replied.

"No, listen," Cadence objected. "We have to get to the cemetery. Where's Josh? We have to tell Josh." Then she remembered. "Dustin!"

"We found Dustin in your wreckage," Amber replied, her voice barely human.

"Where's Josh," Cadence insisted.

Except for the sounds of her being dragged and soft, cautious footsteps ahead and behind her, silence loomed. She inquired once more.

"He's dead," Amber replied and then said no more.

Cadence didn't believe it. It was a trick. She was dreaming.

Natalie continued to drag her along in the dark. She couldn't seem to get away from the black lately. Still, it was better than daylight.

How was Josh dead?

"Natalie," Cadence asked, knowing the guardian couldn't answer. "What's happened?"

"Shhh," Amber's voice crept as gently as the command of Death's own. "We're being hunted."

For the first time since waking, Cadence felt it wise to listen for a change. She heard the sounds of muffled fighting somewhere far in the dark. Voices roared snarls that should have deafened the tunnels. Humans yelled back their own war cry.

Then, from the opposite direction, another voice cried.

"Up ahead," he announced. "They're coming in. How did they find it?"

Book of the Fallen

8 ~ Uncertain Ground

They played with their drugs, drank more liquor and had an illegal tattoo needle running in one corner. Naturally, they all saw Harvey and his dog enter the bar, and he quickly realized he should have obeyed the sign.

The dream came fast tonight. Josh liked when the dream could actually take him to the good places, the good remnants of his life that made him forget about his troubles. Here, he saw his wife, and she was beautiful. Here, her face was the full glory that it had once been. In reality, she was more gorgeous to him with all her scarring. Josh knew that, but in his dreams he could see her in the state that he knew she wanted, the beauty unmarred by wolves or poison. In dream, she had no bandana, no exposed jaw nor missing flesh.

Amber had been silent when Josh recounted how Jasper had saved their lives. She didn't say it, and he could tell that she still wanted her justice. Deep down, so did Josh, but he couldn't deny that both he and his wife were able to see each other once more because of what Jasper had done for them when he beheaded the inquisitor. That was Josh's reality.

This, however, was dream. In this dream, Amber held out her hand to her husband and, without saying a word, looked over the field that had once been their schoolyard when he was younger. The field grew into the grassy hill where many lunch bags and foam trays had been left carelessly behind as the sound of the bell rang to remind students that they had all lost track of time. Only, no students filled the grounds, just Amber, Josh and a smattering of lunch garbage.

Josh held Amber's hand, and they walked towards the hill. He liked this. Their fingers slid in between each others' as love ought to.

He didn't often hold her hand in the real world—in the dreams this was a holy activity, and immediate anger usually followed when he awoke from such holiness.

Amber stopped at the foot of the grassy hill. It was only now that Josh realized the grass was long and uncut. Their strands of green sepulchers stood straight and still. Amber stared up towards the top of the incline, and Josh somehow knew that his time had come to leave her here.

"Protect them from me," Josh said.

Amber tried to smile, but failed to make Josh believe it. She stepped as she did when she climbed the sky, but she remained grounded. No wind existed to hold her here, and her foot returned helplessly to the ground. She remained earthed. "No one can protect them from you," she said.

Josh tried to argue, but Amber was no longer before him.

All was still, and Josh stood a few paces up the hill, lost in green.

He looked up, hoping to see his wife hovering over him, but she wasn't there neither.

The sky was split, arguing with itself whether it should be day or night. To the East, the moon swayed as a pendulum, keeping time and place against a black tapestry speckled with inferior lights. The day held the other half of the earth. Dozens of long arms with golden sabers reached out from the sun and held the night in check. Each time the moon swung close, the sun swiped with its swords.

The sun and all its armament motioned for Josh to continue. Josh started up the hill, and the only sound in existence was that of the long grass opening into a red path a few feet before him. The red grass made his hike easier. It closed behind him, hiding the trail he had previously followed. As he climbed, he heard the whispers. What the whispers were, he didn't know, but he heard them and he knew the grass was watching. No, not just watching, paying him obeisance. Why?

The crown of the hill drew open, as a curtain, revealing a darker Plattsville—not just Plattsville, but the entire world. He now stood above all civilization, and it smoldered in the dying embers of mass devastation. At the center, Josh saw Plattsville, untouched by the ember.

Fire hadn't taken his community. No smoke rose from destroyed and barren buildings. Nuclear remnant left no mark. The buildings simply stood taller than usual. The skyscrapers of the world were here, among the hospital and the college. He knew these buildings, some from movies and pictures, some from experience and study. He wasn't sure how it was, but it was all Plattsville, yet more than Plattsville.

Presently, he noticed red that attempted to cocoon the buildings just as though a spider had spun the stains herself with her own bloody silk. Only now, did he realize the bodies used to construct the buildings and skyscrapers of this world and city. Atop these buildings gloated their architects: monsters all. Corpses constructed the roofs and floors; the skulls of earthly beasts made their precipices; even the bright chandeliers beyond the windows were of human bones, lacquered in the color of smoke and destruction.

They were living bodies that made the building blocks and supports of these structures. They cried, laughed even, at their hopeless situation. Some still wriggled to escape their mortar prison made of bleeding paste, while others had already succumbed to their fate and had lost hope and fight. Yet, not all faces were human. Some appeared with green eyes and thick lion-esque manes—the bodies were all packed into every inch of roof, window and alley, and they watched Josh. They all watched Josh. The buildings swayed from their own inner turmoil, but did not topple.

A loud clamor shattered above, and Josh looked in time to watch as one of the sun's golden sabers holding the night back shattered. Its broken shards fell to the ground, stabbing into the earth and surrounding the paladin. The other blades and arms of the sun repositioned themselves to brace against the unpleasant attack of Plattsville's approaching dark slumber.

The night laughed. The pendulous moon swung faster, beating the black sky farther against the day. Tick-tock-tick. Shatter! Another sword broken.

Josh stepped from among the broken bits of blades before he realized he had a spectator. The stranger had spawned several yards away within the equator of the shadow cast by the night and the sun, and he watched Josh. The sun revealed half of the man's face, which stared back at Josh with a sincere hatred.

Somehow, Josh knew this person.

Chronos, a white wolf said, now standing behind the observer in the equator. It didn't speak aloud. Rather, it was into Josh's mind. The white monster leapt over the observer in the shadowy equator and placed itself before Josh. Its silver eyes peered back into Josh's. Josh knew these eyes. Within them, he saw an ally glaring back at him, mouthing, perhaps cursing, some sort of instruction to fight or run or not to be so stupid. Josh saw his own self arguing back. He saw himself fall into a rainbow.

Josh thought he knew this white wolf's voice, but he failed to find his own ability to respond as he would have wished. Suddenly, the white monster dashed off, circled Josh and then poised itself beside him.

The sky rang out again with the shrieking of broken blades and their giant pieces. These were closer to Josh's height, but still taller and wider. They rained down once more around the paladin, and only one of the sun's arms remained holding the night from conquering the entire stratosphere. Now, in his success, the night began to chime with meteoric explosions as its pendulum, brighter than any moon had ever been, beat against the sun's remaining blade until it too crumbled apart, forcing the sun to roll out of the sky. The night seized the whole of the earth.

Josh began to realize that where the broken bits of blades had fallen, white wolves now stood. They took a formation as if a wall before the approaching figure riding the creeping nightly equator. Suddenly, the dark side charged for Josh. It was swift. The white wolves at Josh's side were just as fast, but the attacking stranger, encompassed in night, threw the white wolves about, and as many as met his strike fell still at his feet.

Call it, the wolf standing beside Josh said, and it looked back to the hill with its long grass. Only, now the hill wasn't made of grass. It was flat, dirt and all seeded. Just then, each seed sprouted into a thousand wiry generals, and they stood in their starving hieroglyphic form and looked to Josh. An entire army stood at his command, and he knew they were his.

"Kill the monster," Josh shouted, and then stood his ground against the wind of his newly-grown army as it raced past him. On the paladin's order, his generals attacked the assailant figure and tore down his corrupted buildings until they, all the creatures within them and the bodies constructing them, blew away as dust.

As he watched the razing, Josh called forth his blades, but he was not wearing them. He wished for them anyway, and something else came forth. His own claws tore through the tips of his fingers.

Prince of beasts, the voice demanded of Josh. *Awaken.*

Before he could call for more strength, the strange observer was upon him, staring and, in a quick and violent contortion, his head was suddenly that of one of the white dogs. It yelled. Josh yelled back. The monster took quick offense and bit into Josh's throat.

The wound burned and boiled madness into his veins—not madness, but order. For once, he was confident in his thoughts. He was calm. The darkness had given him peace. It had given him strength. It had given him realization.

Josh turned to the white wolf beside him and tore its throat open. Here, a face began to appear, someone familiar. The observer laughed, then, with a single point of his middle finger, he ordered Josh to finish killing the white wolf. Josh did, and he watched the face of Amber take form before him.

The observer gloated without smiling and, in disconcerting hallow, said, "Even here, you are mine."

* * *

At this, Josh awoke, screaming obscenity at an invisible foe. Sweat ran down his face and filled every inch of his clothing. He clenched a fist that would have extended a sword from his wrist, but that sword didn't currently clothe him.

Amber hovered over him and tried to hold him down while saying anything to alleviate his screaming. Slowly, he began to accept that his surroundings were not dream anymore. It was reality again.

This was worse. There was no more order over his thoughts. He knew where he was, back in the junkyard. To be exact, he was in the rusted building set in the center of the steel field.

For as rugged as the outside of the dominant building appeared in the junkyard, the inside was surprisingly appealing and comfortable. It was warm, warmer with Amber staring down at him.

Natalie was the first to the room. When Josh saw her, he tensed. He wasn't prepared for her image so abruptly. She filled the doorway, overfilled it even. The house was a little too tight for Natalie, but it was the safest place for her during the sunlit day. Josh had done well to block out the ultraviolet rays from sneaking through the windows and harming her.

Thomas soon appeared, followed by Kenny.

"He doesn't need an audience," Amber snapped.

Natalie grumbled, and Thomas ignored her, but Kenny took the hint and disappeared down the hallway. Natalie stayed and watched Amber hold the man that should have been her husband instead.

"Another concussion," Thomas asked, grabbing Josh's foot, which wore one of Amber's Windriders. "Stop letting him play with your shoes. Why aren't you watching him?"

"I did watch him," Amber snapped. "He had them on before I even woke up, which I wouldn't have done were it not for the 'thud.'"

"Watch him better," Thomas said. "He's valuable."

Natalie huffed something additional.

"Mind your own marriage," Amber yelled sharply.

Natalie roared.

"It's almost time for our shift," Thomas said, ignoring Amber's annoyance.

"I'll be ready," Josh said.

"Lucid or other," Thomas replied. "We need the paladin, not a brain-dead Tinkerbell, as Speatsh would say."

The room suddenly fell silent, and Thomas disappeared down the hall, unapologetically.

"I don't want you experimenting with the Windriders anymore," Amber said breaking the silence. "You could break your neck."

"That didn't stop you," Josh replied.

"I did most of my practice over a swimming pool," Amber continued. "Stick to your strengths."

"Yeah," Josh reluctantly agreed. He stared at Wolf's Breath hanging off the edge of a desk across the room. The swords, the fangs and his gloves were all piled beside it as only a tired person interested in sleep could drop them. He had a sudden thought of falling with all that gear on and decided he was wise for never wearing it when he played with Amber's moccasins.

"How long was I out this time," Josh asked.

"Not long," Amber replied.

"I had another dream," Josh said bringing himself up to the bed and beginning to unravel Amber's knee-length moccasins.

"What was it about," she asked.

Josh thought and finally answered. "I don't remember."

Natalie grumbled and poised herself before Josh. She looked deep into his eyes, and Josh reached for his head at the sharp pain that began to stir.

"Don't," Josh yelled.

Natalie stopped. Why did she do that to him?

Amber's own annoyance appeared. She yelled at Natalie for a right to a little privacy in their own room—her room actually, but more than just her room now. It wasn't as large and luxurious as what she'd had in the bunker, but it was refreshing to be back home in her own bed, even if it was a little dusty from the lack of care while she was gone.

Natalie retreated out of the room, kicking the door off its lower hinge as she did.

"Thomas is right, Josh," Amber said after a moment of chiding Natalie's lack of respect for her home. "You need to stop messing around with the Windriders."

"We need eyes in the sky," Josh replied. "Someone needs to be up there when you can't."

"You don't have the balance," Amber said and suddenly dropped herself onto the edge of the bed next to Josh. She sighed long and deep and drooped forward a bit.

"No one has the balance," Josh replied, then added, "any better today?"

"Not really," Amber said. "I threw up a little is all earlier. Don't think anyone noticed."

"How long you plan on keeping this secret?"

"You know they wouldn't let me fight." Amber began to return her enchanted moccasins back to her own feet.

"That's something I happen to agree with," Josh replied.

"And I happen to agree about you not killing yourself playing with my toys," Amber snapped. "A dead father's not a father."

"All right," Josh replied. "I'll stop, but we have to tell them before it's too late. A dead baby's not a baby."

"If we finish this soon, we won't to have to worry about it anymore," Amber replied.

Kenny suddenly appeared, his knuckles rapping on the door jam. "Bullet's back."

"Alone," Josh asked.

"Leading in a truck," Kenny replied. "Could be what we've been waiting for."

Josh stood, and his every muscle tore at him, screaming for more rest. Still, he stood and started scraping the bits and pieces of his paladin shell together. He suggested that Natalie fix the broken door.

* * *

Children frightened Bear. He had to be nice to children. They didn't cry at his appearance anymore. He was no longer scary. He was interesting. They were mystified. He was magical, and this was dangerous, not to mention annoying, to creatures like bear. He was used to Speatsh keeping people away from him. Children were practically impossible to hide from. Anywhere he could fit, it seemed a child could fit—and they did fit, grasping for him with paws deadlier than his own. They were bigger monsters than wolves.

He yelled at them, they didn't care. He threatened them with sharp teeth, they giggled as though chasing him was a game, and he had to be nice about it. Speatsh would have scared them away. Speatsh would have squashed them all under his boot, but, without Speatsh there, he had no one to fend them off. However, while Speatsh may not have cared about frightening children, bear hated the thought of it. They had too many nightmares to worry about in their lives and didn't need his face as one more.

Currently, he did hide. It had taken him awhile to find this new place. It wasn't perfect, but it seemed safe for now. This corner of the junkyard was dark, but it would probably disappear by tomorrow morning. The walls expanded in any direction at almost every hour, and razor edges continued to stretch over the new sections several times throughout the day. A maintenance crew, which Reggie had selected, worked all hours to strip apart the cars for their steel, aluminum and other precious metals. They melted and molded the ore into the walls that now made up the compound for the refugees: some from the hospital; some from the school; some who fled to the junkyard. Bear had also watched many more hunters appear over the past couple of days. They had come to help the paladin fight, several came through the gates barely alive from being chased.

Josh had ordered spotters on the compound walls to watch for people who sought sanctuary. As a refugee or hunter appeared, those within the walls set out to bring them in. So far, their success rates of retrieval had proven valuable. Many new hunters had proven to be deadly allies, but Josh's team was efficient, intimidating to even the most seasoned of hunters. Typical doubt towards the youth presented across many brows new to the compound, but they quickly disappeared upon witnessing the fury of the paladin either within the heart of a fight or leading the charge towards it. Josh wasn't just a hunter. He was a brawler. If there was a center to a fight, he was at it, berserking all directions at once in a flurry of blades and fabric. The other hunters struggled to deal with the outlying stragglers to his deadly reach. The wolves even began to stay clear of Josh as he escorted new faces into the growing, human sanctuary. The beasts had become wise about choosing their fights, as though another chose for them. Someone knew Josh epitomized annihilation.

The civilians, on the other hand, saw little, if anything, beyond the walls. They saw only a tyrant in Josh, a dictator who controlled the refugees.

That's what they all were, in the eyes of the civilians—refugees, and Bear knew that children were the worst of them. Bear wasn't sure what was worse to fend off, the monsters beyond the high compound walls or the refugees within them. He certainly knew it wasn't the adults. They kept their distance. The smart ones all stayed behind the protection of the walls. Some tried to escape. They failed. Even now, Bear could smell their remains festering from outside of the ever-growing compound. A few lucky ones fled back to the compound, where they were forced to acknowledge the true nature of their situation.

Only the Silver Bullet was able to manage leaving the compound grounds when it needed. The wolves were still no match for its bladed nose; deadly artillery; and deafening horn. Bear wondered how long that luxury would last and that they would be safe. He knew that even the Bullet had its limits. Regardless, most the people inside the compound walls seemed in better spirits since the yard had practically tripled in size and continued to grow. Despite the expansion, the community was still cramped, especially in the sector that was cordoned off for civilians or non-hunters. For now, a gate allowed passage from the civilian sector, but when battle was announced, civilians were to return to their own area within the compound.

The patients from the hospital and the children from the school had mostly become too scared to complain against their protective surroundings. Reggie had some rusted playground equipment for scrap that he enlisted a team of volunteers to clean up and prepare for the children, anything to keep them occupied and out of everyone's way. For the adults, he opened up as much space as possible to let them recreate however they could, usually through work.

Others had shown up as well, not just people who had been freed from their slavery. A few people from Plattsville had come, mostly individuals who, for some reason or another, figured out that not all was what it seemed in the world lately. Several hunters had come too. A large number had reluctantly poised themselves in the outskirts of the county watching and listening for news in Plattsville after word had reached them that a new paladin would require help. When the town blacked out, these hunters chose to believe the call and followed the wolves and the glow of the compound to the far reaches of the city. They claimed that a few had chosen to come into town days before, but no one seemed to know where they were. Some of the hunters were wise and powerful forces to be reckoned with. Many were new and would probably get someone killed, even Bear knew that. To be fair, he still thought Josh was new and that one of his buddies would get someone killed.

Still, the hunters came—some in large groups, many trickled in alone or with a friend or two. Bear didn't understand how some of these hunters had even survived the journey to join the new paladin. They were too unskilled to fight and too stupid for luck. The animated pelt felt that he'd hardly had a moment of rest since Speatsh had been murdered nearly a few days before.

What bear really wanted right now was sleep. However, he was well aware that he wasn't going to get it as he watched how events were unfolding in the compound beneath him. Not only that, but the incessant rhythm of Acotactac marching around the catwalks pinged through his sensitive ears too loudly for him to ignore. She never stopped making rounds. It wasn't even her shift, and she kept at the catwalks, non-stop. For now, Bear tried his best to enjoy the comfort of the deteriorating soft-top convertible that had been dragged in from the exterior wall a few days ago and stacked for future assimilation into the compound structure.

The wolves hadn't allowed the compound residents to retrieve the vehicles openly. Only the best of the hunters had been able to cut their way through the multitude of wolves to claim steel supplies from the exterior junkyard. As the wolves numbers grew, it became impossible to obtain any metal reinforcement. Even Josh had given up trying to lead a charge to reclaim them.

Reggie had a more subtle approach to get what he needed from outside the junkyard walls. They started with what steel they had already within the compound and then continuously extended the walls out to the exterior yard and swallowed up more piles of heaps. The entire process was loud, dangerous and precise.

Loud as it was, Bear listened. Others didn't know he listened. Or maybe they did, but they didn't care. Or maybe noise wasn't a big deal to them.

Speaking of which—just now, the compound below Bear's hiding spot suddenly filled with commotion. The clamor wasn't that of battle or even sound for that matter. It was the energy of those people around the compound choosing to show that they weren't loafing. Friendly chatter had died, labor grew to a more a serious level. Even those watching the catwalks above the compound appeared to work more at standing straight and watching where they were supposed to.

Bear didn't have to look to know the stir of such focused and immediate attention. He knew it by now. He also knew the sound of the door into Reggie's living quarters opening and closing. Josh and Amber marched out into the compound where Thomas and Acotactac were both ready to greet him.

Josh held his side for a moment. It was subtle, but Bear noticed he did it. He did that a lot more since his return from the Taichomée village.

"Still hurting," Bear heard Thomas ask.

Reggie looked up from a battered and oil-stained clipboard.

Nick and Dustin attentively approached, most likely willing to operate once more on him.

Josh brushed them off by pretending his gloves needed to be pulled tighter around his fingers. He wore them everywhere nowadays, and he always seemed to be concerned with their snugness when he didn't like the topic of discussion before him.

"If the dogs put something back together wrong, we should get you to Bogi," Thomas said. "I'm a lot of things, but I've never had to teach a dog reconstructive, internal surgery."

Josh took a straighter stance as if to reiterate that he was fine.

"You lying," Amber asked.

Josh tugged on his thin, silky gloves once more.

"Incoming," the large man cried over a system of loud speakers situated throughout the compound. He could have been mistaken for a lump of clay poised dead-center over the front gates. No one knew this post better than he. He turned on his stool, which set atop the catwalk over the steel doors leading into the compound. He waved his crippled hand over his head to signify that something or someone friendly approached. Bear wondered if Josh ever felt bad for giving this doorman his injury.

A woman dressed in colorful cowgirl attire, long brunette hair dropping from beneath her red hat, stayed posted with the doorman. She peered through a set of binoculars and made hand gestures to another girl who could have passed for her twin except for her blonde hair.

The blonde appeared to say something to the doorman.

"It's the Bullet," the doorman announced.

"Good," Thomas seemed to sigh. "I hope that means the shipment got through."

A small group of young thugs with skateboards strapped to their backs and sides joined a burly man in denim and leather shoulders at the front gates.

"This better be some good gear," Reggie said. "We're low on glycerin rounds."

"Then you should be happy to know that's exactly what I ordered," Thomas replied.

"Tell me, Monsieur de Soleil," Amber said. "Just how does someone order a shipment of diamond bullets and explosive juice?"

"Think I've lived this long to be poor," Thomas replied and, after a moment of realizing no one understood, added "I believe in contingency plans, and caches of supplies that know how to roll out and find hunters when extraordinary events take place."

"Not what I asked," Amber replied.

Thomas sighed at the lack of understanding with the young hunters, but did his best not to show it. "Among other things," he explained. "Mister Revlon is the owner of a facility that manufactures diamonds for oil drills, of course that's simply a cover story. Naturally, we have a manufacturing facility with fantastic shipping abilities nearby—however, not in town because we're not stupid."

"We own what," Amber asked.

"I thought you knew," Thomas said. "It's all a part of how we fund our hunt."

"I thought that was through my uncle's antique dealing," Josh replied.

"Oh, that's right," Thomas said insincerely. "Sure."

"And just who supervises these fundraising events," Josh asked, completely ignoring the topic of ignorant wealth.

"Thug supervises the revenue from the various hunter havens, there's money in food," Thomas explained. "Speatsh, I suppose you might conceive, took over research and development and, after Richard died, Josh's dad took over acquisitions. I oversee certain manufacturing processes. To answer the question you have yet to ask, Mister Revlon and his family, you, are the major share holder of it all."

"Josh was never notified of any inheritance," Amber pointed out.

"He just was," Thomas replied. "We have an excellent legal team."

"I don't get it," Reggie said. "Hunters have been around longer than Richard's been alive. Why would the Revlon family own so much?"

"That is true," Thomas replied. "But Richard was the one who developed the most efficient financial networking systems, and he did use his contacts and money for the most part to make them start working. Before Richard, hunters were nothing more than unequal cells of robbers and identity thieves. Richard's connections and ideas made us disappear from the radar."

"My uncle was a cop," Josh rejected. "He's not exactly business savvy."

"When your uncle organized the hunter underground, wolf slayings increased nearly two thousand percent," Thomas replied. "He made coordinated efforts possible."

"Yeah," Amber said. "Who needs the Internet or cell phones when you're a hunter?"

Thomas glared coolly towards Amber. "Who do you think manufactured cell towers, making them cheaper to put up? And who do you think developed the business model to get phones into the commoners' hands? I'll give you one guess who the silent partner of that company is and who inherited it. By the way, what are your thoughts on R.R. Communications? Think about it."

"You're not serious," Amber said.

"Did Richard ever tell you about his friend who worked at the National Science Foundation," Thomas asked. "A good guy, ran into a wolf once while on vacation and felt he owed your uncle a favor. He allowed Richard to convince him and a few of his intelligent buddies to expand an unrealized networking system into satellite hubs at universities which would eventually tap into nearly every household in the world. So yes, I'm very serious. Would you like to hear about patents you currently own concerning this coordinated attack system that Richard helped to realize?"

Amber wanted to call Thomas a fool and a liar.

The doorman hollered once more. The compound walls then grunted and whined as the old, perspiring hydraulics groaned through worn hoses and gaskets. As the gates started to peel away from each other, several skaters drew their boards and perched themselves atop cement and steel walls on opposite sides of the entryway. It was a simple design really. From the outside, it appeared a straight-forward entrance, but it was actually an elongated skateboarding half-pipe, wide enough for large vehicles to pass through, but narrow enough for the skaters to hew down any monster that tried to get inside. Any time the gates opened, skaters stood nervously, crossed themselves in prayer and prepared for the possibility that this ride would be their last.

In the catwalks directly above them, the doorman, in his leather, barely budged beneath his own weaponry. He grunted and spit. Then he stood, gripped a pole leading to the ground and rode it like a fireman to the earth. The rodeo queens took his place at the gate controls.

Bear didn't like the gates, but he appreciated Josh's and Reggie's work here.

The doorman joined two other skaters at the edge of the half-pipe inside the compound. He checked his sawed-off antique and prepared to take on the brunt of the attack that might funnel past the other skaters and get into the compound.

Josh and Thomas situated themselves close to the half-pipe, ready to rush through to the other side, while Amber climbed up an invisible staircase into the sky.

Kate and Petruchio each took one of Thomas's sides. The vampire chose Petruchio, which meant that Thomas had already planned on a flanking maneuver. Pretty impressive, in theory, actually. Thomas had assured everyone that under the right circumstances, and if needed, Petruchio could easily scale the nose of an oncoming tractor, then clear the wall and its razor wire, setting Thomas in the rears of any monsters immediately trying to push through the gates.

Thomas would then cut off the retreat of one group of monsters; follow them and any vehicle into the compound where the gates could close and seal potential enemies inside. Then Josh's hunters could destroy whatever was foolish enough to enter the compound while Thomas and Petruchio attacked from behind.

The twins posted themselves near Josh.

Acotactac had fled the catwalks and assumed a different role. She ushered non-hunter adults and children back into the civilian sector of the compound.

Bear noticed Josh sneer. Josh didn't like the children in the front area with the hunters and the wolves.The hunters had even come to call this section of the compound the kill zone. However, Reggie had convinced the paladin that letting them play here help stamped out the weeds and make the terrain friendlier to fancy footwork.

Like the other hunters, Bear either followed Josh's lead or took interest in his watchful eye and approach. The paladin gripped the fangs and stood ready, looking for something other than the Silver Bullet that might try to enter the compound. Bear waited for the time being. When Josh moved, he would too.

The blade-nosed, battle diesel rolled into to the compound. A red rig with its longer trailer followed.

The doorman yelled once more as both vehicles cleared the gate. The gates began to close. The Bullet made its way to a familiar parking place stretched before Acotactac and the chain link gate that she guarded. The cab of the red diesel shook as it stopped where Reggie directed it to, along the northern wall of the compound.

In a moment, the driver's door of the Silver Bullet opened, and Thug stepped down from the passenger's side of the vehicle. Bricktain stepped from driver's seat rather than in his usual manner through the backdoors.

Josh might have asked about any problems they had encountered, but Bricktain would have most likely replied with, "We're back aren't we." Instead, Bricktain simply shrugged his metallic shoulder without being asked anything.

The gates finally sealed, the hunters maintaining their original stances.

"Told you we wouldn't have to put up a fight," Thug said, slapping Bricktain on the shoulder. "They want us in here."

Bricktain pulled away from Thug, glaring, wanting to punch him if it weren't for the fact that he respected the man too much.

The driver from the red tractor climbed out. He stepped about five feet from his rig before he turned back to the cab. A few moments later he appeared with a clipboard and few papers. The papers fluttered to the ground, and the driver caught only a few of them before he dropped everything that he was able to hold.

"Not one of ours," Josh asked.

"Safer to contract out," Thomas replied. "Stupid is always safer."

The driver suddenly collapsed, even as he marched his way towards the person closest him, which happened to be Reggie.

"Catch him," Reggie yelled, spotting the wobble of incapacitating fear before it could strike. Josh rushed for him, even reached out to help before thinking better about the damage that Wolf's Breath would do.

Bear was faster. He appeared out of nowhere and quickly rolled up his body to cushion the man's head from striking the hard, child-stamped dirt. Only, the dirt wasn't as hard as everyone had believed. It crumbled, and Bear and the driver fell through the earth's fragile crust.

As a plume of soil and dust erupted into the air, Josh holstered his weapons and unhinged his four blades around his arms.

"No guns," Josh ordered. He listened to the familiar sounds of friends and allies clearing away from his fighting space. He wasn't sure what had just happened. His first thought was that the wolves had tunneled their way beneath the compound.

Amber made no sound, while Bricktain's arm clattered and clanked into his own sword.

Josh waited for whatever might have been hiding in the dust.

Speatsh had warned not too long ago that the compound had likely been armed with traps prior to the hunters' arrival. Was this one of them?

Josh waited and, for a brief instant, might have felt sorry regarding whatever creature tried leaping from the dirt into his deadly melee. He was more than ready to perform as he did best. He heard no screams from the driver, nor any growls from Bear. That was a good omen to some degree.

But nothing came out of the earth.

Now, Bear roared.

"Get it off me," a voice cried from within the cloud.

Bear's voice burst with an even viler snarl, and a second person voiced his own surprise. For some reason, Josh thought he remembered this tone, but he wasn't sure why.

Josh neared what had become the ledge of a pit and watched as several faces gradually appeared through the dirty cloud.

"Generals," Bricktain yelled and aimed his sword as he would his gun upon one of the men, but Josh stopped him and called for some rope.

"You're dead," Josh called down into the chasm. "Jasper killed you."

"Clearly," said the man holding the fallen truck driver.

A one-eared teenager in a Levi jacket and a skateboard strapped to his back appeared with rope, and Josh lowered it into the earth. With the help of Bricktain and the one-eared skater, they hoisted three men and an unconscious driver out of the pit. As a fourth newcomer climbed from the pit on his own, he brushed himself off then rose to his feet and held out a hand to shake.

"I might hug you, but I've heard what you can do," the man said.

Josh gestured towards the vampire. "Might I introduce you to Monsieur de Soleil."

The man appeared as if Josh had threatened to drive him over with a steam engine locomotive. Thomas stood with his hand stretched for gentlemanly greeting.

"Thomas, meet a fan of yours," Josh said. "My friend, Michael Banks."

Michael continued to stand and say nothing. He didn't return the handshake, just stood there. He caught his careless insult soon enough that an apology would still hold effect.

"I didn't expect you to be so real," Michael added.

Josh, Michael and Thomas joined in helping to pull more people from the pit. As the dust finally settled Michael's allies kept appearing in the bottom through what finally appeared to be a small tunnel at the base of the pit.

"How many you got in there," Bricktain asked.

Bear roared and clawed his way over the ledge.

"Bear, we're sorry," Bricktain acknowledged. He reached to help the pelt. Bear scampered up Bricktain's arm and then leapt off towards a pile of cars. Children began cheering and chasing after him. Acotactac tried to slow their charge upon the poor creature as she made her own way back to the catwalk to resume her relentless marching.

"So how is this possible," Josh asked.

"It took a lot," Michael replied. "I have a greater appreciation for my master, eh Jasper now."

"You're a wolf," Thug said appearing at Josh's side. He aided up another person after realizing he was about to climb straight into the hem of Wolf's Breath.

"Jasper freed us, somewhat," Michael said as Josh began escorting his and Dustin's old, one-time savior away from the commotion of the growing audience. Thomas and Thug followed, which caught the eye of Bricktain. He started to follow Josh as well, allowing Michael's own to help each other out of the earth. This seemed to give Amber and Reggie permission to accompany Josh and the newcomers as well on his conversation.

"We saw you dead," Josh said.

"Did you," Michael asked. "Do you know what kind of hibernation a body goes through to convince a master of Jasper's that he's been stripped of all his servants?"

"This is the guy who told you about Thomas," Bricktain asked, but was left to his own to gather an answer.

"You gave him back his life, paladin," Michael said. "And he gave us ours. I don't know how he does it, but there's so much more going on in that mind of his than I realized."

"I don't buy it," Josh replied. "Why didn't he free my sister."

"I thought he did," Michael said. When he realized that his answer didn't seem to satisfy Josh, "She's not with us."

"We have her," Josh said. "She's still a dog."

"So are some of us," Michael replied. After an awkward moment, he continued. "He's in danger, Paladin," Michael said. "He needs help and he needs it fast."

"Jasper," Bricktain asked. "He's a big boy. I'm sure he can ride it out."

At that, Michael suddenly turned. He bent Bricktain over backwards, holding him at the throat. Bricktain's arm whirred and clicked as the barrel of a gun took shape, but for naught. Michael seemed to have no problem with holding the barrel away as well.

"You owe him a debt of gratitude," Michael replied calmly, but through gritted teeth. His face filled with red, and his eyes might have burst from his head had he not stopped to breathe in. "Your insults end here by choice or my hand."

The others drew weapons, but only Josh noticed the sudden interest from Michael's companions as well. He placed his silk hand on Michael's shoulder.

"Let him go, friend," Josh coaxed. "That steel limb you're holding is the only kind of courtesy my friend's known from Jasper."

Michael's face softened and then softened even more as he took in a better look at Bricktain's monstrosity.

"You have to understand," Josh said, not just to Michael, but to the others as well. "Jasper may have suddenly found God, but he left us in hell."

By now, Michael had fully released Bricktain and allowed him to his feet.

"He's redeemed himself," Michael said, the corners of his mouth still holding traces of anger as he spoke.

"We understand redemption, Michael," Josh said. "But he hasn't repented with us yet."

"Amen," Thomas added.

Michael held out a hand to Bricktain and, after a few words of kind common interest, received a gentleman's understanding and resolve.

"In that case," Michael said. "We need your help. I ask for a favor." He placed his hand on Josh's shoulder and then winced and pulled back. "My master's in danger. He will die. Help him for our sake."

"That's not surprising," Amber said. "Considering he betrayed the rogue."

"Forgive me," Michael said. "The rogue. What's that?"

Josh couldn't answer, not because he didn't know how, but because he hadn't considered this fact before. He wasn't a rogue to his slaves, not all of them perhaps.

"The rogue is the ultimate master of your own," Thomas explained, apparently understanding Josh's sudden revelation. "He's the ancient."

"Ah, yes, Jasper told us about him," Michael announced. "That's not why he's in trouble."

"Go on," Josh said.

"Jasper has a strong mind," Michael explained. "He freed those of us he thought he could trust and, those he couldn't, he released entirely."

"You mean he killed them," Thomas observed.

Michael nodded.

"Smart move," Thomas said. "Nicer than I would have been."

"He couldn't relocate us with all the eyes on him," Michael explained trying not to think about the implications of Thomas's previous statement. "And he couldn't relocate our holding area after he had convinced his own that we were dead without raising questions. You don't typically stay in the den with your dead, but we had to."

"Hence, you've been tunneling," Josh said.

"Ever since you came back more than a year ago to face Jasper and killed that other general," Michael said. "We added his body to those Jasper could not trust and let their decay and stink help convince the other generals to keep away from the dead."

"You've survived down there all this time," Josh asked. "How?"

"Bugs and roots mostly," Michael explained. "We found enough while digging. Took us awhile. Tunnels kept collapsing."

Bricktain snorted.

"Forgive us," Michael snapped. "We've never dug one before and we lost a few good friends doing it. Jasper thought it could come in handy if things happened the way he thought they might."

"What's it all for," Josh asked.

For a moment, Michael's eyes might have flashed with anger, but it was quickly gone.

"Does it matter," Thomas said. "We know it's here and the rogue doesn't."

"Exactly," Michael added.

Josh, however wasn't convinced. What about when they did discover it? Would it be a direct path into the compound for the rogue's armies? For that matter, is that what its real purpose was? However, Josh believed Michael deserved the benefit of the doubt, even if Jasper was questionable. After all, Michael had helped him before. Josh decided he wouldn't say anything about it just now; too many people were listening and the last thing he felt he needed was to inspire more mire among the people of the compound.

Josh tried to put the pieces of this new puzzle together. He kept his memories from his previous visit to Taichomée, but every time he started to see some kind of structure appear to a bigger picture, he kept seeing his old teacher take in his last breath.

"I saved two lives once," Michael said. "I call—I beg—you to return the debt."

The conversation had recaptured the new paladin's interest. He knew what needed to be done. Despite Jasper's presence, he had been forced to trust that the villain would take care of Cadence. Josh should have been with her. He was sworn to protect her, but in a single fight, a man's meaning and understanding can change. Jasper had Cadence now. He protected her the other night. Josh believed, for some reason, that he did so now, but what if he decided to change his mind?

Speatsh had taken it upon himself to protect the queen. Josh had promised as much himself, and Jasper seemed to take on that role the moment he leapt into that hole in the ground with Cadence. Despite Jasper's intentions and own conniving, he would be stronger than Josh at protecting anyone. What's more, with the constant growing panic and numbers of people around him, including Michael's own, Josh had a new responsibility within this compound.

He couldn't leave. Yet, in staying, he stewed in vengeance. He had found a new focus of hate and it was directed towards the rogue, the rogue and Genre.

Genre.

Every day, a new danger in monsters seemed to appear. Genre wasn't even the worst of them, as far as Josh knew. What other kinds of monsters had the rogue created? First, Jasper: as vile a creature of strength and cunning in a body that Josh had learned not to underestimate. Then there was the inquisitor, one who may have very well authored all that any military knew about psychological warfare and torture, and he'd had the army to back him. This much Josh wondered, as he felt whatever was stabbing his chest from his insides with each aspiration of breath, had he experienced how much Genre still had to frighten him?

Genre toyed with Speatsh as easily as a ping-pong ball being batted between the Right Arm and Left Arm. Speatsh was strong, and Genre killed him. They would kill Josh too. For a moment, he wondered if he could get Genre to slow down enough for him to sew the separated twins back together. Of course, if he could get them to stand still for that, why not just behead them.

Dumb idea, Josh, he told himself.

His quick thoughts turned to the rogue, whom no one knew nor his ability to fight. Surely, he'd have to be mightier than Genre. How was Josh to prepare the others for that? Even Thomas hadn't caught up with the rogue, and he was the most legendary of hunters.

"Please," Michael requested once more. "He's not as strong as you think."

"He's stronger than any of us," Amber said.

"He's starving himself," Michael said. "To break his link with the one master and to help your friend."

"I don't have to tell you things are complicated here," Josh said. "Can't you help him? You're already stronger than us."

"If we're discovered, any one of us can be used against Jasper," Michael replied.

"Then why did you bother coming here?" Josh felt his face turn hot and presumed Michael's reaction meant he saw it.

"We made you a backdoor," Michael said. "Think about that."

"I can't leave this place," Josh said.

"We can help here in trade," Michael said. "No one can see us here, and—if we must—we can retreat to the tunnels to stay secret."

"And how do we trust you among our troops," Bricktain said.

"Right. The ones who have been severed from their supernatural powers are the monsters in this haven."

Josh felt he should respond, but felt too stung.

"Can you promise that none of your clan can give us away," Josh asked. "Or that it won't be tempted by the sudden supply of flesh after all those roots and bugs?"

"I've been allowed to fast the power and most of the link away, so I think I can," Michael said.

"But you don't know," Josh said. "And the others?"

"Some are still struggling. The others lost their connections already. He allowed me to be the last. In fact, I thought I'd lost the full connection until recently. He doesn't just block his mind. He blocks all of ours too." Michael replied and, after a moment, added, "Maybe we won't have to think about blood if you happen to have a home cooked meal to take our minds off of it." He laughed a little, and Josh allowed the courtesy.

"That is," Michael asked. "If you have any to spare."

"We have it," Thug said nodding out towards a couple of diesel trailers parked in the distance. "That part wasn't hard to come by,"

"I don't like it," Bricktain said in a hushed voice directly next to Josh.

"I have to say I agree," Thomas added.

Michael couldn't hide the insult from showing on his face any more than Josh could hide his own doubt to the proposal. Still, Josh did owe Michael. He couldn't deny that.

"They've demonstrated their faith in us," Josh said. "Perhaps if we both show it, we can all go home again."

No one objected.

"What can we do to help," Josh asked.

"Only this very hour did I hear him tell us to seek you out for help," Michael explained. "His voice was gone, and then it was there. It was weak, but it was there."

"How do I help him," Josh asked. "Have you seen what we're doing here?"

"Yes," Michael said. "We've been beneath you since you got here. Until he spoke to me, we've been debating whether we should risk joining you or not."

"Then you know the danger," Josh said.

"There's more danger than you realize," Michael said, as if an order. "Jasper will grow hungry, and the only blood near him is your friend's. Do you understand? He's fighting for his sanity and health to protect you all, and your friend is a tempting food supply. Make of his request what you will. He asked for help, I have no one else to seek out."

Again, Josh fell into thought and stayed that way for some time until—

"I'll go," Bricktain said. "Give me some lanterns and the twins, and I'll do it."

"You'll go into the water," Josh asked. "Aren't you the one who needed water wings last time you got in that river?"

Josh recognized just one solution and knew only one of his allies who would be happy to hear it. He scanned the catwalk until he found the figure he was looking for making her rounds, watching beyond the compound for any activity that might suggest the attack might be coming. Only she knew the forest well enough not to get lost. As if she knew he was looking for her, Josh found her peering down at him.

"No," Bricktain snapped. "You're not sending her."

* * *

Of course he hated the decision. It was a bad decision, but it was also the only decision.

Thomas continued to suggest that Josh go as well.

"I can't," Josh replied. "My place is here now."

"You gave your word to protect her," Thomas said.

"I'm keeping my word," Josh said.

"Maybe, we can take a different approach," Thomas continued. "Follow the river from the school."

"You can't," Josh replied. "The ceiling's too low. It would be more dangerous for me to try to swim that than to be here."

Much to Josh's chagrin, Thomas continued his efforts, making some rather moving arguments. Bricktain had even joined in.

"This is my place," Josh insisted. "There's more than one way to protect her, and this is the best place for us."

Bricktain started to argue the situation further, but it suddenly ended as soon as Amber joined the efforts to convince Josh that maybe he should be the one to go.

"I'd like everyone to look over those walls and tell me what's out there," Josh demanded, pointing off past the gates. "They are out there, which means they aren't around her."

"If you go, they won't be around you either," Thomas urged and Bricktain echoed, only Bricktain suggested he go as well still."

"And what good will a close-combat paladin be, in an underground cavern if any should follow us down there," Josh asked. "Don't you get it? The way I fight is claustrophobic. I can't protect anyone down there. I belong in the open."

"Coward," one of the newer hunter's voices mumbled as he walked past the group performing whatever task he was performing. "If you have a weakness, you practice that weakness."

Josh turned quickly on him, but Thomas distracted him immediately with the argument that the biker with the wolf bandana made a valid point. Josh grabbed a stone and beaned the biker square in his bandana.

The paladin said nothing more on the topic, but called Dustin and Nick to his side. The two Dobermans quickly obeyed. One looked to Josh as if waiting for instruction. The other leapt into the pit without requiring an order and nearly disappeared down the small tunnel.

"Nick," Josh called after him. "Wait for the others." He turned back to Dustin. "Help Jasper. Keep an eye on him, but help him all the same."

The hum of Reggie's chair crept upon the group. A high-quality, black backpack rested in his lap. "Here's some food and some other items," he said. "It's not a lot, but it's more than they have right now, I'm sure. Maybe Michael's right. Having something to eat might help keep Jasper's mind off something other than feeding." He held the bag out for someone to take, although it appeared that he wasn't sure who he was handing it off to.

Acotactac took it. She appeared grim, even anxious, but not angry. She even managed a sort of friendly smile to Josh and patted one of his cheeks before nodding her understanding of her work. She might have wanted to hug Josh, but he stayed his cloak. Bricktain, she hugged and encouraged him with soft caresses over his left temple.

"Hurry back this time," Bricktain said.

Acotactac smiled at Bricktain, but then glared at Josh. Tears of anger welled in her eyes. She pulled her backpack over one of her arms and ensured her arm cannons were secure. She held an arm towards the earth, and the hydraulic-like pole shot straight down and into the pit. Then she hoisted herself over the pole and let it lower her casually into the tunnel entry way.

"I'll show you the way through," Michael said, then jumped into the hole where the twins and the Taichomée woman waited. His other companions had already returned to the hand-carved cavern.

"I need you to go with them," Josh said to Thomas.

Thomas started to protest and might have won this debate. He was wiser than Josh.

"Just enough to get them to the water hole and make sure they're not followed," Josh said. "Then come back."

"That I can do," Thomas said. He too leapt into the pit and called to Thug. "Make sure he gets sleep when it's his turn. Knock him out if you have to."

"I'll tell him a bedtime story and let him play with the moccasins," Thug returned.

This time Josh started to protest, but quickly lost the argument.

"And take Amber with you," Josh suggested.

"Don't think so," Amber said.

"Thomas might need your eyes," Josh explained. "Just come back."

Amber reluctantly agreed and stepped softly down to where Thomas was speaking to Michael about the size and structure of the tunnel.

Michael disappeared into the ground first, and Thomas ushered the others to follow. He whistled.

The black-and-white splattered Kate was down fast with barely enough room for her height.

"Think you can crawl it," Thomas asked.

Kate snorted.

"Then let's go," Thomas said and disappeared into the tunnel as well.

Kate dropped to her knees and haunches, then shimmied her way into the opening in the ground.

9 ~ Tight Spaces

"No," one man bellowed. "Keep driving."
The tavern echoed the sentiment.

Thomas wasn't comfortable with the plan. He knew who Josh was. He agreed that it was dangerous to reveal who he was. He couldn't force the new paladin to leave his post. Lately, he wondered if the new paladin had actually planned to ever accompany Cadence on the quest to find the ancients at all. He wondered lots of things where Josh was concerned, but most of them seemed trivial, laughable or simply unsure. If it were up to the British agent, he would have brought Josh along by force, but he'd learned long ago that unwilling traveling companions usually made for dead ones.

Besides, he wasn't feeling too certain of any well-laid plans lately and maybe taking Josh into darkness wasn't what he had previously thought.

The tunnels grew dark fast. They were rounded. Michael explained a little about how they used what supplies they had in their own underground bunker to help stabilize the man-made cavern. They crawled, though they probably didn't have to. They could have walked through in a constant state that might have led to irreversibly poor posture, but Thomas and the others found it easier to travel on their hands and knees. The vampire didn't find it easy at first, with his sheaths stabbing the dirt and creating strange fulcrums against his own body, but, after he rearranged to carry them on his back, he moved much more readily. Why couldn't he think better in tight spaces?

Kate snorted close at his heels. She was agile, and, even though he heard her and felt her breath at his back every now and then, he made sure to encourage her through a gentle stroke to her snout.

Up ahead, Michael announced where a low support beam appeared, and Thomas slowed his crawl until he knew that his girl was safely beyond it. The last thing any of them needed was for Kate to tear out something that could drop the earth on their party. Thomas was pretty certain he could survive digging his way up, but he knew the others couldn't do it. More than that though, if Kate died in this pit, the vampire would kill Michael and every last wolf in these tunnels.

"We'll be turning left, here," Michael announced. "And go down a small incline."

"With a half-ton horse taking up our rear," Thomas asked.

"I'm sorry," Michael apologized, "But they did build a trailer park over our bunker. We couldn't have them hearing us dig."

"How far is the exit," Thomas asked. "The air can't be that good on my friends."

Amber agreed without saying a word.

"Give us some credit," Michael replied. "We learned some things while doing this. Fresh air comes in from the edge of Shallow."

"The edge of Shallow," Thomas spat.

"Well, not quite to Shallow," Michael said. "But close enough. If we had another three weeks, we might be there."

Thomas urged the others to get a safe lead ahead of him and Kate, just in case she slipped down the dark, invisible slope. The decline wasn't as bad as Thomas thought it might be. Kate was probably more comfortable with it than the vampire was. She almost seemed to enjoy the crawl and nipped once at Thomas's rear end when he tried to crawl too slow for her taste. They soon caught back up with the rest of their group after completing their deep descent. Air eventually grew thin. Thomas noticed it. Acotactac moved a little slower. Kate took deeper breaths. Amber prayed the tunnel wouldn't collapse.

"Just a little farther, my dear," Thomas encouraged.

"Actually, we still have a ways to go," Michael countered.

Strangely, even though the air grew thin, somehow, it seemed fresh. Whatever these buffoons had done to build their tunnels, the air was still good.

"Doing all right back there," Michael asked.

"Stop wasting the oxygen," Thomas replied. "I imagine we should use it wisely rather than poison ourselves on carbon monoxide before we have to fight again."

Michael fell silent again, and Thomas continued to follow the sound of the twins trotting leisurely among the path and the group. Thomas swatted them away, ensuring that he was perfectly fine. At least the dogs seemed a bit comfortable in this environment. Then the air began to strengthen. Soon, it wasn't so bad at all. No one seemed to be huffing nearly as much, and even Kate appeared to be doing well.

"It's just up here," Michael said. After perhaps another half of a mile, they were in a place where they could stand. Electric lanterns filled the walls of a huge gathering area with rooms off the sides and hand-formed, earth benches. Tree roots ran through the walls, strengthening them. Even Kate could stand for the most part, although she still had to keep her head low.

They rested for a time, Michael disappeared off into a dark corridor. Thomas couldn't tell how filthy anyone was in comparison to how much shadow the lanterns threw, but everyone looked much darker than they should have.

After about twenty minutes, Michael reappeared and requested that they continue their journey. This time, the twins followed directly behind him, and Acotactac followed before Amber, then Thomas and Kate.

"It's not so pleasant up ahead," Michael said. "Be warned."

"Might I ask what happened to your friends," Thomas asked.

"They're around," Michael replied.

Eventually, the vampire found himself back inside a tunnel and on his hands and knees. Kate occasionally snorted her disgust, and the farther they pressed, the more she snorted. Once they found themselves rounding a larger boulder, they started to smell the rot.

The odor crept in—weak at first, but stronger as the group continued on. The ground had become softer, moister somehow—like mud, only not. Thomas thought he felt movement—not only on the ground, but in his pant legs as well.

He wasn't certain, but he also thought the ceiling was dripping on him—not water, something warm and oily. Perhaps it was byproduct from the roots. For a while, he struggled with the effect of the stench on his body. When he finally started to feel he'd be able to withstand this horrible gas, Acotactac suddenly began coughing. That was soon followed by soft gags. A few seconds of silence followed by the splash of vomit. Then, Thomas followed suit and felt his coat for the vial of blood he might need to fill his stomach if this environment kept up.

"Sorry," Michael said. "We use it to mask our scent from the exit, sort of a line of defense."

"This isn't a tunnel. This is a cemetery," Thomas eventually choked out, realizing what must have loomed all around them.

"No," Michael said. "Smell of rotting flesh isn't enough. It's also maggot and waste. What we can't bury, we build into the walls and ceiling."

Acotactac coughed again.

Amber threw up. "You mean, the stuff falling on us could be corpse."

"Not just above us," Thomas replied, feeling what he knew was the end of a tibia as it popped through whomever's rotting flesh his hand just passed over.

Amber said nothing. It wasn't difficult to do while she was heaving up the remains of what little breakfast she'd had earlier.

"We'll be to air soon," Michael said.

The group continued on and so did the stink.

"Would you be so kind to vomit to the side, my dear girl," Thomas requested after tromping through Cadence and Amber's third evidence of sick.

"You don't want to do that, ma'am," Michael said. "Trust me, down is better."

Kate complained some more.

"I know it's bad," Michael said. "We thought we couldn't survive it ourselves at first."

"You could have dragged most of them out instead of bury them in your tunnels," Thomas coughed.

"Friend," Michael replied. "Try living here."

"If I have offended. I am truly sorry, good sir." Thomas then felt what he believed to be a ribcage cushion his left knee. At first, he thought it breathed, but then made the realization that it merely gave beneath his weight.

The crypt tunnel continued on, and the stench lingered, but eventually, little, if anything, remained in the stomachs of Michael's guests. Thomas tried to ignore the sound of the cracking of bones and old cartilage as Kate passed over the floor. She stirred as if she wanted to stand, run or smash down the walls.

"Perhaps there is an end in sight before my horse panics," Thomas inquired. "I fear the floor is not so designed to hold her weight."

"Don't worry," Michael replied. "The ceiling will fall upon her before the floor gives way."

Thomas encouraged her, realizing Michael was only trying to do the same. The vampire soon began encouraging the twins as well as their comfort had worn off. He prayed Kate wouldn't decide to start heaving as the rest of his allies had done.

The twins' eyes weren't as bright as some of the other beasts he'd encountered. They were hardly strong enough to light any of the darkness, but from time to time he'd catch a slight glow. At least he believed that's what the glow was. It was too dark to tell since they had left the lanterns some time ago.

Then a new light appeared, and Michael fell silent. He encouraged the others to do the same. It seemed much more a mist than rays of light. It lightly painted the floor with long strokes of shadows. Thomas was grateful to realize he had returned to earthy walls and floors once more. No matter though, he still felt rotting corpse. He'd never forget that feeling. The mist of light gradually grew until Thomas could make out the discernible shadows of each of his friends, and grains of dirt threw fat auras over the cavern floors now. Thomas, Kate, Amber, Acotactac and the twins joined Michael in a larger area.

Michael breathed deeply at the ceiling where strands of fierce sun broke through a jumble of roots and terrestrial remnants. He motioned for the others to remain silent. They knelt, still and quiet, for some time. Eventually, Thomas's eyes adjusted, and the den had appeared as if filled with day itself. The room was nothing short of shoddy work: crumbling walls; uneven surfaces at every angle; and a steep slope at one side. Kate's frame, still partially within the narrower portion of the tunnel, appeared twisted

Michael silently signaled that everyone should let their eyes face as much of the light as possible so they wouldn't run into the bright world blind. He seemed quite comfortable with grabbing Amber's head and positioning it to face into the daylight. He attempted the same with Thomas, but recoiled upon gripping Thomas's head and discovering all the spiky balls weaved into his straight and white hair.

"It's crowded out there," Michael whispered.

They waited several more minutes in silence. Thomas watched the cavern walls twist even more around him. He breathed deep and tried to find his center.

"Now," Michael said abruptly standing. "It's clear."

He quickly folded the entire ceiling of roots and limbs to one side. Earth, leaves, grass and debris fell into the unhealthy pit.

"Run straight," Michael ordered in a low volume. "Don't ask. Just go. Go now!"

Nick and Dustin charged up the steep incline first with Acotactac close behind. Amber flew as well and immediately took a more vertical, and silent escape route as soon as she was back into the outside world.

"Don't burn up out there," Michael said.

"That's not how it works," Thomas ridiculed. "Everyone thinks they know what a vampire does."

Thomas leapt out. He was stiff, but he executed the quick exit. Kate joined him, which took a little longer than made Thomas comfortable. He launched himself up onto her back and listened to the blanket of roots reseal the tunnel behind them. He made a quick note of the fallen tree near the entrance.

"Go," Michael demanded from within the hidden tunnel. "While there's time to mask your scent."

"I see them," Amber's voice spoke through the earpiece. "They haven't noticed us yet."

Thomas tried to gain his bearings while Kate and the others sped straight ahead as Michael had instructed. Dustin and Nick kept pace ahead of Kate. Acotactac kept her own pace. One pole launched her into the air and forward, while the other caught her weight and lowered her back to the ground a moment before she blasted herself forward once more. Surprisingly, Thomas was the one trying to keep up with the hydraulic Taichomée and the supernatural twin Doberman pinschers.

A whistle cooed past Thomas. He drew his steel blade and dispatched a black mutt. Upon Amber's return whistle, he watched the brown body of another dog fall.

"More coming," Amber said into Thomas's left ear through his small hearing device.

"Perhaps they should try their luck in the woods," Thomas replied.

"You catch up," Amber said. "I'll keep 'em from following."

In a few more paces, Thomas was at the edge of the Shallow Woods. Amber's whistling death of her orbits had started a second verse behind him. She was competent. These scouts couldn't hold against her higher elevation. Even if they should find the numbers to coordinate any high-jumping attacks against her, by the time they pulled any off, she'd be fleeing the scene; Thomas would already be gone; and their foes would most likely become lost. The vampire and Kate rode into the woods.

Thomas had heard much about these woods, but the truth was, he didn't know these woods himself. He'd had opportunities in his life for many things, but meeting the Taichomée was not one of them. However, he knew they were Acotactac's home, and she seemed quite in faculty concerning which direction they should flee. These were her woods, and she knew exactly which direction to move. If only she was more conscientious of her slower allies.

"Can you see where they went, Kate," Thomas asked, finding himself now surrounded by trees in all directions. He remembered the stories of the leaves and the vines that could ensnare intruders. "Don't get caught in the vines."

Kate grumbled back to Thomas after he asked too many times whether she knew which way to go.

"Then I leave you to your chase, my dear," Thomas replied, then trusted his steed to carry this leg of the journey.

Thomas had understood to become one with his own beasts. He had learned every muscle along Kate's back and knew what each tightening or softening meant. Sometimes, he should lean. Sometimes, he should hug, and sometimes he should jump off, or allow himself to be thrown off. He rode well with all of his horses, but Kate was most subtle. She was most in tune with Thomas. Every horse had their strengths. Where Petruchio's movements were more boisterous, sometimes predicting to throw Thomas rather than give him leverage, Kate's movements were harmonious. Thomas trusted and knew when to let her take control, and she knew that when Thomas moved back, it wasn't to break her.

He hugged her, his head pressed tight against her neck. Trees and branches whipped past him, and he adjusted only for a moment as she leapt an obstacle hidden beneath ivy of some sort. Then she altered direction and continued her flight. Here she stopped. She switched her head from one side to another. Her ears twisted like miniature radar dishes, flicked, and her head snapped in a new direction. Then she was running again in that same direction. Thomas leaned as she curved around a particularly unmoving tree in her path.

"Where is she, Kate," Thomas asked.

Acotactac suddenly appeared to Thomas's left. She stood still. Nick and Dustin perched on each side of her. Her face had been what he was used to seeing, but it instantly filled with an unrecognizable fear, as Thomas drew closer. She started, appearing to scream, and chased towards Kate as the canyon of shale suddenly opened its jaws before Thomas and swallowed him and his steed.

The duo charged over the ledge and flew straight into the depths of the shale ravine that notoriously masticated any who entered it.

Their landing was rough, striking the walls of the pit and skidding deeper down towards a long narrow throat. With Thomas barely still poised on her back, Kate fought the current of platelet-like rocks valiantly. They drew to a skid, and finally a stop. Kate's muscles now worked feverishly beneath Thomas to keep them both afloat of the rock slivers. Thomas egged her on to climb out.

The shale was fast, flaky and too much. It rolled down upon them like hour glass sand, and, yes, it fought to bury them. Still, Kate railed her hooves against the shale, keeping her weight on top. She and Thomas, of one mind, plotted a course up the side of the canyon. She plowed at the path before her, trudging, climbing, fighting and probably succeeding at gaining more ground than any other victim had done with this death trap, the very reason no one ventured into the Shallow.

Suddenly she stopped, stiffened atop the waves of shale. Both she and her rider entered a step-less dance to keep them balanced, while they listened to strands of stone-leaves meander around her legs.

Thomas contorted in the ways that he knew would help Kate keep her still footing. They waited, let the canyon have its fun. Gently, the canyon trickled into silence. Kate stood still and breathed in unison with her rider, her back muscles preparing Thomas for their next strategy. Then she took a step. Thomas arched his back, then straightened it. He felt Kate struggle to stay standing, stumble but not fall. She stomped out yet one more step. Her front legs wobbled, and her rump suddenly squatted, causing her and Thomas to slide backwards and lose a few paces. She grunted. She was tired. They worked together again to regain balance.

"We can do this," Thomas urged. He continued his waltz with his companion. Together, they worked to inch their way to their friends. Kate sat a time or two more, each time taking a little longer to find the energy to pull out of the slide and regain footing.

The stories about Shale Canyon had been eerie before, even to Thomas. However, as he and Kate lost another pace and gained three, he found them not frightening enough. This was no canyon. It was death itself. Deep, wide, perhaps a quarter of a mile across is all. It appeared to resemble the concave and sinking structure like that of a copper or lithium mine. He couldn't see the end of its length in either direction, for the tree line, but he imagined it must have continued on for several miles just as the rumors had told.

Thomas thought of leaping off her back to lighten Kate's load, but he thought of other variables as well, such as wondering if a person of his size and weight helped her create any additional leverage that she needed to grip the wall of stones with her awkward and straight hooves. He also knew more feet on the ground, even if they were his own, would only rain down more shale upon them both. Had he a rope, he could have moved quickly enough to tie a few knots and at least anchor them in place, but he had nothing.

Amber appeared, interrupting his thoughts upon the variables. She planted her feet against the turbulent breezes created by the millions of falling stone slivers. She hugged at Kate's neck and stomped against the airflow rushing around all three bodies and over the canyon skin. Amber's face felt hot. It felt red. Suddenly, she stumbled, let go of Kate and hobbled deeper into the canyon herself, catching her footing before fumbling against the shale.

Thomas felt Kate's instinct to turn and run to aid Amber.

"No," Thomas ordered. "She's in control."

Amber returned to Kate and Thomas, who ordered Acotactac not to do something stupid like jump in to save them.

"You'll only bring more down upon us," he explained.

Acotactac paced in frustration.

"We'll do this," Amber said. She grabbed Kate's neck once again and, this time, swung beneath, saddling her underside, her feet pressed firmly against an unseen lever that only Amber could use to help alleviate Kate's struggle. Kate's body suddenly seemed less tense beneath Thomas.

"It's helping," Thomas said.

"Heavy," Amber grunted from beneath Kate's head. Her feet poised hard against whatever breeze she could find. "Can you reach the orbits?"

Thomas could. Although he didn't want to throw his Kate off balance, he tore one of the orbital whips from Amber's left side then maneuvered himself around Kate's neck and took the one from her right.

"Use them," Amber tried to muster but could only groan.

Thomas understood. His time had come to lighten both his comrades burdens. He leapt and threw out one ring. It didn't sing like Amber could orchestrate, but his point was to sink the ring into anything that could act like an anchor. It sank, chipping into shale and holding only the slightest of leverage to allow Thomas one more leap. It had lost its hold before Thomas could finish that jump. He landed in a squat in the wall, and held his pose. He slid back a few feet and used the orbits as best he could to act as braking mechanisms. The slide stopped. He heard Kate and Amber struggle with the residual farther down the chasm. He leapt again, same maneuver, same outcome, but with even less anchor than before and a little more slide back.

From here, he spotted a tree root breaking through the stony lip of the crevasse. He thought it might be close enough. He wasn't sure. It was a rough call. He felt his footing start to slip. He was on his back now, but managed a roll, threw an orbit and gained enough hold to pull out one more leap. He threw the second ring of razored sharpness out towards the tree root, father away this time than when he had first estimated the distance.

His ring fell short. He tossed the other ring, knowing it would fall short too, but this one did find an anchor. Rather, Acotactac had caught it on one of her telescopic posts. With one arm, she held the trunk of the same tree to which Thomas had hoped to anchor into its root.

It was enough for Thomas to bound his way out of the chasm and begin searching for a way to save his friends still down the gully of stone avalanche.

Meanwhile, Amber continued to do her best to give Kate leverage. Sometimes, she thought Kate was making ground, but then the horse would slip back more paces than she could recover, and she dragged Amber down with her. Amber, to her credit struggled to keep her footing out of the shale. She thought a moment of finding a better position, but the ground was close and if she dipped a moccasin into the shale, she might not get out herself. Truth was, she was afraid to let go of Kate for just that reason right now. She felt safer here.

"Get out of there," Thomas yelled when Amber's foot dipped once and Kate helped to break it free.

Amber wanted to brush off his order.

"She's dragging you with her," Thomas yelled. "Let her try on her own."

Amber didn't want to, but Kate yelled as if to agree with Thomas.

"She can't use her head with your fat arse holding it down," Thomas yelled. Despite the storm of falling stone flooding out his physical voice now, Amber understood common-sense yelling through her crackling earpiece.

Somehow Amber broke her grip from Kate's neck, and she climbed away from the torrent before it could swallow her.

With this, Kate charged with a fresh burst of energy, taking the shale head-on. No more dancing, straight up the side of the canyon wall. For a moment, she fumbled, but continued to maintain her dignified, standing stature of integrity and regality. She stood still again and turned not once, nor did she whinny as she continued to slide down the slope, despite her continued rigid stance. She maintained that she was still the master of grace and exception.

"That's right, my dear," Thomas yelled after her as she slid farther into the vortex of deadly shale. "Don't struggle, find your moment."

She heard him and squared her head with the danger before her just as she had done many times before. She reconvened her rampage, her overheated breaths now screaming throughout the canyon as she continued to lose ground and slide deeper away.

She slipped into a cloud of brown dust and the storm of falling rock.

Thomas watched. He should have flown. He knew that, but had already contributed enough to her fall. However, she was his friend. She was strong. She deserved to be rescued.

"I'm so sorry, Thomas," Amber said.

Thomas drooped. He probably didn't realize or he might not have allowed it. He slouched and stared down into the chasm. The others let him.

Amidst the settling dust, a silhouette appeared. She stood tall and firm atop the fragile skin of the canyon, again, waiting her moment. The stone had settled. Kate waited. The dust was receding. Five minutes she held her statuesque ground, except for her movements of deep breaths. If ever a champion horse was so picturesque, it could not compare with the determination and composure of Thomas's Kate as she stood erect near the bottom of the gully, her head defiant just as with any other enemy.

If Thomas cheered, Amber couldn't hear it over her own.

"That's right," Thomas yelled. "Catch your breath, dear."

Several minutes passed.

"If she can stay standing, I can get something around her," Amber said as she retrieved her weapons and began coiling them. "We could pull her out."

"You mean rope," Thomas said. "Already thought of that."

"We have vines," Amber replied. "They're all over."

Kate grunted.

"I don't think she's waiting," Thomas said and shouted for Kate to wait, but his driven horse had made up her mind. She would stomp this enemy as she did all other foes. The shale fell once more like angry dominoes. This time, she ran along the length of the canyon. It was a farther run, a greater distance, but the ground didn't move against her until she reached it, and, by the time she had unsettled it, she had run over it entirely. After some distance, she suddenly switched back, climbing the walls with each step.

Thomas knew her. He found her after all. He trained her; made her; broke her and molded her through wars that no other creature could have endured. She was, above all, stubborn and right. He admired her as he watched her kick up shale behind her.

"What is she thinking," Amber asked.

"Of course," Thomas said. "She's trying to make a break, she's going to use the flow of rocks against each other. It might slow the flow, give her a better chance."

After a ways of running into the gorge, Kate suddenly switched back, hard to her right. She continued her arduous climb and suddenly switched back once more, stamping lightly at the gravel beneath her. She held her head as if staring an enemy in the face. She switched again, higher up the wall now. Though she seemed not to notice, the others watched a vortex of stone now nip at her heels as she continued to carve her path up the canyon.

"She's staying ahead of it," Amber realized.

As the flow began to subside behind her, Kate switched back once more. Small slivers fell around her hooves around the turns, but she pulled out of them before she could be overtaken. She continued her charge back to her vampire who now stood perhaps two hundred feet up the slope from her.

She cried and her whinny filled every crevice of echo. Her will overflowed the canyon, this and every other one around for continents. She fixed on Thomas's face each time she switched her trail back across the canyon skin. She planned her next turn. Each switchback pulled her higher up the face of her foe. Three, five, six more switches, easily bringing her within perhaps 50 feet of the forest grade and her friends.

Then, at the next maneuver, she didn't switch back. She charged straight up the hill again. She was close, she could do it. She knew she could.

"No, no, no," Thomas said softly and to himself, then yelled, "Use what's working."

Kate ignored him.

"Don't do it," he said again, keeping anything that might shut down Kate's confidence too quiet for her to hear.

"Come on girl," Amber cried.

"No," Thomas shot back at Amber. "She's going to jump."

"That's good," Amber replied.

Thomas drooped once again.

Suddenly Kate did it. She readied herself, raised her front half and drove her rear legs against the ground to launch.

The shale quickly swam around her hooves, stealing her leverage and strength. She managed a small leap, but her momentum was gone now. Instead of progressing, she was struggling once more to swim the slide of rocks. Above it all, a cracking sound, unlike the colliding rock filling the cavern, erupted as thunder. It was followed by Kate's horrified scream as she rolled on her side like a capsizing vessel.

Amber started to step back in, but Thomas held her arm. She understood. She knew a broken leg on a horse when she heard one.

Kate continued to cry. Here, she fell sideways, the shale speeding her back towards the bottom of the canyon. She continued to fight, kicking herself back to her feet. She could make it on three legs if she could get back on her toes. She knew she could. She'd do it on two if she had to. She waited it out once, she could do it again, but her feet sank. Her captor pinched her in now, cut her, pressed against her. She felt as though a million locusts bit at her, each hitting an intense mark.

Her fall stopped, but the shale kept swimming in around her. She struggled to breathe, sealed in by horrible broken rock and heavy dust. She felt nothing beneath or around her, nothing to press against, nothing to stamp against, no leverage, only a broken leg, perhaps two now. The pressure built around her chest. The rock fell.

Still, she was strong. She had conquered greater mountains than this and, as the air fell thin, the dust grew annoying, and the weight of shale around her tried ever more to smother her, she could no longer move.

"Save me," she cried in a language that Thomas understood all too well.

Thomas watched his lovely Kate, her head, the only extremity to prove her existence, barely staying afloat at the bottom of the canyon in a sea of snare. Her cry for rescue carried up the canyon and would soon invite the beasts of the wilderness, and worse, down upon her and her friends.

Dustin, anxiously examined the ledge of the canyon, clearly thinking of something daring that might help Kate. Nick kept his distance and stayed poised at Amber's side.

"No," Thomas ordered. Dustin stopped his plotting.

Kate screamed again. She cried. She begged Thomas to come down and pull her to safety, which Thomas would have gladly done if it would have done her any good. With every scream, her chest drew tighter and her lungs took in less air.

Thomas drew a small, single-shot pistol and a chrome lighter. He lit a fuse and steadied an aim, even while smoke sputtered from its top and blocked his sight. A single shot fired into that one place that God had created to free any fallen and broken horse from unnecessary torture.

Kate stopped crying, stopped struggling and finally let the avalanche of stone take her.

Thomas returned his single-shot pistol into his breast pocket, then buttoned up his dirty red suit before he turned to Acotactac, who could only watch the fallen horse's ambush.

"I believe you know the way, my lady," Thomas said. "Lead on."

10 ~ Boot to the Head

"I'm thirsty," is all he could think to say, and the tavern filled with laughter.

The stink of death was strong. He'd smelled the stench before, in wars, more than any soul should have to know, but not in a very long time. Over the years, mankind had become better at burying their dead. This was the stench of massacre.

The vampire of the royal guard was silent. He had nothing to say, and none of his comrades knew any comfort to give, so he continued to follow Acotactac without uttering a word. The twins appeared somewhat strangely at ease. Thomas still didn't know which one was Dustin and which was Nick. He pointed, he ordered and one, or both, of the twins followed. Come to think of it, he didn't know who they were as people at all, maybe at the next full moon. One Doberman seemed intent on pressing forward, and the other seemed more interested in the sounds of the woods surrounding them.

Occasionally, the one who liked to listen put the right mix of energy into a belly sound that even Thomas believed might be dangerous. If anything, Thomas spent his time listening to the forest. At least, it gave him something to do other than think about Kate.

The stench had clearly festered since Jasper had destroyed the inquisitor and his army. Thomas was grateful the stench of their bodies was nothing like he had suffered in the tunnel, but it was different somehow. Although Thomas knew the aroma, he still hadn't discovered where it emanated from.

They walked now, and Acotactac took great care to show Thomas how to step on the large leaves covering the forest floor. They had already begun to scuff and cut his black shoes. He wondered if they'd stay on his feet long enough to get out of the razor-sharp mess. Every so often, Acotactac made sure to point out some unique landmark that Thomas could easily recognize upon his return to help him navigate his way back out of the forest.

Then the bodies appeared. Sprawled everywhere and surrounding a large clearing where tall redwoods hid almost the entire sky away. Hundreds of corpses had fallen here. They were bloated, one without a head. Thomas wondered if he actually searched the area if he wouldn't discover a thousand or even more corpses in the surrounding woods.

Acotactac surveyed the area herself. She peeled back a section of her wrappings from around her wrist, and a bracelet of beads fell. She rattled it and then hid it away again. The sound of wood scraping startled even Thomas. It took him a moment to realize an opening in a large tree where three faces peered down from above. One of the faces rattled a similar chain of beads and more trees opened with more scraping sounds.

The strange tribe began to gather to Acotactac and her conspirators. Children peered out from openings, too afraid to leave their hiding. The Dobermans each ran towards a different group of children, and the youth poured praises upon them and hands upon their heads.

An older man, whom Thomas believed to be the elder of the hidden village, began speaking to Acotactac. Thomas knew the language, but only from hearing it from Speatsh. He didn't know what Speatsh had taught him, but this was clearly not the same language he knew.

Acotactac signed back. Thomas had picked up several variations of sign language during his lifetime, but this was new to him as well, and he watched closely to see if he could decipher it. He managed to make out the term, or what he believed was the term for general and then a lesser emphasis of the same sign meant guardian. He wasn't sure if he saw a sign for the soldier or scout. He'd lived long enough that he felt he should know.

Had the circumstances been different, Thomas might have enjoyed visiting this place. He had heard the stories, and even promised Speatsh that he would visit with him some time, but that never happened. Speatsh would have been good company right now, even if he had been too young for his own good.

It was about this time that one of the younger tribesmen appeared before Acotactac. He held a brown bag with vines and leaves woven into its skin. They seemed quite intent on the bag's contents. Acotactac directed the bag holder towards the vampire. Thomas reached for the bag, but the tribesman recoiled. Acotactac clapped at the bag bearer. Thomas received the bag, and reached in to withdraw a legendary head with a familiar face.

"Ha," Thomas burst, and quickly recovered his composure at the sight of the inquisitor's head. "I know precisely what to do with this."

He stuffed the head back into the bag. "With your permission, I'd like to keep this." He awaited a nod from the chief, which he took as approval. Thomas threw the bag over his shoulder, thanked the Taichomée and then turned his attention elsewhere. Thomas then politely pressed through the group of tribal people, towards the signs of melee that still lingered among the camp. He knew these people weren't really tribal. They held no claim to an actual clan of any North American tribe. These people were a society in their own, with a general who had granted their freedom.

These were once some of the most ferocious monsters on the earth, and now they hid. Centuries ago, he actually tried hunting them, but the stories he knew about them now deserved an unspoken respect. Perhaps that's part of why he'd stayed away from this forest for so long. Anything as valiant as a community of monsters controlling their hunger deserved a sort of reverence, provided they abided peacefully. Thomas may have been the oldest living human, a vampire, a person whom he believed God had forgotten—but he was still a human, and blood did flow through his veins. Why tempt such an honorable clan with any sort of fleshly visit?

They were more than he realized still. They protected an entrance, and he wondered: had he known about it, would he have had the strength to endure whatever torture might have drawn it from his lips? The chief of this group was indeed a brave and clever strategist.

Thomas's interest was in secrets. It was hard to explain sometimes why, but so far he'd only had one student who truly picked up an eye for it, and that was Richard. Richard had always been the best at discovering secrets, but Thomas was the best at keeping them. Richard saw things. Not as much as Thomas saw, but where the vampire saw them, Richard had a knack to see through them. It's what made him such a remarkable investigator. He was puzzle-solving, even Thomas hadn't developed the knack as Richard had. Here, Thomas began wishing that Richard could help him solve yet another enigma.

Thomas stepped carefully. The tangling leaves that had covered the floor of Shallow previously were absent, but he was still in the habit. Other leaves were prone to cover the ground, leaves of the redwood trees. The entire setting was still more magnificent than he had imagined. How did such a place go unnoticed? Then he remembered the treacherous canyon and quickly pressed Kate out of his mind to begin searching for imprints in the ground.

Thomas had seen Genre once, he recognized his footprints immediately. Strangely, the Taichomée had avoided coming out of their hiding—presumably, to preserve their being in case any other monsters came. He'd thought about so many possible ways to divide and conquer Genre: kill the left half then hunt down the right, but the two had proven impossible in just that. Even if he could draw them apart, they were still conjoined mentally. Thomas was impressed that Speatsh had lasted as long as he had against them.

The vampire kept searching; found several more imprints; and eventually discovered the larger footprints with deep jagged treads. They laid out a dance of majesty, despite the impressions of the brace on one of the feet. Then he found the spot where the dancer finally fell to his knees and died.

"I would cut my hand," Thomas said, squatting and pressing his palm upon the place of Speatsh's death. "You understand why I can't." He bowed his head.

"Father," he prayed. "Forgive this man. We both know he needs it." Thomas stood and stomped at Speatsh's spot, blotting out the image of his disrespectful death. "And please forgive the vengeance I swear to return with as much blood as possible."

He turned suddenly and with conviction that seemed to frighten Amber as she met his hateful gaze.

"Are you okay, Thomas," Amber asked.

"All of you made him lazy," Thomas replied. "You will not find the same mistake from me. Do try to keep up." He marched past Amber, ignoring her question.

Amber chose not to press for an explanation.

"Where is it," Thomas asked, interrupting the conversation Acotactac and the Elder were currently having.

Acotactac pointed, and Thomas saw nothing more than a plank or a log resting nearby.

One of the Taichomée joined Acotactac in moving the plank that revealed the hole in the earth where the sound of running water softly filtered out and above ground.

"You should have told us what this place protected long ago," Thomas said returning a disdainful look to Acotactac.

She returned a quizzical look.

"Your secret keeping got Speatsh killed," Thomas replied.

He saw her shoulder move. He reacted, but not quickly enough. Her palm struck powerfully across the side of his face, a force Thomas knew could only be driven by fierce anger, and more, much more. He regained his posture and found the Taichomée elder standing before him with frosty eyes and steel-like jaw muscles.

"Taichomée protect hole," he spoke slowly and with a fat tongue so Thomas could understand his English better. "Beneath hole, our water. Rest forbidden. Why tell you? Do no help yet. You need, you came, now you know. Now good time to know. Better chances for vampire."

Thomas apologized, mostly as courtesy. He found a pebble and tossed it into the chasm. He waited for its reply to tell him how far down the drop was. Scanning the area, he discovered a small stockpile of rope, a bowl tied to one of them, but he doubted any of it could hold any weight. Before he could make the suggestion, one of the twins leapt into the hole. The other twin cocked its head at Thomas and sang a low rumble.

"Josh will be fine," Thomas replied. "He's made strong allies."

With that, the second twin leapt into the pit.

Acotactac shared some more signs and words with the eldest man in the group. She turned to Thomas, and he apologized once more. She hugged him.

"Don't worry," Thomas added finally pulling away. "Your husband has Josh."

Acotactac rolled her eyes, whatever that meant.

She smiled and leapt into the hole. An instant later, she was gone. The sound of the poles catching Acotactac's weight popped from beneath the hollow of the earth below.

He yelled for the crew to wait and pulled a small LED flashlight from his suit pocket. He turned it on before dropping it down the way his allies had ventured. He didn't use it much, usually for closer examinations in dark places. It wasn't great, but he hoped it would assist them.

The Taichomée resealed the entrance.

They didn't return to hiding immediately. They tried a time or two to communicate with the vampire, but he simply didn't understand, and he had more important issues at hand.

"We could use you at the bunker," Thomas requested.

Amber attempted to translate, which caught Thomas off guard. The chief replied and confused Amber.

"He says, they must reside with the down-below," Amber said. "I think."

"Down-below," Thomas asked.

The chief spoke more in the Taichomée tongue.

"He was just speaking in English," Thomas said.

The elder appeared confused now as well.

"Very well," Thomas replied. "I won't press. We all have our jobs." He doubted the Taichomée understood. The chief clapped his hands, and more of the villagers withdrew from the trees. As the sun had little strength left to offer, they began preparing several torches;

sitting around an empty fire pit; or huddling in small groups around the camp, where they ate out of baskets. They offered Amber and Thomas to join. He was grateful for the invitation, but his dinner was more than what he believed they deserved to smell. He did need the blood, but the pouch remained in his inside pockets where the cooling system could preserve it until he was ready for it. He'd simply have to manage his hunger. If these people could do it, surely he could honor them in denying this temptation.

Even with the canopy of thick leaves overhead, he could tell that the night was upon them. Thomas ran his hands over his side arms and the various dangerous goodies hidden throughout his uniform. He let his hair smooth itself and finally decided the time had come to return to the compound.

"I'll leave you to your work, good sir," Thomas said, bowing fully before the old chief of the village.

The chief smiled and wiped his fingers across his bare chest, cleaning them of the juices from the berries he'd been eating. He held his wet and sticky hand out to Thomas. The vampire didn't hesitate to return the courtesy.

Then the chief made a new gesture, pointing Thomas towards one of the reaches of the village. At least this motion Thomas believed he understood and followed the chief.

"I am grateful of any direction out of here," Thomas said. "I'm not sure I can find the landmarks your Acotactac pointed out."

The chief said nothing, but merely began marching. He seemed to know that Thomas didn't quite understand his intent. As he led Thomas and Amber towards a hidden area of camp, the truck appeared out of nowhere. It was dented. The windshield was cracked in several places. One of the side windows had been blown out. The decorative grill was gone. The hood had been smashed in, and its side seams turned up. The red light on the roof had been broken off, but the blue appeared in good condition still.

"Josh said it was a small accident," Amber screeched, as she caught sight of the police truck with its crumpled roof that appeared to have been popped back up since the wreck.

Thomas thought quickly to the police officer that had entered the compound two nights ago with Josh. What was his name again? This must have been his vehicle. Could it still work?

The chief pulled at the driver's door. It dropped on its hinge, but didn't fall off. He reached inside, turned a key, and a moment later the vehicle started.

"I do believe there's more to you than meets the eye," Thomas replied.

The chief smiled and spoke in a language that Thomas didn't know. He pointed off in the distance.

"That way," Thomas asked.

"Panu danna," the chief replied, pointed and spoke again. "Panu danna."

Thomas felt obliged to bow a second time before climbing into the truck.

"You coming with me," Thomas asked.

"I'll walk!" Amber spat and had already started climbing high. "You'll need my eyes."

"Don't be too angry with him," Thomas said. "I'm sure he didn't want you to worry."

"That's a stupid excuse."

Thomas knew better than to argue. This wasn't his fight. He placed the truck into gear and drove away from the camp.

The engine seemed a little rough, but it ran, and that's what Thomas cared about. If he had the time and tools, he might have been able to smooth out its rattle a bit, but it had been a long time since he looked under an engine bonnet.

He steered the truck between a set of trees, eventually turning on the loosely-mounted spotlight on the side of the vehicle to show his path since both headlights had been smashed out. Should he be ambushed, both the windshield and the door were weak enough that they shouldn't interfere too much with his escape or attack.

The truck crept slowly through the dark forest, and Thomas pushed Kate out of his mind. Well, mostly, he pushed her out. When he approached the shale canyon once more, he parked the truck and stepped out.

"What are you doing," Amber asked from somewhere hidden in the dark sky.

"Paying my respects," Thomas replied. He opened the leaf bag that the Taichomée had given him and pulled out the inquisitors head. "So great a day as this is cheaply bought," he said, and, with that, he dropped the inquisitor's head against his foot and punted it into the canyon where a distant, rocky landslide whispered an angry cheer. "Bloody cur!"

Thomas returned to the truck and didn't bother attempting to answer Amber. She didn't attempt any follow-up questions.

Out of curiosity and a need to be entertained, he turned on the vehicle radio and tried to boot up the laptop. The radio turned on, but the laptop screen stayed black. Although, the small printer did startle Thomas a hair as the carriage rattled to life. He threw the printer and the useless laptop out the window. Then he started his drive home.

He dodged the trees, hoping the vines he'd heard so much about wouldn't tie down his truck. For that purpose, he drove much more slowly than he preferred. He was even starting to think that Speatsh had exaggerated his story of ever bringing the Silver Bullet into this area.

Had Amber not been providing some direction, he would have abandoned the truck and all faith in Speatsh's stories. Every so often, she would come back to earth to help him cut his vehicle free of the strangling vines.

Once he finally watched the tree line open up back into the outskirt fields of Plattsville, he was tempted to leave the truck and proceed on foot, but he wasn't quite sure where he was. It was too dark to tell. He turned off the spotlight and watched for any of the reflective green dots that he knew would belong to the guardians who were sure to be alerted to the sound of his engine.

He had seen black cities before. Even in the light of the stars and growing moon, the black could seem overpowering. But it had been a long time since he'd seen this much black over any city. He remembered the debate he had held once with an old friend about how electricity had killed the night. Right now, even he would have felt more comfortable with a brighter town. This would have meant some distance between him and the rogue. As it was, he couldn't see the town, except for a soft glow off in the distance hidden in the deep black.

"Why do they have lights," Amber asked.

"Who," Thomas asked.

"The college campus," she replied.

"Could be back-up generators," Thomas replied. "Or a new farm."

There, the rogue had entered his mind. Even Thomas had his fears. Tonight demonstrated that.

Without Kate, he wondered if he could fight well enough to fend off the worst attacks that could come at him.

Here, he noticed the blinking light. He might have noticed it sooner, but it was faint and barely yellow. He might not have noticed it had any other light been around. It wasn't high enough for stars, but it was unnaturally off the ground. Then a sudden burst of brightness accompanied it, that of electricity breaking into a downpour of sparks.

"I see it," Amber said. "How do you want to do this?"

Thomas thought a moment before, "Head back to the compound. Tell them I might be running in fast."

Amber acknowledged the suggestion.

Thomas dropped the gas pedal and felt the truck dig ruts behind itself as he turned the spotlight back on. In a moment, he had control over the vehicle once more, despite it pulling heavily to the left, and he dodged what strange protrusions in the ground he felt so inclined to avoid.

The tower appeared out of nowhere. Had the guardians not been focused around its base, he might have smashed the truck headlong into the tower's footing and made the rest of his journey back to camp on foot. Instead, the truck stopped; the driver's door flew off its hinge; and Thomas launched himself into a mob of at least twenty or so guardians.

He drew his diamond blade and then his long sword.

"Get back in your truck," a man's voice cried from high into the cage of the electrical tower. "There's too many of them."

Guardians were easy. He'd fought so many, and they all had one tactic: growl, swipe and puke on you if they were going to die. Maybe they might attack in force, unless they had mastered the elements. If they had, then they could actually be fun despite their chaotic bumbling around to slap at anything they wanted to kill. These guardians fell upon him instantly.

Thomas's approach was a little more refined: sidestep this one, stab that one, cut off this one's paw and let him bleed out. Now, whip the hair. Careful. Let the head's turn carry the momentum of the miniature morning stars so that they rip open the monster's faces, but not his own. Then, while his clumsy opponents reel from the shock, sink the long blade down, past its soft fleshy area of the clavicle, to puncture the lungs and heart. Meanwhile, his short diamond blade slices another monster's eye, any eye would do. He'd take advantage of the blind spot later in the fight. Then he'd recoil quickly in case one of his thrusts didn't quite hit the mark. Do this all while making sure to withdraw his blades without allowing them to break off while still inside the falling and twisting bodies of the monsters. Diamond was quite brittle that way.

Somewhere in his precise footwork, some of the wolves might have taken a swipe at him. Most couldn't keep up. Not with him, at leas—uh oh!

The gurgle started. Thomas thrust out a leap that threw him over their heads. He listened, discovered the kamikaze venom-spitter and maneuvered his way to the beast's back. Then he grabbed the guardian's ears, ignoring the stinging quills lining the monster's mane which stabbed through Thomas's uniform, but not his Kevlar lining beneath. The monster erupted, and Thomas aimed its head over the faces of four creatures that hadn't the sense to stay out of Thomas's line of sight as they charged for him.

The venom-spitter tumbled below Thomas, and the vampire left the fool to corrode into his own acidic juices with his four sprayed allies screaming and dying without the need for any more of Thomas's attention. While he was at it, take advantage of the blind spot with that beast with one eye, now no eyes. He'd come back and kill him in a moment, but first he had highter priorities.

As he regained his footing, he whipped his hair; stuck his diamond blade; threw his steel blade; then tore a patch of quills from his pants and drove them into a snarling guardian's throat. He retrieved his steel from his fallen target.

He said nothing. He knew some people, like Speatsh, felt better swearing at the monsters between blows. Maybe it was therapeutic for them. Some people thought grunting gave their attacks power. He had tried it a time or two himself, mostly in the presence of grunters and cussers. However, Thomas found silence made his opponents uncomfortable and brought out second thoughts and mistakes.

In a few more strokes and nasty maneuvers, Thomas was searching for any more adversaries left alive to fight. Ah, yes, the blinded one. He'd almost forgotten. There! Dead too.

With the guardians all down, Thomas peered up the tower and sheathed his weapons.

"Are they gone," the deep voice cried from above.

Thomas moved quickly, leaping from one galvanized beam to the next until he came face to face with the scrawny fellow who continued to hug one of the rails in the power-line tower.

"You should probably try and keep quiet," Thomas said. "We wouldn't want to announce to the wolves where you are."

An instant later, Thomas broke the man's hands loose from their safe cradle. The man now screamed as he dangled by nothing more than Thomas's strength and firm grip within the center of the tower.

"Don't drop me," the man cried while clutching his fingers as tightly onto Thomas's hand as he could.

Thomas peered upon the man, ignoring the several hundred feet between his cargo and the earth.

"Wolves make for excellent climbers," Thomas explained. He ensured his tone was polite, calm and gentlemanly. What, after all, if he was wrong in his assumption? "Why aren't you dead?"

"I thought I was until you appeared," the man replied.

Thomas let go, watched the man fall. He quickly leapt down and to the opposite side of the tower, catching the man by the scruff of his fuzzy collared jacket. The man drew in a breath and began his begging at the sight of the ground far beneath him.

"Are you a general," Thomas asked.

"Am I what," the man asked. "I don't under—"

The man fell and once again stopped short. Thomas regained his grip perhaps ten feet lower than his previous post now. Again, Thomas had anchored himself to another wall of the tower.

"If you think for a moment you can ambush me," Thomas said, "you've made a gravely error."

Thomas hoisted the man up and flipped him before he caught him yet again by the toes of his thick black tennis shoes.

"Please," the man yelled. "I don't have much. You can have it all."

"I don't want what you have," Thomas replied.

"My kids!"

"What would I do with goats," Thomas asked.

"Please," the man wailed. "Don't drop me."

"Your trap failed," Thomas said. He released the man. The man swore once and then fell silent. His arms flailed down below him as he surged towards the ground, and Thomas waited for him to make his move.

No move came. Thomas quickly set his feet and began racing head-first down the giant Erector Set of brackets and giant bolts that had once conducted power. With each step downwards, he launched himself faster towards the earth than he could move by simply falling. He twisted his way down the tower, chasing the man.

Make your move, he thought; his hands alternating back and forth between clutching the electrical tower walls and the hilts of his blades to help steer his descent.

The man did nothing. The man said nothing, simply fell. Before the man's head could splatter against the earth, before his arms could mesh into a jelly of goop and splintered bones, Thomas caught him once more by the ankle, careful not to make the stop so abrupt that his brain didn't jostle over the countours that lined the insides of his skull. It wasn't a lot of room to do the maneuver, but he executed it without killing his prey. The man suddenly began screaming again.

"I see now," Thomas said. "You're all right. Put your hands down now, and I'll let you go."

It took a few moments, but the man stretched his arms until they pressed against tall grass and earth. His body tumbled safely to the ground.

"Why," the man finally asked through hollow gasps.

"I don't like surprises," Thomas said. He helped the stranger maintain his balance until the man was able to find the strength to do so on his own. "How'd you get out here?"

"Huh," the man asked. Although, Thomas was certain the man didn't realize he'd said anything.

"You didn't walk out here, did you," Thomas asked.

"No," the man replied. "I have a truck."

"Where is it," Thomas asked, trying his best to find the outline of anything that appeared to be a better vehicle than the broken police cruiser the Taichomée had given him.

"One of the doors is over there," the man said while pointing off in the distance. "And I think the bed's over there."

So much for the vehicle upgrade.

Thomas urged the man into the passenger's seat of the battered police truck. The man, though hesitant to follow the vampire who had nearly killed him, obliged.

Thomas situated himself behind the steering wheel and let the starter grind itself before he realized he had left the engine running.

"Exactly what were you doing out here," Thomas asked, as his truck began to speed off once more.

"I was sent to inspect some of the local towers," the man said. "All the cellular traffic suddenly stopped on them."

Thomas was about to acknowledge the sense this would make when he was interrupted in a way that made even him jump.

"Base to Eight-twelve," a woman's voice crackled to life. Thomas decided she had either come from a previous job as department store employee who thought she had to swallow her microphone while talking, or she was buried in the dashboard.

"Eight-twelve, go ahead, Base," a man's deep voice replied.

"What's your twenty," the woman asked.

"Where else would I be," the man replied. "I'm watching the log."

"Is it still just him?"

"Isn't he enough?"

"Please notify us if he tries to leave that graveyard," the woman promptly said.

Thomas snatched up the radio mouthpiece. "You're out at the graveyard all night. Right, Eight-twelve," Thomas asked into the microphone.

"Or if anyone tries to go in," the woman ordered as if Thomas hadn't said anything. "Let no one else go in."

"Are we arresting that brute or what," Eight-twelve asked.

"No," the woman said. "Shoot him if you must."

Thomas dropped the broken microphone into the center console.

"Your funeral," Thomas said to himself then turned to his passenger. "We better get you to safety first, sir." He took a moment to get his bearings and searched for the distant lights of the junkyard.

"You mean that junkyard out there," the newcomer asked. "The one with all the dogs? Hasn't anyone ever heard of spaying or neutering around these parts."

"Only the ones that don't deserve it," Thomas said as he shifted the vehicle into a bumpier gear. "Better hold on, we'll be driving through a rather large breed, sir."

"Through them," the man asked. "Isn't there a back way or something? Something without any of those dogs?"

"Funny you should ask," Thomas said, continuing to unleash the full power of the damaged vehicle.

11 ~ Look into My Eye

"Once is courtesy," said one woman, larger than most bikers in the room. She pointed her half-empty mug of Coors menacingly at the intruder. "Twice is in case you're deaf. Keep driving."

So many monsters!

He couldn't remember the last time he had felt fear. This was close, but he wished it actually scared him.

Life had lingered for so long that he wished sometimes he could move on to meet his maker. If he died before he could bury his blade into the gullet of yet another black, quilled guardian, then he'd have lived a full life. Yet, he felt unsure. Speatsh wasn't around to pick up the slack anymore. Not to mention, most of these hunters were still green. Josh was strong, much like his uncle, Richard, had been. Given time, Thomas believed Josh would surpass even Richard's capacity. But how could Josh possibly be prepared for the danger that approached? If Thomas should die now, who would keep watch over the queen's child? The protector, although skilled, was not skilled enough. He wondered if Cadence ever would be. Speatsh was a fool to put the heir in the open as he did and lie to him about his true heritage. At this thought, he felt the dark carriage of knots begin riding through his stomach. Perhaps, Thomas did fear this openness.

"So many," the tower technician spoke, mostly in disbelief, but Thomas knew what the sound of fear really was.

Nevertheless, he agreed. In the black, they were just sets of countless green dots floating as demonic fireflies. However, under the glow of the single spotlight mounted on the driver's door, they had become a flurry, like insects huddled together, for whatever reason insects mass together. He recalled such sights from the mass graves of his past.

"We're not going in," the technician asked incredulously as Thomas started the truck forward.

"Have no choice," Thomas said. "Have to get you to safety. You might need medical treatment."

The first monster's head bounced off the bare radiator, and the truck bounded past the rest of its body and probably several other bodies.

"This is different," Thomas observed.

"What is that," the passenger cried.

"That's a guardian," Thomas explained quickly and then, "That's a scout. Don't worry, this'll all make sense."

A dirt path slowly opened before the truck.

"That's not a good sign," Thomas said, although this was what he had expected. He continued to speed into the ocean of monsters without hitting a single one.

The compound drew close, and the steel gates remained shut.

"Open the gates, please," Thomas said. He might have cursed about losing his earpiece if he were the cursing type. How did he not notice? "You knew I was coming," Thomas mumbled. "I hope you made it back, my dear."

"You talking to me," the technician asked.

"What color are your socks," Thomas asked.

The man in the passenger seat took a moment to realize the question. "White."

"Wave them out the window," Thomas ordered.

The stranger quickly dropped his black tennis shoes and tore off his socks. An instant later, he shoved his hand through the window, letting his socks wave in the force of oncoming wind.

The gates began to open, and flashes of light blasted from atop the walls and also within the front gates.

"What in God's green ocean is that," the stranger asked as he pointed off towards the figure of a man in black leaping into the middle of a cluster of monsters. His body puffed out in ribbon and rope, and monster after monster dropped before him.

"That's the boss," Thomas replied. "He's going to adore you."

The truck sped into the compound. By the time it stopped, and Thomas had stepped down from the vehicle, the steel gates had all but closed behind him.

"Amber told us," Josh said approaching him, surprised at Thomas's appearance. "I'm so sorry."

"Not here," Thomas said respectfully.

"And who's that," Josh asked, taking notice of Thomas's new guest-companion.

The new visitor quickly reacted and politely too. He rounded the truck, holding his hand out to Josh. "My name's Sam, sir."

Josh stared at the newcomer's hand and instinctively took a step back. He nearly released the blades from his right arm to strike at the man.

Thomas, however, reacted differently. He stepped quickly, faster than Josh had seen the vampire move before. The British guard gripped the stranger under his jawline and peeled him back and down, onto the hard dirt. Sam coughed out what might have been the only air in his body. Before he could take in another breath, Thomas dropped a knee onto his chest and held his diamond blade to the man's neck.

"You're a good actor," the vampire explained. "However, I'm so much better."

The man struggled only a moment, nearly bucking Thomas off of his chest. It didn't matter though; Thomas adapted and maintained an elegant balance and grip on the man.

"I've done this longer than you," Thomas said. "You will lose. Now please stop so we can have a nice little chat about your shoes."

Sam stopped his struggle and said nothing.

"Very clever," Thomas said. "Of course, you know who I am, but how could I have left the compound without being seen, right?"

Sam said nothing, but—

"Don't do that," Thomas said suddenly wiping his face dry. "I've killed creatures who've done less than spit on me, sir."

"He's a general," Josh was about to say, but it was Bricktain who blurted it out first.

"Amber," Josh asked aloud.

"I heard," Amber's voice replied through the earpiece. "Natalie's on her way."

Thomas held his position, hardly blinking, hardly moving. "When you put together a costume to play construction worker, you should consider the role of steel-toes. And you might want to learn the difference between cell towers and power lines when you reference them."

Josh stepped alongside Thomas and glared at the newcomer. "Where is he?"

Sam stared back at Josh with sharp, deep hate. Josh imagined a scenario where he'd have to fend off the general if Thomas couldn't hold him.

"That's what I thought." Josh drew one of his silver-purple fangs and fired off a cylinder through the man's bare, left foot.

The general convulsed but held back any sounds of pain. Still, Thomas held his poise and power over the monster before him.

"He's not going to tell us anything," Thomas said.

Sam seemed pleased. "That's the best you have?" He crackled. He might have laughed, but the vampire against his chest and the sword against his throat might have kept it from sounding like one.

"Oh no," Josh leered. "We can do better."

Thomas stood. Sam tried to react. He managed a tiny leap to his feet and even smaller kick at Thomas while maneuvering for Josh, but he dropped back to the ground, this time landing sprawled out and on his chest. Thomas stood over the general straddling him.

"There's that agility I was looking for earlier," Thomas said. "But I assume you knew that."

Thomas stepped against Sam's hand. He twisted it under his sole until the palm rolled upward. Then he stretched the arm straight down the side of Sam's body, where he stepped his sharp heel into the palm. He secured the other arm in similar fashion, pinning the would-be-spy in place. Next, Thomas gripped the man's head by its hair and folded his body backward until he came face to face with the black beast before him.

Natalie squared her massive guardian head with the general and drew close to him.

"A guardian is your best," Sam asked. He laughed for a moment and then suddenly screamed. The guardian screamed back, bearing all the rows of her spindly teeth within its shark-like, lunging bite. After she had finally silenced Sam, she returned to her gaze, this time appearing more intent on what she had in mind.

Sam fell limp in his newfound silence.

Several moments passed and then minutes. After about twenty, Thomas carefully switched the hand that held the general's head. When a crowd began to form, Thug, Ty and the mayor quickly helped remove the noisemakers.

"How long does it—," Bricktain started, but fell silent on his own.

After a half an hour, Josh carefully traded places with Thomas, but Thomas stood with his swords, prepared to behead Sam should he rediscover his strength.

At a little more than an hour, Bricktain took his turn holding Sam in his strange position, while allowing Natalie to do whatever it was she was doing.

Suddenly, Sam's body stiffened, and his eyes widened.

"I've found him," Sam said without breaking his gaze with the guardian.

"Found who," Josh asked. He held a small crossbow to Sam's head.

"It's her," Thomas said, gently pressing Josh's aim away. "Fascinating."

"Her," Josh asked and then "Nata?"

"He's on campus, Josh," Sam continued. "There's stacks of pedestals, like what you might see in an exhibit. It might be a warehouse. I think he's in the art department."

"Art department?"

"Try the museum," Sam explained. "It might be in a back room of the museum. That would make sense."

"Nata," Josh said again. "Are you OK?"

"She's a bimbo, Josh," Sam screeched.

"Bimbo," Amber's voice cried into the earpiece.

"Bimbo," Sam yelled.

"Focus," Thomas said, trying not to yell.

Sam's body tensed. "He's aware of me," Sam said. "We're done with this one."

Sam's body fell, and Natalie stepped back just as the general leapt to his feet, throwing Bricktain off his back.

Thomas moved quickly and once again had the general subdued, this time holding Sam from the back with a blade at his throat.

"You should kill me now," Sam said. "Do it!"

"You were meant to come in here and discover how we got out without your noticing," Thomas said. "You failed your master, and now we know where he is because of your incompetence."

"All the more reason for you to kill me," Sam cried. This time, he spia at Josh.

Josh wiped his face and gave a moment to the thought of how he should kill this general. He smashed his palm into Sam's face and nearly let his swords staple his forehead before he realized there might be a better punishment.

"Throw him to the wolves," Bricktain suggested.

"You can't," Sam cried, but Thomas began dragging him back towards the steel gates anyway. "Kill me! You have to!"

"Open them," Thomas ordered. The immediate clank and hum of moving hydraulic and steel replied.

"You open those gates, and they'll flood in here and take your haven," Sam said.

"For some reason," Thomas replied. "At this moment, I don't think they care about this place."

"I deserve death!"

"Wrong," Bricktain yelled back. "You deserve to live. Get rid of him, Thomas."

"My thought exactly," The vampire replied. Thomas pushed the general through the gates and kicked him out to the mob of creatures on the other side. "He's all yours."

One particularly large guardian grunted at Thomas, snapped its jaws in Josh's direction. Then, it quickly latched onto Sam's bloodied foot and dragged him away into the sea of so many beasts.

Before Josh knew what he was doing, he was out the gates and chasing the creature that held Sam in tow. "This is not how we do things."

Josh's blades finally leapt from his wrists as he punched his arm to his side, knowing this movement would throw the folds of his cloak into the three monsters suddenly to his right. Then, he buried a set of blades into the creature that held Sam. He shot it first with his crossbow cylinder, and, as it turned upon him, stabbed right into the thief's mouth and down into its throat amidst its threatening cry. Josh withdrew and ripped a gash across the creature's left shoulder. He could have gone deeper. If the human being beneath this tough skin couldn't appreciate what Josh had just done for him, he wouldn't be so merciful next time.

"Get up," Josh yelled down at Sam. Somewhere in this chaos, he parried, snapped his cloak and tore open another creature's neck just enough to send it reeling.

"Stop playing and kill them," Thomas demanded as he dropped two creatures in his path to Josh. A louder-than-normal gunshot announced that Bricktain had taken post in the Silver Bullet, although the diesel had not left the compound. Then, just now, Josh knew to step to the left. The whistle, as well as the pang of the steel cable, became easier to hear with each use. As quickly as it appeared, spinning on the end of the whip, the razor disc snapped back to its thrower. A silvery-black beast fell dead.

Josh ordered Sam to his feet once again.

"Kill me," Sam screamed. "You have to kill me."

"Your wish is my pleasure," Thomas said and then stepped for the injured general.

"No," Josh shouted. "Take him back."

The familiar sound of hunters and their various weapons grew more numerous around the paladin.

"Kill sparingly," Josh ordered and hoped the others heard him. "They still deserve saving."

Thomas, began dragging Sam back to the compound by his leg. Were he the cursing type, he might have been doing so now.

"You can't protect me," Sam cried.

"I just did," Josh replied and used his blades once more to parry another attack from his left, allowing Bricktain to compensate for the assault on the right.

The gates began to seal even before the hunters made their way back inside the compound. Josh made sure he was the last one through.

He limped into the compound, his body aching even more than earlier. He hid this little fact and suddenly—

"Are you out of your mind," Thug yelled. He gripped Josh through the collar of Wolf's Breath and pressed him against the sealed gates. "What is wrong with you? We kill them. We don't save them." He slammed Josh against the gates again.

"I'm following your advice," Josh replied.

Thug slammed him again and then shrugged off Bricktain with a quick elbow to the stomach then a head-butt.

Josh tore the earpiece from his ear and clenched it in his fist.

"He's expendable, and he knows it," Josh replied softly. He'd never seen any side of Thug that was uncaring, but everything in his godfather's face, right this moment, told him why this man was dangerous.

"He was sent on a suicide mission. He failed," Josh explained. "We're his only friends now."

Thug slammed Josh again and ignored the blood now seeping between his clenched fingers and Josh's cape.

"He's the only one who Natalie's been able to conduit successfully," Josh said nearly a whisper now. "That means she can do it again."

Thug appeared unmoved.

"I think he let her in," Josh said.

Still, Thug said nothing.

"He's still a human being in there," Josh replied.

Nothing. Thug's breath cursed out heavy huffs.

"I own him," Josh replied. "And he knows it."

Thug grunted.

Josh didn't understand, but it seemed he was supposed to.

Thug grunted again and slammed Josh one more time, but not as hard as he had done before.

"I'm the only one who can drive the Bullet," Thug whispered. "And make sure I can still flip a steak."

Josh didn't respond, but still stared into Thug's angry face, no longer hateful. He understood now. He felt the eyes of the hunters and civilians upon him. Speatsh's counsel to appear mean rang through his ears. He had to punish his godfather. He had overstepped his authority.

Without word or nod, Josh replied his refusal.

"You have to," Thug whispered.

Josh knew how to do it. He clenched his jaw until Thug realized he was supposed to do the same. He clenched, stiffened his neck as well.

Josh ripped Thug's hands away from his collar. He smashed his head into Thug's and uppercut into his jaw, making sure Wolf's Breath steered clear of cutting his godfather in any way. Thug stumbled backward. Josh's blades leapt from his right wrist and drew down against the top of his godfather's ribcage, lightly cutting skin.

Thug stumbled, fell and pretended to lay unconscious on the ground.

The eyes of the mob, hunters and civilians, who stood watching Josh, were different and somehow afraid.

"Get back to work," Josh ordered and began his march back into the compound, leaving Thug to decide when to appear to return to his senses.

The mob quickly dispersed. Reggie disappeared into the house shaking his head and possibly laughing, but Josh couldn't be sure.

Josh made his own way to Bricktain and Thomas, who continued to subdue the newcomer general. Thomas had stuffed Sam's sock into his mouth. Bricktain created a quick noose out of the rusted steel cable. Reggie regained his composure and returned outside to order a crew of people to move a tow crane into position to hold it.

"Well, Mister Revlon," Thomas said as he monitored the binding of the infiltrator. "Now we know where he might be. Shall we go hunting now?"

12 ~ The Elemental

The third time meant guns, not brandished, but clearly hidden and well-within reach. Who would even know with that lake of motorcycles between him and the road? The Schnauzer yipped, pranced up to the woman and peed on her foot.

No. He didn't want to hunt. All this time, Josh had been driven to avenge his sister, driven to find and kill Jasper. He knew the rogue was out there, knew he was a force beyond dangerous reckon. Funny! After everything, he had almost forgotten that he was a hunter. Lately he'd felt like he was supposed to be more of a strategist. He brought the people here. It was his idea that saved those patients from the hospital. Most of them were unruly now, angry that they couldn't leave. Some were disruptive, believed that they could find a way to negotiate with the generals. One man in particular was especially eager to raise his voice against Josh, a man with a magnificent chip on his shoulder and a deep gunshot wound in his butt, thanks to Speatsh's ever illustrious patience. It took everything that the mayor had to keep the peace with the people—he was a good diplomat, Josh gave him that much.

Only now, did Josh stop to ponder if stepping through the gates would have been the end of him.

"We can't tear the hunters away from this place," Josh finally answered. "We need everyone we have here."

Thomas agreed.

At this, Thug returned to the scene, his jaw bruised and lips crusted in blood. Reggie trailed behind him in his motorized wheelchair and was trying to wave off the technical questions of Kenny, the compound technological genius.

"What's this about hunting the rogue," Thug asked. "No. No!" He shook a bloody cleaver in Thomas's face, careful of having to stage another confrontation with the paladin. "He doesn't go out there."

"He's the only one," Thomas replied.

"I agree, Josh stays here," Amber said. Josh hadn't even heard her step out of the sky and take a stand beside him. "Let's just wait for the rogue to come to us."

Thomas waved off similar objections from Reggie and Bricktain.

"We can't wait," Thomas said gently, but firmly enough to silence the others. "When he comes, it will be on his terms. Something's holding him back, right now."

"Yeah," Thug shouted. "It's not a full moon."

"He doesn't need the moon," Thomas replied, sharply enough to pierce Thug, for he should have known better. "He's got enough to start this war."

"The entrance," Josh said. "He hasn't found it yet."

"Maybe," Thomas replied. "But I don't think that's it."

"Why not," Josh asked.

"Scouting parties," Thomas said. "We haven't seen any. And the Taichomée village hasn't seen battle other than your last visit. These aren't signs of someone who's looking."

"So you think he knows something we don't," Thug said.

"I know I don't want to invent some way to appear alpha wolf with you again," Josh replied.

Thug acknowledged the paladin's right of thought, and returned his gaze to Thomas so as to appear angry with him to anyone out of earshot.

Natalie breathed in heavily, which wouldn't have been unnatural, except that Josh actually noticed it.

"Restrain Sam in a safe place first," Josh replied.

"Why," Bricktain asked.

Josh returned the earpiece to its proper place. "Because I said so."

"I'm sorry, Mister Revlon," Thomas replied. "Where should we hold him?"

But before anyone could answer, Bricktain asked "Does it suddenly seem windy to you?"

Josh hadn't really noticed until just then. It did seem to howl for some reason. It wasn't exactly windy, Josh didn't think, but the steel walls were high and strong. Maybe they had been withstanding it. While he was pondering how sturdy the walls actually could be to natural elements, the air around them spoke.

Sam laughed. Reggie's crane held him and his noose off the ground, a second steel binding wrapped about his feet and stretched him to the back of a tow truck. It was enough to keep him, but not kill him.

"Can we get something more humane on him," Josh cried.

"On it," Bricktain replied.

"Uh, boss," the doorman called down from his chair above the steel gates. The sight of him and the frightful appearance of the rodeo queens at each side was all Josh needed to run towards the steel stairs that led to the catwalk. "I ain't never seen this one before," the doorman added.

"Impossible," Thomas said, looking to the skies as if expecting them to respond.

"Wind," Amber asked. "I'm sure wind has some scientific history."

Sam laughed from his bound position. "You didn't think he hadn't taken your presence into consideration did you, Vampire?"

"Mrs. Revlon, watch more than the ground while you're up there," Thomas said. He turned to Bricktain and his small crew of civs trying to improve Sam's prison. "If anything comes for that general, shoot him in the head."

Bricktain soon held his barreled arm against Sam's temple.

Thomas sprinted up the steel stairs close at Josh's heels.

"Give me all the light you can on the gates, Kenny," Josh demanded, now approaching the top of the wall.

"That's a lot of juice," a high-tone, male voice replied. "If you need any of the defense weapons, or UV, we'll trip the power."

"Just the regular lights then," Josh replied.

The ground before the compound exploded with brightness.

"Judas monkey," the doorman said at Josh's approach. He gripped the ledge of the wall before him. Who could blame him? They were everywhere. Guardians outnumbered the scouts at least five to one, drowned them out, dwarfed them. Their numbers, congested and swarming, bled into the black where green dots appeared and could have easily been mistaken for the sparkling of city lights in the distance. "Where do they keep coming from?"

Josh gripped the ledge as well. Although he couldn't see them for the silk gloves over his fingers, he was sure his knuckles were white as he stared off through the curtain of razor wire before his face. "That's a lot of dogs," he muttered. "There weren't that many earlier."

"I've seen worse," the doorman said.

"When have you ever seen worse," Josh couldn't help asking.

"I used to teach."

An immense army of dogs stood before Josh, and an entire line of hunters filled the catwalks looking out into the swarm of dog packs. Josh realized a new danger seemed to be lurking, and, for some reason, the only question that intrigued him enough to ask was, "You taught?"

"That surprise you," the doorman asked.

"What subject?"

"Auto shop."

Josh didn't know why he laughed. It just popped out.

"You think that's funny," the doorman asked.

"Not any more," Josh replied and suddenly remembered his proper place. He didn't need to apologize. He remembered establishing authority over the doorman in his godfather's dim café, but he wondered if he really wanted to offend this man tonight. He wondered what might be a way to redeem himself respectfully.

"How does a shop teacher become a hunter," Josh asked.

"My mom," the doorman said. "When I was little, we were attacked on a camping trip. That was the last I'd seen my parents."

Josh didn't know how to respond. Actually, he didn't want to. He remembered the woman in the doorman's arms at Thug's. Josh said nothing.

"Lived in a few foster homes, after that. Therapists convinced me I was infatuated with horror stories. Grew up wanting to help the youth myself. Then met a guardian at a student competition," the doorman said. He didn't sound cold nor reserved. "Killed a student. Ty was our principal."

"Get the wolf," Josh asked.

Doorman nodded. He scratched his waist and adjusted his weight back onto his stool. "Eventually ran into your godfather, and he hired us to work on the Bullet, said someone big was coming for it some day." His eyes scanned Josh, "Not the big I was expecting."

"We have chains," Bricktain's voice crackled over the earpiece.

"Chains," Josh asked.

"Big buggers," Bricktain replied. "Reggie had 'em. Sam's not going anywhere."

"For now," Josh said. "But he'll turn. We should probably build something to hold him."

"I'm breaking out the torches now," Thug joined. "If I can get one of these links around his feet, that's a start."

A micro-burst slapped across Josh, nearly throwing him off the catwalk and turning Wolf's Breath berserk. The surrounding hunters rallied to the railing to keep from blowing away themselves. The doorman planted a foot behind his stool and struggled to keep his balance.

"Something wicked this way comes, Bricktain," Josh said using the railing to pull him to his feet.

"Isn't Shakespeare above your reading level," Bricktain asked.

"That's Bradbury," Josh replied.

Bricktain broke into a tirade about Josh's ignorance.

"Bricktain," Josh replied, hoping the wind didn't interfere with the earpiece quality. "I'm joking."

Another gale bashed into the wall. This time, Josh was more prepared to withstand the attack. He fought to keep Wolf's Breath from flapping uncontrollably as the wind persisted to strengthen. It was at this that he understood how suddenly useless and unarmed he had become.

"You might want to let our residents know to take cover," he instructed Bricktain. "And make sure your kids are prepared for wind."

Whatever reply Bricktain gave was unclear.

Thomas stepped beside the brunette cowgirl and made a few hand gestures to her. She appeared to take confidence in whatever it was that he said. Yet, Josh seemed more interested in the way Thomas gripped the hilt of his long blade when he had finished speaking to her.

"What is this, Thomas," Josh asked, and the wind seemed to echo Josh's question well enough that it caught the attention of all who heard it.

"Soleil," the night suddenly shrieked.

The wind blew hard into their faces. Josh had been so focused on discovering this new mystery that he hardly noticed the wind, but when his eyes began to dry and the tears blew away, he rubbed them. Then he noticed.

"Parley," announced the voice, soft, a whisper, yet everywhere.

The doorman propped his shotgun against the wall, and the fat curve of a zulfiqar appeared in his hand.

"Now, there's a slow sword for you," Thomas said.

The doorman snorted and sighed.

"It's a fake, you know," Thomas added.

"Give it time," the doorman answered.

Maybe later, Josh would ask the doorman where it had come from. The doorman rested the curve over his shoulder and gripped the pommel, although one hand didn't quite seem to be able to grip as tightly as the other.

"I thought them gone," Thomas said.

"Curved swords," Josh asked before realizing Thomas was talking about something else. He then watched a gap begin to appear within the sea of monsters surrounding the compound.

"I'm afraid I must make my leave of you," Thomas said and quickly disappeared from the catwalk and into the compound.

"New, young paladin," the wind spoke again. "I request parley."

"You must accept," Thomas's voice replied into Josh's ear. "They sound reasonable tonight."

"They," Josh asked.

"They're quite wise," Thomas replied. "Quite impartial to the cause—and dangerous, choose their fights rather unpredictably. Present yourselves well, and they may not get involved, or they may."

"That's not comforting."

"Do not provoke them, Monsieur Revlon," Thomas explained.

"The Sun," the voice shrilled. "I hear you, Thomas of the Sun."

The walls of the compound shook and began to waver at the strength of the gusts of wind. "Give me the Sun."

"You heard the vampire," the doorman bellowed as he kept himself from toppling headlong into the coil of razor wire. "Agree already!"

"I'm not giving whatever that is, Thomas," Josh said.

"Parley," the wind shrieked, and Josh blew over backwards, staying safe on the catwalks only because of the handrail his luck offered him.

"I agree to your parley," Josh screamed, and the wall suddenly stood still.

"I welcome parley with the paladin," the wind spoke strangely and softly.

Josh soon realized what seemed to divide the beasts before him. It had been so dark and subtle that he hadn't believed to have seen it at all. It crept forward, biting into the earth, sucking the remnants of its dust and rock into its skin—and yet, it didn't spit anything back out.

From the catwalk, it didn't seem all that large as it blew its way forward like some footless atrocity, but Josh wondered if it would have appeared the same way were he fully on the ground. However, the closer it drew, the exponentially larger it appeared.

He'd never seen one before. They didn't do well in this area, yet here one was.

The wind drew harsh, but not unbearably so and, for a moment, Josh thought he saw a face appear within its Goliath skin. It rolled gently from one side of the wall and then rotated around to the other before disappearing entirely.

"I'm sorry, Mister Revlon," Thomas said through the earpiece once more. Josh glanced over the compound to find the vampire, but saw nothing of him.

Reggie and his small construction crew continued to hold his own on Sam. Natalie now stood poised to kill the traitorous general if anything wolf tried to take him.

"It shouldn't be possible," Thomas said.

"I didn't imagine it would be so big," The blonde cowgirl said from her post on the other side of the doorman.

"You were expecting it," Josh asked.

"I've just never seen a cyclone before," the woman replied.

"They're wolves," Thomas corrected.

"No," The doorman replied. "Wolves are cute little creatures—cuddly—you shoot them, they die. That's a tornado."

Josh robotically parroted his agreement.

"I'm not shooting no tornado," the doorman said. "Who knows how mad it'll get."

"Do not shoot the tornado," Thomas instructed. "Her patience is short, but she is honorable. Or she used to be before I unfortunately killed her sister."

"What are you talking about," Josh asked.

"They're elementals," Thomas said. "Masters of the elements. They'll tear this place down if you offend her in any way."

"Elementals," Amber's voice followed, cold and quivering. "Umm?"

"Yes, please stay where we can catch you," Thomas said.

"They're supposed to walk on wind, not make it," Amber said.

"Wind, no—but turbulence, yes. Manipulated properly, turbulence becomes wind." Thomas replied. "Someone's made an impression, whether it's you or the rogue or someone else. They shouldn't be here."

"We are," the wind continued to speak softly.

The dark, slab-funnel of wind closed in upon the walls of the compound—and the face Josh had thought he had seen, he now knew was so. It appeared again, this time along with a decrepit figure. It rolled from the left of the twister, faced Josh for a moment, inquisitive, and then faded to the right. Several moments later, it appeared from the left again.

The wall of gust and debris now blocked the front gates entirely. The sky was no longer visible. Josh believed it powerful enough to tear the compound off the earth if it so chose, yet it threw little more than a harsh breeze into Josh's face now. Josh gripped a crossbow beneath his cloak. Maybe these would still work in a pinch, since Wolf's Breath clearly was of no use in high winds. The cylinder of air pressed tightly against the wall of the compound.

The next time the gruesome image appeared in the cyclone, a twisted hand reached out. It maneuvered through the spiral of razor wire, and gripped the ledge of the wall with a set of fingers that bent unnaturally backwards. Then she pulled herself free of the swirling mix of wind and filth, through the coils of razor and onto the catwalk.

She wore black stretch fabric, perhaps spandex, from neck to ankle. A gray shawl fell down her sides. It had hugged her crooked form as she gyrated through the razor wire, but now, standing on the catwalk, it drooped freely to her sides. She was barefoot, her nails thick and long. Josh might have feared them as weapons if they weren't so obviously rotten and brittle. She hunched forward and to the side, standing nearly straight on one leg, but propped against her other. The heel of this leg twisted outwards and locked in bend, forcing it to stand unnaturally on its toes. Her head seemed oddly out of place, as if disjointed from the spine. It was beautiful, crowned in short, shiny black hair. Her face would have drawn Odysseus from the mast. Here, Josh realized that her eyes were white and after a few nods of her head, he made the assumption that she could not see. She cocked her head quickly and took in a shallow, quick sniff.

"I never forget a smell," she said through a raspy and withered voice.

It was more distinct than what had carried in the air before. Josh was certain that it was the same voice.

"I doubt I'll forget yours, young paladin," she said, and suddenly her face locked as if looking upon Josh. "But it could be more."

She grinned through sharpened teeth, not sharp like an animal, sharp as if filed down on purpose. "Let me get a look at you," she said and limped towards Josh, each step appearing to be deeper and more awkward than the previous.

The doorman readied his blade, only to have it whisked out of his hand and thrown over the catwalk into the compound by some unseen force. Then he, himself, fell over backwards and blew along the catwalk, toppling over the blonde rodeo girl and two other hunters.

"Dishonorable," the woman said. "I came to talk." She inched towards Josh until she set before him. She stood as tall as her broken body would let her and then motioned for Josh to hunker down to meet her awkward gaze. "I am my word."

Josh knew his place. He held his ground. He stood tall. His own allies couldn't see him appear to bow to the enemy.

"You'll bend in respect or fall without your throat," she added, suddenly sounding as a young woman would with a voice of silver. Her hand was upon Josh's neck, barely demonstrating enough strength to show Josh's flesh the jagged blades of her fingernails.

Josh bent enough to square off with the woman's white eyes. She slid her hands up to his face, and her knuckles crackled as they bent from backwards to forwards. She pulled his face close to hers and appeared to be staring directly into his eyes, never blinking. Without warning, she blew into Josh's face. Her breath was strangely sweet, and she waved her hands as if to cast off some foul smoke.

"Oh you're a handsome one," she whispered while she breathed in deeply. He barely noticed her soft touch as her hands removed his grip from his drawn crossbow and slid the weapon back onto its waist-clip.

He didn't even remember drawing the weapon over her seductive touch.

"I can take her," Amber's voice spoke into Josh's ear.

"No she can't," the disfigured woman replied.

"What do you want," Josh finally found the courage to ask.

"Do you know who I am," she asked.

Josh didn't—only that she was an elemental, according to Thomas.

The young woman, or so she appeared, drew near Josh as if to embrace him. She drew back sharply after a moment of silence. "No," she asked. "Very well then," and, in one grasp, she had hold of his hand and drew with him into the air. Her strength overpowered Josh's, and, as she tore him away, over the compound razor wire, and into the twister, he felt his brain darken to the sudden change in elevation and G-force.

Josh's allies made their characteristic objections behind him. Amber appeared the fastest, speeding towards the tornado and twisting her body to give it the momentum it needed to launch a powerful silver disk at Josh's captor. A guardian wolf suddenly leapt from the skin of the tornado and knocked the orbit away before disappearing once more. Josh felt the filthy wall of swirling dirt swallow him. He shielded his eyes from the instant sting. When the pain subsided, his friends and the compound were gone. All was quiet. It took a moment for him to realize that he was standing on earth. Another moment passed, and he realized Wolf's Breath had been removed from his shoulders entirely.

The wall of wind rushed all around him, and yet it was silent. It was filthy, and yet, here, in the center, it was clean.

The twisted woman stood some distance away from Josh.

"How did you do it," her voice asked from within the wind all around him.

Josh spoke, but no sound came out. He yelled, but the silence was stronger.

Her brow sharpened, and she took several steps forward. "How did you do it," she spoke once more through the spiraling gust.

Josh hadn't noticed, but his swords had obeyed his call and were both extended from the metal cages around his forearms. She stepped back suddenly. He corrected the situation. He shouldn't have summoned nor put away his blades. He knew that much, but she made no move to attack. He couldn't help his habit that quickly.

He bowed a false apology. It seemed the right gesture. Suddenly she was standing straight, elegantly poised and even slightly taller than Josh. The twisted person who had faced him only moments ago had disappeared. She returned a gentle bow.

In an instant, she was upon him again, hugging him in her arms. Josh felt himself whisked against the wall of wind. His feet left the ground once more, and the force of motion against him spiraled Josh around and up the gusting storm until all that was before him was the black of the nightly sky. Above, were glittering stars. Below was the barrier of the cyclone's deep, hollow eye. A billowing flat floor, spiraled beneath their feet, spewing contents from the drain in the center. Josh and his host hovered above the storm.

The lady, once more withered into her appalling and deranged shape, continued to embrace him. He did his best to embrace her back, mostly out of fear of falling. Her limbs, fingers, even head seemed to sway in all sorts of directions, rarely in unison. Then it struck him. She was feeling the wind, much like Amber did in her windriders, only this woman used every one of her extremities to maintain her stability. She was the master up here. True, he was close enough that if she should try anything, it would be an easy dig for his blades, but it would be a long fall after. He wondered if he might be able to catch sight of Amber hiding somewhere in this nightmare. He doubted it. These were stronger gales than anything she had mastered before, strong enough that the woman before him needed every limb to stay in control.

This strange being was fluid. Fluid enough to strip Josh of Wolf's Breath. He felt the gravity tugging at him, but the woman overpowered it and held him aloft in the air while they circled the eye of the storm below them. Then he noticed that all the glitter that he had taken for stars a moment ago were the eyes of guardians hovering above him.

Here, despite the rampaging cone of destruction below him, all was silent. He was neither above nor below the storm. Where was he?

"You silenced him," she said. "You frightened him, and he has left our consciousness. How? Tell me. How strong are you?"

"Does it matter," Josh began yelling, but adjusted himself to a softer volume when he realized his voice wasn't as muffled here. "If you're going to kill me just do it already!"

"We must be quick," She said, and her face filled with what Josh took for fear. She appeared stunned, as if caught in an overwhelming choice. "He can't know we spoke."

"Speak then" Josh ordered.

She kissed him, drove her lips against his and sucked on his sealed mouth until Josh could feel her saliva drain through and bead down his chin. She pulled away and Josh sank his face into her shoulder to wipe his face dry.

"Stop it," Josh cried, pulling away, but afraid to push himself to his death.

"Don't," she replied and kissed him once more, this time licking her way to his neck. Suddenly she stopped. "Now I can find you."

"Do you taunt all your prey this way," Josh asked.

"You're not my prey," she replied. "But you'll want to impress me soon."

"Why?"

"I can't tell you that," she replied. "But you have something I want."

"Freedom," Josh made another observation. "You can't fight him on your own, can you?"

"That's a part of it," she said. "I want Thomas Sun."

"I don't know who that is," Josh replied.

"Don't try me," she snapped, but then laughed. "You don't know the language. All your valiant credibility, and you still lack culture." She hugged Josh tighter. "I want Thomas de Soleil. The man who murdered my sister."

"Why now," Josh asked.

"Because he can't be predicted," she said. Her face was suddenly nose-to-nose with her prisoner's. Her eyes, once white, rolled forward revealing bright purple irises. Perhaps it was the dark, but they were purple. "He doesn't answer to you."

"He's an ally."

She laughed. "He was ours too." Her face grimaced. "He's a liar."

Josh could call the blades right now, let them shoot straight into her body. One less general and her army to fight, but could he survive the fall?

"You'll die before you can," she said. "And I'm not amused."

Josh didn't realize he'd spoken out loud. Curse this place.

"You will deliver Thomas of the Sun to me or I will destroy your pathetic playground down there," she explained, maintaining her soft, yet welcoming tone. "Deliver him to me, give me my justice, and I will give you my strength."

"Not a chance," Josh replied.

"My power surpasses Soleil," she said. "One life, we can save the world."

"We clearly couldn't stop you from taking him if we wanted to," Josh said. "But I'm not giving him to you."

"My powers are not to be trifled with," she said. "I bring an army of destruction that can raze the rogue's filth from these grounds. Give me one man, and it is yours."

"I thought we just established that you can't beat the rogue on your own," Josh sneered. "I don't betray my own."

"But will they betray you," she asked.

Josh clenched fists and felt his blades draw above and below his wrists, but suddenly he was falling.

She applauded at Josh as she quickly fell away above him. She remained unmarked by the blades.

Josh dropped, but then felt himself pushed back up towards her. This time she kept her distance, and hovered around him.

"You have humanity," she said. "You have loyalty, but can you survive?"

"What does that mean?"

"Our time is nearly gone." She now appeared frightened, more so than before. "He is returning. I'll have to let him back in soon. He won't know our meeting though. That much I can help."

Josh tried to question her, but—

"You have what he wants," she said. "With ten thousand, he can rebuild one. I truly hope you survive so you can stop him from doing so."

She suddenly screamed, and the wind just as abruptly died. The wall of dirt, once racing, holding him up, now exploded against his face as his flailing body burst through its skin. The wind sucked at his ears as if to remove the drums themselves. He heard nothing, but the torture of vacuum, which caused his head to hurt. Immediately, he felt no pain and once more he could hear her voice whispering, "I hope this conversation is not over."

An instant later, all was clear, the dust washed away. He rushed towards the ground, but then the wind picked him up again, this time clean, free of debris. It launched him towards the compound far below him. He flew high and rose to a new apex under his own momentum. For a brief instant his stomach felt strong, calm. In this very second, he was weightless. He was in control of his body again as he wavered and relaxed just enough to breathe deeply once more. Then his stomach screamed, clenching itself into a fist and punching out the air in Josh's chest. He instantly plummeted back towards the earth, this time blinded by two spotlights from within the compound.

Despite his best efforts, Josh was mentally about to say that one single word any grown person would find himself shouting as he helplessly flailed mercilessly to the ground. Anyone who's suddenly found himself falling to the ground knows this word. Josh let this word last perhaps fifty feet worth of plunge, perhaps a hundred. Who knew how many hundreds of feet he had left to curse. Maybe he'd use the same word for all of it.

Again, his head began to fall dark.

Then the whistle came. That sound could pierce any danger, yet Josh wondered if it had come fast enough.

He felt the ring clasp over his foot, and his body suddenly jerked.

Josh screamed, a new word this time, or maybe the same. He couldn't be sure of which obscenity he was singing anymore. His tongue and bowels currently controlled this level of vocabulary.

"Stop struggling," Amber yelled.

"It's cutting my foot," Josh yelled back.

"You wanna do this?"

Josh dropped once again, his foot now free of the ring. Amber's dark figured sped alongside Josh. She pulled on his ankle, and Josh watched the earth dissolve and the sky appear as his torso flipped upwards. Amber hugged him into her.

"Stand on my feet," she ordered.

Josh fumbled, but couldn't seem to find his wife's toes.

"If you can't find my feet, you can't find the wind," Amber replied, the two of them now spiraling downward, feet first together. "You wanted to learn how to use them."

"Not like this," Josh screamed.

"Would you rather splatter?"

Josh found her moccasins. He didn't know how, but he didn't care about that technicality right now.

Her feet contorted beneath his boots, and she grunted in his ear.

"What is it," Josh asked.

"Shut up," She growled, holding Josh until he couldn't breathe. Her feet moved as an unbalanced figure skater's might. First, they turned this direction, then that, then this angle where Josh's foot almost slid off. She grunted again as Josh consciously repositioned his boot back on top of her curving foot.

Something popped within Amber's frame that shook the core of Josh's spine.

After an extensive and shallow breath, Amber released him, and Josh felt the hands at his back. He allowed himself to fall into them so they could escort him safely to the floor of the compound. He eventually tackled his breath and used Bricktain as a crutch to regain his composure.

"Forget something," Thomas asked, placing Wolf's Breath around Josh's shoulders. "That's two you owe your wife for tonight."

"What happened up there," Bricktain asked, but Josh ignored him.

Josh found Amber crumpled on the ground. She made no sound, but she sobbed and grasped at her leg. Thug was already at her side.

"What is it," Josh asked.

"That's a lot of stress for a knee," Thug said. "You're one tough chick you know that?"

"She blew the knee," Thomas asked.

"Twisted her ankle too, I think," Thug replied. "Could be broken, can't tell."

"Can we fix it? The knee," Josh asked, carefully sliding beside his sullen wife. He dropped Wolf's Breath, this time on purpose, and held her. She cringed a moment, but then gripped him back and clenched his arm that had once been broken, but still carried her from danger not so long ago.

"The twins are gone," Thomas said. "She'll need a hospital."

"What about you," Reggie asked.

Natalie huffed.

Josh had hardly noticed that the guardian wolf had stumbled onto the scene.

"Of course," Amber replied weakly, but controlled. She tried to laugh but cried instead.

"Who else," Reggie asked. He tried to reach for Amber but rested his hand on Josh's shoulder instead.

"I'm not a doctor," Thomas replied. "I couldn't talk her through it."

"How does a man live to be older than dirt and not learn medicine," Reggie asked.

"Why? Because my physiology is so similar to yours," Thomas asked. "You're how old? Why don't you know this stuff?"

"So we have no dogs, we have no doctor and no one knows what to do," Bricktain said. "I wish Speatsh was—" and then he stopped himself.

"That's not entirely true," Josh said. "Natalie was a pre-med student."

"So, she knows medicine," Thug said. "That's good."

"Yeah, about that," Josh said. "We mostly just took the lower level anatomy classes."

"That's not pre-med, Josh," Bricktain said. "That's art appreciation. All you do is look at picture books!"

"She had it all memorized."

"Josh, no," Bricktain said and lifted one of his hands into the air, palm-side down. "See, way up here, that's med school—so, people like your dad. Down here—seriously, look at me, Josh—college. Those are finger painting classes where people still get fascinated that the bellybutton can hold lint."

"She needs treatment," Josh argued.

"Yeah," Reggie snapped. "But not the werewolf-surgery-for-dummies kind."

"Never mind that," Amber finally exploded. "Do something."

Natalie appeared at Amber's feet.

"Am I the only one who seems to remember that Natalie hates Amber," Bricktain asked.

Natalie roared.

"What are you yelling at me for," Bricktain screamed. "I didn't marry him."

Natalie yelled again, huffed at Bricktain's fright and then raked her nearly invisible claws across the front of Amber's leg.

13 ~ It Begins

"Wait," Harvey cried, as guns drew. Knowing what he knew, what he'd seen with other dogs: their power, their speed, he doubted even Chandler's bullets could stop them. Above all, he remembered Chandler's words to catch the dog off guard so as not to alert any other monsters. "Cylinder owes me a favor, and I want a drink."

Black.

Too much black.

Too much dark. Always dark! Black creatures. Dark night. Black monsters with black hearts and dark minds. All dark, and too many chasms. Too many times they faced the bottomless pit of dark, black chasms where no light of hope exists. Always dark. If it's not one darkness it's another. If it's not black, it's still black and always dark.

Yet, here, a puddle of bright, red blood stained the dirt, and it didn't appear to be any better than the drudge that the new paladin had grown to live and despise.

Amber hadn't noticed it yet, but at least she stopped screaming. Natalie even stopped yelling back, and she only had to start over five times.

As she tried to stand, Amber wobbled and caught herself. then trembled perched atop her bent knees.

"Where does it all come from," Amber asked, finally seeing the new color herself.

No one said anything for some time, even to answer. Finally, Thug spoke up and pontificated about how he'd seen worse. Somehow, he found a way to blame Speatsh for it. Then, he fell silent again.

Still, no one said anything.

After some agonizing time, Amber forced herself to stand.

Reggie's chair sputtered alongside her as she tried out her repaired knee. She almost appeared sturdy once more. She asked for water a time or a dozen before Ty finally appeared with a squat plastic bottle.

"That fever's murder," Ty said.

Amber peeled back her black bandana, and even Josh cringed at the swollen edges of skin that appeared from beneath the patches of gauze, which had peeled away from her gold-plated jaw.

"Have you put on your salve today," Josh asked, then quickly dodged the half-empty plastic bottle.

A siren erupted from the compound walls.

"Better get up here," the doorman cried.

"Now what," Josh yelled. He fumbled with Wolf's Breath, ensuring every button was properly sealed.

"Two on foot," the blonde rodeo queen called.

The brunette signed something feverishly to the blonde.

"One now," the blonde amended. "They're not playing nicely anymore."

"Open the gates," Josh ordered. Before he could arm a new earpiece, the properly and Britishly-dressed albino-vampire was at Josh's side.

"I'm offering aid," Amber announced. already back in her hidden perch in the black sky.

"I'm on my way," Josh replied. "If you think the knee's not ready—,"

"Oh, trust me," Amber replied. "Don't you worry about me."

Thomas said something, but Josh ignored him, which was fair since the vampire had actually been speaking to Petruchio before leaping to his back.

The gates opened, and the paladin was quickly outside, pausing only a moment at the sound of cheering children as they realized the soaring parachute over their heads was Bear leaping from his hiding place and towards the gates.

"Hey," Bricktain yelled. "You kids know you don't come out here when the gates are open! Get back of the fence!"

The children obeyed and rushed back to the civilian section.

Bricktain hurried to the Silver Bullet, then swore about the back being locked. Thug yelled something about forgetting the keys and, at that, Bricktain tore the unique diamond glasses from his face and ran off, trailing behind Bear, towards the now closing gateway.

The former cop's strange arm began ratcheting and twisting until a gun barrel appeared. . He was the last one to clear the gates, feeling them seal behind him.

"Gates secured," the doorman announced.

"What are you doing, Brick," Josh shrieked into Bricktain's ear.

"Apparently, we're waiting for a locksmith," Bricktain replied.

Josh might have lectured him if he wasn't too busy grunting out some weird attack. When Bear's flat body suddenly leapt over the crowd of enemies, a monster bit up at him. Bear snarled, wrapped himself around his attacker and then leapt off a moment later, allowing the monster to drop back into the crowd.

"I see you," Bricktain replied. He kept taking aim upon dogs, but none seemed interested in the mechanical man.

"We have him," Thomas's voice informed.

"Cutting you a path now," Bricktain cried. "Watch your feet."

"Don't hit us," Josh pled.

Bricktain open fired, his gun-arm chirping like an army of morning treetop twittering. Meanwhile, deafening, high-tone pangs popped from above everyone's heads as the orbits helped widen the footpath even more.

Several monsters turned on Bricktain. Now, they were interested. He fired, dropping none at first, but slowing them down. Amber ended three that Bricktain had already injured.

"About that path," Thomas asked.

"A little busy," Bricktain replied. He finally downed a guardian. Another leapt from behind it. Bricktain fired. Dead.

Another leapt from Bricktain's side. Another shot! Also dead. A silver disc wrapped around the monster's snout, and he yanked sideways, thrown into a group of attackers trying to flank Bricktain. Most of these monsters crumpled as Amber's attack toppled into them.

One, however, did not. It raced for Bricktain and seemed too unconcerned for Bricktain's return fire.

Suddenly, Bear was on the monster, scampering up his chest, around his mane and over his forehead, where he clawed out its eyes and leapt to another guardian and then another, each time launching himself higher and higher before dive bombing one more monster that had almost overtaken Bricktain.

"Opening the gates," the doorman announced a moment before Josh and Thomas appeared, Josh fighting and Thomas dragging a third person with him.

As another beast focused on Bricktain, Petruchio leapt over its body and stopped short of running into Bricktain. Petruchio kicked back, leapt once more over Bricktain and through the now open gates, leaving a monster felled from a broken face.

Bricktain retreated into the compound, firing off shots despite Josh and Thomas racing into his line of fire. Bear zipped from beneath the onslaught of grey monsters. Bricktain avoided Bear's screaming human cargo, which he now carried to allow Josh and Thomas to perform their fights better now.

Guardians and Josh's small crew flooded through the gates. The half-pipe came to life with skaters and their decapitating steel boards.

"Closing," said the doorman.

Several more wolves burst into the pipe.

A lot happened at once. Hunters open fired. Josh ordered them to push back only if they could. A chariot of gold came to life. Amber's whips sang. Josh unleashed his deadly fury, while Thomas finessed his own battle with blades and obedient hair. Natalie wrested one opponent from the group and began her own melee.

Bear weaved in around legs of creatures and humans, yelling in some of their faces enough to startle them before running off for another monster. He didn't usually kill anything. He wasn't strong enough for that, but he could blind, trip or surprise them, and even incapacitate them long enough for someone else to finish the job.

Speaking of which.

Bricktain fired, and Bear left his current dead opponent. Bear then pulled himself into his familiar log shape and slipped straight between Bricktain's legs. He scampered up Bricktain's back, launched himself to the shoulder of the vampire and smashed his head against one of Josh's targets from behind. In that moment, the wolf turned on Bear, and Josh blasted the beast with a shot from a purple-steel crossbow.

"Gates closed!"

Finally, the Silver Bullet blasted its horn. The guardians and scouts froze, as if paralyzed, which was all Josh and his companions needed to end the skirmish.

"Found the keys," Thug said into his headset. "Left 'em by the stove."

"All clear," Josh asked, unable to find another opponent.

The others replied that they were also free of any adversaries.

Children rushed back into the area screaming, once more excited for bear, immune to the sight of the fallen wolves and humans that now littered the entrance to the compound.

This time Bear fled to Bricktain, caught hold of his leg and quickly scaled up the ex-cop's back. The pelt finally rested himself across Bricktain's shoulders, careful—it seemed— to prop his weight off his friend's bionic attachment. Bear began to pick quills with his teeth out of his pelt body.

"Come on guys," Bricktain said as he scratched his friend's head. "Leave Bear alone. He's not a toy."

* * *

The man should have been dead. His bicep had been torn so that no doctor would have classified it as any kind of appendage. Whatever had once been recognizable muscle or sinew had been mangled into an unworkable mash.

The newcomer shrieked as Thomas tightened a shoe lace high around the man's bicep to create a tourniquet. It might not matter if Thomas saved this limb, the stranger was losing even more blood through his lower leg that used to have a foot attached to it. They should have let the man die.

Yet why was he there? Draped over the hood of the old front end of the gray and rusted sedan? Keeping him alive long enough to find out might be worth some entertainment.

Thomas cinched the tourniquet tighter around the soldier's arm. Amber now pulled one at the leg as well. Thug and the doorman held the man down. Josh tried to calm the patient with angry words, which led to Thomas handing off his tourniquet to Josh and trying to calm the patient instead.

Natalie stood close, but had been denied trying to help out of fear that this much blood getting in her system would be too much for her.

The man, who was dressed in black military garb, cried.

Thomas bent over him, shoved a large cylinder into his mouth. It might have been wood. It might have been steel. No one could tell.

"If the pain goes away before we can fix it," Thomas said. "That's good news."

Reggie's chair sputtered towards the sedan operating table. A single-burner camping stove in the junkyard owner's lap sprouted a blue ring of propane. An empty fry pan danced on top of it as the chair bounced over the uneven ground. Not one of the blue and clear threads of flames seemed deterred from heating the pan.

"Did you find any thread," Amber asked. Her sweaty hand struggled to hold the tourniquet under the soldier's wild dance.

Reggie handed the small stove off to Bricktain and gripped the frying pan by the handle. "No time," Reggie said. He immediately pressed the round griddle against the man's severed ankle.

Strips of smoke rose from the injured soldier's leg, and ghosts of his dead nerves rose from their third-degree graves in black, malodorous wisps.

The black-dressed man continued to scream, and Amber wrested every ounce of her strength into keeping the tourniquet in power.

"Hold him," Reggie yelled struggling to synchronize the man's kicks to strike the bottom of the frying pan.

Amber buried her nose into her shoulder and did her best not to let the smell of burning flesh help her throw up.

Finally, Reggie pulled the pan and its liquefied trails of skin and other tissue away from the red and black stub.

"That should help for now," Reggie said. "We gotta cover that bone better than this and do something about those veins."

Reggie set the pan back onto the campstove, which Bricktain had now set on the hood of the sedan next to the patient. Reggie's chair sputtered to the demolished arm.

"We saved all these people from a hospital, and none of them are doctors," Bricktain said. "How did we manage that?"

"We still have you," Reggie said.

Bricktain appeared confused.

"Right then," Thomas said, however, understanding Reggie's meaning, and directed Josh to stretch the man's shredded arm out to the side, ignoring the man's pleas for mercy. "Go ahead, give it a good whack."

Bricktain stared at the mutilated arm, its bare bone sticking straight from the bicep, broken and sharp like a shovel handle that had cracked its spade. It didn't take a skilled surgeon to know that the appendage needed to be cut back. Bricktain's steel arm rang out with the familiar and eerie series of metallic and cable. His metal digits disappeared into his forearm and his long thick blade unfolded. Yet, he paused.

"Do it," Reggie ordered.

"Wait a minute," Josh cried and then repositioned himself as far out of the way as possible while still holding the Tourniquet.

"Think past the bone, Mr. Morris. Don't swing twice. We need a clean cut."

"And don't hit me," Josh added. He watched his wife disappear into the cold, steel house and office in the center of the yard. She continued to limp. She hadn't complained, but Josh knew something still wasn't right with her leg. He knew that wasn't why she was going into hiding though.

Bricktain's arm snapped down fast and straight. The wasted pieces of the man's arm flipped into the air, and Josh landed on his butt.

The man screamed.

Reggie drove the frying pan into the pink and fleshy end of the bicep. The man screeched even louder until all the nerves had finally given up their wills to live as well. "Let's get him a bed and thread now," he finally said.

"Not yet," Thomas said, once Reggie had finished his life-saving torture.

"You're in danger," the man insisted.

"That's not news," Josh said. He wiggled his fingers to help revive their blood flow after holding the tourniquet for as tightly as he had.

"Inside my pocket," the man said as he attempted to reach across his body to the pocket without a hand to accomplish the goal.

"What is this," Reggie asked, being the first to answer the call and withdraw a small black gadget with a plasma screen.

"The location of a platoon," the man explained softly and nearly inaudibly now. "I was supposed to tell you to—

He fell into slumber.

Amber had barely returned on the scene when she recognized the look from Josh that was really an order, or in her case a request, to get an eagle's eye view going.

"Probably not a good idea, Hon," Amber objected.

"They sound like soldiers," Josh said examing the green screen that currently flashed a gps location.

"Mercenaries aren't my favorite allies," Thomas said.

"We can use soldiers," Josh replied. "Let's go get 'em."

"And if they're already dead," Amber asked.

"Then at least we tried," Josh replied. "Sure wish we had our crack-shot."

Amber would rather have gone after the rogue, now that they had an idea of where he was—but she agreed, they needed the numbers.

"I wish we had Speatsh," Amber said, and she wondered what it was about this injured man that wasn't sitting right with her.

14 ~ Pit Stop

"What you mean, Cylinder owes you a favor," one man from a far, dark corner asked.

The Knosh family had to pull over to let Adam, make pee. The town was dark as they passed by on their way south. Even if they'd wanted to stop for gas, bathroom and refreshment, Jim wouldn't have been able to see the main turn-off nor be able to maneuver the unfamiliar city streets. Adam couldn't have picked a worse stretch of highway to go to the bathroom. Even if he could have led the family minivan down the right streets, it was clear the town had no power for neither gas pump nor restaurant. Jim knew a town was nearby because the signs all pointed to one. Otherwise, he would have passed the entire county none the wiser.

Jim hated to pull over at all. Two daughters slept in the back seat, and, for once, the bickering had quieted down. Jim might have suggested they keep driving, but his wife, Trudy, had been behind the wheel for the last three hundred miles and Adam's nagging that he was thirsty and hungry and had to potty had devoured the last of her patience. It was time for a switch.

The minivan drew to a stop. The hollow ping of the blinker didn't even come close to coinciding with the orange flash erupting out the left side of the vehicle.

Jim had never seen anything so dark. The stars were bright, and the moon was nearly full. The orange flasher seemed eerie in such a black hole. As Trudy slid into to the front passenger seat, Jim stepped down, and opened the side of the van. The interior dome light was eaten quickly by the dark surroundings, which were made even blacker by a coat of dark trees encapsulating the road.

"Come on, bud," Jim said.

Adam stood at the skin of the van and spent some time deciding that it was too far to the ground for him to hop down on his own.

"Need some help down," Jim asked.

"Yah," Adam replied as he hugged his blue elephant into his chest. "Ah need hewp."

Jim helped the toddler to the ground. "How about we leave Mr. E in the van."

"No," Adam said. "I need Missow E."

"Don't go too far," Trudy said as she reclined her seat fully back and nestled into a pillow. She didn't show it, but she was really most excited for the trip. She'd been planning on it for the past five years. They had saved for four, but nothing had ever lined up. They almost went every year for the last four, but she worried that an ill-timed trip might interfere with Adam's adoption. It might not have happened this year as well, but after she was laid off from work, she decided that it was either now or never. The kids were excited, not about the drive, but about the coasters and costume characters that awaited them at the end of this nine hundred mile journey.

For now, Trudy looked forward to sleep and the quiet road. She hoped she could get better rest than Jim got with all the sibling quarrels that took place during the daylight hours.

"We won't go too far," Jim said.

"No, we won't," Adam agreed.

"What a time for you to be in training," Trudy said.

"Yah," Adam said. "What a time."

Jim urged his only son towards the black trees. Even though the street was empty, save for the headlights of his humming van, Adam still sought greater privacy to do his business.

The forest gave up the lives of sticks and unfortunate weeds as each of Jim and Adam's footsteps took them farther away from the van.

"OK," Adam said. "Hode E."

Jim held the blue elephant.

"Tone awound."

Jim apologized and turned to face the van where his daughters and wife slept. He listened to Adam make his noisy potty song.

"How do I fwush," Adam asked after the sound had quieted.

"There's no flush out here," Jim said.

"Oh," Adam said "Fwussh. Now it has one. Fwussh."

He returned to Jim's side and took his blue elephant. Jim made sure Adam had redressed himself all the way.

Then something roared. Trudy screamed, the girls screamed and before Jim could look back to the minivan, it skidded down the street, on its side and in a trail of sparks. Jim started to run after it, but came to his senses enough to quickly retrieve his son. He'd never find him out here if he left him. The minivan disappeared into the distance off the freeway and the screaming from within suddenly stopped.

Jim yelled after his family to no avail. All evidence that he had ever had a family suddenly disappeared. Not even the eerie orange flasher betrayed where the van was now hiding. Jim and Adam stood at the mercy of the stars, among the black earth and the immediate woodland area. Before Jim could have known what to expect, two monsters appeared before him. He might not have seen them were it not for their glowing, green and red eyes. Their silhouettes set upon him and his son. Jim clenched his fists and stepped between the monsters and Adam. A moment later, the closest guardian destroyed Jim, tearing him in so many directions even the dark couldn't keep track. The second guardian was quickly upon Adam, glaring upon him for the fresh morsel of food he was.

Suddenly, the guardian was flat on his back.

"Those were mine," Adam shrieked. He held the beast by the throat and glared back into those demonic eyes. "Where's your master?"

The second guardian leapt for the child, but Adam, without losing his gaze on the beast that was already in his hand caught the fresh attacker's snout and crushed it, along with its jaw. Then, just as easily, Adam tossed the dog away.

"There's your master," Adam said still peering past the first monster's eyes and into its brain. Adam flipped the guardian into the air as if it held no weight. Without a sound, the creature never returned to the ground, simply disappeared into sky.

"I'm coming for you next, general," Adam said then began his journey towards the woods, careful to take up his stuffed elephant along the way. "They were not yours to take!"

"Ba-roo!"

Adam chuckled to himself. "Really," he asked. He smelled the air and waited for the creatures to make their presence more fully known.

"Hello," Adam welcomed the five creatures, "Someone's not sticking to the script." He then quickly began to tear the five creatures apart one at a time. Three more guardians reinforced the group, but wished they hadn't. Adam took up his elephant. "Idiots."

Then the little red dots appeared on his chest. He saw them waver over his heart and imagined they might have been on his head as well.

"That's more like it," he said. Then he watched the soldiers. dressed in black, clear the trees and approach the road. Each knew his and her respect to formation, and the moment Adam leapt for their leader, the gunfire opened—each bullet missing its target, as it was choreographed.

Adam seemed to dance on the bullets, dodging them as he disarmed each soldier and broke their automatic weapons to pieces. He drew down on the leader of the human militia, stretching for his throat. The other soldiers reached for more weapons, the leader using his last bit of breath to fend the toddler-like general off.

At that moment, Amber's whistle broke the air—Fast, too. A silver ring pierced the pavement beside Adam and stuck in the hard blacktop. The weakened military leader had already appeared to succumb to the inevitable defeat.

Adam actually flinched just enough to avoid having his arm removed. His eyes followed the steel whip from the pavement and up to the shadow hovering in the air. He reached for the embedded cable and recoiled as a second silver flash nearly took off his hand. Chunks of pavement began breaking apart as Amber directed her disk over and over to dislodge her other weapon from the pavement. Each time it struck, Adam reached for it, unable to completely grapple it. Then he teetered backwards as a steel bolt nearly took his foot out. A second and third bolt followed, and then a wave of black ribbon streaked past him.

Adam realized he was now bleeding. He gave chase to Josh, who stopped suddenly; dropped to his knees; and drove a blade straight for Adam. The general leapt to dodge the blow, but Amber's whip coiled around his leg. She heaved the scoundrel off towards the trees where several small side arms erupted.

Josh's swords snapped to attention, ready to impale whatever might come charging back for revenge.

He listened. He was good at listening now. Soldiers rustled on the balls of their feet as they aimed military-issued sidearms or readied blades. Josh silently chided them and returned to staring at nothing, simply relying on his ears.

Leaves crumpled somewhere beyond the black of the barrier of freeway foliage.

"Crack it," Josh said.

A high-pitched twang popped the air.

A beast cried, and Josh's aim was fast. One set of swords already retracted, and one of his fangs emptied its contents. The toddler-general cried again, this time in pain. Josh was already halfway done reloading his weapon before the creature fell silent and Josh stood again, listening.

"I think we're clear," Amber's voice crept into Josh's ear after what had become too much quiet for her.

Josh continued to listen for some time before he finally turned to the group of militants. "Bricktain?"

"Can't see him," Bricktain replied. "Think he ran off."

"I have a truck," Thomas announced. "Three guards, automatic weapons, not much ammo, a bazooka—one shot. We're coming out."

"Wow, one bazooka round," Josh said approaching the fortuitously unwounded leader of the soldiers. "You must be the dumbest hunters in the world."

"My name is Lieutenant Colonel Dee," the leader, a clean-shaved, yet filthy-faced man announced. "Who is in charge here?"

"Are we clear ," Josh asked, ignoring the soldiers.

"Yep," Thug's voice acknowledged through the earpiece. For several minutes, the freeway fell quiet. A car or two passed quickly through without any knowledge of the human figures hiding from view. Then a soft hum, almost electric-like, rolled from the woods, cutting through small trees with its bladed nose, while maneuvering around larger ones. Its soft blue lights might have surprised the soldiers were their lenses not so subtle. Had Speatsh been driving, he would have used the natural-sun high-beams to intimidate the soldiers, but Thug was a little more conservative, at least in this approach.

A second diesel, on the other hand, announced itself the moment it started and took significantly longer to clear the trees. Josh had to help remove some of the barriers himself with a few strikes of Wolf's Breath. It was a new sleek rig with a common trailer. A motor home followed. It was battered—new, but battered. The side looked as though a buffalo had charged it into a huge boulder. Three armored military Hummers soon appeared.

When the albino swordsman appeared atop Petruchio, the mercenaries hushed.

"You're real," one of them said.

The vampire paid no response until he towered over Josh.

"If they were forced off the road by an attack, where is the path they took," Thomas asked.

"A topic for another time, perhaps," Josh replied.

"Or a topic for the present," Thomas said in his ever-polite tone.

"They made it this far," Josh replied.

"So did the rogue," Thomas replied. Petruchio began his pace again and carried his white-haired rider into the back of the Silver Bullet where Bricktain had barely lowered the ramp.

"I believe I asked a question," Dee said, rubbing his bald head.

Amber wondered if it was meant to be an intimidating move. If it was, she wondered what morons it had worked on before. She laughed a little as she helped seal up the rear of the Bullet before positioning herself on the roof of its armored trailer.

"We have more important matters," Josh said to Dee and his men, before disappearing around to the passenger side of the silver diesel. Amber stayed atop the vehicle until the Bullet and other vehicles were loaded. When the motorcade finally began moving, she dropped through the hatch to join the rest of her comrades inside.

* * *

The Silver Bullet led the convoy into the compound. Once they had parked, the military squad all dressed in black, loose-fitting outfits emptied from the vehicles. They were armed once more with automatic weapons. The compound gates closed without a fight.

Several men stepped forward, following Dee. In the new light of the compound, besides his shaved head, he now distinguished himself with only half a nose.

"My name is Lieutenant Colonel Dee," the shaved man announced. "And I believe you'll answer my question now. Who is in charge here?"

Thomas would have stopped him, but the mayor stepped forward a little too quickly to greet the leader. "I'm the mayor of this city. I guess I am."

Dee looked the mayor over a moment and punched him square in the chest. "Don't insult me. You're not the one the man told us about. Where is the paladin?"

Josh started but was suddenly stopped.

"Is it you," Dee asked of Josh.

Josh said nothing.

"You're not prepared to dodge bullets," Thomas mumbled into his headset.

"Then pray I don't get shot," Josh replied. He stepped out to help the mayor to his feet.

Amber had already moved to take position above the group of soldiers and held both orbits at the ready.

Dee examined Josh as he aided the mayor. A moment later, Dee crumpled to the ground, grabbing his side. Before Dee's men could react, Josh held one small crossbow in their leader's face. "You'll find I have very little patience for disruptive guests in my home."

Dee's eyes narrowed. "Hunters don't kill humans. Aren't those the rules?"

Josh directed the aim to Dee's right eye to help him see his response more clearly. "Are they?"

"I needed to know it was you," Dee said. "Your father told us you could use some help."

Josh had nothing to say.

"We're here to help," Dee said. When he realized that Josh was unmoved, he added, "Hunters don't kill hunters."

He was right, and Josh hated that in this second.

"You attacked our mayor," Josh said. He held out a hand as if to help Dee up from his crumpled position.

Dee held up an unwavering hand expecting to receive help, but Josh gripped the folds of Wolf's Breath and envisioned the movement that would remove the hand that struck down the mayor.

"Allow me to help you to your feet, friend," Thomas said, suddenly gripping Dee's hand. "Our generosity to fellow hunters is only equal to our devotion to the fight." Thomas helped Dee to his feet and shook his hand firmly. "But make no mistake, those dogs are smart to fear the paladin."

Dee's face flushed as Thomas nearly crushed his hand. To his credit, Dee didn't acknowledge the pain, only clenched his jaw and waved his fellow hunters back.

"My choice would have been to cut your hand off," Thomas said, throwing Dee's handshake away. "Suppose that could be why I'm not in charge." Thomas composed himself, placing his palm over the hilt of his long blade.

"I apologize for any offense," Dee replied, not nearly as gentlemanly as Thomas sounded. "We're not usually among friends. Sometimes a good hit helps establish who those are."

Josh said nothing. He understood, but he wasn't telling this man the like.

"We're all ex-military," Dee said.

"Still use your rank," Josh asked.

"Helps us maintain order," Dee replied. "We came to offer our skills and our tools to help you win this fight."

"Did you bring enough," Josh asked.

"I don't know," Dee replied. "Never seen a fight like this before, but we're orderly, and we recognize authority where authority is due, sir. Heard you could use some help. Mind if we join?"

* * *

The newer catwalks wobbled. Dee squeezed past one of the sentries easily enough. It was a man in a black duster and a set of triple barreled shotguns, but Josh had been more casual about the uncertain ground.

The gate sentry yawned, it was the biker in the wolf bandana, a man whose company Josh hadn't enjoyed since he met him at Thug's café. Something bothered Josh deeply about this man and didn't want him anywhere near him. However, the biker could fight, and the doorman did need to sleep from time to time. Josh also didn't like the rodeo queens who seemed to never leave the biker's side. Despite how much he didn't care for them, they had put in the longest shifts and slept less than anybody else. They were annoying, but clearly reliable and driven by the wolves.

At least the blonde queen wasn't running laps around the catwalk for the time being. That one was a little too sporty for Josh's taste. Maybe it reminded him too much of how Cadence used to run laps around the swimming pool in the claustrophobic bunker. The brunette was too quiet. Although, Josh kind of liked that part about her.

Dawn hinted at breaking. The birthing horizon marked the change in shift for the beasts beyond the compound walls. The silvery guardians had already begun to thin out, leaving only scouts, those monsters under the guise of common dogs.

"They never go away," the sentry mumbled.

"They will," Josh replied.

"Oh yes," the biker replied. "They will."

"Interesting set up you got here, kid," Dee acknowledged.

"Paladin," Bricktain corrected taking up the rear of the tour, which currently consisted of Josh, Dee, three of his fellow soldiers and then Bricktain.

"What's that area over there," Dee asked.

"Those are the non-hunters," Josh explained. "We found it easier to let them have their own living area. Lets us work."

"You have a problem with them interfering," Dee asked.

"We have a few unpleasants," Josh explained. "Mostly those who don't fully understand the situation. The mayor deals with them for the most part. I'm not quite as patient."

"Why are they here," Dee asked.

"Rescued from farms," Bricktain said.

"What keeps the wolves from attacking that area instead," Dee asked.

"Walls are stronger over there," Josh replied. "And electrified."

"How about that area, there," one of Dee's mercenaries asked, changing direction of his interest. He was older than Dee, friendlier.

Josh took a moment to follow the direction of the merc's hand to an area of the compound lighter than the rest, even in the waning dark.

"Playground," Josh said.

"Right," Dee straightened up. "I saw you brought children here?"

"Had to," Bricktain replied. "Couldn't leave them in the farm neither."

"A green move," Dee sniffed. "Bad place for kids, and my men aren't babysitters."

The older merc patted Bricktain's arm as if to say, "Don't worry, we're here now."

The merc suddenly grappled at the handrail to keep from falling over.

Bricktain's steel hand clenched tightly into Dee's shoulder. "If children are a problem for you, your men are welcome to leave," Bricktain replied and would have said more had Josh not waved him down.

"I would expect a man who fought for liberties of others to understand that," Josh said.

Dee nodded and acknowledged the truth in Josh's words.

"Where do me and my men fit in," Dee asked.

"The mayor acts as a liaison between the non-hunter community and the rest of us. Keeps them more pleasant to be around." Josh explained. "Bricktain here has been duly appointed and sworn in as sheriff of this city since our local law enforcement can't be trusted now."

"Sheriff," Dee asked. Josh couldn't tell if he was pouting or lightly amused.

"We do have the elected authority of the mayor in here," Josh replied. "Technically, any police that you run into outside of these walls have been relieved of authority. Most of them are manipulated by the wolves now. You and your men can swear in as deputies until these wolves are remedied."

"If it ever ends," the sentry with the triple-barrel shotgun added.

Josh turned on the sentry. "You think it won't?"

The older sentry said nothing, just stared out into the fields beyond the walls of the compound.

"Get off my wall," Josh ordered and then yelled to one of Dee's own men to replace the sentry's post.

Dee's mercenary looked to Dee for approval.

"Now," Josh yelled to the slow-of-hearing mercenary.

The mercenary immediately responded.

"And your position," Dee asked as his subordinate and the sentry raced to change places.

"I go where I'm needed," Josh replied. "And if you ever call me kid or green again, I'll have to fix that." Without explaining himself further, he motioned for Dee to continue his way along the catwalk. Eventually the small group of men approached a pole and took turns sliding down it back to the ground.

They returned to the rest of Dee's men who were currently getting a rather rude orientation from Thug and Thomas.

"Their ammo's garbage," Thomas said.

"And we're not wasting ours in their automatic weapons," Thug added.

"Great," Amber said from her high perch, where only those connected to her could hear. "Useless hunters."

Bricktain agreed.

Josh made note of the sky. The day shift was nearly upon him. Perhaps the laborers could do something about getting some shade up today. Natalie could use it.

Nata?

"What is she still doing out," Josh shouted. "Get her inside before she burns up."

Reggie was the first to react and held open the door to his cold, steel house. He waited for Natalie, who appeared from the shadows of a pile of plastic and fiberglass vehicle bumpers.

"Dog," one of Dee's men cried. A barrage of automatic weapons drawing into their hands twittered within the compound.

Natalie roared and prepared to attack, but held her ground.

One gun fell into two pieces. Another soldier grabbed his face from the many leather and braided ropes that slashed across it. Two more men dropped, grabbing at injuries, before Josh had finally gained their attention. He now held a fang to another man, pressing the tip of the crossbow into his throat.

"Hunters don't kill hunters," the mercenary said. He seemed bemused, or maybe Josh only saw that he was.

In this moment, Josh saw the danger of these men. They were militant, respectful of only one code, Dee's. Their leader had given too many clues. He didn't respect the civilians. He didn't respect the children. They clearly had hunted dogs so long that they only understood the law of the alpha.

Very well.

These men were going to get people killed, or kill his allies. Josh couldn't allow that. He held far too many lives to be responsible to let these few men put them in harm's way. However, he also couldn't in good conscience turn them back out to the wolves.

That was twice now that Dee and his men had rallied around the excuse that hunters don't kill hunters. They had abused the code. They tried to kill one of his comrades, and he had no action.

"You think you're a hunter," Josh asked. He suddenly smashed his crossbow against the side of merc's head.

The soldier fell, grabbing at his injury. He might have whimpered an apology, but Josh heard the drawing of a sidearm to his left from another mercenary. Before it could draw aim, Josh had this idiot in the sight of his crossbow.

Dee's men were encircled at once by armed hunters that would have given them no chance to survive any retaliation.

Josh wanted to tell the soldier not to do it, but he feared the soldier might see that as the opening he needed to fire upon Josh.

Neither man blinked.

"I'm on him," Amber's voice came through the earpiece.

"Don't chance it," Thomas's voice replied.

Then the soldier did something stupid, he squared his eyes. Josh rolled onto his heels. He could have fired, but he rolled out of the sight of the gun.

The sidearm fired.

Josh's arm—hand, still clenching the crossbow—climbed in the elegant, but controlled motion that he had spent far too long practicing. Wolf's Breath obeyed his command, extending his lethal touch and slicing through the arteries, muscles, bone and windpipe of his opponent.

He felt the head roll into the ribbon of his cloak and drop to the ground before he had drawn back into a fighting stance with his crossbow at the ready again.

The headless body finished dropping nearly at Josh's feet.

"Was the paladin not clear," Thomas asked before Josh could further complicate the situation further.

Josh drew aim on another soldier.

"What did I say about my patience and disruptive guests, Colonel," Josh shouted. "Your people seem to be confused as to whose blood gets spilled in my compound."

He heard Speatsh's voice reminding him to appear mean. He hated what he'd become in that moment. This wasn't appearing mean anymore. This was worse. He had taken human life. True, it was a life that was about to harm his own, but was life nonetheless. This was the role of passing judgment to remind others that the lives of all allies were sacred, that no attempt on any of their lives would be permitted. This was not the role he had desired to take up, yet he had seen this new group of mercs already disregard too much when it came to preserving the human race. He saw their disregard to know their place as a threat to the lives of others. Again, he ordered Natalie indoors and waited for the house to slam that hard metallic bang behind her.

"Please tell me if you're still confused so I can clarify the answer," Josh announced.

The mercs looked to their colonel, who returned a nod.

A soldier suddenly grabbed at his arm, which had instantly severed at the wrist. Two companions began rushing to his aid.

"Is anybody else under the impression that I need your colonel's permission," Josh cried. "The next time your head nods permission in my compound, Dee, I'll take it off too. If I see a head nod towards you, I'll take that one as well. And the next time any mercenary in my compound raises a weapon to any ally, I'll raise mine." He kicked the severed head to punctuate his law. "Understood?" Josh clenched Wolf's Breath, afraid he'd have to follow through with this threat, realizing the truth of Speatsh's counsel that not being mean could indeed cost lives. Would Thomas step in to stop it this time? Would Thug? Could Josh take another head? End another life? Or could he be lenient and allow these mercs to put more allies in danger? No, he had to have control in his compound.

He waited for the nod.

Dee stood still. "Sir!" Dee cried. "Yes, sir!"

Josh relinquished his attack. "Aggon," he cried finally turning his attention on the amputated soldier.

It may have appeared to be nothing at first sight, but the golden chariot with the face of the sun, which had been parked casually beside the central structure, suddenly jerked. The large-statured, spectral driver appeared out of nowhere and cracked a long whip over his head. Six horses apparated. Even those bystanders used to his appearance were taken a bit off by his sudden outburst.

"I be to slap da boo-hoo about anyone dat wants to beat on me," Aggon cried. "Where's my cripple?"

"Not this time," Josh said. "You're just taking out some trash. I don't need blood stirring up the dogs."

"No cripple," Aggon said. "No me."

Reggie's chair whined to the back of Aggon's chariot. The gold pommel of a swordless blade appeared from a bag hanging over the back of his chair. "Don't make me puke this time, ghostboy."

"Load," Aggon ordered. The spectral horses pressed back, and the chariot tipped down for Reggie's chair to drive up and into. "Okay, cripple."

"Stop calling me cripple," Reggie said before driving his scooter into the chariot. "What are we doing, Son?"

"This man needs a doctor," Josh said.

Thug had already torn the shoelace out of the maimed man's boot and had begun lashing it around his wrist to stop the bleeding.

"And, unfortunately, our chief surgeon can't be trusted with these poeple at the moment," Josh continued

Aggon made note of the dawning sun.

"Something wrong," Josh asked.

Aggon chortled, "Not for da me."

"Up," Josh ordered the injured man. "You're going too."

"Not da oozy one," Aggon cried. "Dis gold chariot, not for da bleedings, makes my aura all greasy."

"He will die," Josh said. "You're the fastest."

"Cook da hand as other soldier," Aggon said.

"No," Josh replied. "This one's friends all need to understand where the next closest help is if they're not going to play nice with the rest of the team, here."

Dee and two of his men helped the injured mercenary into the chariot.

"No," Aggon cried. "Arm hangs outside."

"He'll fall out, you moron," Reggie snapped.

Aggon started laughing. "Cripple is funny."

Josh dropped the severed hand, dirt and all, into the back of the chariot and told the dying mercenary to find something to hold onto. When the soldier appeared to border on passing out. Josh smacked him awake. "It's your choice, die falling out or find something to hold onto."

"Now is all bleedy," Aggon complained. "Bleedy is not what I does."

"Just drop him on the steps of the E.R.," Josh said and, when he didn't hear any complaint from his comrades or Dee, continued. "It may be a farm, but they go through a lot of trouble to preserve their meat. We can retrieve him later."

"I understand," Dee replied.

"Do you," Josh asked.

"You have a better chance living where the doctors are than you do here," Dee encouraged his soldier. "You'll be taken care of."

Josh ordered Aggon away.

Aggon cried. The chariot spun and, in a mighty leap, the horses carried it and all of its passengers over the steel wall, crowned with deadly wire.

"Don't make me repeat myself," Josh said. "You and your team have no authority here. Until I see your worth, you answer to everyone else in this place."

Dee acknowledged the comment.

Josh returned to Bricktain who had been watching the rest of Dee's men carefully. "Have 'em start digging trenches around the base of the walls and bury the razor wire," he said in a hushed tone.

"Bury it," Bricktain asked.

"I imagine the rogue will launch an attack before too long," Josh said. "Let's cut a few knuckles that might try digging under the walls."

"I get the feeling you're leaving me the game, boss," Bricktain said. He inconspicuously drew a bottle of white pills from his pocket and chomped down on two of them.

"Thomas and I are going after the rogue," Josh replied.

"Then I should come with you," Bricktain urged. He tucked his bottle away.

"And leave our new friends without someone serious in charge," Josh asked. "I need you in the Bullet to keep an eye on our new comrades."

"I don't trust them," Bricktain said.

"Then I guess it's your turn to be the mean one," Josh said.

"You mean to be the killer."

Josh felt the sting.

"What would you have done?"

"I guess we may find out," Bricktain replied mournfully.

"I don't want to come back and have to reestablish order. Until then, you may have to be mean. Don't feel bad for shooting any mercs that get out of hand."

"I'd rather not," Bricktain said. "But I'll do what I have to. You really should take more help though."

"I'm coming with you," Amber's voice carried both in the earpiece and in the area as she floated gently to the ground.

"Of course you are," Josh answered.

"We're all split up now," Bricktain said and Josh watched the man try to keep his face straight.

"Acotactac's going to be all right," Josh said. "I know she is."

Bricktain faked a smile. "It just doesn't feel right."

"If something happens," Josh said, turning now to Bricktain. "If I don't make it back."

"You're too reckless to make that promise," Bricktain said.

"You've been a good friend," Josh said then made a handshake with the robot man's healthy arm.

Amber said something about Bricktain watching after her dad and moved in to hug the compound's sheriff.

"Doorman," Josh said. "You up yet?"

"Do I sound up yet," the gruff voice yelled. The volume rang in Josh's ear, but it seemed even louder from his sleeping bag beneath the trailer of a parked diesel.

"There's too many itchy trigger fingers starting to fill the catwalks," Josh said. "I would take it as a personal favor if you would take post to guard the house and Natalie."

"Yep," The doorman replied. "Jaws can fill in for me until I wake up."

"Jaws," Josh asked.

"The man with—," the doorman started to say, but never finished.

"It's that new biker who's been watching the gate," Thomas replied.

"You call him Jaws," Josh asked.

"Because of his teeth," the doorman said. "Don't know what his name is."

Josh called a few orders up to the biker who currently held the doorman's post over the gates. The biker took up his gear and, in the process, the brunette somehow got pinched against the railing, and her silver revolver blasted off a shot, embedding its bullet into the heel of Josh's black sneaker.

After a few dance steps of retreat, Josh realized he hadn't been shot.

"Are you stupid," Josh shrieked.

"Easy," Thomas said. "It was an accident."

Josh considered Thomas's words, then screamed. "Make those stupid women get some sleep before they kill someone."

At that, the brunette stumbled and nearly teetered off the catwalk.

Thomas flew to catch her in case she fell.

Josh was several moments behind him.

"Careful," Josh ordered.

She replied with a rude gesture.

"Get that cow off my catwalk," Josh demanded.

The brunette queen nodded and slid down the pole, rather than use the stairs into the compound. She rushed off with a trembling lip.

The blonde took the stairs and glared at Josh as she walked past.

Josh might have punished her publicly if he hadn't had his fill of appearing the brute for the night.

"I know it's not in your character," Thomas said. "But you might wish to consider apologizing to those two."

"Why," Amber asked. "The last thing we need around here is a klutz."

"Because they've put in more hours since they've gotten here than you have," Thomas replied. "That's worthy of respect."

"I don't have time to argue," Josh replied.

"Agreed," Thomas replied. "No changing your mind? Sure you want to do this?"

"I want that rogue," Josh said.

"Then let me go alone," Thomas suggested.

"I'll go alone before you do," Josh sneered, and then moved to one of the Hummers. He pondered how far one could make it trying to get out of the compound without the Bullet. It had been successful in plowing the road out, but he wondered how long that could last before the wolves learned how to bring it down. It was probably best to conserve the field trips. Josh wasn't fully certain either that it was a good idea to leave the silver bullet behind, but he needed to leave Bricktain his firepower in case the soldiers decided to behave brashly again.

On that thought, "I think we should park the Bullet in front of the house," Josh said. "Shoot anyone who comes near it or Natalie."

"You taking a Hummer, out," Bricktain asked.

Then Josh noticed the flat tire on the rear of the vehicle. He chose another Hummer and found it too had a flat tire. The third vehicle he checked had two flats, another had three.

"You've been driving on rims," Josh called to Dee before deciding to abandon the idea of using the military SUVs. He leapt down into the new hole in the ground. "The tunnel it is," Josh said. Thomas said nothing. Amber mumbled something about being glad she hadn't eaten. Josh called for a flashlight, and Bricktain appeared with an electric lantern.

"Have you given any thought to what you're going to do if you actually find the rogue," Bricktain asked.

About a dozen replies jumped to mind, one was a pretty funny one, two or three might have made a good catch phrase for an army-of-one movie, but he settled on "Why? Should I?"

"I mean it, boss," Bricktain said. "It doesn't feel right. Something's just wrong here."

"Yeah," Josh replied. "Started the day you got involved in this." Then he disappeared into the underground tunnel. A moment later he reappeared. "You know what I mean."

Bricktain nodded.

Josh disappeared again.

"Don't let him go, Thomas," Bricktain urged. "I just got a feeling he needs to stay here."

"He'll be fine," Amber chided as she climbed into the ground and followed after her husband.

"You do your job, and let me worry about mine, Mister Morris," Thomas said, leaping into the ground and giving room for Petruchio to follow. "I hope you're wrong," Thomas added. "But if bad comes, give it fight worthy of remembrance. Because remembrance raises new warriors to your cause."

Still, as Bricktain Morris watched his friends disappear, he couldn't shake the nagging feeling that he had failed in some way.

15 ~ Tainted Blood

"We were two kids, helped him hide about twenty years ago," Harvey Bruce replied. "Said if we ever needed something, come find him. And now, I'm hungry."

Somewhere between hiking onto campus alongside a vampire on a horse and himself dressed like some anime cowboy, it occurred to Josh that he looked like an idiot. Amber, who sat behind Thomas upon Petruchio, appeared the only normal one in the group, supposing you looked past her leather duster, which currently concealed her whips.

It was here that Josh also realized that he smelled worse than a garbage can. He was certain it would never wash out. It hadn't dissipated in the air, even after their walk to campus, which seemed to be more of an extensive game of hide-and-seek. What should have normally been a two hour walk at most, ended up taking the day. All of this meant perspiration. The tunnel was a nightmare in itself with stench. The odor was only made worse by two days without a bath since there was no running water in the compound as of yet. They had plans to get it going, but it hadn't come to fruition yet.

What he wouldn't give to be in the bunker shower right now.

His feet hurt too. Hickerbilly might have been an even more welcome blessing. Josh took a moment to curse Speatsh for the lack of a vehicle as well as his pain. Unfortunately, aching wasn't an option. He was hunting the rogue now. On that note: "This would be a good time for a higher view," Josh said.

"That's what we need," Amber said. "Reports on campus about an unidentified, flying girl. I wouldn't chance it for another thirty minutes, at least. Should be dark enough by then."

"View wouldn't be any good with a rooftop in the way anyway," Thomas replied. "Hope you remember your close-quarter training, my dear."

Here, Thomas stopped Petruchio. Amber swung off Petruchio and stepped down an invisible staircase of air. Thomas then dropped to the ground himself and urged the horse to find a good hiding spot.

The trio made its way into one of the lesser used parking lots.

Not long after, students began to rush past with bags in hands, over shoulders and on wheels. They weren't the normal young students that Josh was used to seeing during his day at the university. This was the older crowd that came with the setting in of the evening. A few texted while they walked. One complained about car problems Into his Bluetooth. Another student sat on a green-brick wall and tapped away on his tablet.

"How do they not know," Amber asked. "And they even have electricity here."

"It makes sense. People retreat to where there's power," Thomas replied. "Where better for the rogue to do his work than among a community whose noses are trapped within the walls of study. Ironic, isn't it?"

"But how is it possible," Josh asked. "They're everywhere. People have disappeared. The power is out all over the city. How can they keep living like this? How can they not know what's happening?"

"Do you think it was any different when you didn't know," Thomas asked. "You think the wolves waited for you to become wiser? Besides, ever see a college student who noticed anything other than their own ego?"

Now, Josh realized that he really did look like an idiot walking in his strange garb, which concealed crossbows and swords. He envied the students. He suddenly missed his studies; missed having lunch in a cafeteria; joking around with Dustin over a burger; and making weekend plans with Natalie. He pushed those thoughts back as soon as he understood where they were taking him.

"The art museum's this way," Josh said, and he turned down a set of cement stairs, which led towards the commons sidewalk and out of the parking lot. They moved towards the three-story building.

Thomas wondered how secure of a hiding place Petruchio had found. Thomas's stallion usually hid well, but it didn't stop the vampire from wondering all the same.

Not long ago, Thomas worried whether his cutting horse would be captured by animal control, but when he returned to find Petruchio fending off a small group of officers, he knew his four-legged companion's capabilities. His horses knew when to hide and when to appear, but that didn't mean that tranquilizer guns couldn't still be effective.

"Not to seem the doubting Thomas here," Amber said. "But there's three of us. Do we really think us capable to take on the rogue?"

"He won't show himself today," Thomas replied. "He has a plan and he'll stick to it. He's not going to show himself on our clock. We're just looking for clues today. See if we can get an idea of what he's up to. If we find anything, we'll come back with a more appropriate response team."

"And if we happen to find the rogue instead of clues," Josh asked.

"I doubt that will happen," Thomas said. "We haven't been watched once, since we got here. But if it makes you feel better, if we run into him, you two return to the compound, and I'll buy your escape."

"Why you," Josh asked.

"I'm better than you," Thomas replied.

"Can we make it fast," Amber asked through what could have passed for dreary blush. She needed a bathroom, but kept her stomach down.

Josh glanced at Thomas. Thomas read the glance, looked to Amber and fully stopped in his tracks.

"You pregnant," Thomas asked bluntly and didn't need a verbal response. "You should not be here."

"Great idea," Amber replied. "We'll just ignore that you need what I can do."

"You should have both told me," Thomas complained, stabbing a disdainful finger between Josh and Amber. He then continued walking.

They meandered their way around the art building. Thomas held one of the main doors open to his companions, which somehow unnerved Josh before he reminded himself that Thomas was simply being polite

The three comrades entered the foyer of the building. The large double doors to the right, which led immediately into the art gallery, were sealed shut. The brass placard next to one of the doors left no question as to the room on the other side of this wall.

Josh took in his surroundings. Thomas appeared to do the same. A few students filled the foyer, one sat at a table with his back to the doors. Three more sat at a table, more interested in their tablets than they seemed to be in real life. A man, probably a faculty member, disappeared down a set of stairs into the lecture hall.

Josh shifted his weight, and a surge of pain fired up his leg from his heel.

"Hurting," Thomas asked.

"I'm getting used to it," Josh wanted to say "yes", but lied instead.

Thomas didn't believe him. The vampire approached the set of reddish doors and peered through the crack between them. The light was on. His hand gripped the pommel of his long blade and politely pushed Josh behind him.

"A door," Thomas chuckled. "All this time, and it's quite possible that he's on the other side of a door." He started to pull at the latch and suddenly stopped. "If elements suddenly get away from us," Thomas said, but didn't finish.

"Yes," Amber asked.

"It's nothing," Thomas replied. "Just, it's been an honor."

"Thought you said, we wouldn't run into him today," Josh said.

"I did, didn't I," Thomas said.

Before either Josh or Amber could respond, one of the tall doors burst open, and Thomas sidestepped its launch. Two guys and a girl came through talking some gibberish.

"Excuse you," the girl said as she passed Thomas.

"My apologies, madam," Thomas replied.

"Madam," one of the guys repeated and broke out laughing.

The girl wasn't amused, however. "Oh my gosh, it's a herd of nerd," she replied.

Amber over-faked a laugh. "Says the girl coming *out* of the art museum," she added.

Josh pondered his own response, which might have normally been on par for hunters, but was a little more inappropriate at the moment. The instant his blades shot from his arms to teach the cretins a lesson, he realized his mistake.

The girl gasped, and her male companions seemed to step away.

"You should see my crossbows," Josh said.

"That's disgusting," the girl cried.

"Not as much as you think, actually," Josh replied.

The girl's face twisted in repulsion.

"Does that mean no kiss," Josh asked.

Thomas abruptly apologized and lied about being part of the show, which, for some reason, the gaggle of idiots believed.

He ushered Josh and Amber through the door and pulled it shut. He would have locked it as well to provide the freedom to search for clues uninhibited, except that a class was in session reviewing a large silver mural of the woodland scene where a wolf of some sort seemed to be in the process of devouring some being in its path.

The room was tall with white walls, ceiling and bright recessed lights. Lanky figures surrounded the exterior room and were all too unsettling. Josh knew at once what they were.

"They're ancients," Josh blurted. Many faces from the class turned away from their lecture in front of the large, metallic sculpture. Josh thought it looked a bit like an image from a Little Red Riding Hood scene, except with dead bodies and the form of a guardian standing over them. This time Josh apologized for himself, and the class returned to its discussion. "Aren't they," Josh asked in a softer tone.

They looked almost like the ancient in the trophy room back in the bunker, except these stood erect under the support of black metal posts. They appeared taller than Speatsh's mother might have been if she had been standing, and they seemed to have given way to starvation and decay.

"He kept them," Thomas whispered. "This is unexpected."

"How could anyone expect this," Amber asked finding herself squaring up against the torso of one of the shorter creatures.

"Go figure," Thomas replied then caught himself. "I'm not sure one could, milady."

While Thomas and Amber seemed entranced by the presence of the taxidermy of old white wolves, Josh was too busy contemplating the people in the room.

"Don't fret," Thomas replied. "They're not generals."

"Can you be sure?"

"Yes," Thomas said. "Eyes never lie. They're all hearing the professor and none learning."

"Then I guess we should leave them to their lecture," Josh said. He then felt himself drawn towards a podium with a book on it. Thomas followed, his dress shoes clicking away at the high-gloss sheen of the marbled floor with black and white tiles.

Josh tried to appreciate the art that showed on the page of the book, an image of a carriage of some sort with faces pressed against the glass.

"Impossible," Thomas muttered and then he gripped the paper. Gasps erupted behind him until he held up his gloved hand and wiggled his fingers at the class. "Always bring my own."

Thomas examined the page with the drawing of the carriage, then the one before and the one after it, then examined them all again. He continued to turn pages until he found an image of a circle of creatures. He suddenly pulled the pages out of the book without raising alarm.

"Where is it," Thomas asked. He turned around and inspected the rest of the open gallery for something more, something that seemed to be missing.

He immediately found the podium with stones. He compared the pages with the stones before folding the papers and placing them in his suit pocket.

He honed in on the largest object in the exhibit, the metal mural behind the lecturing class, which was silent now. Most of the students sat on the floor and examined the steel art. Thomas stepped through the collected students and drew near the mural.

He'd barely noticed that Josh had done the same.

"Are those sewing pins," Josh asked.

"Uh, yeah," one of the students replied before Thomas could, and several snickers filled the room.

"He made this," Thomas said.

"He," Josh asked.

"He's definitely here," Thomas added. He scrutinized the mural, drawing close enough that the professor felt inclined to caution the vampire. Thomas felt inclined to thank her and almost seemed embarrassed that he had let his manners get away from him.

Josh drew close to Thomas. "Something you want to tell me?"

"That text," Thomas did his best to whisper. "It's written in the tongue of the ancients, Speatsh showed it to me once. The text is about passing on power. I'm not sure, but it seems to suggest a ritual among the ancients. When they are gathered in a circle and face within, they pass on a part of their power to their living target. It's how they select the different roles they each have: who protects, who serves, even who rules."

"Speatsh said the queen was the oldest," Josh said. "He didn't say anything about a ritual."

"Excuse me," the lecturer pleaded. "Do you mind?"

Thomas politely stepped away from the crowd to the far left of the mural where Amber had finally approached. Without touching the paladin, he prompted Josh to follow. "She probably was the oldest. That's what I always thought." He withdrew the pages from his pocket, careful to keep them from public view and directed Josh over the writing. "But this text suggests that roles and callings are distributed through this circle of judgment, if you will. I think the rogue wants to force judgment, give himself power. The more that stand in the circle, the more power they have to give."

"I guess it's a good thing these ones are all dead then," Josh said.

"No," Thomas said trying to stay hushed and drawing up the picture of the carriage. "There used to be talk about a hearse or some kind of cart that was empowered to gather souls. I don't remember all of it, and I don't understand all this language. You hear so many rumors in this business, you don't know which ones to disavow and which ones to dignify sometimes."

Josh was lost, and the sound that Amber made suddenly to his side, announced that she was too.

"If my translation is correct, this hearse, or whatever it is, can use the souls it gathers to return life to another," Thomas explained.

"Like a soul bank," Amber asked.

"You're saying there's a wagon that can kill someone, steal the soul and then bring one of these things back to life instead," Josh asked, and a realization hit him. "And grant the rogue more power?"

"No," Thomas replied. "It takes more than one to restore a life."

"How many does it take the—," and then Josh stopped.

"What," Thomas asked.

"With ten thousand, he can rebuild one," Josh recited as it had been told him. "That's what the elemental said."

"Just curious," Amber asked. "But how does the wagon gather the souls?"

"I'm not certain," Thomas replied, examining the pages for an answer. "I think, perhaps, one must die in a close proximity of the hearse."

"So where is this wagon," Josh asked. "He's got to have it, right?"

"I should think that if he had it, they wouldn't be dead on display," Amber suggested.

"Unless he's not ready," Thomas said. "But I think he knows where it is."

This time, Josh made a sound, one that seemed to catch Thomas's attention more than it should have.

"You know something," Thomas said.

"Maybe. I'm not sure," Josh replied. "I think—"

A student suddenly spoke to ask their lecturer a question.

"I think it's time we get out of here," Josh said. "I can't think here."

"Wise idea," Thomas replied, and quickly buried his stolen pages once more. As he turned to leave, Josh and Amber followed, which would have normally been a simple practice. However, in turning, Josh had given little account to the inanimate surrounding, and a lower fold of Wolf's Breath swiped away a chunk of sculptured tree trunk.

In an instant, the entire mural of pins began to fall apart, as if water bursting through a dam. The pins fell fast, the entire museum turned into a sound which was uncanny to that of white water. Students who tried to stand and run were quickly buried in the downpour of the gigantic mural.

Despite the cries of those students stuck by sewing pins, Thomas remained silent. Josh and Amber followed suit, waited for the commotion to end and then carefully climbed out of the pile of steel slivers that had grown around their ankles.

"And we were so close," Thomas said. Strangely, he didn't appear angry to Josh. He appeared something that Josh hadn't seen in him yet, but it was unclear what it was. Josh hadn't seen it in Speatsh, Thug or Bogi even. "We have to go now," Thomas said, kicking his way from beneath the pins, trying his best to remain cordial and apologetic to the professor and students who were now screaming at him about his museum etiquette. Although he didn't quite understand how it was possible, doubt began to fill Thomas. He needed to remember something. Perhaps it was the absence of Kate that blinded his ability to think. Regardless, Thomas was fearful. As Soleil stepped out of the pile, Josh follow his lead.

"Check for pins, Josh," Thomas said. "You'll flee faster without them finding their ways in your heels."

The small band's interest quickly turned to making sure no unaccounted pins had disappeared into any shoe or crevice where it could sneak in an unfortunate attack during an inopportune fight-or-flight moment.

The lecturing professor had taken to her phone to report the vandals, cursing its lack of service. The students took photos of the fallen art and the stupid criminals who were now also emptying their shoes and folds of their odd clothes.

"Great," Thomas said.

"It's okay," Josh observed. "They don't have service, right?"

"They have cameras," Thomas replied. He stretched out his wrist to reveal a Rolex with four different colored stones at each quarter. He pressed on the face of the glass.

The students began complaining at their phones for going dark.

"How does the emergency service not work, either," the professor cried into her cell.

"We've lingered too long," Thomas said. "Go, now."

Josh pulled his shoe back over his foot after ensuring no stray needle remained.

"Why are you people even here," Amber asked the class as she raced with Josh and Thomas towards the exit.

Josh arrived to the door first and pressed. "It's locked," he quickly observed and prepared to cut the doors down.

A loud locking mechanism of some sort crackled from the far corner of the gallery.

"It's too late," Thomas replied. "He knows we're here."

"You said—," Amber started.

"That was before Josh destroyed his art," Thomas said.

"So I just forced his hand," Josh said. "Great."

"This may just be to taunt us," Thomas said. "Whatever happens, I'll make you an exit, and you get back. That's the plan, got it?"

The wall in the back corner of the museum slowly began to open. A blonde woman dressed in professional, black skirting stepped through. She assessed the damage of the sculpture. "Ladies and gentlemen, the museum will have to close now. Thank you for coming," Loraine said. She turned to Josh and his friends. "Security is waiting. This way, please." She gestured for Josh's group to follow her through the back of the museum. The other guests applauded and cheered as Thomas chose to lead the group towards the newly opened exit at the back of the gallery where Loraine waited a little too smuggishly.

"The rest of you may please exit the way you came in," Loraine informed. The towering doors that led to the museum, locked a moment ago to Josh's party, now opened on their own for the class to exit.

"I think we'll decline your offer," Josh replied. He even turned to make his way back. His chest ridiculed him, reminding him he would rather not test how much more injury he could incur this week.

"That's your choice," Loraine replied. "But I can't guarantee you'll have anything to go back to if you leave now."

Josh stopped and watched the last of the students file out of the gallery. The doors banged shut.

"Putting everyone in that tinfoil trap like that, are you sure that was a wise idea," Loraine asked. She then turned to enter the backdoor when she realized that Josh had decided to follow her.

Thomas followed Loraine closely, with Amber behind him. When he made his move, Loraine would die first. Josh cautiously took up the rear. When Thomas casually drew his weapons at the sight of the two black, one-armed generals that had killed Speatsh, Josh forced out his own blades.

He'd seen Genre fight. Josh felt that he and his friends were skilled, but he feared the harmony of mind that The Left Arm and The Right Arm held. This monster had proven too much for Speatsh. It had proven too much for Josh. The paladin still ached from his last beating Genre gave him.

"Don't worry," Loraine said from the front of the line. "They won't hurt you."

Loraine led deeper into a plain concrete room, where mobile walls lined up awaiting to be removed for future exhibitions. Bad lighting and paint splotches betrayed their integrity. Suddenly, he was there. Josh knew it was him. He held himself majestically from many millenia, maybe more, of looking down on other creatures. Thomas's actions stiffened as well, and his frame took stance to fight.

The rogue was shorter than Josh by only an inch or two. He was well-groomed, appeared young to middle-aged, or so Josh thought. He wore a brown turtle neck with a yellow suit and black accessories. He glanced over Thomas, showing no emotion nor interest. He scrutinized Amber a moment before allowing his gaze to fall on Josh. Then he abruptly turned and disappeared around a corner farther into the warehouse. Genre slinked past the group and followed its master.

"Please," Loraine pointed out their expected path as she, herself, forged after the rogue and his protectors.

Thomas, Amber and Josh maintained their formation. Amber clenched her orbits and had already made note of the ceiling height and one wall that she'd tear down if she had to give herself more attacking room. She located a beam that should bring down enough of the ceiling to buy some time for escape, provided Josh knew not to run beneath it before she could make her move. She'd step in his way if she had to. For now, she was poised between the two best point guards she could ask for.

Around the corner revealed four more ancients, but these were different from those in the gallery. Each stood on a black podium with a tall bronze pole, to which each had also been bound and wrapped in heavy rusty chain. Only their heads and feet showed through the bulky, blankets of chain.

"They're alive," Amber said. "He's got living ancients," she prepared to launch an attack. What did she have to lose? Surely, one of them could fight alongside her group if she freed it. What if she could free all of them? A glance from Thomas told her it was a bad idea. He was probably right. She wasn't certain how precisely she could cut the thin layers that bound them without tearing their flesh open.

The Yellow-dressed man now sat back against a shop stool, while Genre poised himself on both sides.

"Your rogueship," Josh greeted. Rogueship? Really? That was the best he could come up with? He'd faced off against other generals with better insult than this.

The rogue seemed unaffected by the comment. Thomas, however, glared Josh into silence.

Suddenly, Josh hovered high above the others. His swords collapsed as he grasped at the chain around his neck. His face grew hot with trapped blood. He coughed once and then wished he hadn't as no air returned to him.

Amber's eyes immediately followed the chain into the rafters where a black Scottish terrier held the other end. She launched an orbit at the Scottie, but found herself down, on her side upon the cold concrete, her face warm and brain pounding from the impact.

The Left Arm pressed its foot against her head a moment, but then withdrew. Amber scrambled to her feet, and found Thomas and the rogue each with one of Thomas's blades at the other's throat. Thomas held his steel, the rogue the diamond blade. The rogue remained emotionless. Thomas returned the cold stare of one hiding his annoyance, in that one of his own weapons had suddenly been stripped from him. Amber rushed to Josh and tried lifting him, anything she could to give him breathing leverage.

Josh flapped his cloak helplessly over his head, but to no avail of cutting the chain around his neck. He stopped upon realizing the danger he recoiled down upon his wife.

"My wrath if he dies," Thomas said.

The rogue twisted Thomas's diamond tip. Thomas pressed his own blade back at him. He balanced the balls of his feet so that they might launch him in whichever direction the rogue might prompt.

Loraine moved to a workbench and opened a clear plastic tote.

She withdrew a silvery envelope and opened it. She said, "You know, I never knew that hanging took so long to kill people. I always thought it was like fast. But now that I see it, it's like eww."

Amber hit just the right leverage, and Josh drew in a quick breath, but not much. The Scottie pulled him higher into the air.

"Can an ancient be hung," Loraine asked.

"What are you talking about," Amber asked.

Loraine produced an antique, three-ring syringe as she walked towards one of the podiums, where she drove the needle between two of the creature's toes. A small amount of black appeared within the vial as her thumb pulled back on the plunger. She moved to the next podium and filled the syringe a little more with the second beast's black blood. She continued to visit each ancient and filled the glass a little more each time.

She approached around the backside of the rogue. Genre instantly poised himself for retaliation against whatever action Thomas might be considering. Loraine looked for a vein in the rogue's throat. "Excuse me," she said as she pierced near the point of Thomas's sword. Again she filled the syringe, this time with something redder.

The rogue remained emotionless still, but maintained his point upon the vampire's neck.

"Thomas de Soleil," she said, mocking the need for time-consuming small talk.

Josh grappled with the chain around his neck and made the sound of a duck.

"The boss is a huge fan of your work," Loraine said as she waved her syringe like an in-tune composer until the needle was only inches from Thomas's eye.

"Your turn," she cheerfully announced.

Thomas could have fought. It was a matter of simple execution, really: cut off Loraine's head; step back and right, sinking his sword into The Left Arm's chest. The rogue would most likely create distance.

Judging from The Right Arm's stance, Thomas could expect a clean rotation, allowing the creature to pass him, allowing Thomas to the back of his neck for a spinal attack—not the easiest of offensive maneuvers, but Thomas had done worse. That would leave the rogue and only one of his guards to deal with.

However, he allowed his mind to regroup. Even upon injecting this cocktail of blood into his system, blood was still only blood in his veins. Sure, it became contaminated with his disease, but blood was blood to him, despite its power within. Wolf blood didnt' affect him, just fermented in his veins. Let her inject him. That was a good plan. The rogue was clever, but he didn't know the vampire's biology.

Thus, Thomas developed his plan: fake the pain of turning into one of the rogue's minions. That conceited cur, he'd expect Thomas to cower to his sudden weakness. It would be enough for Thomas to get some greater foothold than he had now and to lower the rogue's expectations.

The rogue's plan became apparent. Hang Josh, poison Thomas and then perhaps devour Amber? Or turn her? Excellent play on the rogue's part, but again not at all perpetual to the physiology of a vampire.

Thomas allowed Loraine to stab him. Whatever advantage the rogue thought he was about to gain, Thomas knew better. He knew what his attack was now. When the rogue was caught up in believing

Thomas was dying from the poisonous injection of the ancients, the vampire would show him otherwise.

However, Thomas's plan fell apart the moment Loraine drew back on the plunger rather than press upon it. She withdrew the needle, her syringe now full, partly with Soleil's own blood. Before Loraine had stepped away, Thomas realized that the rogue's stance had shifted. How did Thomas miss it happening? It was now Thomas who had been played into position to be beheaded. More than that, how had Thomas been so foolish to disregard this most important detail? Just now, a memory appeared, nothing vivid, a shadow mostly, but he remembered it. It grew in his mind. Something from not-so long ago. Stronger now. He'd have cursed himself out loud if he didn't think the rogue would use the moment of weakness to his advantage. Now, he understood.

Could Thomas have changed his stance to protect Josh, he would have.

Check mate!

Finally, Loraine stepped in front of Josh. Amber, still insisting and struggling to help Josh find air, dropped a ring into the palm of her hand, but couldn't seem to swipe it effectively at Loraine without losing her hold.

"Wakey, wakey, paladin," Loraine said and suddenly stabbed the needle into Josh's leg, pumping every drop of blood straight into him.

Josh seized. Amber struggled to hold him once more.

"You're free to go now," Loraine said, turning away from Josh.

The rogue stepped down from his opponent and politely returned Thomas's blade to him, properly, pommel first. For a moment, the vampire thought of leaving the rogue with a wound in his palm, but Thomas was cautiously aware that the rogue may have previously prepared for such an impulsive act.

The rogue had made his play. Now it was time to see if Thomas could manage an equally clever parry.

Thomas sheathed his blades, nodded honor to the rogue and ran. The rogue was no longer priority.

Amber screamed her protests as Thomas struggled to break her grip, despite the greasy blood that now stained her arms thanks to the bottom edges of Josh's robe.

"He'll live," Thomas urged. "But we won't."

Josh's body fell from the rafters, forcing Amber to release her grip whether she wanted to or not. The paladin writhed on the floor and burst into screaming. His tearful shriek blasting like an elk warning of hunters. Here, Amber took her shot. The orbit screamed across the room, intent on the rogue's chest. The rogue snatched the ring in his hand, preventing the attack.

"Bet you can't do that again," Amber shrilled and yanked back on her weapon.

The rogue's fingers toppled into the air like broken glass. One instant, he seemed angry. Another, he smiled. Then he appeared to be bending over to pick up his lost digits. Amber lost sight of the rogue after that, as Thomas began forcing her towards the emergency exit through a nearby cinder-block wall. They quickly escaped into the now dark of night.

Thomas called for Petruchio, and hooves clattered in the distance. The cries from the back of the art museum grew more violent. The vampire now felt he was carrying Amber more than guiding her as they fled into the black parking lot. Despite her kicking and screaming, once she might have smacked him with the side of her orbit, he carried her towards the sounds of Petruchio's approaching clatter.

Only the few cars belonging to those who attended night classes lingered, so Petruchio was easy to spot.

He strode up before Thomas. Thomas thrust Amber onto the horse's back. A cry, inhuman, not wolf, carried from the museum. Thomas caught sight of a few students who couldn't help but to notice the sound.

"The secret's about to be out," Thomas said, drawing onto his horse.

"We're not leaving him," Amber screamed.

"I doubt that's his plan," Thomas retorted. "Ride, Petruchio."

Petruchio raced off, and Thomas yelled for anyone, who may have heard the monster, to hide. Before they were out of the parking lot, Josh, a newly cursed beast, was out of the museum.

Thomas chanced a look and chilled himself at the sight of Josh's new form: dark, lanky and spry. Wolf's Breath, still attached to him, flailed in the high wind as he quickly spotted Petruchio and gave chase. "I should have listened better," he said. "I should have written it down."

"What are you talking about," Amber asked.

Josh charged through a motorcycle, sending it into the air where it finally got itself wrapped up in power lines. Showers of sparks announced it was there to stay.

"Show him what you can do," Thomas ordered Petruchio, realizing Josh was gaining ground. He then instructed Amber to keep her eyes forward and prepare for a rough ride. "If we can lead him back to the compound, we can catch him. Maybe Natalie can get through to him."

"And if he catches us first," Amber asked after realizing a smidgen of hope in what Thomas just said.

"I don't know," Thomas said. "This is a new one for me."

Amber felt something shoved into her hand, the pages from the book that Thomas had stolen.

"These are safer with you now." Thomas said. "I can no longer worry about their safety and yours."

Amber tucked the wad of the old, folded pages from the museum into an inside pocket of her trench coat. As she zipped the pocket, a four-door sedan skidded on its side past Thomas, its occupants screaming.

Josh's next screech resounded at the heels of his own friends, causing Petruchio to wail and twist at the same time.

16 ~ Death by Chaos

"Cylinder's dead. Your favor's dead," the dark corner replied. "And he's a cop!"

Amber took to the air the first chance she got, despite it not being by her choice. When Petruchio suddenly jerked beneath her, Thomas spun and she involuntarily went flying. She caught her balance well enough and took Thomas's advice when he yelled at her to stay out of this fight. So she ran, she climbed into the right crosswind and used it to lengthen her steps above the ghastly city below her.

Thomas returned to the back of Petruchio for several strides, then dismounted once again. The two coordinated an attack, Petruchio launched a side kick into Josh's shoulder while Thomas swiped at the underside of Josh's opposing bicep. Thomas returned to his riding position, and Petruchio continued his race against the darkened paladin. The duo separated once more to dodge Josh's next attack, which was one that would have torn out Thomas's spine had the vampire not been so nimble.

Amber struggled too often with the decision to help, but any time she thought of taking a shot, Thomas kept reminding her to get to the compound alive and ready the others. Still, Amber felt inclined to hurl at least one attack. But how, without causing permanent injury to her husband?

Once again, carrying Thomas, Petruchio charged down residential streets. All at once, he scaled up a car, leapt to the roof of a single story house and continued to bound from one roof to the next.

Josh, smashed through one roof trying to keep up, then threw shards of another at his prey. Amber, herself, barely dodged a plywood wall of shingle and roofing nail, realizing Josh hadn't forgotten about her.

"Let it go," she heard Thomas's voice, shaky, out of breath, in her ear. "Get back and ready the others. I promise I'll only slow him down."

Amber watched, Petruchio launch himself to a higher roof. Thomas leapt through a bushy, spindly tree, bending it as far as his weight could take it, and then allowed it to whip back into Josh. As if planned, Thomas was back with Petruchio, pounding pavement once more.

Josh had lost a few paces, but, after a few city blocks regained, them.

Petruchio charged straight for another rambler and leapt for its roof, but decided it was more important to separate from Thomas once more to avoid another of Josh's attacks. It was a hesitating move that allowed Josh to grip the painted horse's rear leg and hurl the beast like a shot-put through the large picture window of another house.

Amber glimpsed the image of Thomas dodging into a small alley between two homes. He scaled a fence; grabbed an eave; and twisted himself onto a roof. Josh joined him, and Thomas's silvery, white hair fanned. Josh fumbled from the roof, cursing. Thomas leapt for another, and when he leapt from this roof to the ground, Petruchio had appeared below him once more favoring one of his legs and maintaining his escape on the other three.

"Amber," Thomas said, his voice barely connecting the syllables. "Make everyone listen. They won't, but you have to make them."

Amber didn't understand what he was saying and started her descent to help Thomas.

"Stop," Thomas said. "Do your part. Protect the others."

Petruchio disappeared from beneath Thomas and, while Thomas somehow found his own footing to keep running, Petruchio was skewered over a mailbox post, his race lost. The needle-nosed, and sharp-toothed Josh complained that his victory wasn't enough.

Thomas ordered Amber listen to him, and she watched Josh's dark, slender figure glide along the pavement, which had been made silver from the night. Thomas parried an attack, ended up behind Josh and sliced at him. Josh back-handed at Thomas. Thomas dodged, rolled on the ground, regained his footing and lunged.

Then Josh tucked and spun on his heels just like Amber had seen him do so many times before when he was surrounded by monsters, but this time he was the monster.

The folds of Wolf's Breath fanned out, its leather-braided hooks, like a hundred small blades, all unsheathed in one deadly motion. Thomas stopped, held his side and tried to deflect Josh's open palm blow that followed, but pencil-like claws shattered the albino's diamond sword.

"Save him," Thomas's voice whimpered. From above, Amber could no longer see them. She was too far ahead, too high and it was far too dark. Thomas had stopped responding.

Amber wiped her eyes, the cold clouded them with water. She drew a set of rounded goggles over her face to fight the tears, some forced by the wind in her face. Now wasn't the time to lose sight. Thomas was right. Natalie could save Josh, but Amber didn't know how exactly at the moment. She continued to flee, keeping sight on the growing light in the distance that was her home.

The monster-Josh screamed. It was ferocious, dry, high, deep and pristine all together. Then something struck Amber's shoulder, and she stumbled slightly, recovering well enough to see that what she had just been hit with was Thomas's torso.

A hissing alley cat flew past her next, barely missing her head, followed by a blue and grey fire hydrant. The sound of hissing water erupted from behind and below her. She climbed higher, first against the wind and then into a side current until she found another, leading somewhat in her desired direction. She couldn't run and watch Josh, nor anticipate his attacks, as he continued to hurl objects at her, so she changed her strategy. First she climbed, then fell, then caught a current that would pull her in an entirely different direction. Josh couldn't possibly predict her movement because she didn't know what it was herself. Somehow her blind-fighting style seemed to work.

Yet, being Josh's target practice wasn't her biggest danger anymore. She drew in as long of breaths as she could take as the air grew cold, sometimes painful. What she took as sounds of breaking wood, she realized were her ears popping under the wind.

"Who is that," a voice crackled over her earpiece.

Amber had hardly realized how close she had drawn to the compound, and still Josh was beneath her. He lobbed massive stones, large chunks of earth and pavement, even power poles that bungeed back on their dead power lines. Although a pipe scraped the side of her thigh, nothing else connected.

"Bricktain," Amber cried, but remembered it was time to change currents almost too late.

"Where are you," Bricktain asked.

"I'm coming in fast," she explained. This time, she forced tears back. She could barely say it. "Josh is turned. He's killed Thomas, and he's after me."

"What? How? What is he?"

"I can't be certain," She said, then spun through the air as something blunt struck her hip. She fell fast and struggled longer than she should have to find her footing. When she finally found it, she fell and barely dodged Josh's paw in her recovery. She climbed again, over the heads of the huddled guardians entrenching the compound. This time she did cry. "I can't make it," she said.

"Yes you can," Bricktain shouted. "You get here!"

The exterior compound lights blazed, and Amber complained about getting them out of her face.

"There's no way that's Josh," Bricktain's voice trembled.

"Ready a net," Amber said. "We have to let him in and catch him away from the guardians."

"We can't," Bricktain replied.

"We have to," Amber snapped back.

"We can't hold him," Bricktain explained. "I'm sorry, he's gone. I can see that from here."

"Natalie can get to him," Amber explained. "If you fight me on this, Brick, I will end you."

The gates opened, and Amber felt that wave of relief, which comes with being home, seep into her heels and flood towards her head. She allowed herself to fall onto the roof of her house.

Gunfire erupted.

"I said catch him, don't kill him," Bricktain cried.

Amber tried to stand, but found her strength less than what it had been a moment ago.

The hollow sound of a net cannon swished its echo over the top of the compound.

"Take the other end," Thug's voice trailed upwards as Amber pulled herself to the ledge of the roof. Here, she watched a netted Josh send a young hunter to the earth with a wound down his back that clearly branded him as Death's. Four more bodies took on similar brands, one of them, or maybe it was two, fell into pieces strewed across the courtyard.

Four hunters, including Bricktain, fell back on a rope. Six hunters, including Thug, held the other end, forcing Josh to the ground by his shoulders. Ty rushed to Josh's head and fixed a rope around his neck before stretching it to the bumper of a Hummer. Thug moved to his feet and began lashing the tie-down while Ty held it.

Josh screamed from beneath his Gulliver strapping.

Amber finally recuperated the strength she needed to launch herself back into the fight, but her knee refused to cooperate. She forced, it wouldn't bend. It spasmed instead.

A man's voice cried. Amber scanned the compound a moment before she realized it was Dee's. Before she could interpret what he was trying to say, the soldiers drew weapons upon the hunters and the compound.

"Kill the mercs," Reggie shrieked, suddenly realizing Dee's betrayal. His wheelchair sped towards one of the mercenaries on the ground. He swung his golden pommel, its long glowing blade suddenly appeared from the hilt and swept deep into the soldier's torso before disappearing as the blade stopped its motion. The merc fell.

The next gunshot burst down its long barrel, fueled by fire, not glycerin. Before Reggie could speed towards another mercenary, the bullet spun down into the compound and twisted itself into the old man's chest. Reggie's sword rolled out of his fingers, and his chair slowed and turned to a stop. The old man sat still and empty, a red dot grew from the middle of ribcage.

The firefight was immediate. Hunters, trained to fight monsters, suddenly found themselves dodging the attacks of humans and their fast bullets. Some fell from the walls, and many on the ground barely had time to take up their weapons. The rodeo queens seemed to respond first and fastest, dodging aim, attacking soldiers in range and using dead bodies as shields until opportunity allowed them another killing blow.

The blonde's lasso wrapped around one merc, and he clenched as the sudden jolt of electricity burned his internal organs. He toppled from the wall, and Dee ordered his men to shoot her. Her brunette partner fired off several rounds to give her cover.

"Help the rodeo prats," Amber cried, and instantly became an open target to Dee and his soldiers as well.

They had accomplished walking right into the graces of her husband and now surrounded the entire community from its very own walkways.

Amber knew where to attack. She tried again, stood, but fell under her wobbly knee. She couldn't trust to stay atop the wind, her enchanted shoes were worthless in this moment.

Moccasins or not, she still knew this game. She leapt from the roof to the crane cable that still dangled Sam. Now, she found a set of chains also held his feet to the ground so he couldn't try any fancy dexterity to knock his noose loose. She slid down the cable, listening to ammunition pop and whiz around her.

"Don't even think of joining this fight," she warned Sam as she climbed past him and set her own feet on the earth.

"Shouldn't you be in the air, please," Bricktain's voice shrilled as he continued to help several other hunters hold Josh down in ropes, all while somehow firing off a shot or two when the monster permitted. Two hunters had fallen on Bricktain's line, and he felt the weight of Josh's strength gaining ground against the fewer number of people holding him in place and trying to shoot back at mercs.

"It's my knee," Amber replied and raced, despite her injury, over the front of the stable compound floor. As she took up her orbits, she felt herself for any wet spots that might be bullet wounds. Then she saw her father.

She heard herself screaming; rushing to her father's lifeless body and suddenly cowering behind his chair as more gunfire rained down upon her.

"All right," Dee ordered. "Now, open the gates! Do it now!"

"I think not," The doorman cried from his new post in front of Amber's home. He fired off his shotgun in Dee's direction.

"Do it," Dee demanded.

The gates began to open. Guardian faces appeared through the opening immediately.

The bandana biker in the doorman's usual post now defended the controls to the gate, trying to reseal them.

Just then she felt it. Amber knew exactly what she needed to do.

"Bricktain," Amber called. "Get off Josh, and do you what you do best."

Bricktain immediately apologized to his fellow hunters and gestured for another to take his place at his line that held Josh. The rodeo queens responded first. Bricktain ran off, making the motion of pulling a set of glasses over his face. One soldier shot towards the hunters holding down Josh, but the brunette queen fired off her own blast, ending the mercenary's life.

"Someone get those gates closed," Bricktain's voice came across clearly in Amber's ear.

The Guardians ran into the compound, and as many hunters as could met them with fight. For a moment, Amber expected to hear Josh's voice dictate how to start organizing the buffoons, but she couldn't think of that now.

"I'm on it," Amber reported and ran out from the cover of her father and his chair. "Get the skaters in the pipe."

She hadn't noticed Dee's attention on her as she ran towards the front wall. He fired a shot, and it shredded through her ear, which she would have noticed if she easily gave in to such little facial pain nowadays. She palmed an orbit and readied her own attack. Dee took a second aim at her, and missed. Amber suddenly leapt to the banister of the stairs up, towards the catwalk and quickly scaled her way to her target, her knee driving scream the entire way.

Meanwhile, the Silver Bullet came to life, rattling off shot after shot at every monster that made its way into the compound and eventually turned upon those who even tried to enter.

Bricktain's bellowing eruptions caught Dee off guard. Before he could regain his senses, Amber threw her orbit. It shot straight past the mercenary leader's head, barely missing the wolf-bandana biker's as well. It sliced through the hydraulic hose feeding the piston and snapped through the razor wire behind it. Some of the wire snapped apart, leaving a small opening that Amber hoped no monster would notice.

One half of the steel door suddenly slammed shut. Hot fluid shot into the air and splattered Dee's back.

He groaned and, at the recoil of Amber's weapon, Dee's neck ruptured its artery. She launched another orbit to finish him, but he made quick use of the new opening in the razor wire. He rushed the biker, wounded himself in the process and leapt through the new opening to the outside of the compound where he disappeared among the onslaught of monsters.

Amber then watched as the doorman appeared at the other side of the gate and blasted its hose with his shotgun.

"You're supposed to be watching Natalie," she scowled.

"Figured all the ones who want to kill her are already making their move," the doorman replied. "Might as well watch her from out here."

"We could use Natalie," Bricktain said.

"Not until we secure the compound," Amber replied, reaching for the fireman pole that could carry her back to the compound floor once more. "We can't risk her. She's our only chance to—"

Just then a bullet tore through Amber's thigh. She gripped the pole and fell down it rather than rode it.

"She's shot," the biker yelled.

"I'm fine," Amber replied scornfully.

Above her, she watched the massive figure of the doorman rush the catwalk towards a mercenary. He hefted his shotgun, aimed from the waist and blew out the merc's foreleg. As the merc fell uncontrollably, to his credit, silently, the doorman grabbed his curved sword and hurled it down the catwalk where it sank into the chest of another merc.

"The wife is down," the doorman announced.

"Guardians on the catwalk," The bandana-biker yelled.

They'd found the opening in the razor wire, probably thanks to Dee.

"Heads up on the catwalk," Bricktain announced and turned his aim on the second level walkways.

The Silver Bullet erupted, and the mercenaries began to fall alongside the Guardians that had made the mistake of breaching the gates or the walls.

A mercenary bullet hit one of Josh's captors. The surprise of the attack weakened this strain of hold on Josh, and his other jailers suddenly crumbled beneath Josh's strength.

Josh now stood.

He wasted no time. He gripped the first hunter he could and wrapped him inside the net that had been used to capture him. The hunter, strangled, was left lifeless. Thug's own body presently scrambled out of the way of his godson.

"Better get in here, Thug," Bricktain cried. "I could use a driver."

Thug climbed to his feet and ran for the silver trailer. Several hunters opened fire on the black creature that was Josh, no one hitting him. Josh kicked at Thug's back, throwing him to the ground.

Thug rolled. Josh stomped for him, but the chef somehow drew a bronze cleaver and hurled it with such speed that it sank into Josh's left shoulder.

Several hunters who had formerly held Josh's reins ran to Thug's aid, but never made it, as the new monster quickly destroyed the would-be-saviors.

"Shoot him, Sheriff," one dying hunter pleaded.

The Silver Bullet fired, missing Josh.

"Don't shoot him," Amber ordered.

"Think I want to," Bricktain asked.

Thug was back to his feet and fleeing Josh, but was soon face-down in the dirt again.

More voices pleaded for Bricktain to fire.

Thug, on his back, wielded a second cleaver and a knife and fought to fend off much of the physical, maniacal insult that Josh thrust down upon him.

Josh's almost metallic teeth bit into the cleaver, sheared through. The monster spit the chunk back into Thug's face.

Amber knew. She understood the lesson now, and she hated Speatsh for it more than ever before. Somehow, she brought herself up, knowing what had to be done. Josh had done too much already, and his opponents were no match. Thug couldn't be next. After Thug, it would be someone else, maybe even her. She knew it. She hated it. But she had to do it. For once, she believed she felt the pressure Josh had faced too often.

She launched her orbits just as Josh bit down for Thug. Both discs wrapped around his neck. Even the paladin seemed surprised at the stealthy attack, no whistle this time. He screamed at Amber, but continued pressing for Thug. Amber pulled tighter at the reigns until Josh could no longer make sound, until Josh was choking.

Meanwhile, Thug swiped an empty attack with his small steak knife, and Josh smacked the futile weapon away. Thug tried backing away.

Josh pressed forward still, pulling Amber behind him as a plow drags a farmer. Josh snapped his arm forward, and Wolf's Breath sliced Thug's bicep open. Thug's face screwed into something tearful that denied the satisfaction of a scream, and he now did his best to flee what could be a final blow.

Josh drew his wrist slightly. Amber knew this move. It inevitably ended with a lost limb or decapitation. He was going to cut through the lines of her own weapon, and, after Thug, she'd most certainly be Josh's next victim. She couldn't allow it.

"I'm shooting," Bricktain insisted.

"Don't," Amber demanded.

"He's gone," Bricktain cried. "We lost him."

"Get Natalie," Amber ordered.

"It's over," Bricktain screamed at her. "How many lives lose for his, Amber?!"

Josh made his move. Thug rolled, barely saving his life. Josh anticipated and drew to repeat the maneuver.

Amber snapped back on her cable whips in the manner that would normally have called the orbits back to her, only this time she pulled straight back. Instead, she felt them do just what they had been created to do, destroy. The orbits tightened around Josh's neck; loosened for only a moment; and, at Amber's command, quickly came straight back to her.

For a split second she wanted them to strike her down, end all the torment she now felt and would feel, but she had to stay alive long enough to know she had protected the compound. She caught up her weapons before they could harm her, and she watched Josh's body fall straight on top of Thug.

Josh's monstrous head landed several feet away.

The job was done.

The danger was gone.

Now, she screamed and clenched the knots of her whips so hard in her fists that she nearly broke bone. All the energy she had left, now surged through her veins and vocal cords. It pulled at every ligament and tendon, dropping her as though she were a discarded clump of useless limbs. Her cry cursed its vocal damnation over all it fell upon. This fallen compound was indeed hell, and Amber couldn't stop screaming her recognition of the curse.

She threw both orbits again, this time with only one intent. They flew, reached their full extension and suddenly snapped back towards her, not to be caught, but to bury themselves into her own chest.

The whips tore away from her hands wrapped in a bundle of brown fur and snarling teeth.

Bear scampered away with Amber's deadly tools before they could accomplish their task. The living animal pelt ran towards the back of the Silver Bullet where Bricktain stood, clear with his emotion that he wasn't losing any more friends this day. Bricktain snatched the cables out of his new partner's grasp and began to coil them.

Here, only now, did Amber realize the fighting had ceased.

"And I had such high hopes for the paladin," The elemental queen's voice called out above everyone's heads. A large vortex had come to surround the entire compound. The elemental queen's twisted form swayed like a flag on a pole within the cloud that held her. "I thought he might actually survive."

Long dust devils shot up from within the civilian sector of the compound. They honed in on individual groups of people and sucked them high into the air, where the vortex swallowed them and their screams. Many civilians fled, but the twisters chased with greater speed, stealing up any human that got in its path.

"You force my hand," the elemental general's voice carried softly within the thick wind. "That which you stole from the master will buy his forgiveness towards me."

"Get those people out of there," Amber found herself automatically resuming orders, but was suddenly dodging falling tires and metal debris that had been caught up in the invisible fists of the wind.

That's right!

Wind! Let's see her friends stop her where they can't reach her.

Amber leapt into the air, fought her knee, stumbled, fought it, let the tears of physical pain drown out those of sorrow. She drew herself near the elemental queen and made the motion of throwing her weapon, only to realize it was nothing more than muscle response.

The queen turned quickly in Amber's direction. She appeared amused. "Do you still not understand," the queen asked. "We must survive too."

Amber almost lunged for the elemental general but she knew her strength and skills were no match for this master of wind. Even if she were, she only now realized just how many guardians filled the sky and watched from above the walls of the vortex. She glared at them all from their high reach, watching, controlling the winds to steal the humans back that had once filled the rogue's farms. Only now, did Amber understand just how outnumbered the hunters were.

She understood why Josh was dead.

Amber could simply let herself drop now from her high stance above the earth and join him, anything to avoid his same monstrous fate.

However, she also considered that she had one more move to make first. This elemental general would most likely take her out, but Amber's hatred suggested the beast should have to work for it.

The windriders caught the right angle of wind, and Amber twisted around the elemental general. Amber called upon what she knew about this general: polite, honorable, maybe that was her weakness. She let the wind spiral her around the twisted woman. The queen blew into the wind, sniffed and kept herself facing Amber the entire time.

Amber drew closer with each cycle around the twisted woman, she had to draw attention from it. "He didn't have to die."

"You should have saved him," the lady shot back, anger showing for the first time. She floated in place, her joints bending disproportionately to maintain the whim.

Wrong approach, Amber thought. *She has to have another weak spot.* She circled, drawing closer still. *Look, Amber,* she told herself. Speatsh would have seen her bane. Josh would have found it. Cadence would have nailed it from two hundred feet away. It had to be here somewhere. She searched. She watched. A twist in the shoulder? A rotation of her knee? Where was the weak spot of a rubber general.

I'm sure she'll just bend around me, Amber thought to herself. Amber reflected desperately on this fact that the elemental queen would surely have centuries of experience in maneuvering this environment. She imagined the queen simply twisting out of the way of any attack, and, if she was anything like the other generals, she's be eager enough to clout her excellence over the simple human.

"Ah, screw it," she mumbled.

Amber bit her toes into the wind and rushed the elemental. She grasped for the throat. The lady twisted around Amber's back and suddenly appeared in front of her again, her hands now strangling at the mortal's neck, which is exactly where Amber hoped for her to place herself.

Amber quickly drove the wood-puzzle blade straight into the elemental's chest, calling upon the energy of despair that still charged through her veins. She twisted the handle, and her enemy's chest echoed with the sound of sharp edges flaring from its smooth blade, allowing the flowered knife to completely destroy the woman's heart.

"Your master will die," Amber replied and used all her adrenaline and strength to tear the expanded knife out of the elemental's chest. Now, Amber could let the elemental fall to her death.

Only, she didn't fall. She caught herself, appeared surprised, and laughed up blood.

"It's over," the elemental queen said. "But I'll give you a headstart."

At this, Amber fell backwards. She let her despair control her. It had owned her far too long anyway. It was time to meet her true master. The fight was lost. She rushed to the ground. She didn't just fall, she was pushed. She could feel the pressure of the wind upon her chest as clearly as if they had been hands upon her, ready to smash her into the dirt below.

"That's how you make someone fall," the elemental winds cheered after her.

Amber was glad. She'd tried and failed. Someone else could do what she had been denied. She'd gotten her fight, and now she could finally rest. She waited for her impact with the earth to end this silly debate with these wolves.

Gold glinted to her right, then her left and then completely encased her.

"Lose cripple," Aggon roared. "Not lose cripple's daughter too."

Amber screamed, kicked the side of the chariot and screamed some more.

"Watch for da bump," Aggon warned.

Suddenly, Amber was looking up at small fluorescent bulbs. She climbed to her feet and began to move again.

"Where are you going," Bricktain asked from beneath his glasses and staring at the wall of television screens. His toy guns were poised at them.

Amber limped quickly for the back of the silver bullet trailer. She knew what was happening and wouldn't be part of it.

"We're not leaving," Amber ordered, but Thug was at the back and restraining her.

"We can't stay here anymore," Thug replied.

"We can't leave him like this," She cried, unable to tear her eyes from the body of her husband.

"We will mourn the fallen before you die," the elemental general's voice announced from the heavens. "It's honorable. We will leave you to bury your dead, then see if you can escape."

Suddenly, it was on her just like it was every night lately. She tried to run, and when her friend continued to restrain her, she threw up on his and her own feet. Then she remembered what she had to live for, but she wasn't quite sure if she cared about that now.

* * *

"We should get to Oliver's," Bricktain said. He stood over Amber as she sat on her feet next to her husband. Really, Bricktain was babysitting her. He took every weapon from her. Her orbits hung at his side. "They're toying with us."

Amber hadn't spoken since she'd thrown up. Thug had spent the time wrapping Josh's body in sheets from the house and was now beginning to drape Reggie as well.

By the time Amber had returned to her fallen family, Natalie had joined. The guardian searched the area, investigated the bodies, sniffed them and suddenly screamed at Amber. Amber said nothing. Natalie backhanded Amber. Amber lunged at Natalie, hugging into her quills and punching the guardian.

Natalie drew the first blood, quilling Amber and tearing her shoulder open. Amber retaliated by spitting in the wolf's face.

"Do it," she screamed at Natalie. "You worthless bi—,"

Amber fell to the ground, with Bricktain on top of her. He held his rifle-arm in Natalie's face.

"Look at him," Bricktain demanded and forced Amber's face towards his friend's corpse. "What's he saying now? Look at him!"

Amber did look. She tried not to. The blood seeped through the sheets more heavily with Josh's corpse than her father's had done. Bricktain's voice yelled in her ear once more, but this time it was warning Natalie to stay back or he would shoot her.

Natalie screeched.

"I didn't see you out there having to make the tough decisions," Bricktain yelled back. "He's dead. You can stop being a jealous skank now."

Amber wriggled her way out from beneath Bricktain, who somehow ended up on his face and cursing. She pulled her way to Josh's corpse and drew him into her lap. Here she hugged him as tightly as she could, letting his red stain carry into her clothes. She wailed at Natalie to stay away and continued to clench her husband.

Eventually, Bricktain and the doorman helped Amber to her feet, which was a greater chore than it should have been. Amber had barely noticed the feeling in her legs Josh's weight had left her.

"I've been thinking," Thug said, finally daring to intrude. "Maybe it's time to leave."

Amber's eyes, narrowed and she'd just now realized that her gauze and bandana had fallen off as Thug handed her fresh covering, tape and a small jar of petroleum jelly. It was time to redress her face.

"We don't like it neither," the doorman said. "But maybe retreat's not the wrong idea here."

"Give us time to regroup," Thug said. "And mourn."

Amber had no answer.

"If I may, folks," Kenny's voice announced to those with earpieces. "I think we should stay. Here, we have security."

"Can I just point out that computer nerds always get eaten," Thug said. "You call this security?"

"OK, let's regroup," Bricktain said, realizing Amber wasn't going to answer. "But we're not retreating. We've all earned better than that."

Bricktain surveyed the compound once more. All of them were gone. All the energy they spent to save those people from the hospital; the children from the school; even the mayor was wasted. All that effort to guard them, and they simply floated right up into the sky, maybe even returned to their farms. How could they fight against that.

"I'm so tired," Bricktain said.

"We could all use some sleep," Thug admitted.

"I mean old," Bricktain said. "I feel like I've always been doing this."

Maybe a dozen hunters remained. Three manned the walls. The rodeo queens seemed to be reading Bricktain's mind. It made sense. He believed he knew what they were thinking. They'd failed. They'd all failed.

Thug was right. It was time to regroup.

"Ammo up," Bricktain said. "Let's take what we can from the new shipment and get out of here before the elementals decide our time is up."

Amber chugged in shallow breaths between throaty tears.

"You don't cry until this is done," Bricktain scowled. "Somebody get her on the Bullet and make her sleep."

"You don't tell me what to do," Amber said. She wiped her nose on the leather sleeve of her trench coat. She broke away from the grip of the hands trying to support her, which now only consisted of the doorman. She knelt once more to her husband's corpse. The fangs, Wolf's Breath and the swords laid on the ground near his feet.

She quickly sliced an opening in the bandaging near his waist and reached inside. They were torn where his claws had broken through, but they were still there. She withdrew the gloves from Josh's fingers and ignored how cold his hands had become. She held them one last time, until she was able to push the tears back.

Finish this, she could hear him say. She stood, holding all of Josh's gear. She tucked what she could into her trench coat and then pulled Wolf's Breath around her shoulders, careful to hold it by the inside collar as she had seen her husband do.

"Fine," Bricktain grumbled. "Destroy yourself. You clearly want to."

"I'm taking it to the Bullet," Amber rebuked. "It's easier this way."

"Everyone stay away from the wife, she's a death trap," Bricktain announced via earpieces.

"Hasn't she always been," the doorman's voice asked back.

"All right," Amber said. "We bury him and then what's the plan?" She was looking to Bricktain now for his input.

Bricktain looked up. The sky was clear, and dawn would once more awaken in a couple of hours.

The moon waxed, almost full. Only a small sliver of dark appeared on its left, hardly noticeable unless you were looking for it. Bricktain for some reason felt hesitant to speak out loud about any plans. He wasn't sure what the elementals could hear, but he couldn't underestimate their power right now. All Bricktain believed was that the elementals were busy escorting their humans back to their farms, and that he didn't want to be in this deathtrap when the moon brought out the real monsters.

"They weren't farms," Bricktain said to himself. "Just more bodies." For some reason he kept looking to the sky.

"Brick," Amber asked. "What?"

"Huh," Bricktain replied. "Oh, I feel like I'm forgetting something."

Yeah, your brain, he half expected to hear Speatsh suggest.

"We need to limit their options," Bricktain said. "We need to get underground."

"The bunker," Amber asked. "You want to hide again."

"The tunnels, maybe the cemetery," Bricktain replied. "They're underground, no wind."

"They'll dig us out," Thug said.

"Yeah, but maybe we can plan in private at least," Bricktain explained.

Bricktain fell into thought once more.

"May I make a suggestion," the blonde rodeo queen asked, suddenly appearing in the group.

Bricktain, like the others, seemed surprised at the interruption. He ignored her. "I say we load up Josh in Aggon's wagon and take

Josh to the cemetery. Maybe there's something more respectful we can do than leave him here."

"Respect is letting him pass," Amber replied

"No one let me pass," Bricktain shouted. He brandished his metal hand to emphasize his own involuntary resuscitation.

"No freaking way," the blonde lauded.

"You got a problem," Bricktain asked.

"I can't believe I didn't realize this before," the blonde replied, and before Bricktain could demand someone to get her out of his face, she walked off calling after her mute partner. "You're never going to believe this one."

"I don't care what vehicle those women ride in, but keep them away from me," Bricktain yelled. Then he made it official. "Everyone off the walls, we're moving out."

"Guess who's back," the doorman said, his gaze not only towards the sky, but to the elemental woman now circling overhead in the walls of a funnel that hadn't quite touched down.

"Clearly, the time for mourning is over," the elemental general's voice whispered to the ground.

As before, the air fell silent.

"Oh come on," Amber complained. "We haven't even dug a grave yet."

"Get Josh on board," Bricktain ordered as he started running for the trailer and firing off a few blind shots upwards, hopefully towards the elemental terrorist. He armed his eyes. Thug was already several paces ahead of him.

The Bullet suddenly lifted into the air, twisting like an angry cobra before finally lifting off into the sky.

Bricktain shot at the treacherous diesel, as it spun above their heads. "That's it," he cried. "I quit!"

Gun shots burst from around the compound, and several voices started yelling, but then fell quiet. The man with a three-barrel shotgun blasted off his full force. A moment later, a guardian flew past him and pulled him into the sky. Another hunter flew off the wall to Bricktain's left, the shadow of another guardian running off into the dark with her.

"You who talk about dishonor," Bricktain cried.

"Open the gates," a familiar voice suddenly cried through the earpieces.

"We're a little busy right now," a male's voice screamed back.

"Cadence," Amber gasped.

"Amber, I'm shooting whoever that was when I—."

"Get out of here," Amber demanded. She watched a guardian strike for the doorman. She reached for her orbits, but found none.

"It's not safe out here," Cadence replied.

Amber felt the ground disappear from beneath her feet, torn away in the vile grasp of another guardian hidden in the wind. Bricktain released a barrage of bullets into the monster trying to carry her away. However, the beast didn't drop her until Amber ejected three cylinders from Josh's crossbow and into her attacker's shoulder.

Amber dropped and nodded her thanks to her companion.

The Bullet suddenly flew back to the ground and towards the front gate, breaking through the wall and exposing the compound to the frenzy of monsters that had waited patiently without all this time. A SWAT truck, which the bullet had just sheared off its roof, flipped forward and into the compound.

Acotactac's body fell from the truck, and Bricktain instantly responded. He fired off several rounds towards the opening in the wall before any invaders could press through. Two hunters flew into the air, and another was suddenly mauled. One guardian leapt for Bricktain, but a steel lasso wrapped around its snout, and its entire head jerked before a blast from the brunette rodeo queen's gun put an end to its attack.

"Into the ground," Thug cried as Bricktain took a breath of relief at the sight of Acotactac brushing off any injures she might have obtained and quickly joined in the fight. Bricktain's sword appeared, and he cut Cadence's unconscious body out of her seatbelt.

He nearly jumped out of his skin when the small boy's hand reached out from behind Cadence's chair. He handed off Cadence to the rodeo queens.

The sound of Aggon's whip, cries and chariot dust told Bricktain the ghost and his team had his back.

Bricktain soon located the boy's mother, who stumbled to her knees, lost in her own head injuries. He handed her to the doorman before she could see the body of the teenager who had clearly not survived the accident and laid halfway through the backdoors of the truck.

Bricktain bit back his anger.

"We're done here," Bricktain said. "Everyone into the tunnel."

Thug dropped into the ground. Amber now stood inside the pit, where the wind couldn't throw Wolf's Breath around and she could move slowly enough to not throw it dangerously.

"What about Sam," Bricktain asked.

"Leave him," Amber replied.

"Let's go," Bricktain cried to the remaining hunters. "Where's Kenny," he asked, looking to the top floor of the house.

"He's out already," Thug cried back.

The rodeo queens lowered Cadence's limp body, the last of the injured, into the pit and then followed down to the tunnel themselves. The biker with the head bandana followed. Acotactac surveyed the area with Bricktain one last time to ensure no one was left behind.

"We have to hurry," the biker said. "We'll need to close the tunnel behind us or they'll suck us out like a vacuum."

Bricktain realized someone was missing. He knew who it was too—Natalie. He soon caught glimpse of her dragging Josh's wrapped corpse out of the compound and into the tunnel herself. An elemental attempted to attack from various angles, but, Natalie gave back as well as she received.

Acotactac slapped Bricktain and then hugged him before leaping into the opening herself. Bricktain was the last in the compound, he noticed the mob of guardians maintain its place outside the wall.

"You were never going to come in, were you," Bricktain cried and then leaped for the pit, but never touched the ground. He flew straight up into the air.

"No be takin," Aggon's voice blasted through the wind. He cracked his ghostly whip, and it wrapped around Bricktain's leg. "No be takin." His horses and chariot held strongly upon the ground and against the wind.

One brave guardian emerged from the spinning dust and smacked Bricktain, followed by a second and third monster, each delivering a potentially deadly blow and then cowering back into hiding. Bricktain's sword-arm flailed to hit anything and nothing.

"You to be shooting," Aggon cried. "Not swording."

Bricktain's gun materialized, and he fired off a shot, but retaliation came in the form of several guardians smashing into his side—their quills sticking deeply into his one fleshy arm, blood quickly draining from their piercings.

These monsters too disappeared back into the wind, and Bricktain prepared to fire again.

The next guardian emerged, attacked Bricktain and suddenly dived back into the cyclone. Acotactac appeared next to Aggon who continued to concentrate all energy on allowing his ethereal whip to hold Bricktain.

"Don't make me waste it," Aggon cried from the back of his chariot. "Might need later."

Acotactac launched herself into the air where she fired off her poles into another monster. She fell back to the earth, her telescopic weapons carefully catching her fall. Then she launched herself once more up to her husband's side in the atmosphere. This time, she twisted her body, unleashing a cone of steel-pipe attack, and fending off more of Bricktain's attackers. Again, she fell to the ground, and launched herself back up a third time for another fight. Try as they might, her Taichomée training and agility met them fiercely.

"We need more help," Thug's voice cried.

The doorman climbed the side of Aggon's chariot and leapt to Bricktain to help weigh him down.

Then, in the midst of the rescue attack, the Silver Bullet emerged once more, this time from the walls of the cyclone and smashed a wall of its trailer full-on into Bricktain's helpless body.

17 ~ Bricktain's Aim

"Please," Harvey replied. "I came here in good faith. I'll leave."

"Don't forget your dog," one gang member, shorter than those around him, said. He kicked the Schnautzer at the detective.

Bricktain awoke. The strips of eight-feet lights overhead were like shards of glass beneath his eyelids. His head hurt.

He heard the sounds. They echoed among the sculptures. When he finally realized they were the noises of unpleasantness, he forced himself to sit. He knew this room, but not how he got here. Last he remembered, he was being struck by the silver bullet. Somehow, he'd made it to Oliver's stone-carving studio.

Kenny bled out onto the floor next to Bricktain. Bricktain felt; there was no pulse. The skater-leader with one ear sat next to him against a slab of untouched, red stone—dead, as if his last action had been to save and look over Kenny.

"Well, I'm not done," Bricktain growled.

When he heard gunshots, despite his pounding concussion, he forced himself to kneel. When he recognized the voices that he heard screaming, from beyond this room, were those of his allies, he stood. Pain pulled heavily at his chest, neck and shoulder where his steel armament melded into his bones and flesh. He reached for his bottle of—well, he didn't quite know what pills were in this bottle. It had said "pain relief" so he took it.

However, his bottle was gone. He ran to the door, cursing.

His arm transformed into its gun, excruciating heat burned into his lungs and brain. He had no choice but to let it, and he pressed open the door that led out of Oliver's workroom.

His first glimpse of the graveyard was a bleeding Jasper who squared off against a mob of wolves and other dogs. What caught Bricktain's attention most was what appeared to be a swarm of giant bees, which flew from one attacking monster to another. Their coordinating attacks allowed Jasper the time he needed to maneuver against his own targets.

Where did these come from?

Feeling there was no need to intrude in Jasper's fight, Bricktain left the jerk to die on his own terms. Currently, the old man was helping. At this point, Jasper was kicking a giant barrel into one guardian's face while burying his blade into a decent-sized scout. Bricktain doubted his own skill could add to that precision anyway. There were other mobs and other hunters who were likely worse off than Jasper.

He made his way into the dark cemetery, searching for which fight deserved his attention the most.

Cadence's sniper-like music staccatoed in the distance. Good! She was alive. Where Cadence fought, Acotactac would surely be near. He stumbled towards its orchestra and immediately stopped. Dogs, guardians and scouts alike, suddenly withdrew some distance.

"No," Jasper yelled as a few of the newer hunters tried to give chase.

"Stay together," Cadence's voice added.

The beasts began to fall to the earth, in few numbers at first, then in droves until every one of them was gyrating in agony, turning from its monstrous wolf and dog form into that of human. They were at the mercy of the fullness of the moon as it released them from their servitude while simultaneaously re-enslaving their masters. Easy targets! Bricktain wondered how many he could take out while they were down. Only, it seemed unfair and immoral now. This wasn't their choice, after all. He couldn't dwell on this. This entire activity meant generals would be coming soon, also because of the moon.

In fact, they spilled onto the field, charging for Bricktain's allies. Some hunters began attacking those slaves that had earned Freedom for the night. Death, it seemed, now too. Cowardly, Bricktain thought.

Yet, the sounds of one battle farther out caught Bricktain's interest. He saw Oliver. The giant spun two large stones over his head before striking The Left Arm and then yelling at his counterpart. Genre coordinated an attack that Oliver seemed intent on avoiding.

Then Bricktain saw her. He almost didn't. She was crumpled behind a knee-high tombstone. She was alone. He'd only seen her from the photo that Josh's father had given him the night this whole nightmare began. She looked just as he remembered, except for her now missing hair. She huddled in the alcove of a hedged, family plot: bald, naked. He ran to the child. As he reached for Bear, the animal pelt's scruff stretched into Bricktain's fingers, anticipating a call to action. Bear stretched himself around the young girl's bare shoulders.

"You're changed," Bricktain observed.

Cracey nodded. "He said I had to. He said to hide."

Bricktain's eyes shot to the moon. It was full in a light blue sky. He'd been unconscious longer than he realized.

The cemetery erupted with screams that turned more human with each.

"To me," Jasper cried.

The blur of a familiar, unfriendly face ran past Bricktain. "Are you still alive, Brick Face?"

Bricktain stumbled over finding the words to respond to the voice of Speatsh Cheatham's ghost. He was certain he was only imagining seeing the old grump.

"Are you crazy," Speatsh yelled. "You're barely old enough to be here, what makes you think she should? Get her out of here."

Bricktain, stole a glimpse of the graveyard, scanning for wherever a person could hide. Back to Oliver's hall of stone? No. Jasper stood before the doors, and the others fled towards him. Too much danger there, too many eyes upon it. He watched Acotactac catapult herself over a bunch of generals now hunkered in the dark. They gave her chase, but she somehow outmaneuvered them enough that Bricktain felt confident she'd find support among their friends. As much as losing her frightened him, he understood by now that his being near her in a fight only got in her way. Strangely, he couldn't imagine a fight where she wouldn't come out the victor.

Then Bricktain saw the stranger. He might not have noticed him except he was one of only two people who didn't seem to be making any movement in the battle whatsoever. He wasn't writhing in agony at that moment. He wasn't changing, wasn't screaming, and seemed uninterested in joining the fight. Genre left his confrontation with Oliver and returned to the stranger's side. Oliver rallied to Jasper's cries.

Bricktain tried shouting an order before realizing he was without an earpiece.

The stranger pointed, and Genre charged towards a gigantic shadow. Together, Genre pulled the item, an old carriage, deep into the battalion of slaves turning human.

Genre screamed, and then many more cries filled the air.

"Oh no," Cracey whispered.

"What," Bricktain asked.

"More generals," Cracey replied.

He heaved Cracey against his chest and charged into the dark, away from the climaxing massacre of hunters.

"Why isn't Jasper turning," Bricktain panted.

"He got help," Cracey replied.

Bricktain would have asked, but his questions could wait. For now, Cracey needed to hide, and he thought he knew just the place.

It had to be here somewhere. The story of this entire graveyard centered on it. He knew this was the oldest part of the cemetery. He searched for the place that had given birth to the graveyard.

Bricktain suddenly pressed against a near-black hedge. He felt the wall of briar, and pulled back a pricked thumb.

No time to search for the gate! His arm ratcheted into a sword, and he began hacking away at the small branches, each time spreading a sharp wave of pain through the spider web that were his nerve endings. He then proceeded to lead Cracey into the crevice he created. He carved through several feet before emerging into the other side. It was dimly lit, but no one would have known it from outside, from the dense wall of briar and shrub.

Dark roses plastered the walls, while trusses of small blossoms grew into large wedding podiums around the lot. In the center, a white stone building, not a mausoleum, but a cottage set.

"I w-will watch the child," an unseen woman's voice submitted. "You m-must return to your friends, Bricktain M-Morris."

Bricktain trusted the voice. It was friendly. It reminded him of things he'd lost since this fight had begun. The voice recalled other details, things he knew he never wanted to remember if he was to keep his edge. Memories, long forgotten suddenly flooded to him.

No, he told himself.

He forced the memories back. They shouldn't be there, not now. Why did they have to come out now? He couldn't bear reliving them at the moment. Right now, because of this sudden burst of memories, he might possibly be the most dangerous person in this graveyard.

Focus on the fight, he convinced himself. He remembered the enemies in the wind. He thought of his training. *Fight! That'll occupy your mind.*

"Go to the house," Bricktain encouraged Cracey. "You're safe there."

Cracey ran to the cottage. Bricktain was already back through the hedge when Bear scampered back up to his shoulders.

Bricktain expected to leap into battle, but he found no battle—only screams of humans, those that had littered the cemetery only minutes ago. Gold generals now slaughtered them and gave the hunters no thought at all. Across the graves, his own allies appeared to be preparing their own defensive strategy for when the gold werewolves decided to change their minds. He watched the enslaved humans try to flee their own masters. Their cries for help, brought slaughter from them instead. As much as he wanted to help, he knew the only chance he had in saving any of them was to rejoin his rank with his allies. Then rain came in the form of humans. He knew some of their faces almost instantly, they were the civilians that the elementals had whisked away from the junkyard earlier. Now they all fell around the feet of the rogue's army. Bricktain ran back towards his rallying allies, praying no body should land upon him.

"You can't stop it," a woman cried from the silent stranger's side.

Bricktain wasn't exactly sure why he did it, most likely because it seemed like what he should do to change things up. Josh would have done it. He was certain of that.

Bricktain shot. The woman fell. Not because Bricktain intended to hit her, but because he missed the stranger whom he had assumed was the rogue. Bricktain shot again for good measure and lowered his head just a few inches, imitating a charging bull. It seemed, he learned, the maneuver kept him from blacking out.

Genre shrieked. The stranger glared out towards Bricktain, and the area suddenly began swarming with more golden generals who leaped from the shadows and aided in slaughtering those humans who had once been guardians just moments ago.

Make a fight, Bricktain ordered himself. He'd tangoed this chaos one too many times for his taste already. He was now looking to the sky, wondering when another unseen attack would come.

Genre charged Bricktain as the robotic sheriff fled towards his own companions. Bricktain fired off a few shots, but the general halves seemed to anticipate the attacks and remained unscathed.

How did they do that?

Aggon's chariot sped towards Bricktain and turned sharply, kicking dirt at Genre.

Bricktain took the opportunity to jump in where Nick, in his human form, stood poised to snap a kick into a monster's face.

"All is comfy and speedy now," Aggon said before cracking his whip and racing towards Jasper. "You was all dead before."

Suddenly, Genre stopped his chase and huffed at Bricktain's escape like he was no big deal. He returned to each of his master's sides.

That was okay with Bricktain, for now. His goal was to get to his own number of friends now. Aggon returned to the group, and Nick quickly joined Cadence who stood with Constance Chandler, who was poised in full SWAT garb and held an automatic weapon.

"Glad you weren't dead," Jasper said in a tone that Bricktain found inviting of a chirping bullet.

Instead, Bricktain found the inquiry leaping from his mouth of, "Why aren't we retreating?"

"We were feeling a bit short-handed without you." Jasper drew a lid over his barrel of leeches and sealed it.

"You're not changed," Bricktain said and noticed the tears streaming down Jasper's twisted and angry face. He fought his instinct to shoot it, for it belonged to the man who had inflicted so much pain upon Bricktain.

"Not changed yet, no," Jasper replied. His attention fixed a moment on Bricktain. "Something different about you, though. Can't quite put my finger on what that is though."

Bricktain refused to bite.

A general shrieked. Bricktain turned, fired and hit nothing, and nothing returned any retaliation whatsoever.

He'd fired off a few more shots, but only one shot struck a monster. Why couldn't he seem to hit anything? This wouldn't have happened if he had the Bullet. He'd have hit everything if he had his trailer.

"Why aren't they attacking us," Bricktain cried in frustration.

"I no can to answer that one," Aggon replied. "I can't see. All my questions were gone before all."

"Questions," Amber asked, suddenly appearing on the ground. "You were an oracle!"

"You don't have to be an oracle to use your brain," Speatsh's ghost stammered. "Even I can answer this one." He looked out across the field of blood and tombstones and reached towards Bear, but the animal pelt rested now upon Bricktain's shoulders.

Bear whined.

The cemetery had indeed become a field of the dead as the generals continued their massacre of humans who had once been guardians earlier.

"He's playing with you to the end," Speatsh replied. Then he yelled out towards the rogue, "And this is why no one ever likes your posts."

If the rogue heard him, he didn't give any clues as to doing so.

Speatsh turned back to Bricktain. "He's not attacking, because he's too busy killing his own right now, God knows why."

"If he's not interested in us, why aren't we running," Bricktain asked.

"Why?" Speatsh asked. "Think he won't find you? Perhaps if someone had asked me these questions instead, I could have told you."

"I thought you were the oracle," Cadence asked looking to Richard who, until now had been standing still and watching the scene.

"I was," Richard replied. "But my three questions got used up, and then Speatsh here took the role when he died."

"So you have three questions," Cadence said, careful to make a statement.

"Nice try," Speatsh replied. "But Oliver got my three. I'd have been a zombie mind still if he hadn't."

"Can I just point out that you're answering questions now," Bricktain said.

"Jealous," Speatsh asked. "We're not dumb," Speatsh finally blasted back. "We just can't see beyond our own abilities anymore."

"What did Oliver ask you" Amber asked.

"I asked questions," Oliver replied, his gaze was fixed in another area of the graveyard when he suddenly hefted his staff. "Here comes first now."

From across the graveyard, a roar, not a wolf's, erupted. A sabretooth appeared from the treeline at the boundaries of the cemetery. It raced fast for the group. Cadence had barely pulled her rifle to her shoulder, but Oliver had already hurled his staff like a spear. The rod flew for the approaching cat, but suddenly curved from Bogi and carved into a tombstone at the side of the sabretooth's path. The staff now stood poised as a tripping hazard.

Bogi hit it. Unaware that Oliver had already planned his trap. Bogi stumbled only a small step, but it was all the error he needed. Oliver was suddenly before him, a huge a slab of stone hovering over his head, gripped in both hands. The giant smashed the slab and the sabretooth cat's head into the earth.

Oliver recovered his spear and began beating its body.

"Bad kitty," he cried over and over. "You is getting spanked now."

Oliver finished his punishment, and his allies watched speechless.

Jasper finally couldn't contain himself and started laughing. "That's right," Jasper cooed. "George was naughty, naughty."

"No more talking kitty," Oliver said upon returning to the group with bloody staff in hand. He glared at Jasper. "His name not George."

"What else did he ask," Cadence asked.

"He asked how to win," Speatsh finally answered.

"That's what mine to ask was too," Aggon said.

"Wait a minute," Bricktain re-entered the conversation. "If Oliver asked Speatsh how to win, who asked you?"

"Hims," Aggon replied extending a long ghostly finger towards the one person in the graveyard who seemed most amused in the presence of so much death. "Rogue."

"They both asked how to win," Bricktain replied. He broke out laughing, couldn't stop. Then he fired off as many shots as he could towards the massacre, knowing that once the mob of generals had finished their work, they would turn on the remaining hunters and friends. One general grabbed its shoulder and didn't seem to give a second thought to Bricktain's feeble attempt after that.

"So who gets the trump," Bricktain asked.

"We to find out now," Aggon said.

"No," Bricktain said. "Bury Josh. Couldn't he be the next oracle then?"

"We can't," Cadence said.

"Sure we can," Bricktain replied.

"We lost him," Amber replied coolly.

"How do you lose Josh's body," Bricktain shrieked.

"You were out the long trip to get here. It was either bring his body or yours," Amber seemed to hiss out.

Bricktain stayed his tongue.

The sound of human screams stopped, as their countless corpses littered the cemetery.

Silence blanketed the area.

The generals appeared still now and took to watching the group of remaining hunters. The number of Bricktain's allies had dwindled: Bricktain, Jasper, Cadence, Amber, Natalie, three ghosts, Oliver. Bricktain noticed that the rodeo queens were still here, the biker with his wolf headband also. Chandler's wife and children stood with Cadence. Thug, Ty and the Doorman tended to a handful of injured hunters who Bricktain really didn't know, but had seen around the compound running Reggie's chores.

The rogue bowed a slight nod towards Bricktain's group, although Jasper was perhaps the only one who realized the nod was for him. Jasper readied his leech barrel and his blade.

Instead of attack, the rogue helped his companion to her feet. Loraine, stood as if to laugh off Bricktain's horrible shot from earlier.

Several police officers began carrying in white bodies of ancients towards the same red and turquoise Conestoga wagon that Cadence had discovered in the bunker and somehow the Rogue had claimed. Chandler led the officers with orders and they began setting the ancients inside the back of the carriage. Constance suddenly appeared anxious to charge in to the rogue's army and pull him out.

Cadence urged her to wait.

"I can't believe they took that wagon from you," Cadence scowled.

"Did you need it for something," Jasper asked.

"The question is, what does he want with it," Cadence inquired.

"There you go," Jasper replied. "That's the question."

"I hate to sound like a broken record, but you know what would be a good suggestion here," Bricktain asked. "Running away."

"We're holding a discussion," Jasper replied.

"Oh good," Bricktain said. "Cuz if there's one thing that holds off a werewolf, it's sitting around holding a discussion."

Amber clenched down on her weapons. "We found something about a cart at the museum," she said ignoring Bricktain. "Something about bringing others back to life."

"Back to life," Jasper asked. "Are you sure?"

"I'm not sure about anything," Amber replied. "I wasn't fully listening. Wait!" She reached into her trench coat pocket and withdrew the wad of papers that Thomas had given to her for protection. "Thomas took these."

As she withdrew them, Bricktain realized that Amber had her weapons and was no longer carrying Josh's.

"Where's Wolf's Breath," Bricktain asked.

Amber turned slightly to reveal a tattered backpack over her shoulders. He believed it more likely to be one of Oliver's aprons, from his tombstone work room, folded to be a backpack.

Amber handed the pages to Jasper.

Jasper took those pages and quickly scanned them. Speatsh and Richard's ghosts peered upon them as well. He folded them up and handed them back to Amber. "I do believe you and those papers just became our highest priority," Jasper said. He suddenly seemed lost in thought.

"Can we please just run the hell away, right now," Bricktain complained.

"Not what we do," Oliver chided. "Lizard's not run. Hello!"

"Then what," Cadence asked trying not to appear as though she were disregarding the giant's juvenile comment.

"I'm not just sitting here for my health," Bricktain said. He fired off more shots in frustration. All missing their standing marks. The targets continued to taunt Bricktain with their bemused interest in his danger to them.

"Will you stop trying to escalate this," Cadence cried. "Or at least hit something."

"I'm trying," Bricktain complained.

"I thought you said you never miss," Cadence laughed.

"I wasn't allowed a lot of training on the gun range," his tone suddenly fell sullen. "That's right," he said in instant realization. "I've been looking through diamond glasses for too long. That needs to change."

"At least the wind's dead here," Amber said watching the sky.

"Think the rogue wants to blow his own army away while they're changing," Jasper asked.

"I need the Bullet," Bricktain said.

"Well, we don't have it, do we," Cadence responded.

"I hope you asked some good questions to get us out of here, Oliver," Amber said.

"Gotted three answers," Oliver said. "Trip talking kitty then bash over there and wait for giant lizards; where new home is; and there are lots and lots of pants."

"Pants," Jasper asked.

"Jeans," Oliver replied.

"Why would you ask something like that," Jasper continued to wonder, then started chuckling at the giant's innocence.

"It secret," Oliver said rearing back and pretending to lock his lip with an invisible stapler.

Across the graveyard, Chandler shouted orders for his officers to hurry as they carefully slid the still white bodies of decaying ancients into the back of the Conestoga.

"At least that's all the ancient corpses he has," Cadence said.

"For now," Jasper replied. He stood in a trance-like state, staring at the ground.

After Chandler's officers loaded the last body into the carriage, the rogue, himself, shut the front gate to the cemetery.

"Captain," Loraine called.

Chandler approached. The rogue pointed towards the mausoleum where the rescued ancients hid.

"He knows where they are," Jasper scowled.

Chandler ordered some of his men to open the stone hiding place.

The rogue approached the carriage. He inspected it, walking around as if looking for some secret. Finally, he waved Loraine to his side. Genre assisted her.

"It's not the carriage," the rogue's pet woman announced.

The carriage exploded against the rogue's hands; he tore it to shreds and then knelt over the pile of white bodies that remained within the splinters.

"Where is it, Captain Chandler," the woman demanded.

POP!

Just then, she hunkered forward, grasping at her throat.

Chandler ran towards Bricktain and his allies. The officer had hit his target, but now fired his gun blindly behind him as he retreated the rogue.

"That could have been played better," Jasper laughed, but not really.

Genre howled. The rogue caught Loraine in his arms and gently laid her onto the lawn.

Now, the generals attacked.

Amber took to the air. Cadence and Constance began to take positions to fire upon the wolves and help Captain Chandler escape.

Even Aggon appeared anxious to get to fighting.

"No," Bricktain ordered. "Don't split up the group this time. Everyone stays together."

Bricktain raised his weapon and fired several shots at the beasts chasing the captain. Most of the monsters dodged, but the gunshots were enough to give Chandler some running space.

Cadence aimed her arsenal upon the generals and the rogue. Although her shots were a bit more successful against striking their targets than Bricktain's were, she couldn't land a shot on the rogue.

One of the generals tackled Chandler. Cadence shot it off. Chandler, now out of bullets, whipped the general in the eye with his sidearm.

Bricktain fired a shot and, this time, clipped the captor's shoulder. Cadence struck it in the chest. Two more generals took the fallen one's place. Bricktain fired and missed again.

"I'm no good at this range!" Bricktain shrieked.

"You sound like a pencil pusher," Jasper said, he kicked his barrel over, and his leeches immediately flew at Chandler's attackers and the wave of wolves rushing towards. "Can't imagine why they didn't let you train."

"That's it," Bricktain cried. "That's what we need!"

Bricktain took aim once more, slowly this time. He breathed patiently and waited. Chandler stood under the commotion of the leeches and ran. Bricktain refined his aim, inhaled and—

CHIRP!

Chandler grabbed at his chest a moment before crumpling forward.

"You idiot," Cadence screamed.

Constance shrilled louder and turned to open fire upon Bricktain, only to be stopped by Amber who quickly used an orbit to destroy Constance's weapon.

"How can you be such a dead-eye from a diesel and miss the simple shots," Amber screeched, suddenly dropping out of the sky before turning in anticipation of a vengeful widow focused now on Bricktain.

Here, Bricktain finally realized that Amber looked different. She had become hate since Bricktain had seen her last.

While Cadence and Amber cussed him out, the brunette rodeo queen opened fire from the second huddle. Bricktain ordered her and the others in her group to stop. She may have thrown an obscene gesture Bricktain's way, but he wasn't sure.

"Time to get out of here," Bricktain cried. He fired off random shots, just to occupy his mind.

More wailing erupted from Chandler's family as they were forced to huddle with Thug's group of hunters without their father and husband.

The wave of generals raced towards the huddle.

The wind suddenly grew.

This time, Amber cursed.

"Please tell me someone has a good idea," Cadence said.

"Don't be dumb." Jasper shouted. "Of course I have." This time he whistled in the direction of a mausoleum with a strange shadow atop it. "Get us out of here, What."

"And what do I get," a voice heckled from an unseen place.

Jasper pointed towards the second huddle of hunters with the injured, the rodeo queens, Thug and others, including Constance and her children. More specifically, he pointed to the blonde rodeo queen, "You can have that blonde bimbo."

The blonde rodeo queen objected.

"And," What asked. "What needs more."

"Fine! And the children," Jasper relented. He knew who What really wanted. "You'll get your dead soon enough if you help us first."

Constance questioned what Jasper meant.

"You don't get to make that deal," Cadence screamed.

A horrific tune sang over the graveyard. Its notes stabbed the ears like daggers with fast high notes, a bludgeoning low note and then back to high-pitched blades.

"It's either them or us," Jasper replied.

The black, ash-children erupted from the ground, leap-frogging into one another until a large, burnt wall towered over the group of hunters. From the other side of the barrier, general's howled, cursing that they couldn't reach the group of allies.

From this side, the sound of children giggled as they do from too much tickling.

In an instant, the protesting blonde rodeo queen raised atop a mound of ash towards the pinnacle of the mausoleum. By the time the biker or her partner got into range of protecting her, What had leapt down among the group of hunters, still playing his angry tune, his caged head now atop the blonde queen's shoulders, her head completely devoured and replaced with his cage. He reached down and pat the Chandler boy's crown before dancing jigs to dodge the blows of many hunters at once.

Both the brunette partner and the biker flew at Jasper, the biker screaming that he didn't care who Jasper was, he didn't deserve to live.

Black bars shot up from the ground around Bricktain and his small group. Another set appeared around Thug and Aggon's huddle. The two parties now stood in what appeared to be black prison cells.

What blew his flute, laughing, fresh blood streamed down his, or was it her, chin. A mound of laughing ash broke from the wall and hefted him atop the solid ceiling over the heads of Jasper's group.

The wall exploded, revealing an even larger army of generals than had before been there.

"Where did they come from," Bricktain panicked.

"Where else," Jasper said. "The shadows."

The ash that had once made up the wall protecting the remaining hunters from the rogue and his generals suddenly melded into two giant black creatures. Their long wings unfolded, revealing the frames of dark, silky dragons with smooth wing-backs. Three feathered tails slapped away generals that tried rushing the scene before What could accomplish his rescue. The dragons' snake-like necks and spindly joints reached to the skies as if being pulled by a marionette master. They screamed the million joys of children frolicking in a playground.

"I think I see where this is going," Speatsh said as What's music suddenly turned into long heavy notes as if cannons blasting. These notes were far too powerful for any normal flute to sing. "This is where is where ghosts can't go."

"You is pansy ghost," Aggon screamed from the other cage.

Each ash dragon clenched a cage filled with hunters and hefted it into the air, the screams were joined by cheers of rescued hunters.

From below, Speatsh laughed as the cages flew out of reach of the headstones. "Look! Lizards!"

Even Cadence couldn't help but to celebrate the escape by firing off several shots at the generals who continued to leap after the cage.

"Use the children to fight, not flee," Amber shouted.

"They're innocent," Jasper replied. "They won't shed blood." Then he turned his attention to the biker and the brunette rodeo queen who seemed to think they were capable of arguing with Jasper over his decision to sell off their blonde friend. Jasper slapped at both in one motion to silence their endeavors. The biker dodged, which Jasper found interesting.

Jasper believed his reflexes must have already been getting slower.

Meanwhile, amidst the lake of pursuing monsters, the golden generals swarmed to construct their bodies into a giant pyramin. It built high and climbed quickly into the sky towards the fleeing cage. The entire structure of wolves gave chase, it didn't remain stationary. Up one of its sides, raced one figure faster than all the others. This figure was human. He didn't even bother changing form until he finally leapt from the top of the monster-made structure. He leapt towards Jasper's cage. With the wind of the elementals now pressing at his back to throw him farther, the rogue easily caught grip of the floor.

He grappled for the bars. He was fully white now and peered into the cage with his bright silver eyes. His claws had grown at least two feet long, stretched from his fingertips, and still grew. He slashed at the group. The ash bars gave way only momentarily, enough for the rogue to lose his grip. The cage quickly repaired itself.

The rogue gripped another section of the cage floor.

Bricktain took aim on the rogue. "We're coming for you."

He fired and missed, not because of his terrible aim this time, but because of the speed of the rogue. The monster dodged Bricktain's point-blank blast and leapt higher up the cage, but as he reached for another bar, it too disintegrated before his hand.

What laughed while he continued to play his dark melody.

The biker suddenly appeared with his pistol shotgun and blasted. Yet in that same instant of fire, somehow the rogue spun the barrel backwards upon the biker. The blast blew away the biker's wolf headband and all that it covered. Then the biker fell, the brunette catching him and realizing her face was sprayed with what had once been the biker's head. The brunette shoved the biker's corpse at the rogue who once again hung from one of the bars.

The biker's body toppled through the cage bars, breaking the rogue's grip. Both bodies fell away, but the rogue's was caught up in the wind. The speed of the dragons made of child and ash picked up as the gust and rogue continued pursuit. The rogue standing high in the sky, gained ground under the strength of his wind-master elementals.

The brunette drew her pistols and fired off every shot The rogue dodged each one. She stomped, threw her pistols and withdrew a small cannon she hadn't considered using since Speatsh Cheatham had given it to her. Suddenly, she ran for the rogue and leapt off the cage. She fired the single blast which caused a small explosion at the rogue's chest. She punched at him once before falling to the earth, dragging the rogue with her in a calamity of fists and fury from both opponents.

What's tune picked up even more speed, and the dragons began to flap harder.

The rogue and elementals disappeared into the black that quickly consumed Plattsville and all the land about it.

Finally, they were free of their dungeon.

"Oh no," Oliver suddenly cried. "She's lost."

The cage teetered in the dragon's clutches as oliver rampaged his realization. What, now sitting atop the dragon carrying this cage, stumbled with his own playing, but quickly recovered.

"My puppy gone," Oliver cried. "Man said to take care of her." He ran to the side of the cage and whistled. "Here puppy, puppy." He whistled again. "Here, boy!" Tears streamed down his cheek.

Bricktain felt the shudder. "I forgot!"

"What did you do," Amber asked.

"Everything was happening so fast," Bricktain said. He couldn't believe his own self. For a moment he thought of rushing the bars and throwing himself to his own deserved death.

"You lost her," Cadence asked screaming. Her face turned to the bars and looked down. "Cracey? Again?"

"I left her in the hedge," Bricktain said.

"The cottage," Oliver asked with greater excitement and a smile broke across his face. "My doggy in safe place. No one care go in there."

Bricktain had no choice but to trust the giant as their cage flew higher, and the air grew thin and cold.

Still, What's music played on, and the dragons' wings kept beat.

After the adrenaline had worn off, and the feeling of safety settled in, Bricktain felt himself of enough mind to finally take bearing of his surroundings. Jasper and Natalie were the only other ones awake now. Oliver's head rested in the back of the golden chariot. Aggon might have argued for the giant to find a better pillow, but he was silent now. Amber and Cadence, once huddled together in tears, now slept beneath Wolf's Breath, which Bricktain couldn't imagine gave very much protection against the cold air.

Bricktain searched for Speatsh, he could use advice now, but Speatsh was not in either cage. He called for him a time or two, hoping he might materialize as Aggon did, but Jasper told him to get some sleep too. As he found a spot on the cage floor, he noticed Acotactac watching. He eventually fell asleep with her head in his lap, she too crying herself to sleep. Bricktain did his best to let bear replace his lap as her pillow when he felt the need to stand some time later. Bricktain simply couldn't sleep. He was afraid to. There were things he had started to realize, things he should not. They were hints of forgotten memories at first, but now, it was possible they could start making sense, too much sense. He had to stop it.

Natalie sat perched at the back ledge of the cage looking into the distance. She shivered beneath various pieces of clothing others had volunteered to her human form.

A few feet away, Jasper stared beyond the bars as well.

"I think I need your help," Bricktain said approaching Natalie.

"Don't know what I can do," Natalie replied. Her voice had numbed with loss.

"You wounded," Jasper asked, suddenly standing behind Bricktain, startling him.

"I think I've put us all in danger," Bricktain said. "Either you need to tell me if we can fix it, or I need you to kill me."

The Book of Eulogies

18 ~ Twenty-Five

The Schnautzer rebounded off of the Detective's chest. Bruce fell, while his dangerous companion tore out the little man's throat before a single gang bullet fired.

The island was a living volcano. A refuge. Their home now. This is where Oliver told What to fly them after their failure in the cemetery. Here, they'd found sanctuary, where they'd remained hidden now for more than twenty years.

The skylight that held Nick's attention looked down into underground river of lava. The red and stringy orange flowed slowly beneath the rock shell under his feet—slow, but quickly enough to show the lava would devour anything that might have decided to swim within it. Nick tossed in his empty Vienna sausage can and watched the yellowed label burn before the container itself turned onto its side and began drinking in the lava before it too lit on fire, began to sink and disappeared from view of the skylight. Then, as he had done with the rest of the sausages, he chewed the last link, savored the meaty taste, and spit out the masticated mash into the flow. He found peace in the small bursts of flames in the lava that followed.

He missed meat.

He didn't have to turn around to know someone had approached him. Nick had heard him some time ago, walking slowly across the lava ropes. If this messenger fell through the hard, but sometimes brittle lava crust, it would be at least another hour before another gopher was sent for him. However, Nick wouldn't wish that upon him. Nick cracked open another can of Vienna sausages and wrestled the pruned link from the center. He hated when they tore, which this one thought about doing, but didn't.

"Sure you don't want one," Nick asked.

Natalie huffed her disgust from beside him. Her head finally turned slowly to look upon the messenger. She already knew though, she knew everyone's scent, but she didn't always trust it around the lava nor its gases, which was part of what helped to mask that humans hid within this island.

Nick sighed. "Let him be."

He chewed his sausage and spit it out as he had before—watching it flickering into ash against the lava, pimpling the orange with combustible acne.

"I'm sorry, Sir," the man submitted, sneaking cautiously upon Nick.

"Douglas," Nick acknowledged. He threw another link into his mouth.

He heard Douglas's feet creep closer behind him. He put Nick between himself and the monster Natalie.

Nick spit.

"Look, then walk, officer," Nick suggested, still not turning to properly greet Douglas. "The rock might be thin."

The young officer apologized.

"Tell the captain I'm busy," Nick said.

"She said if you said that to tell you it's not an order."

"Good," Nick said. "Then tell her to go to hell."

"The chief said it is an order though."

Natalie yelled at the messenger. Douglas jumped at the sudden outburst, and Nick grabbed the front of his shirt to keep him from misstepping into the skylight.

"Look," Nick grumbled. "Then walk."

"Yes, sir," Douglas replied.

"You didn't make it this far to fall into fire."

"Yes, sir," Douglas repeated.

"What a waste," Nick said, staring at his can of uneaten sausages. He dropped it, and its contents into the skylight, where they too drowned in the thick ooze only inches below a black crust. He drew a glove from his jacket pocket, gripped up his curled walking stick that he had found washed upon the shore. He turned his head to scan a path before deciding that it was safe to proceed around; the hot rock peeled away at the liquefying bottoms of his thick firefighter boots. He left behind small imprints of what appeared to be filthy water behind him.

He closed his eyes and breathed in the last outside air he knew he was doomed to enjoy for the rest of the night, perhaps month.

That's how it was for him anymore. He was fasted, free of his wolf addiction for far too long, twenty-five years too long. Twenty-five years of hiding since the night they had fled the rogue. Twenty-five years since they'd had real electricity or hope.

Occasionally, he thought he felt his master, or what he thought was his master. Sometimes he'd be reading and felt as though someone were with him, watching him, or rather the pages of his book. He'd come to enjoy reading. They had developed a fair library on the island, but people fought over the classics. The residents had become tired of the fantasy of ignorance created by people who knew nothing of real monsters and felt they needed to change them. Although, some popular vampire and werewolf books from his era had become excellent comedies with long lists of people waiting to read them. *Frankenstein* was still deeply respected, however. Don't ever knock *Frankenstein!* The presences he tended to feel seemed attracted to Shakespeare and Homer, but he assumed it was just shadows of memories linked to when he felt her. He would much rather read right now.

That was his original plan: taste his canned meat and then sit down to a good book. Someone had brought in a copy of Hesiod's *Theogeny*. It should have been a simple read.

However, the captain wanted him, again. Probably more orders to spend more time in the gun range. He didn't mind the shooting, but Cadence had become a vile teacher. Any gun they picked up now, she made sure to learn every aspect of its character. She expected Nick to do the same, but he just didn't have her eye. That's not to say that he didn't develop one. That is, he could hit the same distant targets as Cadence, just not as accurately. He could still outshoot the chief though. At least that was something—but really, who cares when all you shoot are targets in an indoor firing range.

In the distance, he could hear the numerous explosions of sea water and fire hose leaks somewhere near the growing bench. Nick was annoyed that he wouldn't be able to watch if it should fall today. Sometimes, he wished he hadn't decided to enter the police training, not that he had a choice really. A lot of good it did him too, since he never got to actually leave the island. Practice, practice! He hated that gun range. Punishment for no longer being human, he guessed. What he really wanted was to join the other catchers at the cliffs who netted the lava and debris that shot out of the sides of the island. He hated their fat lava suits, but, in watching them catch debris that might become future bullets, he thought they looked like they were having fun.

Natalie snapped her teeth, and her heavy feet plotted the path ahead of Nick and away from the lava ropes.

Finally, Nick's eyes popped open, and he followed his sister. This time he pushed past the rookie.

Natalie coughed at a patch of rock. A pace later, Nick's cane swatted the ground. "Careful of that tube, Douglas," Nick said, and continued to press towards the colder lava.

A mile in, the sound of children playing caught his ear. He stopped and found several scurrying around the edge of greenery. He might not have picked up on where they were, but one of their little heads popped from behind a tree, and another suddenly gave chase. Natalie poised, ready to bellow.

"Get away from there," Nick shouted, then turned to Douglas. "Get them out of there before they blow themselves up."

Nick left Douglas so they could each follow their orders. He continued his way towards a path, which led safely through foliage that no longer set atop hidden rivers of lava. Here, he straddled his chainless mountain bike and pressed himself inland. Natalie kept pace, or she allowed Nick to.

After a short ride farther into the tropic, they found themselves before a set of glass doors to a building that no one would have ever expected sat upon an island hiding the human battalion of forlorn. Thomas had designed it to be his vault, but it had grown into a military base and refuge of sorts. Speatsh told Jasper where it was, and Jasper directed What to bring everyone to the island. Here was the source of Thomas's supply of diamonds. It had taken some time to convince the facility guards and staff of everyone's status.

They had decided that Amber should inherit the vault as it had rightfully been passed to Josh, but she preferred hunting and had no time to operate it. Jasper too felt the desire to spend his talents elsewhere in the fight. Oliver became the likely choice to manage the operations as his father had. This quickly helped create order among the disgruntled.

Mostly, no one wanted to argue with the giant. Stan might have, but he had yet to set foot on the island. He was too busy still being off on his own. Only now, he seemed to hunt survivors and storehouses of supplies to be brought back to the island. With a little redesign and reallocation of facilities—not to mention Oliver's approval—Bricktain had decided it was the best choice to center a headquarters upon what had once been the central weapons research and development site for hunters in Speatsh's circle.

After Washington fell to the rogue, this island became the center for organized law enforcement, if you could call it law enforcement. It wasn't exactly a known place, and only those who were invited to flee to it even knew it existed. It was more accurate to call it a center for people who could aid human survivalism. Still, it was easier to refer to it as the police department. Everyone who lived on the island contributed to it in some way.

For that matter, the entire population of the island, the few thousand who lived there, were all mandated to learn the hunter trade. No one was excused. You fought. You trained. You did your part to preserve the human race or you found yourself swimming out to sea, or worse.

Nick hated it. It reminded him that his last sanctuary was a small set of islands off of who knew where. If he ever got to leave this particular island, he might know exactly. Before being allowed to join the population himself, he was forced to wait in an underground jail until he learned to control his hunger. His master could have probably freed him sooner than fasting had, but never did.

What Nick was allowed to know, and only because of reconnaissance reports he was allowed to read, was that the world had become a wasteland. Entire countries were dominated by wolves, and the purpose of the human race had become feed for the monsters and to breed more feed. He knew they searched for something. They expanded their numbers over the globe and had yet to find it. Many cities still remained, from what Nick had read and photos that he had seen on Cadence's desk, but the only governing force in the world now belonged to the rogue.

India was the last to fall. The rogue infiltrated all militaries within less than a year. Rebellions naturally arose, most fled inland, but they fell quickly. Others retreated to ancient tombs around the globe. Pyramids, underground tunnels and mausoleums all became cemeteries for those who continued to hold a spirit to fight. Power grids fell. Satellite signals became lost, some fell. Those that remained in orbit aided hunters in communication, but they could have just as easily helped the wolves. As this clearly put discovery of their island in danger, small troops of hunters were dispatched to locate as many satellite controls as possible and shut down all the eyes in the sky as they could. They didn't just seek out satellite power, they brought down cell towers as well. They weren't many, but give them time and they might have the western part of the U.S. brought down within a few years.

Tanks became mobile tombs to any who thought they offered longevity in survival. Planes always needed to land, usually in a mob of awaiting devastation. For hunters, all military tools of destruction had become materials for research and development of new weapons, gear and transportation on the island, so long as that transportation was silent and easy to bring across the ocean or by What and his dragons. Communication took place mostly on paper and digital cameras.

Only those humans who learned how to hide in the shadows, where wolves had no problem seeing, stood a chance of getting rescued and taken back to the island.

Supplies were still strong, mostly thanks to Jasper's and Bricktain's ideas. The island camouflaged the hunter's police department. This place was completely alive. The one thing the rogue couldn't stop was the growth of the earth. Noise erupted here every day at its coasts, where gases gathered beneath everyone's feet and rivers of lava flowed nonstop beneath an ever expanding crust. Here, hunters could hide. Wolf scouting parties, elementals mostly, couldn't hear the humans over the growth caused by flowing earth. The land was fertile; the greenhouse crops were healthy; what supplies they couldn't grow had their own systems of entering the island.

Nick wished that bicycle chains would make their way to the island, but they were not allowed for their noise.

Other facilities existed too, but Nick wasn't familiar with anything that wasn't written on paper: books mostly and gun manuals. To help hone his investigative practice, occasionally he received an old supply of murder files, which hunters had salvaged from defunct police buildings around the world—generally, nothing vital to the Island. The powers-that-be hid everything from Nick.

He'd watched his friends and allies move on; patrol the other islands; even get assigned missions to kill wolves, but Nick had been relegated to the gun range, which had been buried as low into the oldest part of the island as was safe. He cleaned and fired weapons, tested and even authorized some hunters on them, all in the loud confines of enclosed concrete walls. It was as if they didn't trust Nick. They didn't say it, but Nick felt it. Bricktain went out of his way to keep him out of any missions or planning.

Even Natalie was allowed more freedom to take part than he was. She often disappeared for a mission here and there. Mostly with Jasper and Amber. Nick, however, saw mostly the gun range. When he pleaded for responsibility, Bricktain made him the gun range overseer and firearms trainer for hunters.

Despite all, even though many thought, and many still argued, that Nick should be forced to leave, his friends remained true to his staying. Usually, Cadence would too.

He once loathed the bunker below Richard's garage, but he found himself in much worse now. Even the shafts of light that flooded down into the range, much like those in the bunker, refused to let him escape his failed hopes of anything better.

He did get his nightly hour outside with his Vienna sausages at least, provided they felt it was safe for him to have his hour.

"Lieutenant," the receptionist welcomed as Nick entered the stone-carved building. Nick ignored the man's masked disrespect, the kind that suggested his rank was more novel than real.

Natalie did not ignore the receptionist and now posted herself across his desk where she rumbled long and low. She remained this way until the man on the other side could only look down at whatever paperwork he had on his desk.

"In case you're wondering," Nick said. He had changed his mind about ignoring the curt man. "She offered to have you reassigned to a hunting party."

The receptionist fell into a deep state of paralysis, and tried not to make eye contact with Natalie, who now began drooling over his deskwork.

"I'll leave her with you so you can both talk about it," Nick said, and then left his sister to maintain her intimidating watch. Nick happened to believe she enjoyed this activity with disrespectful staff.

Nick passed the lobby and then climbed the stairs to the second floor. This was the newest portion of the building, which was actually, a rather well-constructed facility—if you could see past the stucco, mud and forest that had been used to encapsulate and disguise it, necessary in case any satellites caught image or wandering elementals passed over it.

This facility was where candidate hunters came to get training. Ex-military trainees were rare, so Bricktain insisted on the law enforcement standards that he had learned to abide by. One or two military-backed hunters attempted to convince change, but when they realized how noisy their training approaches were, they had to adapt as well. The fact also remained that many of the most experienced hunters on the island lacked trust for real military-type soldiers or mercenaries. The highest ranking had not forgotten the damage of betrayal by their own kin. Militants and mercenaries were required to endure a three-month-long, break-in period before being allowed to train.

The period mostly consisted of living in dark quarters and offered food by hunters until they realized their dependency upon them. If they didn't adapt, they were discharged, allowed to swim off the island—if they could, which they never could.

Rookies, for the most part, were the worst. No one gave hunters a hard time, but Nick faced ridicule from the most pathetic of newbies with every new class. Even when they realized his inner wolf still gave him some strength, they seemed to push his buttons even more. He was, after all, a liability and icon of what had killed their world.

Jasper and Natalie were too, but they were belligerent and well enough to silence any who dared challenge them. They were powerful. Nick was just Nick.

His fast hadn't been easy. Natalie had helped him, Jasper too. In truth, Jasper had become perhaps his greatest supporter. It turned out that being forced to live on a secluded island actually promoted the fasting that cleansed the blood, which gave power to the wolf inside. It nearly drove Jasper mad after a while, but he never lost his mind. He had to leave the island frequently to stay the madness. Nick, however, didn't suffer as deeply.

Natalie hadn't even bothered to fast. She hunted mostly with Amber now; Nick rarely saw them and, when he did, they hardly had time for him. Acotactac and Bricktain never worked apart. The demon, What, worked a great deal with Jasper or Bricktain and Acotactac. What's job was to locate supply warehouses of various sizes and bring their contents back to the island. Nick wondered what his payment was supposed to be for his continued involvement. It happened in secret, but Nick had noticed it coincided well with the disappearances of people on the island who refused to contribute or to adapt.

Although they never said it, Nick assumed Bricktain spent most of his travels with What and Acotactac, observing and developing strategy. Sometimes they flew off in What's flying cages with large groups of soldiers and returned fatigued, usually with more supplies, often with newer hunters. That's when Nick felt left out the most.

When Jasper was around, he helped Oliver oversee the mines. He came out the most to speak to Nick, tried teaching Nick how to close his primitive, wolf-touched mind. Nick felt it served no purpose, but Jasper was good company. Strange he should become Nick's best friend. Through Jasper's fast, his age crept upon him. However, it hadn't lowered his formidable character. He could still frighten the rookies when he needed to.

Nick's partner, however, drained his strength more every day. Lately, with Jasper gone on assignment, he noticed it more. *Lately* was an understatement. Nick hadn't seen Jasper in over two years, not since Bricktain sent him on his own mission. Perhaps he was dead. No one spoke of it, nor Jasper. When hunters died, the community tended not to talk about them. It was a means to respect that perhaps they might still be surviving, but haven't come home yet. More than two years was a long time for the great Jasper to not come back though. Nick liked to think he was still hunting. The point is, without Jasper, Nick's only real and constant friend on the island was the one who hated him most. He hated her, especially when she summoned him from his rare private time.

"Lieutenant," Cadence greeted from behind her desk, its corner splintered from where she smashed an insubordinate officer's head against it. Her face was etched with lines that were eager to swallow shadows that made her appear older than she would have liked. She peered down at a pile of papers. Oil lamps decorated her wall and desk, yet they were all unlit as light still came through the window and sun-tubes. Sparse strands of silver weaved through her graying-red head. She gathered her papers together and slid them into a desk drawer.

"You can't even call me by my name anymore," Nick asked.

Her walls were otherwise clean. Nick understood why, she never came home early. Nick had begun to call the small hut his because she became more and more interested in longer work days.

"I'm not in the mood," Cadence replied.

"Oh," Nick replied. "Well, I'm certainly sorry about that."

"Can we not do this," Cadence asked, still not looking up from her desk, despite having removed anything of substance upon it to look at.

"What? Talk," Nick replied.

"I do not have time for childishness, Lieutenant," Cadence shouted.

"Funny you should mention children," Nick fired back.

"Just stop!" Cadence stood now pumping a fist against her desk. "I told you! Not with that piper on this island."

"Enough," Bricktain's voice commanded, not loud, but enough to maintain his respect and order. Nick had seen it bring the cockiest of hunters to tears. "What is it every time I come home with you two?"

Bricktain entered the room. Every trip out from the island had brought more and more discoloration to his hair. White now filled his head, and his beard would soon be the same. He walked slowly, limped more upon each visit.

Retire. It was time for him to retire. He was more than sixty now, yet he was still the most dangerous hunter, bar any comrade monsters, and he still had the strength to wield that contraption on his shoulder.

Acotactac, on the other hand, still appeared young in comparison to Bricktain. Bricktain often joked that the day would come that her gray would eventually show, and that's when he'd know it was time to retire.

"When her hair's gray," Bricktain would say. "That's when I'll know my job is affecting both of us."

Nick hated it. He, himself, appeared as though he were still in high school.

"I should have made you both take a vacation years ago," Bricktain said, pressing his way past Nick.

Cadence walked out from behind her desk to greet Bricktain in a hug and allowed him to have the first seat in a hard-looking couch against the wall. He originally offered the seat to Acotactac, but lost the argument. He then sat in a way which disguised that he was really falling, and he failed to hide his wincing.

Cadence drew a can of orange soda from her desk and offered it to him.

"Oh, I want this," Bricktain said through a smile crossing his face of yellowing, even browning teeth. He quickly cracked open the top of the can, took a long drink and belched. "How did you find this?"

"A group found a frozen warehouse—Anchorage, I think," Cadence replied.

"Remember when they used to be cold?"

"Give me one generator, I'll make it happen."

"No," Bricktain politely shut down Cadence's request. "Not worth the noise." He finished his drink. Then he turned his face to Nick.

Here it came: Hello, old friend. Train more, and will you excuse us now so we non-monsters can talk behind your back?

Acotactac had now taken a stance beside Bricktain and massaged the flesh around his robotic shoulder.

"How you doing, Nick," Bricktain asked.

"Good to see you, Chief," Nick returned the usual courtesy.

"I've been reviewing your log," Bricktain explained as he pulled a small notebook from his pocket and began rifling through it. "I told you I wanted you in the range a minimum of forty hours a week."

"If you'd give me a mission, I could get that time in," Nick replied.

"You can't follow the orders that you get here," Bricktain replied. "What makes you think you can follow them out there."

"Then give me something to do here then," Nick requested, more as an order.

"You've been given something to do."

"Yeah," Nick complained. "Wake up, shoot. Shoot all day. Shoot all night. Teach other people to shoot. Classes, all day, all night. Get out and exercise, shoot some more. Oh, and don't go home until you've solved at least ten sudokus and three logic puzzles. I can't remember the last time I had a dream that didn't involve a target."

"You ungrateful snot," Bricktain finally shouted.

"You oppressive, forgetful tissue," Nick shouted back.

Bricktain sat stunned. It had been far too long since any had dared challenge him.

"I'm more capable than you in every department, old man," Nick said. "I can outthink and outrun you. Give me some blood, and I'll show you what I can do."

"Yeah! Blood." Bricktain rose to his feet faster than Nick had anticipated. "You think I've been oppressive? You don't know how lucky you are." Now, he squared himself with Nick. Even though Bricktain was a little shorter and a little more human, he still stared him down better than anyone. "You are here because that's where you're needed. I've lost enough friends out there."

"Amber and Natalie," Nick started.

"Are not as clumsy as you," Bricktain finished.

Cadence snorted.

"You better check that attitude, Captain," Bricktain said turning his wrath upon Nick's mocker, almost with more ferocity than he had towards Nick. "If you think you've been doing everything right yourself, you haven't been paying attention." He sat once more, this time against Cadence's desk. "Is treating a person like a human being beneath you now?"

"I'm sorry," Nick said. "I'm just tired."

Bricktain chuckled to himself. "You're tired?"

"I'll put in the hours," Nick said.

"Oh, you have no idea." Bricktain rubbed his head. "My aim is horrible," he finally said. "Know why? Because my old chief thought the best place for me was behind a desk, reading and analyzing. He thought it would keep my brain too busy to cause problems for my co-workers. If he had never been my chief, we might not be in this mess right now. What I would have given to have your aim. Maybe none of this would be happening right now if I had. Which is exactly why I—," Bricktain trailed off before realizing the others were waiting for him to finish. "I'm giving you better than I got. Our lives would have been better if my chief had never been involved."

"At least you were allowed to think," Nick replied.

"The only thing I learned," Bricktain suddenly paused in his anger, as if he had said something he shouldn't have. "Was to focus on shutting others out," Bricktain took a swig from his orange can. "I was so focused, nothing interrupted my thoughts that I didn't want to." Bricktain smacked his head for emphasis. "Great at analyzing and blocking out the world, bad with people and bad with firearms."

"That's not true," Nick retorted. "You single-handedly gunned the Bullet."

"Artificial aim! People died because of my aim when I was outside that trailer," Bricktain snapped. "Sure, in the Bullet, I could hit anything. I wasn't a klutz, and believe me, my ex-wife was pretty good at pointing out how much of a klutz I was." He suddenly glared at Cadence, who appeared ashamed and avoided looking at Nick. "I didn't get that time to practice shooting. I need your focus, but I need your aim to be second-nature, subliminal even. You've got to be better than me. Perhaps if my old supervisor had been killed in the line of duty sooner, and I'd gotten a boss more like me, one who'd let me get away from pencil pushing, I might have been as good as you are." Bricktain seemed to barely have enough air to squeeze out the last of his rambling.

"Are you all right," Nick asked. He knew Bricktain enough.

"Do you still have your mask, Captain," Bricktain asked.

"Yes," Cadence replied.

"Good," Bricktain said. He somewhat smiled within a wince as he once more dropped onto the simple brown couch.

"What do you need me to do, Brick," Cadence asked and shot a familiar glance of policy towards Nick.

"Don't worry," Nick said. "I'm going."

"Stay," Bricktain requested. It was still an order, but it was softer, friendlier.

This was new.

"Twenty-five years ago, we left someone behind in Plattsville," Bricktain explained. "It's time to go bring that ally back."

"You mean Cracey," Cadence asked. "How has she—

"I need you two to accompany Acotactac back to Plattsville," Bricktain explained.

A grumble came from the doorway. Natalie had sneaked into the conversation. Nick had hardly heard her.

"I wouldn't dream of keeping you away from your brother on his first time out," Bricktain said.

"That's not protocol, Brick," Cadence replied. "You're Acotactac's partner."

"Not this time." Bricktain said, and breathed. Just now, he looked almost unreal, like a man ready to stop fighting. Ready to stop doing everything. “You’re going back to the bunker. You’ll be briefed on your assignment when you get there.”

“Do we know if she’s alive,” Nick asked.

Bricktain became lost in sigh. “Thats a question that has haunted me for twenty-five years,” Bricktain said. “Just get your gear. We have a bigger fish to catch.”

19 ~ The Farmer's Son

Another biker fell, his ribs torn open.

Even living on an island in the light-forsaken ocean was brighter than this. Nick was stunned. As far as he could see, the only lights that shone on the earth belonged to the stars and the slivered moon that reflected upon any bodies of water they flew over. His fast had returned the beauty of black to his mind.

When he was younger, he'd gotten a window seat on a flight to Los Angeles, and the entire world below was splotched with yellow city dots and street grids, but here, in his flying cage with What flying his dragon, the earth could not be seen.

They had traveled for three days straight. At night, the cage opened to reveal the black night, but, in the day, it became a black box, sealing the deadly rays of sun from wounding Natalie. Nick was grateful for this night.

"You knew about this," Nick asked, peering down upon what he believed had been a river. "You couldn't tell me."

"You knew it was all gone," Cadence said, staring out beyond the magical bars.

"I still had hope," he replied. "I'd like to be told these things."

"I'll take that into consideration." Her thick coat and hat muffled her words only a little. "Besides, do you really think we could have stopped this?"

Nick was grateful that Bricktain had reminded them to dress up. After living on a volcano, this high altitude was all the more freezing. "We would have been dumb enough to try," He said.

"We were driven," Cadence said.

"No we weren't," Nick replied. "Josh was driven. We just wanted to help."

"Josh wasn't driven," Cadence corrected. "He was insane."

"Would we be here without that," Nick asked. Then wondered about his small mind for posing the question.

"He did have a way of getting things done," Cadence said.

"He had a way of getting lucky," Nick replied curtly.

The balance of the floor shifted beneath his feet. Natalie moved away from this conversation and joined Acotactac on the other side of the cage. Here, they held silent conversation about their loved ones who had not joined them on this journey.

"Still," Cadence said. "I wouldn't mind having some of that luck again."

For a moment, Nick's chest felt as though it were suddenly tearing. It lasted only a second. It didn't floor him. It just happened sometimes, and his reaction didn't escape Cadence's eye.

"That night, when you saved me," Cadence said.

Nick didn't want to talk about it.

"That's when I saw you," Cadence explained.

"And yet, here we are," Nick said, distant, alone practically.

"I can't see that again," Cadence continued. "I can fight. I can defend myself, but you'd die trying to save our child who couldn't."

"That's your reasoning," Nick blurted. "Our marriage in the dirt, and that's your stupid reasoning?"

He fell silent as he heard the rustle of Acotactac and Natalie at the other end of the cage, pretending that their two friends actually had some privacy. The two eavesdroppers weren't even silhouettes against the black sky. They were invisible.

"If keeping you alive means losing you, then that's better than having you die again," Cadence said, mindful of her volume. "I know it's cheese, but not to me."

At this, Nick decided his mute friend would probably make a much better conversational companion. He stood and nearly tripped over his own feet just to join Acotactac on the other side of the cage.

Cadence snickered. "You're still so clumsy."

The rest of the flight was mostly uneventful, some small inquiries about whether another passenger felt cold or not. Otherwise, it was silent until Cadence announced she thought they were back in Plattsville. To this, Nick peered over the ledge, looking for landmarks that were so familiar that even the black of night might not be able to hide them all.

"Why are we going this way," Nick asked, realizing perhaps all his supernatural vision had not fully left him. He could see, he thought, the edge of a familiar forest. "This is the way to the Taichomée, isn't it."

Natalie approached, took a better look and huffed agreement. Even now, as the dragon flew closer to the ground, even Cadence could see the trees.

"Hey," Cadence screamed up to What. "We don't want to go to the forest."

"It's all forest," What replied quickly between note playing. "Boss says to take you to the hole in ground."

"Not a chance," Cadence complained. "We're going to the bunker, take us to the bunker."

"The chief said hole in the ground," What replied. "We're going to the hole in ground."

"You take us where we want to go, or we'll walk there on our own and make sure the boss knows you betrayed us," Cadence said. "How many more deals will you get then? Think the wolf population will have a desire to feed your bargains?"

The dragon slowed. Air was still except for the whispering lull of the ash beast's wings.

"Where," What finally asked.

"Fly low," Cadence said and pointed back the direction they had flown in from. "We'll tell you when we see something familiar."

Nothing looked familiar. It was all buried in growth. She watched for green or gold eyes, but the town, it seemed, had been derived of even that.

She spotted what she believed was her farm, now twisted with the black of what were most likely trash trees.

She'd gone on a mission once or twice before, seen still towns, but this unsettled her most of all. Even her most precious of memories were now shattered. She'd at least thought she'd have seen familiar framework for nostalgia, but twenty-five years had built a forest over all. For a moment she thought she had seen the stone structure of a mausoleum, but she couldn't be sure.

"There," Nick finally said, pointing down.

Cadence looked. "I don't see anything," she said. "But I guess that's your thing, not mine."

"Wow," Nick replied. "You said that and the demons didn't come screaming out of you."

"Over there," Cadence ordered to What.

The cage hovered over a grove of tall overgrowth. The cage floor disappeared from beneath them, surprising a sleeping Acotactac. The three friends slid to the ground atop a soft hill of ash and hushed giggling. Once they were safely on the ground, What's dragon absorbed the ash from the ground.

"Boss says your transportation back has already been arranged," What called down between notes of playing. Then he was gone, carried away by the set of heavy wings and fading flute music.

Cadence shed her coat, revealing what remained of her magnetic suit. It was mostly a chest plate now that barely held enough ammo for a single fight. Her arsenal had reduced itself to an old, tarnished Glock, an updated rifle and the two shotguns at her side. She hoisted her rifle, rubbed her shoulder and took her first step with a limp, but then carried herself as though she were without injury. Nick was now foolishly admiring her as he had done many times before.

"Stay close," she said, killing the admiration. "You're not exactly armed to the teeth anymore."

Nick drew his own handguns in defiance.

Acotactac rustled softly behind Nick. Now, in this moment, he missed the advantage that blood could have provided in this situation.

Cadence peered through her night scope and studied the area. "Unbelievable," she finally said, scanning her green eye over a field of black. She stepped into the trees. Nick and Acotactac followed for several paces, until they found themselves standing at a weathered door, rusted and flaking. Ivy grew over it.

"Think it works," Nick asked.

"If the generators still work, maybe," Cadence said. "I assume. If they're inside, maybe they got it working."

She holstered her rifle and asked Acotactac to hold a small flashlight on the area. She tore at the vines and leaves that webbed the door. It had turned brown. She began prodding at the ground, pulling long grass and heavy ivy out of her way.

Nick followed her lead and accepted a duel with an angry thistle. He found the ceramic pot first. Other than a thick coat of dirt, it was still fairly pristine, unlike the rusted door. Whatever tried to live inside the pot was mostly dead now. Cadence drew a knife and began stabbing the dirt out.

Something white finally caught her eye, and Acotactac caught it before it could fall and get hidden in the unkempt ground clutter.

"I can't believe it didn't rust," Nick said, taking a white key from their silent ally's fingers and eventually holding it out to Cadence.

"It's aluminum," Cadence said. "It doesn't rust."

He was about to toss the flower pot away.

"Hey," Cadence scowled. "Don't break that! That's from our first real date out of this underground hell-hole."

Nick paused and investigated the flower pot. "I'd almost forgotten," Nick said.

"Yeah," Cadence said. "Well, we bought a flowerpot and reburied the key in it. You don't have much more memorable dates than that."

"I remember the moon was full," Nick said.

Cadence snapped a gun cleaning brush from within her coat and ran it over the key a few times, peeling away some of the white dust that had appeared.

She slid the key into the lock.

"The question is, if everything else still works, or if we walk to the watering hole afterall," she said. She pulled out a small aerosol can. "I hope this works or I brought it for nothing." She sprayed the deadbolt then the edges of the frame. She kicked the door and brown, rust scales fell.

She slid the key into the deadbolt. It turned, but then nothing else happened.

Nick kicked the door, and it swung open revealing the steel secondary door, which was much more preserved than the exterior. The entry way beeped, and a keyboard appeared.

"Password," the door seemed to shout.

"Let's hurry this up," Nick said. "I'm sure if there are any wolves out there, they all heard that."

Acotactac nodded agreement.

Natalie too seemed a bit on edge now, even for a wolf.

Cadence approached the keyboard and typed in the last password she could remember for the place, M-e-a-d-e.

The steel door dropped straight into the ground, making an even louder noise than Nick remembered it making.

They stepped into the dark garage, where Cadence entered the code to reseal the place. The door was a little slower upon closing. It moaned, as if in pain.

Nick searched for a light switch, while Cadence looked through her scope. One light in the entire strip of bulbs sprinkled with power until a steady staff revealed the empty garage and elevator entrance.

"Have you seen anything as beautiful as that," Nick asked, taking in the majestic view of outdated ballast and white tube.

"Ask me that again if the shower works," she replied.

Cadence called the elevator, and Nick wondered out loud if two-and-a-half decades had been kind to the elevator mechanics. It whined its way up the unseen shaft, and the doors rolled mostly open.

Despite their reservations about its maintenance, all four entered the small box and allowed it to lower them once again into the solitude of the bunker. As it descended, Cadence snickered before recalling the story behind the hole in the ceiling. Nick enjoyed the story as well, once she announced why she was so humored.

The doors opened. The sounds of whistles told them to hug against the side walls. They would never forget this training. The orbits sank into the back wall of the elevator and pulled back.

"You mean that still works," Amber cried.

"Seems to have," Cadence replied.

"We took the river," Amber complained.

"We had a boat," a familiar, old voice called from the kitchen. Jasper had his back to the group and was working on something at the counter. His voice sounded older. His hair had thinned into small white threads over a pink scalp with brown continents of age and centuries of sun finally catching up.

"We *took* the *river*," Amber screamed.

"Well, but" the voice said back. "It was a perfectly good boat."

"Welcome home," Amber said, now glaring. A leather patch adorned the side of her face. It had been sewn into her skin not long after they arrived at the island. Her blonde hair now held streaks of white. It was pulled back as it had been so many years ago. "Hungry?"

"We made salad," Jasper announced as he emerged from the kitchen area with a plate in one hand; the other hand bore his weight on his trusted cane much more than it had before. Had he been injured? The lines on his face had grown deeper too, his cheeks hollower.

Nick and Cadence practically raced each other to the settings on the dining table. Cadence paused. She hadn't seated herself at a proper dinner table in such luxury in ages. She decided to respect the moment more properly. She dropped her weaponry and armor on the floor at the side of her chair, then watched Amber recoil her steel whips from the elevator and tuck them beneath the folds of Wolf's Breath.

Their eyes met a moment, and Cadence felt as though she had committed a crime in doing so.

"It's clean," Cadence said making note of the lack of decay in the room.

"You remember how boring it got in here," Amber replied. "We were even thinking of clearing the yard so we could mow the lawn soon."

"How long have you been here," Nick asked, dropping in front of a plate of fresh tomatoes and then inquired about them without asking.

"The garden," Amber explained. "And a little seed hunting."

"Is anyone else here," Cadence asked.

"Should there be," Amber asked back.

"She's asking about Cracey," Jasper said. He dropped a slab of pink and furry meat in front of Natalie, who now sat at the head of the table. She quickly began gnawing at her food. "Do you really think she could have survived out here?"

The room fell awkward until Nick requested a slice of Natalie's meal.

"Are you eating blood again," Amber asked.

"He spits it out," Cadence replied.

"Mind if I answer for my own self," Nick snapped. "I'm still capable of doing that, aren't I?"

"You tell me," Cadence answered.

"I see you're talking to each other again," Jasper joined in. "How's that chest of yours, Nick? Still hurt?"

Cadence slammed down her utensils and picked up her plate. "I assume the bedrooms are still in good condition?"

"Single or double bed," Jasper asked.

She stood.

"Sit," Jasper ordered, his voice almost monstrous, not human.

Cadence, might have protested, stared Jasper down, but the old man was better at it, and he didn't even have to look at her to win the contest. She knew his age was trying him now. It came quickly upon him since his own fast had mostly cleansed him, and she knew he desired to see the rogue fall before he should die. Cadence sat.

Jasper reached to the side of his seat and drew up a blue mask with a garden hose attached to it. He held it over his face and drank in a few long breaths.

"What is this," Cadence asked.

"It's a toilet plunger with a garden hose," Jasper replied. "Obviously, I'm sniffing poo."

"Don't be dumb," Cadence reprimanded. "You a liah."

"Then use your head." Jasper replied. He breathed in a couple of more drafts. "This is what old looks like. Seems age is finally catching up. You know what I'm talking about. Is it still easy dating a teenager after 25 years." He slapped the table. "I thought you two were smarter. Did you stop to think what you were going to do if that garage door didn't open for you? You've forgotten who you are."

"That happens when you get locked in a basement for the rest of your life," Nick replied.

"You think I liked the close quarters," Cadence snapped. "I was there too."

"Waah," Jasper said. "Twenty-some years having to do things you don't want to. How would it be?"

"And what have you been doing," Cadence asked. "I haven't seen any reports from you in, what, two years?"

Jasper dropped his mask back to his side and turned his attention to his salad. He bit into a sliced tomato and grimaced. He gnawed at it anyway. "Does spitting it out help," he asked through everything in his mouth.

"It's tempting to swallow," Nick replied. "I find it's easier with canned meat."

"That's disgusting," Jasper replied. "I thought you meant real meat."

Acotactac rapped her knuckles against the table.

Jasper rapped his knuckles against the table back at her and then against his plate, then his silverware, even a leaf of lettuce.

Acotactac glared.

"All right," Jasper acknowledged. "Now's as good a time as any I suppose." He stood and returned to the kitchen area. He dropped his food in a plastic box with the words *for mulch* written in black ink across it. "Many years back, I heard an interesting story. One of those things you brush off because you find no use for it, nor sense.

"A young farmer's son is working his father's field when he spies a young woman stumbling through the tall grass," Jasper began telling.

"Farmer's son," Cadence blurted. "Why does that sound familiar? Wait a minute! You don't mean What's farmer's son, do you? His treasure?"

"The same," Jasper said.

"I thought that was my treasure," Cadence scowled.

"I convinced him to tell me," Jasper said. "May I continue?"

"By all means," Cadence said. "Tell us about my pound of flesh you stole." Cadence raised her sleeve to show the large pit in her arm.

"Psshh," Jasper blew. "I've seen worse. Remember that time, Nick, when you had claws in your chest?"

Acotactac threw a cucumber slice at Jasper. He didn't catch it.

"Anyway," Jasper continued, wiping his face where the cucumber had struck. "The farmer's son spots this girl stumbling through his field, and faints. So, he rushes to her and finds her on the brink of death. Kind of like that one time I rescued you from the dog claws in your chest, Nick."

"You put them there in the first place," Cadence screamed.

"Why you getting nasty," Jasper asked, then continued his story. "He took her away and hid her in a nearby shack and nursed her back to life.

"Secretly, the boy had fallen in love with her. On the day she prepared to leave his care, he confessed that love to her. She broke into tears and told him she could not love him until she saved her brother. She told him of a story—"

"Oh geez," Cadence interrupted. "A story within a story? Really? You can't just simplify this?"

"We'll go faster if you stop interrupting," Amber replied rather callously.

"I'm sorry," Cadence replied, matching Amber's coldness.

Amber turned and disappeared down the hall.

"I know you're throwing up," Cadence yelled after her. "You're not fooling anyone. It's that virus Thomas gave you when he fed on you."

"Yeah, that's what it is," Jasper laughed. "You're daft aren't you? Let's see how well you hold up when you're sick."

Cadence thought about apologizing, but decided not to. "Finish the story."

"She told him of a story," Jasper backtracked in frustration, trying to ignore Cadence. "She and her family had been traveling to a distant kingdom to meet her brother's future bride, for they were royalty, and her prince-brother could only marry a princess. However, along the way, a group of bandits, attacked them," Jasper suddenly stopped and glared down upon Nick. "I'm sorry you're bored. Wake up!" He threw a wooden spoon across the kitchen counter and struck Nick in the head.

Nick apologized for letting his eyelids grow heavy.

"Her parents were killed," Jasper continued. "She was left for dead, and her brother was stuffed into an urn, along with all of his riches, and was carried away by thieves. She could not think about loving anyone until her brother was saved."

Jasper returned to the table with a half-gallon carton of ice cream and failed to offer any to his ungrateful companions.

"The farmer's son wanted to show his love for the woman even more now," he continued. "And he vowed to help her find her brother so the woman could feel free to move on with her life."

Jasper stopped a moment trying to chisel out a mouthful of his ice cream, bending his spoon a time or two.

"Is that Rocky Road," Cadence asked. She might have drooled; her lips hadn't done it in so long, she couldn't remember what it felt like.

Jasper pulled the tub protectively into his chest and continued to chisel away at the hard cream.

"And so," he finally started again. "They searched three years before they found him, still sealed in an urn, opened only to drop food in to him. He and his urn had been locked away in the house of a money lender who was under the employ of the bandit gang that had killed the princess's family and stolen her brother. One night the farmer's son and the girl snuck into the money lender's home.

"The young farmer tried to free the brother from the urn, but the brother had another plan. He desired to find his bride, but he was afraid if he disappeared that the bandits would seek him out before he could reclaim his dowry. He promised the farmer's son half of his kingdom in dowry for his sister if he promised to help.

"The young farmer vowed to find the prince's bride, but the brother said only he knew how to sneak into her prison tower—because being in the urn allowed him to overhear many conversations, including how to find and save his bride. He suggested that the farmer's son take his place in the urn until he could save his bride from the tower. You see, every day the money lender would tap the urn to mock the trapped prince. If the prince inside the urn didn't knock back, instead of food, the lender would pour in a saucer of hot oil."

"Wait a minute," Cadence asked. "They only opened it to feed him?"

"Was that part over your head," Jasper asked. "Here, I'll draw the story in pictures for you."

"I don't need pictures?"

"Then why are you interrupting?"

"He was in an urn," Cadence asked.

"Yes."

"And they only opened it to throw food in?"

"Yes! Again!"

"After more than three years? Why didn't he drown in his own bathroom?"

Jasper groaned. "Maybe there was a hole in the bottom."

"He must have had good aim," Nick said.

He and Cadence broke out into laughter.

"Fine," Jasper, bit out. "It was a magic urn."

"Oooh," Cadence said. "A magic poopoo urn. I've always wanted a magic poo—"

This time the cucumber slice hit Cadence, and Acotactac readied an entire handful for future bombardment.

"Ha! That's what you get," Jasper cooed. Then took another huff on his oxygen mask before starting into his story again. "The young farmer's son agreed to help, freeing the prince from his pythos coffin.

"No sooner had the young farmer made the vow, than the prince was freed, but the farmer's son was instantly swallowed by the urn. The prince and princess fled, laughing at the foolishness of the naive, love-struck boy. The two never returned, for the prince was not a prince, and the princess was not a princess. They were, in fact, a husband and wife who had once robbed a powerful being, a being who dealt out an eternal curse upon anyone who dared steal from him. It was the curse of giving back to others. It was a curse of servitude as djinn.

"The woman, having been freed from her own curse first, had helped trick the innocent farmboy into taking her companion's place and becoming the djinn himself. Here, the farmboy would stay until he should be freed."

"Please tell me, we didn't come all this way to hear you tell us you believe in genies," Nick said.

"You wanted to know what we've been working on," Jasper asked, and stuffed a mouthful of chocolate and marshmallow into his face. "Do you want to know or not? My ice cream's going to get soft."

This time Cadence apologized.

Jasper started again. "Josh's father—"

"Josh's father was a traitor, like his mother," Cadence continued to complain.

"Josh's father was no traitor," Jasper returned sharply, stood and then fumbled for his mask. "They're misconceptions like that, which kept him from ever finding solace among his own kind and people who should have been his friends. He and Dustin's father single-handedly brought you an army when you needed one. Don't devalue that."

"Our army died," Cadence replied.

"Not because of Stan Revlon," Jasper explained. "But because the rogue was smarter than you. He knew everything about you. He was in Josh's head. Josh was a wolf, and no one stopped to think that the rogue could connect to him."

"But Josh wasn't awake," Cadence said. "And Speatsh said the heir had to be awake to create the link."

"Speatsh was wrong," Jasper said. "The rogue's always held a link. That's why you never succeeded. That's why he was always one step ahead of you."

"Like the tunnel," Amber said.

"What tunnel," Cadence asked.

"You were in it the night Josh died," Amber explained. "It's how we escaped. Josh was in it too, and that's how the wolves knew where we'd exit."

"Oh, yeah. Sorry. I forgot," Cadence said. She suddenly remembered the sound of slaughter and a long night of fleeing. She still wasn't sure how they made it to the cemetery. Perhaps it was because the rogue was playing with them.

"But here's the good news," Jasper cut in. "I know the rogue, and I know he hasn't won. In the last hours of our fight, I thought about What's words in the bunker that day and recalled the story of the young farmer."

"Why," Cadence asked.

"Because it suddenly climbed up the ladder of importance of remembering, along with other rumors we hear, such as magical carriages that might interest the rogue," Jasper replied.

"Please tell me that hunters aren't dying while rebelling against the rogue, while you're chasing genies in bottles," Cadence ridiculed.

"There are no hunters fighting the rogue," Jasper replied. He took a deep breath on his toilet plunger mask. "We've been helping Stan. Of course we had to find him first."

"Hold on," Cadence replied, angrier that her plate was empty than she was at Jasper's revelation. "I've been sending hunters out on false missions?"

"Sorry," Jasper said. "We couldn't risk you blabbing."

Nick laughed.

"I wouldn't laugh too much," Jasper said. He dropped his mask once more. "We found Stan in hiding. It took us three years after Josh died, but we managed to find him in some kind of human preserve."

"You mean a farm," Nick asked.

"No," Jasper said. "Believe it or not, some wolves don't stand with the rogue. In fact, many wolves are devoted to protecting hunters and humans, it was among one of these factions of wolves that we found him."

"At least he still has Eric," Cadence asked.

"No," Jasper replied. "Unfortunately, that's not true anymore."

Cadence took a moment to process the news.

"Umm," she finally said. "We seem to be pretty loose with talking in front of our leak here."

"Wait, what," Nick asked upon realizing Cadence was referring to him.

"I can fight any one creature from getting into my head," Jasper explained. "But they all stopped trying to get in years ago. Natalie proved early on to be adept at not only blocking out thought, but getting into other wolves' heads. They stayed out of hers, I imagine, because they feared she'd use it against them. Her mind's not blocked, just, they don't want her knowing anything in their heads either. It was an unintentional lesson on my part, but she's a danger to them. The rogue knows we're still out here, and he knows were up to something, but he's not willing to try Natalie to find out. She's dangerous to locating him."

"How do you know they're not in there," Cadence asked. "Josh didn't know."

"Because Josh didn't have Natalie's perception." Jasper then turned to Nick. "She's known for some time. In fact, she's quite privy to about everything we've hidden from the rest of you." He patted Nick on the hand in strange apology. "However, you don't have that ability. Eric—well, we don't have to get into that topic. But you were a liability, Nick. You were open and could have destroyed us.

"We had two choices to protect ourselves from the rogue: hide you from anything that could help the rogue identify our location and plans, or kill you. Most thought we should kill you. I thought setting you on a cruise ship into the ocean would be humane. Aggon suggested we hide you in the open with everyone else on the island until you weakened the link," his face drew cold just now, "And you should know better anyway than toying with meat of any kind, even if it is canned. Your link is not gone, but it's so quiet that anyone wanting into your head will have to be looking for it. Your mind's not blocked, it's just sitting quietly on the back row. It's not the best way to block out the rogue, but it's something. I thought I could help you learn to do on your own, but your mind—well—has a mind of its own. I blocked you as long as I could, but I couldn't do that forever. I was needed elsewhere. So we had to hide yours in other ways.

"Anyway, even if the rogue were listening to you now, he couldn't get here fast enough to affect our plan in a way that would save him. We've secured the underground entrance. Alarms will let us know when someone comes near that back way."

"Then tell us what you've been doing," Cadence asked, seething that she had been tricked all this time.

"After we found Stan," Jasper continued. "We sent him out to do what he did best, find things."

"Alone," Nick asked.

"Aggon accompanies him," Jasper said.

"You sent Stan to find the farmer's son," Cadence suggested.

Jasper answered with a sly smile.

"Did you find him," Cadence asked.

"No," Jasper replied. "We did come across a story of a heart-broken genie, trapped inside an urn through trickery. The story is that he refused to work. Did you know that a genie who refuses to serve, dies. We also learned that there are only three ways for the curse to be broken: get someone to take your place; gain forgiveness from the being that cursed you in the first place; gain another's trust to free you."

"Or you could refuse the work," Nick asked.

Jasper nodded. "Right. So, no farmer's son. That tale is dead."

"Who knew genies could be so suicidal," Cadence joked.

"Of course, you understand why a genie is rare then," Jasper explained. He stood once more with a near-full carton of ice cream and made his way around the table towards Nick's seat. "Whether the genie we heard of was the farmer's son, who knows? And then it hit us."

Jasper held the ice cream carton to Nick. "Want some?"

Nick reached for the carton with such eagerness that he couldn't possibly have thought that Jasper's next move would be to suddenly slam the hard container against the side of his head. Nick fell over in his chair, caught suddenly by Acotactac who glared at Jasper.

Cadence too was on her feet.

Natalie was strangely uninterested.

"That's about as much as the rogue knows anyway," Jasper said. He helped settle Nick's unconscious head against the dining table.

"The rogue knows about the genie," Cadence asked.

"It's not news. A lot of us old timers heard the stories," Jasper replied. "It's always been a daydream for human and wolf alike, kind of like looking for that one briefcase with a million dollars that someone left on the street." The old man moved into the living room and past the red couch, which was now weathered, torn, brown. Jasper opened a cabinet and dug inside.

"So, if he finds this farmboy," Cadence started to ask.

"Good luck," Jasper interrupted. "We've searched a long time for the boy in the story and came up empty handed, except for a story of a djinn who refused to grant wishes, and, as I said, that's death for a djinn."

"So what you're saying is that you wasted our resources on a fairy tale," Cadence said.

Amber huffed. Jasper smirked.

"You should know me better than that," Jasper said. "So I thought, what about the girl?"

"What girl," Cadence asked.

"The girl who helped trick the farmer's son into releasing her husband," Jasper stopped a moment to let Cadence catch on. "Surely, you can figure this one out! If she was cursed, and she was out, who had taken her place? If the farmboy took the place of the husband djinn, who took the place of the wife?"

"That's a lot to assume," Cadence replied, embarrassed at her slow realization. "She could have been forgiven or wished out."

"Our thoughts too, but we looked anyway," Jasper said. "And we found her, or Stan found her."

By now, Jasper had returned to the table with a large plastic bag. He opened it and removed a black pouch and a book. Cadence recognized the book at once, it was the same she had seen in the bunker the night they had fought Barbara.

"What's book gave us information we already knew," Jasper said. "But then he was kind enough to draw us some maps, which really only told us that she wasn't in the U.S."

"So it was an easy search is what you're saying," Cadence asked.

"It wasn't at first, but then that behemoth of a gravedigger kept crying because the person who told him to ask about pants would never get his answer for one of his three questions from the oracle.

"It took me a while to realize that pants meant jeans, because he didn't understand the word djinn," Jasper stopped to take a breath from his plunger. "Once I convinced him to tell me what the answer was, we were able to take What's book and his maps and at least get to the right continent. Then it was just a matter of following history, common sense and a few hunches."

Jasper set the book aside and opened the cloth envelope. He withdrew a red-paper, gift cracker. It was a simple wrapping: no bows, no tinsel, no glossy sheen, just paper.

"You're telling me, you found a genie wrapped in a Christmas present," Cadence asked.

"The genie can change the appearance of what it hides in. Those who don't wish to be found, perhaps tired djinn or djinn who wish to be left to their woes, might bury themselves. Some might wish to help others and make themselves easily found. When we found this one, she was in a Chinese puzzle box. Luckily for us, we had someone who had developed a little bit of respect for Chinese puzzles."

Amber set her wooden, vampire-killing knife on the table.

"We found her in a museum of sort in Dingcun, China," Jasper said presenting the cracker in front of him like some fragile trophy. "She wasn't so nice at first."

"Of course you did, and of course she wasn't," Cadence replied and laughed at the incredible idea.

"We explained the situation with the djinn and came to an arrangement," Jasper explained. "After a lot of work and thought, there are two wishes left. You will be required for one of those wishes."

"What about the third wish," Cadence asked.

"This is the third wish," Jasper said.

"I thought you got three wishes," Cadence replied.

"Look who's been reading her genie text books," Jasper grinned. "You do get three, but I got us a freebie."

"How?"

"Have you met Jasper," Amber asked, breaking her silence.

"I have," Jasper said.

"You tricked one out of her, didn't you," Cadence asked.

Jasper's face demonstrated that he was rather pleased with himself.

"Alright. What's the third wish then?"

"It's a surprise," Jasper said. "But I've given my word, that it will be the last wish she has to grant, or I will take her place."

"You," Cadence suddenly realized. "Become the djinn? Oh, you a liah!"

"Hopefully, we'll never know," Jasper said, then he suddenly grabbed the ends of the red cracker and broke it open.

Upon the cracker popping, she leapt from inside the wrapper and landed a full-sized person in the center of the dining table. She looked over the group, finally setting her attention on Amber. What appeared to be a glowing, evening gown gradually changed into what Amber was wearing, including the leather patch over the side of her face. The Djinn's Rapunzel-length hair fell back into braids, each braid a different color, and disappeared back into the broken cracker.

"Hello again, Amber," she greeted.

Amber nodded.

The djinn turned to Cadence, and suddenly her clothing became that of Cadence's flimsy magnetic breastplate. "Cadence."

As she greeted Acotactac, her clothing changed once more. They changed again as she looked down upon Nick. When her eyes eventually fell on Natalie, her body spurred a black quill mane and fur coat.

"I've learned not to trust those who promise my freedom," the djinn said. "Do not fail me." She looked sharply to Jasper and took upon his suit. "Are you ready to take my place?"

"Not quite," Jasper said. "Amber?"

Amber left the group a moment and returned with a dirty folder. She opened it and set it on the table. Some strange, creased pages filled it.

"When we were in the museum, before the rogue attacked us, Josh seemed to think he might have known something about the carriage," Amber said. "Our mission is two-fold. We need to get him to finish his thought process, and we need to find this carriage if it exists."

"Why," Cadence asked. "The rogue's already destroyed the world."

"So you can save Josh," Amber replied.

"So wish him back already," Cadence said. "As much as I'd like to see him again, though I can't say what good it will do us at this point."

"Contradictory to popular idiocy," Jasper replied in a rather impatient tone. "Djinn don't grant impulsive wishes. They are masters of time, who can alter an outcome to bring a person's desire into reality."

"Shoot me," Cadence requested. "Just put me out of my misery now."

"I will open the fabric of time and give you a thread to bring about this desire," the djinn explained. "What you do with that thread to achieve your desire is up to you. Shoot yourself if you must. But if you want to retrieve your friend, you must get him. All I can do is mediate your travel unless I were free. That is my part in the wish." She glanced to Jasper, then around the room, changing her appearance as she glanced over each person until her eyes set upon Cadence once more.

"Better idea," The djinn and Cadence said in unison. "Send us back to when the rogue was born. I'll shoot him, and we'll live happily ever after."

By the end of the request, Cadence was glaring.

"You want your life back," the djinn asked.

"I would like a life again, yes," Cadence growled.

The djinn smiled. "And how would your being or relationships evolve without this influence of the one you call the rogue," the djinn grabbed a fistful of air and pulled up. Nick's limp body drew up from his chair by his shoulder. He drew towards her, and she placed her hand on his chest. He winced, cried in pain even, and then set gently back into his chair once more.

"You could be his wife again and a mother," the djinn explained. "But when will you see him as such if there's no wolf to draw his sacrifice for you?"

"There could be another way," Cadence said.

"No," the djinn replied. "I've seen all ways, and I know."

Cadence wanted to dispute the matter.

One of the djinn's braids reached towards Cadence and flared open. One strand of hair drew apart from the rest.

"There are many ways a thread can stitch through time," the djinn explained. The hair began to rebraid itself. "And many ways for other threads that cross it to give it strength, or break it. Josh is one of those threads. The carriage is another. The rogue is yet a third, and there are many more that you can't see." With each example, a new strand of hair removed from the braid, floated before Cadence and wove out many patterns before her. "There are more threads than I desire to see, but I have seen them. I can count enough of them to find your solution. I have studied the possibilities of your timelines for an eternity in years, as you understand them, and I have decided again that it will take several threads to seam the desired tapestry that will save you and the ones you love."

Suddenly, all of her hair unraveled above her head, each strand glowing with some form of bright color that had once been in braid. "I am a keeper of time and know how each thread falls to create history. Rearrange a single thread thus, and your history and chance at a better today are over."

Three strands of hair separated themselves from the unraveled explosion above her head. They broke away from each other and now reached towards Nick, Cadence and Acotactac. "My calculations will allow you to walk among your fallen comrades once more and aid them, but remember that confusion can interfere with a fight. Knowing who you are, may inhibit your allies and your former selves' actions."

"What good are we then," Cadence asked.

"Present options to save Josh where you know he will fail," the djinn replied. "But don't interfere in what you know he will overcome. In fact, it is best that some of you don't know the others' roles so that the rogue can't discover them, even if he discovers you. Your appearances will change, you'll understand why when you get there. You three will have new lives, be new people."

The djinn then looked towards Amber. Amber glared at Jasper. Jasper smacked a fist against the table.

"We're not debating this again," Jasper yelled, and put his face back into his mask, a little longer than he had before.

"Don't seek each other out," the djinn lectured. "Do not undermine my calculations, or your agenda could unravel. Although this decision is yours, there is a greater threat to revealing yourselves:

it could show this plan to the rogue. This must not happen or I could be used against you."

The djinn once more took on the appearance of Nick's clothing as she peered upon him.

"If this creature named Nick learns of this sneak attack, your enemy may decide to use his resources to find me too. I have seen your fall if he does." She leaned gently towards Nick. "This one presents the greatest danger of all, for your rogue can still reach his mind, but he is necessary to your goal—and for this, he must be hidden more. For he is a truly strong ally and has prepared himself even better."

"What are you suggesting," Cadence asked.

"She's suggesting how to win the old world back," Jasper said. "But this is the only way. We have to help Josh find that carriage before the rogue can."

"Maybe you should have searched for the carriage instead of this genie," Cadence grumbled.

"We tried," Jasper replied.

"Maybe you should have wished to find the carriage or to kill the person who built it in the first place," Cadence screeched.

"And who says not having a carriage will have prevented this war," Jasper asked. "The existence of a carriage is a way to win. What you're not realizing is that Josh may be all we need. Save Josh, we could find the carriage and end this war, maybe kill the rogue. It's the only way that we can accomplish all of these things."

"And you know all of this," Cadence asked.

"No, but she's seen it," Jasper replied. "And I believe her. Will you believe me one last time."

"Like you've never lied before," Cadence fired back.

Jasper's face suddenly frowned. He took in a long drag from his mask.

"You know I didn't mean it," Cadence said, nearly frowning as much as Jasper. "You know I didn't mean it."

"The Jasper more than twenty years ago would have agreed with you," Jasper replied. "But those scruples have done enough damage."

"I'm sorry," Cadence said.

"Besides," Jasper added. "Even if I'd wanted to, the wishes weren't mine to make."

"Who made them? And what were the first two wishes?"

"Truthfully," Jasper said. "I don't know."

"How is that possible?"

"Again, I don't know," Jasper said. "All I know is when we found her, she said I had been given voice to execute the last wish. I didn't like that plan. I didn't know that plan, so I got another wish out of her, say I tricked her if you like. But I don't know all of it, not entirely."

"Well I know how it works," Cadence tried to enlighten. "Use one of those wishes to get Josh and the other to get the carriage or to end this war."

"What did I just say?" Jasper shook his head. "I spent most of my life imprisoning others to my will and destroying lives. If I make a selfish final wish, she must hide again for someone to find her. Could you live knowing you sentenced a person to an eternity of slavery? Isn't that what Josh fought against?"

"You and your scruples, old man," Cadence complained. "You can have anything with that wish, and this is what you want—"

"Don't tempt me!" For this, Jasper and the djinn shouted in unison. "You think this is easy on me? That there aren't lives I wouldn't go back and save, that deserve to be saved every bit as much as Josh's or this djinn? Josh is your kin, not mine! I don't have that luxury to choose someone else over him. Josh may know how to stop this once and always. After this wish is made, I need to set her free and I'm not sure I'll have the strength to do that. So can we please stop talking about hypothetical wishes that would serve only your happiness right now?"

Acotactac was first to Jasper's side as he toppled sideways out of breath. Amber was close behind with the mask, but it was Cadence who had found herself clasping his hand and apologizing.

"I know," Jasper said, then patted Cadence's hand back with his bony white fingers of purple spots and suffocating veins. "I've been overcoming this temptation for two years as we've been planning with the djinn. And for two years, I've been trying to see the bigger picture and help develop who should play roles in this wish. Personally, I'd like to spend another year working out the kinks with my new magical friend, but I'm not stupid. I'm cleansed and old, as I should be. My body was ready to die before I became wolf, now I'm fasted and it's been hundreds of years longer than I should have lived. I have to be able to free her. I can't prolong it anymore."

Cadence couldn't find her voice. Was Jasper's life waning? How had the time flown? They were all old. Brictain's head was gray, thin. Amber's head had begun to carry flock. How much of her own silver had Cadence learned to ignore in the filthy mirror in her drab office.

"It's time for you to get Josh back, and maybe he'll get that carriage for us," Jasper said. "A lot of people need you to be ready now. I need you. I've done my part, and I'll keep doing it until it's time for me to finish it properly. Give me this one, last, good thing I can do in this world of evil I've helped build. Please."

"I can do that," Cadence said, finally understanding that her part in this wish was her old friend's last fight to preserve that humanity that he had nearly forgotten so many years ago.

"Let us begin then," the djinn said.

"Wait," Cadence asked. "Will you tell us who made the first wishes?"

"That is not for me to say," the djinn replied.

"The wish is officially presented," Jasper said, his voice strained now with an emotion that the others hadn't heard before. "As we have worked together to plan, as well as according to your judgment."

"And you will keep your word to free me," the djinn asked.

Jasper nodded. "After this wish is executed."

"Or you could break your word," the djinn said.

Jasper appeared stung, as if caught in deception.

The djinn began to pet Nick's rich head of hair. "I will now cloud this one's mind. You are wolf, and your mind threatens this course of action. You must forget yourself. Your memories must be altered, and for this, your friend has suggested that we find a vessel that will help suppress them and protect your mind from other wolves. I will put you in a place where your own memories can be drowned out by severe and traumatic fresh ones. You will know agony unlike any you've known before—and you will become a mighty weapon because of it, one that will preserve many allies and your friend, the paladin. Constant and severe pain will be your ally to guard your mind. Any who enter your mind will feel the pain you endure and will desire to stay out. Don't give them an invitation to find reason to resist. Remain ignorant of who you are."

At this, the djinn lifted Nick's head, and a blue strand of her hair fell gently upon his forehead.

Nick's body came to life once more. He grabbed his head and screamed.

Although the others could not see it, Nick's insides burst with black pain. He cursed Jasper, then screamed as heat and tearing nerves thrust through his entire body. The djinn's glow diminished before him, and Nick's brain fell into burning blackness. For a while, he heard voices he knew asking if he was all right, but then he forgot them. It was as if his memories were folding up, locking away into depths that Nick couldn't recall. Something more powerful and hidden began to stir deep in his mind.

"No," Jasper's voice yelled from somewhere in the disappearing void of his own recognition. "That wasn't part of the plan!"

"Jasper," he heard Cadence scream, if he could have remembered who Cadence was. "Jasper? What's wrong with Jasper?"

The voices fell silent, and Nick's conscious and being disappeared into the shrinking galaxy of his mind until black swallowed him. He heard no sound nor friends. He no longer knew himself.

No anyone existed anymore. No self of Nick remained at all.

It was dark. Nick was aware of the emptiness and nothing. His brain hurt. Other memories began to open to him, memories that weren't his but now were. He didn't know them, but now he did. He had known them from the outside-looking-in, but now knew them from within. They were overwhelming. He felt himself become one with new illusions of a self he didn't fully know. They flooded his mind. He couldn't understand them all as they filled his brain as though a fire hose blasted them into his head all at once

Suddenly, he was sick. His stomach twisted. He couldn't breathe.

Then he could, and breathing was a stabbing torment across his back and chest, then into his shoulder. His shoulder! It was eating him alive.

His stomach untwisted, and he sat straight up spewing whatever he'd eaten earlier all in his lap. His arm burned and grew hotter still. He shrieked, tried to squash the pain of his shoulder by slamming his hand against whatever surface he was currently laying upon, but there was no hand to pound nor fist to make.

"Hold him down," a familiar and unfriendly voice hollered.

Suddenly, Acotactac was over him. She stroked Nick's head. Whatever happened, he was glad he was among friends. A familiar hand-carved moon dangled from around her neck towards him. He remembered making it for her. How he loved her. He felt stronger knowing she was there, caressing him through the pain he was now bearing. It had been so long since he'd felt such a loving touch, as he felt now with her finger tips raking gently over his scalp and through his hair. Something had gone wrong, he knew that much. What though, and why?

Like an electrical surge, the pain arced from his head to his right shoulder. He fell back, rather Speatsh shoved him to the ground. His entire body ruptured in one agonizing surge of hellish hurt and torment. Acotactac stroked his head. None of it helped, Nick screamed until he passed out.

He awoke, still in agony. Or maybe he dreamed. He wasn't sure anymore.

Trees? Familiar. Torches too. Taichomée village? How did he get here?

The pain!

He couldn't help it. He screamed more; he cried; he inhaled his own tears and choked on them until he could find strength to cough them out, nearly passing out in the attempts.

Speatsh appeared over him.

"Speatsh," Nick blurted.

"Good," Speatsh replied, he seemed happy about it in a way. "Do you know your name now?"

Nick croaked, finding himself thinking of only the pain and numbness that all ran through his body at the same time.

"Careful. You've been injured," Speatsh tried to comfort. "Just your name."

"Ick," Nick moaned. He knew his answer was weak. He could do better. Nick thought. The pain jumbled his brain as he tried once more to pull his name out. His agony was so deep that he couldn't even draw his name out to say it. Wait, a moment. Yes he could.

"It's," he forced out from between his feverish lips, and then drew in a long crackling breath with enough air to blurt out, "Bricktain."

20 ~ Stolen Identities

Harvey fled the bar, as gunfire also turned on him.

First, the djinn appeared before them on the table. Then they each grabbed a strand of hair; then there was—whatever it was—that took Cadence from the bunker to this new place. This new surrounding caused her stomach to twist and unwrench vomit that fell up—only it wasn't up, she was hanging upside down.

Cadence realized she dangled from a passenger seat. The person who should have been in the driver's seat was halfway out the windshield, sprawled onto the pavement—her body twisted in a way that certainly meant a broken spine, her blood pooled along her wounds and over the roof panel. Outside, over the pavement, more blood continued to drain from her mouth.

What had just happened?

Cadence reached for her knife, but found none. She remembered she had left it on the floor in the bunker for dining. Maybe she had something else on her. Perhaps there might have been if these had been her clothes, but she came to the realization that she didn't recognize anything she was wearing. She struggled to find something that could cut her seatbelt. Pressing the release button didn't work, neither did twisting in her seat—if anything, that made it more uncomfortable.

Cadence almost screamed for help, but her first thought fell to who or what might hear her. The sun glared down on the asphalt outside and reflected across shattered bits and blades of windshield. She tried not to let it blind her.

Her next resort was the glove compartment, which unloaded paper, a fat book and a tire gauge.

The broken driver suddenly lurched, screamed and spit up blood along with stomach contents. The driver pressed herself up from the gravel and untwisted her body. She took a moment to take in her surroundings, then drew in from the window. Eventually her eyes drew up to Cadence. The driver appeared stunned before suddenly screaming.

She felt over the various stains and fresh springs around her body and clothes that signified where blood had spilled out of her.

"It's okay," Cadence tried to assure.

The driver continued to cry, even seemed to speak a little before realizing that doing so spouted more blood from her mouth. She spit it out; spit out more; then reached into her mouth and discovered a mostly severed tongue.

"I think you bit your tongue off, lady," Cadence said.

The driver glared, but then seemed to understand Cadence's situation. She took a moment to locate a dashboard cigarette lighter, finding two of them in a console between the front seats of the RV. She punched them to heat up. Next, she reached up and tore the broken tip of her tongue out of her mouth. As if a piece of worthless garbage, she tossed it through the broken windshield.

Cadence watched the driver's cheek puff to the side. The driver bit down, apparently oblivious to the same popping and tearing sounds, which had erupted from her mouth, as Cadence heard. The driver spit out another large chunk of tongue.

Now, she searched her own surroundings and ended up finding a small blade upon the set of keys hanging from the ignition switch. It wasn't the sharpest or the fastest at slicing, but the driver used it nonetheless to shove it into her mouth and begin sawing. Occasionally, she stopped and spit out blood and smaller pieces of her shredded tongue.

The lighters erupted from the console in readiness. The driver spit once more, snatched up both electric lighters and held them coil-first into her mouth. As she bit down on the lighters, her tears flowed until she couldn't stand the pain anymore. Finally, she spit the lighters out and screamed, but couldn't make words.

"Acotactac, I presume," Cadence said. The bloodied driver seemed somewhat relieved, but then appeared confused. "A little help."

The new form of Acotactac quickly turned her attention upon Cadence's situation, trapped upside down in her passenger seat and pinned against gravity within her restraint. Acotactac soon cut her free of the seatbelt. Getting Cadence to her feet was a bit clumsy, but she came away with only a bump to her knee and an elbow in Acotactac's face, which wasn't entirely accidental.

"Who," Acotactac signed inquisitively.

"Cadence," Cadence replied.

The two friends wandered the roof of the flipped-over motor home and took in their surroundings. Acotactac seemed a little faster at it. She rattled the side door trying to open it, but it was stuck. She suddenly startled at the sound of Cadence kicking inside the hall of the motor home.

"No," Cadence shrieked. "This isn't even funny!"

She had torn down one of the interior doors, which revealed a bathroom in shambles. She then yanked open another small closet a little farther down the hall. "You've got to be kidding me," she continued to complain. Then she started kicking at anything that was in her means: walls, doors, cabinets, anything, and let slip a few obscenities in the process. Finally, she reached down into the closet, and her arms gobbled up a handful of overly pastel clothes. "You're not going to believe this!"

When Acotactac finally decided it was safe to approach her rampaging friend, Cadence's arms spewed a pile of decorative western clothing across the ceiling of the toppled motor home.

"This is some serious bullshuuuhhh!" Cadence caught her breath and tried to speak calmly, but instead screamed, "We're those stupid, moron rodeo queens we hated so much!"

Acotactac's face turned pale as she looked at the floor of hideous western-wear. She was about to kick the walls herself when the door to the vehicle burst open. The man, dressed in leather, stood on the other side and yelled something foul at Cadence and Acotactac. When the door fell on his head, he yelled the same thing at the door.

"Which one of you lunatic floozies just ran me over," the biker screeched. He hefted his big black boots, with their full-length zippers, over the head trim of the door frame and stomped down into the RV. Blood squirted from their leather seams.

"Unbelievable," the biker complained noticing the effect of his foot. "I did not come all this way to get run over by a bimbo driver." He stopped his march to shake his foot and make a realization. "I'm bleeding? Thanks a lot!" Suddenly, he looked scared and started searching his pockets. "Oh no," then he stopped and looked at his hands in their fingerless leather gloves. The cuffs of his denim shirt peeped through the sleeves of his black and worn leather jacket. "Where is it?" He began patting down his well-pocketed attire. "You better hope I didn't lose it!"

"Are you—," Cadence started to ask.

"Don't point," the biker said. "It's rude." And a loud pop burst from Cadence's forefinger. The biker was so fast. Cadence recoiled a hand with a finger now bent sideways in its socket.

Relief passed the biker's face, and he pulled a red Christmas cracker from a deep pocket at the side of his black leather BDUs. "Thank you," he said and kissed the Christmas present.

Cadence fought back her bent-finger scream and started looking for a weapon to beat the biker with.

"Jasper," she screamed through a gritted jaw.

The biker's face fell dead as he stood holding his wrapped djinn. For a moment, he looked like he was about to cry. "Is it you? Aco—uh. Who are you?"

"Cadence," she screamed.

"What are you doing here? Those aren't the bodies we planned—Crap," the biker finally realized. "That was your trigger finger." His face told everything as he sealed up his genie once more into his clothing. Just as quickly as he had pulled it from its socket, he returned Cadence's finger to its rightful position. "Might want to ice that."

An instant later he embraced Cadence, smothering her in brawn much larger than Jasper's old spindly frame. His face turned to Acotactac, well not Acotactac, but whomever Acotactac had come to possess. "Don't," he said suddenly standing back. He wiped his eyes dry. "He's difficult enough as it is to keep out of my head." Suddenly he stopped. "We found each other!"

"Geez," Cadence shrugged off the comment. "You sound like you haven't seen us less than five minutes ago."

"Did you just get here," Jasper asked, astonished, then chuckled. "I've been here over a couple of years."

"A couple of—what have you been doing here all that time," Cadence asked.

"You probably don't want to know," Jasper said. "Once I took care of my business and realized I shouldn't probably interfere too much, I thought, 'What the heck, might as well see the sights before everyone starts bleeding.'"

"You've been playing," Cadenced screeched.

"Yeah," Jasper said. "It's been fun." He suddenly spun Cadence around and patted her down before ripping out a driver's license from her back pocket. "Apparently, your name is Lisa," Jasper said after scanning the license photo. "She looks good on you."

Acotactac searched her own pockets and found a slim wallet. She held it out to the new Jasper. He searched it and discovered a debit card, a few small bills and another license.

"Your name is Winter," Jasper said. "So Cadence is Lisa and you, Acotactac, are Winter. Might as well get used to calling each other by these names, because we already have a Cadence and an Acotactac in this time."

"What's your name," Cadence, rather Lisa, asked.

The biker grimaced, noticing how still the highway was next to them. "Everyone out of the camper. We should probably get to work."

Jasper stepped out and then offered a hand to the others. "Anyone else in here," he asked. When no answer came, he joined his friends in the shoulder of the country-side road and surrounding fields. He checked the adjacent roadway. It was a narrow, straight stretch, clearly not Plattsville, and no one seemed to be traveling it from what he could see.

"What are you doing here, Jasper," Cadence-turned-Lisa asked.

"I stopped asking that," Jasper said. "When we last saw each other. I was ready to die. That's why we moved when we did."

"You did die," Lisa replied. "Right there in front of us, and then we were here," Lisa realized what she'd just said. Jasper caught it too.

"I did not know that part. I assume it was the only way to save me. I see what she did there." He patted the pocket with the djinn's cracker. "Suddenly, I'm feeling a little cautious to save my other wish for an in-case emergency."

"Why haven't you freed her," Lisa asked.

"She's been waiting this long," Jasper said.

"You might as well use it then," Lisa said.

"I told you to stop tempting me," Jasper replied.

"Well, if you're not going to use it, then keep your word and let her go!"

"I'm thinking about it," Jasper grimaced and then walked to the side of the RV.

"Haven't done something like this in a while," Jasper said, gripping a ledge of the roof to the RV. The vehicle quickly rolled back onto its tires.

"You've eaten," Lisa said.

"No," Jasper replied.

"I'm confused."

"So was I," Jasper explained. "Keys?"

Acotactac-turned-Winter, checked the pockets of her white, blood-stained jeans and threw Jasper the bloody set of keys with their small, useful blade. Jasper, started the RV, backed it up to a fallen motorcycle, that he lashed to the back wall. Lisa suggested simply leaving it; they didn't need it.

"No chances," he said climbing back into the camper and found Lisa and Winter seated on a couch before a small television screen rampant with sitcom.

"That works," he asked.

Neither answered.

"Suppose I'm driving."

"Sorry," Cadence said holding up her hand. "Finger injury."

Acotactac pointed to her empty and burned mouth.

The biker flounced himself into the driver seat. Then, as an afterthought, he searched his pockets and discovered a bill-fattened wallet on a chain. "You might want to have a look-see for any money sitting around."

A small bag of white crystals fell from his wallet.

"What is that," Lisa asked, jumping up from her couch, then regretted her painful decision.

"It's called income," Jasper said. "And we need it to get you armed up."

"Not that way," Lisa complained.

"All right," Jasper said and then concealed the wallet, "No need to start your morality march in here."

He tossed the crystals out the front of the windshield, then began to check every last pocket for anything that didn't need to attract the wrong attention from his traveling companions. He left the camper once more and returned to his bike, checked all the compartments, dropping all white powder, green grass and misty blue crystal he could find as well. He drew out several fat rolls of elastic-rolled cash and sealed them in a gallon-sized freezer bag.

"The last thing we need is jail getting in the way, Jasper," Lisa said as he returned to the motor home.

Again, Jasper retreated to the driver's seat. "Bean," he said. "Better call me Bean." he scowled.

Lisa bust up laughing. Winter smiled, but winced.

"No way, that's your name," Lisa cried. "You a liah!"

"You'd think I'd been something awful in my previous life," Bean-Jasper said.

"Well," Lisa replied. "Weren't you?"

The next portion of their history is rather inconsequential, mostly it was filled with complaining about certain pains that Winter and Lisa had received, most likely from their host bodies' causes of death prior to their possession. Bean assured them that they were healing. Winter's body had already even clotted over the many mortal wounds.

Bean was upset that the radio had so few channels. Lisa was more upset that no one seemed to know how to stock the RV refrigerator with food. That was until Bean steered into a lone gas station. Bean fueled. Lisa and Winter bought food with Bean's money. It was here that Lisa realized she was ignorant about one small detail and chose to ask the cashier for an answer.

"What year," the gas station attendant asked. He might have thought about laughing, except that he was probably smart enough to realize that Lisa didn't appear to have a sense of humor on this particular matter. So, the attendant told Lisa, and she thought better of busting his teeth out of his head. Then she and her companion left.

"I didn't realize we had to start so soon," Lisa complained, climbing back into the trailer.

"Speak for yourself," Bean fired back.

Once they returned to the road, they rested a little and held a few sparse discussions. A few conversations covered theory in time travel, which was really just speculation and nothing but theory.

"You do realize that most nerds who speak authoritatively on time travel have never done it, right," Bean pointed out.

The friends also shared a few ideas about how to proceed with helping Josh, but really none of those approaches panned out to the level that would be of interest in this history.

However one point worthy of note is that Winter, while exploring the vehicle, discovered a set of silver polished revolvers, Colt longs. She also discovered evidence to show that her host was a performance shootist. Lisa, of course, was pleased with the news. She was the marksman, after all, and felt safer with firearms in her grasp.

Then she thought perhaps that, if they weren't taking chances to give away who they were, she probably should choose a different weapon and let Winter learn how to draw instead.

"Bad idea," Bean said. "You should stick to your strengths."

"I have other strengths," Lisa said. "Aco—Winter can use the firearms. She needs to learn something new and fast. It's not like she has her poles anymore."

Bean laughed, but eventually conceded that Josh's present-time Cadence already had the role of keeping an eye on the paladin. Perhaps, choosing a different role for Lisa might actually fill a defensive role that could serve to protect Josh all the more.

Lisa agreed. She wasn't really happy nor comfortable with trying to play a new weapon, but she had already felt it was the right approach if she wasn't going to let her mannerisms give herself away. Even if Josh didn't notice it, the rogue or his minions might find two hunters with the same drawing and shooting tendencies of interest. He might not guess how it could be, but what if he did? It might unravel their plan. Lisa had to remind herself that the purpose here was to catch the rogue off guard. Josh had put so much trust in her to protect him from a distance. She hoped she could ignore that instinct now.

These thoughts happened to occupy her mind as she came across the farm supply store on the outstretch of road near a ranching community. Had she not been driving, they might have passed it. She parked, and they all too happily went inside to stretch their legs.

It was almost closing time. Had they been ten miles back down the road, this part of history might have upset the balance of the outcome to follow. Lisa was glad she stopped.

"What are we doing here," Bean asked.

"Getting armed," Lisa replied. She wasted no time scanning the farm supply. "Get as many forty-five hollow points as you can get."

"That's your plan," Bean asked.

"You're right," Lisa replied. "Maybe they sell glycerin, diamond bullets here?"

"Don't waste money on ammo you know won't work," Bean argued.

"She needs practice," Lisa said. "Besides, if we can pin them down, then perhaps enough slugs concentrated on the same spot might actually break through and do some damage."

"Interesting thought," Bean said. "All right, I'll bite," and he followed his companions out of the battered vehicle.

Once inside, Bean and Winter proceeded to the guns and ammo rack. Lisa went straight to the hardware section where she ordered several feet of steel cable and clamps.

"Anything else," the elderly salesman asked.

"Cattle prods," she asked. "Strongest you have."

"Where you got cattle," the old man asked.

"Not cattle," Lisa replied.

"What you using it for then?"

"Wolves," she said.

The old salesman studied Lisa long enough to make her uncomfortable.

"Wolves," he asked. "Hate 'em."

"Only good wolf's a dead wolf," Lisa replied.

"Amen to that," the salesman said. "But I don't understand the cattle prod. Why don't you just shoot 'em?"

"I—uh," Lisa explained.

"Yeah, my aim's not so good neither," the salesman said. "But you're going to have to get up close for the cattle prod to stun them."

"Don't want to stun them," Lisa said. "I want to kill them."

"Cattle prod won't kill them, and you've still got to get close."

"Want to make a lasso," Lisa said.

"Lasso wolves," the salesman asked.

"And fry 'em," Lisa answered.

Again the salesman seemed to ponder Lisa. "Horrible idea. Come with me."

He led Lisa back to the cable aisle and cut her several feet of smaller gauge. He coiled what he had cut and handed it off to Lisa. Then he led her to another aisle and grabbed some rubber mats. He rolled those and dropped them in Lisa's arms before leading her towards the back of the store. Along the way, Lisa pointed out another item she thought might come in handy. The clerk grabbed it for her and tossed that on top of the rubber mats. He stopped at a wall of rubber tubing on spindles and in containers. He pulled some out of a cardboard box, clipped it, then wrapped that up as well. This he held onto himself.

"This way," he said, before walking in a new direction.

A few more paces and Lisa entered into a caged-in area in the back stockroom.

"You can toss a lasso," the salesman asked.

"It's been a while," Lisa said. "But I imagine it'll come back to me."

"What have you roped?"

"Used to rope rabbits before daddy taught me to shoot—tried to teach me to shoot," she quickly corrected.

"OK," the salesman said. "Rabbits." He reached for Lisa's supplies. "The problem with your lasso idea is you'll need weight behind your cast, and you don't have any with the cable. And you're going to need two lines to create the circuit. So we'll lay you down two cables and insulate 'em with this rubber mat and tubing. That should solve both problems."

The old man broke out a blade and started slicing the rubber mat into thin strips. Meanwhile, he had Lisa start sliding the cable down, into the rubber tubing. "The hose won't protect you from the shock, but we can anchor it to some insulation that should be able to."

After he cut the mat into strips, he fired off a torch and melted them together. "How long you want," he asked.

"Fifteen, twenty feet," Lisa replied.

"Short," he said. "Good. Don't want too much coil left over or you'll have problems keeping it off the ground, and you'll keep better potency."

He went back to the store to restock on rubber mats. After about an hour, he had finally put all the pieces together, and Lisa was just finishing her part on her second cable. Maybe it should have gone faster except the rubber tubing got too difficult to push through, especially when it started bunching.

The old man had already had his staff close the doors and go home. Except for Bean and Winter, all other customers were gone. These two attempted to help stuff cable into the hose, but they were more of a nuisance so they mostly explored the stockroom and left the store clerk to his work. The salesman began to weld the rubber tubing to the strips.

Again, he returned to the store then came back with some heavy elastics to bite the lasso. He kept adding insulation to the eye of the lasso until it was large and fat with rubber. "If that's not enough, I guess you'll know," the salesman said. "This is going to be heavy for a little thing like you."

"I've carried heavier," she said.

"How much you want to spend on a prod," the salesman asked.

Lisa signaled for Winter, who, after a moment of realizing what she needed to do, handed over the credit card she had found in her newly obtained wallet earlier that day.

"Whatever that will cover," Lisa replied.

The old man returned to the store and spent a few minutes at the register. Then he returned to the warehouse and disappeared farther into the back. When he reappeared, he carried a black wand.

"Thought you might like this," the old man said. "Sell these to the local law enforcement. See if it still has a charge."

A round, white blinding light burst from the end of the stick. The old man smiled.

"Five-and-a-half-million volts of electricity," the clerk said. "Great stun baton, but won't kill anything yet. Flickers too fast to do any lethal harm, and this is a lot of cable for those little bursts to travel."

He set the baton on his work bench and took out some small tools to disassemble the unit. He removed the battery and set it to the side. "But if we take out this regulator here and replace it with this."

Lisa was just letting him talk now. She didn't understand any of it nor could she see what he was doing. Several minutes later, he was stripping away rubber from the end of the new lasso and inserting the cable leads into the stun baton. A few more welds of solder, and he seemed pleased with his work. He returned the battery and sealed up the unit.

"Now look, there's not a set of gloves I can sell you that's going to insulate you from what this thing will put out—not a set that's going to let you wield this thing with accuracy, that is" the salesman explained. "The good news is, unless you're on the receiving end when you discharge it, you won't need to worry about gloves."

He imitated rolling and throwing the weapon.

"Lasso, trap, then fire," he explained. "And make sure no part of it's coiled when you fire it off. Might mean you having to run away to take up the slack. I can put a cap over the trigger if you want. It already has a safety set up, but do you really want to take chances," he said in afterthought. He went about setting up the added safety mechanism.

It was nearly three hours after Lisa had entered the store.

"All right, let's try it," the salesman finally said.

He set a wooden sawhorse several feet away and hooked one end of the lasso to it. He began adjusting how well it should slide through its own eye. He applied some quick-setting resin to make it a little more slick. "Might break, might not. Treat it well."

Once the resin dried, he adjusted some more and seemed pleased again. He stretched out the lasso as taut as he could. Before attempting to announce what he was doing, he fired off the weapon. Smoke rose from the sawhorse.

"Like I said," the salesman said. "Didn't think the tubing would insulate well." He began recoiling the weapon. "This kit comes with a car adapter and extra battery. Charge won't last long, that's for sure. Will there be anything else?"

"Yeah," Bean said. "How many more of those stun batons do you have?"

Again, Lisa and Winter's debit cards were able to cover the cost of their items: several boxes of .45 caliber ammo, Lisa's new lasso, and five modified stun batons for replacement and batteries for inevitable reloading. After a little more prodding, the salesman directed the small group of hunters to an open gun range about twenty miles out of the way.

It's worth mentioning here too that nothing really happened at the gun range worth mentioning, other than they discovered that, although not as great as Lisa's, Winter's talent with her revolvers weren't all that bad. They also learned that Bean had acquired a sawed-off shotgun from beneath the arms counter where the farm supply owner had hidden it. He also pocketed several cases of cartridges for it. The three allies decided that the best hunter tactic for them might be to let Lisa rope the target and hold it in close range for Winter to shoot multiple times, hopefully breaking the skin, or for Bean to finish off in some way that wouldn't fry him.

It was a crude plan, but they couldn't risk their old habits.

Lisa did, at this time, complain that she didn't see what the big deal would be to reveal their identity, but Bean explained that he thought if they revealed who they were, they might cause their historical pasts to second-guess themselves, and, at least now, they knew what those decisions were. They took some comfort in the fact that they did have a history of surviving the majority of their decisions. Although Bean would have preferred a different approach, himself, he did defy every suggestion to help their former identities when they had the capacity and history to save themselves.

"We don't want to save Josh at the cost of losing someone else," Bean said. "Let them work until we need to step in."

"Someone could still die when we do," Lisa said.

"You're right," Bean replied. "Just because we're helping doesn't mean we still might not lose allies. We know where they will survive though, so we should let them do that. And we also need Josh to think out whatever it was Amber saw in him at the museum."

From here, nothing truly eventful or important happened, with the exception of further hypothesizing plans that never took fruition, until they finally returned to Plattsville after several days of driving.

Upon realizing their blood-stained clothes reeked, their discussion finally led to deciding that Winter and Lisa should wear the bright nasty rodeo costumes with gold hats. Bean was adamant about the two dressing up as he believed it would make them easier to locate each other when the fighting broke out. Neither of them liked it, but they agreed nonetheless. They didn't have their earpieces to talk to each other like they had when they fought alongside Josh so many years ago. Once Lisa and Winter had changed, they really only knew of one place they could go to find safe haven and information.

An hour after arriving in Plattsville, they sought out this haven.

"What d'ya want," the doorman grunted from the other side of Thug's steel door, his eyes glaring down on Lisa, his shotgun aimed at her stomach.

"We hear you have a werewolf problem," Lisa replied. "We're here for news."

The doorman grunted. Lisa thought about using one of her stun batons through the eyehole, but was afraid with the modifications, it might kill her ally.

"What do you want, a tip," Bean scowled. "Feed us or shoot us already."

Now, had the doorman chosen the latter, perhaps Lisa wouldn't have done the stupid thing that she did.

21 ~ The Room of Geniuses

He scrambled past the parking lot of bikes. He ducked behind one, knowing no one would dare to shoot up another member's ride.

As the doorman's usual routine sounds of unlocking the door proceeded, Bean took the opportunity to make one last suggestion that they keep their actions low-profile.

"And we probably shouldn't sit together," Lisa quickly observed as their demeanors and appearance seemed to clash.

"If you say so," Bean replied.

The door opened, and Bean shoved his way past Lisa and Winter to enter the café first. "Cowgirls," he complained loudly.

The doorman looked as though he had been insulted, not at Bean, but at the bright and shiny rodeo queens that entered afterwards.

A gang of young skateboarders, all wearing denim and white arm bandanas, filled the two booths at the far end of the café. Silver skateboards leaned against the sides of their benches. One of the skaters wore the bandana of a wolf on his head. In the final booth sat a man in a suit. For a moment, Lisa almost flew at him, before realizing that even he had a role to play in giving off clues that would save Josh and maybe Thomas's lives. She pushed her disgust down and pressed into a barrage of catcalls and whistles from the immature skateboard gang.

"Not happening," Lisa said, failing to squash the rude mating calls of idiots.

"How many," Thug called from behind his kitchen window.

"Three," Ty replied.

Lisa winced, fighting back emotion ignited by the sight of her old comrades. She made her way to the only seats left in the café: barstools at the opposite end of the counter where Bean had placed himself. Then she felt the hand on her, grabbing that piece of her backside that brought the death penalty in her old future. Lisa reached for one of the stun batons hidden beneath her vest just as an almost-forgotten sense of humor appeared. Lisa nodded that Bean shouldn't, but she only half meant it.

"Oh, Is this an icebreaker game with hunters now," Bean cooed. His hand gripped the culprit's butt, clenching and lifting him onto his toes.

The young man tried a few times to make words into a threat, but each time screeched instead as Bean tightened his grip.

The skater's wolf bandana identified him quickly as one who would someday soon have only one ear. Lisa took a little pride in knowing she could keep that secret to herself.

"Did I win," Bean asked, twisting his grip. "I'll bet I didn't. I'm new to this."

The skater screamed.

"I'm sorry. I'm just not as good at this groping thing as you are. When do I know my turn's over. Was I supposed to roll a die and count? Or do I just keep going?"

The other skaters jumped from their seats to attack the biker who had dared make the assault on one of their own.

"Foul! I think that's a foul," Bean cried as he grabbed the elastic of the their leader's underwear and yanked so hard he hefted the brat off his feet. "That means I get a free bounce right there, unless you get back to the dugout." He bounced the skater in the air, pulling higher on his waistband.

The skater screeched apologies, all of which Bean mocked because none of his moaning words came out clearly. Bean dropped the skater captain and smacked his other backside half.

"How sorry are you," Bean asked.

"I'm sorry," the skater cried over and over.

"You sure you don't want another turn," Bean asked. "You can have another turn."

"I'm done. I'm sorry."

"Offer the ladies your seats," Bean suggested. "That's what I win, right?"

"Give them your seats, guys," the skater said to his friends sitting at the booth next to his.

"Excuse me," Bean scowled, refreshing his grip, but lower the back of his thigh. "They didn't even play!"

"They can have our seats," the leader of the skaters escalated in his cry.

The skater's partner from his own booth stood.

"You can take your plates," Bean suggested. "I'm not a greedy winner."

The partner made a few trips to the bar to set their food and drinks, then took up the two metallic skateboards from beside the booth. Lisa and Winter slid into the booth.

"Better," Bean said, and then tore the leader's bandana from his scalp before letting him go. He made sure to take his time tying the bandana onto his own head without once taking his eyes off the leader, who now sneered at the bold biker. Bean's hand suddenly caught the skater leader by the nose and twisted his head sideways. "Got your nose!" Bean dialed the biker's head to the other side. "This is just because I thought it would be funny." Then he released the skater. "I was right, it was."

The skater wiped tears from his face.

"Are you okay," Bean asked the skater. "Do you feel violated?" He pushed the skater away. "Then sit down and stop acting like puberty held you back in class ten years."

The leader sat, and Bean waited for him. He was careful to smile politely upon the young man throughout the entire process. In an instant, Bean turned on one of the three skaters at the second booth. One had tried to draw a black, double-barrel, shotgun-like pistol. Bean snatched it away; drove it under the skater's chin; drew back the hammers. He held the pistol as though the weapon were made for him.

"Now this game I do know" Bean said. "But you're only supposed to have one bullet in the chamber, so we need to get rid of one."

This skater too started spouting apologies.

"You're not forfeiting are you," Bean asked.

The skater shook his head.

"I guess I get to keep the game ball then." Bean withdrew the weapon; lowered the hammers; left the frightened set of hunters and took the shotgun pistol. He returned to his seat at the far side of the bar where he could watch both the leader and his friends on the opposite end, as well as the lackeys in the booth next to Winter and Lisa.

"How stupid of me," Bean said. "I forgot to take your holster? Would you be a sport and toss that over?"

The skater stripped himself of a holster beneath his armless, denim jacket. He tossed it to Bean, who armed himself with the leather carrier and its gun, hiding it beneath his leather jacket. "Good game," he said. "Get those two at the end of the bar some more food on me."

"Food," Thug announced. Soon after, Ty dropped a plate of potatoes and steak in front of Bean. Bean grunted his thanks.

"Food," Thug cried again as he dropped down two more plates for the skaters. The wounded leader glared at Bean until his partner convinced him to eat. He threw a scoop of potatoes into his mouth and began eating, and suddenly Bean had the image of children squabbling around the breakfast table. What the heck! Why stop the fun now?

Bean slammed his fist against the counter. He was mostly showing off now, and he knew it. It had been a while since he'd been able to play like this. He'd forgotten how fun it could be. "Chew with your mouth closed."

"Oh, what," the skater complained. "You don't like the way I eat now."

"I don't like you," Bean replied. "And stop looking at me." He snatched up a glass of water, expecting he might have the opportunity to throw the cup itself at one of the followers who might attempt to charge him, but, unfortunately, the leader waved off the attack. Bummer too! Bean was already developing a great verbal jab. *So much for low-profile*, he thought. He drank his water and sleeve-wiped his beard, hoping some rookie would take that as a good time to invite more Bean-bashing of his or her own.

"Settle down," the doorman said calmly from atop his stool.

Thug dropped two more plates down in the window for the rodeo queens, but didn't announce it, as a knock came at the steel door, and the doorman went to his duties. Ty delivered the food to Lisa and Winter.

A series of commotions broke out at the entrance. Bean, however, kept his view on his new enemies until he realized their attention was now on the door more than him now. He was about to risk a look when he suddenly fell onto his back. His head flared hot and with impact of the concrete floor. He drew his new gun, and, had his choice of weapon actually been the sawed-off that he acquired from the farm supply, he might have failed his mission right there, for hovering over him was the new paladin with one of those purple-glinting crossbows held right to his face.

"You're in my seat," the young man said. Bean had never seen the boy's hatred this close. Even he found something behind the new paladin's eyes that frightened him. Or maybe he'd just forgotten. He had a tendency to do that. Still, he couldn't help feel that he was glad he hadn't been this close to the hunter before.

Bean lowered his gun, hoping Josh wouldn't take the movement as an invitation to take the old general's head off. Even dodging would give away that Bean wasn't merely a hunter. Besides, he wasn't sure if he could dodge the paladin anymore. It had been a while since he'd used that reflex. He found himself praying the man he was sent to save wouldn't actually kill him first.

When the skaters cheered at Josh's triumph, Bean was somewhat pleased with Josh's quick reply for silence. Here, Bean suddenly realized that this simple college kid had stolen command of the room from him. No wonder Jasper had enjoyed toying with him so much.

"We gonna have a problem," Josh asked, his weapons still aimed on Bean.

Bean assured Josh he wouldn't. Josh holstered his weapons; his sleeved, black cloak rippled as if it had a mind of its own. Bean hadn't fully realized just how attuned Josh had become to the physics of deadly fabric. He'd seen Amber wear it, but she still mostly kept her fight in the air. She didn't rely on the cloak as

Josh had done. Even in his simple movements now, Josh's actions were as though he were the cloak, not that the cloak was only his weapon. Simple motions of Josh's created just the right openings in his wardrobe to give him access to holsters. Bean couldn't help but admire this man once again. Josh turned and sat in Bean's stool. He allowed Bean to stand and eventually retrieve his food.

Thug shared greetings with the new party. The skaters tried to get bullish with the dark hunter. Then Thug announced that more food was ready. A few moments later, the cook entered the restaurant area and demanded the new paladin follow him, leaving Speatsh and Amber in the café with the rest of the hunters.

The café fell silent, and Bean now shared the bar with Speatsh several seats away to one side, while Amber sat two stools away to his other. It was smart planning. Josh was perfectly positioned for brawling in the center of the room. He could start and end a fight without warning with just one of his maneuvers, and no one would question his capability. Amber was seated where she'd have room to hurl her decapitating whips at anyone who miraculously dodged Josh's footwork. Speatsh was a force in himself. Bean dared not stir any contention with this creature, not here at least. Although, he had to admit, it seemed tempting in this moment, yet he stayed his tongue.

Bean, felt it appropriate to keep his interest in his own food and continued to shovel the atrocious meal into his face. It was best not to become confrontrational right now.

"What's your problem," Speatsh asked Bean from behind a mountain of potatoes. "Don't like your steak?"

Well, Bean tried.

Here, Speatsh was taking on the role of deciding who Bean was. Bean knew who Speatsh was, but he was certain the other hunters filling the room did not. Speatsh was marking his territory.

It was still difficult for Bean not to eat the meat. Every day, he still longed for the blood to return to his gullet. This host, however, had eaten meat. Bean could feel its strength growing in him. He'd been fighting the urge since taking on this body. A few more years, and the physical gnawing would turn into remembered habit, but, for now, it still gave him strength. It was like he was still in the beginning withdrawal stages of his fast.

Bean decided he could throw Speatsh off the hunt by taking a bite. However, with the blood in his system, Bean would need more of his strength to keep his mind closed. He needed to reserve every last drop of strength for fights to come. The last thing he needed was for any chance he would risk arousing the rogue to his presence, let alone two of his presences. He had just barely started to feel himself start to age again since he took on this vessel. He wasn't ready to stop fasting now. On the other hand, hunters ate meat. The only ones who didn't were typically traitors.

Still, Speatsh was investigating now. Bean knew everything about predicting how Josh would behave, but Speatsh was a loose cannon. He could be read generally—but now Bean needed to manipulate him specifically, and Bean's mind wasn't what it used to be. He hadn't practiced his quick wit in far too long.

"You're one to talk," Bean replied. He prepared to dodge a blow from Josh's wife to his left.

"I know why I don't have steak," Speatsh announced. "I just don't know why you're not eating yours."

"Too hot," Bean replied. "I like it cold." His next action seemed only natural. "Here, if it's that important to you, blow on it for me!" He grabbed the steak off his plate and tossed it down the counter, where it landed in Speatsh's dinner, exploding potatoes down Speatsh's front and across the two skaters sitting next to him.

Bean silently cursed his aim and realized a confrontation was surely coming, one which was bound to end with Bean having to swallow his pride in the form of a beating. Bear smiled subtly. Others may not have seen it, but Bean hadn't missed it. At least he wouldn't be caught off-guard by Bear, as so many others who never learned he was more than just an animal pelt decoration. However, that didn't mean Bean wanted to face off with Bear either.

Speatsh hadn't said a word yet when the skater leader leaned suddenly against the counter, apparently refreshed with the illusion of having an ally who could probably stand up to Bean.

"What is your problem, man," the lead skater asked and then made the mistake of spitting on the steak.

Speatsh spun on his barstool, the thick slab of beef flopped limp in his hand. It smacked the skater captain across the face, knocking him off his stool. When his partner stood, Speatsh slapped this skater three times with the same piece of meat and finished off the attack with the foolish kid's own plate of food, full in the face.

"Keep your spit off my plate," Speatsh yelled down at the fallen leader whose body was hidden by the counter. Speatsh drew out a long loogie and hacked it at the floor. "You're gross," he continued to rant and then dropped behind the counter where his voice ordered the leader to eat Bean's steak.

The partner charged Speatsh. Speatsh swore, and the partner fell. The three skaters from the booth stood. Whatever Speatsh did behind the bar, the three skaters suddenly sat back down, clearly content with this safer maneuver.

"Why you crying," Speatsh continued to rant unseen behind the far end of the counter with the hidden skater captain. "I'm giving you free steak? Everyone likes free steak. You can do better than that. Take a big bite. The fat's the best par—chew your food dummy."

Finally Speatsh returned to his stool. He slapped a half-portion of Bean's steak on the counter in front of him and then switched his plate with thc leader's.

"That'll be five 'Hail Marys' and ten 'bite mes,'" Speatsh said, then laughed at himself until he realized he was the only one. He dropped the leader's plate on the floor and the leader moaned.

"More food please," Speatsh said. "I dropped mine."

Ty nodded before sauntering back into the kitchen.

"I know you," Speatsh said pointing a long, hairy, open-gloved finger at Bean. "I never forget a face worth punching."

Bean couldn't help notice that Winter suddenly appeared as uncomfortable as Bean now felt. Could he see Lisa's face, he might have wondered what she gave away. They'd discuss that later. Of course, he knew him! He had met him before in Richard's house after Josh had gone into hiding. Now was not the time to recognize him. He had hoped Speatsh wouldn't have been able to recall the details of when they had met at Richard's dark, living room. Even if he did, even Speatsh couldn't be so dumb as to announce it.

"You were in Austen," Speatsh burst. "That was you."

"Maybe," Bean replied. "I've been known to pass there a time or two."

If this were a test, answering "yes" might tell Speatsh that Bean was a liar, especially if Speatsh made the location up. Answering "no" might tell Speatsh he was a liar if the location was real.

"You're that idiot, drug-dealing, Harley hunter that overdosed his own crew right before a full-moon," Speatsh cried standing.

"All generals," Bean replied. He wondered how Speatsh had been aware of that event.

"I knew, I knew your stupid face," Speatsh crowed. He grabbed the rest of Bean's steak and threw it back at him.

Bean deflected, and the steak flew sideways, striking the man in the suit who sat alone and, up until now, kept to himself, in his own booth.

The man in the suit drew two guns, one silver and one black, and held aim on both Speatsh and Bean. Even Speatsh appeared to be taken off guard at the suit's speed, and prepped his fork for an attack. The suit's triggers began to wrench the hammers back. The man said nothing and barely looked at either of his targets. But before his hammers could fire off any bullets, two Glocks suddenly appeared at the man's head.

Bean, hadn't even noticed her. He was so caught up with the skaters and then Speatsh, that he hadn't even seen her lingering in the farthest shadows. How did he miss her enter with the rest of the group? She was better than he remembered.

"No," Cadence said pressing the points of her barrels against the side of the suit's head.

The suit settled his hammers back gently. For a moment, his head began to turn to Cadence, but the sound of her own hammers snapping back faster than he could move turned his eyes white. He bowed out and holstered his weapons.

"Bang-bang," Cadence added. "Remember that."

The skater leader had now returned to his seat and immediately began wiping meat from his mouth and out of his nose. His partner sat next to him and pretended to ignore his friend's humiliation.

Ty dropped a plate of potatoes in front of Speatsh, and Cheatham laughed as he dug into the tall mound.

"You may not realize it," Speatsh said while eating. "But we just saved your lives. The paladin wouldn't have been as forgiving for such idiocy."

Stupid, Bean shouted at himself. He suddenly remembered who the suit was.

About here, Josh returned to the café—his face flushed.

"Ah," Speatsh cried, spitting potatoes into the face of the skater leader. Bean almost laughed. It was one of Speatsh's more intelligent jabs. "Our beloved hero returns. What's wrong?"

Josh didn't answer, his stone face threw a cold glare at the man sitting alone in the booth. Whatever Josh saw, Bean had missed it.

Bean knew who the man was, for the most part. He was a tapper. Generals hired tappers sometimes to infiltrate or destroy hunter havens. Bean knew the man's purpose. He, himself, had hired him, after all—not to infiltrate, but to get caught, althought he man didn't know that.

The man, whatever his name was—generals rarely cared—was called the suit. He was good, skilled, thoughtful, but versed in hunting human hunters and not wolves like Speatsh. Somewhere beyond the walls of this café, Jasper had suggested the suit kill Josh, but to get to Josh, he needed to take down his protection. Jasper had made sure to drop the imbecilic hint to poison Thomas, who the man easily believed to be Josh's most powerful ally. All the suit needed to do then was to make his move on Josh, and hopefully alert Speatsh to Jasper's design to establish trust with the paladin—that is, if Speatsh was capable of such brain power. Jasper's mistake was assuming he had that cognitive ability.

Sure, it wasn't the best of Jasper's plans, but it had played out well enough. Too bad Josh had been too stupid to take a hint and run when Jasper had offered it to him bluntly.

Although, Bean didn't know what had transpired here in this bar, he did know that Speatsh eventually caught the suit in time and picked up on Jasper's clue. Still, Bean wondered what it had been that had caused Josh to take notice and square off against the suit just now. He disguised his curiosity with another bite of potatoes.

After a few accusations, Josh suddenly punched the suit in the throat, surprising even Bean. Bean was too familiar with dodging Josh's projectiles, not his pugilistic impulses—well, not ones that weren't followed by flying razor cloth.

Josh then set himself above Winter and glared her down. Winter, played it smart, looked nervous, but it was here that Bean saw what the others, even Speatsh, had missed: a simple nod between the lead skater and the suit. Jasper had hired the suit as a means to tip off Josh and his allies, but even he wasn't aware of this alliance. Yet, he couldn't say anything about it, right now. He had to let this play out.

This cooperation was not part of Jasper's original plan here. This didn't bother him so much as that he hadn't been aware of it. The skaters must be in employ to the suit. That's why Speatsh didn't figure everything out sooner. The suit's secret employees had executed Jasper's plan without fault. What that meant, just now, is that Jasper realized there were potential loose ends that he hadn't considered.

Strangely, Bean was beginning to feel anxious. As the suit's hand discreetly made its way back to his pistol, Bean found his own hand preparing his own new shotgun. He watched without looking like he was watching, studied as though he wasn't studying. He evaluated the suit and each skater to see if any of their actions would betray who they were.

The suit was going to make his move. Bean wondered if his own actions had somehow altered the timeline. He prepped his gun.

A shot rang out from Winter and Lisa's booth, surprising Bean and everyone else in the room—including the suit, who realized he'd lost his opening. Cadence and the doorman both had drawn weapons and were too close for him to finish his maneuver. Winter's face was wide and scared. Bean quickly assumed she was upset that she had let Speatsh get under her skin enough to make her draw one of her Colts and fire upon him. Surely, she knew Speatsh's abilities.

Immediately, Speatsh produced a small blunderbuss and blasted off his own shot that threw Winter's gun out of her hand.

The suit's face suddenly changed and again, Bean attempted to not be paying attention. The suit removed his hand from his weapon and his weight settled back into his booth. He glared down at his nearly empty plate and began, stabbing away at his remaining food.

Bean's hand remained on his gun. He figured he could have taken the suit without it, but he kept reminding himself not to betray who he was, that meant sticking with his own weapon.

Speatsh began to verbally insult the hunters. Bean watched each of their faces, even those of his own friends, twist in offense. Bean wanted to laugh at some of the comments, but he made sure to squint and glare appropriately as well.

"We need a hunter like Brogan O'Kieth," Speatsh announced. "There was a hunter. Best pugilist there was."

"O'Kieth's dead," the suit said.

You idiot, Bean thought and wanted to yell, but then he saw the soft and hardly noticeable smirk on Speatsh's face as he stood and held up a bottle of beer. Actually, he had taken the skater leader's beer.

So, Speatsh knew more than he had let on.

"May he rest in peace," Thug said. Bean assumed the tone of his voice and the look on his face was confusion. Bean also assumed he didn't know any better, but he had become accustomed to following Speatsh's lead. No wonder Speatsh's friends were able to have accomplished so much in their tyranny against Bean's old master.

Bean wasn't sure if he should be impressed with Speatsh's brain here yet. Did Speatsh know who the suit was, now? Not likely. Or he might have ended the entire charade right here. This didn't sound like the story of the suit dying that Bean had heard before. Surely, Speatsh knew something was amiss, but was he certain what it could be? Maybe that's why, when the second clue came later, he knew to finish Jasper's hired pawn. In the end, Jasper had picked the suit for this task because he knew Speatsh could take him easily.

Thug rang a bell, and Speatsh screamed at the room, "You people don't know the first thing about hunting." He then threw a quick threat at Winter.

"Do it again," Josh ordered. "Drinks all around, Ty."

Ty began filling glasses with liquor except for one, which he filled with water for Josh. Josh proceeded to toast, demanding everyone participate. Bean stood with the rest and toasted, one hand on his glass, the other in quick grasp of his firearm.

"Other hunters may be better," Josh ended his toast. "But you're the ones whose help I need right now." Without another word, Josh made his way out of the café. His companions followed. Speatsh, however, paused a moment to hand some items to Winter before he followed after Josh.

Once they exited, the suit casually stood from his booth, ensured that he had all of his belongings and then left the café as well.

Bean thought a moment about giving chase, but then realized why he was exiting. If, things were the way he remembered they had gone, the suit was actually on his way to communicate with his old Jasper-self in a nearby parking lot. However, he had an impulse to kill the suit for keeping his cohort's secret.

So why not give the old Jasper a clue? What could that harm.

"I'll bet the paladin kills that man," Bean said, slapping a wad of bills on the counter. "Two-hundred bucks says he dies walking to his car."

The crew of skaters revealed too much interest in Bean's proposal.

The leader nodded to the three skaters at the table. One of them took out a phone and played with the screen.

"He's fine," the one with the phone said.

"How do you know," Bean asked.

"I'm looking at his satellite image, if you must know," the kid with the phone snapped.

"You can do that," Bean asked, playing stupid. "Which phone is that, I want one."

"This isn't a store-bought piece of junk," the skater scoffed. "Our friend custom-made this. You can't buy it."

"Did he custom-made the satellite too," Bean mocked.

"He didn't have to," the skater said.

"Ask him how much he'd charge to build me one," Bean said.

"I think we're done here," the leader said and stood. His lackeys followed him down the bar and past Bean. The leader stopped a moment to take up Bean's wad of bills before moving towards the doorman's area. They each collected an aluminum backpack from beside the door and locked their skateboards to the frames. Then they were gone, and the doorman was latching up the exit.

He grunted at Bean. Bean wondered if it was a compliment.

Bean finished his food and left as well. He waited about five minutes for Winter and Lisa to join him outside in the dark alley.

"You learned something," Lisa asked.

"We don't leave this spot until Speatsh kills the suit," Bean said.

"We're not going to look for the death wagon," Lisa asked.

"The skaters are working with the suit," Bean explained. "I want to know how I didn't know. Something slipped through the cracks here."

22 ~ The Great Bed Sheet Debate

A body crashed through glass that had been painted black. It stood, tried to run, but was bowled down by a fresh cadaver.

Winter stood at a dark window and watched across the parking lot to the narrow alley that led back to Thug's.

"Josh left himself open to the skaters," Bean explained. "The suit called off their attack, probably because he realized they wouldn't make it out alive if they'd tried to take that opening to kill him tonight."

"Speatsh would have put an end to that fast," Lisa said.

"It was your younger self that stopped him," Bean refuted. "That man's fast, faster than I realized when I hired him in the first place."

"Which you shouldn't have done," Lisa replied.

"That clue saved your lives," Bean replied. "But I didn't realize he'd hired the skaters. My guess is he figured that, while that gang took on Speatsh, he could handle Josh and the rest of you. He found an opening to take out Josh tonight, but he underestimated Cadence's speed. When he saw that, he called off his attack."

"And Speatsh didn't see it," Lisa added. "Which explains why it took him so long to figure it out."

"I'm not so sure," Bean replied. "He has the scent, I'm sure."

"Care to explain?"

"Brogan O'Kieth."

"The suit said he died," Lisa replied.

"He wasn't a real person," Bean explained. "He was only a legend that had come to epitomize the deeds of numerous, historical hunters. Some wolves even believed long ago that the wearer of

Wolf's Breath was just an evolution of O'Kieth, until entire packs started turning up dead with the same wounds." Bean stopped a moment to think. "The last time I think I heard a real hunter refer to O'Kieth as a real person was during the Revolutionary War, when a good storyteller was all you needed to get some fortune-seeker to set out to find the monsters of the new frontier. Most hunters today are too self-absorbed in their own accomplishments to care about O'Kieth stories, and, if they do, they don't tend to realize he never existed."

"Your point," Lisa asked.

"A hunter who knew about O'Kieth would have said he wasn't real when Speatsh mentioned his name," Bean said. "A wolf would have kept his tongue, like I did. But an impostor, say for instance, one who might have heard his name after poor research, would have heard a story of O'Kieth's demise and spouted back that little piece of trivia to sound knowledgeable."

"Speatsh was testing them," Lisa suggested.

Bean nodded.

"It was probably a hint that helped him know later to kill the suit and see him as the clue I sent him to be," Bean replied.

Winter motioned for the others to join her at the window. Bean and Lisa did so and looked down on the alley across the parking lot of their hotel. The suit had returned to the walkway to the café. He stood for several moments, as if inspecting his surroundings.

"What's he doing," Lisa asked.

"He's learning," Bean replied.

Bean made a quick round to turn off the cheap, pregnant hotel lamps before returning to the window to continue watching.

The suit's cell phone turned bright for a moment and then disappeared into his pocket.

"Don't want to stray too far from your hit-spot," Bean said. "Don't want to be seen cohorting neither, do you, Mr. Suit?"

Lisa asked what he meant, but Bean just kept watching.

"Don't know why we're bothering," Lisa said. "We know Josh survives this."

"I'm curious how I didn't know," Bean said. "I want to see how many helped him."

Nearly twenty minutes later, a group of people appeared.

"Can you see who it is," Lisa asked.

"The punks from the café: the leader, his right hand man and a new face," Bean said. "Don't recognize this one."

Winter's jaw clenched, and she wrangled Lisa's arm.

Lisa didn't understand, but Winter insisted that she must be able to. "Too bad I don't have a night scope," Lisa said as she continued to squint into the dark. She didn't understand why Winter was now pacing away from and back to the window in frustration. Her mute friend barked a moan, but didn't make any sense. Bean could probably see the person, but didn't recognize him.

"I can't see who it is," Lisa scowled at Winter's impatience.

Winter tripped in the dark. She stood, then made a commotion of yanking an end drawer open. Paper tore, more fumbling bellowed, and the sound of scribbling came next. Lisa felt the piece of paper shoved into her hand.

The writing was bad, hardly readable in the dark room. The fresh paper cut stung, then smarted even more once Lisa could finally read the name scribbled on the gray note.

"I'll kill him," Lisa said, her head snapping back to the scene in the alley.

"Who," Bean asked.

"I'll bet that worm's their inventor you asked about," Lisa replied. "A whiz with technology."

"How do you know," Bean asked.

"Because he handled ours too. His name's Kenny Kenny."

"Kenny," Bean asked, taking another look. "I *do* know him. I recruited him to break into your bunker—don't look at me like that—it was back in my 'I-hate-you year.'"

"What are you talking ab—oh, he's how the wolves got into our bunker," Lisa replied. "Hold on. I'm confused. Didn't you say once that you got the code from Natalie, except for the last digit. Why would you need Kenny for that?"

"Why did I need Kenny for that," Bean asked, then fell silent in thought again. "Oh!" He startled even himself. "Well, first there was the key."

"What key?"

"You needed a key to open the door to get to the second door with the keypad," Bean said.

"The door doesn't have an outside keypad," Lisa said. "It has a full keyboard."

"I know," Bean cried. "I discovered that when I finally uncovered it on my own. I got most of the code from Natalie, all except the last digit. I figured I could guess the rest of the code in a few tries."

"I didn't realize Natalie had been in the bunker before that night," Lisa said. "She never told me about it."

"She didn't," Bean replied and sniffed angrily towards the window.

"She was dragged away before she ever got to the garage," Lisa said. "She never entered until Thomas brought her back. So how would she have been able to give you the code if she never even saw how to get in, in the first place."

"She didn't," Bean almost snapped, but kept his tone. "Someone helped her lie to me."

"From inside her own head," Lisa asked.

"Exactly," Bean said. "Her maker put the images in her head, even made Natalie believe she had memory of seeing it, which, in the confusion of all Natalie had gone through that night, would have been easy to do. If there's one thing I should have known, it's that psychology teaches traumatic events often create false memories, and, in my arrogance, I thought I could tell traumatic from real. Pshh! Shows what I knew.

"I thought I had gotten most of the code, but I found I needed a key. When I discovered that, I tried tearing the place down, but Richard knows the material to use that can stand up to even wolves.

"Natalie gave away nothing about a key, not even a glimmer of a memory. Naturally, I brought in a locksmith. Funny thing though, the locksmith's tools kept breaking. Turns out the deadbolt breaks anything other than the correct key and discharges its remains.

Ingenious, actually. So I searched for the real key, which wasn't always easy with Speatsh and your security cameras roaming the grounds, but I made due.

"Eventually, I found one in Richard's house in a safe that someone was kind enough to break open for me."

"Did it have a hole in it," Lisa asked.

"Oh, you saw it too," Bean asked.

"I saw Josh put it there," she said.

"Well, I sure did appreciate his help," Bean said. "So I finally find the key and a full keyboard, not a keypad for entering simple digits. That's when I realize I'm being toyed with. So I decide to kill Natalie at the next full moon. Luckily, for both of us, Thomas showed up. Also, it was a good thing that I didn't know about the back entrance. Although, I doubt I would have survived getting through it to be honest.

"Anyway, that's when I started looking for a hacker and eventually found Kenny." Bean fell into his silent thought again. "So, why is that technological worm with the suit now?"

"Apparently, to die," Lisa seethed.

Winter had stretched her pacing to reach between the bathroom door and the window now.

"Hmm," Bean said, then left his two companions hanging on that verbal thought for far longer than either of them liked. "How does he join up with you?"

"Let's see, we met the rodeo—I mean, us—tonight. So, if memory serves, I think Josh rescues him tomorrow night, from the junkyard," Lisa explained, mocking this idea of rescue.

"From the junkyard?"

"Josh was scouting for farms. It was infested with wolves," Lisa continued to explain. "Kenny was being delivered. He broke away and—it was a set up, wasn't it?"

"I remember meeting with the suit, so I guess that was tonight," Bean said. "But I don't recall if that was before or after I met with the inquisitor, I'm assuming before. It was the only time that I wouldn't have been home or near the junkyard at some point during the day.

That might explain why I didn't know. He was careful to hide that from me, wasn't he?" Bean's face suddenly lit up. "Oh! I just realized I could kill the inquisitor again, can't I?" His dark smile turned into an even darker frown. "It's the thought that counts, I suppose."

The group had dispersed. Kenny now remained alone.

Winter's finger suddenly pressed against the glass of the window, her face long, pale. She glanced to Bean.

The others followed Winter's finger towards a well-groomed couple and their black Scottish Terrier. They approached Kenny.

Bean suddenly pulled Lisa to the floor beneath the view of the window. Winter was already waiting on it.

"What is it," Lisa asked.

Bean held his finger to his lips. He closed his eyes a moment, saluting for no sound. Suddenly, his eyes popped open. "Hide," he mouthed and leapt over one of the beds, carrying Lisa with him.

Winter took up a hiding spot behind the second bed. They all remained from view of the window. Bean quickly disappeared into the bathroom, leaving Lisa in her hiding.

Water gushed from the distant shower head, and Bean began singing, badly.

Lisa was about to object, but drew back as the large black general's head appeared in the window. Its shadow loomed over the far wall like a silhouette art projection. A second appeared, nearly identical to the first.

The window rattled and then the exterior walls scratched as the shadows disappeared and their beasts quickly ran across them. The patter of their feet trailed into silence.

Bean continued to sing. After several hallelujah choruses of—well, who knew what song Bean was singing—something Scotly and pub-ish, he finally stopped and crept out of the bathroom. The shower-head still thundered. From the rays of light breaking through the bathroom door, he motioned for Winter and Lisa to stay hidden as he ventured out. He eventually walked into the room, up to the window and nonchalantly drew the curtain across.

"It's time for bed, kids," he said. "See you in the morning." A few moments later and the bathroom was dark and quiet. Bean disappeared through the connecting door to his own suite.

Winter and Lisa each crawled into one of the double beds, let their heads hit the pillows and remained unable to nod off for most of the night. When Lisa awoke, Winter was already out of bed. In fact, she was out of the room.

The walls were dark from drawn curtains, but daylight leaked from their edges. She allowed herself a few minutes to run her routine of waking up, which involved a few grunts, curse words and cracking of joints from her new host body, which were still fewer than she used to have in her old one. She made her way to the sink to wash her face and reached for a gas lantern, before realizing power was still abundant enough to waste on a morning ritual. She turned on the electric lights and basked in the wonderful practice of morning wastefulness that came from more than just bathroom lights.

She framed herself up in the mirror.

She would have preferred her own face. This one was rounder and practically had no lips. Exploring her reflection was a little adventurous: a fleck of a mole below her right eye; perfect cheeks, but too white of teeth; ears elegantly pierced with rhinestone boots spurred through them. Her nose had been broken and clearly rebuilt, perhaps a couple of times. Her pores were abused by too thick of make-up, most likely for stage, maybe from pride—based on her nose-work, Lisa assumed the latter.

The worst discovery was that her hair was bleached. She could see the brunette reeds clearly in need of a blonde touch up. Perhaps, the real queens did this to appeal more to distant arena audiences? She didn't care for it, but it had been awhile since she had long, young hair so she didn't wast thought on cutting it.

However, what moron treated this new head?

Lisa hated this face and wanted her own back. As long as she was stuck with it though, she might as well plan a stop or two for more appropriate supplies to treat it better. Then, she remembered where she was. Now, was not the time to stroke pride. Why the sudden interest in appearance anyway? Maybe because it was something forgotten?

Oh, but her hair was greasy and still had splotches of blood from the accident in it. Wait a minute! Was this a bit of brain matter?

"I'm taking a shower," she announced.

"If you insist," Bean's voice called back.

Lisa showered and enjoyed the salt-free water. After years of bathing in the ocean, she had forgotten how sweet the aroma of treated water had been. She enjoyed what the hot tap had to provide; enjoyed the discovery of the sauna controls even more; and then relished following it up with a quick burst of cold spray before leaving the glass and stone closet. She returned to a steamed mirror. Her recently-acquired, blonde hair seemed darker when wet. At least its roots seemed less noticeable, and it was clean of blood stain now. She dried herself, wondered about her other friends, worried about Nick and convinced herself that they would be fine.

Still, Nick was prone to stupidity. She missed him.

Then she dressed back into the same clothes she had been wearing. It was time to discover what her companions were up to.

Both were in Bean's apartment hunched over his king-sized bed, staring upon it and lost in thought. The pillows and unused bedding sat piled over a small round table before a drawn curtain.

Only a plain off-white sheet remained over the mattress. It had been vandalized with red and black scribbling. Bean leaned over the sheet and marked on it further with a mascara brush.

"I just had a question," Lisa announced. "How exactly does getting back to our time work?"

Bean continued to lean across the sheet and complete whatever he was painting. He returned the mascara brush to its bottle and shook both, all without losing focus on the sheet. "You thought we were going back," he asked.

"Only makes sense," Lisa replied.

"Mmm, no," Bean replied. "This is one-way for us. If we accomplish what we came here to do, there shouldn't be a place for us to return to, and the old us should have a better outcome than the one we know."

"Don't you think you should have told us that before we came here," Lisa asked.

"Why? Did you want to go back," Bean asked. He looked up from his strange mural. "You'd have come anyway," he said. "Josh was your friend; our time stunk; and you're unselfish that way." He threw his attention back to his sheet.

"OK, assuming then that we rewrite the future," Lisa said. "The genie—"

"Djinn," Bean corrected.

"Djinn," Lisa said loathingly at Bean's need to correct. "Your secret plan was to send people back in time, change the future and free the djinn so the rogue couldn't counter our plan."

"Well, and it's the nice thing to do for her," Bean replied.

"And where is the djinn now?"

"Safe," Bean replied again. He patted his fat cargo pocket. "Yeah, she's still there."

"So you brought the djinn we don't want the rogue to know about with you," Lisa explained. "And if you don't free her, anyone can come along in the future; find her after you make your wishes; and counteract everything we do here."

"Oh they don't have to wait until then," Bean answered. "Her concept of time isn't linear liker ours. Anyone can find her at any time."

"What," Lisa blurted in confusion. "All I'm trying to get at is: if we come back and change the timeline for our old selves, what happens to us then? Won't we—I don't know—disappear, or something, because the we that we are now won't exist anymore because we won't have been made. Won't we adapt into other versions of ourselves? And if we're the future selves now of a past that changes and, let's say, we just evolve into the new selves, won't our being here do something to the us in the time where we should be. Oh my gosh! Are we going to cease to exist if we succeed?"

"What are you talking about," Bean asked.

"Isn't this just basic timeline philosophy?"

"I love Star Trek too," Bean said. "But you know it's not real, right?"

"Don't make fun of me," Lisa replied.

"Okay, look," Bean replied. "We, you and I, comprehend time linearly. We only understand forward. It's human, but djinn encompass time. There's no linear. They manipulate time because they happen to just be there, see it all. To a djinn, moving us from our time to this time is as simple as moving a chess piece on a board. To us, however, past, future, we remain who we are because we are in a constant state of progressing, and memory follows. Our past is what it is, and our future is what we have yet to make. If our time disappears, it won't matter because, as to our understanding of time, we have already progressed beyond that, and the djinn's understanding of time, potential future or not, we're simply here. There's no 'oh no, we're going to fade away, Mcfly' going on here. We exist within progression. Time—as we're capable of understanding it—doesn't undo that. It only moves forward with what happens to enter into it. Yesterday is always gone, yet we always continue to exist.

"There's no, 'if the old me dies in the future or the past, I will cease to exist here' because time is progressive to us, just as life is progressive, always moving forward."

"Until you die," Lisa pointed out.

"Well yeah," Bean replied, "But you still progress, whether in decay or passing on energy to the cosmos."

"But how can you progress when somewhere along your past timeline, even though it is in the future, you may cease to exist," Lisa asked.

"Well assuming that it's possible for your to simply cease to exist in one frame of time," Bean continued. "That sudden non-existence would have to be capable of progressing into any direction of time to catch up with the part of you that can progress, which is our current state, and, when something no longer exists, it can't progress because it doesn't exist, whereas we do, so we get further and further away from the state of non-existence."

"What," Lisa blurted in exasperation.

Bean huffed at Lisa and held up his mascara stick. "Let's say this is the future us." Now, he held up the mascara bottle next to the stick. "And suppose this is the past us. Both of these points continue to proceed at the same pace along the timeline. They're always the same distance apart. However far this little brush progresses, the bottle has also progressed that exact same amount. If we somehow cease to exist back here—I don't know, maybe God decides to toss our bottle in the garbage." Bean tossed the bottle into a wastebasket near the nightstand. "Then it doesn't matter because future us continues to progress, therefore continues to exist. For us to simply disappear, the past where we ceased to exist would have to somehow progress along the timeline at a rate fast enough to catch up with future us on that timeline. If something doesn't exist in a timeline, it can't progress in the timeline. It would stop progressing entirely while we, where we do exist, would continue to move forward in time, moving us actually farther away from that point in time where we did cease to exist.

"It's a race we can't lose. Kind of like if the hare had a headstart and then suddenly turned and shot the tortoise dead. The rabbit could sleep all day; buy a new house on the race track; move into that house to retire and die; and then hire a taxi to drive him across the finish line a hundred years later, and the hare would still win the race. No matter what, the dead tortoise is never going to catch up with him. In other words, you can cease to exist in the past, but still exist now because there's no you in the past to run up to you in the future, or now even, and say, 'sorry, but you can't be here.'"

"Ah," Lisa began to inquire smugly. "But what if we progress into the frame of time where we cease to exist, shouldn't there be some sonic boom or black hole or something to cancel each other out?"

"No," Bean shrilled incredulously. "Impossible!"

"Why?"

"Because if we no longer exist in that frame of time, there's nothing for our progressive selves to collide with to create such a destructive force," Bean replied. "Not to mention, hopefully, we're not going back to that future anyway and won't have to worry about taking that same path. That's just how our time works. And before you ask, no our existence in this timeline doesn't cause a problem with our existence in the past timeline because, even though we may appear in this timeline with our past selves, we are still progressing according to that of our future selves. It's like we're on the same race track as our past selves, we're just on the second lap. Our past selves may be beside us, but we're still a full lap ahead of them. We may be in this time, but we're still progressing according to our own moment in time."

"And the djinn's interaction with time doesn't work that way," Lisa asked. "Hers doesn't progress, so if we cease to exist as she sees time, it doesn't have to catch up with progression. We just cease to exist to her?"

"Yes and no," Bean said, "Since she sees time in all possible outcomes, we will always exist to her and always not exist to her. The only way we could cease to exist entirely to her if she ceases to exist herself."

"I see," Lisa said. "Any more confusion you'd like to damper me with while we're on the topic?"

"Always," Bean said and returned to hovering over the bed sheet. "We're locked in this finite of inertia, if you will. That's your body now. I'm young again. Our mute friend—okay, she's still mute—but the point is: will we return as ourselves to the better life we wanted all this time? No, but we can give a better life to our former selves, and they'll never know our agoney. The world will still be a better place if we succeed. So, we can move forward in our own ways; take part in that; and potentially leave our bad memories behind.

"Look," Bean said in frustration, realizing that Lisa didn't fully approve of his approach. "We can only be where we are; go where we're going; and have been where we've been. A djinn is always there no matter what time is possible."

Bean fell silent as he seemed to spend a bit of time on a small section of mascara detailing on the bed sheet before him. Lisa was about to ask him to focus when he suddenly pulled away from drawing to retrieve the mascara bottle from the wastebasket.

"Still confused," he asked as he closed and shook the container some more. "Our djinn has no future, no past—well, except the events leading up to her being tricked into trading places with the djinn before her, but now we're talking supernatural events and that's a whole new theory the application of time, I'm sure. She is simply there, among all possibilities of time and historical outcome, and when she's not there—laced in time—there will be no djinn for the rogue or anyone else to find, past, future or present."

"You're saying that even though we have her, the rogue could still find her somewhere else, because technically she exists in all time," Lisa asked.

"Unless we free her."

"If we free her," Lisa asked. "The rogue can't find her."

"Right,"

"What if he finds her before we do in the future?"

"Won't matter," Bean said. "Once she's freed, she disappears from her perspective of time and becomes a permanent fixture of our linear time. In other words, she'll become progressive."

"But you're taking her place," Lisa said. "He could find you instead. You'd still be there."

"We'll see," Bean said.

"I don't understand," Lisa replied.

Bean laughed to himself. "Remember, trading places with the djinn is only one way to free one," he explained. "When you sacrifice a wish to break their bond with time, you're, in essence, making their ability to thread time incapable so they have no choice but to progress on the timeline they are freed upon. So a wish can do it too."

"But you plan to free her," Lisa asked.

"Yes," Bean said, and he returned to examining the bed sheet with all his scrawlings upon it.

"So free her now," Lisa said.

"Can't," Bean replied. "We might need that wish. You can only call on a djinn to free them, wish on them, or plan a wish, but that's part of wishing on them."

"So you've been saving her for in case you need to use that wish you tricked out of her?"

"I would rather keep myself out of an eternity of servitude," Bean replied. "But if I have no other choice, then I will honor my word."

"Because you've so humbly agreed to take her place and become the djinn?"

"Yep."

"So then we'd get three more wishes because we already have you."

"You'd have to find me first," Bean said. "I believe you're required to hide yourself so you have to be found. You know, no playing Pass the Bottle among friends."

"But the rogue *could* find you."

"Not just the rogue," Bean replied, his nose pressed up tight against the sheet.

"Anyone could find you?"

"Yes."

"From any timeline?"

"Yes."

"And mess with our timeline even more," Lisa said. "Perhaps they're already doing it now."

"Kind of screws with your brain doesn't it," Bean chuckled.

"That's not funny!"

"No one else is messing with the timeline," Bean encouraged.

"How do we know that?"

"Because she's still a djinn," Bean replied. Then he patted his pocket just to make sure. "And she's still in my pocket. If someone else had found her, she wouldn't be there anymore."

"That's reassuring," Lisa said.

"Not really," Bean replied. "Because then we'd have to find her again to take her back and make our final wish."

"You're saying at any moment someone from any time could find her and she could disappear on us and none of what we do here is guaranteed to stay," Lisa complained. "We're just hoping we can use her before she goes off somewhere else like some inter-delusional timebomb."

"Time bomb," Bean guffawed. "That's funny! I wouldn't worry about someone finding her. Look how difficult it was for us. No one else has ever found her."

"How do you know that," Cadence asked.

"Because she's still in my pocket," Bean replied.

"You're very casual about this," Lisa said. "We should end this."

"A good plan requires patience," Bean said. "Besides, it's not your wish."

"It's not yours either," Lisa said. "You said so yourself. Someone else made the wish."

"Someone else gave me permission to help plan and execute the wish," Bean replied. "But this last wish is mine. I stole it from her fair and square. I know my part."

"And what's that," Lisa asked.

"Not sure yet," Bean replied, then dabbed the sheets some more.

"All right, so we're stuck here in new bodies." Lisa said trying to ignore Bean's lack of interest to answer anything straight. "If these bodies are ours now, how are you still wolf?"

"I'd have thought you would have figured that out by now," Bean said. "The answer is, if I understood her correctly, we took the looks so we wouldn't be recognized, but the real us, our essence, who we are: our insides, blood, organs and souls needed to come with us. That's what rebuilt and strengthened those internal bits and pieces of our hosts that caused their deaths."

"You mean, we're still old," Lisa asked. "If my old heart replaced this young one, I could still have a heart attack any minute now?"

"No," Bean replied. "Okay. Maybe I said it wrong. Think of it this way. We, you, me, us, our organs, brain, blood, didn't replace anything here, we acted as glue, held everything together, help it heal. Since I was infected with wolf, and my essence was used to repair this body, that infection is now in this body. You're young again. Your old parts repaired your new, young parts. That's good and bad, bad because your body now might not have the ability you've been used to having if your host didn't upkeep it. The good news is, you're young again."

"So you're saying I have to start training again," Lisa asked. "To get my strength and flexibility back."

"Maybe not," Bean replied. "Your hosts are performers, rodeo athletes I'm sure we can assume. You may be more fit than your old self, but finding out wouldn't hurt."

"I do need some new clothes," Lisa replied. "Suppose I could get some by way of a run. I'm not wearing this crap."

"I thought we decided you should wear them."

"The hats," Lisa said. "Not the showy theatrical junk."

"We have a different agenda, and we need to stay in character," Bean explained. "That means looking the part for when we join your old companions and selves. Those ugly, bright suits might be the only communication we three are going to have between us."

"If we have to wear it, you have to wear it. You're harder to see than we are."

"I have a wolf bandana on my head." Bean returned to his mural, shaking his bottle of mascara.

"And what are you doing," Lisa asked at last in frustration.

Bean stopped just short of drawing. "Finally, a question of value," he said. "We're trying to see how it all fits. Well, I am. Some people just make you work to find out for yourself."

Lisa decided to actually study the marked sheet. Dates and years littered its face with short phrases and a detailed description or two. Badly-drawn pictures appeared every so often. "What is this," she asked.

"An equation," Bean replied.

"Why mascara," Lisa asked already knowing her answer would be treated as ludicrous.

"Because I ran out of red nail polish," Bean replied as he looked at her as though she were a fool.

Well, she called that one.

"There's probably a pen or pencil in a drawer here," she said.

"Didn't show up well on the sheet."

"There's paper."

"Too small," Bean replied.

"Where'd you get the mascara?"

"Found it in some ugly woman's purse."

"Will you just tell me what you're going to tell me anyway," Lisa blurted.

"Where's the fun in that," Bean replied. He smiled as he shook the mascara bottle. "I have to work for it, why shouldn't you have to?"

Lisa did not smile back.

"I'm trying to understand Kenny's role," Bean replied. He pointed a gruff and swollen finger at the sheet. "Here's where Josh rescues him tonight, this is what we saw last night. This is my dealings with the inquisitor."

"What does that have to do with Kenny?"

"Everything is always interlaced," Bean explained. "You have to look at the bigger picture if you want to understand a plan. If I can see why Kenny's involved, I might see what I'm missing. If Kenny was in your compound, he may have played a role in Josh's death. That's worth considering changing."

"What's that," Lisa asked, pointing to some strange markings.

"That's seven-hundred years ago, it's hard to explain."

"Seven-hundred years ago would explain Kenny?"

"Seven-hundred years ago explains everything."

"Okay," Lisa said. "I thought you were coming up with a real plan."

"This is a real plan," Bean complained. "If the inquisitor had done this, he might still live."

"I don't get it."

"The rogue put a lot of effort into bringing Josh down," Bean explained. "He's very selective about humans he uses. If I can find something that makes sense, I can help predict his moves. Seven-hundred years ago, the rogue wiped out a den of hunters without raising a finger, I thought it might help me understand how he plans."

"Did it help?"

"I don't know yet. Look." Bean began pointing to different places on the sheet.

Acotactac helped stretch the sheet so some areas could show better.

"David Gin steals Cracey, accidentally uncovering Josh's ancient ancestry and making the wrong momma mad. I save Cracey, only I don't save her," Bean explained. "I accelerate them."

"Because Bricktain couldn't find her," Lisa replied.

"No," Bean said. "Because I think I sent her into a coma of sorts."

"Huh?"

"Something to do with mixing virus with virus. Too inappropriate to explain right now," Bean said. "The point is, this forces a growth spurt of inexperienced hunters, you, who come knocking on my door looking for Josh's little sister, which I believe will upset the rogue if he finds out because this is hallowed ground. My job is to keep generals out of Plattsville because that's what the rogue wants. Ha. Ha. Joke's on me."

"It's not a good joke," Lisa observed.

"My job, I thought, was to destroy any insubordinate general who tried to set up shop. Apparently, I was here to keep generals from uncovering the ancients. I thought I was his eyes and ears," Bean replied. "However, my arrogance and personal vendetta allowed hunters to discover me. I kept my agenda hidden from the rogue until I tried to use a mental connection with Natalie to learn the code to the bunker you were hiding in, but that plan backfired and alerted the rogue to my failures. Or perhaps started the entire war completely."

Bean's finger slid to another section of notes written upon the sheet.

"His response was to assassinate me, but you killed my assassin, which doesn't bother me, really, because it's not the one I was expecting the rogue to send, and now another must come, the inquisitor, to get me back in line. Then your small group of hunters defeats two generals, and, in doing so, the rogue is now aware of your abilities, and he decides it's time to bring all of his followers to Plattsville. Why?" Bean finally asked.

"Before the cavern, I would have said because he discovered Josh was the heir," Lisa replied. "But now I have to say because Josh was made aware, he was on the brink of waking up."

"Wrong," Bean replied. "He could have manipulated that at any time and with less confrontation from Josh. Barbara's assistance was evidence of that. Why after all that time of my guarding Plattsville, did he decide to appear now?"

"Do I look like I understand," Lisa asked.

"Carnage," Bean replied. "The cat was out of the bag. Speatsh turned Josh into the paladin to become a beacon to attract both hunters and slaves to him. The rogue allowed Speatsh to bring them all into one place where they can all be slaughtered in one move. Speatsh defined the battleground."

"And set us up to be trapped and killed by the elementals," Lisa said, shuddering.

"I'm not so sure that was the rogue's doing," Bean replied.

"Then whose?"

"I haven't figured that out yet. My theory is all I can give you, but it's incomplete," Bean said.

"Give me what you can."

"Thomas came back to Plattsville," Bean said. "Speatsh raised hunters, and that invited others to make a stand with them. The most elite of hunters who ever lived were backing Josh and calling others to him, which is exactly what the rogue wanted. Even Thomas was finally seduced by Speatsh, or so it appeared. Do you see, yet?"

"No," Lisa blurted. "And neither do you, or you wouldn't be stealing mascara to write on sheets."

"All this time, they've been preparing you for war," Bean explained. "Hunting me was just convenient practice. They knew generals weren't allowed in this crappy town, which is why Speatsh never stayed here, and why Thomas never stuck around. They didn't need to. The rogue had me watching the city, and Speatsh had Richard and Oliver watching the queen. I have my assumptions that they knew something was off with the queen, or either Speatsh would have been in on it with the rogue or he'd be dead. He had his own game, and I haven't figured that out either. From Thomas's history with Speatsh, I don't think he ever knew how much to trust Speatsh neither. So Speatsh hid what he did well. Either way, The city was safe, despite my being here. When Josh's sister was taken, Speatsh and Thomas probably thought it was a general working from the shadows that I hadn't been able to catch. When it turned out to be one of my own, Speatsh fueled Josh to take on the fight, maybe to watch how much he could trust Josh. My people told you about finding Thomas—

Bean suddenly stopped and wrote some more on the sheet.

"That was an unexpected for everyone's part," Bean said. "But it played into the rogue's hands nonetheless."

"I'm still not following," Lisa said.

"Think," Bean said. He appeared angry now. "Hunters were gathering in one spot. The rogue started gathering his army in one spot."

Lisa wasn't seeing it.

"You studied the pages Amber recovered from that book at the museum," Bean shouted. "A carriage that feeds off of death, reviving others? The museum had bodies of ancients. He has some ancients he wants to revive, and that's not counting the ones we found in the cave."

"He needed everyone together so he could massacre them," Lisa finally realized.

"Yes," Bean praised. "Ten thousand will bring back one, as Amber said Josh told her."

"He didn't build an army to fight the human race," Lisa said. "You think he built an army out of the human race so he could kill it, and bring his family members back."

"And, I'm not sure what this circle means in this other picture, but I think it's some sort of coronation ceremony," Bean said. "I think he wants the ancients alive to exalt himself. I think he somehow needs them to receive their approval or power. He even convinced his own sister, the queen, to help him."

"That theory doesn't work," Lisa said.

"Of course it does," Bean said. "What part don't you understand?"

"A couple reasons," Lisa explained. "When the elementals wiped us out, they didn't have this revivification carriage. Why waste those lives?"

"I agree with you on that one," Bean said. "That's got me stumped."

"Not to mention, the rogue turned Josh on us," Lisa said. "If the rogue needed lives to fuel the carriage, why turn Josh and send him to kill his allies?"

"And that's the million-dollar question," Bean explained. "If the rogue kills his army, what's to keep some other branch from rising against him in the future? Remember the generals in the graveyard? They butchered the guardians. Why?"

"Perhaps, the rogue thought he had the carriage," Lisa answered. "It didn't work though."

"Yes," Bean agreed. "But he didn't have the carriage when the compound was attacked. Remember what I said last night about the rogue being selective with the humans he chooses to turn? I babysat Plattsville. The inquisitor broke humanity. Genre was hand-picked to protect the rogue. The guardians were fodder for fuel and so, might I add, were his generals. Anyone can be a general. Any general can bite and turn guardians and scouts. Anyone can raise an army against the ruler of the ancients. He did it himself, and it took him a really long time."

"I'm lost again," Lisa said.

"I believe the rogue turned Josh on his own camp, not to kill them, but to turn them into something so powerful that no other ancient would dare dispute his power," Bean said. "I think he was sent to turn the wisest and most skilled of killers in his world into a new kind of wolf army, one that would protect the rogue into his rule. They would be servants of Josh, mixed with the blood of ancients, and they would all answer to the rogue. They'd all have ancient blood in them. That's not just the power of one master, that's the power of many. No one would have dared challenge him ever again."

"But Josh did kill," Lisa reminded. "Thomas and others."

"Ah, but Amber beheaded Josh before we could have found out if there was a link there, didn't she," Bean said. "And I don't think Thomas can be turned. That's his curse. Blood is a meal to him, just fills his veins. So Josh had no other choice but to kill what would be the rogue's most powerful adversary after Josh had turned all the hunters. The only ones who did die that night were those engaged in firefight with the mercs, which I believe was a result of simply trying to keep Josh free so he could run his attack."

"Oh my gosh. You're saying the goal was to let Josh build a new breed of superwolf," Lisa said finally understanding.

"And after Josh built it out of his own allies," Bean explained. "They would be powerful enough to conduct the rogue's full slaughter of all scouts, guardians, even his generals within the presence of the carriage. Enough power to wipe out entire armies of wolves and hunters, revive the ancients, and provide the rogue his own personal guard more powerful that even Genre."

"That's a genius plan," Lisa acknowledged. "Looking back, it's a wonder it didn't work."

"Because the merc's made one teeny, tiny mistake," Bean explained. "They killed Amber's dad. Remember when I told you that it takes showing someone what they've lost to make them dangerous? Murdering her father made Amber dangerous enough to deliver the killing blow to Josh. Amber, a simple human, put an end to the rogue's superwolf. Then, later, Chandler didn't deliver the carriage, and that destroyed everything the rogue had built for just that moment. All this time, we thought we had lost the war, but we actually foiled the rogue's strategy. We just didn't win, but neither did he. Now, everything the rogue does is to build an army to find us for his own vengeance."

"So how do we go through that again without losing Josh or our own army this time," Lisa asked.

"We have to secure Josh, secure the carriage and figure out how to use it against the rogue," Bean said. "Otherwise, we end up back where we ended before, flying away in What's cages and watching humanity eventually waste away. Because there will be no other choice."

"What's your idea then," Lisa asked.

"I don't know," Bean shrieked. "As brilliant as I like to think I am, I can't think around what I don't observe. I wish I knew more about Speatsh's approach. I need to know what Josh was going to say about the carriage."

"There's a problem with that," Lisa pointed out. "If Josh thinks it, then the rogue will know too, won't he? If the link with Josh was how the rogue knew our plans all this time, he'll just out-maneuver us once again."

"So you see the problem there," Bean said. "We need Josh to reveal, but the second he even thinks about it, the rogue knows. Our only option is to be able to act faster."

"Wait a sec," Lisa said. "What does any of this have to do with understanding Kenny? It thought that's what your bed sheets here were all about in the first place."

"This part, right here," Bean said pointing to a section of sheet heavily condensed with notes. "I imagine Speatsh could have killed Barbara while she was in the bunker or even earlier, but he didn't, maybe because he had plans for her. I imagine it was because she was his mother. I happen to have reason to believe that he convinced her to lay low."

"How so?"

"I kind of hinted at it with Speatsh the night you all went into hiding."

"Wait, you what?"

"For whatever reason, maybe he convinces her that if Josh should awaken on his own and learn the truth of her treachery, Josh would kill her out of feelings of anger and betrayal. Plus, being a new wolf and all, maybe Josh would be hard to control. Anyway, somehow, Speatsh convinces her the best way to protect herself is to hide. Barbara's an ancient, she spent who knows how many millions of years living in isolation before she decided to leave the den, a few years of severed spine, would be so simple for her."

"But we've already established that doesn't break the psychic link," Lisa said. "The rogue still got into Josh's head."

"Yeah, and I'm pretty sure it's because Josh was inherently an ancient. He's linked to the circle by blood," Bean said. "But you know who's not?"

"You really expect me to know this," Lisa screamed. "I hate your puzzle—Bogi! Bogi's not an ancient! Severing her spine wasn't to cut off the link with Josh. It was to cut off the link with Bogi!."

"And the Taichomée," Bean added.

"Speatsh found a way to keep their general ignorant and committed treason right under their noses, at least I think that's what must have happened. They think he's weaning Josh for the rogue so they can't see what he's really up to, and Speatsh lies so much to everyone that no one, not even Speatsh himself, can tell what is reality and what is truth through his own inherited connection. Speatsh even confuses the situation more by making Josh believe that you, my dear Cad—Lisa, are the heir. He gives Josh information to complicate Speatsh's approaches even more. Every time Josh asks a question, Speatsh has to lie his way through. I would not be surprised to find out that Speatsh's defense to keep the rogue out of his own mind was to constantly lie so much that the rogue avoided his link because it couldn't be trusted."

"What about the farms," Lisa asked. "Josh knew about the farms."

"And just how much interference did you get rescuing people from those farms," Bean asked. "A small fight here and there? Enough action that you felt like you were actually planning something out and even succeeding?"

Lisa wanted to voice her sudden realization.

"That's right," Bean cried. "You were played! The rogue, Barbara, Bogi. They played you. They played Thomas. They played Speatsh. You had the clues the entire time and didn't even need Speatsh to see them, and you still didn't see them."

"What clues could we possibly have had," Lisa cried. "I didn't even know we'd been betrayed until you and I stumbled into Bogi's secret cave."

"Who gave Amber the blade to kill Thomas with," Bean poignantly asked

"Bogi, but it didn't work," Lisa replied. "It was a prank."

"Was it," Bean asked. "Or was Thomas simply prepared for it?"

"I don't know," Lisa said. "I never thought about it. We've always been so busy. One day we're happy-go-lucky in college, the next we're taking guidance from a werewolf, a cat and a vampire. How were we supposed to know anything?"

"Enter my individual interests and keen insight," Bean said. "What I suddenly see is Josh and his friends go into hiding. Then Speatsh goes inside that bunker after someone turned his friends into wolves, and that someone who turned them wasn't me. My job is to keep generals out of my town, remember? So who is in that bunker with you? Maybe I can use that to unwittingly help me defeat the inquisitor, who, as we mentioned took his sweet time getting here. Have I lost you?"

"No," Lisa lied, but only a little.

"I needed into the bunker," Bean said. He grabbed a handful of sheet and held it up to Lisa as though she should be able to understand what he was talking about.

"We know you needed into the bunker," Lisa bellowed. "You told us, you tried to get into Natalie's head. I think we've established that you tried getting into the bunker."

"Right," Bean replied throwing down the sheet and pointing to another section covered in the text of blue eye shadow. "What you're not getting is that I breached the bunker."

"I get it, you let the guardians in," Lisa said. "Thank you, I remember that day."

"I didn't have the codes," Bean said. "Weren't you listening last night?"

"My brain is fried," Lisa said. "Just say it already."

"Who do you think had the technological expertise to get me inside?"

Lisa slowly understood and released a sigh of frustration just as gradually, "That little turd."

"Yes! Kenny broke us in—and afterwards, I sent Kenny on his way."

"So why is he back," Lisa asked. "He could just break in."

"How," Bean asked. "When he let wolves in before, you destroyed them in a bottle neck elevator. Even I knew to abandon that fight and just wait for you to come out. Had I known you were going camping with the Taichomée for a month! All that time I spent trying to get in, and you just let Kenny in on your own."

"We were already suspicious of Kenny after he joined us," Lisa said.

"Yet, despite that suspicion, you still let him in," Bean replied. "You let him stay. Why do you think he stayed? What was his purpose?"

"Infiltrate the group?"

"Weak," Bean said. "The rogue hardly needed him, he had Bogi and Josh's mother for that."

"Protection," Lisa said.

"Still weak," Bean replied. "Come on! Give me something that adds up here."

"I don't know," Lisa said. "Maybe he wanted to switch sides? Move up the ranks? We did put him in charge of our security system at the compound."

Bean entertained himself with the thought a moment. "Meh. You guys were desperate for technology, he proved his ability in the compound. No, he wanted inside the bunker. Why? I can't see it."

"To communicate with Bogi," Lisa asked.

"There's a thought," Bean said then, "No, still doesn't add up. Something's missing, or else I'm just not seeing it."

Lisa stared at Bean's strange equation drawn across the sheet, even helped straighten it out on the mattress to help him read it more clearly himself. She wished she understood it as much as Winter seemed to, but she just didn't. Or maybe Winter was really just asleep on her feet, bored to death of Bean's overthinking. Apparently, she was. Lisa let her stay that way.

How difficult this must have been on Winter. Josh wasn't the only person who discovered family was treacherous. Winter had lost her own tribe as well. Lisa stirred her emotions, remembering the deaths of her own parents. In this moment, she felt guilty that so much time had been spent empathizing with the treason of Josh's family, yet little had been spent on the betrayal of those who adopted Winter.

"If we have no next step prepared," Lisa suggested. "I'm going for a run and see what this body can do. Anyone care to join me?"

No one answered.

"Take a stun baton," Bean said.

"I doubt any wolves are watching for me."

"Who said it was for wolves?"

23 ~ The Crosswalk

Gunshots!

Any hope that the RV might have some workout clothes went out the broken windshield as well as the missing and unlocked doors. They all expected it, actually. What had once been inside the motor home, was now stretched over the hotel parking lot that sat across the street from the silent neon bull. Had they left the good stuff like the weapons and munchies behind, Lisa might have been more upset, but neither she nor her friends were that stupid. She was happy about the theft because now she had an excuse to go shopping, which meant returning a moment to her room and retrieving some of Bean's cash, in case the debit and credit card in her newly acquired wallet didn't work for her.

She felt foolish walking around in her ridiculously-tasseled, pink and white western wear, but it was sure to be temporary.

It wasn't too far down the street to a little thrift store she remembered. She chose to walk the distance, not because she thought she looked stupid running in her gaudy costume, but because she thought she sounded annoying in all her crunchy dress leather and dangling cymbals clamoring into each other. This led to thoughts about how her pink, leather pants would announce any attack she might make in the future, and that led to her realization that the only way to silence the leather was to oil it up and break it in for more of her fighting style, which meant treatment and running.

What a nightmare!

She chose a black backpack to store her current gear in. Then she found a pair of jeans to replace the pink pants, only to discover they didn't fit. Mostly, she gathered some light workout gear. She was about to change into the workout clothes when she reminded herself once more that maybe all she needed was to put the ugly leather pants through a rigorous workout to make them more comfortable. So she simply purchased a white sweatshirt and the backpack. Returning outside, she tied the sweatshirt around her hips.

She was a bit proud that she had made the costume pants look more like bright, neon warmups beneath her new, hideous sweatshirt. After leaving the thrift shop, she tried her debit card at a convenience store to see if she could purchase some bottles of water for her pack. Lastly, she stopped into a small pawn broker and purchased a pocket knife to aerate her leather by slicing the knees open.

Next, she cut into the side of her pack and slid the stun baton in so she could hide and retrieve it easily. Up until now, she had concealed the weapon under the back of her pink jacket. She thought it would have been smart to cut out the long sleeves and make it a vest, but she also realized that long leather sleeves were still some sort of shielding against wolf attacks. She had to consider this stuff since she was going to be in the thick of fights now and not watching them through a scope.

She could handle the long sleeves, but it reminded her that she needed to get familiar with her gear. She started her run.

Two miles down the street, she stopped into the first department store she came across and bought a pair of white jeans off the rack and a can of pink spray paint from the automotive section. She disappeared into the restrooms after the checkout stands to change out of her horrible, smoldering leather. Right there, she painted her jeans to match the bright-pink, plastic cap of the spray can. Leather or not, Bean was right. She had to keep her higher visibility with Bean and Winter, which she still happened to hate the idea of.

She was used to staying in the shadows. That was her entire purpose. Now, she had to stick out like a full-fledged target. She kept her black boots with sparkly whatever-they-weres spackling them. She didn't know what the sparklies were. She didn't care, but strange as it may have seemed, she didn't find them all that uncomfortable to run in, probably because her host had actually known something about cowboy boots. They were Ariats. Sure, they were violated with plastic jewels and decoration for show, but they were a perfect and comfortable fit all the same.

She stuffed her pink, leather pants into the restroom trashcan and continued outside to resume her run. She might have found the leather jacket a little too hot as well, but she still couldn't bring herself to give up that protection. She kept the jacket and continued her workout. She wanted to run more, but decided that this particular show queen must not have been much of an athlete. Lisa walked mostly; ran when she had her breath; and pushed herself like she remembered Speatsh would have done.

Although no wolves actually gave chase, she still moved as though they did. She didn't slow down unless she had to catch her breath. Sometimes it was difficult to remember that she wasn't as fit as she had been when she was younger; also that she was no longer as old as she used to be; and she couldn't decide if this body felt slower because it was recently in an accident or just wasn't what she was used to. She also supposed, after a fit of coughing, that her healing interior must have been doing some serious work on her new body's lungs.

Despite all the difficult nuances, to some degree, she was actually enjoying personal time that wasn't found behind an old cruddy desk; in a stinky office; on a living island for once. Still, she walked and ran when she felt up to it.

She did wonder if she would find herself sore later, but, even though her host hadn't been great with the respiration, she was, however, limber. Lisa didn't seem to have too much difficulty stretching and warming up, which was a big help right now. She might have even been more flexible than her old self, come to think of it. Then a new sensation seemed to develop. She'd felt it since yesterday actually, just passed it off as new host jitters. It seemed more evident now though. Among all the walking, running and discovering her physical abilities, she was feeling anxious, like her body needed something to keep her from shaking—probably the healing process, she thought. Whatever it was, it was a new sensation. As she passed a tobacco shop, she found her body desiring to gravitate towards it to find some relaxation.

She fought the urge.

Along her route, she somehow ended up near her old campus. Why not? She'd come this far already. She hit the button at the intersection leading into the main parking lot and waited for the little white silhouette to appear in the sign across the street. She jogged through the slatted crosswalk and through the front campus lot.

Maybe it was time to turn back. Maybe she'd come too far. She imagined Bean chiding her and Winter giving her the extreme silent treatment, but she ignored the need to return home.

In time, she was standing before the glass and aluminum doors of the art building. She remembered the place well. Their café had the best waffles on campus: the right match of crispy and soft; the perfect hint of vanilla; and unlike some waffle places, no hard chunks of sugar to remind her she has no need to enjoy syrup.

Somehow, in a few days, Josh would uncover a clue in this place that he would carry to his grave, unless she and the others could change that outcome. She didn't want to think about his last living moments, prided herself somewhat on not being around during Josh's demise so she didn't have to blame herself nor remember such a gruesome fall. Of course, hearing the details of the event probably hadn't been much better. She wondered if she could handle living through it now after all these years of mere storytelling. What's worse, Amber would have to relive it.

Strangely, she was presently missing Amber.

And Nick?

Idiot. Where was he? Too much had been asked of him already. She missed him when he wasn't around, and she missed him when he was around, hidden by the shadow of the idea of raising children together. Maybe she'd have felt differently about it in a better world. Maybe this was her chance to set things right for him now, or how she repaid him for watching over her most of his life. Yeah, he had still done that. They fought, but he still made sure she wasn't killing herself in her work. He brought her lunch. He interrupted her heavy workload for a good fight and a breath of fresh air. Maybe she couldn't fix her own future with him, but she could change Nick's possible new future so he could smile more and fight less with her former self.

Change? What a concept! What change? Don't give away anything to the rogue, but change the past. How? Wasn't that their purpose in the first place? To change their history?

How?

Leave a message Josh was going to die? A hint! For whom, though? Where?

And how?

How could she clue any of her past friends in on something they might understand, but that others would not? How about a warning? Should she drop a note in the museum for Josh and hope the enemy doesn't find nor understand it?

Wouldn't have done herself any good to try anyway, the building was locked. She kicked the glass doors in frustration at her ineptitude and smacked the sign that indicated the building was supposed to be open. How did she leave a clue in these circumstances? Bean would have known. Sounds of construction came from the other side. As she turned to leave, she heard the rattle of the pink spray paint in her bag. How long would it take to clean the word "Beware" off of the tall doors leading into the museum?

"Beware" was a little blunt, obviously, but something should be able to say it without advertising it. A symbol? What kind? Something that Thomas, Josh and Amber could all know, or at least one of them.

She wondered which route her three friends would take to enter the building, suddenly attuned to the painful realization that this was the place where her friend had lost his humanity, where he had truly died. This was his coffin, but it didn't have to be. She had to leave a clue, any would do.

Her allies hadn't had a symbol, not one that they all stood behind any differently than the average person would stand: a flag, a logo, school mascot. How about initials? "J.R. for president!" Would anyone translate that into Josh Revlon running? And where would she put it so her friends were sure to see it? And no one would remove it? At least immediately that was.

Graffiti, that was the way. The university was always slow to remove graffiti. The grounds crew and maintenance staff were kind of inept in that way, kept arguing over who's responsibility it wasn't to clean the outside of buildings. The campus paper had a huge write-up about it. Then the semester ended, and no one seemed to care anymore. When fall came back around, the graffiti had finally disappeared.

She missed Josh. She didn't just mourn him and his last venture. She missed him, who he was before the fighting and wolves. For a moment, she remembered having fun and double-dating. She missed Natalie, Dustin too, her boyfriend before Nick came along.

Here she was back to thinking about Nick again—Natalie's broken, jock brother with Cadence's name written all over his raging hormones. She missed teasing him and whom he had become in the face of all their peril. Even now, years into his fast, she still expected to see him in his Doberman form: protective, jealous.

Who knew where he was? Maybe he was already dead. Maybe they were all already dead and were just too stubborn to know it. Who would ring the tavern bell in their honor?

Just then, she knew the symbol they might understand. Lisa made a quick glance around the area, waiting for a time to quickly break out her pink spray paint, long enough to shoot out the curve of a bell that should be familiar to her past friends. If this didn't insinuate the symbolic ring of death in their ears, she didn't know what would warn them. It was fast and her can was back in the bag before anyone noticed. Surely, one of her old friends would see Thug's bell to honor the dead in this image.

She began to leave again.

Still, what if the campus staff did clean the graffiti before Josh arrived? What if her friends brushed off the symbol? Maybe another? Maybe something to tell them not to ignore the warning.

Her knife!

She returned to the glass doors and drew her new knife. It wasn't much, but it was sturdy enough to etch the aluminum door. This time she did something with straight, fast lines. It wasn't the bell, but it might work too. It was a simple shape, that of a syringe. It needed more, something for a keen mind like Thomas's. Perhaps a sun behind the syringe. No. The rogue might get that. Not a sun, but maybe the syringe could be the sun instead. She carved some straight lines around the syringe to give off the impression that it should be illuminating light like the sun would. Might still be too blatant still. It needed to look like it's only purpose was vandalism. Her mind was blank. She remembered an old slogan, something before her time, but still occasionally appeared every so often. "Just say 'NO,'" she quickly etched into the metal. Maybe Thomas—he was smartest—would pick up on it.

It was time to go now; she still had to run back to her hotel.

She realized she was feeling stiff. If she wasn't careful, she'd be sore, unable to fight. She mixed her pace with jogging and walking now and returned to the crosswalk sign she had used earlier. She approached the signal button, but someone else had stepped up to it before she could. A couple: he smiled cordially. His partner seemed to glare at Lisa's horrible roots, even snickered to herself most likely about them. A little, black Scottish terrier appeared between the man and woman.

Lisa thought she should know them, probably people she'd seen before but had forgotten over the years. Then she was filled with the electric jolt of their familiarity. She had seen them once before, the night in the graveyard and then again last night.

The rogue's blonde companion mustered a smile, fake and insincere, afraid in some ways. Lisa wished for a gun, or Bean, or Speatsh. All of her friends would have tried be as nice too. Instead, she returned the courtesy back to the couple, wondering where Genre currently watched her from. The rogue didn't know her. Did he? Or had they seen her leave her warnings to keep Josh out of their grasp.

Her body fell cold. What if her warning kept Josh out of the building all together? What if they didn't retrieve the pages from that book now?

Stupid!

She wanted to return and erase the clues. But how? Whatever she did, she couldn't enact here. The rogue was too close. He could return before she was done. Or she could do something insanely worse.

Lisa could end this war now. Or could she? All she had was a worthless stun baton. She could probably take the dog or the woman, but she'd seen the rogue's abilities. She stood no chance.

Don't give anything away, Lisa thought. *Keep jogging, get away. Look normal. You'll figure something else out.*

They inched closer towards her. She stepped sideways to give them room to the crosswalk. Were they inching towards her again?

The walking silhouette appeared, and the sign across the street chirped.

Go, she told herself and propelled herself forward into a tired, yet anxious jog.

Suddenly, his hand was on the back of her neck. It was strong, tight and bruising. Her first notion was to pull the stun baton.

The blurred advertisement of public transit bus screamed across her face by what seemed to be only inches.

When she finally caught her breath, she realized she was sitting. Her shoulder still hurt, but the rogue now stood over her. He held his hand down to her. The Scottie yipped in her face and licked at it.

Lisa pretended, with hesitation, to find the dog cute. She allowed further insult to herself by taking the rogue's hand and climbed back to her feet.

The window of opportunity to cross the street had passed. A big red hand now denied access to the walk.

"Thank you," she said.

The rogue nodded.

"So stupid of me."

The rogue shrugged, but smiled.

"We like your jacket," the rogue's companion said. "Are you a performer?"

"Thank you. Yes," Lisa lied, but, as she found herself standing in conversation with these two villains, she wondered if she might not be a performer yet. "It's all I had to wear today."

"Watch out for oblivious bus drivers this time," the woman said. "Hate to ruin that jacket."

The rogue reached to the button to call the white walking human outline again, and as the sign began chirping from across the street a few moments later, she knew what Bean couldn't see.

She seemed to find no trouble running a great deal of the distance back, but as a black and green taxi appeared, she summoned it.

* * *

"Where have you been," Bean chided, as Lisa entered the suite.

"He lets them in," Lisa announced.

"What are you talking about," Bean asked.

"Kenny," Lisa replied. "He lets the wolves into Thug's café. Richard and Thug hunted together. They were practically family, he's Josh's godfather. I'll bet that somehow the bunker and Thug's place have a linked security network."

"You think Kenny manipulates the network to let the wolves into Thug's the night they attack the café," Bean suddenly burst.

"It adds up!"

"If he'd come in any other way, suspicion would have been too high to let him near a computer," Bean said methodically.

"Right," Lisa replied. "But a technology wizard, that we just happened to rescue, who could pretend to strengthen our bunker security, while actually hacking it, would be in place to use our technology in ways we didn't even understand ourselves."

"We can't be certain," Bean replied. "We can't assume."

"It has to be him," Lisa argued. "You hire the suit, the suit hires the skaters, who somehow have connection to Kenny, a person the rogue knows about because you used him—by such coincidence, he happens to be readily available in Plattsville."

"Maybe roguey hired the people who knew about Kenny," Bean suggested. "Maybe Kenny was just a fluke to happen for the rogue."

"Regardless," Lisa continued. "Kenny makes the diversion possible. He lets the wolves into Thug's. Maybe he bypasses alarms, or enables the elevator, whatever! A huge fight starts. The suit kills Josh in the midst of it, the skaters kill Speatsh and now the rest of the hunters are fodder for wolves, skaters and suit alike." Just then she stopped in contemplation. "Only that can't be, now that I look back on it."

"Why?"

"Because the only reason we were alerted to the attack at Thug's was because the compound was a set up, and Kenny was with us. Son of a b—," Lisa faded into defeat.

"He was with you the entire time," Bean asked.

"We even locked him in the trunk of a car at the compound when Speatsh thought it was a setup. We had assumed Speatsh was just being overly paranoid so we allowed Kenny to stay even after that," Lisa said. She frowned and realized her epiphany was for nothing. "I thought I had it figured out."

"Did he have a phone," Bean asked, and then became lost in thought once more.

"Could have had a phone," Lisa replied. "I don't really remember paying attention to that."

"What's wrong," Bean asked.

Lisa took a long time to answer, mostly because she didn't realize that her face had given away so many clues.

"Something doesn't settle," Lisa said. "Why the elaborate diversion? Why not just attack him? You had the generals, the wolves. Your master could have overpowered us and killed us at any point. Kenny knew where we were. We could have been wiped out at the compound. He could have discovered the security door out to the cemetery and let the wolves in that way. Why race us across town to the compound and then back across to Thug's to kill us? Not to mention, if the rogue's plan was to use Josh to turn us into an army of super wolves, why would he allow your goons to kill us at all? I'm sorry. I thought I had a piece of your puzzle."

Bean didn't respond. He stared down at his sheet which had developed more marks since Lisa had left to go running.

"No. You raise a good question," he finally said.

After several minutes of silence, Lisa finally decided to do something productive and order some food: burgers for her, cheese pizza for Winter and imitation crab salad for Bean—she thought he might appreciate the meat, even if it was only soy.

While they waited, Lisa jumped into a hot shower and gradually turned the water cold to help her muscles become more reasonable a few hours from now.

The food came, they hardly touched it.

"It's been an hour," Lisa said.

"Thank you," Bean replied. He looked at the clock. "Remind me again?"

"We always do," Lisa answered. She had too. After twenty-five years, she'd gotten used to helping Jasper keep track of time. He said time moved differently for him. She wasn't sure she believed him, but time did get away from the old man. She remembered that once she had left him in thought in her office, and two days later, when she came back, he was still there. He'd even seemed startled that she hadn't gone home yet.

Winter and Lisa finally broke down and ate. Lisa stuffed a plate of food into Bean's hand, and he ate it as if performing a simple-programmed automaton. He finished his dish and became surprised that it was empty. Lisa took the plate and dropped it in the trash. She reminded him another hour had passed.

"Thank you," he replied. "Remind me again?"

"We always do," she said. She realized she needed another shower, as her muscles started to tighten once again. She was halfway through it when she heard shouting from the other room. She rinsed the soap off and climbed into a hotel bathrobe. As she rushed back to Bean's apartment, the phone began to ring.

"I stepped on a tack," Bean yelled into the phone and then, "I do apologize for the noise, but I'm bleeding here! I should sue you for your lack of care of these facilities." He hung up and turned to his allies. "I got it."

"Really," Lisa asked. "A tack?"

Bean began pointing at his strange map. "This day, the day you went back to the yard, tomorrow night. You rescue Kenny tonight, right? Take him to the bunker, right? And then you return with him tomorrow, right?"

"I think so," Lisa said, but she wasn't entirely sure. "No, Kenny was with us a couple of days, I think."

"You sure about that?"

"It's been so long, I—not tomorrow, no. At least another day. Had to be at least one more, but I'm not sure."

"Then, I believe one of these next few days, the inquisitor shows up."

"OK," Lisa replied.

Bean pointed. "Look. What's missing?"

Lisa finally relented that she didn't know, and Bean stumbled through the apartment looking, for something to write with, he settled for a piece of pizza. Tearing off the toppings, he dipped a hardened fingernail polish brush into the tomato sauce and began writing on the sheets again.

"The mercenaries," Bean replied.

"OK? I'm sorry," Lisa said. "I don't see it."

"What's Stan doing right now," Bean asked.

"Gathering hunters," Lisa replied.

"Among other things," Bean said getting more excited with every word that came out of his mouth. "Kill Thomas, kill Speatsh, kill Josh, kill you—or turn all of you, the hunters are still going to come and be betrayed by other hunters."

"The skater punks," Lisa said.

"Aha," Bean shouted. "Infiltrated by the skaters, their own kind, an entire gang hired by the suit to set up the hunters, maybe even throttle them all in their sleep, except."

"Except?"

"Except, someone hired mercenaries to attack you from within the junkyard walls," Bean said. "Who?"

"I don't know."

"Did the skaters ever betray you?"

"No," Lisa replied after a moment of thinking. "Some died fighting, if memory serves."

"The mercs are the clue," Bean said. "Think about it, if you had infiltrators already, why call in more? We saw the suit and the skaters, but where were the mercs last night? How did they get here so fast and into your compound?"

"Something happened," Lisa replied. Now she was deep in thought too and suddenly burst with, "The skaters didn't do what they were supposed to do. They changed their minds."

"They changed their minds," Bean agreed. "They didn't do what they were supposed to do and joined Josh. Why?"

"They got scared?"

"Or smart," Bean replied. "We're the missing piece."

"Huh?"

"We're here," Bean explained. "Speatsh's warning bells went off inside his head when you brought in Kenny, right? When Speatsh discovers the compound empty, I'll bet his mind started reeling. 'It's a setup, isn't it?' Speatsh is paranoid. He races to Thug's to join a fight, a fight where the suit fully gives himself away. Speatsh wouldn't have noticed this clue if he hadn't been in a paranoid state of mind already."

"We need to work on your simplification skills," Lisa said.

"You're not listening," Bean said. "We three sat in this room twenty-odd years ago, er, right now and realized by the time Speatsh picked up on the suit, unless we did something to help him, it would be too late."

"I don't know if I want to hear this," Lisa insisted.

"The reason Speatsh didn't unmask the suit and his entire gang completely last night at Thug's was because Speatsh was paying too much attention to all the rookie hunters, including us. The skaters were dumb, we were acting conservative and stupid, trying not to blow our cover, and he mistook that for us being green. He had quite an enjoyable time mocking you two. It kept him from even paying full attention to the suit. Probably thought he was an amateur too.

"But I saw the suit, and I saw the skaters. They were prepared and willing to kill Speatsh." Bean clapped his hands into fists and shook them triumphantly over his head. "That's why Josh saw the suit do something, and Speatsh missed it. I'm sure of it. But the suit wasn't working alone. Which brings us to what I missed."

"Good, Lord," Lisa said. "I thought that's what you were talking about already."

"No, I was talking about what Speatsh missed," Bean said.

Lisa groaned.

"I had to point out what he missed so you'd understand what I missed," Bean explained.

"K, this yammering of yours is what puts razor blades in high demand," Lisa announced.

"We have to get the suit to work alone so his behavior will betray him," Bean said.

"He does that," Lisa said. "Speatsh sees it when Thug's gets attacked."

"No, he won't," Bean said. "He would have last night at Thug's if we hadn't been there, but we messed that up and probably changed the timeline. If our presence hadn't distracted Speatsh, I'll bet the suit would have been dead about now."

"You're saying our coming back and being there delayed Speatsh's realization," Lisa said. She got it now. "But that's okay, because Speatsh still uncovers him."

"We have to make sure he does, or he might not live long enough to save Josh from Genre so we, in turn, can actually save Josh from his wife tearing his head off later on," Bean said. He lowered his excitement of the situation as he watched Lisa cringe at Bean's insensitivity.

"We messed this up," he said more calmly now. "I think we have to fix this. I think we sat here just like we are now realizing that we may have killed Josh and Speatsh and had to do something to stop that without getting too involved."

"All right. Fine. Let's turn the skaters on him," Lisa said. "How? They didn't turn on him before."

"Do you remember them trying to kill you before," Bean asked.

Lisa didn't.

"Then we must have succeeded," Bean said. "So what do you think we did?"

"I give up," Lisa said.

Bean's face smoothed into a wicked grin that Lisa hadn't seen since before Jasper had revealed his true intentions to support Josh. "I think I can scare them."

"Seems simple enough," Lisa lied.

"I'll bet my life that their plan was to attack Thug's all along," Bean thought some more and then started again. "The phone call," he finally said. "The suit ignored it last night. Might have been a text, I don't know. What did I need a phone for? I kept a Rolodex and a land line. I barely stood those."

"Fine," Lisa said. "The phone call, let's get back to that. Better yet, let's call Speatsh and leave him an anonymous call."

"Know Speatsh's number?"

She didn't.

"What about the phone," Lisa cried. She fell into an uncomfortable soft chair in the corner of Bean's suite and stared at the green shag floor.

"The suit met with me right after Josh left. What was it he said? 'There was a technical glitch.'" Bean kicked the bed and threw his pizza. "A glitch? I should have seen it then. The suit? Technical glitch, and I didn't see it. He had brainiacs helping him, and I didn't see it."

"Anyone could have overlooked that one," Lisa replied.

"Not me, and you don't get it," Bean snapped. "It was supposed to happen last night, and it didn't work."

"What are you talking about," Lisa moaned.

"What I missed," Bean replied. "Haven't you been listening?"

"I'm trying not to," Lisa replied, then shot up straight in her chair. "Wait! We still haven't gotten to what you missed, yet?"

"I wanted to make sure you understand," Bean said.

"You crazy old bat turd," Lisa shrieked. "God himself doesn't understand what you're saying! Tell us already. What did you miss?"

"But you won't understand," Bean replied.

"Try me!"

"Kenny was trying some technical voodoo to attack Josh last night, but it didn't work," Bean said.

"Kenny," Lisa asked. "You missed Kenny?"

"He was there," Bean replied. "He was somewhere in the shadows trying to unleash the attack of wolves on Thug's last night, and it didn't work. That's why they all met outside Thug's after Josh's appearance," Bean explained. "The suit says 'what happened, boys,' the skaters say 'we don't know, let us call our man Kenny.' Kenny shows, and they have the meeting we witnessed last night."

He fell silent, then chuckled.

"Now what," Lisa asked.

"That dodgy, little worm," Bean said. "I figured something out, ladies."

"Aco—Winter went for a walk a half hour ago," Lisa said. "It's just me."

"I hire the suit," Bean said, as if speaking to himself. "The suit hires his skater gang, and they hire Kenny." Bean fell silent.

"It's been an hour," Lisa said.

"Thank you. Remind me again," he requested, placing his hand on Lisa's shoulder in gratitude only to realize that Winter had returned. "Oh, you're back."

Winter nodded.

"Got it," Bean shouted. "The rogue needs a technical genius to shut down a city of this size: towers, power and all. Kenny's already working for the rogue, and the rogue is aware of him because he already helped me. Meanwhile, the skaters also recruit Kenny."

"Popular guy," Lisa interrupted.

"When the plan failed last night, Kenny shows up to the little meeting we witnessed. He says, 'hey, some sort of security network link between Thug's and someplace else kept me from getting us in, and I think I might know where that is, because I was hired to break into it a while back. But not to worry, I can get into it before morning.'"

"That's a lot of assumption," Lisa said.

"It's not assumption," Bean said. "It's what I missed."

"Wait! What," Lisa screamed. "You still haven't gotten there yet." She drew an angry, shaking finger. "The next words out of your mouth better be what you missed or I'll leave you lost in your thoughts until someone else finds that woman in your pocket!"

"All right," Bean said. "I'm sorry. It's how I am. What I missed is Kenny's superiority."

"That idiot? Superior?"

"Remember the stories we were told," Bean explained. "Josh attacks the compound. His allies capture Josh. The mercenary leader orders the gates open."

"That sounds about right," Lisa said.

"Who opened the gates," Bean asked.

"I had assumed whoever was at the gate controls," Lisa explained.

"Stories say the doorman was at the house guarding Natalie from trigger-happy mercs," Bean said. "The stories say I was at the gates when the doorman was not."

"So it was you," Lisa said. "There, easy answer—except you wouldn't have taken orders from a merc."

Bean shook his head.

"So who opened the gates to let the wolves in," he asked.

"It would have to be done by someone who had access to the controls," Lisa replied. "Controls were at the gate, or in the main control room." She felt the realization setting in.

"That means Kenny," Bean replied. "I hire the suit. He hires—"

"Enough," Lisa screamed. "I get it! Kenny's bad. The suit hires the skaters, the skaters hire Kenny, and all this time the rogue's smarter than you."

"Don't get snotty," Bean replied. "And you're wrong."

"Please don't explain why," Lisa said.

"The suit didn't hire the skaters," Bean said. "He hired Kenny."

"Wait," Lisa said, but knew she was about to regret the next, "What are you talking about?"

"You're still not listening," Bean blurted. "Kenny's not some employee. He's calling the shots. He's one of the mercenaries. He is a trained killer."

Lisa tried to understand, but not fast enough for Bean.

"The suit needed an assassination play," Bean explained. "Knew he couldn't break the bunker, nor the Bullet. The only other place his target would most likely be to drop his guard would be Thug's.

He couldn't attack anyone in the open because Speatsh would hear it, Natalie would hear it, or you would see it with your night vision. Like all smart assassins, he investigated Thug's and found a backdoor that was beyond his technological expertise to escape or sneak into, or something. If he had tried any attack on his own, he would have failed. My plan to clue Speatsh in would have worked from the start."

"But that's not what happened," Lisa said.

"No," Bean replied. "The suit found the one tech who had the clout to draw in an entire platoon of mercenaries at his whim."

"What does that mean?"

"Mercenary leaders choose the assignments," Bean said. "We know they were working together now. The suit hired skaters. The skaters hire Kenny, who's already working for the rogue, why? Because he has mercenaries. People who would appear to be skilled hunters, and they came at Kenny's request."

"You think Kenny led the mercenaries," Lisa asked.

"I do," Bean replied. "And I unwittingly played my part. So, let's recap: I hired the suit; the suit hired the skaters; the skaters hired Kenny to help assassinate Josh and his allies. Kenny jumps at the job and tells the suit, 'wait at the haven and I'll bring the paladin to you.' Only he doesn't bring the paladin. He brings wolves. Why?"

"Is there any clue on my face that suggests, I'm even listening to you anymore," Lisa said.

"Really," Bean responded. "Nothing?"

Nothing. She didn't even try to get something.

"Kenny works for the rogue," Bean blurted.

"He's a general?"

"No, if he were a general, Speatsh and Thomas would have recognized it at once. He was an employee. That's why he met with the rogue last night. You remember, the man with the shopping cart?"

A pang filled Lisa. Did she dare tell Bean about her warning? No. He'd rattle on about something else for five hours, and she'd be in a coma.

"The rogue piggy-backed my own workings. The rogue devises a means to get his own guy into Josh's circle. He gets eyes on Josh and sets the stage to perform Kenny's abduction into a farm."

"But how would he have known Josh would go to the junkyard," Lisa asked.

"Because he urged Josh to go to the junkyard," Bean replied.

"Their psychic link," Lisa finally understood.

"Josh probably thought it was just an idea that came to him," Bean explained. "I wouldn't be surprised if the rogue hadn't played with many ideas that Josh had. Probably taunted his dreams too. As soon as Josh followed through, the rogue was able to have his own minions in place and ready before Josh ever left the bunker."

"How?"

"The elementals," Bean said. "They could have flown Kenny and others anywhere in the city with time to set enough stage to convince Josh to Kenny's kidnapping.

"The rogue convinces Josh that Kenny is good, and he gets that worm into the bunker so he can figure out how to open Thug's to an attack, because that will shut down the haven and force the hunters to retreat and gather in the open—not to mention that when word gets out about the destruction on Thug's tavern, all really good hunters will come running to Josh's side all the more."

"Why doesn't the rogue just use the river and get word to Bogi to open Thug's security system," Lisa asked.

"You're not listening! Because the rogue didn't want the suit to kill Josh," Bean said. "He wanted to infect him to make his army of super wolves."

"You think the attack was all to get hunters to rally to Josh," Lisa asked.

"Could make sense," Bean replied. "Rallying to the sight of of a tavern destruction would bring bodies to the rogue."

"Wouldn't being involved with the suit mean the rogue knew your plan to kill the inquisitor?"

"I doubt it," Bean replied. "Or he would have stopped it. The inquisitor had a large army. And I had my special skills."

"So we save Kenny. He gets what he wants, then convinces us to return to the compound," Lisa said.

"Most likely to prevent you from stopping the attack on Thug's before it happened," Bean added. "Which is exactly what you would have done if the attack had actually taken place last night when they had planned it, and the suit might very well have accomplished his task during the commotion. So, either you got lucky, or the rogue did on that one."

"If the rogue had special plans for Josh, your hitman would have interfered with that," Lisa said. "Maybe the attack on Thug's was to take out your hitman before he could sabotage the rogue's own agenda."

"That's a possibility," Bean said. "But I'm not fully sure."

"Kenny literally opened the backdoor to Thug's while we were being sidetracked to the compound," Lisa finally said, and felt stupid for not realizing it sooner. "And if he had the technology, he could have monitored the situation even locked in the trunk. He probably set it in motion without us noticing before we ever got to the junkyard."

"And when you all returned to him still locked away in the trunk, you were convinced he was no longer a threat, so you eventually trusted him with full security and control of your defensive facilities," Bean explained. "Especially, now that Thug's had been breached and he had already given the facade of improving the bunker security."

"Just one flaw," Lisa explained. "As you know we went to Thug's that night too."

"Do you remember why," Bean asked.

"Someone called Speatsh," Lisa said. "And we went."

"Who called Speatsh," Bean asked.

"I assume Thug," Lisa said.

"Really? You think the doorman and Ty somehow gave Thug time to call all his buddies while being attacked by wolves, the skaters and the suit," Bean asked. "I don't think so."

"You're forgetting we were there too," Lisa said. "Maybe we gave Thug time to call."

"I wasn't there."

"I mean us," Lisa asked.

"Oh," Bean replied, this time slow to his own realization and sheepish for not seeing something so simple. "Us, future us. Okay, so we discovered the plan to pop a backdoor into Thug's, just as we're doing now. So we warn Speatsh! That's a solid clue that works for us. Meanwhile, perhaps I should give some thoughts to persuading the skaters to support Josh."

"Why not the suit," Lisa asked.

"Because we'd still need him to tip off Speatsh," Bean explained.

"Why not just tip off Speatsh ourselves," Lisa asked.

"Why not just tell everyone our plan," Bean said. "Look. An anonymous phone call crying for help is one thing, but we can't have him know he's got allies in the shadows or he'll question, which will make the rogue question. We can't go dropping any kind of clue. It could alter behavior. What? What is it?"

"It's nothing," Lisa replied, and quickly returned to the topic. "It just seems like we're over-complicating things."

"Welcome to the art of manipulation," Bean said. "The key here is to keep Speatsh from overthinking the clues we throw his way."

"Okay," Lisa said. "I'm not arguing. You're right. The problem is, we don't have Speatsh's cell number."

"How is that possible," Bean asked.

"We never needed it."

"All right," Bean said. "We can work with that. Got it! The attack's within the next day or so: we get a phone, and we make sure it gets into Thug's hands to make—."

"No," Lisa ordered, and tore the sheet away from the bed.

"I'm not finished with that," Bean objected. "I'm still missing something."

Lisa tried not to shudder. "Jas—Bean, you're a brilliant tactician, but you overthink."

"I have to," Bean replied.

"I know," Lisa said. "And we can miss our entire mission sitting in this room listening to you hypothesize. But we're here to act."

"I have to know everything," Bean explained. "It's important to winning this."

"I get that," Lisa said. "But you said it yourself. The three us sat in this room before trying to come up with a plan to save Josh and it failed. We know what we can fix. You've identified that, but we have to do something differently this time. And this seems like it would be different to me. Sometimes, you have to stop thinking and simply react."

"This is a little more complicated than that," Bean said.

"No, it's not," Lisa said. She pulled the sheets away as Bean reached for them. "It's very simple. For whatever reason, Kenny's bad, and the skaters are working with the suit, but we know they help us. So let's just turn the skaters against the suit and use that."

"And how do you suggest we do that without a plan," Bean asked.

"You're you," Lisa laughed. "Be you. Trust me, that'll scare 'em."

"All right," Bean said. He reluctantly turned himself away from his mattress with its comforter, which was scarred with make-up bleed-through from the sheet that had been above it. He moved towards the window and complained about being too old. He hesitated a moment before opening the curtain.

Dusk had begun to bronze the city street.

"The rogue can predict reaction better than I can," Bean said.

"I'm sure he can," Lisa said. "But he doesn't know we're here."

"I certainly hope not," Bean replied. He continued to stare out the window. His mind still whirled with opportunity and explanation, but he chose to keep it to himself this time.

Then he watched a shadow of a vehicle creep into the hotel parking lot. The street and city lights glistened against its skin.

"Now, that's a beautiful piece of machinery," Bean said.

He had liked trucks, never got into keeping or restoring them because they changed too much and parts disappeared far too often to keep up with. Besides, it had never been his job, all his while in Plattsville, to play with cars. He had his own older pickups over the years, but nothing like this. This one had six wheels and some sort of hardshell camper attached to it. He knew instantly it was an early 40s Power Wagon, perhaps 42, not really a feasible vehicle for driving around town, but, unlike most cars that claimed they could get you where you wanted to go, this one would definitely get you to your destination. True, a little slower perhaps, but it would conquer the terrain.

As the driver stepped down, Bean was tempted to race after him and ask if he could get behind the wheel himself. The driver walked around to the back of the vehicle; opened the door to the hard shell; and a golden dog joined him outside.

"Is he insane," Bean cried. "What in hell's black flame does he think he's doing here?"

24 ~ Dangerous Alley

Gangsters, gunshots and fear spilled into the parking lot.

Lisa fumbled with hiding an extra baton within her jacket. Her lasso was already coiled securely within her new backpack. She'd put so much time into getting the weapon built that she didn't even stop to consider how to carry all the extra supplies and pack them on the fly. Bean grabbed the extra baton and found a place to hide it on his own person for now.

By the time they were outside the hotel, Winter's figure was dashing down Thug's alley. When they finally reached the entrance into the tavern, Winter was smacking it. Soon the doorman's shotgun appeared.

In one motion, Bean pulled Winter out of line of the shotgun, and shoved the baton against the door for a quick instant.

BLAM!

The doorman's body and shotgun disappeared from the door. Some sort of commotion of voices erupted from within the café.

"Is that the right password," Bean yelled through the open slot.

The doorman grunted, and Bean could see a few faces through the slot, they mostly belonged to skaters standing to the sudden commotion. Ty's voice inquired of the guard to the café. Eventually the doorman returned to his post.

"Well, don't leave your gun on the floor," Ty suggested.

"Yeah! Yeah," the doorman replied as though he didn't quite know why he needed it. His eyes finally squared with the small opening in the door. "Who is it?"

"Who is it," Thug's voice questioned from farther inside the café. "Take over for him will ya, Ty?"

A little coercion, as well as a few inaudible words and grunts later, and Ty was standing at the door. A new shotgun appeared through the small opening, halfway up the door to anyone on the outside.

"What," Ty asked.

"Little pig, little pig," Bean asked rather than replied, while concealing the stun baton once again into his jacket.

"Oh, it's you," Ty said, and the door finally whined open.

"Leave the door. We're not staying," he instructed, preventing Ty from closing it behind him.

The same skaters filled the booths, along with two additional faces. The suit was also sitting, glaring at Bean, even as he rushed inside. Bean let the suit know his hand was also ready to draw and fire a weapon if it needed to. For now, Bean's interest was beyond the suit. He paid the hitman little attention as he passed him, then he leaned into the booth, upon the man sitting with his golden retriever.

"You don't find things by making stupid mistakes, Doctor" Bean whispered. "Now, follow me out."

Stan Revlon stood from his booth.

"Leaving," Thug asked.

"Not hungry," Stan replied.

The two men and the golden dog exited the building.

A short trip down the alley later, then across the street to the parking lot, and they were back in the hotel suite.

"And you don't see a problem with you being here," Bean asked.

"I wanted to check in," Stan replied. "I don't know what you're getting angry about. I haven't told anyone about you."

"Wait a minute," Lisa said. "He knows?"

"Better than that," Bean replied. "Let's change the subject!"

"But he knows!"

"What do you think he's been doing all this time," Bean replied.

"First, we thought he was dead and then we found out he was rounding up hunters."

"Yes," Bean replied hesitantly. "Rounding up hunters isn't easy."

"You're looking for it," she suddenly realized and turned on Stan.

Eric growled.

"He and Eric, here," Bean corrected.

"So the rogue does know about our plan," Lisa said. "All this fuss about closing minds off to the rogue and this entire time this scout knows about the—"

"Will you shut up," Bean belted.

Lisa fell silent, startled at the sudden outburst.

"You are making very loud and vocal assumptions in front of his canine companion here," Bean explained.

"How," Lisa screamed. "They're traveling partners."

"So you understand his dilemma, and why we're not taking chances, don't you?" Bean said. "You've always been the smart one. My explaining everything's making you lazy."

"Your explaining things kills me slowly," Lisa argued.

Lisa fell quiet, and, for several minutes, the room followed suit. Stan helped himself to a glass of water and scoffed at the empty ice bucket and the unopened plastic bags inside.

"Then, are you ready to give me your name yet," Stan asked.

Lisa bust up laughing and left the room to continue without an audience.

"You can't be here," Bean replied.

"I was passing by," Stan tried to justify.

"You shouldn't be anywhere near here," Bean retorted.

"I had no choice," Stan argued. "There's talk."

"What kind of talk," Bean asked.

"A massacre of some sort. Reports that my recruits weren't getting here," Stan said. "I ran into a hunter, a hockey player. She said her last kill had revealed some information to watch the paladin's home for some sort of demonstration. She wasn't sure what it meant, but she got the impression to avoid us."

"Coward," Bean replied.

"Not just her," Stan said. "Hunters seem to know who I am before I even walk into the taverns lately."

"Strange, I hadn't heard anything," Bean replied.

"Phew! I thought the world might stop spinning," Stan replied. "Thank you wise and powerful Noctor Flea."

"Hey," Bean snapped. "Don't think I don't know your surgical slang."

"You think the rogue is looking for you," Stan guffawed.

"Of course not," Bean replied, and could almost remember the sharp teeth he concealed as he clenched his jaw at the ignorant insult. For an instant, he recalled his spite and wanted, would it have done any good, to bite the man as a demonstration of his power.

"Then, I suppose I should get on my way," Stan replied. First, he made use of the shower and shaved himself before reappearing in his same grungy white shirt and brown jacket with leather elbow patches.

"You can't just go," Bean said. "They're not just going to let you out of here. You'll be in a farm or dead before dawn. You can have the floor in my room. Might as well sleep. We'll get you into hiding until we can get you escorted out of town."

Stan thanked Bean for his offering and tried to appear less grateful than he really was. He disappeared into Bean's room with Dustin's dad, Eric, Stan's mighty golden retriever, at his heels. The lights turned out almost instantly.

"We need to talk," Lisa demanded.

Bean shushed her and motioned her to follow him silently. He led the way to the door out of their suite and into the hallway. Winter, seemed quite content to stay, relaxing on a couch, and did not follow. Bean guided Lisa through the hall and its several turns, then down a flight of stairs before stopping at the guest counter where he requested some stationery and a pen.

No ears, he wrote. *Eric's vulnerable.*

Lisa took the pen. *You want the rogue to see that he's recruiting hunters!*

"Not me," Bean replied. He made some gestures with his hands and mouth to mimick talking but no sound came out.

"You mean Speatsh?"

Bean tapped the pen.

When were you going to tell us that Stan was a general, Lisa wrote.

Bean glared. *He's not,* he jotted back.

Then who made Eric, she scribbled.

Me, Bean wrote and quickly began to tear up the paper into pieces, which he then ate.

You a liah!

You're smart, Bean replied. *What gave it away?*

Speatsh said they weren't yours, Lisa replied.

"Blabbermouth," Bean vocalized.

Nick and Dustin too, she wrote out this time.

Bean nodded in the negative.

And Natalie, Lisa added.

Again, a negative shake.

He ate this sheet of paper too.

"Who then," Lisa asked, then returned pen to paper and scribbled out, *Because we all saw the same white ancient attack them.*

Bean refused to answer and simply shook his head in a way that said, "and don't ask again."

"Speatsh obviously knows who made them then," Lisa suggested. "He had them."

Bean nodded disagreement.

Only what they are, he wrote. *I didn't tell him everything.*

"How," Lisa asked. "When did you talk to him?"

I've been here longer than you, Bean replied. "Remember?"

"And you didn't think that was taking a chance on the turnout?"

"Think about it," Bean replied. "What made it possible for us to survive the confrontation in the cave? What protected Stan?" He put pen to ink once more. *Who located the rogue?*

Josh, Lisa answered.

Bean nodded disagreement

Natalie, Lisa corrected.

And who bit her, Bean asked.

Lisa snatched up the pen one last time. *Not you, it was the white dog. I know your form. I've seen it, remember?*

You haven't seen it since, have you?

Bean ate the paper.

If not you, and not Barbara, and it wasn't Stan, Lisa wrote and suddenly blurted, "Then that means," she trailed off.

Bean looked as though he wanted to nod from behind a start of a smile.

"Someone's been hiding in the shadows," she said, then wrote, *And hunting the rogue*, and finally realized, "We have another ally."

Bean nodded. Lisa took a few breaths to let this information settle in before saying,

How are we going to get Stan and Eric out of town, Lisa asked. "It took all of us to get him out last—Oh!" Her realization set in once more as it had been doing more commonly lately. *So how are we going to tip ourselves off?*

* * *

If Lisa's memory was correct, they should be here, or near here somewhere, provided that they hadn't already come and gone. Bean slid into the shadow of a power transformer box and watched the station across the street.

Several police vehicles pulled up over the next two hours. Some left. Most were driven by stupid people. This was entirely too easy. Bean watched the sky. If he couldn't spot one, he should be able to at least see the other overhead, but she might as well have been an invisible being in her environment. She was spooky that way.

He looked at his wrist, Lisa had made him pick out a watch from the hotel gift shop. He missed his pocket watch. He grabbed what they had. It was a cheap, piece of pink plastic and fairy turtles or something else really overmarketed and stupid on the face. Two hours had passed. Still, he watched, and saw nothing. Thirty minutes passed, and he groaned at the idea of having to keep track of time. He dwelled a couple minutes on that thought.

"Check your watch often," Lisa had ordered. "Every time you blink or look in a different direction."

He checked. *That was another thirty minutes*, Bean marveled. *How do humans survive this slow crawl?*

He was about to check his watch again after this thought when something nudged him forward. He turned. Until now, he hadn't been too concerned with needing too many armaments. He was wolf after all. Then again, how was he supposed to fight without bringing attention to the fact that he was a general? He was pretty certain many complications loomed before him still.

He turned slower than he normally would have, drawing his shotgun.

Upon the sight of this, the horse that had snuck upon him stood tall on its back legs. It didn't make a sound. A second horse appeared to Bean's right. Its head nodded and took a strange stance in a parking stall between a minivan and white luxury sedan.

The rider on the back of the closest horse peered from above the heightened creature's shoulder. Even in the dark, his white hair seemed to radiate. His hand held something that appeared to have no substance. Bean had been a general a long time, yet he was strangely willing to believe this could potentially become a deadly fight if he didn't play his part smartly. Although, somewhere deep-down, he found his curiosity wanting to check the mettle of these three, but their fourth and invisible ally would have been too much of a wildcard.

Bean cautiously holstered his weapon and hoisted his hands into the air.

"Thomas de Soleil, I must speak with you privately," Bean announced with careful tone. "I am not your enemy."

"I know a general when I see one," Thomas said from his high position. "You are my enemy."

"I bring a message from Stan Revlon," Bean replied, and attempted to lower his hands.

"No, stay where you are," Thomas replied kindly, and it took Bean a moment to realize the order was not made towards him, but to the unseen companion looming in the air. "Keep your distance."

Thomas withdrew the earpiece from his ear and clenched it in his hand. It was here that Bean noticed the small lines of discoloration along his wrist. Cuts, they seemed. Old scars? How many had this hemophiliac acquired through his years?

Kate lowered herself to the ground, again without making a sound.

"Very well. Privately," Thomas said. "What do you want, general?"

"He felt compelled to come to town," Bean explained.

"He cannot be here," Thomas replied.

"I know. He's with us and safe—for now—but we don't have the resources to help him escape."

"How did you know to find me," Thomas asked, after a moment of thought.

Bean had no answer. Actually, he had one, but he couldn't give it. What a remarkable feeling to be left speechless.

"Who are you," Thomas asked leaning forward.

Bean felt the point of a diamond blade against his throat.

"I am Bean," he replied. "And believe me there are things I cannot tell you, but I am no enemy to the paladin. Stan Revlon is not safe here."

"Thug's is a haven for hunters, he can wait there."

"Thug's is not an option," Bean explained. "You must trust me, defeating the rogue depends upon it. Or did Speatsh not tell you that he had a visitor the night he arrived in town?"

Thomas returned the earpiece to his ear. "Are there any among you who still have family? Who?" He withdrew the earpiece once more.

"Take him to the parents of Natalie and Nick Meade," Thomas instructed. "Tell him to wait until he hears from us and to be prepared to leave upon our arrival."

"Our thoughts as well," Bean replied.

"Ours," Thomas asked.

"We needed you to know where you could find him," Bean said. "I'm certain we can all find the place."

Thomas bowed in cautious gratitude. "Then good evening, friend."

Had Bean's eyes been human, they may not have seen the lighter lines of flesh that etched into Thomas's brow. They had healed for the most part, but their depths couldn't hide from Bean. Thomas, Bean thought, was quite ugly for a supposed gentleman. How could humans, or Thomas not see this?

Bean bowed back, and then remembered something he'd heard once, but paid little regard to.

"Wait," he shouldn't have said anything, but he just couldn't help himself.

"More?"

"No," Bean replied. "Wait, yes."

"Speak."

And then Bean saw his response. He leapt at the quivering within Kate's neck, punching her throat before diving beneath her legs. She raised into a stance, and Bean used her momentum to build his own, launching him highly enough into the air to take aim with his little shotgun on Thomas's face.

"Bang," he said, before kicking off of Kate's neck to let him flip backwards and land once more in the shadows and upon his feet.

"I hope you'll give more thought to how you'll protect the paladin than that," Bean said, holding his ground.

Thomas said nothing, but settled Kate back to her feet. Petruchio had drawn almost entirely upon Bean before he stopped.

"I expect the great vampire has gotten fat," Bean suggested. "I know the effects of a monotonous life when I see one. You've forgotten how to take a stand."

"Shall we test that," Thomas asked.

"There's an idea," Bean said. "I once heard a story of the infamous Thomas de Soleil."

"Infamous," Thomas appeared intrigued.

"He hunted a general," Bean continued. "Louis the Demented, I believe they called him."

"He was hardly a challenge," Thomas said, less than amused.

"That's what I heard too. I could have taken Louis the Demented. However, I wonder if I could have snuck into his pack and shaved seven of his guardians without awakening any as you had. A warning that you would be back, I believe?"

Thomas smiled, barely noticeable in the dark, but Bean's general eyes saw it. "Can you still do it?"

"Too easy," Thomas said.

"The rogue isn't," Bean replied. "Might be time to step up your game to something a little stronger."

"Unfortunately," Thomas said peering up to the moon a moment. "No generals to shave at this time. And if there were, I'd have more than I could handle, which is too much even for me."

Bean sniffed. "And here I thought you of all people would understand that there was more than one way to shave a cat. Do you know any cats that might be a challenge to shave, Mister Soleil?"

Thomas's face drew cold.

"Surely, you could use the practice," Bean said.

Kate snorted.

"It would serve no purpose," Thomas said.

"You never know. You might discover something long forgotten," Bean said. Then, he knew he shouldn't have said it, but it came out, "But if you're a coward these days then—"

Thomas leapt from his horse, now with both weapons drawn.

Bean decided not to prolong the event and suddenly fled. With as much as he wished to convince Thomas to step up his game, Bean knew that he too was less than he used to be. He flew, barely dodging Thomas's first thrust, and not dodging his second, which caught Bean across the thigh. Thomas was toying with the general. Bean elbowed, twisted, leapt to Kate, to Petruchio and used their own close-quarter confusion to put distance between him and the vampire.

"Hold," Thomas cried after him.

Bean dove into the shadows and around several corners of buildings and alley ways, where he had hoped horses could not navigate. Thomas, however, pursued on foot.

Around the next corner, Bean suddenly found Amber standing with her back to him. She had barely heard him sneak upon her, and Bean stealthily scaled the brick wall of one of the buildings into a high shadow. However, she turned to the slight sound of the scrambling and screamed as Thomas suddenly appeared before her. In a frantic chain of movement and confusion both in herself and Thomas, she drove her hands against his chest. She withdrew, and a wooden knife hilt remained in his chest.

"What are you doing down here," Thomas coughed out.

Amber broke into tears and cowered. Thomas tried to console her. Bean remained still and prayed neither would look up to see him hanging like a plaque from an art museum wall.

"It's OK," Thomas said. "I'm fine."

"I thought I saw something and I couldn't reach you on vox. And I didn't know." With that, she began to shake at what she had done.

"Don't be afraid," Thomas replied, and led her out of the alley. "It's my fault for growing fat and letting my ego get bruised. Come. We have another job to do."

Once they were gone, Bean waited a few more moments to decide that it was safe to make his flight back to his hotel.

25 ~ Forgotten Leisures

The Miniature Schnautzer bit into the tire of the Shadow, and swung the entire bike, smashing it into one of the gangsters legs, then again into his arm, then his chest, then eventually, there was nothing more of the biker worth smashing.

The hotel was upset with the eyesore of the vandalized RV and its contents that vandals had strewn all over the parking lot. Lisa and Winter spent most of the day outside cleaning up, they stopped only to take a walk and run.

Bean, however, scoured the town for a new vehicle. He spent half of a roll of his cash purchasing a beat up cargo van. It wasn't a good vehicle, a blue rust wagon really, with a poorly unfinished paint job of an eyeball on one side. It was enough to hide Stan and should be enough to last the few days they would actually need it, nothing that could withstand a wolf attack though.

They had argued how Stan already had a vehicle. Bean argued that his vehicle stood out and wouldn't make it out of the city. Shame too, such a gorgeous piece of machinery.

Bean stopped to fill the crappy van with gas and used his debit card before returning to the hotel.

"Do you know the PIN to your card," Bean asked, returning to the suites to find Winter and Lisa recouping from their workout.

"I've just been punching in two-two-seven-one," Lisa replied. "Seemed like a reasonable number to try."

"And it's worked?"

"Why," Lisa asked. "Need a loan."

"Funny how we know that information," Bean said.

"It's magic, ooh," Lisa mocked. "We know stuff from the brains of the bodies we possess."

Bean laughed slightly. "You're so stupid," he said, and then made his way to his room to ensure Stan and Eric hadn't wandered too far away.

"And what's with the eye-mobile," Lisa called after Bean, who ignored her. "You know it looks like a target, right?"

When Bean returned to the room, Stan and Eric were with him. Eric's head had been blinded by an entire roll of toilet paper over his face. The five made their way outside and to the hideous van. The trek to it was long and tedious. Bean had to scout every stretch of the trip until he was confident no eyes were interested in him. He had parked the vehicle out the back of the hotel, near dumpsters and not far from the unloading area. This stretch of the hotel had fewer windows, and a lone steel door could practically open right into the back of the vehicle. There was no sign to say it was a no parking zone, but Bean believed it most likely was a tow away area. Unfortunately, he worked with the tools he had, and they worked. Stan made it into the back of the van unseen. Eric made it blindly.

The trip to the Meade residence was pretty much uneventful. They dropped off Stan to Natalie and Nick's parents and watched him long enough to ensure that he could be invited in. All the parents seemed pleased to see each other.

Then the eyeball van returned to the hotel, where the three comrades finished cleaning up the parking lot. By the time they had finished, the RV had been towed away by some old, walking tattoo with about a thousand calluses. He was willing to pay $50 for the heap, but Bean was feeling a little superior and talked the buyer to $125, $10,000 for Bean's bike.

The day felt uneventful, but what could they do? No one liked it, but, short of interfering, what else was there? Lisa felt compelled to train some more. Winter joined her, and together they ran along as many populated streets as they could. Knowing human farms already grew within the city, Lisa suggested that populated streets be the best means of avoiding becoming inventory themselves. When the sun started to wane, Winter turned her jog back towards the hotel. Lisa thought it wise to follow.

After a shower and dressing back into her same clothes, Lisa suggested they eat. They returned to Thug's, where hardly anything happened except that Bean observed how the skaters, more of them this time, were a little skittish at the sight of him again. Still, they gave him room to dine. The additional skater faces didn't quite understand, but they followed their boss's lead. The suit made no motion for weapons. Thug fed Bean.

The rodeo queens joined a few minutes later, and Thug fed them too. Several skaters promptly offered their seats to Lisa and Winter. The café was more than full. Several young hunters stood in corners or squished into booths to enjoy their meals. Bean and the queens dropped some of the RV money at their seats and left, again at separate times.

"Now what do we do," Lisa asked.

"We wait," Bean replied.

She didn't wait though. After a few minutes, she felt restless and decided to take to running in the halls, which is how she discovered the hotel gym. She set herself to a quick pace on the treadmill. Her lungs felt stronger today. She didn't shake as much. She still felt anxious, but she had more focus not to drive it out.

Really, nothing else significant happened except that she realized the gift shop around the corner from the gym sold books. She made a quick trip back to her room and coaxed Bean out of some cash once her debit card no longer worked. Likewise, Bean became suddenly interested in the idea of books and accompanied her to the shop. However, he mostly complained upon seeing the poor selection the store offered. It was mostly modern junk, he finally selected what appeared to be a crime novel of some sort as well as some woodworking magazines. Lisa chose something more biographical and political, but she also bought a shirt and a pair of sweat pants so she could wear something clean. Winter, who joined them several minutes later followed suit in the end.

"Do I stink," Bean asked, making a spectacle of himself and drawing a strange look from the evening shop manager. He thought about getting something new to wear, but decided on a bar of deodorant and cheap cologne instead. He left his allies to browse the store further.

When Lisa and Winter returned, they found Bean in his suite reading one of his magazines and asked them to close the door.

Despite her best efforts to read and pass time, the combination of bad reading material and the approach of night outside, Lisa fell asleep before she had passed the first chapter of her book. When she awoke, morning light filled the room once more. She found her clothes had been laundered and returned. They were now hanging where Winter had left them, over the edge of the open dresser.

After waking and a short discussion about being tired, Lisa let Bean convince her that it might be a good idea to try the hotel breakfast buffet.

The buffet itself was okay, overpriced, but not entirely bad. That's not true. It was awesome! She felt somewhat spoiled since returning to Plattsville after far too many years of coconuts, bananas, fish, bugs and whatever edible leaf, root or can of expired food that presented itself.

Lisa sat with her face full of pancake and boysenberry. She sighed. Or maybe she moaned, she wasn't sure what kind of sound she currently made as she let the flavor stay on her tongue and absorb into her cheeks. Bean admitted that he understood and began to tell some cockamamie story from his glory-gone yesteryears as a delusional general who once stumbled on a rat after starving for two full moons, which was a long time for a hungry wolf.

She drowned his voice out with the sounds of her own mastication in her ears, followed by swallowing her loot and chasing it down with long, deafening chugs of milk. She slathered an English muffin with raspberry jelly and popped an egg yolk all over it. Then she dropped in a cheap link of sausage and bit into it, realizing halfway through this course that she was full, but that didn't stop her from visiting the buffet bar two more times.

She returned to her hotel room fat, bloated and happy. She dove into her crappy book once more. Winter peeled open an adult coloring book and a large box of colored pencils, which she picked up the previous night from the gift shop, and began coloring.

By the time Lisa reached chapter seven of her own book, it was almost time for lunch. Meanwhile, Winter had finished all the pictures in her own book then paced for all of chapter eight. Lisa suggested that Winter watch some television. Winter's attention drew suddenly to the large, black flat-screen hanging on the wall, as though she hadn't realized it was there.

In a few moments, Winter had discovered the remote control and figured out how to turn it on. Once she mastered the power button, she discovered a wireless game paddle and stared at it for several moments.

"You play games with it," Lisa finally said. "There's probably a channel for games, but you have to sell your child to the hotel to play them."

Winter took great interest in flipping through buttons on the remote and scanning channels on the television until a brightly colored screen appeared with thumbnails of available games to play. She figured out how to activate the game controller and began scrolling through all the thumbnails until she finally settled on one and flounced onto the ledge of the bed.

"I know that game," Lisa announced and had the urge to play as well.

The screen flickered with lightning, leaving a little man behind. "Let's kick some butt," the screen called. A few moments later, it screamed "you suck," as the little man died.

Winter stared in amazement between the paddle and the television. Lisa laughed and suffered the consequences of the glare that Winter shot back at her.

"You have to use the buttons to fight," Lisa suggested. "There might be a guide that shows you."

Lisa returned to her book and made it three more chapters, reading much more slowly as half of her attention was on Winter's performance with the little man who picked his nose between battling monsters.

Finally, Lisa couldn't stand it anymore. She groaned in a manner that soon had Bean asking if everything is all right.

"I'm so bored," Lisa replied.

"That's all that's bothering you," Bean scoffed from his suite. "Finish your book."

"I'm trying," she replied. "It's one of those boring parts that doesn't go anywhere, and the characters aren't doing anything but waiting and talking and talking and waiting, and you wonder why it's even there—other than to be boring, or to kill you softly but may actually be important."

"I hate those kinds of books," Bean moaned. "Burn it already. The authors of them all need to be punched in the throat at least three times."

"You suck," the television screamed. Winter threw her game paddle and began scrolling through channels instead.

"Why aren't we doing something productive," Lisa asked.

"You want to discuss philosophy," Bean asked.

"I'd rather birth an orca," Lisa replied.

"What do you want to do?"

"I don't know, something besides this," Lisa suggested. "Let's go help Josh."

"Wrong," Bean said. "We don't do anything. We wait for now."

"Then why were we sent to this time?"

"Most likely to give you time to adjust, or maybe to save Stan," Bean replied. "Think he would have gotten out of town alive without us helping him? Now your younger selves can help him escape, and he can save Dustin."

"Lot of good that does!"

"I hate to bring reality into check," Bean said. "But we can't risk Josh by trying to choose Dustin too. Sorry. Dustin dies."

Even now, the pain of his statement cut her to the core. Lisa wanted a loophole. She sat thinking for far longer than she wanted to.

"Why were we at Thug's when the wolves attacked, and the suit tried to kill Josh," she asked.

"Don't know," Bean replied. "I'm sure we'll find out."

"Well, maybe we should at least plan on how to save Speatsh from Genre."

"No," Bean responded harshly.

"We could use Speatsh," she was almost shouting. "He could be the key to rescuing Josh. He's the strongest of us."

"No," Bean responded again. "We're not here to save Speatsh. We're not here to save Dustin. We're not here to save Thomas. We know Josh survives Genre. That's one thing we know for certain. If we try anything else, Genre could change his tactics and manage to kill Josh. Then what? We know what decisions lead to Josh's death. That's what we need to alter."

"But Speatsh—,"

"Could get Josh killed," Bean refuted. "Josh lives through Genre, and until he's beheaded. Do you really want to gamble that certainty just to save Speatsh?"

"Why did you do this," she screamed. "I'm sure there were a lot of places she could have sent us to stop this at the source. Why not send us there? Why not send armies?"

"You think we didn't think of that," Bean asked. "Do you have any idea how many plans we drew out? I picked the most reliable people I trusted not to botch this job, and you already want to run off and possibly jeopardize Josh. What would have happened if we'd have sent back every miner and staff on that island to save Josh? You think they would have appreciated the situation with him and not done something stupid to mess things up? They'd have been running off to try and save their own families and friends, possibly blowing our plans."

"Could have sent us somewhere more entertaining than this place," Lisa continued to complain.

"Where would you like to go to," Bean asked.

"We could kill the rogue, like I said before," Lisa said. "He's born, we kill him."

"And brush off any potential future with Nick?"

"You mean the wonderful future I have now with him," she snapped.

"Okay then," Bean countered. "Forget Nick. You want to kill the rogue when he's born and start a war between humans and ancients before they know his danger to the world? What do you think his family will think of humans when they kill one of their own innocents? Think they'll respect life then?"

"Then after he leaves his family," Lisa suggested.

"Before or after their civil war," Bean asked. "Whose parents do we kill? Speatsh and Josh's? Your adoptive parents? Which of your friends do you want to risk never existing? Can you make that decision? Choose the most appropriate battle? Do we abandon moral ethics and introduce a smarter breed of human for thousands of years more of evolution?"

"Anything would have been better than this," Lisa asked.

"Wrong," Bean snapped. "We're not going back to our time or that island, and I hope that time never gets to exist again. Can we trust that if we go back to the first ancient that we won't stir an even more oppressive relationship with them? Because if you can, then you're a better god than I am."

"I just can't believe this was the best plan you could have possibly come up with."

"Well, it wasn't the best plan," Bean acknowledged. "The best plan didn't involve me being here, but here I am, and I'm certain it was for just this moment to keep you from doing something stupid during your boring section of your book."

"I'm not sure that's a comfort," Lisa replied.

"This is the fight we're familiar with," Bean explained. "It's with the people we know, and we just have to save one of them."

"And then what? He'll save the human race? If we've already been here, what did we do. Wouldn't that have been something you should have discussed with the djinn?"

"I was told what I was told," Bean replied. "Believe it or not, I didn't orchestrate this whole mess, just authorized the wishes."

"But you helped plan this."

"Yeah, this wish," Bean explained. "Not the previous ones."

"Then break her out," Lisa replied. "You have the djinn with you, break her out, and let's ask her."

"I told you," Bean said. "You can't just drag her out of her bottle to shoot the breeze. Are you saying you want your wish to be to know if Josh will save the human race?"

"No," Lisa replied grudgingly.

"Well, that's the contract. You find, you get wishes. The djinn hides again, or you free it. Besides, I may decide we might still need our last wish, and God help us if we do."

"I know. I know," Lisa said.

"Better for me to be here with you than lost where the rogue can find me and get his own three wishes," Bean said.

"Better for no djinn to be out there at all," Lisa realized.

Bean nodded, but no one could see it. "I will make a fourth wish if I must, but only if there's no other choice because at least there could be a chance to finding her again."

"But if you left us a clue, we could find you as the djinn," Lisa realized.

"It's possible," Bean said. "But there's too many unreliable variables. I might not know where I am. I might never be found. I may cease to exist as the person you know. In leaving a clue to you, I may leave one to the rogue. I tend to believe I'm of greater service being here right now, than going into hiding, or wasting a wish we could use later."

"But why wish us here," Lisa moaned. "I just don't get your logic."

"Because no one has ever been able to find the hearse, and, if Josh knows where it is, it could tip the scales in our favor. If we had it, we could revive the strongest of allies. No one's come this close to the rogue, and Josh is going to flush him out. This is the best time to get him. Believe me, I've spent a long time hypothesizing and letting that rainbow-haired djinn get lost in theoretical time options. Sometimes, I don't even know if I'm really here or still looking at her visions, but I do know this is the only place where anyone has voice and inkling of a clue that they may know where the hearse is. We don't know who made it. We don't know its power, and suppose, for a moment, we did something like go to the source and kill the rogue at his birth. How do we know the hearse won't still be invented or used to bring him back? And then what? No rogue, means no hunters to keep him at bay. He could still create his civil war—it'll just be postponed—and he could still manage to bring desolation to the world."

"Well, can't the djinn tell you any of this," Lisa asked. "I mean, she is all-knowing in time."

"Sure," Bean said. "She could tell us, if I was the person who actually got the three wishes and if my wish was related directly to finding the hearse creator, but it's not. It's related to Josh."

"So you decided this was the best plan," Lisa asked beratingly.

"Josh lives, that's what we need to make sure of."

"And if it doesn't work? Or if it turns out the hearse still isn't here?"

"I don't think the best pastime for time travelers is playing sliding doors," Bean chuckled. "Just stick to the plan, remember our goal."

"Fair enough, but one more question," Lisa asked. "How do we get that information from Josh without the rogue knowing, if he really does know Josh's mind?"

"That's the challenge," Bean said. "I thought about knocking him out and trying to close his mind."

"And what if you can't find the right flavor ice cream to do that," she asked.

"Then I have a free wish, don't I," Bean replied.

Lisa stood and decided it was time to go to the gym once more. She left her book so she'd have something to do when she got back. As she walked for the door, she suddenly stopped.

"What were the first two wishes," Lisa asked.

Bean smiled, and, for a moment, almost appeared as his old trickster self. "I wish I could tell you."

26 ~ Bull by the Horns

"Gut him," the large woman from inside the bar cried. She flipped a rather effective-looking knife open.

And the Schnauzer heard her.

Evening came again, and with it hunger. The dinner buffet sounded more appealing, but Bean felt that perhaps it was a good idea to stop into Thug's again to check its pulse. Lisa hid her disappointment well, but agreed all the same.

The neon bull greeted them from across the parking lot as soon as they exited the hotel and made their way towards the alley. Lisa adjusted her backpack. She had cut a new slit into the layer that pressed against her own back. It allowed her to grab an additional stun baton and power pack without disrupting access to her other tools that the pack also concealed. It wasn't the quickest access to her weapon, but if she needed, Bean could open her bag, allowing her faster capacity. They had practiced the maneuver a few times before leaving their apartment. The bag held two batons. Three more stun batons affixed to her belt under her leather jacket: one under each arm, another at her back, each capable of being able to attach and detach to her lasso as more power was needed. She stowed spare power packs in the side pockets of her new bag.

"Not much down that way," said a man in a white, open vest over a T-shirt with a red face of the snorting bull on it.

"We're fine, thank you," Lisa replied.

The thin, aged man could have passed for a used car salesman, except they had no time for a sleaze ball of his stature.

"Wait," he called after them and ran to catch up.

Bean gave a thought to kneeing him and letting him on his way.

"Hunters," he whispered.

They stopped. Now he had their attention.

"That man recruit you too," he asked. "Thought so. You can tell. You dress like real hunters."

All three remained silent. Clearly the man had not noticed the women were wearing show costumes.

The man asked, "You came for the haven, yes?"

"We heard it was around here," Bean played along.

"It's this way," the man said.

Lisa appeared ready to protest, but she trusted Bean's lead and followed at the heels of the hustler as he led towards a set of brown doors beneath the neon bull, Bean followed a step behind her, ready to open Lisa's bag if needed.

Two security guards showing their hick more than the cowboy they probably thought they were portraying stood as the man and his recruited party approached. True, Winter and Lisa looked ridiculous in their rodeo garb, but Lisa had lived farm life enough to know the difference between the quality of her hand-crafted Ariats as opposed to these buffoons' Fakemart brands that are made of more crap than any manure they'll never step in. Their guide waved off the guards, stating Bean's party belonged. The hicks let the trio through the doors.

"Tell them Scott sent you," the recruiter called after them.

The lobby was filled with red, leather couches, chairs, curtains and walls under dim yellow lights. It was narrow and trimmed in fake ivy, which advertised nothing country-style at all. A woman in her twenties, and with twisted buns on the back of her head, smiled at them from behind a podium perched before a set of brass and wood-slatted doors. Through the glass, the trio of friends could see diners beneath dark, bronze lamps. Gold candles flickered before them as people ate and gave no thought to anyone coming to interrupt their over-priced meals.

"Do you have a reservation," the greeter asked.

"The dweeb on the street showed us in," Bean replied.

"The dweeb on the street," she asked, confused.

"Scott sent us," Lisa added.

"That would be this way," the host said and aimed a remote towards a set of crimson curtains to the side of her podium. The drapes hummed apart and revealed an aluminum door, which opened on its own for the party of three.

"Enjoy your dinner," the host said.

Bean took pause to notice that the hidden door had been situated so no one from the restaurant could see it. He imagined the guards at the front kept anyone from walking in upon the revelation. Interesting—to degree, Bean thought—but mostly entertaining.

The three made their way through the new opening of the curtain. The next room was less inviting than the previous reception area. Cold, heavy-gauge, zoo-animal cage created a slender hallway within a larger room lined floor-to-ceiling in polished sheet metal. The silver door sealed behind them. A chain-link curtain drew over the door.

"Take your weapons," a man who could have passed for a butler named Lurch asked. He stood behind a steel counter built into the a wall of zoo-cage materials.

"We're good," Bean replied.

"Take your weapons," Lurch asked, again maintaining the same cordial welcome, but this time his hand rested on a large power switch on the wall. "No weapons of any kind allowed."

"Maybe we just take our business elsewhere," Bean said.

"Your choice," Lurch replied. "Weapons are allowed outside."

"All right," Bean replied, after a moment of friendly observation of the room.

"Are you crazy," Lisa contended.

"We're not being forced to be here, and I seriously doubt we'll like being electrocuted," Bean said motioning to the metal floor and nodding to the power switch. He pushed his shotgun through a window in the cage separating Lurch from the customers. Lurch tagged the weapon and handed a small silver bullet through the window to Bean. A set of numbers had been etched into the shell.

Bean laughed. "Silver? That's a good one."

"Are you not hunters," Lurch asked.

"Yes, sir. We're hunters," Bean replied more seriously now. "Are you?"

"I guard the weapons," Lurch explained, friendly, but advertising too much that he found Bean and his allies a joke.

"Get a lot of guns with silver bullets back there," Lisa asked, stepping up and pushing one of her disconnected stun batons through the window.

"We have a lot of hunters here," Lurch said, after a moment of looking over the weapons. "So I would assume yes."

Lisa stuffed two more batons through the window. When her pack wouldn't fit, Lurch opened a larger security bin that could accommodate the size of her weapons. Lurch handed her back her own bullet with engraved numbers.

"Anything happens to those weapons, and I'll be back to put this thing in your head," Lisa threatened.

"I'll make them a priority," Lurch said, surely saying enough to appease Lisa.

Winter stood before the opening now and set her silver show revolvers through the window, she turned to leave.

"I see another weapon, ma'am," Lurch said.

"Are you scanning us," Bean asked.

"It's protocol," Lurch replied.

"You should be proud of the greatness you've attained in your employment," Bean explained. "To imagine, convicts get free room and board for doing for what you do."

Now, Lurch glared.

Winter dropped the small cannon that Speatsh had given her on the platform and through the port. As Lurch reached for this weapon to tag it, Winter suddenly gripped his wrist and pulled him through the window up to his shoulder.

"I assume you understand the danger of violating the constitutional rights of an American," Bean suggested. "Especially an American who happens to hunt monsters."

"It's my job," Lurch replied.

"Do you like your job enough," Lisa asked.

Bean tapped on the cage with his bullet. "Do you ever wish you didn't have to come out of there sometime?"

Winter released Lurch, and he said nothing, but reached under the counter and appeared to press something that caused the far end of the steel hallway to open to loud music and a bunch of drunken idiots.

Tables outlined the next room with the same red, yellow, brass and ivy motif as in the lobby. The dining area was set on a rim of boardwalk that circled the entire room, creating an arena of sort in the center. The entire setting was large.

One step down from the dining boardwalk was another level of hardwood floor with pool tables, bad dancers and large beer kegs posted around the loop. The far end of the circle held a concave glass counter that burst with flames whenever some sort of celebration seemed to take place. On the other end, the kitchen and cooks in white yelled at servers in jeans and plaid shirts.

As they entered, the steel door to the weapon-check room closed behind Bean, Lisa and Winter. Another red curtain covered it, most likely to blend in with the motif of this restaurant.

A bouncer, a young, short and muscular kid, greeted the trio. While Bean didn't return the nod, Winter did and Lisa verbally thanked him.

The arena in the center held a ring of dirt and a squared lot of cattle fencing. A mechanical bull sat within. It seemed an odd contraption to Bean, but held his attention while he tried to figure out what it was exactly. It didn't take long for some dumb thug with only one arm to climb the fencing and take a seat on the mechanized contraption, which sat abnormally close to the steel corral panels.

"My money's on the bull," Lisa said.

"Why," Bean asked.

"I always bet on the one with brains," she replied.

A large man appeared, straddling the fencing and holding a large black box with wires. The audience cheered for him. He held up a hand and shouted, his voice amplified through a lapel microphone.

"Who's gonna throw him," this ringmaster asked.

Several women's hands flew towards the black box, and a thin brunette with half of her head sheared won the honor of whatever the item brought.

The ringmaster climbed down from the fencing and stood with the women. He started a countdown, and a unison of voices from around the arena joined in. A buzzer blasted, shaking the slats of the boardwalk. The room erupted with cheers and other uneducated cat calls and floor stomps.

The rider's body suddenly jerked back and forth, riding out into the center of the ring. He spun, bucked, twirled—all atop a six wheeled stand that raced around the inside of its perimeter. The bucking mechanism sped forward then suddenly backward. Once it moved backward, the rider toppled forward and off.

The ringmaster pointed towards the ceiling where a Jumbotron replayed the ride, and a set of numbers showed the clock at 5.7 seconds. Some of the crowd groaned. Some cheered Some laughed.

"What kind of garbage is this," Lisa asked, taking a seat at a wood-slatted table that had once acted as a spindle for thousands of feet of electrical cable of some sort.

"Must be the slow class," Bean said as he and Winter joined her.

"It's not so bad," a server said, dropping slender water glasses in front of them. "Break the record, and your dinner's free."

"Where's the line," Bean asked suddenly standing again and making his way towards the center of the room. "What's the record?"

"Record," the ringmaster cried out. "Do I hear a record challenge?"

"I hear free dinner," Bean shouted back. The crowd cleared, and a posse of employees helped reset the mechanical bull within reach of the steel rodeo panel. Then they allowed Bean up and into the saddle.

"What's the record," Bean asked.

"Fifty-seven seconds," one of the staff replied.

"I have to stay on this thing for a minute," Bean cried. "Your cooking better be worth it!"

The ringmaster made a spectacle of Bean's remarks. The guests cheered.

"Who's gonna throw him," the ringmaster asked. The same set of women's hands shot into the air. A short dirty blonde won this round.

The countdown started; the buzzer blared; and Bean's body lurched into the middle of the arena. The six-wheeled platform sped around the ring once, then reversed for an entire lap. All the time, Bean's body bobbed back and forth and spun.

The crowd cheered as he broke the eight second buzzer, then again at twenty seconds.

"Stop," Bean shouted.

"Stop," the ringmaster questioned and then announced. The crowd moaned. The replay started.

"That's too bad," the ringmaster cried taking up the black box. "Never saw the challenge end like that."

"You mean this thing was actually turned on? My grandpa's wheelchair bucks more than this thing," Bean cried. "I thought this was supposed to be a challenge."

The audience roared at the insult.

"This is what you get when the woman drives," Bean cried.

Women booed. Most men laughed.

"The man has thrown down the gauntlet," the ringmaster cooed. "Do we have someone who can throw this pig. Free beer if you can."

"No," Bean complained. "I can't sit here all night awarding free bimbo booze. Give me someone who can do this." He pointed out across the arena to Lisa, who had been caught off guard in her own amusement. "Her. I know she won't hold back."

"You heard the man," the ringmaster cried. "What do you say?"

"Give me that thing!" Lisa could hardly contain her excitement to amuse herself further at Bean's expense with the black box.

The staff began to reset Bean and the bull.

"Done this before," the ringmaster asked.

Of course she hadn't.

"Left and right are here," He explained pointing to a large silver lever. "This one controls forward and backward. This is rocker on, spin left, spin right and power. Goes to ten but don't go above this red area here. We don't want to kill the man."

"Don't turn the dial to ten, and don't kill the man," Lisa replied. "Got it."

The countdown started once more. The buzzer blared, and Lisa turned the dial to ten.

"Not so high," the ringmaster shouted.

"Yeah-yeah," Lisa replied, pulling away from the ringmaster's hands as he tried to intervene. She spun Bean to the right, then to the left and used the moving, mechanical bull to carve a sharp circle in the layer of temporary earth before suddenly ordering the vehicle backwards, spinning the bull left and speeding back then forward. The crowd cheered. The bull smacked into the fence.

Bean cursed, then cried, "That all you got?"

The crowd cheered, and suddenly, dead center of the arena, the bull stopped completely.

Bean screamed, "I'm not finish—"

The vehicle shot forward once more, the bull slammed into another section of fence head on, spun on its axis and drove sharply to the right. The vehicle toppled to one side of its wheels and slammed back down on all six as Lisa rediscovered the center of gravity for the device. Mostly she just got lucky. She assumed Bean offered some help in that area.

"What was that supposed to be," Bean screeched.

The crowd hollered.

"I need to throw up," Bean cried, speeding past Lisa's side of the fence. On the next time past her, "I'm not kidding!"

As he approached the next section of fence and its crowd, he feigned a vomit and then laughed at the spectators who cringed for cover.

A horn blasted.

"And that's a new record," the ringmaster announced.

Lisa kept at the controls, tossing Bean in every direction, each time raising the volume of cheers throughout the room.

"Turn it off," Bean ordered. "I'm bored."

"That's got to be the cockiest hunter I've ever seen," the ringmaster said, turning to Lisa. "Throw him off."

"What did he say," Bean asked, amidst the middle of a powerful backwards spin.

"He said you're cocky," Lisa yelled back. She wanted to laugh. She actually found herself having fun waiting to see what the agile general would do next.

The next time the mechanical bull came near the fence, Bean was standing in the saddle, stepped onto the fence and hopped to the ground. The crowd erupted with cheers. The ringmaster egged them on and applauded. Bean squared up with the ringmaster.

"I win," he screamed in the poor man's face. "I win!"

"Now you're just showing off," Lisa said.

She handed the control box back to the stunned and somewhat laughing ringmaster.

"Let's eat," she laughed.

"That's right," Bean shouted, then danced dramatic side-steps as he followed Lisa back to the table. "I won the fake bull. Who has a selfie-stick? Is there a photo I can buy?"

They set themselves back into their chairs and watched the rest of the replay on the Jumbotron as it announced a new record at eighty seconds. Their server appeared before them.

"That was the funniest thing I've ever seen in here," the server said. "Would you like a few minutes before you order."

"Bring me an egg salad sandwich," Bean replied.

"You went through all that for an egg salad sandwich," Lisa asked.

"Put a pickle in it?"

The server laughed. Lisa laughed. Winter wiped her own face free of tears. It felt good. Lisa kept laughing. Bean joined in with a faint chuckle.

"Egg salad all around," Lisa replied, laughing even harder. Winter and Bean erupted in suit.

The server shared in the laughter as she jotted down her notes. "All, right, I'll have those out in just a few minutes." The server turned about and made her way to the order-entry computer that sat in a booth several yards away. She continued to laugh as she walked away.

"All right," Lisa said turning back to Bean and no longer laughing. "What did you learn?"

"Very good," Bean replied, suddenly serious as well. "I told you, you were the smart one." He scanned the arena to see if anyone could appear to hear him and then continued. "About ninety people here, easy. Call them hunters if you want, I wouldn't. Not many scars. One or two who might actually be any good."

"Mostly idiots," Lisa added. "Hunter roadies? Safety features on the remote control? Hunters amazed at quick-thinking footwork?"

"You'd think most of these people hadn't seen it before," Bean replied.

"The goon on the street probably mistook our show costumes for being rookies," Lisa added. "They're all dipwads."

"That ringmaster's not," Bean pointed out. "He's a profiteer. Think Thug knows what's going on here? Because I sure didn't."

"That happens when you free your army of eyes to help us," Lisa replied. "But, I'll bet he'd prefer to let this place keep the rejects."

"Still," Bean added. "Every hunter is an able warrior."

"I can attest to that," Lisa said, then, "I have an idea."

"No timeline risks," Bean said.

Lisa contemplated Bean's caution and then decided, screw it, what could it hurt to lie this one time to the old man. "If I remember correctly," Lisa started. "Tonight's when we help Stan get out of town. I think, tomorrow's the attack on Thug's."

"You're thinking of bringing these guys into the fight," Bean asked.

"Why not," Lisa asked. "They're here. They'd be a big boost to our numbers."

"It's another gamble with Josh's life," Bean replied, maintaining his hushed tone. "The suit could change tactics and get lucky."

Lisa wiped the cold sweat from her glass of ice water. "So we wait until the suit is dead. Bring out the hunters let them finish up the guardians and we take them with us to get a head-start on prepping the compound."

Bean nodded. "I don't know."

"You know Josh can handle guardians," Lisa argued. "Put some trust in him. That's one thing you never got to learn, you know."

"I believe in Josh," Bean replied. "I'm just afraid one of these tourists would get him killed, though."

"Look," Lisa replied and knew she needed to add deceit to her fraud to bolster Josh. "You weren't there during the fight anyway. Maybe this is why. Maybe this is what we were trying to do last time."

"I wasn't there?"

"See, your being there could change tactics," Lisa replied. "I remember the rodeo queens, but I'm certain you weren't there. This would make a logical sense as to why."

"You're certain I wasn't there?"

"This would make sense," Lisa answered. "Besides, Josh leaves the group to go to the farm. Time it right, and these people won't even be near him while we make our escape. All you have to do is convince them this place is a tourist trap for noobs."

"All right," Bean finally relented. "It would add up that I would try to recruit people, even these noodle-heads. If Josh does survive without me there, I must have been doing something somewhere else to help. This seems to be the only helpful idea we've encountered that would hold my attention." Bean pondered the plan a few more moments before Lisa interrupted him with a little white-lie peer pressure. He supposed, for a moment, it would prevent Speatsh from remembering seeing him in Richard's house, which could actually be detrimental to their entire task. He should have thought about that before, but he had been certain Speatsh wouldn't have recognized him.

"All right, we go with your plan." Bean said.

Lisa made a non-verbal toast with her water, and the others returned the gesture.

"Could have sworn I heard I was there," Bean said.

"I don't remember you being there," Lisa returned carefully not to give herself away.

"Another night at the rodeo," Bean replied scanning the room and watching a new bozo climb aboard the mechanical bull. "I don't know if I could stand the torture of doing this again tomorrow."

"Oh, you wouldn't have to do this tomorrow," the server said dropping a sandwich down before Bean. She sneaked in a wink, which Bean wasn't sure what he was supposed to do with it. "Tomorrow's brag night."

"Brag night," Lisa asked.

"War stories," the server said. "They're mostly pretty stupid, but some are entertaining. It's going to be a very popular night. I'd love to hear what you got, Hun." She exited the table slyly brushing Bean's hand.

Lisa and Winter tried not to raise too much attention that they had taken notice themselves.

"Is she sick," Bean asked. He bit into his sandwich and frowned. "It's like there's a party in my mouth and everyone farted."

27 ~ Teeth

She stabbed once.

"Your cell phone," Lurch asked from within his weapon crib. Tonight he wore a gray tuxedo that was a little too small for him.

"You didn't ask for that yesterday," Bean said.

"You didn't have one yesterday," Lurch replied, and snugged at one of his silver and black cuff links.

"I just bought this," Bean objected.

"No phone policy," Lurch replied. "We don't need viral hunter haven vids."

"Huh," Bean asked, but then dug it out of his pocket, "Fine. Take it. Don't know who you have to call on it anyway." He tossed the cell through the small opening before Lurch's steel counter.

"And where are your friends today," Lurch retorted.

"One of us should have someone waiting for him when he leaves here today," Bean politely replied.

Lurch stuffed the phone into a small chain link bin with Bean's shotgun. He handed Bean his bullet, just as he had the night before. Bean thought about smashing the casing against the steel counter and seeing if he could fire it off just to watch Lurch flinch, or duck, or whatever these kinds of cowards do.

"If it rings," Bean said.

"We'll let you know." Lurch replied. He chuckled.

Bean chuckled with him, then guffawed, then broke into a guttural laugh, which came from his entire life of knowing how easily he could destroy Lurch. Bean took control of the laughing conversation, smacking the cage jovially. He watched Lurch's humor diminish into a silent, doubtful fear that Bean had stirred many times in his life. He found an old, familiar enjoyment executing his power to manipulate Lurch into distress, even though this weapon-check moron was safely sealed within a cage—that is, safe from Bean's current dormant condition.

Then Bean stopped laughing and simply stared and allowed a grin to thin across his lips, still chuckling. Lurch's smile disappeared. Bean stood a moment, tapping his bullet against the locked cage door besides the steel counter. "Is this the only way out of that little room?"

"We'll notify you if it rings," Lurch replied.

"I'd be ever so grateful," Bean replied and stared and grinned.

Lurch allowed the entryway into the hunter's restaurant to open as it had done the previous night when all three allies had visited. Bean took a while to turn away from his encased host. He waited for Lurch's eyes to freeze in fear against his own gaze.

Finally, Bean made his way towards the restaurant.

So much for the new throw-away phones that Lisa insisted they get so that she and Winter could contact Bean when the wolves attacked Thug's. Lurch better come get him when they rang.

He really wanted to be with his allies now. He wasn't too comfortable with this plan of Lisa's. It made sense, now that Bean had time to look at the situation more closely. It was so simple too. After looking around the room at all the amateur behavior and decoration, it wasn't a surprise that they were so easy to spot on the street and even easier to rustle into this establishment.

All the naïve hunters would enjoy a place like this. So someone, probably the rogue, sets up a false hunter den right under everyone's noses. Hunters come to this joke shop and, when the attack comes at the real haven, against the most experienced and vicious of hunters, the rogue can laugh at his own irony of having many of Stan's foolish recruits just around the corner and unaware. It would discredit Stan, and no hunter would take him seriously to send any professional to Plattsville anymore.

Then what was the rogue's plan?

After the rogue's guardians tear Thug's place apart and kill off the best hunters, maybe even Speatsh and Thomas, would the suit or one of the surviving skaters stumble into this phony hunters' rodeo ground and shout, "Someone killed a whole bunch of hunters?" Is that how the rogue gets the word out fast? Scare them so badly they run off to all ends of the earth and pass the bad news to hunters who could be reliable? Or would it rally the best hunters here for revenge for their fallen brothers? Bean had to remind himself he wasn't there to consider possibilities. He was there to recruit, even if they were idiots.

Still, it was rather brilliant for the rogue to destroy this most renowned hunter haven of Thug's with an army nearby that could have helped to protect it.

Yet, why didn't Bean discover the plan himself? Why didn't it all completely settle with him? To be fair, nothing settled with him, most of all Lisa's plan to be here, but who was he to argue on a matter that she'd remember better than he?

"Back again," his server from the previous night asked, rushing by with a plated order of food set upon her shoulder and palm. "You can have the same table if you like."

Dodging her tray of steaming dinners, Bean decided the best response would be to follow her advice and simply take a seat at his familiar table and let her do her job.

He watched her empty the tray at a nearby crowd of leather-wearing beards. They laughed at her jokes, and she barked like a hen, laughing, but rolled her eyes as she walked away and shrugged off the act as she realized Bean was watching.

"Can I get ya," she asked.

"Water," Bean replied.

"Boring," she returned. A snap behind her lips betrayed that she was trying to hide gum. "Anything else?"

"Cheese omelet? Pancakes," Bean tossed out.

"Sausage?"

"Eww," Bean replied. "I only like to taste my meat once, thank you."

The server laughed. "Nothing else, you'd like?"

"I could use this," Bean said reaching up for the pen behind her ear.

She let him pull it out of her shiny hair and blushed a little.

"I don't really need it anyway," the server said, then walked off. She glanced back at Bean for a moment, which he only noticed because he happened to be looking her way while he wondered if she might be rolling her eyes again about him.

Instead, she winked.

Bean did something. He wasn't sure what it was, but he felt the necessity to hide his face in what might have been shame for getting caught staring. Weird.

He took up a paper napkin from the center of the table and pondered its uniqueness for a moment before concluding that hunters probably didn't care for real fabric ones. He began to write upon the napkin. The ink didn't roll out. Bean grabbed a few more napkins, setting a stack before him. He doodled many small circles until the black ink started flowing out of the ballpoint tip.

He filled up the top napkin with as much of the bed sheet collage that he could remember from staring at so much the past few days. He couldn't help but commit it to memory. He started filling a second napkin.

"You an artist," the server asked.

Bean laughed.

"Don't laugh," the server said pulling up the napkin and inspecting it, clearly no idea which way was up. "It's very hieroglyphic. I like stick figures, those I can draw." She handed back his napkin and set Bean's glass of water far enough away from him to protect his canvas from accidental water seepage. "Have your dinner out in a moment," she announced. As she walked off this time, she gently squeezed his shoulder.

The leather beards glared.

Bean grinned, but only because it made the beards seethe more. Maybe they'd start something. He could use some sparring enjoyment before the main event. On the other hand, he didn't exactly need to injure any potential allies.

"Who's got a boast," the familiar voice of the ringmaster shouted into a microphone. The room was still. Just now, Bean noticed the bull ring and dirt had been cleared entirely from the center of the arena. A black-painted floor remained. A black stage, large enough to hold perhaps a dozen people at most, stood in its place now.

"Come on," the ringmaster urged. "Every time you do this. This is our chance to honor the dead. We're warriors. Let's do as warriors of old and bear our tales. Anyone? Someone?"

He waited in silence for an answer. He appeared uncomfortable, a poor master of ceremony. Completely unlike the man of confidence that Bean had seen only the night before.

"No one," the host asked.

He sighed. Then he appeared shocked. "Oh that's right," he shouted. The room began to murmur with light chuckles and chatter. A few customers began snatching napkins from the small silver boxes set in the centers of tables around the boardwalk. Servers began marching into the room with stacks of empty plates and segregated bins of silverware.

"Hope you're hungry," Bean's server said, dropping a stack of gleaming, square, white plates in front of him.

"I forgot," the ringmaster cried into his microphone. The speakers registered the mid-tone gravel of his pompously-developed, announcers voice. His dumb image broadcasted in high-definition insult from the cube of televisions above his stage. "What's boasting, without a little fire?"

Four rings of flames suddenly burst from the floor and nearly reached the ceiling. The room filled with cheers, and hunters began standing as the flames slowly lowered to a few feet above the floor, revealing white-dressed cooks, wielding heavy tongs and long roasting forks. Then, large cauldrons rose through the freely-burning propane, until they appeared to set sail upon the flames. Each black pot held a mountain of barbecued meat. The flames fizzed as juice drizzled out the bottoms. The heap of ribs before Bean was both savory and gut-wrenching at the same time. He wanted them. He wanted them fresher though, but he still wanted them.

"All right," the ringmaster tried again. "Now who has a boast?"

"If it'll shut that void in your face, I've got one," One of the beards from the table near Bean cried. He was a large man wearing orange outdoor hunter's colors. He marched away from the wooden ring of tables and towards the stage. He snatched the microphone from the ringmaster who tried to ham up the event and receive a round of laughter.

"All right," the orange-dressed beard said into the microphone. "Delaware, three months back. Chuck and me heard there was something to see there. So we went, and we found it." The orange man's hand settled at his waist, and his finger tapped at an empty, brown-sheen holster.

"It was a big mother too," Orange continued. "And it was just as I remembered, since the day one killed my brother, only bigger."

Bean went back to his doodling to avoid the temptation of calling this man, with his shiny unblemished holster, a liar.

"We found it preyin' in the woods on a couple camping," Orange bragged. "I didn't even know there was camping in Delaware. But we caught it. Chuck bashed it with an axe, and that piece of—," he caught himself from choking up. "Them claws ripped Chuck apart. So I shot it. I shot it good! Bam! Right there in the eye-yam! And I kept shooting it there until he was good and mad and then I took one of Chuck's grenades and I said 'this one's yours Chuck.'"

The table of beards stood and cheered.

"He'd be proud of you, Lewis," one of the them hollered.

"Shoved a grenade in the eye-yam did you," Bean laughed to himself and kept to his artwork. He stopped a moment and inspected his thought-map more.

What was he missing? His mind simply couldn't get past that.

He looked back to the doorway out of the restaurant. He worried that Lurch wouldn't notify him. Bean wasn't the most reliable with telling time. He reached for a pocket watch that he no longer carried and groaned. He turned his wrist to ask the pink, plastic fairy turtles instead.

The beards fell silent, and Bean felt them staring.

"What can I say," Bean said. "You're setting a trend."

Bean realized then that too much time couldn't have passed because his food hadn't arrived yet.

"No barbecue for you," his server asked, as she sneaked upon him with his omelet.

"At this hour," Bean replied. "I'd have to pay you rent for one of your toilets tonight."

The server walked off laughing, but returned shortly with a free drink, which Bean hadn't ordered.

He pushed the smell of meat out of his head. He still craved it. Luckily, the horrible scent of mesquite-sugar coating helped mask the scent.

"My buddies and I came across this dog, a boxer," a new man boasted into the microphone. He was a gangling creature who looked like he belonged on an episode of *Heroine Addicts Power Diet*. "We was hiking Yosemite when it appeared. There was no one around, and we just thought it was, you know, a dog. But then it dragged my friend off. I ran. I was scared. But now I know monsters be out there, and I won't rest until I find the one that took my friend."

Bean stopped listening again when he noticed the man's hands shaking too much to hold the microphone, let alone a steady blade or aim. The server stopped by to ask if Bean's food was okay. The next time she stopped by, she offered to spoon feed him.

"I need to stretch my legs," Bean said. "What do you recommend from the bar?"

"Ask him for the wolf's bane," the server replied and then asked if she should clean up his food.

"Just need to stretch," Bean replied. "I'll be back."

"Okay, Hun," she replied then held out his napkins of drawings. "Don't forget your pictures. Someone might take 'em."

He thanked her and made his way out onto the floor, towards the bar across the room.

"We found two of 'em," said a husky man that Bean quickly recognized as another one of the beards. He practically swallowed the microphone. "Heard they were there and we went out for a good, old werewolf bamhammer."

Bamhammer, Bean wondered. *That's a new stupid.* He approached what turned out to be a blue glass bar.

"Shoot," the bartender, a young man, perhaps in his late twenties, early thirties, asked.

"You guys must have changed management," Bean blurted. "This place doesn't sound like the tavern I heard about."

"Tavern," the bartender laughed. "No tavern around here! Just fine dining, good drink and fine hotel living."

"Hotel," Bean asked.

"Only the finest comfort a hunter could ask for. Everything a hunter needs under this roof. Keep your profiles low and safe."

"Finest comfort? You're not a hunter, are you?"

"Me? No, just work here. But even hunters have money," the bartender said, and then appeared to recognize that he might not have been so vulgar to his customer.

"You're a novelty," Bean asked.

"No way! I believe in the same gray wolves you do," he laughed a little. "What's your poison?"

"Let me try a Wolf's Bane," Bean replied, ignoring the innuendo of lunacy the barkeep gave up.

"Wolf's Bane!" The bartender yelled, then reached up and yanked a heavy chrome-plated chain. A steam-whistle blew, then waned and silenced the room. "Wolf's Bane," he cried again, repeating the entire ritual.

The room erupted with cheers, and the people started chanting "Bane" as if preparing to drink a swimming pool of fruit punch and then sacrifice a virgin. Bean quickly caught the mischievous shrug of his server across the room. She egged on more chanting from her immediate customers.

The bartender cracked an egg, mixed it with salsa, poured in a few ingredients from some liquor bottles, then dropped in some mint leaves and a pickled egg. Finally, he drew open a refrigerator and took out a glass filled a thick grey wax.

"Hog fat," the bartender said. He drew a paring knife, cut out a chunk of the waxy congealment and dropped it into his concoction. He blended the ingredients together, poured it into a glass and lit it on fire. A blue flame rolled around the top of the gloopy beverage.

"You know the rules, folks," the ringmaster cried. "If his story runs out before the flame dies, he has to drink it. It's what separates the real hunters from the kids with popguns."

The restaurant filled with cheers and jeers.

Several customers ushered Bean to the stage and quickly abandoned him. The ringmaster directed Bean to the microphone, but when Bean didn't approach, the emcee moved the microphone to him.

"A story," Bean asked. "What kind?"

"He asks what kind," the ringmaster asked.

"Just drink it," Bean's server shouted now lounging in a chair at his table.

He nodded concession to her manipulation. She kissed her hand and waved at him.

"You people are amazing," Bean said after a pause. "I have to admit I'm in awe. I've never heard such tales in my life. You're real hunters."

The room cheered.

"In fact, I haven't been this impressed with a group of people's escapades since those meddling kids and their Scooby Snack addicted dog unmasked Mr. Wickles."

This time the room booed.

"This isn't a haven. It's a nice pub though," Bean continued. "If I wanted to get fat and lazy, and only dream of becoming a real hunter someday, I'd never leave this place."

He received some jeers and a, "What do you know about it?"

Others called for him to drink.

"No story," the ringmaster said. "You gotta drink."

Two bouncers approached the stage with his flaming hog fat in a glass. They reached for him to help him answer his drinking duties, but with slight-stepping, alluded the men.

"Come on," the ringmaster said. "You're the champ, the record holder, that's you! Don't be like that."

"I still have a flame," Bean replied. "And I've just begun."

The ringmaster motioned the bouncers away. The room groaned and whistled.

"Grey wolves and boxers," Bean started. "Ooh! You've picked some awe-inspiring fights there."

"Like you've done better," one of the beards roared. The server hushed them.

"Tell me." Bean shouted back. "When you stuffed your grenade into the dog's eye-yam, did you bring your bone saw to bore it wide enough so it would fit, or did you inbred buffoons take a more rectal approach? 'Like I've done better,'" Bean mimicked back, then, "I have, and so have all the real hunters at the real tavern next door who wouldn't be caught dead in a place like this for fear they'd kill all of you just knocking your heads together to spark a little common sense."

The room uproared.

"Let him speak," one man shouted. He was easily in his fifties, large and scars down the side of his face. A bad comb-over dropped a straight wall of brown hair down to his shoulder.

"There's a hunter," Bean recognized pointing his own hardened finger out towards him. "You can see it in his face. Scouts, guardians, you know there's worse, don't you?"

The hunter nodded.

"You've seen the gold ones," Bean said. "The boys on the street made a mistake letting you in here, didn't they?"

The hunter's face tightened.

"Like I've done better, you say," Bean repeated again. "What real hunter hasn't? Don't believe me, you can march next door right now to that real tavern and ask any of the gnarled and scarred brutes in there: perhaps the woman who had her face burned off by wolf spit; or another who has a robotic arm because one monster tore his real one out from the shoulder. Or Speatsh Cheatham, a man whose name any real hunter fears because he is also one of those monsters.

"And if you look around this town you'll find another man," Bean regaled. "He bites people, collects them, gathers them to be his slaves. They help him watch this town for intruding monsters and feed him to keep his power up. He built a great army of dogs, all types of regular dogs and great, big, grey and black wolves."

The scarred man's eyes stayed locked on Bean, other hunters rolled theirs.

"One day," Bean continued. "A dumb, punk boy discovered the man and his army, but the man showed the boy that these little gray wolves and domestic looking dogs, although strong to the boy, were absolutely nothing compared to what made them.

"You see, these dogs were merely a security wall for the man. He controlled them all. And every full moon, this man lost his humanity and turned into one of the most vile creatures unknown to this ignorant species we pride ourselves in calling man."

Suddenly the room was no longer filled with mockery. It was still.

"In turning into this vile monster, the man lost power over his poisonous wolves and domestic dogs," Bean explained. "So once a month, he'd call his army of almost a hundred and he locked them inside the ground so they'd be safe from his own inner beast. Once a month, they became the humanity he lost. They turned human. while their master turned beast.

"But the punk kid discovered his work and sought to destroy him, still does. Eventually, the two fought, but the boy couldn't kill him, not even with the help of many allies and a broken arm. He may have been a boy, but he could tear trees down with just the wave of his hand, and he still couldn't beat the general who made all these other monsters." Bean smiled at the confusion that crossed too many faces. "You see, generals make your little grey wolves and boxers look like a whack at a piñata."

Bean pointed to the gangling wretch who had spoken previously. "This man saw a boxer, and that man saw a grey wolf." Bean drew his finger upon the table of beards. "That whole table of bearded ladies saw two guardians."

The table of biker-beards took their usual offense, this time a couple of them standing to do so. They booed. Three bouncers silenced them.

"Oooh," Bean mocked, and, with a salute of his burning glass, made sure the beards knew he was targeting them. "You killed wolves." Bean broke into laughing a moment. "What you don't realize is those monsters you so proudly hail as conquering are the babies of the family. There are much worse, the generals who made them. And even more dangerous is the one who made the generals and directs this entire war that has brought you all here today. This monster or man, however you want to see him, has eluded the best of hunters his entire existence, which you'd know if you knew anything useful. He works from the shadows and laughs at the feeble challenge you all pose. Hell, he managed to herd you all in here while your help is needed only yards away.

"His babies push you to your limits, while I've seen and fought and killed monsters that make those limits look like a friendly food fight. And I'm supposed to be impressed with how you 'bamhammered' Old Yeller?"

Now all the beards stood, ready to rush Bean, and he saw it.

"I know you're too stupid to know this," Bean continued. "Otherwise you wouldn't be here, because an ancient war is about to break loose in this very town, and none of you are leaving until you're dead or you've won the fight. You're so impressed by your war stories for bumhammering the babies, you have no clue what it is to fight a real monster, or to fight alongside real hunters. You're not worthy of eating at my table, and I won't drink at yours." With that, Bean threw his burning drink at the feet of the master of ceremony.

The crowd was silent at first and then called to throw Bean off the stage.

"Who is this elusive creature, then," one man called above the ire of the crowd.

"They call him the rogue," Bean yelled over the group, hushing them once more. "He belongs to an ancient race of wolf, peaceful until he decided he wanted more power. I'll bet many of you were recruited by a stranger to come to this town and help the paladin."

The room now gave Bean his full attention, yet he could see they hadn't grown any smarter.

"Have none of you wondered why the paladin isn't here," Bean asked. "It's because he's in that tavern around the corner waiting for your amateur assistance and teach you better."

"You lie," one of the crowd called out while others agreed.

"It's not a lie," Bean's server cried and continued to shout until she had conquered the volume of the entire room. She was marching her way towards Bean. When she got to the stage, she snatched the microphone from Bean. "I knew you were a real hunter," she said.

Bean wondered how he gave himself away, but, then again, he did spot the other hunter in the crowd.

"I've heard the stories too," the server said. "Many ancient and weak masters tried to hide, but there was one who set out to gather them back together because they knew the secrets to gaining the greatest of power among them."

"Get off the stage," one of the beards cried. "Let's get back to real stories here."

Bean's server sighed.

"It never ceases to amaze me," she said, mostly to Bean. "The stupid ones are so easy to train. Wait on them long enough and you can spot them in a moment." She opened her mouth to speak into the microphone again, but something chirped from her pocket. She pulled out a phone.

Why did she have a phone?

"I don't know what I was thinking coming here to find support," Bean said. "I don't have time to recruit nitwits."

"Good," the server replied handing her phone off to the ringmaster and asking him to take care of it. Then she turned back to Bean and said, "Because I need them." Suddenly, she was gone before the microphone could fall to the ground and dent itself bouncing. The server leapt from the center of the arena into the boardwalk, and Bean understood that Lisa had lied to him.

A male screamed. Bean's server, now standing before the man, screamed a mocking human war cry back into his face and then bit his chest for easier access to infecting his heart. Surprised cursing blasted from the table of beards. One by one, they convulsed in pain; grabbed at their chests; dropped to the ground; and cried the sound that Bean had known from turning so many people into monsters himself.

Bean started for the server-general who continued to drop customer after customer, blood ran from her jaw and into her uniform. The hunter in his 50s, whom Speatsh had identified as real, had already made a dash for the weapons room—yep, definitely a real hunter.

"You're a brilliant one," the ringmaster said stepping in front of Bean before he could race after his rampaging server. The ringmaster tapped away at the screen of the server's cell phone. "But you're done now." He tucked away the phone and straightened out his suit and warmly smiled to Bean. "Please be a challenge."

Bean sniffed at the ringmaster's insignificance and started after his deadly and flirtatious server instead.

The ringmaster grabbed Bean's arm and then punched for him with a strength that only a general could hold.

So, she wasn't the only one, they hid it well. Must be the room lighting. Probably why they didn't see him either.

Bean matched the ringmaster's strength and speed with his own, which wasn't what it used to be after so much fasting, even in this younger, biker body. Perhaps if Bean had allowed himself to feed more since he arrived, he'd be more potent. He had fed a few times after taking his new host, but he'd been fasting about a year now. He felt the slight drain on his abilities.

The ringmaster bit for Bean, but Bean was quick enough to step back a little and gain the leverage to crack the ringmaster's head between his palms.

Bean floundered to his back and rolled away to avoid a pounce and another bite. He reached for a familiar sword that wasn't in his grasp and air fled his lungs as he smashed into the ceiling and then fell back into the ground. He forced his heart to beat his lungs back into rhythm and then rebounded to his feet.

He deflected one punch, avoided a bite and was then thrown into a railroad-tie ceiling support. After he hit the ground, he stood again.

"You're a new breed of hunter," the ringmaster asserted and flew quickly for Bean. Bean dodged, then dodged again, managed a strange aerial assault of his own that ended with the emcee's fist thrust back into his own throat. The emcee cursed Bean. Bean drew the server's pen; stabbed it into his opponent's eye and then retreated several paces. A moment later, Bean was avoiding the pen as it was hurled back at him with deadly speed.

A couple of hunters attempted to aid Bean, but each fell to the ground harder than the first, never to fight again.

Now, the first guardian appeared to fight, the first of the turned—confused somewhat, but still dangerous, strong and under the control of Bean's server. She continued to fight her way through the customers, biting each and calling forth their transition into monsters. She passed the curse faster than Bean had ever seen. The change was never this sudden, his own poison took his own slaves days even to adjust. He'd have to ask her how she did it before he killed her.

Just then, the ringmaster pinned Bean.

"Open the door," he heard the scarred hunter's voice demand from the bouncer at the red curtain.

Bean and the emcee traded blows once more, each with the potential to debilitate any other opponent.

Suddenly the scarred hunter was helping Bean beat the ringmaster with his bare fists. He punched at the side of the general's head, dodged some blows, absorbed others. Bean did the same, a lot better than his new ally though.

Then, the first group of newly turned guardians attacked. The scarred hunter disappeared from the battle as one monster started dragging him away. The creature, however, cried more than the hunter did throughout the event. Bean continued his fight with the ringmaster. He felt awake, vivid. He kicked away a guardian, dodged the ringmaster, kicked another guardian and punched the ringmaster in the knee.

When the next guardian attacked Bean, he grabbed it by the throat and held him to block one of the ringmaster's punches. Then Bean shoved the guardian's head into the ringmaster's and bought himself enough time to gain a better stance, which he used to finish off two more of the dark-maned annoyances.

The entire room either waited their turn to get bit, convulsed now, tried to fight or had turned into new combatants. Bean realized here that the only dead hunters were those that had tried to help him. The scarred hunter still held his own, smacking one wolf with a plate and then driving a shard down through its clavicle. Another of his adversaries had a half a dozen dinner forks jammed in his neck.

The server shrugged nonchalantly to Bean and then continued her massacre. The ringmaster resumed his assault. This time Bean was backed against the wall opposite the door that led into the weapon check room.

His new hunter ally now yelled at him to finish the general.

Bean sidestepped, fast. He hadn't used this maneuver in so long, he'd practically forgotten it, but he was spry enough to pull it off still. He grabbed the back of the surprised ringmaster's head and dribbled his face against the concrete wall with enough force to stun his adversary. Just to be sure, Bean punched just below the back of the base of his enemy's skull, hoping it would break the ringmaster's spine and not the bones in Bean's fingers. He punched and continued to dribble. He jackhammered his fist into the general's spine until he finally heard and felt the crack. He couldn't help wonder, at this moment, how weak humans had ever brought even one of these creatures down.

The server applauded and turned her attention on the last living hunter, Bean's companion, who now held his own in the center of the arena with five guardians and no weapons. Unfortunately, his ally fell the moment the server bit him.

"Find my teeth," the hunter yelled only a moment before he too broke into a familiar seizure that Bean had seen too many times. He threw something silver towards Bean a moment before falling into his own convulsions.

Bean ran, snatched the silver bullet mid-air and kept charging back to the door into the weapons locker. He could have fought, probably could have beaten the server, but he saw the bouncers running for him now, fast too. They, like the emcee, were clearly generals. The task was finished, the server had bitten and nearly turned the entire room and now brought the full house down upon Bean.

Yet, his own server seemed more interested in watching Bean rather than fighting him. She observed from afar off. Why did she wait? Did she really need to evaluate him this much?

These were too many generals, even for him perhaps, at least without weapons.

He ran for the red curtain that hid the steel door to the weapon-check room. He kicked every creature away that came near him. The short bouncer grinned at Bean's approach and then realized his reward as Bean strangely tossed him back into the other bouncers that gave chase. Bean ducked behind the red curtain covering the door out of the restaurant, and quickly discovered a green mushroom button next to the bouncer's chair.

Bean hit it. The door slid open.

He pulled the button out of its box; grabbed a bare wire and snapped it out so it couldn't be used after him. He drew into the weapons room just as the steel door shimmied closed once more. Bean kicked the door and knew at once he'd done enough damage to slow down his pursuers.

Lurch was already laughing as Bean approached the weapon cage. He threw the switch.

The magnetic hum of electricity filled the walls. Bean now directed his hate towards the man in the cage.

"It was a brilliant plan, actually," Bean mocked as he stepped towards the small opening in the cage where they passed weapons through. "Most likely effective on everyone except for firefighters, electricians and bikers wearing boots with big rubber soles."

The steel door leading to the restaurant jerked and slammed inside its framework. The sounds of claws scraping the other side made Lurch smile even more.

Lurch reached under the counter to press his button to open the door. The door jerked but remained unopened. The scratching of claws and thunder of kicks rampaged even more against it.

Lurch frowned. He hit the button again.

"Doesn't quite work when the door's jammed in the track, huh," Bean asked.

Bean kicked the wall of cage. Lurch hit the button again. Bean kicked and left not as much as a dent in the meshing. However, Lurch's eyes did grow wide at the sound of his barrier reverberating under Bean's kick, but then he smiled upon realizing Bean couldn't get to him, and Bean didn't appreciate the joke.

"Oh, yeah," he said glaring gleefully back at Bean. "Forgot, safety precautions."

Lurch flipped the power-surging switch on the wall off. The hum of current stopped.

"Can't go frying the boss, can I," Lurch laughed. He reached back to the counter and smacked the button.

The door jerked open—only a little, but enough that the sounds of his attackers grew in volume through the crack that appeared. The monsters began tearing at the edges of the door to get a better hold to tear it out.

Bean knew he was done if they got in, unless he could arm himself. Even then, the room was small. It was too small to engage battle and survive. Yes, it was a bottle neck. He could take advantage of that, but a bottle neck that fills with bodies becomes a grave for the ones stumbling over them. The server's wolves would take him by numbers alone. The door to the lobby was sealed, locked most likely. He could try to open it. He could try to kick this cage apart too, but he knew either action would take more time and effort than he had.

The door popped in its track a little wider.

Lurch's cage seemed to be the only protection, and if it was designed to withstand generals and a mob of wolves, how could Bean infiltrate it by himself?

That's it! Bean wasn't by himself, was he?

The door to the restaurant suddenly presented a gap that was wide enough that several guardian and human general arms had breached and began to find better leverage to push the door open.

Bean reached into his pockets and pulled out the only weapon he had to persuade Lurch to open the cage. He shoved both hands through the small opening over the counter top where weapons slid through. He clasped the Christmas cracker tightly between his hands and broke it apart.

An explosion popped; Lurch stumbled backwards from the surprise appearance of the rainbow-haired djinn now standing inside the cage with him. She quickly took on his gray tuxedo.

"A wish for your freedom," Bean announced.

The Christmas cracker burst into flames.

The djinn stood slightly fazed and off balance.

"Now, help me," Bean ordered, pointing to a barrel of a gun that wasn't his. "Hand me that thing right there."

The wobbly djinn grabbed up the barrel and shoved it towards Bean, who took the grip and quickly took aim on Lurch, "Open up."

Lurch moved surprisingly fast, and a section of cage opened next to the counter. The steel restaurant door flew open, and two bouncers, followed by several guardians, charged in. Bean dove through the gate into the weapons cage, firing off a shot into a general as he did so. The bouncer recoiled just enough to let Bean get the advantage he needed to seal the gate and lock himself inside the cage with Lurch and the freed djinn.

Bean's first instinct was to feed off of Lurch. With blood, he would be strong again to fight. He knew his old strength. He knew what he could do if he had it back. He needed any edge he could get. Yet, what the server had said rang in his ears. He was a "real" hunter. They didn't realize he was a general. He was just a real hunter. He hadn't given himself away yet, had he? If he fed, the others would inform the rogue of a general hunter and the rogue would go looking for his mind. Bean couldn't feed. He'd done well to hide from the rogue so far, no need to give him reason to look harder. He'd have to fight, perhaps die, in his fast.

The djinn was free now, but there was still too much at stake to reveal any kind of upperhand that could save and help Josh. What advantage might everyone lose if the rogue did, in fact, suddenly sense two Jaspers? Strangely, Bean and his allies were stronger and safer with him in this human form. However, that didn't mean he wasn't going to lounge here behind this cage with the djinn and Lurch. He had to find another way to fight back.

"Where is this," Bean asked, shoving the scarred hunter's silver, claim-bullet into Lurch's face.

Lurch pointed to a tall locker.

"That all of it?"

Lurch nodded, and then Bean shot him center-mast.

The djinn flinched, but made no sound. Instead, she appeared to visually inquire of the falling and surprised man.

"Don't say anything," Bean said, stealing the djinn's attention away. "Stay with me."

A hall of guardians now filled the other side of the cage, clawing at the steel, but to no avail of bringing it down.

"I knew you'd be the challenge," the server said, appearing amidst them. She gripped the cage and rattled it. "Create protection for my staff and I end up protecting you." She glanced to the djinn, "And where did you come from?"

"Where do all hunters come from," Bean replied.

"Love the hair," the server said.

The djinn pulled at an end of a colorful braid that now only reached to her waist. She slid it back and forth through her hand, confused.

The sound of crumbling rock crept from the restaurant.

"You're going to attack Thug's," Bean realized. "It was all you."

"Don't stay in there too long, Hun," the server said before the hall quickly emptied of guardians. She followed, leaving the corridor empty.

Bean rummaged through the bins until he came across his own gear. He drew out his phone.

Broken!

The djinn still played with her hair and inspected the floor as if to discover where the rest of it had fallen.

Bean drew out his shotgun and blasted more red freckles down the already-dead-Lurch's blood-stained shirt. He reloaded and holstered his shotgun, left the broken cell phone and then moved to the tall locker that Lurch had pointed out.

"Please be a sword in a cane," Bean pled at the locker before pulling at the handle. He reached inside and drew out what appeared to be a shawl of leather, outlined with metal, but it grew into much more.

"I love hunter ingenuity," he said and pulled the leather shrug over his shoulder, his arms sliding into a set of sleeves. Both had been sealed with leather tassels. At the end of each sleeve was a gas-powered chainsaw with a blade about three feet long that had been encased in a black motorcycle chain. Three, uneven rows of small white blades protruded from the chain, and bronze welds secured each triangular chip to the chain. Upon further inspection, he realized these white chips were shark teeth. Two cylinders had been welded to the outside of each blade. One cylinder was shiny, but Bean could hardly inspect it while wearing it as the blades were too long to bend back at his elbows for a good view. The other cylinder was lackluster. Bean set his hands into the chainsaws at the end of his leather sleeves and felt a handle set into each that felt much like a set of brass knuckles. He carefully held the blades away from the djinn and pulled at one of the handles.

A restraint of some sort snapped around his wrist, followed by a mechanical brace jetting from each chainsaw glove and cupping his elbows. A set of rods dropped from his shoulders. He aligned them with what appeared to be receptor holes within the elbow brace. At first he cursed the odd design.

"How am I supposed to do this with my hands in here," Bean complained then, "Aha!" He aligned the rods and receptacles and slammed his arms on the counter to allow the two sections to connect as if building a brace for each arm. The pieces spun and reversed as Bean moved his arm. Finally the protracting bracing locked down, and he found the setup rather supportive and form-fitting.

He couldn't use his hands, but he might not need them with this new device. He felt within each chainsaw glove. In addition to the brass-knuckle handle, he felt two switches, a gun trigger and two buttons all within easy reach.

"This could be fun," Bean said, smiling slyly to the djinn who now wiped her wet eyes with the ends of a couple of her colored braids.

He supposed he could have comforted her, but he had more pressing matters at the moment. He pressed on a button within the right glove, and a steel pike lunged from within the shiny cylinder and ten inches beyond the tip of the shark-toothed blade. The spike disappeared just as quickly upon depressing the button. Bean was pretty sure he could figure out what the gun trigger controlled, and, if he was right in his assumption, he'd save that for a less concussive testing ground than this metal box-of-a-hallway.

He tried the first switch, and the black chain burst into a frenzy of spinning shark teeth. He turned the device off and flipped the second switch. Fumes puttered out the sides of his sleeve, and the deafening sound of a gas-powered engine erupted.

Bean killed the sound.

"A green hunter," Bean laughed. He switched between the electric blade and the gas engine to test how well they could alternate. He couldn't help but feel impressed with the chainsaws and leather that enclosed the ends of his hands and arms. Later, he'd dig into this device to study it further, but now he had to put it to work and hoped his own abilities would blend well. He made a few practice lunges, as well as he could inside his confining cage. It was time to get out of his close quarters. He knew how to turn it on. That was good enough right now.

"I miss my sword," he said to himself.

The djinn now kneeled over the body of Lurch and had taken an interest in the blood that leaked onto the floor. Her hands were red and greasy from examining the gunk.

"Is this death," she asked.

"You don't know death," Bean asked.

"Images only," she replied.

"I see," Bean said. He familiarized himself with the feel of buttons and switches in the second chainsaw sleeve, without executing any of their functions. "All right. Would you mind opening the door for me, my hands are a little full."

The djinn stood, and Bean coached her through using the mechanism that opened the cage back into the hallway.

“Stay close to me,” Bean said “But not too close.” He demonstrated the reach of his new weapon. “And always where I can see you.”

“Stay close to you, but don’t let the windmills see me,” the djinn replied, then reached for the door leading out of the cage.

The djinn opened the door.

Bean dashed towards the restaurant, which was now silent except for a bit of sound growing from a fresh hole in the arena floor where concrete had been shredded and a long drop appeared into the basement.

Remembering the last time he threw a woman down a hole in the ground, he instructed the djinn to hold onto him so he could jump.

Then he leapt through. Now, he was ready to fight.

28 ~ This is New

The Schnauzer bit the knife from her hand, whipped his head and sent the blade straight into her lower leg.

Bean's knees recovered a little more slowly than they should have after the twelve-or-so feet drop. He and the djinn had landed in what appeared to be a storage room. The mechanical bull from the previous night stood in the shadows along with its fencing and some other items that Bean really didn't care about giving a second thought to. This story mentions the bull at this time only because Bean recognized it and scoffed at its presence. He soon discovered another hole carved into this concrete floor near where he had landed. In fact, had he tumbled just a few feet to his left he would have fallen through it as well.

Again he leapt, a longer drop this time, twenty-five or thirty feet perhaps. He paused upon this landing to wonder if he'd made a mistake, but then he stood.

"I'm getting too human for this exercise," Bean said, and he helped the djinn release her grip from around his neck.

Lights blazed overhead of what appeared to be an underground loading and unloading dock area.

Three roll-away doors sat high on unloading bays upon the three remaining walls. The entire enclosure was easily large enough to fit a tractor-trailer or three. Yet, one of the doors appeared differently from the other two. Where the other doors were designed of the average thin steel that could roll up and open, the third was made of one heavy slab that currently swung inwards. Bean recognized the material at once. It was the same metal that Richard had used in the bunker to withstand the sharp claws of wolves from digging through. He was sure all of Thug's walls were probably made from it as well.

"So you did open it," Bean said to himself.

"So you did open it," the djinn repeated.

"Stay close," Bean whispered. He then stepped cautiously towards the loading bay.

"Stay close," the djinn repeated, and followed Bean up a small set of steps into the warehouse area of Thug's tavern.

The next room was even larger. Oil stains plastered the floor, yet no cars took up any room. Two metal cabinets stood between pillars and a tower of tools. Small cranes and winches sat against the wall to Bean's right. To his left sat an elevator, its doors destroyed, which opened to an empty shaft and several cables. Bean could already hear guardian growls and gunfire from within the shaft.

"A dragon bellows," the djinn said.

Bean ran for the elevator.

"Don't fight unless you have to," Bean instructed. "Otherwise find a place to hide until this is over."

"What style," the djinn asked.

Bean didn't understand the question.

"What style of fighting should I use," she asked again.

"I don't know," Bean replied. Suddenly, he stopped a few feet shy of reaching the elevator. He laughed. In all their rush, the wolves missed it. Bean almost missed it.

It stood in a darkened corner, somewhat hidden by a concrete upright support. It was black, shiny, had glass all around and was definitely old. Its carriage wheels looked new, well-restored or preserved. It seemed tall, as though built for a larger stature than the average human. Bean would have taken a moment to inspect it, but the noise of gunshots from the elevator shaft started him moving again.

Is that it, he wondered.

"Once more," Bean instructed, and the djinn wrapped her arms around his neck again. This time he had to remove his arms from the sleeves, which took a little while to figure out how to accomplish, which he did by simply twisting the knuckle-like handle inside his sleeves.

Once he discovered the routine, he carried the djinn and the rest of his cargo up the greasy elevator cable. The elevator revealed a hole shorn in the floor. He grappled any surface he could in the shredded floor. Here, he realized that he could have fallen into the abyss below him, but he doubted that would keep him from climbing up again, unless Thug and his allies had thought about putting a floor of spikes at the bottom of the shaft—which, knowing them, he didn't think was too far-fetched. He chose not to give falling a chance, however, as he doubted the now-human djinn could survive.

Finally he helped push the djinn through the hole torn from the bottom of the cargo elevator, all while balancing the leather set of sleeves and their long chainsaws around his neck and maintaining a tremendous grip on the oily cables.

"I have chosen a style of fighting," the djinn said before Bean had pulled himself into the elevator car.

"Don't be stupid," he groaned, even while he was in the process of climbing through the hole to the floor.

However, the djinn was already through the elevator doors.

Bean rearmed his shrug of chainsaws, quickly losing patience at the sounds of battle and the ignorant djinn disobeying him. The elbow bracing aligned much faster this time, and Bean rushed into one of Thug's back hallways where he found two dropped guardians and the djinn standing above their bodies. She hovered over an injured Thugh and held a large meat cleaver in each of her hands.

"Get 'em outside," Thug's voice cried. He hunkered against a wall, blood ran down the side of his arm.

The djinn turned slowly at Thug's voice.

"Is this also death," she asked.

"What," Thug wondered out loud. "No, and I don't plan on being dead."

Bean ignited his blades. He toiled a moment between powering them with gas or the electric and thought he should use the electric so as not to pump carbon dioxide into the small space. However, he had confused the buttons and started the gas engine anyway.

A guardian, then two more, rounded into the hallway. The djinn was still hovering over Thug, strangely observing.

"Get down," Bean announced, rushing the group of attackers.

Bean chose a target, one sneaking upon the djinn's back, the closest to her. The djinn wheeled around and buried one of her square blades into its neck. With the second, she hacked the jaw off of another creature. An instant later, she removed the blades and quickly sank them both into the chest of a third beast. The three monsters joined the two guardians that had already fallen near the djinn's feet.

The hallway now appeared free of attackers. A few sounds came from the café, but they resounded in familiar death.

Thug stood dumbfounded.

Bean realized he, too, was confused.

"Thank you," the djinn said handing the large cleavers to Thug. "That was fun."

Thug took the cleavers, unable to take his eyes off the strange woman.

"Where did you come from," Thug asked.

"Bean," Lisa cried, before Bean could answer. She and Winter appeared at the end of the hallway. "How did you—," her face turned confused at the sight of the djinn as well.

"I am ready to hide now," the djinn said. She knelt down with the fallen wolf bodies, half human now. Her hands, glazed with red, smeared her cheeks in blood. "I've seen them do this," she said. "It brings out the feminine lines?"

"This is new," Lisa said. "What happened?"

"You have to ask," Bean cried, the teeth at the ends of his hands came to a standstill.

"You rub your hands together forty seconds like this and it makes them clean," the djinn continued massaging her hands in pooling blood as though it were soap.

"Stop that," Lisa chided, and helped urge the djinn to her feet.

"I've seen you," the djinn said, then acknowledged that she'd seen Winter, although she wasn't necessarily the same person she remembered seeing. She also pointed out that she knew Thug and several others who had begun to fill the hallway, including the suit and the doorman.

"This isn't right," Lisa replied.

"What did you bring into my place," Thug asked.

"Now, this is more like it," the server's voice announced from the elevator behind Bean.

Bean turned and watched the first guardian appear from the hole in the elevator floor. It joined the server already standing inside.

"We waited for you at the bottom," the server said. "But you didn't fall." She smiled.

Bean didn't.

"You're good," the server said as several guardians began to climb through the elevator floor.

How did I miss it, he asked himself. The chainsaw of teeth came to life once more, and he leered at Lisa. "Don't let anything happen to her," he demanded and nodded towards the djinn who had suddenly started puddle hopping in the red pools spilling over the hallway floor.

Bean ran for the server and her guardians, his blades of shark teeth humming back to life. He cut one beast open. Others rushed past and into the café where Lisa and her own surrounding allies yelled strategies amongst themselves. Bean didn't care, he wanted the server's head. If she got through, his friends might not fare so well. He didn't concern himself with the guardians, they were foolish for thinking they should ignore him and attack what they assumed were non-lethal hunters.

"It's an ambush," Thug cried.

"We can't fight 'em in here," a voice Bean didn't recognize announced.

One of the fake haven's bouncers appeared through the hole in the elevator floor and then fell as Bean quickly decapitated it between stabs at the server.

"Generals incoming," Bean yelled, as another bouncer leapt past Bean and failed to strike him. The server, however did not miss.

"Everyone outside," the doorman's voice could be heard. "Take it outside."

Bean leapt back, barely dodging another kick from the server. Like ants, the monsters erupted from the elevator floor. Despite their numbers, they stopped attempting to land blows on Bean. Now, they ran past him into the café of hunters. So did the third bouncer, and Bean was unable to strike him. Though, he did try what he could.

A trickle of blood ran from Bean's left temple. Black quills stuck from all sides of his skin and clothing, yet he still held against the onslaught of guardians and their master.

The server swiped at Bean, slapped at him with her long French-tipped nails. It didn't seem too dangerous, but each attack she landed took more and more fight out of Bean. His saws tore at the walls, wolves and anything that got in the way of his wide swipes.

The wave of wolves suddenly stopped.

The server laughed off a trail of gashes up her arm and used Bean's speed and weight against him, allowing him to stumble into the freight elevator and nearly through the floor.

"Catch your breath, darling," she said, grabbing his collar one time and keeping him from dropping. "You've earned a better death than that."

Bean rushed her into the hallway. The sounds of wolves, gun shots and an angry doorman came from the other room. Only Bean and the server remained in the debris-filled corridor.

The server flew at Bean once she regained her posture. She dodged one chainsaw and then the other.

Bean kicked her, and, this time, she was the one who fell off balance. He followed this with a left chainsaw and cut at her leg. She retaliated with a quick slice at Bean's neck. Blood began to trickle instantly. Bean dropped, but stood again

"That's more what you deserve," the server said.

The two tumbled into the main restaurant. Bean regained his footing, and the server took a stance to pounce.

"I knew you weren't just any hunter," she gloated.

Bean watched her muscles tense as they do to give away movements. He predicted the next maneuver; she'd lunge head-on, he'd jump straight up and hold both saws up for her chest. That should impale her.

She jumped for Bean. He leapt up, chainsaws poised, and she deflected one saw into another, causing Bean to fall once more. She was good!

Why? Why couldn't he keep up anymore? Sure, he didn't have the blood, but Speatsh had pulled it off, why couldn't Bean? Before he could stand again, the server was over him. Her strength was great, pinning him to the ground.

"Even the best hunters fall," she said and drew back her arm to strike when—

"Ma," the doorman asked.

The server's face filled with memory, a realization she hadn't expected. It was something from long ago, not a voice. The voice was different. A lilt. She treasured that lilt. The one part of her she never lost. She turned.

"Ma," the doorman asked again.

The server's face turned a sudden confusion.

"You," the doorman said. "You look like you did."

"B," she asked.

"It's you," the doorman replied. "You said you'd come back."

"B," she said. Her eyes and sockets fell red, and she embraced the man that towered over her by two heads. They stepped over the fallen bodies that littered the café. "I wanted to come back."

"Someone found me," the doorman said. "Right where you said they would. Someone found me."

"I couldn't come back," she cried.

Just at this moment, Bean, who had climbed to his feet once more, restarted his right-hand saw blade, but somehow unintentionally hit that last button inside his glove, the one he had yet to test. The blade leapt off of his hand and buried itself into the server's side. She drew silent and fell heavily into the doorman's arms. The Doorman cried. He dropped to his knees, still holding her.

Bean didn't try to say anything. He knew nothing could cover it. He'd screwed up. Rather, he was too surprised at the sudden attack to know what to say. And she would have made such a wonderful ally too!

The doorman cried over his mother and after several sobs said, "You're better now, ma."

A phone chirped from within her vest, startling the doorman and Bean both.

"Check it," Bean said.

The doorman grunted.

"It's a hunch," Bean shouted. "I have to know."

"You check it," the doorman replied coldly.

Bean held up his encapsulated hands. The doorman took out the phone and looked it over.

"A few texts," the doorman said.

"She probably didn't hear them over the fighting," Bean said. "What do they say?"

"All the same," the doorman said. "They say 'the paladin's coming.'"

Right then, the steel door leading into the café tore off of its hinges. Bean had been so caught up in the recent events that he hadn't realized that the café had been sealed shut, nor that only he and the doorman remained inside to fend off the wolves.

Where was the djinn? He cursed that she had left him.

Then a familiar and dark figure walked in.

Bean found himself fighting to bite back his own unexpected tears as he watched his old nemesis, draped in his paladin robes and full fury, appear in the doorway and share words with the doorman. Despite that he had seen him the other night, Bean was overcome that he was alive. The sound of battle ripened fresh from behind him. As quickly as he entered, Josh now left the café, but not before glaring off to Bean. For a moment he wanted to laugh at Josh's futile attempt at intimidation, but Josh had earned this moment. Bean pretended to be scared.

Out of respect to the doorman, Bean allowed him to leave the café before he attempted to recover his blade from the fallen general's body.

Once Bean ventured outside, Josh was gone. Sirens sang in the distance. He caught sight of Lisa and Winter standing atop a barrier wall and helping surviving hunters up and over. He quickly spotted the suit, fallen in battle. As Bean ran towards the wall, he kicked the dead assassin for good measure.

"Where is she," Bean cried as he approached his rodeo companions and quickly removed his sleeves, once more so he could scale the cinder-block wall.

"She's already over," Lisa replied. "She's playing in the dirt."

Bean helped the remaining stragglers over the cinder block before leaping to the other side himself just as red and blue strobes began to light up the sky. Bean collected the djinn, who had bitten into a ball of dirt and was just then spitting out the undesired results. Together, they followed after the line of fleeing skaters, who, in turn, trailed the guardian that Bean could only assume was Natalie, as she wasn't actually attacking anyone. She seemed to growl orders every so often.

"Was it the waitress," Lisa asked. "Was she the general?"

"Yeah," Bean suddenly stopped in his tracks. "How did you know?"

"I've waited tables before," Lisa said. "She was a little too happy in her job for me. You kill her?"

"Yes," Bean replied. "That was your plan, wasn't it?"

"They didn't die," Lisa replied.

"Who," Bean asked.

"You killed their general, but her slaves didn't die," Lisa explained.

"They'd only been enslaved this evening," Bean replied. "It takes longer than that to build that deadly level of a withdrawal."

"Well, regardless," Lisa said. "We let her survivors get away and now we're vulnerable with those guardians out there."

"Their general's dead," Bean replied. "And they'll change back soon. Their connection with her wouldn't have been long enough to shock their system." Then Bean noticed. "What happened to your lasso?"

"Josh cut it," Lisa replied.

"Why'd he do that?"

"Because he's stupid that way," She snapped. "He doesn't stop to think. You of all people should know that. I was changing battery packs, and his majesty did his own thing without even attempting to consider the situation."

"You're unarmed?"

"My former gave us some guns, but I'm about out of ammo," she replied.

"Don't say that too loud," Bean said. "Her hearing is still excellent." He gestured towards the dark wolf bobbing in and out of traffic lights and leading the exodus of hunters through the dark streets of the business district. Eventually they came to the fields, and Bean believed he had let enough space creep in between Natalie at the front of the line and his small band taking up the rear before he decided to speak.

"We'll fix it," Bean said. "And don't you ever play me like that again."

Lisa tried to play innocent.

Bean suddenly stepped in front of her. "If you want something from me you ask. I would have done it if you'd been honest with me."

"Honest," Lisa laughed. "You."

"Is that what you still think of me," Bean asked, and abruptly left Lisa so he could join the main group.

"No, of course not. I—"

Lisa ran after Bean.

"I'm sorry," Lisa said softly. "I thought we should try something different. We can't fail again."

"This is definitely different," Bean replied. "Think you can get us through the night without totally defacing what we're here to do?"

"Is this night," the djinn asked. She looked up to the skies as if trying to embrace them. She bobbed on the balls of her feet, waltzing forward instead of walking.

"What are we going to do with her," Lisa asked.

The djinn suddenly stopped. "Give her a name," she said. "We can't belong until we are named."

"What do you mean," Bean asked.

"We cannot remain free unless we are bonded, else we return," the djinn explained.

"Bonded?"

The djinn nodded. "Our thread must be anchored to one time," the djinn explained. "It's time that lets us grow old. I must be named or I must leave."

"You need to be named or you return to your—," Bean caught himself, "line of work?"

"Names are that," the djinn answered.

"We can't let her slip back to where she can be found by someone else," Lisa said.

"We," the djinn asked. "I cannot be mate to all of you."

"Mate," Lisa asked. She wanted to laugh, but held it. "The person who names her becomes her mate, Bean?"

"It's what keeps her here," the djinn explained in slow realization. "She must be bound to one."

"Why did you set her free," Lisa asked.

"Because you lied," Bean replied. "Now, she's free, and we lost our backup plan. I couldn't use the last wi— Look! No matter what I'd done, she'd have been alone, and you would have had one less ally right now because I'd be off hiding or dead—and we both know, you need all your allies."

"How soon do you need a name before you go back to being what you are," Lisa asked.

"I don't know," the djinn replied. "Your time is confusing." She pointed up to the sky. "When those become blurry."

"The stars," Lisa asked.

"Yes," the djinn said. "Stars."

"That would make sense," Bean replied.

"How," Lisa asked. "They're constant."

"No, and neither is the earth," Bean explained. "If she starts perceiving all she has before, they might all appear to move to her."

"She'll be seeing multiple images of the sky," Lisa acknowledged that she understood.

"Not different skies," Bean corrected in an even more hushed tone, barely audible to Lisa. "Different times."

The djinn turned towards them, blinking each eye in turns. "Does this mean that there are two different yous?"

Bean prodded her to continue walking, which she did in more of a dance than a hike.

"This, we do not need," Lisa said.

"Then you shouldn't have lied," Bean replied.

"I knew she would," the djinn replied.

"You did," Bean asked, now he felt his own pace falter. "You knew."

"Freedom is rare," the djinn replied. "You might not have kept the promise."

"What do we do about the skaters," Lisa asked changing the conversation upon wondering if they had lingered too long for eavesdropping.

"Nothing," Bean replied. "We were wrong about them. They weren't meant to help the suit kill Josh. They were meant to die, or at least be added to that lunatic waitress's army during the attack."

"And Kenny," Lisa asked.

"We'll get him," Bean replied. "We know where he is and what he does."

* * *

The steel walls were already open. The entire place remained without power. Oliver stood at the gates and leaned against his steel staff. He welcomed the hunters, asked for a password and then complained that they should have one after no one knew what it was.

The insides of the compound were fairly bright from the rim of spotlights atop the Silver Bullet.

Voices mumbled from the confines of the dark facility, but their words were unclear. One of the voices belonged to Bricktain, that much was certain. Another must have belonged to Reggie.

A dark metallic chariot flew to the group of hunters, which Natalie led. It began circling the incoming group with its majestic and departed steeds.

"We to be having company," Aggon cried, kicking up dust around the group.

The voices in the distance stopped.

"What is it to bring you here," Aggon asked.

Natalie growled and smacked the side of Aggon's chariot, causing it to tumble over.

Aggon stood; flipped his chariot of gold back to its wheels; and began arguing with Natalie, despite her communication gap and uninterested concern.

"Shut up," Reggie yelled. "And stop kicking up the dirt before we die coughing!"

"Who are you," Bricktain asked, approaching the group and paying a little nod to Natalie as she marched past him. When no one answered, either from awe of the sight of ghost-driven chariots; surprise at the appearance of the robotic man; or caution not to give their identities away, he followed up with, "Did you think I was asking myself?"

"I thought you were asking yourself," Thug's voice called from within the group of tavern refugees. He was hardly recognizable from the blood-stained mask he now donned.

Bricktain took a moment to recognize Thug, but knew the doorman who carried Ty on his shoulder a little more quickly.

"The haven's gone," Thug said. "They got in." He suddenly turned on Bean. "How did they get in?"

"They hijacked the visibly, less-experienced hunters when they came to town, and they turned them into wolves," Bean explained. "They were Stan's recruits."

"How'd you escape," Thug asked suspiciously.

"Wasn't easy," Bean replied.

Luckily, Bean's explanation of the hunter's café, minus any revelation of who he or his companions were, satisfied Thug. Most of Thug's disappointment now seemed to stem from his ignorance that another hunter's haven had been open right under his nose.

"Is your waiter alive," Bricktain asked.

"He lost a hand," Thug replied. "And lots of blood."

"I'll get over it," Ty moaned.

"Show off," the doorman said.

Bean shot Lisa a sharp glance, and shame gripped the depths of her gut.

The fog lights above the Silver Bullet suddenly turned blue.

"That's a new one," Bricktain said.

"That's for the CB," Thug explained, then ran for the Silver Bullet. He pulled the door open.

"Break one-nine, Break one-nine," Speatsh's voice called from the cab of the Silver Bullet. "Scurvy Mutt to—well—anyone at the baby, come on back." He repeated the announcement once more before Thug could find the transponder to reply.

"Master Chef here, go ahead Scurvy Mutt," Thug replied.

"I was hoping you'd make it by now," Speatsh's voice replied. "Listen, nine-one-one at the nine-one-one, bring the baby and trigger. Watch for Dracula." He repeated the request. "Come on back."

"Copy Scurvy Mutt," Thug replied. "ETA in—oh hell, you know how long it takes." Thug hung up the mouth piece, "Speatsh needs the Bullet at the hospital." He searched out Bricktain. "You the gunner?"

Bricktain confirmed.

"Well, you're up, Trigger," Thug said.

"I'm coming," the doorman said. He hustled his way past Bricktain to the Bullet's open trailer.

"Get me my guns," Ty said.

"You're not the gunner," the doorman said. "You're missing a hand."

"I can still outshoot this guy," Ty replied, his words slightly slurred.

"Dude," Thug said. "You're dying again."

"He's always dying again," the doorman said.

"I've had worse," Ty replied.

"But, um, just to be safe, Ty. You better find a bandage or something to put over that tourniquet." Thug said. "You're going to infect it."

"Good thing we're going to the hospital," Ty replied, disappearing into the trailer.

"Hope you know how to hold on," Thug said, suddenly appearing rushed and with an outstretched hand. It took Bricktain a few moments to realize he was asking for the keys.

Bricktain tossed them to Thug. "Have you seen Speatsh drive," Bricktain asked, making his way to his station inside the trailer and before his wall of monitors.

"No," the doorman said. "I never met Speatsh until I met you."

"And you wouldn't," Thug replied. "To shield Josh and his sister, Richard turned his back on hunting and forbade all of us from their lives in case any of us gave ourselves away. Last time Speatsh came around before all of this was when he watched the door one night a week. Other than passing on the street or somewhere public, stopped seeing Richard before that."

"I guess that makes sense," the doorman said. "Is Speatsh any good?"

"You mean Miss Daisy," Thug asked, as he climbed into the driver's seat laughing.

Bricktain pulled the backdoor closed behind and questioned how that was supposed to be funny.

"It's not funny," Ty said. He had seated himself in a fold-down chair that Bricktain had never noticed before. The doorman had secured him into an aircraft harness, and Ty had starting digging out a shoelace to tie a clean shop towel over the end of his wrist. "Speatsh can't drive, he doesn't even have his—."

"Wait," Thug erupted laughing. "You thought this was Speatsh's truck?"

"He said it was," Bricktain replied.

"Speatsh said a lot of things," Thug said still laughing.

The doorman burst into laughter as well. "Ty, lend the new guy a hand will ya."

Thug and the doorman's laughter suddenly fell silent, looked at each other realizing their mistake.

"Too soon," the doorman asked.

"Too stupid," Thug replied.

Ty started crowing and drove the stem of his wrist into his face. His eye socket was instantly red with blood that had leaked through his poor bandaging. "Look, I can't even wipe the tears out of my eyes."

"Will you stop moving around so much," Thug announced. "You'll bleed out."

"I am not cleaning that up," the doorman stated matter-of-factly.

"Hey, we're freaking the new guy out," Ty said, as he pointed his handless appendage towards the Silver Bullet's gunner.

They all three looked back to Bricktain, who stood stupefied, and suddenly they bust up laughing again.

"What is wrong with you people," Bricktain scolded.

"Hey, rookie," Thug snapped. "If you have to ask, then you don't deserve to know."

"That's right," the doorman replied. His face stone cold. "Driver's rules."

"Look," Ty announced, gesturing with his one remaining hand at Bricktain's feet. "Speatsh didn't even tell him about the boots."

The three maniacs started laughing again. The doorman stood up from the cab and made his way into the back, stopping at a small locker behind the passenger's seat. He removed two black boots and a bicycle helmet.

"These are called big boots and a helmet," the doorman mocked. "You put them on your feet and your head."

"Make sure you put them on the appropriate body parts," Ty added.

Bricktain, although confused, and suddenly feeling substantially out of his depth, obliged the insults, mostly because he believed he should submit to the urgency in Speatsh's call rather than the desire to crack the doorman over the head with a steel hand. Although, he was sure he would soon regret such an action. He pulled the boots on and realized instantly they had steel soles. He tightened their straps, and the boots snugged to his appropriate size.

Now the doorman withdrew the toy guns from their compartment among the wall of flat viewing monitors and handed them to Bricktain "These are your aiming and shooting devices."

"Gee," Bricktain retorted. "Thanks for that. As if I haven't had them permanenty attached to my arthritis for the rest of my life."

The doorman pointed Bricktain to a set of faded blue dots on the floor, which Bricktain had noticed before, but never really gave any thought to.

"Heels go there," the doorman instructed. "Stomp."

Bricktain stomped once.

"Call that a stomp?"

On the second stomp, a clamp extended from the floor and locked onto the sole of Bricktain's foot. It pulled his foot tight to the floor. The process repeated for the second boot.

The doorman reached up to the ceiling and stretched down what Bricktain had previously believed to be hand-holds for standing passengers. The doorman strapped them around Bricktain's waist and around his shoulders like suspenders. He then shoved both guns into a holster on each side of Bricktain. Next, he drew down a black cable from the ceiling and attached it to the harness over Bricktain's right shoulder and repeated the same for the left. Then he produced four more cables from various places that he connected to Bricktain's belt. Finally, he slipped a soft brace around Bricktain's neck.

"Have you really been doing this without being anchored in," the doorman explained.

"Hurry up," Ty added. "I'm feeling a little woozy, here. Name the movie. Name it."

The doorman stopped a moment to think.

"Scream," Thug replied.

"To release your boots and cables, return the guns to their shelf," the doorman continued.

"We're booted," Thug called and the soft, barely noticeable hum of the nuclear engine took control.

The doorman returned to his seat.

"Isn't this overkill," Bricktain asked. "I've never needed any of this before."

Thug laughed, this time only to himself.

"Speatsh is one person," the doorman said. "The Silver Bullet takes two people to drive."

"And one crash test dummy," Ty added.

Suddenly, the trailer jerked with power that Bricktain hadn't felt from the Bullet before. He began praying that the safety cables would keep his face from smashing into the wall of flat television screens. They did.

"I swear, she's stronger than I remember," Thug said.

"You say that every time, Boss," the doorman replied.

Bricktain watched the confines of the compound race across the monitors in front of him. He remembered to pull his glasses on now, surprised he hadn't dropped them yet.

"Trip check," doorman asked.

"Yes please," Thug replied.

"Trip check," the doorman announced.

"Trip check," Thug and Ty replied.

"What's a—," Bricktain tried to ask.

Several small explosions burst from beneath the trailer, and Bricktain felt his weight shifting beneath him: first forward, the cables holding him snugly from crashing into the screens again; then all blood rushing to his head; then flooding to his back and finally settling where it had started with a loud crash back under Bricktain's feet. All the while, ground and sky flashed across the screens before him.

"Barrel roll complete," the doorman announced. "Three-sixty test?"

"Let's not kill him on his first run out," Thug suggested.

"You got that right," Bricktain screeched.

"What the heck," Thug corrected. "Let's do it."

"Woo-hoo," Ty cheered, then, "But then I think I need a doctor."

* * *

As the chrome, nuclear-powered diesel disappeared into dark and dirt, Reggie finally ordered the newcomers to work. In particular, he needed muscle to start the compound's emergency generator. Bean would have obliged, but felt it more necessary to let the skaters prove their place in the new home.

Aggon spent the majority of time sitting behind steering wheels of junk heaps while Bean, Lisa and a few select hunters helped push cars that could easily be maneuvered towards the recycling smelter. Cars that couldn't be pushed would have to wait until the crane was operational.

Once the generator kicked on, Kenny complained from a second story office window that Reggie's computer was far too outdated to do any good.

Reggie, in truly kind words, encouraged him to stop being a whiny snowflake. Meanwhile, he ordered the gates closed, which worked rather well seeing as they'd been abandoned to the elements ever since he was forced to flee his home. Reggie was more impressed with how many halogens around the compound continued to work under the power of the generator.

"That should keep us up for a while," Reggie explained. "But we could use a tanker of gas to fill my pumps. My supply may have gone bad. Be surprised if this generator keeps working."

He set a few skaters to pumping out the underground gas tanks to test the fuel quality of the current contents.

Oliver and Acotactac continued to watch the gate. Bean picked out a skater: one separated from the group gathering garden hose; one he had tussled with before in Thug's café; one now missing an ear. He grimaced as Bean approached.

"How's the ear," Bean asked.

"Take it somewhere else," the skater leader said.

"Rough-housing is one thing," Bean said. "Ear's a whole other game. You okay?"

The skater said nothing.

Bean acknowledged the silence and turned to find a less intelligent skater.

"They know we're here now," One-ear said before Bean could get too far. "We're sitting ducks."

"They knew we were here before we got here," Bean replied. "If I'd have known what was coming, I'd have stayed in Boise." Then he thought he'd risk one of the questions that had been plaguing him most of the night. "How do you know Kenny?"

"Who's Kenny," the skater asked.

"The kid upstairs running the computers," Bean replied.

"That his name? He worked for that hunter in the suit," the one-eared skater said. "He hired us to help him protect the haven."

"Protect it," Bean asked feigning surprise. "From whom?"

"The paladin," the skater said. "He's a general. A traitor with his own army."

"That's what the suit told you," Bean asked

One-ear shook his head. "Said he'd notify us when he was going to attack the place."

"Not cool," Bean said suddenly in a hushed tone. "Does your phone work? Can you text Kenny?"

"No, sir. None of our phones work," One-ear wrestled broken hose from beneath a tire and decided to drop it.

"None of your phones," Bean asked.

"Yeah," the skater said. "He provided us all phones, said we might need them?"

"And now none of them work?"

"Are you stupid," the skater replied. "The power's out."

"Should still work," Bean said.

"Not if the towers are out too," One-ear retorted.

"Thought you had satellite?"

"Are you kidding? Do you know how much that satellite junk costs? We used an app."

Bean laughed. "What do you plan to do now," he continued to prod.

"We can't have a general in the midst of hunters," the skater said. "You know that. You're a hunter. These people are just lucky they don't know what the paladin truly is."

"How are we going to stop him," Bean asked.

"I don't know," the skater replied. "We?"

"Is this hunt proprietary?"

"I suppose not."

"Go ask Kenny what he thinks we should do," Bean ordered. "I'll stand watch here and make sure you don't get interrupted."

The skater hesitated, but summed up enough courage to slip into the house and compound office. During this time, the Silver Bullet returned with Thug and his bar-mates along with Amber and Natalie instead of Bricktain.

Amber returned to her father, Bean imagined, to update him about the events that had taken place at the hospital.

The skater reappeared, and Bean was quick to inquire. "Job off then?"

"No," the skater replied. "Help's coming. More hunters."

"I was right," Bean said, then caught himself. "How does he know help's coming?"

"His phone works," One-ear explained.

"How so?"

"I don't know," One-ear said. "He has a satellite piece of junk?"

"Nice of him to give you one," Bean explained. "I couldn't work for a boss who didn't trust me."

"What makes you think he doesn't trust us?"

"Why's he bringing in more hunters," Bean replied. "We just downed four generals and their entire armies, and the paladin helped. How do we explain that if the paladin is a general?"

"The paladin was acting?"

"Was I acting when I killed the general," Bean asked. "I can take the paladin on by myself. Why would Kenny have more hunters ready to come in if you weren't good enough." Bean left it at that a moment, waited for any hint of intelligence.

Nothing.

"I'm just saying," Bean continued. "I think it's pretty strange he wasn't around when the haven was hit."

Come on, Bean wanted to scream.

'I mean Kenny didn't even fight," Bean hinted again. "Why is he calling the shots here?"

Bite, fool!

"Well, he did find the paladin," the skater replied.

"A man with a dog told me about the paladin," Bean said. "Said he needed support."

"How do I know that," the skater said. "Maybe you're a general too."

"Maybe you're a general," Bean said. He wanted to punch the kid. How blunt did he have to be? He stayed silent for a few moments, then. "So this Kenny," he finally said.

One ear groaned at the continuous conversation.

"I'm just saying it seems odd to me," Bean continued. "What kind of hunter hides from a fight, anyway? I mean we do all the work, and he's in a cushy booth."

"Now that you mention it," the skater said. "He doesn't seem like any hunter I know."

It's about time!

"I've seen a lot of hunters, and you know when they've killed," Bean said.

"Yeah, Kenny doesn't have that look in his eyes," the skater replied. "Come to think of it, how come his phone worked? Hey, we should have all had phones like him. Wouldn't he get a better deal with all of us on the same calling plan?"

Your intelligence is staggering. "Yeah," Bean dumbed out. "Hey, you know what I think. I don't think he's ever killed a wolf."

"Know what I think," the skater said. "He might be a liar."

"Hey! Yeah! You know. I think you're right," Bean replied. "He could have been lying about everything."

"You know what," One-ear blurted and then let Bean hush him. "I wonder if he lied about the paladin."

"Not cool, man," Bean said. "What do we do about it? Not like we can attack the paladin now without being sure."

"We watch him," the skater said.

"Kenny?"

"And the paladin," One-ear said. "Just to be safe."

"That's a good plan. How do we do that without Kenny getting suspicious?"

"We'll tell him we're waiting for the right time to attack," One-ear explained. "And if the paladin tries to make a move, we'll be ready."

"Yeah," Bean replied.

"Yeah," the djinn's voice replied too.

Bean straightened up at the sound of her sudden appearance and began to escort her off. "I'll tell my crew," Bean said. "You tell yours and if the paladin or Kenny, tries anything, we'll be ready." He put extra emphasis on Kenny's name to help vilify him more.

"And if Kenny tries anything," the skater said. "We'll surprise him."

"I like the way you think," Bean replied. "Kenny will rue the day he lied to hunters."

The rainbow-haired djinn laughed at the skater as Bean escorted her away. Again, Bean found a secluded area of the compound and demanded the djinn stay put. He suggested that they find some water to clean her face, then he quickly located Winter working on helping move cars.

"Someone needs to stay with the djinn, while I do one more thing," Bean explained.

"Yeah," the djinn yelled in agreement. "I have mental diarrhea."

"If you're here, you're working," Reggie yelled from the seat of his crane, where a large magnet dangled from its arm. His voice blared from a small bullhorn speaker at the top corner of his compound residence. "You're not helping,"

"I'm sorry," Bean shouted back. The girl we've rescued is in shock and I need help with her here while I give the big guy a break."

"I'll watch her," Thug announced.

"She doesn't know you," Bean quickly refused as he prodded Winter towards the djinn. "This woman is a grief counselor. She can help her."

"That woman can't even talk," Reggie's voice replied.

"She's not supposed to talk, duh," Bean replied. "She's supposed to listen."

"We don't have to worry about you accidentally naming her," Bean said to Winter once he assumed Reggie's approval. He let Winter take care of the djinn while he continued his rounds of inquisition and manipulation. Then he made his way to Oliver, who stood like a statue, facing the now-closed steel gates as if ready to bash any surprise that might attempt to open them. The little Pomeranian that was strapped to his back warned Oliver of the biker with a wolf bandana approaching from behind.

"Shut that thing up," the doorman cried. Bean hadn't noticed him perched above the gate, taking it upon himself to prepare his watch station.

Oliver turned slowly. "Not pet doggy," Oliver said gruffly. "Not yours."

"I don't want your doggy," Bean replied. "I need a favor."

"You stranger," Oliver trumpeted. "Not talk to strangers."

"What about the people who buy graves," Bean asked. He shouldn't have. He knew it, but he had to know.

"Not strangers," he replied. "Tenant friends."

"I need you to ask Speatsh something the next time you see him," Bean asked.

Oliver glared at Bean.

"Can you ask him something for me?"

Oliver grunted.

"Doggy," Bean said. "I think you called him, Doggy."

"Doggy," Oliver moaned or yelled, whatever it was, Bean was impressed.

"Since you're Doggy's friend, can you ask him something for me," Bean asked once more.

"Okay," Oliver replied. "What?"

"I have to whisper," Bean said. "It's a secret for him."

"I good at secrets," Oliver said. He leaned his head down next to Bean's and whispered, "I've buried a lots."

"Promise you'll ask," Bean asked.

Oliver nodded. "Doggy friend."

"Ask him if there are any more—," he bit his lip, carefully not to encourage Oliver in any way to ask the oracle Speatsh about pants this time. Instead, he turned and pointed towards the djinn. "If there are any more people like that funny-haired friend of mine in this whole world."

"All right," Oliver replied. "I ask next time I see him."

"One more thing," Bean said.

Oliver stayed silent.

"Don't let that dog on your back hear you ask," Bean requested.

"I swore protect her," Oliver railed, rejecting the request.

"She'll have nightmares if you do," Bean lied. "You don't want her to have nightmares, do you?"

Oliver suddenly straightened up. His face turned sullen and he scanned the compound. "Okay," he said. "I hang her on wall before I ask. Nightmares is bad. I haved them once. It was bad."

Moments later, the doorman announced that he was opening the gates. They whined from lack of use. Kate and Petruchio raced into the compound with three figures upon their backs. The Plattsville mayor, his wife and a shaken daughter.

As the crowd of hunters swapped stories with the mayoral family of their previous dealings, Reggie suggested they start extending the walls of the compound out farther and that the mayor prepare to organize leadership among any more civilians that might show up. As the effort grew to clean the compound area, so did the number of people it needed to accommodate.

After the Bullet had appeared with its small crew, Amber informed Reggie that Bricktain and Thomas were escorting a large number of people to them as they spoke.

With this information, Reggie directed many of the available hands to find chain link. He imagined it in the best interest of everyone to keep the civilians out of the hunters', or rather, Josh's way. The work was still in process when Thomas and Bricktain began returning with a parade of weary adults from the hospital and even more ragged children from the school.

After a short discussion, Thomas, a skater, and enough crew to man the Silver Bullet set out to retrieve fuel and provisions. Ty did not join this time. His injuries and wounds had been treated while a mass exodus of humans escaped the hospital through a hole in the floor of the hospital basement. He now slept on the couch in Reggie's living room, enjoying the sedatives that Thug had mixed into his drink before driving back to the compound.

The civilians set to work, and Bean took the moment to have a short discussion with his own cohorts about hiding the djinn.

"The last thing we need is someone inadvertently naming her," Bean said. "We'd have to explain it, and there goes our surprise attack."

"Some places cut out the tongues of liars," the djinn replied, staring off into the sky. "I'm beginning to see the threads again."

"What happens if you're not named," Lisa asked. "Will you disappear on us?"

"I go back and start again," she replied. "All wishes are used."

"Then I'll take your place," Bean said. "I promised."

"Yes," the djinn said. "But I have no container to give you now. It is gone. You broke it. First, I find another container, then you find me to trade. Then we can trade. I must be named, and I will."

Bean rushed the djinn towards the bottom of the stairs leading up to the catwalk. It seemed the place she would least likely be bothered currently. She would be out of earshot and out of sight of most other people for now. He instructed her to go to the farthest reach and watch beyond the walls to appear as though she were helping. If it looked like anyone might approach her, Bean, Lisa or Winter would intercept.

"Listen," Bean said. "If you don't get named, we will find you again."

"Come out! Come out, wherever you are." she suddenly yelled. She now looked upon him as though she were a memory she'd just remembered. She poked her finger into his chest. "When you start to see triple, always poke the liar."

"Incoming," the doorman screamed.

The gates moaned open once again.

The doorman nearly ran Bean and the djinn over as he flew down the catwalk steps. Two figures appeared at the gate, one dragging the other on a make-shift backboard of leaves.

"Doggy," Oliver cried. "Doggy?"

The man, Chandler, pulling Speatsh's lifeless body, fell as though he too were dead.

Oliver took up Speatsh's lifeless body and pet his head and pelts. "Soft," he said. He caught a glimpse of Bean and remembered what he was supposed to ask Speatsh. He suddenly dashed through the gates and into the darkness, towards his graveyard, with the beaten ally in his arms.

The doorman called after him, but he was interrupted by a growling and rustling that now came from beyond the compound. The curious djinn approached the open gates with her finger outstretched.

"Ooh," she said. "Something needs sustenance."

Bean stepped between her and the gates. He quickly identified his chainsaws in a clumped pile near the wall too far for his reach at this moment. He readied his sawed-off and shotgun pistol and mentally prioritized a need to prepare his new weapons for quicker access.

The growling creature appeared around the edge of the open gates. It turned out to be Speatsh's small animal pelt, scrambling for foot holds and dragging another limp body behind him. The doorman cursed and moved quickly to Bear's cargo.

"It's the paladin," the doorman announced.

A rumble roared throughout the junkyard as the doorman lifted Josh to help ease Bear's load, then dropped him in afterthought of Josh's sharp cloak. He grabbed Josh by the hands and helped drag him past the gates.

Amber emerged from the crowd and sprinted upon the sight of her injured husband. Bean wondered whether he should try to restrain her, but when Natalie appeared and roared and charged forward, he decided not to get involved.

That's when he realized the djinn now leaned over Josh along with the doorman.

"You're not allowed to be dead," the djinn said, and then screamed, "Open your eyes."

Josh moaned.

The djinn smacked him. "No sane person would choose to die right now."

The doorman restrained the djinn, but couldn't seem to muster the strength to pull her away. Natalie stamped her paw in the dirt at the djinn. She snorted at her, then screamed. The djinn badly imitated a roar back at Natalie and giggled. Natalie backhanded at the djinn, but missed and seemed surprised at doing so.

Amber now hovered over Josh who was suddenly alert after Natalie's frightening bellow.

"He's fine," the doorman said. He had given up his attempts to remove the djinn, who still knelt beside Josh, and was again blinking her eyes in turns. She appeared amused at how Josh's body jumped back and forth on the ground before her with each blink.

"Help the other one," the doorman said.

Amber took a moment to register that the doorman was trying to distract her to help Chandler who had collapsed after dragging in Speatsh. Thug was to Chandler's side first and called to Amber for help.

"Your husband won't die," the doorman encouraged. "Help the police officer."

"We'll talk about this later," Amber said to Josh before trusting in her other allies and moving towards Chandler who remained unmoving.

Josh's eyes fluttered as he appeared to be trying to focus.

"Don't go anywhere," the doorman urged Josh. Dustin appeared at his side now and began inspecting Josh for injuries.

"Open his cloak," Lisa said when she realized neither Dustin nor Natalie could fully assess Josh safely.

The djinn reached for the clasp of Wolf's Breath, cutting herself in the process. "I am death," she said, looking at the dribbles of blood that quickly seeped from her fingertips. She held her finger to Josh, "Does yours do this?"

"Back off, neon head," Josh mumbled, and it was his intention to call her a neon head, but his words trailed off and out of breath before he could deliver the last syllable of his sentence. He made some strange motion with his shoulder that might have commanded Wolf's Breath to do some harm if he'd had the energy to finish the movement.

Bean froze. He saw the same horror on Lisa's face, as well as Winter's.

"And so Neon is free," the djinn said, placing her hand upon Josh's chest. Josh's torso lunged upwards as though begging to take in more fresh air than his lungs could hold. The compound fell silent as Josh's body arced towards the heavens. He sucked in air and held it. His face flooded with red, his lips spilled over with foaming saliva. Suddenly he screamed, releasing his entire drink of air. He fell back, coughed fluid, breathed deeply and then slowly sat up.

Bean noticed the change in Josh's appearance immediately, Amber noticed it a second later.

"Your hair," Amber said.

Josh didn't understand. Amber presented an orbit with Josh's reflection. A tuft of red, yellow, purple and other colors had appeared above his right temple.

"Now we are bonded," the djinn said, showing that a section of her own hair above her right temple had darkened to that of Josh's. "Josh and Neon are mates."

29 ~ Familiar Ground

The Schnauzer bit the knife from her hand, whipped his head and drove the blade straight into her lower leg.

Bean sat above the gate while the doorman slept. He could see his decrepit house clearly in the distance, posted now in the center of the lot of mobile homes and RVs as though it were some rundown white trash manager's office.

The djinn, Neon, stood with him.

Josh hadn't come out of the house since the previous night when he had been dragged back. Neon had become the target of Josh's full wrath. She stayed by his side until he was healed. Many tried to remove her, but she was unmoved. She insisted that she and Josh remained together, which of course made her the target of Amber's wrath as well; Natalie didn't seem too happy about the situation neither.

To put distance between himself and the freed djinn, Josh had ordered her into the civilian quarters, but Bean pleaded that she was necessary to his well-being. Thug, perhaps out of honor to the rainbow-haired girl for saving his life back at his café, helped convince Josh. Neon moved only when Bean suggested that she was being inconsiderate of her new mate and needed to give him space.

Here, Bean kept watch. Near his feet were his new chainsaws and leather.

Neon played with her new, brown hair. Perched on the opposite end of the gates, stood Amber and Cadence. The doorman balanced himself on the back legs of a metal shop stool.

A number of scouts had crept into the outside area and had already begun monitoring the actions of the compound.

In the distance, Bean could see the dusty storm of what would no doubt be another diesel with a shipment, courtesy of Thomas and some of the new hunters.

Below, the crowd of civilians that had been rescued from the farms booed. Bricktain shouted, and the mayor's voice grew almost as loud, except his seemed to calm the crowd more.

Neon whistled to a bird calling in the distance.

"You lied to me," Bean said, stewing.

Neon cupped her hands over her ears. "Did you know that if you do this, you can hear what you want to," Neon replied.

"Why," Bean asked.

"People who ask 'why' are ignorant," Neon replied.

"You're hiding things from me." Bean said. "You've been hiding things from me the entire time we planned this, weren't you?"

"When children yell 'ollie, ollie oxen free,' the other secrets stop hiding."

"What haven't you told me," Bean said then added on "Ollie, ollie oxen free."

"But you are the one hiding," Neon said. "Only the seeker can say that."

"Who is the seeker?"

"The one who discovers all that hides. Duh!"

"You didn't send me here to help Josh," Bean added.

"You're not going to help Josh now," Neon asked. She was now using the ends of her hair to fill her ears.

"You tricked me into freeing you."

"Freedom," Neon cried.

"Yes," Bean replied.

"Yes," Neon said.

"Why didn't you just tell me."

"You wouldn't have freed me."

"I might have," Bean snapped back.

"No," she replied sternly. "You are ignorant. I was not."

"I was always part of your plan," Bean said. "I didn't trick you out of a free wish, you tricked me into trying to trick you, and, once I made the move, you were able to manipulate your own will, weren't you?"

"I am not ignorant," Neon said. "Or am I now? I should ask the publisher of words."

"You know how things are going to turn out," Bean said.

"No," Neon replied. "But only you were able to be manipulated."

Bean drew silent a moment and suddenly laughed. "You slowed down the planning process until you knew when I would die so that I couldn't fight you when you tried to send me here! You planned how to kill two birds with one stone: save me and free yourself." Suddenly he stopped in realization. "You knew Lisa would trick me into that place."

"I think I did," Neon replied. "I can't remember. Wait. I do. I saw it when the first wish was made. I think. I can't remember. Nothing moves anymore. Everything's too clear. There is," she grabbed at Bean's shirt, "what is this?"

"Shirt," Bean replied.

"And this," she asked feeling his black boots.

"Boots."

"They look different," Neon said. "They are not the same. Like that," she now pointed at the cloudy blue skies. "That does not look bright anymore. It looks like shirt, but not the same."

Like shirt?

Sorry, Neon replied to this glancing thought. *Not our conversation, Josh.*

What the?

"Do you mean color," Bean asked.

"I don't know color," Neon replied.

"Like your hair," Bean explained. "It's different colors."

"I have hair," Neon asked surprised. She began playing with her hair once more.

Bean quit. He knew his conversation was lost.

"I don't know why I'm here," she said after almost an hour had passed. "But I must be good at this game."

Bean complained and would have walked off had his role of filling in for the doorman not been so important right now.

"I am old, but I remember friendship," Neon said. "Friendship is not based on tricks. The one who gave you power over me knew and trusted you. My wishing master was wise."

Bean could have kicked himself for not understanding. He really was out of practice. "Then I thank you," Bean said. "I needed this."

"Yes," Neon replied. "Round things always turn better with black goop."

Bean spent another hour above the gate. The doorman grunted at Bean as they switched their shift at the stool. He grunted again at the sight of the handful of new hunters that had trickled in during his break. He glared at the biker as if to chide him for his irresponsible opening of the gates, and Bean took that as his cue to make his leave. Lisa and Winter, who had already been relieved by some new hunters themselves, now awaited Bean and Neon at the bottom of the catwalk stairwell.

Reggie, in passing, suggested that they get some rest before efforts commenced in the next hour or two to extend the compound walls again. He also suggested that they take advantage of some of the camping gear that had come in on one of the last shipments. The trucks that had brought them in were quickly stripped of their tracking components. Thug and other long-haul drivers kept watch over the vehicle's communication to misdirect dispatchers who didn't have a clue how the real roads worked. Drivers, it turned out, seemed to appreciate their rescue more than civilians from farms. They were happy to contribute to the work.

Thug sat in the diesel and typed, "Confirmed," into an onboard keyboard.

"Need a pick-up in Crepid, two hours," the text read back.

"Have something that can get me home this weekend," Thug typed back. "I think I might need to see a doctor."

"Take a load from Chicago to Omaha," the text asked.

"Confirmed," Thug replied. "Be there tomorrow."

Five minutes later, he burned the onboard computer and demolished any tracking components.

"We could use that to communicate, you know," Bricktain suggested.

"And anyone out there can use it to send more people looking for these trucks," Thug replied. "Need to keep that from happening."

As far as Bean was concerned, Thug's coordination of the vehicles was a smart move, predictable, but he also believed such action allowed them to acquire several more shipments without raising any concern.

The small group of time travelers secured tarps from one trailer, enough to build a shelter for some privacy. They also helped themselves to some mid-grade sleeping bags. Then they ventured off towards a bare area between a pickup truck bed and an unattached wrecking ball to set up camp and hopefully not be bothered.

"No sign of him today, then," Bean asked, finally letting himself inside his flimsy shelter.

"Haven't heard a thing," Lisa replied.

Bean wanted to nap, but decided to take opportunity to check in with his skater companions to learn that the unrest he had stirred with One-ear, now festered with the surviving members of his gang. Nothing much came out of their conversation except that Bean felt more confident that they wouldn't make a move against Josh without Bean's support.

More hunters continued to venture into the compound, some on foot. Some came in vehicles, which were quickly put to work to tow in the junkers from outside the wall. The less reliable vehicles were either stripped for material or were parked along the chain link which now separated the civilians from the kill zone.

Bean returned to his new tent with some food and water. He suggested his allies eat before they'd be called on to exert more work.

Eventually, Josh made an appearance, but only after a new shipment came in. By now, the majority of hunters and a few supportive civilians had begun moving one of the walls outward.

Bean's shift started once more, this time on one of the newer catwalk sections that looked over the civilian area. The walkway swayed against its tossed-together, chain-and-cable suspension-design. The mayor appeared to be running about as if without a head and trying to maintain the peace among the ignorant and less enjoyable humans. Bean felt sorry for the man somewhat.

Lisa took post near Bean. Winter now stood across the compound, and, as expected, a large hole leading to an underground cave suddenly collapsed within the floor of the compound, frightening a trucker and startling even Josh.

"I hate this part," Lisa said. "We should go this time. We know what's coming."

"We know what's coming here, too," Bean replied. He noticed the lasso in Lisa's hands. "You fixed it?"

"Reggie had a few ideas how."

"That was nice of him," Bean suggested.

Lisa agreed. "We don't let him die either."

The time finally came where Lisa watched several old friends drop into the earth and set out to help Cadence and Jasper. Lisa wanted to chase after, to change Josh's judgment about sending Dustin to his death. She noticed Bean clench the rusted chain handrail as his section of catwalk swayed beneath him.

"Shame," Bean said.

"We can't let them die," Lisa suggested. "We shouldn't let him go."

"So you can die instead," Bean asked. "Maybe even me?"

"That's a selfish attitude," Lisa said coldly.

"Get used to it," Bean replied. "Whether you like it or not, we're the greater good and more experienced people here. If Dustin doesn't go, he won't save a killing blow. Who'll find What then? Who'll learn about Neon? Who'll expose Bogi and Barbara?"

"What if more people go to help," Lisa asked.

"The more who go in to save Dustin, the fewer are here for the bigger fight," Bean said. "Who's to say sending more won't mean more people in the way of your fight with Barbara? I'm sorry. I told you. Dustin dies. The thing about sacrifices is, it's not always about ending a life, but living with the consequence of your decision after."

Both he and Lisa resumed their posts in anger.

Several minutes later, the catwalk shook under the weight of an approaching hunter.

"You," Bricktain Morris greeted. "Orders from my white-haired friend. You and Miss Acid Trip have been assigned to help guard the paladin until further notice. Our chef says he trusts you to protect him."

"Yes, sir," Bean replied. He wished, just for a moment, that he could pull off the incredulous man's other arm.

"You hesitate to protect him, and I'll destroy you," Bricktain said.

"I forgot how big of a jerk you were," Lisa mumbled.

"Excuse me," Bricktain asked.

"I didn't say anything," Lisa lied, acting ignorantly.

Bricktain didn't buy it, but he had better things to do. "Keep your harem under control."

"We will protect my mate, I promise," Neon said.

Bricktain suddenly stopped from leaving. "She doesn't talk to the paladin."

With that, Bricktain made his exit.

Lisa braved creeping back towards Bean's post. "How did that ever turn into our boss."

"You're missing the bigger picture," Bean replied. "We've just been given permission to guard him without having to keep our distance."

"So now what?"

"What else can we do," Bean replied. This time, he maintained the poise of a hunter, this time watching inside the camp. So Thomas must have seen and remembered him from the other night. "We wait."

30 ~ It Was Tails

She retreated on her butt, drawing a gun and firing, then screamed as the bullets had no effect.

Forgive my transition here, but I see no need to regale what you have already been told. As the historian, it is not always so simple to separate many stories. I see them all, or I receive them all as one, yet I may choose one from within such perception to focus upon. That is my right and authority. I suppose if you don't like it, you could take it up in an angry letter or contact customer support, but, as to date, we do not have such a department, nor do we have any particular and future plans to create one. So, I suppose you'll just have to deal with the fact that I'm not getting fired any time soon for telling what I choose.

Don't like it? Perhaps you could sing a song of complaint at one of Tolkien's dreary slumber parties to find affirmation.

Regardless, to fully fit the meaning for this book within our larger history, I must now inform you that nothing new had changed since our previous look upon the occurrences that preluded the night of Josh Revlon's destruction and what is happening right now. That is, there were no further alteration of events from those you are already aware of.

Of course, Lisa had taken several opportunities upon herself to prevent the paladin from returning to the museum. Winter, herself, had punctured holes into several vehicle gas tanks and tires to keep Josh from finding transportation. She even thought about shooting Josh in the foot to injure him, but came to the conclusion that Josh would still need his foot to fight if he survived the rogue's attack. She did, however, decide this at the last moment and, luckily, the bullet barely missed his foot, but you probably already realized this, so I'm preaching to the choir. Forgive me.

Bean, having the appreciation of the bigger picture, had concluded that at least they knew Josh should return to the compound alive and therefore did not insist on interfering with the operation. Whether Josh could stay alive in the compound, once he returned, was another argument completely. He suggested they prepare what they could to capture Josh without raising too much awareness.

So Josh, Amber and Thomas with his valiant steed, Petruchio, set out for the museum as before.

Although, he had full confidence in Thomas's ability to change history based upon Bean's interference, the reincarnate of Jasper couldn't help but doubt, to some degree, whether Josh would still return to the compound safely, or alive for that matter.

It was here that he voiced his concerns with his allies. It was also here that Lisa decided she should come clean about the clues she had left on the art museum. As always, Bean was quite supportive of this foolish decision and kept his lecture to a reasonable ten minutes before storming out to interfere some more, but only as a means to undo any potential damage they may have already contributed to.

Thus, Bean convinced Bricktain to allow him to sneak out and provide extra support to Josh at the museum. Originally, Bricktain denied the request, but Neon had become quite attuned to annoying Bricktain into submission, which she did through many pointless conversations that often baited Bricktain into actually debating her one-sided thoughts with her.

Upon the topic of whether Bricktain resembled a guppy more than a turkey fish, Bricktain couldn't help, but to defend that he was certainly more majestic than a guppy, which led to a turn of events where his own time-line companions took great pride in comparing him to other types of fish and animals, but that's beside the point, really.

It was during such argument that Bricktain finally relented to Bean's request to join Josh and his companions at the museum. However, to Bean's chagrin, Bricktain wouldn't hear him concerning Dee and his mercenaries.

"Believe me," Bean tried to persuade. "Don't put them on the wall. Don't trust them."

"Think I trust you any more on the wall than them," Bricktain fired back.

Rather than chance a redaction to the permission he had received to go after Josh's party, he held his tongue. He should be able to deal with Dee and his men when he returned.

Bean and his allies decided that it would be best for the others to remain at the compound in preparation to face off against the mercs—well, most agreed. Neon wasn't happy about having to stay behind, but she did, under the care of Lisa and Winter. As a final bit of instruction, he suggested they try to get a little rest before all hell broke loose. They did even, and Neon observed them for some time, until they awoke so she could inform them that they had performed their nanny duties well.

Bean dressed himself in his chainsaws and made quick travel through the underground tunnels. Michael Banks appeared impressed with Bean's speed and ability to maneuver the tunnels.

"You're a general," Michael said as Bean prepared his exit out the other end of the cavern. "Why are you hiding it?"

Bean laughed. "Do I look like a general."

"Yes," Michael replied. "I may be fasted, but I can still see the gold of your eyes in these tunnels."

How could he have forgotten? Did the server know? Had she seen it? Even now, in hindsight, he realized he had seen it in her eyes himself. He really had gotten too old. Too forgetful. He'd been planning this return far too long. What if the rogue was aware? All the more reason to rush to Thomas's aid.

"You should probably forget that detail," Bean said seriously.

"Yeah, I should probably," Michael replied, emotionless. Then quickly came back with, "Well, God speed my friend."

Bean ignored him and then made his flight towards town. Realizing he might be a little too obvious as someone dangerous, he rolled up his large chainsaws and, upon entering the closest residential district, stole the first truck that allowed him to—nothing flashy, something from what appeared to be a house on vacation. It was a black rust bucket from the early 80s, most likely something no one would report stolen right away, not that any police would actually care about the theft under the current circumstances, anyway.

Evening drew near. Josh and his companions had nearly a day's start against him, and he still had to catch up. Finding the university was easy enough, locating the entrance to the parking lot near the museum was another story. After several attempts at turning around on pointless roads, to find the correct area, he finally drove over a small browning and grassy hill, where students may or may not have been sitting leisurely. He really didn't care to notice. He spotted Petruchio grazing in the shadow of a pine. This was good enough. He drove back onto pavement, parked and located the museum at once. He wondered if Petruchio gave him any notice.

Afraid of attracting too much attention, and, against his better judgment, he left the set of chainsaw teeth in the cab of the truck. Knowing this would be a race rather than a fight, he figured he might serve better in offering hands for escape instead of shark teeth blades. He still took his firearms, however. Besides, he knew he was fast enough to get to his weapons if he really needed. For now, he believed escape was the true focus here. The rogue's plan wasn't to fight, but to turn Josh into a killing machine. At this, Bean realized that Josh was on the verge of his own death. He also doubted any more meddling on his part would prevent Josh from getting back to the compound alive. However, in this coming hour, why not try and save the vampire? What could he possibly have to lose.

He walked his way around the side of the art building. As he did, he pitied the person who might try to tow his weapons away. He hoped no one would spot the stolen vehicle, but just to be safe, he had already scuffed the license plate letters a little to help them read differently to any police who might glance over them.

He made his way around the building, found the entrance and grimaced at the graffiti. A little obvious on Lisa's part, but he wondered if he could have thought of a better clue. He decided he could, but now wasn't the time to remedy the situation. He entered the arts building and then the museum gallery where he found a class listening to an instructor. Josh, Thomas and Amber stood before what he thought looked like a mural of a silver wolf stalking a small girl in a forest of dead bodies.

Everyone's heads turned as Bean made his entrance and let the doors slam behind him. The class glared. And, for once, Bean realized he had marched in without thinking about what should come next. What now?

What else? Be Jasper.

Might as well get this over with, he thought. *Rogue's going to do his thing no matter what tonight.* He turned to the exhibits of ancients.

"Those are beautiful," Bean bellowed, half surprised at the sight of the ancients standing on podiums, but also realizing he was among artists and, just for giggles, he really wanted to slap every single one of them. Not that he hated art or artists, he enjoyed art. He just had a sudden urge, perhaps from old memories, to make someone cry. It was the principle of the thing, he needed some sort of satisfaction and soon. He'd lived a really rotten last few years, and he realized just now that he hated these students and their teacher.

He approached the closest ancient. "What kind of mixed media is this?" He yanked a small tuft of aged, white hair from the leg of one of the slender creatures standing like sentinels. "It's so soft," he said, examining the dry fibers and letting them sprinkle to the ground from between his thumb and fingers. "Was this their first time doing paper maché," he asked when he realized he had the entire class's attention as well as Josh's and his equally displeased companions.

"Cool," Bean hooted, clomping his heavy, leather boots towards his allies. He approached the mural and hated to admit that he was impressed with the patience that must have gone into stacking all those sewing pins into such a fantastic three-dimensional sculpture.

Yet, something was wrong. He pondered the scene a second or so.

"Oops," he cried and pulled a pin from the top of one of the sculptures of a pointy fern. He stuck the pin into a small void in the guardian's shoulder. "That's better."

"What are you doing here," Josh asked, and Bean wondered which answer he should give that would preserve Josh the best.

"What do you mean? I come here all the time," Bean replied. "Though, I'm used to seeing higher-caliber work though."

The professor shushed Bean.

"I believe the correct pronunciation is 'shoo-shay,'" Bean replied. "Latin for, 'Shutteth thou uppeth.' Now go back to pretending you have a real job and 'sshh!'"

Josh glared.

Bean knew the paladin withheld an attack of some sort.

"I'm here to help," Bean said.

Josh's jaw flexed into a square and then softened. "Are you?"

"Oh yeah," Bean replied. "Bricktain thought it would be good for me to help somewhere else."

Josh maintained his scowl, but he clearly believed Bean. Amber seemed unconcerned. Thomas, however, didn't believe Bean. He didn't believe anyone, especially someone who had attacked and then eluded him previously. He had decided it best to hold his tongue in their current location.

Josh started to march away, and, as he turned to exit, Wolf's Breath ripped at the rogue's mural. Even knowing it was coming, Bean wasn't quick enough to dodge the cascading destruction of silver straight-pins.

The students and teacher began filming on their phones as the four allies now weeded pins out of their clothing and shoes. When the students started complaining that their phones didn't work, Bean applauded their scholarly intelligence with the sincerest, "Say it isn't so" he could muster.

"And you, kind teacher, how gracious of you to instill such ability to think among your class," Bean praised and then began to cheer "Hip-hip-hoo-thpbthpbthpb!"

Josh demanded Bean stop it and continued to remove pins from his footwear. He had just finished when the wall began to open, and a blonde woman stepped through.

"Ladies and gentlemen," Loraine announced. "The museum will have to close now. Thank you for coming."

As the students began to clear up their possessions, Bean noticed one with a set of sunglasses hanging out of a pencil pocket. Bean quickly snatched up the glasses and dropped a roll of his drug money into the student's hand. The student gave no further argument.

Bean set the bug-eye shades upon his face.

"This way, sir," Loraine called to Bean, who hoped his eyes were well-disguised. He quickly caught up to take the rear of the group.

The wall-like door sealed behind them, and Bean did his best to ignore the intimidation of Genre as he—they—glared, but made no movement upon the guests.

"Don't worry," Loraine, who now led the front, said. "They won't hurt you."

When Bean rounded a corner in the back warehouse, he constrained his desire to fly at the familiar face that greeted them. It was the face of the man who had taken his daughter, turned Jasper and then given him over to the hands of the inquisitor for conditioning. How Bean truly regretted that he could not behead the inquisitor once again. He might have entertained the thought of doing the same to the rogue right now, but knew better the reality of that happenstance.

Something scratched at his mind.

He stopped it. That was close, he'd almost let his guard down.

Control yourself, Bean told himself, and the mental scratching went away.

"Your rogueship," Josh greeted, now standing before Jasper's old master and Genre.

Bean almost applauded Josh's insult, but held his tongue. He knew the power of the rogue. Josh was too stupid and sure of himself, but dang if that wasn't just funny right now.

Suddenly, Josh was in the air, grasping at a chain noose. Bean lunged for Josh to give him some leverage to breathe, but The Right Arm knocked him to the ground and threatened to snap Bean's leg before grunting and retreating.

Bean watched The Left Arm abandon a fallen Amber in much the same way.

He quickly snugged the sunglasses back to his face, which was when he saw the black Scottish terrier atop the massive crossbeam in the ceiling, anchoring the chain that hoisted Josh. The paladin flailed aimlessly at the chain with his cloak.

Bean reminded himself to relax. This wasn't where Josh would die. He had to trust in history for this part.

"My wrath will be full if he dies," Thomas said as he stood with his blade against the rogue's throat, the rogue stood with Thomas's other blade against its owner's throat. In a way, Bean was a little saddened that he hadn't seen how the rogue had accomplished this disarming feat.

Loraine opened a medical kit, while Amber was able to give Josh some leverage to breathe. She asked Bean to help her, but he pretended to freeze in fear.

He had a better plan. He knew the scenario, he'd heard about it enough over the years. He'd studied the details, questioned time and time again everything. There wasn't a single part of tonight that he didn't know. He knew Loraine would fill the syringe with the blood of the living ancients here in the back room, including that of the rogue's. Then she'd take some of Thomas's blood and inject it into Josh. This is where, Bean would change history. Before Loraine could infect Josh, Bean would reach out and throw an edge of Wolf's Breath into her face and perhaps destroy the syringe as well. It might not be as meticulous an attack as Josh could muster, but Loraine was human, she'd succumb to even the worst delivered pain this robe could cause her. Then he'd crack out his shotgun from under the back of his vest and shoot that little black dog out of the rafters. That should drop Josh and allow Amber to rush him outside to Petruchio. Bean could steal a quick taste of blood from Loraine and take on the rogue. Thomas could take Genre, or at least draw his attention long enough for Bean to face his maker. Hopefully, they could all get away. Maybe, Bean wouldn't, but the others could.

Good plan! Except for the fact that the right arm had just dropped Bean to the floor a moment ago. What made Bean think he could act fast enough to feed on Loraine, avoid Genre and get to the rogue?

Dang!

Bad plan!

"Stop overthinking," Bean could almost hear Lisa scream at him.

Better plan: let history play its course and stop Amber from delivering the killing blow to her husband tonight. Let it ride! Good plan.

Loraine made her rounds, drawing blood from the still ancients on their podiums. She drew more from the rogue.

"Excuse me," she said, reaching towards Thomas.

And now, Bean realized the moment of his own mortality was upon him. He felt he still needed to do something more when chaos broke. To his left was a small pile of painter's poles. He could retrieve and snap the wooden one fast enough to at least get a stab or two in on Genre and the rogue's female pet, Loraine.

Could he do it all and leave the room alive? Perhaps not.

No, in fact not, but perhaps he could stab Josh's leg and slow his pursuit to give enough of a headstart to keep Thomas from dying several, devious miles from now. He supposed Thomas could die, but Josh had to remain the real goal here. Still, if he could manage to save Thomas along the way, that would maintain all the more leverage over the rogue in the future. Even if they should fail at saving Josh again, Bean imagined the years to follow would be a bit easier with Thomas in the picture.

This led to—A ha! New plan. Simple plan.

Stop it, he imagined Lisa and Cadence's voices echoing together now in his head.

But this time, it's good, he would have screamed back.

The plan was simple, forget the painter's pole, he'd simply use Wolf's Breath, not against Loraine, but Josh's leg—not enough to amputate it, just enough to slow his transformation. If he timed right, he might be able to hit Loraine as well and take her out of the picture. After that, if the rogue stayed to the game plan, and assuming Bean knew the rogue, which he believed he did, his old master would hold Genre back just as before because Josh would still be strong, just slower to the kill is all. To be sure, he decided he shouldn't hit Loraine, only Josh.

Bean subtly twisted his back to feel that the grip of his shotgun was where it should be in case he had to go all impromptu on his already impromptu plan.

Okay. He was ready to save Josh, to die if he had to. That was all Bean had left to offer. Instead of escaping with Josh, wound him. He'll still make it back to the compound, his new monster metabolism will surely see to that, but he should be weaker than he was last time. If they can all get back to the compound, maybe they can pull this off. That would be a big improvement from history right there.

Good plan?

Not really. He was still overthinking. Or was he overthinking that he was overthinking?

Go with this plan. It was a bit too Josh Revlon for his taste, but it should work, provided the elementals didn't interfere too much. How to get out of that one. Let's see—

Stop! Overthinking again. Josh first.

Bean watched as Loraine approached Thomas to take her final draw. The time for Bean's move was nearing. He positioned himself closer to the edges of Wolf's Breath. Josh had quit throwing it helplessly. He now gripped at the chain around his neck and pulled himself up as best he could, and Amber kept trying to give him leverage by holding his leg. Bean could see she tried to lift him into the air a time or two, but something was wrong with her knee. She couldn't find the strength. Bean realized that could be an issue.

Loraine searched Thomas's neck and pressed the needled-vial of blackish blood into his skin.

Suddenly, Thomas gripped the syringe and plunged half of its contents into his own neck. The Right Arm kicked Thomas full in the ribs, breaking him away from the needle. Thomas recovered, slashed at The Left Arm, missing.

The rogue now positioned Thomas's diamond blade beneath the vampire's jaw for what would be an easy thrust up and into the brain.

Thomas too, had gained an angle for his own aim upon the rogue, one that would allow him to slice the rogue's head apart if the rogue so much as flexed a muscle to make a move.

Neither the rogue nor Thomas blinked. The rogue smiled. Thomas did not. He refused to give the rogue the opening he needed to.

Genre returned to his post. Bean cursed himself for not taking better advantage of the surprise attack. Loraine appeared shaken and recovered the needle. The rogue patted his Loraine's head and seemed to reassure her. He tilted his head in amusement towards Thomas. Bean knew this amusement. The rogue was tempting Thomas into making a foolishly, slight move to allow the stab up into Thomas's head. Thomas, however, seemed to see through the tactic, he made no response. Again, Loraine stabbed the half-filled syringe into the rogue's neck and pulled out more of the black fluid until the entire vial was full.

The rogue nodded to Loraine, and she moved towards Josh where she drove the needle into his left leg and injected the remaining blood.

"Wakey, Wakey," Loraine said, and Josh started to seize.

Bean decided not to go through with his plan. Any move he made might startle Thomas enough that he might make that mistake to invite the rogue from stabbing into his brain. Perhaps Thomas had just changed history enough now on his own. This was not what Bean knew had happened. This was new too. Things might go differently now. After all, Josh had received only a portion of the blood-cocktail concentration as he had the last time, and Thomas's was not among it. Bean chose not to fire.

Of course, this didn't mean Bean wasn't aware that Josh couldn't still destroy his own friends.

"You might want to run now," Loraine said.

The rogue removed himself from Thomas's range. Thomas swiped his blade, which missed the rogue entirely. The rogue bowed slightly to his opponent and returned his blade to its owner.

It wasn't the opening Thomas perchance wanted, but it worked for Bean.

Bean stood back, and let his shotgun scatter a blast. The black Scottish terrier stumbled out of the ceiling. Thomas, with his fast reflexes sliced through the dog.

Together, Bean and Thomas fled with Amber through the door amidst her own protests. They forced her to run under her own will, although her senses hadn't all returned yet.

Thomas ordered Bean to his horse and drew his swords as though to make a stand.

"I have my own transportation," Bean replied, then ran off towards his truck.

Nearly twenty minutes had passed since he'd arrived at the museum, which Bean only realized because he felt it was time to follow Lisa's advice and look at his pink watch once more.

Bean felt himself jolt at whatever that sound was that came from within the museum walls. Even he wasn't immune to the shock it sent through his frame.

By the time Bean had returned to his stolen truck, Thomas, Amber and the horse had fled away from the museum.

A black monster, tall and spindly, appeared in the parking lot lights. He stumbled and seemed caught in a trap of some sort. Bean eventually recognized that Josh was stumbling over his own shoes. Eventually, they fell off his elongated feet, and he gave chase, barely noticing Bean at all. Wolf's Breath, still attached to Josh's changed form, didn't seem to slow the werewolf paladin down at all. Bean raced after, but gathered the abandoned shoes, thinking Josh might prefer them later, should the paladin survive this time. He climbed back into the truck and gave chase.

Now, Josh noticed Bean and backhanded a motorcycle in his direction. Only he must not have realized his new strength as the bike flew high over Bean's vehicle and became a shower of sparks in the power poles above. In these sparks, Bean caught the glimpse of something shiny on the ground, one of Josh's crossbows, which Bean quickly took a moment to retrieve while he continued to give chase to Josh's monster.

"What other presents do you have for me, Josh," Bean asked, as he wondered a moment if stunt driving might be worthy of adding to his life-long scholarship.

He pushed the thought back in effort to keep pace with Josh.

Josh swung at Petruchio and his cargo, missing barely. Then he swatted a roadside tree straight back for Bean, shattering the windshield of the stolen truck.

"Okay," Bean shouted. "Now you're just being ironic." He punched out the windshield and the tree, then tried his best to gain any ground he had lost.

After several turns, he was on a straight patch of residential road.

"That's better," Bean said to himself, and let his truck accelerate as only straight roads allowed. He began to catch up.

Then the headlights at the stop sign on his right pulled into his path. He pulled his truck hard to the left, sparks flew down the side of this vehicle, and he watched a reflective bumper drop behind in his rearview mirror.

Bean might have complained, but he seemed to remember this part of the story when Cadence had told him about her own adventures. He ignored the SWAT truck and tried to locate Josh, all while regaining control of his swerving vehicle. After a block or two, the road turned sharply to the left, but he found no sign of Josh nor those he chased.

"They wouldn't have turned," Bean said to himself and tried to find any kind of path made of debris and destruction. He found none. He sped into a residential driveway and through a fence behind it. A different yard, then driveway, quickly appeared into the other side of the residential block. As he exited back onto the street again, he smashed into Josh's side, his figure appearing out of nowhere. Josh instantly smacked the truck and toppled it onto its roof.

Bean crawled out, catching a glimpse of Josh disappearing once more down the road.

Tires screamed an "oh crap" warning as they squealed upon the accident. Bean could smell the smoke of rubber.

"Get in," Cadence called down from her driver's seat in the SWAT truck. Bean quickly retrieved the teeth and Josh's gear that he had collected. He climbed up into the vehicle, stuffing his stash of goodies into Cadence's hands and pushing her out of the seat.

"I'm driving," he said. He realized the back of the truck was empty. "You forget someone?"

"We flipped a coin—how did you know," Cadence asked.

"Everyone knows," he replied, realizing he had to think fast to take attention off his blunder.

Bean sped away once more after Josh.

This would have been so much easier if Bean had his strength back, or if he still had his own army. He burst through another fence, sending wooden slats in various directions before catching sight of Josh again.

Bean used the straight stretch of road to pick up speed once more.

Just then, she came out alongside him. Bean didn't see her at first, only the black horse that appeared at his left, overtaking the truck in full gallop. It's stride was unlike any Bean had seen before. A white mark as though a single thick paint stroke wiped from the horse's shoulder past its ribcage. Its rider barely gave Bean and his passengers a second look as it sped past him, also in pursuit of Josh. Long, white hair flapped behind this horse's rider, as did her black cloak, which Bean thought looked an awful lot like Wolf's Breath.

"Who is that," Cadence asked.

"I don't know," Bean replied. "Vampire groupie?"

Bean let the newcomer pass and kept at her heels—partly out of intrigue, mostly out of caution. He didn't know this person, but he had the impression to learn something about her before he might have to fight her. He didn't get a good look at her face, but he couldn't help wonder if it was perhaps one of his hidden comrades. Amber? Not Amber from the past, she was riding with Thomas at this moment, but Amber from his time. How could that be? She wasn't supposed to be involved with coming back to aid Josh. Jasper had been adamant about that.

That's right! He remembered now. Amber wasn't part of the plan to come back. How many times had he and Neon prepared in Josh's bunker to make the wish the perfect rescue operation? She was too connected to the target they were trying to save. She couldn't be trusted. Yet, Bean suddenly remembered Neon's hair touching

Amber, though. He hadn't remembered, but he did now. It did! It touched her. He saw it.

First, he saw it touch Nick and then it touched Amber, and he suddenly remembered realizing his work unraveled in the stroke of one strand of rainbow-colored hair; his realization that he had sent his friends to their deaths because the djinn had altered the plan. He remembered realizing she had betrayed them, killed them. He also just now remembered his heart stopping, feeling his chest tighten that night they all embarked from the bunker to fulfill one more wish. He remembered the sudden loss of hope, of failure and his heart gave out. All because the djinn's hair touched Amber.

Neon was more devious than he had thought. Her manipulation of him was flawless. She had even sent Cadence and Acotactac to different hosts than he had planned. She hadn't given an extra wish to Bean. He'd promised the wish would be her freedom and she manipulated the way to gain it. She had used her wish makers. She prolonged the planning, to Jasper's frustration. Only recently did he realize that she had done so to last until he should die, but she didn't just know when his heart was going to stop. She had stopped it.

That's how she did it! Neon accelerated his heart attack with one simple blow to his greatest efforts ever, his greatest design to bestow vengeance on the rogue. On his own, perhaps this wouldn't have happened, but he wasn't alone now. He'd had more than twenty years of friends, of rediscovering he could belong to the human race once more.

Stop overthinking, old man, Bean screamed at himself. He watched the black horse and its white-haired rider meter closer upon Josh's dark form.

Another thought entered his mind, however. Of course! Why didn't Bean realize it? Perhaps this wasn't Neon. What if this was Thomas. Bean had warned Thomas, after all, two nights ago. This was Thomas's doing. It had to be. Thomas deviates from history by taking half of the injection.

Why?

Perhaps because he has a fellow ally working from the shadows. Could it actually be possible that ally is Amber? Curse that Neon!

Bean! Stop it! He finally pushed the thoughts out of his head. It was difficult. He wanted to understand this newcomer's role. It would explain so much.

Bean watched Thomas's figure suddenly leap from Petruchio into Josh. His attack was brief, but he broke away cleanly. Suddenly, the rider on the black horse leaped straight up and immediately changed her angle of attack jump mid-air. She attacked Josh next, briefly as well, before kicking away, but she didn't fall away back to her black horse, she seemed to run back down to it in Amber-like fashion with her windriders.

"Who is that," Cadence asked. "What is that?" She was poised with her rifle upon the monster.

Bean slapped it down. "Don't! It's Josh!"

Josh turned for the new white-haired assailant, who sped quickly past him. He screamed as he missed at striking her down. Bean took advantage of the situation and drove his new vehicle into Josh's backside. Then, remembering Josh's speed, quickly veered the vehicle past him, nearly taking on a telephone pole in his arrogance.

Josh stumbled in Bean's rearview mirror. Bean wasn't comfortable with being chased, however. He preferred chasing. He wanted to fall behind, but perhaps he should have thought of that before he made that stupid maneuver.

Again, Thomas was at Josh a moment before quickly releasing his hold and escaping another deadly blow. Thomas returned to Petruchio once more, and they both raced forward. It was here, that Bean realized Amber was no longer on the horse's back. Bean hunkered forward in his seat to see if he could find her dark form above his windshield. He couldn't.

Josh now raced past Bean, in pursuit of Petruchio who kept steadily ahead of him. Thomas, again seated and riding, held his gaze straight forward. Once more, the white-haired woman was attached to Josh's back. This time, Bean realized her face was buried into Josh's neck. As she pulled away, Josh swiped. Cadence's hand struck a switch that blared overhead trucklights into Josh's face, an attempt to blind him temporarily. The white-haired woman used the moment to launch herself backwards, towards her black horse with its white stripe. For a brief instant, Bean saw the woman's face. Her mouth appeared to be dripping with the dark contents of Josh's veins.

Before Josh could turn his fury upon either the woman for her attack or the SWAT truck for blinding him, Thomas had returned and buried his face into Josh's shoulder. It was only for a moment, and then he was free again. Josh unleashed another attack after Thomas. Missed! The woman took yet another turn at Josh's opposite shoulder before returning the baton to Thomas, who then took another opportunity to bite into the back of Josh's neck. The three continued to fight with each other and Bean allowed himself to speed ahead of the group and give them room to conduct their strategy. Whoever the new stranger was, two vampires appeared now. For once, Bean felt he was actually in the way of a fight.

Bean felt an unfamiliar joy and hope creep into his brain as he watched a new future unfold even now. Nothing was familiar to the stories he had heard any more.

The monstrous ballet continued towards the gates that led to the courtyard of the compound. Everyone in the SWAT truck did all they could to signal the doorman to open the gates. Bean honked, flipped his lights on and off and plowed through any of the guardians that got in his way, which none did.

"Open the gates," Cadence yelled into the handset mounted to the dashboard, and her voice echoed through the exterior speakers.

The gates opened, but not due to Bean's SWAT signals, Amber had already returned to the compound. He watched her form disappear behind the compound walls. Here, Bean performed a brilliant move, on his part.

He allowed Petruchio and Thomas to race past him. Then Bean swerved directly into Josh's path and stopped the truck. Josh tripped over the back of the vehicle, he took several steps over the roof and face-planted onto the hood. Josh yelled at Bean, stumbled off the hood and gave chase to Thomas de Soleil. Bean thought, Josh seemed to be running more slowly than before.

Yet, where was the second vampire now? The stranger was gone, she hadn't followed into the compound. Bean used any angle his driver's seat afforded, but found no sight of her nor her horse. Petruchio raced through the half-pipe, and Thomas leapt from his back and prepared to receive Josh.

Josh stopped before the entrance to the compound. He peered over the skaters who held their positions at the tops of the half-pipe trap. He leapt for one. A silver flash, accompanied by its familiar whistle sliced at Josh's shoulder, but not enough to kill him. Josh withdrew from the gates and turned his attention on the one who threw the attack. Amber raced above the compound walls, and Bean realized Josh's next execution.

"He's jumping," Bean cried, before realizing no one inside could hear him without an earpiece. "He's going after Amber."

Then Bean saw Lisa making her own move. Her figure ran along the catwalk, straight towards Josh's path. Her lasso waved angrily over her head.

Josh leapt, clearing the compound wall. Then, just at the apex of his attack, Lisa roped his back leg. A second later, she flew over the side of the catwalk, pulled by the short length of the lasso.

By the time Bean sped through the gates and into the compound, Josh was on the ground, motionless. Amber hovered above the ground a few feet before him.

"Tie him down," Amber shrieked. "Use a net."

Josh stood, roared. His body then clenched and fell to his side.

"Shut up," Lisa screamed. She dropped a battery and began to reload her modified stun baton. Thomas stood on his guard. Amber stepped cautiously before Josh. She reached down to his monstrous head.

"Only if you want to get zapped too," Lisa asked, pulling her rearmed lasso taut.

Amber stopped reaching.

Lisa loosed the line, and Josh's body remained limp. He inhaled deeply, nearly frightening another zap out of Lisa's lasso, but nothing more came.

"All right," She announced. He's stunned."

"Tie him up," Thomas ordered. "We got him. But get off if he moves so she can stun him again."

Bean enjoyed a breath of relief and used the time to start rearming himself with the teeth. Josh was trapped all too quickly. Lisa stood poised to zap him again if she needed to. Thomas and his companion in the shadows had drained Josh of blood, enough to weaken him surely. Then, all too late, Bean remembered his work wasn't over.

A gunshot belched, and Reggie's chair toppled backward, a bloody tulip blooming from his back.

While the others froze in distraction to the sudden attack, Josh suddenly lunged.

His swords snapped forward. He screamed and buried his blades into Amber's belly. Her body tightened, and her shriek of pain became trapped within her paralyzed lungs, neither capable of exhaling nor inhaling. Her face went through the motion of making a tormented sound, but none came.

The blades snapped back. She fell into Thomas's arms, and Lisa fired off her lasso once more.

Bean was fastest. He turned to the catwalk. He launched off a chainsaw blade and ran after it, up to the catwalk. He found it next to a mercenary bleeding out of a thigh severed above the knee where the chainsaw blade had chewed straight through. Bean started the electric hum of his remaining blade and leapt to finish the murderer off. He didn't complete his attack. Pain suddenly surged through his own leg. The mercenary leader, Dee had shot him. The fool! Dee took on what would once again be a perfect aim, this time on Bean's head. Bean rolled out of the way of the shot. The catwalks rattled under the weight of a few skaters who were running to Bean's aid. More gunshots rang, and Bean forced himself to his feet, which was surprisingly more difficult than should have been for him. Dee shot one skater, then tossed him over the wall.

Bean made a quick lunge that finished off the now one-legged merc who had killed Reggie. He was aware of the gunfire that suddenly erupted around him, but he focused now upon getting at Dee.

The mercenary leader suddenly rose off of his feet. He hovered a moment, his face growing uncertain before instantly snapping off into the sky.

Then every other mercenary suddenly rose from where they stood openly throughout the compound and whisked off into the air. Bean had hardly noticed the heavy wind, but it was clearly there. After all of the mercenaries were cleared from the compound, the wind suddenly stopped, and, in the dark distance, human cries careened from the heavens ending with soft earthly thuds beyond the walls of the compound. Dee's cursing body, however, fell into the half-pipe and became instantly unrecognizable

The doorman and one of Bean's rescuing skaters helped him down the catwalk to the sound of more of Josh's commotion. Bean could have made it on his own, but his attendants insisted. Lisa had drained yet another battery on Josh while his friends helped Amber escape his further attacks. Now, Josh tore the lasso from Lisa's hands and charged for her, tripping over his own bindings.

Bricktain fired a shot into Josh's leg. Josh barely noticed. Bean fired up his chainsaw once more. He could see the other hunters preparing to follow his lead.

"Don't kill him," Bean cried. Despite his own bindings, Josh leapt and pounded into Bean, knocking him into Lisa, causing her to lose grasp of her lasso. Josh drew in arms to snap Wolf's Breath.

Neon suddenly stepped before Josh.

"Stop," she ordered. She held out an index finger, as if it had been a magic wand preparing to snap out a destructive spell.

Josh obeyed it.

"No one will touch your mind now," Neon said

Josh screamed and immediately fell, as if unconscious.

"This is where vampires should roll the dots with black and take a turn," Neon instructed Thomas.

The confused vampire bent over Josh and began feeding off of him. Slowly Josh started to change back.

"Don't kill him," Bean said.

"I'm just taking what isn't his," Thomas replied.

"How?"

"I can taste it."

"Well, don't turn him neither," Bricktain said.

"No promises," Thomas said. He continued drinking and swallowing Josh's blood.

Bean searched the area for Thomas's other white-haired friend, and would have asked where she was, when Amber's voice screeched from beneath a group of allies trying to help her.

"Wake now," Neon said. She was kneeling over Josh's body as it once again took on his familiar human form. "I will guard your mind."

Josh's eyes opened and took a moment to realize where he was. Fear immediately streaked down his face. He scrambled to his feet, doing his best to kick off the remainder of his restraints and raced to Amber.

"It's okay," Amber said through short bursts of breath as Josh reached her side. Then she sucked in three shallow breaths. Her face was almost as white as the gauze appearing from beneath her bandana. "Are you okay?"

Josh shrilled and crawled behind her, dropping his cloak. He pulled her back into his chest. She screamed and Josh tried to calm her with a kiss to the back of her head. "Somebody help her!"

Michael Banks kneeling nearby shook his head to Thug, but Josh saw it.

Amber cried, and Josh tried not to.

"The rogue," she said. "Kill him."

"Please tell me, you planned for this," Bean softly requested as he directed Neon away from the group.

"I don't remember," Neon said.

As the life drained slowly and painfully from her body, Amber's reality became clear to Bean.

"She needs blood, Monsieur de Soleil," Bean cried. "Have any?"

Thomas knelt before Amber and smelled at her wound. "My apologies," he said and drew her shirt up to dab his finger in the crimson that spilled out. He tried his best to shield the view from others, but failed mostly. He tasted the blood and closed his eyes, as a connoisseur of wine would.

"Kenny," he called over his earpiece-microphone. "Check my stash of blood in the refrigerator for any O or A blood."

"Positive or negative," Kenny asked a few moments later.

"Positive preferably," Thomas replied. "At this point I'll take either."

"Either," Cadence asked.

"At this point, either is better than none," Thomas said.

The door to the house opened, and Kenny raced out towards the group.

"I couldn't find any A-positive," he said. Just before reaching Thomas to hand the blood off, he clumsily dropped the, soft, plastic bag and might have stepped on it had Bean not been fast enough to catch it. After ridiculing Kenny, he ordered him back to his post in the control office.

Thomas drew some clear tubing from inside his coat and a white envelope of some sort. He cracked the envelope and drew out a slender needle. Then he handed the bag to Thug and soon had a line of healthy red running down into Amber's arm.

"Do any of you still have your anti-coagulant," Thomas asked.

Josh felt Amber's trench coat pockets and withdrew the small vial she had received in case Thomas had needed it for his own wounds. Cadence and Acotactac both presented similar vials.

"Drink all of it," Thomas instructed handing one vial to Amber. He poured another container over her wounds. They began to smoke.

Josh held the coagulant to Amber's lips one container at a time. She drank the solution down.

"We have company again," Bricktain announced.

Bean felt the wind, and he wasn't the only one. A narrow funnel cloud touched near a sparse patch of dirt. Were the cloud shorter, it would have been nothing more than a dust devil. Down she came. Once she set foot on the ground, the funnel dissipated. Her body, twisted, deformed and bending in ways a normal body shouldn't even imagine doing, suddenly snapped in one loud chord of pops. She now stood in her full elegant frame and approached the group surrounding the dying Amber. When Bricktain decided to stand against her, a burst of wind threw him out of her path. She knelt besides Thomas and before Amber. She sniffed until she appeared poised directly in front of the blade wounds.

"A dishonorable tactic," the elemental queen said and looked to Josh. "You survived. Perhaps you can be trusted."

Josh called forth a sword.

"You misunderstand," the elemental queen said ignoring the blade. "He wanted you. He couldn't claim you, and you survived. That means you can beat him, can't you? No one ever beats him. But you just did. My army is yours." She placed her hand on Amber's stomach.

Amber wept. The queen withdrew momentarily, apologized and then prodded at her wound. The coagulant was starting to hold.

"Natalie," Josh cried. "Heal her."

Natalie huffed at Josh.

"I don't think she knows how," Thomas said.

"Then you heal her," Josh demanded turning to the elemental queen.

"We are scholars of nature, not physicians," the elemental woman said.

"Then turn her," Josh requested.

"Can't." The queen flicked a forked tongue between her lips.

"She can't turn anymore," Bean replied without thinking.

"Punishment for rebelling," she said. She suddenly seemed interested in Bean more than he would have liked. It prompted him to feel his face for the sunglasses once more. He wondered if any of the elementals had seen him yet. He hadn't felt anyone trying to get into his head other than at the museum, so perhaps not.

"You can't turn because your tongue's broken," Josh asked.

"No," the elemental queen replied. "But I believe there is one here who could. You may have blinded the others, but I can smell the blood in you. It never goes away."

Her head tilted, and her finger shot out towards Bean. All faces turned on the biker.

Lisa tried to expose the absurdity of the idea by laughing it off.

"I am not so ignorant," the elemental said, and her face turned sharply upon Bean's face. "Your fast cannot hide who you are."

Josh had already turned his attention to Bean. "Turn her," he demanded. "Please."

Bean refused, he had to. Suddenly, he felt something scratching once more at his mind. The elemental queen knew about Bean, that meant the rogue knew. Bean knew who scratched at his mind. He was searching. Bean had to stop it.

"I'm no general," Bean said. "Perhaps you smell the generals I killed back in the tavern. There was a lot of blood."

The queen seemed disappointed, but not convinced. She stepped towards Bean.

"Stop it," Bean cried. "Haven't your kind done enough to us?"

She stopped. She might have been stung, but she didn't push the issue any further.

"What about him," Bricktain asked, pointing to Sam who was still restrained above the ground by the crane.

"Let him down," Josh ordered.

Thug rushed to the controls and lowered Sam.

"Why," Sam asked as his restraints were removed.

"We can chain you back up if you prefer," Bricktain said.

"No," Sam replied. "I'll do it." He knelt stiffly to Amber. "Okay," he said, looking to the elemental general. "How do I do it."

"You've never turned anyone before," Bricktain cried.

"It's not that easy if he hasn't done it before," the elemental queen said. "We have to walk him through it. He won't be fast enough."

"He could damage her heart," Bean told Josh.

"So you are a general," Josh asked.

"I just know," Bean replied.

Bean knew he could save Amber. He could pop the contents of the bag of blood and drink it, refuel himself and bite her—but this was new territory now. Anything they planned could be discovered if the rogue got into his head. Actually, it wasn't his head he worried about. If he bit her, he'd open a new connection with Amber, and the rogue would wonder who had made her. He'd suspect something sinister against him.

However, there was a bigger issue at play. Bean knew if Thomas's current aid couldn't save her, nothing short of a bite would. Her wound was in her belly. Her own acid was working against her. Turning her now would only intensify that acid, it would destroy her before she could take on her new healing metabolism. She'd melt apart right here in the paladin's arms. Bean was good at turning others, but he wasn't as good as he used to be. He couldn't do this, not in this fasted state. He didn't dare.

Josh continued to beg Natalie to try something, and Bean watched his own partner for the past twenty-five years slowly dying in the paladin's arms. The crowd grew. Josh didn't notice it, but Bean did. Still Josh begged and Natalie refused, afraid. For one moment, Bean nearly caved and almost said he would save her. He could save her. He could, but he couldn't. If he did, she might only survive to die again soon, along with all her loved ones.

Maybe, if he could discover what Oliver had learned from Speatsh as the oracle, perhaps he could chance more. If there was any chance of another djinn existing, he couldn't reveal it.

Too many what-ifs existed now. He couldn't risk it. Maybe he could save her, but how many others would he kill in consequence. What world would be in the future this time? Josh was alive now, that was the mission. Much was still at stake.

"Turn her," Josh shouted.

Amber's face grew whiter and weaker. Josh drew a crossbow and pointed it upon Natalie. Bean wondered how he hadn't lost it. Natalie roared and smacked the weapon out of his hand.

Josh fell into tears.

Bean watched the faces of those new hunters who hadn't fully known Josh. He read their thoughts through their brows, their doubts of such a young hunter to lead them, especially one who had just attacked them, even if he was the paladin. The paladin appeared broken now, crying. Amber's death would destroy him. That's what he said Josh needed so long ago, wasn't it?

Then an idea struck Bean. Maybe he was thinking about this all wrong.

"You," Bean cried, pointing to his former slave, "Your old master is nearby, go find him." Michael appeared confused, and even flinched at Bean's outburst.

"He blocks our connection," Michael replied. "We're supposed to be a secret."

"There might still be a way," Bean replied, and then called for Natalie.

The black guardian frightened Bean, appearing already behind him. He wondered how much he'd slipped that even a guardian had stealthed upon him. How close had she been all this time?

"You can get into his head," Bean explained to Natalie. "He'll cooperate. Go find Jasper. He can get here and save her faster than anything we can do."

"Why doesn't she just find her own general," the elemental queen asked.

"If her general were close by, don't you think it would already be here," Bean asked.

"Go," Bean snapped when Natalie still hadn't attempted to make her connection. "He'll recognize you. You've done it before. If you hurry, he should be able to get here fast enough."

Natalie set off to handle the task, setting herself before Michael's eyes and peering deep into his mind. Bean took the opportunity to put some distance between himself and the group. A fight was soon to besiege his own mind, and he needed to be ready to face it.

"Where do you think you're going," Josh called after Bean.

"To pray," Bean lied.

He returned to his tarp, dropped to his knees, stared at the ground and began his discussion with the dirt. "All you get is dirt," he began to chant to himself and immediately felt her. She was already trying to enter his mind. She'd found Jasper, but not the right one.

"Dirt," he continued to chant.

"What is it," Lisa asked suddenly at Bean's side.

"Dirt," he replied. "You get dirt." Natalie was subtle, quick, almost as he had been many years ago. She had learned fast. She was better tonight than when she had first entered his mind. If she should live as long as Jasper had, none, not even he, could withstand her mental prowess. Her thoughts prodded, and he felt her clawing at his brain as if it was protected by a fragile balloon that could burst at any moment. It couldn't burst, or it would flood the entire wolf mental link with all that Bean knew. The next prodding hurt his mind, and Bean crumpled on the ground. He heard a cry of agony and realized it was him. He pushed back on the balloon. He could see the silhouette of Natalie's destructive form on the other side, trying to pop it to get in.

"Dirt," he groaned. "You get is dirt."

"We have to stop her," Neon said upon seeing Bean as she entered the tent.

"Why," Lisa asked.

Bean didn't answer, but grit his teeth at the next probe. He wrapped his mind tighter. She mustn't see.

Winter was at Bean's side and held his hand, letting him squeeze hers back to the point that bones should have broken, but did not. Tears fell down her face.

"Tears," he said. "All you get is tears."

"They can't know," Neon replied now watching Bean from over Lisa's shoulder.

Thomas suddenly appeared from the opposite end of the tarp-tent.

The tears straining from Bean's eyes were real, worse than any he'd shed in the name of pain. He had to fight the devastation his own betrayal could have upon his friends if his mind gave. Natalie was going to break him soon. He knew it.

"You have to kill me," Bean whined.

"What is this," Thomas asked.

Bean chomped his jaw and his molar cracked, he quickly swallowed the bits and tried his best to use this pain to divert that which Natalie caused. He couldn't answer any more. He couldn't think of answering, or she'd be inside his head for sure. His face was hot.

"She thinks it's him," Lisa replied. "We have to stop her."

"Why would she think that," Thomas started to ask, but didn't finish.

Bean now struggled between fighting Natalie and trying not to argue with Lisa about saying anything that could give them away.

Lisa wanted to divulge everything, but who else might hear through the thin walls of the tarp.

"Farmers' son," she said.

"Farmer's son," Thomas asked. Then the realities of a memory, of a mythical story, melted his face into disbelief.

Jasper, Natalie's voice muffled into Bean's head.

Thomas's eyes flashed to Neon. Confusion filled his face as he looked upon Bean and then back to Lisa as if to ask, "How?"

Bean held back a scream and wrenched down upon Winter's hand. She squirmed beneath the pain he inflicted upon her fingers.

"We need to knock him out or something," Lisa suggested, preparing to punch Bean.

"No," Thomas replied before Lisa could attack. "He could lose control."

Thomas quickly turned away from Bean's tent; ran across the compound; and smacked Natalie out of her trance. She returned sharply with a growl. Her mane of quills flared to its full majestic silver.

"Are you even trying," Thomas shouted and then under his breath silently, in a tone he knew only she could hear at this short range, "Wrong Jasper."

She snapped at him.

"You're going the wrong way. Find a different path," he said once more in a barely audible tone.

Natalie yelled and faced off with Michael once more.

Bean now stared at the sky, or what would be the sky if the tarp weren't in his way. He felt Natalie once more. She prodded a moment and then she disappeared.

Thomas reappeared over Bean and shouted to someone, whom Bean couldn't see, to stay back.

"Better," Thomas asked.

"Yes," Bean replied, mustering the strength to sit.

Then a cry, such as one as had never been heard among allies, pierced Bean's heart to its core. It shouldn't have. He was above such attacks, yet here it wounded him viciously.

"Get the needle out," Thug demanded. "It's affecting her."

"He won't get here fast enough," Thomas said. "Sometimes negative will work on positive, sometimes not."

Bean cursed himself silently for what he knew he had to do. He exited the tent and quickly returned to Josh.

"Give her to me!" Bean scooped Amber's limp body into his arms. He demanded Thug give him the pouch of blood. Thug dropped it into Amber's lap.

Josh tried to follow, and Bean kicked him down. "Haven't you killed her once already," Bean said, knowing it would paralyze Josh in his own guilt. What he had to do now, he needed to do without an audience.

He held his friend tightly and ran towards Amber's house, ordering Josh to stay away. Amber barely had strength to hold onto Bean as they fled.

Bean entered the house, demanding Thomas and Bricktain keep everyone out. He discovered where Amber's residency was from the simple "up," she mumbled as he approached a set of stairs that led up and another down just inside the entrance. He fled upwards, past the office, where he caught a quick glimpse of Kenny on his phone.

Weasel, Bean thought. Now, he truly knew what he had to do.

Bean flew up a second half-flight of stairs and down the hall to the residency. He ordered Kenny, who decided to follow, to stay away if he didn't want to become food for the elementals. Bean entered a living room area with a rather abused four-cushion sofa and matching love seat. Both looked like they might have been from the 60s, trimmed in gold flowers. He stretched Amber upon the sofa and grasped her hand, cold and almost lifeless.

"I'm ready," Amber begged.

"I can't turn you," Bean replied. "I'm sorry."

She cried, and Bean wiped her tears.

"Then, why," she asked. Bean didn't know how to answer, but he prepared something anyway until he realized her question referred to his own tears as she gently fingered one of his wet cheeks. Damn her! Damn them all! Why now?

He'd thought of fighting the tears, but he could not control them. His humanity had been stripped enough that he'd struggled to rediscover any of it for twenty-five years. Amber had been responsible for some of that, urging him in his own laughter and sharing her own tears throughout their friendship, which this Amber would never know.

He affected her in turn, he'd discovered. Over the years, she'd almost become cold as he was, but that was a different Amber, an Amber who'd lived with the guilt of killing her own husband—but an Amber who still wouldn't lose her humanity, and one who still cried whenever she thought about her lost earlier years.

"Because you weren't supposed to die," Bean said and then quietly explained to her all about who he was, which received a cool, but expected reaction. As he continued, her features softened as to why he, Cadence and Acotactac had returned. Her eyes narrowed at the careful revelation of Kenny and more so at the mention of the djinn—but then watered when she realized that Josh wouldn't be alone if her future Amber had yet to reveal herself, an Amber who would refuse to lose her husband a second time.

Amber's breathing continued to fall, and she lingered far longer than she should have. She screamed in pain a time or two. Bean calmed her.

Suddenly, she lurched forward and gripped at her stomach. She fell back into the couch.

"You came back for him, good," She said. "Eulogies."

Bean questioned her.

"You came back for him," she repeated. "Most people just say something nice about the departed, but you came back."

She struggled with her pain once more. "I was tired of throwing up anyway," which startled and confused Bean at the same time.

"What was it like in your time," Amber asked.

"What," Bean asked.

"Our child," she said. "What was it? Was it a boy?"

Now, this she'd never mentioned before, but he understood why. People were entitled to their secrets after all. He didn't know how to respond. As long as he had known her, she had always carried an illness, but a child. She never revealed that. None of her friends revealed that. He was suddenly angry that he hadn't seen it before.

"What was it," she asked again, barely a whisper.

"A boy," Bean lied, certain that she should lose the child soon.

"A boy," Amber approved with a smile. "Was he strong like his dad."

"Like his mother," Bean replied.

She smiled and cringed again in an attack of pain.

"It hurts," she cried, this statement louder than anything she'd stated in a while. "Don't let him be stupid."

Bean wiped his eyes for the last time. "We need him to be stupid."

"Oh," she replied. Her words had become a solid slur or wind, and Bean struggled to understand. "I feel sorry for you."

"Don't."

"And we were friends, you and I," she sputtered.

"The best," Bean replied.

"Then," she said. "End it."

To fill her request, Bean drew Amber's wooden blade from her side and drew it up over her chest. She refreshed her cheeks with tears once more, and tried to wipe them.

The wooden dagger sank deep into her heart, and her breathing stopped. She shook a moment. Her lungs took in a quick, shallow breath and then let it out. Her pain was over.

Bean kissed her forehead and bit back into reality. He stayed at her side until anger and impatient vengeance dried his eyes.

Bean solved the wooden blade, withdrew it from Amber's chest and slid it into one of his pockets. He quickly composed himself; and buried his reemerging humanity. He located the kitchen one room off and popped open the refrigerator.

Less than a minute later, Bean rushed into the office and gathered in his surroundings.

"Open the gates," Bean ordered. "The master's coming."

"Finally," Kenny said and promptly responded. The sound of the hydraulic gates began to pop from outside in the compound.

"I was right!" Bean yanked Kenny out of his office chair.

"Hey," Kenny cried, and struck at Bean's hands as someone who knew clearly how to fight back. He might have broken the grip on a weaker person. "This wasn't the deal. He's supposed to turn me."

"Why would he want you," Bean asked. He punched Kenny's throat. The traitor's windpipe crumpled, quickly swelling to prevent the passage of any air. Kenny's mouth floundered like a guppy's. Bean flipped Kenny sideways and smashed his back against the support that separated two large panes of window. The only sound his victim made was the crackling of his spine. Outside, the population of the junkyard remained ignorant of what happened on the other side of the mirrored glass. There was a little commotion over the gates opening, but the doorman quickly closed them in confusion.

Bean dropped Kenny to the floor. Blood filled the traitor's face and his eyeballs. He blinked at Bean. Bean dropped a red bag on his stomach and stabbed a kitchen knife through it and into his own stomach. Kenny's face rushed with blue.

"Does it hurt," Bean asked squatting down over the injured young man. "Blink for 'yes.'"

Kenny blinked.

"The rogue lied," Bean said.

Kenny's throat garbled with sounds of broken cartilage.

"But I can turn you," Bean said. "Would you like that?"

Again, Kenny blinked.

"Yeah," Bean replied. "If I wouldn't turn her, why would I turn a worm like you?" Bean gripped Kenny's shoulders and flipped him heels over head into the air. Kenny's chest, face and legs slapped into one of the window panes. The kitchen knife handled punched through the glass and the window exploded under his weight. He flew out into the junkyard then down twenty feet.

"Traitor," Bean cried over the yard of hunters, many still poised in confusion at the opened gates. His eyes fell on Josh. "He killed her."

Thug and Thomas were quickly to Kenny's side. Their first reaction was that Bean had attacked their own. Thug rolled Kenny onto his back, the body already lifeless. Red blood had exploded across his front from the clear plastic pouch stabbed against Kenny's gut. The label read "A-Positive."

The Book of Ancients

31 ~ Neon

While other gangsters kept their distance, one, a surprisingly clean-cut man, leapt for the Schnautzer.

Vengeance drew the paladin through the gates. Inhibition had no place in this fight, only absolute destruction. He cared not that his clothing was ragged, loosened and torn in some places from his previous inhuman transformation.

Hate had overtaken his sadness, his grief, his naiveté. His veins were vile with waves of red abhorrence, such fierceness and roll tide that it was all his very soul could do to withstand their forces from breaking him. His entire being surged with disgust for the scouts, those heartless creatures who looked like dogs, fed as such and deserved to die like the mongrels they were. His arteries pulsed with disdain for those guardians with their sharp fur, burning quills and their nail-like teeth—cowards, for they hid from the sun.

His heart pumped revulsion for the generals who made the scouts and guardians. His soul seethed frigid detestation for the earth and the moon, for their loathsome dance together. His bowels festered bile at the thought of weak generals who couldn't bear the communion of these two dancing spirits, an act so overwhelming it forced wicked masters to change from human into vicious, monstrous forms. He drew hate for that same full moon where generals lost control for just one night, one inhuman, yet human night. Prejudice cried against the ancients hidden away while humans fought their battle.

He reviled the insignificant role of man, that incredulous creature who deserved to die, deserved to be turned and killed, who did little to fight for their own survival and who lacked the capability to accept the truth at the door. He'd had his fill of lazy humans who would just as soon allow annihilation of their own species in the name of ethics, rather than stand up and fight for their right to simply be. They would rather die than accept that truth, which predicted mankind was nothing to the rogue. Josh had his fill of wannabe and clueless delegates.

His every pore now trembled with animosity: to Dustin for dying; at Speatsh for leaving him; for his father for hiding from him; to Kenny for his betrayal; and, as he had just learned from Cadence, his mother for her lifetime of deception. Most importantly, he despised himself for destroying that goodness, the sacred holiness, that comfort that had raised him up above all hope anyone deserved to hold, love anyone deserved to share—his wife, Amber.

As for the rogue, emotion held little strength over the cold that continued to grow within the new paladin's black heart, which poured less and less compassion associated to the emotion of being. It pumped the vile hopes and respects of a newborn demon. That's what the rogue had stirred. He wanted to awaken the monster within Josh, but he summoned the very bowels of hell themselves.

The remnant of ancient blood still affected Josh. He was hot. Sweat sprinkled his face, and he held back the urge to vomit where he stood, as if every ounce of him had been healed by that flu-riddled saliva of the monsters.

Josh, evading the protestations of his own allies, had ordered the gates open and flew into the horde of wolves outside of them now. Few tried to withdraw him from his purpose as such an act only fueled his desire to destroy them. He struck out at anyone who tried to stop him, and now he single-handedly dealt justice on these monsters he had vowed to spend so much time protecting. These dog forms masked no innocent humans. They were all wolves, and the more that died tonight meant the fewer that would attack tomorrow—and that would force the generals to show their hands, and then he could kill them too.

One behind you, Neon's voice spoke into his head.

Josh screamed, but turned and sliced a backstabbing coward apart.

"Get out of my head," he shouted.

No need to yell, Neon said, watching the battleground from the catwalks above Josh's head. *I am your thoughts. Duck!*

Get out of my thoughts, Josh thought, while he did, in fact, duck in time to avoid a swipe for his head.

I am your thoughts, Neon replied. *Backwards somersault now.*

Enough! Josh did the backwards somersault anyway and felt his cloak destroy whatever attack he hadn't seen coming.

Josh dove deeper into the mob of monsters and spun that spiral on his heels that destroyed all within that deadly radius of his cloak. He reloaded his fang crossbow. Where was his other one? He must have lost it. He unloaded his crossbow, reloaded and emptied three weaker projectiles the next time he pulled the trigger.

Two jumping from in front, Neon added.

Josh made his fists, his swords telescoped in time to graze the face of one adversary before catching the roof of the mouth of the other on the tips of both blades.

A gunshot chirped, and the grazed wolf fell. Josh threw all his strength into his blades; up through their points; through the roof of his current foe's mouth and into his skull, quickly finishing this foe. The blades snapped back into their housing around Josh's wrist and the creature fell dead at his feet.

To your left, Neon suggested.

Josh, followed her advice.

It won't bring her back, Neon observed.

That's it, Josh's thought seethed. *You're dead too!*

Mob left, mob right, Neon added.

I see them, Josh responded and performed a strange combo of projectiles, eruption of blades and flurry of nasty fabric.

One at your heels, from the back!

Josh's body leapt straight up, and he plunged his blades down into a brave and stupid wiener dog that had decided to sneak up on him. Then he returned to his bigger brawl with larger guardians.

More little ones coming.

Josh swore. He hadn't even realized until now that his feet were bare.

You see now?

What was I thinking, Josh asked.

It's fine, Neon excused. *Help is on the way.*

A streak of gold shot past Josh, its ghostly driver shouting at every monster in his path.

The Silver Bullet blasted the air with its sound that deafened Josh's assailants. It whipped around the onslaught of guardians and scouts, which now surrounded Josh. Aggon orchestrated his own rescue, backing his chariot into the paladin, such that Josh stumbled backward into the golden bucket. Soon, both vehicles were speeding back towards the compound, the bladed nose of the Silver Bullet slicing a path before Aggon's cart. The wheels of the chariot kicked dirt into high walls behind itself, which might have gone unnoticed under lesser lighting than that of the compound. They burst into small dust devils and raced out into the mob, throwing them away from Josh's escape. Above Josh's route, he made out the strange figure of the elemental queen gliding casually through the air and back towards the compound.

Several more small, but powerful twisters stretched up from the ground, laying out a clear road towards the front gates.

"Kill them all," Josh yelled to the elemental queen, but couldn't hear himself over his surrounding commotion.

That won't bring her back either.

What did you do to me, Josh asked, somehow feeling relieved that he was being rescued from his own idiocy.

In an instant of thought, as though forgotten memories, Josh's mind swelled with visions of his death and friends, older than now, coming to save him from a dark and diminishing world. He saw friends with faces of rodeo queens and an enemy with the face of a biker. Other faces he knew were there, but the shadows of these thoughts hid them. He saw hair draw them to places that he could not see. He saw Neon sending them.

What about you, Josh asked, realizing she hadn't fully explained herself.

We are mates, she replied.

We are not, Josh replied.

You named me, she replied. *We are mates. I am needed to block your thoughts. I destined us to be mates.*

Josh didn't understand. He didn't admit it, but he didn't need to.

He is linked to all wolves, Neon explained. *You are wolf. Thinking they could hide your mind by not telling you was ignorant. Thinking if you awoke, you could be strong enough to block him off was arrogant. Your friends failed in this. You named me, and now I have hidden your thoughts from the rogue for that is my power. The sudden disappearance of your mind, will surely frustrate the rogue's own thinking. He has no reliability now. He cannot predict you any longer.*

That's why he knew how to trap us?

Yes, the djinn replied.

And I can't block him out?

Your brain is too slow, Neon replied. *You are not Speatsh nor Jasper. Teaching you would take too long. I am fast. I am the only way to block your mind. He does not know me. He does not own me. I came so you would name me. Only then could our minds link, and you could succeed. Only this could save both of us.*

Whose stupid plan was that, Josh asked.

If you think hard enough, you can figure it out, Neon replied.

Even with my slow brain and all, Josh asked.

It's not that slow, Neon's voice retorted.

Josh didn't know how to respond, and he felt himself gripping the rim of the golden chariot. The gates had closed. Aggon was telling him to get out. Bricktain, having exited the Silver Bullet, was now cursing Josh for his continual lunacy.

Wouldn't a better plan have been to learn how to change into my wolf form, Josh finally asked. *If I'm wolf, I'd be stronger changed. Wouldn't I? If I'm the heir, I should have even more strength.*

You did change. Do you feel you did better changed, Neon replied.

Josh punched the side of the chariot.

"Hey," Aggon screamed. "No does swim in your toilet, don't grunt in my car."

"What," Josh asked trying to understand, but he gave up. He exited the carrier, still wanting to punch something.

His eyes fell on Sam. In a matter of paces, Josh was quickly to him. The angry paladin held a small crossbow to his face.

"I gave you your life, general, and you didn't repay," Josh complained, his finger hugging the release of his trigger. "How could you not know how to create a wolf?"

Sam could have retreated, could have attacked Josh easily, but he held his ground.

"I'm sorry," Sam said. "I don't approve of slavery."

Neon's frame appeared to Josh's left.

"I never saw it as a power to save a life." Sam made no move to flee.

A general without slaves? Josh lowered his weapon.

"Find a way to make yourself useful," he said. He had hardly noticed that Sam moved quickly to obey the order.

I don't want you in my head, Josh thought.

No, but you'll have it, Neon replied. *Protecting one's mind to preserve what was my world, and is again, is a small price to pay for freedom.*

'So it's time for a new—," Josh started to speak out loud to Neon.

"When talking to strangers, one shouldn't volunteer information instead of candy," Neon replied, her voice sounding more infantile and higher-registered than that which he had heard in his head. The voice he heard in his head was gentler, yet more forceful and clearer. *Shall we move the conversation indoors with allies who aren't wolves.*

Josh accepted Neon's advice and took a few moments for himself to first visit his wife and say goodbye.

He found her on the couch.

She is lovely.

Not now, Josh replied.

Might I recommend grieving less and planning more, Neon suggested. *We came a long way to learn what you knew.*

You can read my thoughts, you make the plans, Josh replied.

I can't take what you don't volunteer.

Give me a moment will you?

We already have, Neon said. *And might I say you seem a little ungrateful.*

"I'm saying goodbye here," Josh screeched. "Show some respect!"

Why, Neon asked. *She's dead. She can't answer you.*

"Josh?"

It took Josh a moment to realize this voice was real.

"What," Josh shouted in frustration. "What? What? One minute, please! What?"

"I'm sorry," Bricktain replied unable to take his eyes off of Amber's broken being. "But they're up to something."

"Of course they are," Josh replied. "They're always up to something, and I'm always doing something to irritate them or get someone killed."

Bricktain knelt beside Josh and huffed, "It's not your fault."

"Of course it's not," Josh snapped. "Haven't you heard, I'm the heir. It's never royalty's fault." Josh replied. He sagged back onto his legs. "I killed her."

"You weren't you."

"We had him. We could have ended him and all of this."

"He did this," Bricktain's voice interrupted.

"I brought her into it," Josh rebuffed. "We brought her family into this." Josh slumped forward. "I took on the bully and lost."

"You're right," Bricktain shot back. "This is your fault, but we could have left any time we wanted to."

"We all should have left," Josh said. He stood to end the conversation.

"The rogue's the one who just failed, Josh," Bricktain said. "For once, he failed, and you beat him. And now we have an army that he doesn't know about."

"What are you talking about?"

"The elementals."

"He knew they joined us before we did," Josh said. "He's in her head. Like he was mine."

Josh allowed himself a deep breath and a moment for what Josh had just said to sink into Bricktain's head.

"He knows your mind," Bricktain asked.

"Not any more," Josh replied and glanced quickly at Neon. "I have a shield now."

"Still, for the first time since we've started this, we didn't play into one of those monster's hands," Bricktain continued. "I don't know what the rogue planned by turning you, but it had to have been worse than this. You showed him he was fallible."

Josh tried to ignore Bricktain who now drew a heavy blanket out of the top shelf of a small closet.

"We don't stop," Bricktain said. "She didn't stop. She married it."

Josh would have clocked Bricktain if he hadn't known he would have decapitated him in the process.

"We don't stop," Bricktain said. "Not here. We go out there. We finish him. You finish this and bury her with the honor she and everyone else we've lost deserves."

Josh growled. Bricktain grabbed Josh's arm and, despite all the lacerations that suddenly covered his palm and fingers, ignored the pain. "Don't let that smarmy crud take that respect from her. She's earned that much."

"I've never liked you," Josh said, strangely calm right now.

"Join the club," Bricktain replied.

"Call the others in," Josh said. He flared the blanket out over Amber.

Bricktain got on his earpiece, reminding Josh he needed a new one, if they had any new ones. "Guys. The paladin wants you."

"No dogs," Josh said. "Have them wait. The elemental scary lady too."

"Not the dogs," Bricktain repeated and mimicked Josh's other order into his own headset.

"And tell that biker dude and his rodeo friends to come in."

Bricktain gave pause, but then made the recommendation.

"And I need shoes," Josh said. "I seem to have lost mine. Check one of the trucks."

Bricktain was halfway through this order when, "Seems someone found some of your belongings. They're bringing them in."

Josh continued to dress Amber in the heavy brown blanket, figuring that blanket wouldn't remind him of the blood so much. Bricktain helped him lift her to wrap, and they were just about to cover Amber's head when the others came in. Josh stole a quick look at Amber's beautiful and scarred face before hiding it beneath her black bandana.

"I've seen this," Neon said. "First you drop them in a bag, and then you throw them in the big, black can."

Several people began to spout protestations, but Josh silenced them when he heard what she really had to say in his head. Except for tears, they remained silent for another hour.

After an hour, Bean finally risked straddling alongside Josh and setting the paladin's recovered shoes and crossbow on the back of the couch. He looked one last time upon his old partner. Then he suggested that they bury her and bring her back as an oracle. At least she wouldn't completely be gone then. A debate broke out about how it wasn't a cemetery, to which Cadence reminded everyone that it was because Amber's brothers had already been buried within the land.

"We're not doing that to her," Josh said. "Let her rest. Let them all just rest."

"It would have required a keeper to waken an oracle anyway," Thomas said.

"What's a keeper," Cadence asked, standing on the opposite side of the room, refusing to look upon her friend. Lisa, however had kept looking.

"A keeper owns the dead," Thomas said. "They're not psychic, they don't see ghosts—well they do, but no more than any of us have been able to—but they have a knack with the energies of the dead to let them speak again. Most keepers tend to keep the dead together."

"Like a cemetery," Bricktain asked, but really didn't need an answer.

"Oliver's a keeper," Josh realized.

"Yes," Thomas replied. "Having a father who doesn't die and friends who—well—he's truly exceptional. There's only one other I've ever known, and that was a terribly long time ago. I had to stop him once he discovered his ability, and his first oracle was used to give strength to the rogue." He neglected to inform them that it was the same who called Aggon as an oracle, during a trip many decades ago to Rome. That was another time, however, a time when Thomas's own wife was alive, and Thomas cherished that she would live forever with him. "Fitting punishment that my son be the innocent thing I destroyed so long ago."

The conversation lulled as others had gathered gradually around Amber and couldn't seem to leave her. Josh drew a corner of the blanket that had fallen away and revealed a piece of Amber's neck.

Finally, Josh turned to Bean and asked, "So he can't read your mind?"

"No he—Well aren't you smart," Bean replied, and suddenly he was filled with fear. "How much do you know? He knows everything you know. He's always had a link with you."

"Not any more," Josh replied, confused and angry about issues he had to force himself to dwell on later. "Can he read your mind?"

"What are you talking about," Bricktain asked.

"No, he can't," Bean finally answered.

Josh quickly explained as much of the thoughts that he had seen and identified Bean for who he really was, which sent Bricktain into a flurry of ratcheting parts that ended with a barrel of a gun aimed upon the biker. Josh ordered him to stop.

"What else do you know," Bean asked. "And how can you be sure he doesn't have a link with you."

"I only know what she showed me," Josh replied. "And I just need you to trust me that he's not linked to me any more."

Bricktain and most of the others appeared confused.

"She told you who I was, then," Bean asked.

Josh admitted that she had.

"So you know where the others are," Bean asked.

Josh glanced to Cadence and Acotactac and wondered if they'd truly appreciate knowing the truth about the rodeo queens. He looked to Lisa and Winter and, before he could say anything, Lisa embraced Josh and sobbed into the sleeves of her leather jacket. Winter kept her ground and simply nodded in smile.

"I'm confused," Bricktain said.

"You might find this interesting," Josh said breaking the embrace and then revealed what Neon had allowed him to know. Cadence dropped heavily into the loveseat, but Acotactac seemed quite intent to keep listening.

Bricktain, for once, was speechless.

"Do you know where Nick is then," Bean asked.

"Nick came back too," Josh asked in surprise. "Don't you know where he is?"

"No," Bean replied.

"But you're friends," Josh asked. "I thought—"

"I thought things too," Bean explained. "But I was duped, and we went where she sent us. Don't you know where the others are?"

"What others? She only showed me you three," Josh blurted.

"You don't have to be a know-it-all, you know," Neon said snidely.

"I'm confused," Bricktain said. "And believe me, I was already confused."

"I'm not surprised," Bean replied. He then began to relay many of the precedings of the djinn and his allies, twenty-five years in a future of a worse time. He spared the finer details and threatened that the djinn must remain secret.

After he had finished, he urged Cadence to regale what she had learned back at the bunker and the cemetery. The memory was freshest with her.

"So Nick could be running around out there like some idiot, and not even know who he is," Bricktain said.

"It's possible," Bean replied.

"That's cold," Bricktain observed.

"Could be worse," Cadence said and suddenly started laughing. "You have one wife and they're both in the room, right now!"

Now, Bricktain stood stupefied, "Why is it always me?"

Then he laughed. They all laughed. They needed to laugh and couldn't stop, and they laughed until they stopped and realized it Amber didn't find it quite as humorous.

As he stared at her blankets, Josh felt the strange responsibility to rescue Bricktain fall upon him. He began to piece together the djinn's plan as best as he could. "You were sent to protect me," Josh said.

"No," Bean replied. "We specifically kept ourselves anonymous so you wouldn't second guess—ah, never mind! It's not like this part of history was ever first-guessed." He struggled a moment longer with whether he should tell Josh or not. "They were sent to save you, but I was sent to release her so she could get named and gain her freedom."

"And in doing so, she's able to block my mind," Josh said.

Now, Bean seemed confused. "She can do that?"

"Among other things," Josh replied. He chose not to disclose that she was in his head.

Bean's face suddenly lit up and he said, "So, that's it! I was trying to figure out how she got away with being selfish when her curse was to give. She tricked me into freeing her so she could ultimately protect your mind from the rogue and ultimately—"

"We get it," Lisa scowled. "You don't have to spell every brainwave out for us."

"I know! It's so annoying, isn't it," Cadence replied, then found herself staring silently at herself dressed in a rodeo costume. She started laughing again, but Lisa did not.

"Whatever happens," Josh said sternly. His eyes were still locked on the body wrapped in the blanket on the couch. "We protect Neon at all costs or whatever we plan here goes down the drain the second that barrier between me and the rogue goes down."

"Oh, I wouldn't worry too much about that broad," Thug interjected. Josh had hardly noticed him enter the room. "I've seen her hold her own."

Neon blushed and almost appeared to glow—not metaphorically, she might have actually been giving off light. Josh contemplated turning off the overhead lamp to test that theory.

"So, she didn't show you anything other than us coming here," Bean asked.

Was there more? Josh reached out to Neon.

Yes, Neon replied.

What is it?

You mustn't pull at those threads, she replied. *You might unravel something you should not at this time.*

"No," Josh replied. "I don't know anything else. I assume you came in with a plan?"

"I suppose we did," Bean replied.

"And what is it?"

"Let you make your plan," Bean explained. "And let us do our plan."

"You didn't come in with a plan," Josh ridiculed.

"Not one you're ready to hear," Bean said. "But I think I've discovered one that shouldn't interfere with anything you develop. In fact, I think it will help quite a bit."

"Well, what is it?"

"Nope," Bean denied. "Let's call it a backup in case that brain of yours gets breached. I imagine you can come up with something on your own there."

Stop, Neon ordered. *You must not contemplate that.*

I need to know what I'm working with, Josh thought to Neon.

And what if something happens to me, and my barrier falls from your mind, Neon asked. *You could betray Jasper.*

Josh's glare turned to piercing. "What do you need for your part?"

"It's important that we get to Oliver as quickly as possible," Bean explained. "And we need to make a stop or two."

"He does have Speatsh," Thomas said, rather encouraged.

Commotion from Cadence, Bricktain and Josh broke out until Josh fell silent in remembering Oliver's role as keeper. A few moments later and the others seemed to realize.

"What else do you need," Josh asked.

"Well, mostly we needed you," Bean replied. "I couldn't really plan much beyond that."

"Excuse me," both Lisa and Josh asked as though Bean had let them down.

"We came because the rogue is after the hearse, and you gave us impression to believe you might know where it was. For once, I didn't know what to expect from you."

"That was your plan," Josh yelled. "To see if I knew where the hearse was?"

"You weren't exactly coming up with any ideas, yourself, where we came from," Bean said. "We come from a desolate future. If we lose, you may get a chance to see it for yourself. I can help with the rogue, but we need your thoughts first, and I really hope you have something in that head of yours to make this all worthwhile. We had hoped you knew something about this carriage."

Josh asked Thomas for the pages that he had torn out of the museum book. Thomas produced them carefully, and Josh studied for several minutes.

You're sure he doesn't know what I know, Josh asked her.

I am certain, Neon replied. *I know which thoughts are yours and which are trying to invade. He will never get in. In fact, he can no longer find you.*

"Tell me if I understand correctly, Thomas," Josh asked. "We bring death to the hearse and it revives a dead. One life for every ten thousand killed."

"I suppose," Thomas said. "This is new to me too."

"A hearse that really is powered by death," Josh said suddenly reinvigorated. "So we can bring her back! I mean, really bring her back, not as a ghost. For Real!"

Thomas agreed, and hope might have filled his face.

"And who knows how many deaths it's stockpiled over the years with other users." Josh jubilantly waved the torn page with the hearse on it. He examined the page that depicted the figure leading others to the vehicle. Thomas replayed what he had explained to Josh at the museum to help stimulate his memory of any thoughts he might have had. "And this hearse works," Josh asked realizing that no one knew.

"Based upon what we've seen and you've been told, the rogue seems to think so," Thomas said.

"Then she's not dead," Josh cheered, and he axiously fingered the page within his hands. "Yeah. I can fix her."

Josh reviewed the ancient inked portrait with a renewed energy and even wondered how many artisans and scholars would have sought his life for manhandling this ancient papyrus as he was doing now. Maybe he should have at least put on his silk gloves. Then again, he didn't care. He did, however, care about the detail of artwork. He patted his pocket and was pleased that his torn gloves were there. He decided to pull them on.

The carriage with its almost round, fairy tale appearance was the only completely black object on the page. Yet, Josh could still see the depictions of streams of light radiating from within its doors and throughout the entire sheet of strange paper. Then the page began to reveal its details. What appeared to look like simple dots at first, surrounding the carriage, became more as Josh inspected this particular image further. These weren't just dots. What were they? Eyes? No, they were faces.

Here, a predominant figure grew out of the parchment. It was encased in small pinpoints, which could have passed for floating specks of elements to any eye which was willing to see them as such. Josh, however, saw them for what he believed them to be, subtle drawings of approaching dark images being washed out in the brightness of the rays that had been sketched to shine from within the carriage. Now that Josh saw it, he discovered an image that was clearly a hairy being of some sort with features similar to the lankiness that Josh had seen in the ancients at the museum. This one led others into the shafts of light and towards the carriage. What were these others? Humans? The detail wasn't clear enough.

Humans would make sense; kill the humans; strengthen the wolves. It appeared to Josh that here was a wolf leading the humans to their deaths, to the hearse, the womb of rebirth for whoever sat inside.

He turned his attention to the second page of the ancient book, this one presenting the image of monsters all standing in a circle. The scene was more distinct than the image depicting the carriage. Here, Josh didn't have to look so intently to find evident tufts of fur, fingers and joints on the individuals within the piece of art. What appeared to be beams of some sort of light, drawn in thin lines, shot from each figure's eyes to a single individual standing in the center of their circle. Perhaps the lines weren't rays of light, but representations of the gazes of the monsters instead?

Josh looked over a third picture, the same as the previous except the rays from their faces were completely black, and all figures in the circle appeared to be bound in thick, black and contoured strokes. Some sort of cord perhaps? In the center of this drawing, surrounded by the circle of ancients, stood, not an individual, but a carriage. In this image, more illumination appeared to shoot out from a chariot, perhaps the symbolism of the hearse returning life.

Why surround the hearse with the living ancients though?

"He brings them to life," Josh asked, mostly to himself. "Does he take their power?"

"Come again," Cadence asked.

"Shush," Josh replied, then returned to his own personal banter.

Thomas was taken aback and shared a surprised look with Thug. "You are incredibly like your uncle," he said. "It's quite intriguing."

Josh flipped back and forth between the pages in frustration.

"Hate it when you can't figure out what you're missing," Bean asked. "I've been doing it myself lately,"

"Missing?" Josh wondered what that meant, then "Thank you, Bean!"

He looked down at the wolf leading the humans to their deaths—not humans—no, they have hair. Not deaths, resurrection!

And the rope?

The leading wolf clenched the cord in his hand, while the others had it wrapped around their wrists. Not leading. Dragging?

"What does that look like to you," Josh asked turning to Thomas and pointing out the rope.

"A rope," Thomas said.

"How about you," Josh asked, offering Bean the same view of the picture.

"That's a leash," Bean rattled off quickly.

"You're sure," Josh asked.

Bean snapped the paper from Josh's hand and looked a second more closely then held it back to Josh. "Every dog knows a leash."

"That's what I thought," Josh said. He felt himself smile.

Don't dwell on it, Neon urged.

Shush! Josh mentally snapped. *I'll think any way I want. It's still my brain.*

He felt her laugh inside his head. *Fair enough.*

Josh clenched the papers in his hands. "And we know for certain that the wagon you guys brought out from the bunker isn't the one?"

"That was pretty much when the world ended," Lisa replied. "Because he discovered it wasn't."

Bean and Winter agreed, in similar nods of the head.

"So he doesn't know," Josh said. Now he felt he was beaming. So much was different now. This was new. This could change everything.

"What already," Bricktain asked, and others sustained.

"I know how to beat the rogue," Josh said. "And maybe we can revive our friends while we're at it."

"So you do know where it is," Bean asked. "The black carriage in Thug's basement, right?"

"Wait," Thug interjected. "My basement?"

Bean nodded and, for the first time in many years, suddenly felt a real energy in his hope.

Josh's face lifted to the others. He was grinning.

"We all know where it is," Josh said.

"So what's the plan," Cadence asked.

"The plan stays with us," Josh explained. He went to preparing his crossbows, which he had learned he did when he was ready to act. He made a quick note that he needed more silver cylindrical ammunition. Luckily, Reggie had recently milled him nearly a box of them. "We tell the wolves what they need to know, and only when they need to know it. Understood?"

The others agreed, even though they didn't understand.

"I think we're right." Josh said holding up the first page. "The rogue's plan is to collect all of the ancients and return them to life. The matter of 'why' is what these pictures are all about." He flourished the second page, with the circle of ancients surrounding the individual, so that his companions could see it. "I think this shows some sort of judgment. I think the ancients used to pass judgment freely, or power freely, to collectively assign roles to each other." Josh re-examined the drawing a moment as if to convince himself that his theory was actually correct. "That's how my mom—the queen—got her position. I'll bet she wasn't the oldest like we were led to believe. To them, perhaps oldest is the one with the most authority or power. Regardless, I believe her role as queen was her judgment for standing amidst the power of her own peers. I'll also bet they gave their power freely before she betrayed them."

Josh now held the picture with the darker circle of figures surrounding the hearse, up next to the previous image. "I think both of these show judgment. But only one of these pictures shows the hearse."

Bean abruptly pulled the drawings out of Josh's hands and began examining them.

"What if the hearse is a magnet for power," Josh asked. "If it can somehow power itself with any dead that fall in close proximity to it—"

"The power of souls, for instance," Bean suggested.

"Yes," Josh replied. "Then perhaps it can draw other energy as well?"

"What do you mean," Bricktain asked.

"I have a crazy thought," Josh said. "We've already established that when something dies near the hearse, the hearse somehow feeds off that death and uses what it collects to help fuel itself to revive another life. Rumor is, it takes ten thousand to bring back one. What if that's why the rogue's army is so large, so it can be annihilated to power the hearse enough to revive all the ancients."

"Had that thought myself," Bean said, exchanging a look with Lisa.

"However, what if the hearse can do more than steal energy from the dead," Josh asked.

"Like steal power from living creatures that have it," Cadence and Lisa suddenly realized together.

"One of these pictures shows an individual standing in the center of a circle of others who are free," Josh explained. "The other shows a hearse and those standing around it are bound. What if the rogue plans to use the hearse to bring the ancients back to life so he can then bind them and force them to give him the power that he feels he should have?"

"You mean like whoever sits in the hearse can take power for themselves," Lisa asked, who had joined Bean to examine the pictures.

"It's brilliant," Bean said.

Several of the others quickly argued that point, but didn't linger on it.

"That can't be it," Cadence said. "The need to assign roles suggests a community need. There's only a few of them."

"And I'll bet the community was much larger than we've come to believe," Josh said. "He's been rounding up the ones who died or went into hiding. The more living ancients that have power he can steal, the more powerful he can become himself."

"All this time, he's been collecting them," Bean said.

Thomas grunted something that clearly displeased him.

"The rogue's an antique dealer," Josh continued. "While my mom—," Josh bit his words again at the betrayal that now engulfed his heart. "While the queen imprisons the ones who are still alive, her brother collects those who fled or died in process. That has to be it!"

"Restore the dead to life, restore their power, you have more power to take," Thomas said. "It's possible."

"Perhaps there are more of them out there," Bean said, "but what's in the museum is all he could find."

"That's a lot of theory to base a plan on," Thug said.

"Tell me I'm wrong," Josh said.

"It does complete the picture," Bean finally relented.

Thomas agreed, but admitted he couldn't be certain.

"It adds up," Cadence said.

I think it's true, Neon's voice declared in Josh's mind. *But I can't be certain.*

Why not, Josh asked.

Because I can't remember, Neon explained. *But it sounds familiar.*

"Majority rules," Neon screamed. She shook her fist like a gavel and imitated knocking sounds.

"I think he's gathered all his pieces together, except for the hearse, and he's ready to take that power," Josh suddenly turned to

Thomas. "He won't wait another month. He's too close." Josh spoke to Bricktain now, "He knows we found the cave and he can't have us relocate them. He has the ancients. He has the carriage in his grasp. He's too close to completing his task. He has to act before we stump him. Have Nata use that general Thomas brought in—"

"Sam," Bricktain suggested.

"Let's use Sam to contact the rogue and tell him we have the hearse, and we'll take it to him in exchange for future peace and preservation," Josh instructed. "Something the rogue would believe we'd be stupid enough to beg for in return for his mercy."

"The rogue won't go for that," Bricktain ridiculed.

"Overruled," Neon shouted and smacked her pretend gavel again. A startled Bricktain eyed Neon in bewilderment. Thomas smirked at Bricktain's scare.

"Of course he won't," Josh agreed. "But he'll pretend and show up nonetheless. And he'll bring all his wolves, won't he? He needs them to power it."

"You want those numbers there," Bricktain asked.

"If we can bring her back, we're not taking any chances of shortchanging the hearse," Josh said, pointing to Amber's wrapped body. "I want everything he has. We're going nuclear."

"Mr. Revlon," Bricktain cautiously said. "It might not work."

"It will," Josh replied sternly. "Have Natalie contact him."

"We could simply use Kenny's satellite phone. He's been using it to communicate with the rogue," Bean suggested.

"Nah. Where's the fun in that," Josh replied.

"All right," Thomas said, "But why risk Natalie on Sam. We have that elemental general out there. She could just tell him."

"No. Use Sam," Josh said. "It's good for the rogue to know the paladin's guardian can take control of his creation any time she wants."

Bean seemed to smile. Josh wasn't sure what it meant. It disconcerted him yet strangely gave him confidence too.

"Let him think we're stupid," Josh said. "But have Natalie convince him we'll destroy the hearse and the ancients who are in our care if he tries anything before we hand it over."

"And when shall we hand off the carriage," Thomas asked.

"This evening," Josh answered. He glanced at a window and watched the waning of night draw upon them. He thought better about how late it was and added, "Not now tonight—tonight—later tonight, after day."

"That would be tomorrow night," Bricktain mocked.

"Wrong," Cadence shrieked. "Do it when he only has scouts. Do it during the day."

"No," Josh replied. "Tonight."

"Tomorrow night," Bricktain corrected.

"It already is tomorrow, you moron," Cadence corrected.

"Oh," Bricktain relented.

"Let him think he's got the advantage," Josh said.

"It's full moon tomorrow," Cadence replied.

"Tonight," Bricktain corrected.

Cadence drew an ammunition clip off her magnetic suit and flung it at the side of Bricktain's head.

"He does have the advantage, Josh" Lisa growled.

"No, he doesn't. We have what he wants," Josh said.

"Understood," Bricktain suddenly said at his earpiece and looked back to Josh. "Boss, something's up. The guardians, the scouts, doorman says they're all vacating."

"He's onto us," Cadence asked. "What do we do?"

"Relax," Bean urged. "He's probably regrouping now that he doesn't know your mind and since you've just escaped him."

"Agreed," Thomas added.

"Then let him do his thing for now," Josh said. "It frees us to do our own thing."

"And what is our thing," Bean asked.

"We need more carriages," Josh said. "We need to get in touch with the rogue before he does something we can't see coming." He looked to Thomas.

"I'll inform her now," Thomas answered, then left to deliver Natalie's orders.

Josh went back to thinking, then cried out for Aggon.

A loud static pop later, and the ghost gladiator stood in the room.

"Is nice in here," Aggon said. "Smells like de person of dead though. You forget flush?"

"We need your chariot," Josh wheezed in a burst of contempt.

"No," Aggon cried. "You gets it all bleedy."

"It's not up for debate, but hold that thought for a moment," Josh said. He turned to Bean. "You said you have a plan. What do you need for it?"

"My companions and a vehicle," Bean said. "I also need Acotactac to get us back to the Taichomée river entrance."

Bricktain objected, but Acotactac agreed before anyone else could sustain him.

"And if I could make a suggestion to load up as many abled bodies as can handle a shovel into one of those diesel trailers. We need to start digging," Bean added, ignoring their inquiries.

"Digging," Josh asked.

"I think I know what your idea is. There's another wagon in the bunker," Bean said. "But someone," his eyes fell on Cadence. "Buried the door from the cemetery with an explosion, so we have to dig it out. It should help confuse the situation."

"Are you in here," Josh asked tapping his own temple.

Of course he's not in here, Neon's words seemed to migraine into Josh's head.

"No," Bean said. "I just have experience trying to outthink you."

"Then it's predictable," Josh said. "We need a new plan."

"No," Bean replied. "It's a good plan. I said I have experience outthinking you. The rogue's never had to. He's had the answers given to him—*and*, I learned to keep him out of my head, so he never learned it from me himself."

"You're sure," Josh asked.

"I know when prying eyes are in my mind," Bean said. "They haven't been there in years. So let's just dig out your wagon."

"And we could arm some of those people with weapons from the bunker," Cadence added. "Could be a nice reinforcement army the rogue won't see."

"We should send Michael and the others who used to belong to Jasper to help with that since they've got this tunnel digging thing down," Josh said.

"Yes, good," Bean replied. "But don't expect supernatural support from them. Jasper promised them their freedom, and they might be tired after all that digging. However, get them started on it, and I'll join later. The work will go faster that way. Oh, and our identities stay here. Don't tell Jasper's old wolves."

Josh was silent a moment longer, before, "I need something else out of you, then. Do you think you can create a diversion for me while you're at it," Josh asked. "Something to keep the rogue busy so he's too preoccupied to anticipate us as you just did?"

"Such as?"

"Can you attack his mind enough to stun him?"

"You want me to get into his head," Bean asked. "Natalie almost brought my barrier down earlier, and you want me to risk that again?"

"If there's ever a need for it. You're best suited," Josh said. "You know the rogue's mind. Can you do it?"

"I won't risk my mind or our agenda to that," Bean said. "But I believe I can do something else to catch him off guard and make him feel vulnerable—and if there's anything that distracts, its vulnerability. I'll need Natalie's help though."

"Take her with you," Josh said. "But tell her only what she needs. Don't let her give anything away neither. You'll need an earpiece too."

"Don't forget your own, then," Bean replied quickly.

"Do you need anything else," Josh asked.

"A rubber raft," Lisa said.

"Oh, yes," Bean said. "A rubber raft will make things move faster on my—our end."

"How is that," Josh asked.

"Do you want your diversion or not," Bean replied.

"There might be something in the truck," Bricktain said. "We did have tents and sleeping bags. Maybe there's something else outdoorsy in there."

"All right," Josh relented. "See if there's a rubber raft."

"If we're doing this, we have to leave soon," Bean said. "Sun will be coming soon for Natalie. We have the Hummers. One should get us to Shale."

"After we replace the tires, of course," Lisa said.

Josh acknowledged and then instructed Bricktain to order that a vehicle be prepared for Bean and his crew.

Lisa, Winter and Acotactac followed the biker out of the room. They were soon out of the house and on their way to create Josh's diversion.

Bricktain cupped his ear.

"Thomas says, Natalie made contact with the rogue and we have a deal," Bricktain said, then paused a moment to listen to whatever his earpiece was relaying to him. "I'll tell him," Bricktain said to himself. He looked to Josh, "You should know, Sam's dead."

"What," Josh asked, with a simple confused twist of his brow.

"Don't know. He just dropped while Natalie was in his head."

Josh acknowledged the bad news. "Put his body with the hunters. He didn't betray us. And inform Natalie to go with the biker and do what he asks."

"Done," Bricktain replied and began to relay the order.

"Also, ask Thomas to bring that elemental woman back in here with him," Josh added.

Bricktain relayed both orders.

Josh turned to Thug. "You don't have much time," he said. "Get Jasper's wolves and any willing civilians to the bunker's vehicle access tunnel, and get them digging."

"On it," Thug acknowledged.

"While you're at it load up Aggon's chariot."

"Aggon's chariot?"

"Load up Aggon's chariot and get back to your café," Josh said ignoring his godfather's question. "Load up that carriage that's in your garage and take both back to the cemetery. Let's see if giving him a few choices slows down his plan."

"You wanna play a shell game," Thug said cautiously.

"Should stir some confusion, and give us some much needed control over the rogue right now," Josh said.

"What about the Bullet," Thug asked. "You need her and a driver."

"Aggon can drive for now," Josh said. "The doorman can help him."

"I drive," Aggon cried.

"He can't even hold the wheel," Thug said.

"He'll be fine," Josh reassured.

Bricktain objected, again to no avail. Thug quickly exited after realizing any of his own disagreements would only eat up valuable time to execute Josh's plan.

Thomas returned to the living room. The elemental queen walked ahead of him in her untwisted and elegant form.

"You could have helped us at any time," Josh asked. "Why did you wait?"

"Can you free us," she asked in return.

"I believe I can," Josh answered.

"Then I believe you," the elemental replied.

"I don't buy it," Josh said.

"I told you. You have humanity. You have loyalty, and you can survive."

"You wolves are always hiding something," Josh replied coldly.

"Deception is dishonorable," she said. "I hide nothing. I told you I wanted the vampire. I promised my power for his, and you remained loyal to your ally. I expect we can show you can do the same for us. You also endangered yourself to save the life of Sam, and you survived the rogue's first attack. That means you are a reliable warrior to finally stand with. No human has done what you have."

"You have an odd way of testing me," Josh said.

"I don't trust lightly," she replied.

"And we're supposed to," Bricktain blurted.

"I do not give my loyalty lightly either," the elemental queen replied. "Our only chance of survival has always been to hide or to stand with the rogue. We lost our fight with him, and learned there are worse things than broken tongues for turning on him."

"You want my trust," Bricktain asked. "Die."

"Very well," the elemental queen lowered herself to her knees and bent forward. "If this is what shows my loyalty, take my head. Free my slaves in death. Your justice will be more merciful than the rogue's."

Josh looked to Thomas to ask his counsel.

"They are dangerous," Thomas said. "But I have never known them to be dishonorable." He was silent a moment while he was clearly in thought. "I believe this will be a most useful alliance." His diamond blade drew out towards the elemental. "However, I will find more comfort in hearing her say the words."

"I pledge our loyalty to the paladin if he agrees to honor us with the same devotion as he exercises towards all of you. If that means sustaining his allies beyond our capacity, we will do it."

Bricktain started to complain.

"I have your word on that," Josh asked.

"You doubt my word," the queen asked tilting her head to look upon him with her real eyes once more.

"I've known too many wolves," Josh said. "My own relation, in fact."

"I can respect that." She bowed before him again and held up her hands. "You have my word and my hands. We elementals are nothing without our means to feel the wind. You will have my hands if I break this promise, and my army is instructed to ensure you get them. My army will fight alongside you. Or you can still take my head."

The room fell silent, and all eyes fell upon either Josh or the vulnerable queen.

"I've entertained worse ideas," Josh said. "Stop bowing."

She stood, almost surprised.

"Your kind's been enslaved long enough," Josh said. "How big is your army?"

"In the vicinity, a little less than four thousand," she replied. "Not nearly as much as what the rogue's put at your gates and much less than what he has yet to reveal, but we are the rarer breed."

"That's not so helpful when she turns," Cadence said. "Then we'll have one general and four thousand more humans to protect."

"Not hers," Thomas said. "Hers are legendary."

"You don't control elements like we do without spending time contemplating the spirits that drive us mad," the queen said.

"You can control when you change," Josh observed.

The queen nodded. "I am at peace with the spirits that conflict me. It's what helps me hear the elements. It's also why he cannot control us."

"So you can you block your mind," Josh asked.

"No."

"So he already knows about our alliance."

"No," she said. "He withdrew after your guardian communicated with him. He knows we are in close proximity to you and that you are resourceful. He won't allow you to use use to enter is head, so he has withdrawn as before. He does not want you knowing his mind any more than you want him knowing yours. He could change his mind at any time, though."

"Then please wait outside for further instruction and be ready to act on a moment's notice without question," Josh said. "Forgive us, but what you know, he knows."

"And you too."

"Not any more," Josh replied.

A smile slowly drew across her face. "I can accept that," she said. "Don't let me down." She excused herself so the others could continue planning.

Josh turned to Thomas next. "Take a small group of hunters and one of the diesel tractors. See if you can find us a fuel tanker or two and park them somewhere that shouldn't raise too many questions or interest. If you can't find a full tanker, rob a gas station."

"What kind of attack are you planning," Thomas asked.

"The kind that goes boom," Josh replied. "This time, he turned his attention to Bricktain. "Instruct the remaining hunters to take whatever vehicles they can and direct them to the cemetery."

"You're leaving the civilians unprotected," Bricktain asked.

"Give them whatever armaments we can," Josh replied. "And hide them in Banks's tunnel."

"Josh, that's a death warrant," Cadence submitted.

"Well, unless they want to chance going back to a farm, it's either that or let them fight. Which one do you think they'll choose to do? Besides, I can't think about them when I have a future to protect," Josh explained. "Our priority now is to get an army to Oliver so the rogue can't plant any rotten Easter eggs for us in the cemetery. He can't stand to the rogue on his own. Either the civilians fight, or they hide. That's the choice."

"Actually," Cadence interrupted. "Oliver has an army."

"How," Josh asked.

"We found one in the bunker," Cadence explained.

"You didn't," Thomas said, his tone suddenly not the confidence that he had previously maintained. "There's only one creature in that entire bunker with an army. You let What loose?"

"We had to," Cadence replied. "He's the reason we escaped."

"Explain," Josh requested.

"What did you promise him," Thomas asked.

"Wolves," Cadence said.

"And you gave him a body."

"Explain," Josh requested again.

"What is a creature unlike any," Thomas explained. "He preys upon the afflicted and barters his services. If you can't pay, he takes who is most precious to you. He has been known by many names, the most popular is the pied piper. He is a twisted soul who has learned how to trap the innocent. Children for the most part. Any child you have, any child you know." His eyes suddenly snapped to Neon.

"That's how they found you, isn't it," he cried. "He told them!"

Neon's expressions failed to give anything away.

"But if he gets the wolves, he'll be paid," Josh said. "So what's the problem?"

"He doesn't want the wolves," Thomas explained. "He wants their lives. What will he be paid with if we fail to deliver? Especially, when I have the feeling you plan on using those wolves to power the hearse to raise the dead yourself."

"Many are going to die any way," Josh said finding his eyes locked once again on Amber's body. "Why not take advantage of that?"

"This thing is known for taking entire cities of children when it doesn't get paid," Thomas said.

"So what do we do about it," Josh asked.

"The village who captured him did so at great loss and cunning," Thomas explained. "We were entrusted with ensuring What never regained power. It was a miracle he was ever caught in the first place."

"How is he an army," Bricktain asked.

"He has children," Cadence said. "They fight for him."

"But they won't kill," Thomas said. "They are innocent. They can guard. They can mislead, or create illusion, but they can't kill, and he won't direct them to or else he loses power over them. They must remain innocent. If they shed blood, his power is lost, and he won't risk that."

"Even if he loses them, he is a dangerous foe in his own," Cadence replied. "He can consume a head and take control of a person's body."

"That's not possible," Bricktain said.

"I've seen it," Cadence replied.

"I have selected my opponent," Neon said.

Give me the pied piper, she whispered into Josh's head.

It's too dangerous, Josh replied. *For both of us.*

It should be fun. You should trust me too.

'Neon will take care of this pied piper," Josh said against his better judgment.

"Her," Bricktain cried. "Really?"

"You heard Thug," Josh continued. "She can hold her own."

"I have chosen my style of fighting," Neon said, taking up a rechargeable hand-held vacuum from a nearby outlet.

"That's not funny on so many levels," Cadence replied.

What are you doing, Josh asked.

Not all weapons are steel, Neon replied.

"That's the plan," Josh yelled. "We have to trust each other. You trust me, and I have no choice but to trust her."

"And if she fails," Thomas asked.

"Yeah, what if her vacuum needs a bag replacement or something," Bricktain mocked.

Neon cracked open the small vacuum and poured out dust and hair where she stood.

"It's raining," she sang.

"Then we deal with What after we deal with the rogue," Josh replied. "Until then, let's get to work."

Bricktain cupped his ear once more.

"Repeat that," Bricktain said, listened for a bit. "The doorman says there's no sign of any dogs now."

"Let's go kill us a rogue," Josh said.

As Thomas was turning to do what he had been asked to do, Josh had one last request for him. "Would you ask Oliver to do something before I get there?"

"What's that," Thomas asked.

"Dig up a grave."

32 ~ "Oh, Burn!!!"

The clean-cut gangster suddenly grasped at the hole in his throat and fell as others before him.

The generals moved from before the SWAT truck. Josh had waited longer than he wished. He needed to revisit his plan a few more times, but several of his belligerent friends forced him to sleep while he waited for others to do their parts. They reminded him that Josh's work couldn't happen until all else was done. Now, Josh sat in the SWAT driver's seat and carefully examined the entrance to the graveyard before him.

The moon was full, bright. Josh's time was now.

The golden, lanky bodies of the generals obeyed the rogue's orders and removed themselves from Josh's path. The police, however, were a little less uneducated in the ways of the paladin. They also did not have the rogue's link to receive his orders. Perhaps they were dumb. Maybe they thought they were doing the rogue's will, or possibly Chandler was ordering it himself.

"Five," Josh's voice announced through the vehicle PA system.

While the generals huddled together in groups out of the way of the cemetery entrance, the police took ground behind their blockade of vehicles between it and Josh's SWAT truck. The officers behind the blockade held rifles and various weapons with their aim wholly on the paladin who sat in the driver's seat.

"See him yet," Cadence asked.

"Not yet," Josh replied. He took in a deep breath before speaking again.

"Four," the PA cried from the grill and sides of the vehicle.

The officers made no effort to move.

"I can give a warning shot," Cadence said from the back of the truck where she, Neon and a third individual dressed in full SWAT gear now sat.

"Three," Josh continued. He searched for what he deemed to be the weakest spot in the blockade, but even if he made it through the barrier, he wondered how much speed would be left in the armored wagon to take out the cemetery entrance gates as well.

Still, the generals held their ground out of Josh's path. At least they knew how to honor agreements. Unless, of course the rogue was fishing for Josh's strategic capacity and was willing to let the counterfeit police department die. Was this rogue seeking amusement?

"Give them a chance first," Bricktain's voice requested into Josh's ear.

"Under authority of duly appointed Sheriff Bricktain Morris and the mayor of Plattsville, I am hereby ordered to give you a chance first," Josh said, to humor his friend. "Stand down."

Nothing.

"Let me rephrase that," Josh said apologetically. "I have full authority of the local government to run you over, and I fully intend to. Now move!"

A bullhorn appeared over one of the faces behind the vehicles. Finally, it was the familiar face Josh was hoping to see.

"Found him," Josh said towards those in the back of the truck.

"Took him long enough," Cadence complained.

"Maybe he couldn't find his bullhorn," Bricktain said.

"This is Captain Chandler of the P.C.P.D.," Chandler's voice blared back. "We do not recognize your authority and have received no such order from our mayor. We will gun you down if you do not surrender yourselves immediately. You have ten seconds to comply."

"But we're already on two," Josh resumed his countdown through his PA system. "So, two!"

Cadence drew her Uzis and kicked the back of the SWAT truck open. "Retrieve that captain," she instructed the hunter in full riot gear. "We'll cover you."

"One," Josh finished.

The hunter in SWAT gear ducked out of the truck and charged quickly towards the police vehicles. A rain of gunfire blared down upon him as he ran straight into the heart of the police force. He wrangled one officer; disarmed another; confused several more; and was soon dragging Chandler back towards the truck.

"Take him down," one of the barricade officers ordered.

Cadence appeared from behind the vehicle. Her Uzis exploded with regular bullets that wouldn't be more than annoyance to a wolf, but would surely destroy a human being.

Smoke canisters bounced across the ground, and their sudden trails quickly masked Chandler's and his assailant's escape. The hunters returned to the vehicle, and the large man in SWAT gear tore off his helmet.

"You could have warned me," Nick shouted.

"No. We couldn't," Josh replied.

"What did you do that for," Chandler asked, finding SWAT gear shoved into his hands. "You blew my cover. I had a plan."

"He knows you're with me," Josh replied. "He's toying with you."

When Chandler questioned how he knew, Josh explained that they didn't have that kind of time.

"Your family's safe," Cadence said. She'd neglected to tell him they hadn't actually retrieved it, because a coin toss had come up tails. Besides, his family was probably safer anywhere than here right now.

Josh took up the public address mouthpiece again. "When the smoke clears, you will be out of the way or I will move you."

Gunshots blared again. The passengers of the SWAT wagon ducked down.

"We're not getting hit," Cadence observed. The group returned to waiting for the smoke to dissipate.

The vehicles no longer blocked the gates. One had plunged into the middle of one group of generals. The other was on its side. One lay inside Oliver's cemetery. One was speared on the top of the fence line. Another was being dragged just inside the gates by that bulking giant Oliver. The old, frail frame of Jasper now stood before the entrance. He sheathed his sword into his cane and cleverly retreated back into the cemetery over the pile of corpses, which he and Oliver had just created. Those who had been spared fled the scene.

Still, the generals perched on either side of the gates made no attack.

Josh took up the p.a. transmitter once again. "Told ya," Josh said. He steered the vehicle into the cemetery.

"They're following us," Nick said, as he stared out beyond the window within one of the backdoors.

"Hey," Cadence suddenly burst, smacking Nick's shoulder. "This is kind of like that time you got your butt kicked by that poodle in the back of Josh's car and you were screaming like a baby."

"That's not funny," Nick snapped.

"Remember that, Josh," Cadence continued to egg through her own laughter. "And he was all 'Drive! Drive!'"

"I remember saving your life when that guardian came in through the roof," Nick growled.

"I remember that too," Cadence said suddenly sober. "I remember he also kicked your butt," Cadence bust up again. "Look, here's you, 'Get off of her!'"

This time Josh started laughing. "No," he corrected. "It was 'leave her alone.'"

"That's right. 'Leave her alone.'" Cadence's laugh seemed to shift gear into something more maniacal.

Josh joined her and wiped his eye with his gloved fingers.

"What is wrong with you people," Chandler asked.

"Thank you," Nick complained. "It's not funny."

"Don't worry, we still love you," Cadence said, then quickly stole a kiss, which Nick would have been stupid to complain about, so he didn't.

"Poodle," Cadence suddenly screamed.

Nick dropped to the floor and punched one of the back doors.

Cadence laughed even harder now.

"All right," Josh said, sober now. "Jokes don't bring Amber back. It's time."

Josh took up the police radio.

"Check in," Josh said.

"What are we supposed to say," Bricktain asked into Josh's ear.

"Baby and the trigger are ready," the doorman's voice announced.

"Dracula ready," Thomas followed.

"We've cleared up the obstacles, finally," Thug's voice said a little exhausted. "But we're rolling. Should be there in ten to fifteen."

"They're not ready," Cadence asked. "What do we do without the hearse?"

"Stall," Josh replied.

Oliver and Jasper led the SWAT vehicle deep into the cemetery, almost to the hidden entrance to the underground bunker.

The rogue leaned against a rounded headstone and faced Oliver and Jasper, who stood a little less alert than Josh knew he probably really was. Loraine stood near the rogue. Genre, perched at each side of the rogue and Loraine, wailed at the blinding SWAT lights.

Josh stepped down from the truck and approached the rogue, making note that three other groupings of generals filled various places throughout the cemetery. He joined Oliver and Jasper then seated himself atop a square headstone to face across an aisle of burial plots towards the rogue. He chose this gravestone because it was something he could roll over and use as a shield should he be attacked.

"How are you still alive," Loraine asked, as though her question could possibly pass for something polite.

Josh said nothing. His eyes set upon the rogue, who simply smiled.

"You've learned to close your mind, too," Loraine continued. "It was so small at first that the master didn't see it happening, but you're mind is hidden now, isn't it. How?

That's right. The rogue would wonder about that part. Still, Josh said nothing and pretended to enjoy his silent conversation with his nemesis. He appeared much younger than Josh expected for some reason. He carried no weapon. He presented no claws. His power must indeed be great to keep so many generals under control and carry no weapon. Even Jasper couldn't do that. Yet, how was Jasper not changed? He knew Jasper had no control over his form at the moon. He was there the night he had changed and nearly killed his friends. Had he become stronger? If they both survived this, Josh would ask him.

Loraine continued to babble on about something to do with Josh's lack of appreciation for the situation.

Josh wondered if the rogue could actually talk. Did he talk? Or did he already know what the conversation would be? Did he simply sit and predict every sentence and therefore get bored with the conversation before he had it? Isn't that something an old being might do? Get tired of conversation? Could Josh push his buttons and get him to speak?

The rogue seemed to smile even more.

What could Josh learn from someone whose actions didn't betray himself? Josh smiled back. The rogue snickered.

So, he thought Josh was beneath him? Not allowed to smile?

You might be onto something there, Neon said, nearly startling Josh from his thought.

We need to talk about your timing, Josh replied, certain that the rogue had seen the startle within him.

Just think about it, Neon urged. *He probably does think he's above you.*

He probably did. Could Josh use that? Josh looked casually to Jasper who seemed sincere to follow Josh's lead. What would Jasper say in Josh's shoes? That old man always had some zingers that got under Josh's skin. Josh had even made mistakes when he was foolish enough to act rashly following those comments. Would the rogue make mistakes too? Josh returned his gaze to the rogue, who resumed smiling. The paladin almost laughed as he realized he was wondering what Jasper would do. Josh couldn't be predictable tonight, and he didn't have a lot of leniency to gamble upon mental warfare that might not work.

What did an elite being take pride in? His accomplishments? Not likely too many living beings could outdo this monster in life experience. Money? Would an "I'm-richer-than-you" comment get his goad? He was about to destroy the world, what use would riches have there?

How about power? How do you mock that?

His clothes.

Again, bad timing. But Neon was right. He was dressed rather well. Someone who took this much pride in their clothing line must fancy themselves above reproach in taste. The suit? No, pomp is in the shoe, not the armor.

"Nice shoes," Josh said.

The rogue nodded.

"Madrigals, right," Josh asked. "I think I have a pair of those in the back of my closet. I got 'em at a yard sale when I started school I think. Cost me fifty cents. Everyone has them now. How much were those?"

The rogue's smile diminished slightly.

"Red, huh," Josh jabbed, and hoped it sounded like a jab. "I guess if you like that color."

The smile all but disappeared.

Mention their bloodspot, Neon suggested.

What bloodspot, Josh asked.

On his left toe.

Josh still didn't see it, but what the heck. Trust her.

"Uh-oh," Josh said. "Looks like in all your carnage, you dribbled."

The rogue's eyebrow raised.

"If you'd like," Josh said. "I can show you how to get rid of that bloodstain there on your toe. Oh well, not everyone's fit for fine shoes."

The rogue's smile returned. Did Josh make a mistake? Did he lose his lead?

The rogue leaned forward, and, in a brief moment, Josh wondered if he could tear the monster's head off right then. Josh remembered how easily the master had toyed with Thomas, so he doubted it, nor thought he should try finding out.

The rogue untied his shoes, removed them and set them aside along with his black socks.

So that's how you one-up someone who owns what you own. Toss it away like it's junk. Still, Josh felt he could do better.

"You sure you want to do that," Josh asked. "There's a lot of dogs out here."

The smile began to fade once more.

"You don't know what you might step in," Josh continued.

An amused smirk remained.

"How's your little black dog, by the way," Josh added.

The smile now fully faded.

Genre bellowed, and The Right Arm leapt for Josh, ready to break the paladin. He bore down and prepared to backhand.

"I will destroy it," Josh said, hoping his flinching appreared smaller than it felt.

The Right Arm huffed in Josh's face.

"Try me," Josh spat. He flexed a sword towards Genre's face. "Get back in your run."

The Right Arm retreated, and the rogue applauded.

"Where do you find these rookies," Josh asked.

The rogue smiled again.

I don't think that one worked, Neon said.

"If you're going to bluff, you should at least be good at it," called the familiar voice of Bogi. His small Persian cat-like body walked its way to the rogue and leaned forward on his cane, in what might have been an intimidating position if he had been taller. "Out of respect to my master and your blood, I implore you to think about whose side you're on."

This time Josh said nothing. He had too much he wanted to say to the Persian-cat-looking traitor, about Bogi, about his lies, about Josh's mother's lies. So he said nothing.

"Think, Josh," Bogi said. "You can't beat this army. The Taichomée lie out there as back up."

"Your guardians," Josh asked. "I'm worried about your guardians?"

"Generals, Josh," Bogi replied. "My generals. The only generals created by another general and only I have learned how to do it."

Josh saw it. Took him long enough. Even Jasper would be proud of this one. Josh cupped his hand over his left eye and removed it, then repeated the process.

Bogi's teeth flashed.

"I can't quite put my hand on it, Bogi," Josh said. "But something just doesn't quite look right about you."

"Don't push me," Bogi threatened.

"Do me a favor and say 'Aarrr' just once."

Neon laughed in Josh's head.

"If you squint just right you sort of actually do look like a," Josh dropped his hand. "No. I lied. You still look like a cat."

Bogi screeched.

Josh unholstered one of his small, steel crossbows. He had to test the waters. How dangerous was Bogi? The rogue was no fool, but maybe Bogi was.

Bogi dropped his cane. "You threaten me?"

"No," Josh replied. "I'm just done taking advice from the butler."

Bogi's face swelled, and long incisors protruded out of one side of his head. "I would watch your words."

"I'd like to, but you got that big cat-tooth thing sticking out your head, and it's distracting," Josh said. He laughed at his own joke, then slowly straightened up to stare down on Bogi. "I'm going to rip your head off and use it to bring back my wife, you feline son of a—

Bogi leapt for Josh, fully changing before everyone's eyes into the ancient sabretooth form that he was born into. Josh's blades stabbed forth from his arms, and he leapt.

33 ~ Striking the Deal

The woman called for help, unable to run, pulled the knife from her leg and forced herself to a position ready to brawl with the attacking dog.

Too many people talk about how time stands still whenever they are faced with devastating actions. People on trains that derail, or on planes that hit a nasty bit of turbulence, often talk about how the event seemed to last forever. I once heard of a man who had to perform open-heart surgery on himself in the middle of a white squall—long story. To hear him tell the story, you'd think he was playing golf and just let the storm play through.

One would be inclined to think that the entire world must know when these moments come because it slows down for each individual.

Once upon a time, perhaps I might have felt the same way, but as a historian—and yes, I choose the proper hard sound to say *historian.* Deal with it. The fact that Soleil and his entire culture can find the H in the word *herb*, but not in the word *istory,* is absolutely orrendous.

It's a joke. Deal with that too. Geez! Too many pompous Brits out there.

Where was I?

Ah!

Yes. As a HHHistorian, H-H-H-Historian, HHHHHis HHHHHH-HHHHistorian (I warned you to deal with it)—as historian, I can't remember if I've ever felt that way about time standing still. But I am a bit unique in that I see things differently.

I do know, however, that time does not slow down for a paladin being charged by a werewolf-ized sabretooth cat. In fact, Josh found his adversary moved rather quickly. For some reason, which I'm sure you've figured out by now, Josh too moved rather quickly, leaping behind the large square headstone and recoiling with such speed that he hardly noticed the surprise on even Jasper's face.

Bogi, naturally had anticipated that Josh would have had slow reaction time, but did not calculate on what you and I both know, that the rogue had infected Josh with a cocktail of blood and with it came a few side effects, such as a residual speed and strength. Perhaps the effects would wane in time, but lingered for now. As Bogi calculated his projection to maul our hero, he did not take into consideration just how hard he would strike the giant piece of granite behind a much faster target than he had predicted. So much for unrealized variables.

Bogi smashed into the headstone that had, a moment ago, been behind Josh: first with his knuckles and then with his head. His horns did little to prevent the direct contact to his skull.

Josh waited behind the slab of rock for a reprise, something in the form of Bogi's head appearing over the top of the unbroken tombstone so Josh could take a quick stab. It would be a futile attack, but it would have connected nonetheless.

Still, no head arose. In fact, nothing arose: no sound, no attack, no Bogi.

The rogue stood still, his face motionless. He snickered, then rolled his eyes and applauded Josh.

Suddenly Oliver burst out laughing, long explosions of entertainment broke his lung capacity. "That better than what I imagine doggy say."

No one else made a sound, perhaps due to the tension of remaining intent upon the rogue and his party. Josh, however stole a quick glance and discovered the sabretooth monster face down and unmoving.

"Are you kidding me," Josh asked. He couldn't stop laughing along with Oliver and Jasper.

"Not one of your side's finer moments," Josh said to the rogue, who was currently drawing a handkerchief from his pocket and lightly blotting the corner of an eye.

"What," Bricktain asked through the earpiece. "What happened?"

Josh tried to say, but he kept laughing too hard. "I'll tell you later."

Eventually Bogi groaned. His eyes popped open and tried to focus on Josh.

"Did that depth perception throw you off," Josh asked.

Bogi wobbled to his feet.

"You're right," Josh said. He circled the recovering Bogi, who now stood on all fours, shaking. "You are no cat, but I'll bet you wish you were right now."

Josh aimed his crossbow, the purple sheen lightly glistened, even now, under the cemetery lamps. It was kind of pretty, Josh thought. Bogi's eyes narrowed on the paladin, and he made his move, but all of his weight fell limp right then. A three-piece dart leapt from Josh's crossbow, buried into Bogi's head and never exited out the back of his thick skull.

"We trusted you," Josh said and began reloading his crossbow. He turned back to the rogue. "I presume, you respect my right to have earned this honor."

The rogue bowed slightly.

"Very impressive," Loraine said.

"I am of ancient blood," Josh replied sternly. "Don't presume righteousness over me, you traitorous cow!"

Just now, a set of lights appeared through the gates of the cemetery. A familiar diesel drew itself into the graveyard and carelessly maneuvered down the roads and over tombstones that didn't have the sense to present the concept of "wide turn."

"Lots of work there," Oliver said as he watched several headstones topple under the weight of the tractor and trailer. "Dogs is so bad."

"Show him where to park, Oliver," Josh said.

Oliver grunted and marched his way towards the diesel like a hiker letting his trusty walking stick lead the way. He yelled directions of how to back in the truck.

"Don't think we haven't taken precautions," Josh now spoke to the rogue noticing his refined enemy and Genre's renewed interest in Josh. "We're not stupid."

Now, to some degree, Josh was bluffing, but the rogue wouldn't have known that. The contents of the diesel had yet to be revealed.

"The truck has arrived," Josh said. "You're up, Bean."

"On it," Bean's voice returned.

* * *

Kneeling inside Oliver's studio of tombstones and untouched slabs of rock, was Bean facing an anxious Natalie who voiced her concern that she had never done what Bean wanted of her.

"You don't need the wolf form. You've done it before," Bean said. "You've been doing it since the day Jasper trapped you."

"What do you need me to do," Natalie asked.

"Find Jasper," Bean said. "He's near. You've felt his strand before when you were in Jasper's head. Remember? Search for that. The back of your head. Jasper touched your mind there. Do you remember?"

Natalie shook her head. "How do you know that?"

"I just do, and you have to," Bean said. "However, If I tell you to look somewhere else, you do it."

"How are thing's on your end, Bean," Josh's voice came through his earpiece.

"I said I was on it," Bean replied. He turned his attention back to Natalie and muted his transmitter.

"Just like that, huh?" Natalie said.

She felt Cracey's soft human touch on her hand. "You can do it," Cracey said.

"Your memories from when you did it before will help you find the connection better. Think of how Jasper got in the first time."

Natalie thought back. She pulled up the memories.

Tink!

Shamus.

Tink!

That monkey.

Tink!

Her toes cringed in memory of that awful pain.

Then the cockroaches came to her. She could feel how their hurtful, little feet trampled over every inch of her. They ate her flesh, crawling out of that sewer in droves at the intoxication of those paints that Shamus rubbed into her fur.

Those paints!

Jasper was an artist. That's how he touched her mind. The swirling of thought like color. There! She saw something near, a streak of color, a thread. No, it was a stroke. She followed it to more color, a mix of colors, more than her mind could comprehend. A voice came to her, but not a voice, a thought. It was someone else's thought. The thought seemed to say, "no," the energy was not hers. Nevertheless, she felt it. She followed some abstract thought that she didn't understand, but it felt familiar and close.

Then it stopped. The energy flowed but something stopped it, a wall perhaps.

"What," Bean asked.

"I don't know," Natalie replied. "Something's in the way."

"Can you feel it," Bean asked.

Natalie tried. The energy was fast, feverish, a constant rotation of meditation that moved so quickly that it repelled what did not belong, like spokes on a racing, bicycle rim.

"I feel it," she said.

"Can you match its flow?"

She didn't know. She knew the energy, how to follow their trails. But manipulate it? She felt the barrier once more. Her energy needed to be faster. She tried it, just a burst really, but she felt the energy build speed. Was that it? She tried again. Held it longer.

"I think I have something," Natalie said. "It's not the same. Not as strong, but I have something.

"Can you sense anything other than Jasper there," Bean asked.

Natalie searched. "Yes," she replied.

"Okay. You're almost there," Bean said. "Stay away from the others, for now. Now, find mine, but don't lose sight of Jasper's."

"I've never done two before," Natalie said.

"You're not animalistic now," Bean explained. "That means you have more mental awareness. You're not weaker as a human. You're stronger because you're more in control."

Natalie mentally stumbled a bit; her connection on Jasper seemed to falter a moment as she tried to comprehend what Bean had just told her. She tried reaching out anyway. She felt Bean's mind. His was a little easier to find. He wanted her to find him. Both the minds of Jasper and Bean were practically right in front of her, but Bean's was stronger. The energy faster, more solid. Something about it frightened her. The movements of mental energy were like Jasper's, but they felt more dangerous.

"Don't try to duplicate my energy," Bean said. "You've learned to block out other's thoughts on your own. You started doing it to keep Jasper out of your head. And now we need you to block two more minds. Trust me, your energy is enough. Now, try to encapsulate my energy with your own."

"I can't do this," Natalie said.

"Breathe," Bean encouraged. "Think of it as one balloon trying to swallow another. Encompass my energy first and then Jasper's. But do not encapsulate any other energy. Copy our energy flow if you find it easier, but don't become like it."

"Nothing about this is easy," Natalie scowled.

She stretched her mind further, following the skins of the two streams of energy. She suddenly felt a competing strain of energy tapping at Jasper's wall. Natalie squeezed her own threads between these two forces. At first, the attacking strand attempted to connect with Natalie, but quickly recoiled when it realized it was her.

The rogue!

So the rogue was afraid of her. She continued to carve her own psychic path until she felt both Jasper's and Bean's defensive energies parallel to her own. She felt as though she were a puddle trying to match the currents of two river-ways. She stretched her puddle even more, widening it, curving it around the circumferences of Bean and Jasper's blockades, but no others. Eventually, she felt her own mental flow touch back into itself and she allowed one trail of it to encompas Bean's mind just as he had suggested, one balloon swallowing another. In a few more moments, she created a second ballon to encompas Jasper's.

"I think I have it," Natalie said slowly and softly as it was the only way she could maintain her concentration. Her own brain felt warmer than usual.

"Can you hold it," Bean asked.

"Now that I see what I'm doing, I think so," Natalie replied. "It feels solid."

"Good," Bean replied. "Now, I need you to imagine a tube that runs from my balloon to Jasper's. Create it for me, and I will use this to reach out to Jasper and break his barrier. Both of our defenses will be down. You're the only wall that we're going to have to protect us from the rogue's mind so you must hold your barrier. The second you drop this energy, the rogue will be able to see what I know. You must continue to maintain it."

"How long will that be," Natalie asked. "I'm feeling a little warm."

"All night if you need," Bean replied. "Josh is depending upon it. I'll let you know when to drop the barrier. Do you understand?"

"I think so," Natalie said. She envisioned the tube running between the minds encircled by defensive energy. "I have it."

"You're going to hear a lot of distractions tonight. You can't give in to them. Your barrier must hold. Everything depends upon this."

"I won't drop it," Natalie assured.

"Better test it first," Bean said reluctantly. "Hold that barrier no matter what."

"How?"

"Jasper's basement," He said. "He caught you. He kept you."

Natalie felt a spike of hatred. Her energy warbled.

"You have to hold it," Bean urged, then pressed the issue. "How many times did he break you? How many times did you have to heal? To be allowed to be human for only one day out of the month, only to have that day filled with torture?"

She almost lost it this time.

"You gave away the code to the bunker."

"No," Natalie replied.

"Don't speak," Bean snapped. "Hold the barrier," and he continued to prod. "Jasper was able to get into the bunker because of you. You failed to protect Josh."

Natalie screamed in her head, pushing her own energy out of its wobble. When she recovered, her energy seemed a little stronger.

"And when you finally were reunited with Josh, he was married," Bean continued.

"Stop it," Natalie begged through tears, her head hurting at every edge. It felt hotter now.

"We can't," Bean said. "He didn't even wait for you."

"Why are you doing this," she asked.

"Because if you let go, the rogue wins," Bean replied. "And you're about to get much worse."

"What could be worse," she asked.

I'm Jasper, Bean's voice burst into her brain. Natalie's skull felt as if it might implode, just as she remembered from not so long ago. She might have waivered a moment, but she pushed her hatred out of her mind. She let Josh fill it.

"That's it," Bean replied. "Whatever you're focusing on don't let go of that."

She felt Bean's energy shoot through the conduit she created until it reached Jasper's side of it.

You have to hold it, Bean's energy suggested.

She tried to hold it. She stuttered a moment, and Bean's energy withdrew quickly until she was able to reestablish her own barrier's strength.

"I know," Bean said. "And I'm sorry." *I'm trying to protect you now.*

Natalie gave no reply. She felt the tears on her face. She felt herself screaming everything and nothing at Jasper and Bean all at once.

Bean's energy surged back through Natalie's pathway and quickly attacked Jasper's barrier. She felt him drilling, matching currents and trying to peck away at any defensive thread that frayed. Jasper's energy sputtered and began to wane. Bean's energy strengthened. Natalie tried to contain it all.

And then finally she heard, *Who is this?*

I am you, Bean replied. *It's not a trick.* Then he quickly revealed his circumstances.

So what's the plan, Jasper asked.

Bean showed him. Natalie saw all as well and suddenly understood why she had to double her efforts to maintain the barrier over the three minds.

Perhaps we can lighten your load, Natalie, Bean thought.

Natalie, Jasper asked. *That guardian? You owe me a monkey!*

Can you tell the difference between my energy and yours, Jasper, Bean asked.

It's subtle, Jasper replied. *I don't think so.*

Natalie, Bean asked.

Really, she retorted, demanding all her concentration to even answer.

I'm sorry, Bean said. *I thought maybe we might be able to do this without you, but we can't. It looks like we're all in this together until I tell you drop it.*

Natalie cried. It weakened her energy, but she maintained the barrier. She physically wailed for a moment.

Stop it, Jasper screamed and silenced Natalie. *This is not the woman I remember. Pull it together or you'll kill Josh.*

That's cruel, Bean snapped.

You've forgotten where you come from, Jasper replied.

All right, Natalie replied. The pain was awful. Her strength faltered just to reply, but she didn't lose hold. Josh, her Josh, needed her now. Maybe he'd forgotten her, but he was still her Josh, and if it meant keeping two imbeciles under control long enough for this plan to work, then she'd do it. *I do this, you keep Josh alive!*

We better be fast, Jasper said. *Her brain is already burning up. I know you can feel it too.*

"It gets easier if you listen to the energy, like music," Bean said, finally standing up. Cracey will guard you." He drew his chainsaw shrug over his shoulders and let the bracing connect and strengthen his joints. He unmuted his earpiece once more. "Your distraction is armed, paladin."

"Understood," Josh replied.

Bean left Natalie hidden in Oliver's warehouse of stone and made his way outside; Natalie had only Cracey's company to protect her. Bean had wished them luck and smiled slightly as he watched Cracey try to wrap her bald head with one of Oliver's stained painters' rags. She swore as the strange turban unraveled. Bean hoped she wouldn't have to put any energy into protecting Natalie.

"Keep her safe," Bean said before he sealed the mausoleum doors behind him and unguarded. He believed a sentry here would suggest something important was inside. It was a dangerous gamble, but he could get back here quickly enough if he needed to. He felt the buttons in his strange, leather sleeves simply to ensure they were still where he remembered them being. He was ready to ignite his chainsaws at any moment now.

He quickly gained his bearings. Cadence stood perhaps two hundred feet ahead of Bean and to his left, near four large crypts. One of them seemed particularly blacker than the others. Perched atop one the lighter colored mausoleums, still and gargoyle-ish was the figure of a man with a small cage set on his head. Bean knew who this was. He wondered how much care the rogue had given to What. He couldn't imagine that the rogue hadn't become aware of him.

Likewise, he wondered how much care What had given to the shadowy figure that sat upon another nearby crypt's gargoyle to watch him. She hunkered amidst the stone creature's wings as if in a saddle. She was just as still as What, except for that moment she waved to Bean and then pretended to be a statue once more. He marveled only slightly at Neon's naiveté. As long as she did whatever she thought she was going to do without killing herself or anyone else, that's all that mattered right now. He wondered a moment if he should worry, but then he remembered her with meat cleavers.

Perhaps five hundred feet to Bean's right, in a newly prepared area of cemetery, and near a jagged border of trees and shrubs, stood the Conestoga wagon. The black carriage from Thug's basement rested next to it, and several hunters now carefully guided Aggon's sun-faced chariot out of the back of a semi trailer to join these other carts.

It would soon happen. The paladin had set his pieces.

The rogue, however, had set his own. Bean took notice of the clumps of generals posted wisely around the graveyard. Good and bad. There were fewer generals, even theough they were stronger.

Guardians may have been weaker, but they could beat the hunters on sheer numbers alone. The presence of generals meant, no other wolves to contend with.

Josh might not have seen the strategic placement of vicious attackers upon walls and fencing, but Bean did. Some gathered together, others stood individually, ready to pounce. Bean might have worried that he had more responsibility to protect Josh, if he didn't also realize that the rogue, similar to Josh, couldn't see all the strategically placed allies who were ready to attack as well.

Certainly, priorities would shift and maybe even allow Bean to worry about dealing with some of the groups, but for now, his next concern was Genre.

He'll still be annoying, Jasper announced down that long conduit that Natalie provided for both he and Bean.

The rogue stood near Josh, appearing to enjoy the paladin's revealing of the carriages. But Genre maintained strategic poise against Jasper. Surely, the rogue must have felt that of all the warriors in the graveyard, Jasper, not Oliver, would pose the biggest threat to the rogue. Josh and his human sidekick hunters would hardly present a challenge that the rogue could not handle.

This fight almost seems unfair now, Bean thought.

You're kind of full of yourself, aren't you, Jasper replied.

* * *

Thug and his small group of hunters sealed up the back of the diesel's trailer, then positioned themselves a distance away from Josh and his nearby allies.

Josh's group, which still consisted of himself, Jasper and Oliver, accompanied the rogue, Loraine and Genre to the collection of carriages.

"Are you trying to be cute," Loraine asked as the rogue approached the three wagons. "Which one is it?"

"Just being safe," Josh replied.

The rogue stepped away from the others and began to inspect the different and old vehicles. He stopped at the Conestoga and pointed as if to ask.

"Do you like that one," Josh asked. "I'll give you a fair price, but you get what you pay for."

The rogue turned an amused new gaze upon Josh, one that said he was about to stab the paladin in the back.

Genre howled. A large march of movement chattered around the graveyard among the tense generals. Josh watched the silhouette of Cadence draw her mask over her face and point two Glocks towards The Right Arm. Jasper drew his sword and seemed more intent on The Left Arm.

"Very well," Josh said. Then he erupted into a flurry of black fabric and braids with jagged edges. The Conestoga wagon erupted into a storm of timber and human remains once constructing it. The burst of attack quickly ended, and he regained his composure. "Two left. Fifty-fifty chance," Josh said, positioning himself between Aggon's chariot and the black carriage from Thug's basement. "Unless I already destroyed the correct one. It might be time to consider that issue."

The rogue's face once more etched a smile, and he slightly nodded concession.

"Good," Josh replied. "Then we have a deal. You get the carriage, and we leave each other alone."

The rogue nodded.

"You won't mind if we perform a small test to verify your product then," Loraine asked.

The rogue smiled largely as his blonde mouthpiece dropped the term *product.*

"One test," Josh said.

The rogue's smile faded.

"I'm being more than reasonable, considering all you've brought upon me," Josh said.

Something's up, Neon's thoughts whispered. *Truck at the gates.*

"The truck stays at the gates," Josh said, then poised himself to launch another attack into the black carriage from Thug's.

They've stopped at the gates. Neon said.

What do you see, Josh asked.

A group of generals are emptying the trailer, Neon explained. *I see white packages.*

Good, Josh replied. *He brought them.*

They're coming your way, Neon added. *Should I give the order yet?*

Not yet, Josh insisted.

Soon enough, a line of generals appeared, carrying in the long bodies of ancients from the museum. They were wrapped now in white fabric and bound in twine—most likely to protect them from their transportation bumps and bruises, or perhaps they were meant to be a misdirection for the paladin.

One way to find out, Neon said, as the generals migrated what Josh believed to be the ancient cadavers into the cemetery and lined the bodies upon the ground beside each other. *Now?*

Josh watched the rogue; he seemed intent on Josh's reactions. He appeared less in humor than he had tried to flaunt earlier. The other generals moved. Some groups broke up while new ones formed. Their attacks would be swift, and they were ready. They were changing strategy. Even the paladin realized that the rogue would most certainly come in with alternate battle plans. More importantly, Josh knew their next move was nearly upon him. He was losing his leverage, and the rogue was definitely not going to keep his promise.

I'm certain, Josh thought to Neon. *He's feeling as ready as we are now.*

The last body now entered the area. Only the two generals that carried its length did not set this one on the ground with the others. They waited for their orders.

The rogue bowed slightly to Josh.

"Please," Josh replied, pointing a hand to each of the remaining chariots. "Take your pick."

The rogue smirked, as if he found Josh amusing.

The generals made their way towards Josh's position between the two carts.

Here came the attack. Josh was sure of this, and he envisioned that they would draw close to him in precept of placing a body in one of the wagons, but then they'd drop their cargo and attack before he could destroy another carriage. If he tried to withdraw, he'd remove himself from the destructive radius of the wagons, allowing the surrounding generals to quickly encircle him.

Which was fine with him, and Josh's actual preferred attack.

Josh launched himself backwards, away from his comrades.

Now, he ordered, and his foes jumped in from their shadows to surround him.

34 ~ Dog Pile

The Schnauzer leapt at her. Seeing how the dog had killed by tearing out her friends' throats, she quickly clasped her hands over her own.

At Neon's nod, Jasper signaled the demon. What's melody ruptured from his flute with such surprising power and charm that it nearly cost Josh his own opening to strike at the generals who had indeed surrounded him.

The paladin performed a familiar dance, pointing, spinning, firing a weapon here, stabbing a sword there. He downed two creatures and hoped he had stirred enough injuries to put some ground between himself and the rogue. He did all without damaging either of the two carriages.

He leapt past the two fallen generals, breaking free of the crowd that surrounded him, and praying to behead at least two more.

As he leapt from one batch of master monsters, he flailed haphazardly into another. Here, What blew a powerful and surprising note. His ash children burst from the ground, surprising Josh's attackers as well as the paladin himself, despite his knowledge of this coming moment.

"Keep away," one of the children cried. The little, ash boy grabbed Josh and hurled him over the heads of the confused generals. Josh sailed through the air, hiding his face from his own flapping fabric, which now tried to swallow him.

He landed into something soft, then opened his eyes to see that the arms he felt around him belonged to another ash child, a girl with her hair in the shape of a duck sitting backwards on her head.

"Keep away," she cried, right as she tossed Josh once more up high before another entourage of generals could regroup and land an attack.

Again he fell, and, above him, he saw one of the white wrapped ancients fly over his head before it too would fall and land in an another ash child's hands. She too launched it back into the air while crying "keep away!"

"Keep away," and Josh was also flying again and moments later feeling another set of soft hands around him.

"Keep away," this young boy also shrilled in fun. Once more Josh soared over the heads of the rogue and his confused army as What's conquered and stolen children took pleasure in tossing him, as though he were a beach ball, out of the reach of his assailants.

He landed once more, but felt himself immediately released so hard into the sky that he realized instantly that something was vastly different with his launch. He was far above the ground, ready to plummet back at any second. Yet, he didn't fall.

Had he been more alert, he might have noticed that the wind he felt in his face wasn't just from his sensation of being thrown about.

The elemental queen grabbed him by the front of his black shirt. Grey clouds suddenly swallowed him, and she continued to carry Josh towards the sky and into the walls of a giant tornado that Josh hadn't even noticed had come alive. She breathed him in deeply.

"Found you," The elemental queen greeted, smelling her kiss upon him. "This would be easier without that cloak."

They spun inwards from the gray wall and towards the eye of the storm, where a clear theater of stars suddenly opened a moment and allowed Josh to take a deep breath. The queen meandered back into the wall, and Josh felt himself spiraling over the graveyard.

"This should be a better view," the elemental said.

She was correct. Josh's outlook of the battleground was much different now from his high perch. His currently blind ally still held him by his shirt, but also, now propped his weight on her foot. Below them, several groups of hunters had created their own squads and launched individual strategies to keep as many wolves as possible from the area of the cemetery where the carriages and the rogue stood. Thug and Ty both fought over a fallen human body, a skater, still alive and firing a weapon.

Cadence fired off a nonstop war of bullets at any general, occasionally the rogue, that crossed her line of sight. She was in the middle of reloading one weapon, when Josh realized that Genre had been trying radically to land a destructive attack on her, only Jasper and Bean seemed to be preventing any from landing. Like Genre, they seemed to work just as equal in harmony. When Jasper moved to attack, Bean knew exactly how to deliver a follow up blow. Genre did the same, each time attacking for Cadence, but being blocked by an evenly-matched set of Jaspers, as though they too were psychically linked, which wouldn't have surprised Josh in the least at this point.

Around the cemetery, the wrapped ancient bodies that the rogue had brought from the museum bounced, and generals rushed about to catch them. Children, all screaming "keep away," directed their ancient playthings away from the rogue and his generals.

Strangely, the rogue made little move to join the battle and seemed intent on protecting Loraine, standing guard over her rather than attacking Josh's endeavors.

"He's not interested, is he," the elemental queen said.

"He knows we can't keep this up. Besides, we lose our best bargaining chip if we harm any of his ancients," Josh said, as he watched a child in a round hat catch one of the ancient bodies mere feet away from the rogue and launching it off into a distant reach of the cemetery.

"You want to do something," Bean's voice crackled into Josh's ear. "This game's going to get old soon."

"Can you do anything with the wolves," Josh asked the elemental queen. "Suck 'em up or something?"

The queen laughed, then looked insultingly to Josh. "Do you think if we could, we'd have needed your help?"

Josh apologized.

"Wolves are too good at anchoring themselves," she said. "Trust me. Hunters will fly before wolves do."

Josh quickly pointed out two sets of generals that were not fighting. One appeared to be a group licking their wounds and preparing to rally once more into battle. The other group, larger than all that filled the cemetery, held its position beyond the lawns. Perhaps they waited as the rogue's next wave of order.

"Wise choices," the elemental queen said, quickly spotting the two groups Josh had identified.

"Let's block their lines of sight," Josh ordered. "Drop 'em."

Suddenly a large fuel tanker blew out of the folds of the giant twister. A second spit forth from higher up the black, windy wall. Both fuel tanks fell to ground and struck their marks. The first that struck erupted into a giant ball of fire that rose into the air, nearly as high as Josh's stance upon the tornado itself. The second tanker did not explode. It instantly shed its steel skin, spilling its liquid contents over the ground.

"Light it up," Josh yelled, hoping his order would be received. A rocket fired from the roof of the cemetery chapel and ignited the spill-out into a wall of flames large enough surely to hinder the view or strategy of the rogue. He cursed to himself. He had hoped they could reserve the explosive, which Dee had brought, to fire upon the wolves if both tankers had actually blown.

The rogue's face suddenly turned on Josh.

"Thanks for the bazooka, you shoeless moron," Josh yelled.

The rogue leapt to the diesel that Thug had used to transport the carriages into the graveyard. An instant later, the trailer and its tractor flew straight towards Josh, digging into the tornado and barely missing the paladin, due only to the manipulation of the elemental queen's own skill.

"Get me back down now," Josh said. "Do what you can to keep those other generals from getting in."

"My thoughts exactly," the elemental queen said, just as a large object appeared besides Josh: another diesel trailer, but this time a welcome and silver one.

Thomas's body swung out from the rear of the swaying trailer and grappled Josh's hand in time for the elemental queen to release her own grip.

"Mr. Revlon," Thomas cried, but Josh barely heard him over the wind that rushed about them as they soared hundreds of feet above the ground. Thomas continued to speak, drawing Josh into the back of the Bullet and quickly sealing up the doors.

"Do you think we woke the neighbors, Boss," Bricktain asked.

"Do you think there are any neighbors," Josh asked, and pushed his wrist through a leather handhold dangling from the ceiling of the trailer.

"He's right," Thomas added. "This entire place is a farm by now."

The trailer swayed heavily under the wind that held it up.

"We ready," the elemental's voice asked through the earpiece.

"Do it," Josh said.

"This is the dumbest idea you've ever had," Bricktain cried.

"What is this," Josh asked almost laughing at the sight of Bricktain, finally realizing he was strung up like some strange marionette before his wall of monitors.

"Something Speatsh didn't bother telling me about," Bricktain scowled.

The Silver Bullet suddenly jerked in a new direction and Aggon, who sat in the driver's seat, waved his hands over his head and cheered.

"Dis is driving," Aggon cooed.

The doorman yelled at him to stop.

The Silver Bullet dropped, and Josh suddenly found his feet off the floor and hanging as though to fall straight into the cab. From this perch, and through the windshield, he watched as they plummeted straight for the earth, where a giant cloud of black ash appeared and softened its landing. The Bullet took position about a hundred or so yards away from where the rogue and the horseless vehicles stood.

A loud applause and cheers of children erupted as Josh unlatched the backdoors to the Bullet.

"What's with the kids," Bricktain asked.

"Weird, huh," Josh said and then kicked the backdoors open.

The vehicle abruptly erupteded and shook with gunfire.

"Brick, don't shoot me," Josh cried.

Get ready, Neon suggested.

"They see you, Boss," Bricktain shouted, while his cannons began focusing its fire into a large group of generals coming straight for the paladin.

Where's the rogue, Josh mentally asked.

Can't see him, Neon replied.

"Blast it," Josh ordered.

The Bullet's horns blared, and suddenly the generals seemed attacked by an unseen force. Many fell to the earth in spastic fashion while others merely shook their heads. Others howled in pain. Several others didn't seem affected in the least and continued their approach.

The hunters used the deafening attack to their advantage as best as possible.

Josh dispatched the closest general he could. "Lay it down," Josh ordered. He sliced as much as he could through those enemies that writhed in deafening pain before him. These were the easy kills.

"Duck, Boss," Bricktain announced.

Josh did, the Bullet fired, a general's chest exploded and his lower half fell beside Josh.

"Nice," he said.

"That's right," Bricktain's voice adulated in Josh's ear and over the sounds of more cannon fire. "Everyone wants to be me."

Front of the Bullet, Neon informed.

Josh saw him. The rogue appeared on the bladed nose of the diesel and tore the deafening horns from the roof.

"Drive," Josh ordered.

Inside the Bullet, Aggon had tried to stomp on the accelerator, but to no avail. It was the doorman's foot that finally reached over and made the physical connection.

The rig sped away, and Josh ran after it, hoping his understanding of laws of physics might actually be correct, and that inertia would drop the rogue in front of him. Then again, what did Josh remember of physics?

Stop, Neon ordered.

Josh did. He might not like her in his head, but he stopped. Several yards away, so did the Bullet. It was enough.

The rogue landed with his back to Josh, not by accident, but with grace.

Josh threw an attack just as a group of ash children charged between him and the rogue. They cheered as they tossed an ancient's body off to another group of children. While the rogue appeared to look offended at the sight, Josh thrust. The rogue parried and kicked backwards into Josh's chest. Josh now stared at the stars, unable to breathe, yet he forced himself to his feet only to see the rogue speed for him and strike again.

The rogue's hand flew sideways and off its mark. His attack stopped, and his gaze suddenly turned upon Cadence, the one whose bullet blocked the rogue's offensive. For a moment he seemed conflicted on who to attack first, Josh or the one who had just shot his hand, Cadence.

Cadence it was.

The rogue flew after her, and Josh gave chase, dodging those generals that he could, harming those he couldn't. As he passed Aggon's chariot, he banged its side with the back of his hand. "What are you waiting for," he cried.

From the ground rose a ghostly hand, and up crawled the ghost of Richard.

"We're not ready yet," Richard asked.

"Get ready, then," Josh demanded.

Jump.

Josh jumped and landed with both swords ready for a general, who proceeded to dodge Josh's attacks twice, but then tumbled sideways as Petruchio squared a kick, cracking the beast's skull with one of its front hooves. The general cursed. Josh attacked from behind, Petruchio raced across the path and snapped a back kick to the other side of the general's head. The opponent dropped, Petruchio sat on him, and Thomas appeared from nowhere to finish off the trapped creature.

Josh then took advantage of Petruchio's bare back in front of him. He gripped the horse's mane and rose with it as the steed stood.

"Get me to Cadence," Josh requested, hoping Petruchio would actually take an order from him. The painted horse raced off.

Meanwhile, the rogue had already dived for Cadence several times, but Jasper himself took to fending him off. The rogue was fast, faster than Jasper even, yet Jasper still, somehow found just the right places to step and point his sword to prevent his own death. Bean, on the other hand, now attempted to fend off Genre on his own, but he wasn't nearly as efficient alone as he had been when working with Jasper. In the middle of what would otherwise have been a brilliant attack, the rogue turned instantly and swept the biker's feet from beneath him. Bean forced his chainsaws to shut down so he could attempt to stand without shearing his own bits and pieces off.

Genre stomped and suddenly screamed to his side as a large SWAT uniform raced past and drilled a punch upward into his jaw.

Nick wasn't stupid, he kept running. One potshot was all he'd get in, but it might be enough to help Bean. Genre realized the cheap shot for what it was and stomped down at Bean. Then it was Petruchio who drove his and the paladin's combined weight into The Right Arm, and, before Josh could leap down with his own attack, The Left Arm tore Petruchio's rider off. Josh fell hard onto his chest.

Crawl away!

Josh did, and fast, feeling the thud of a foot driving into the grass and dirt behind him.

In front of him, Cadence drew to her knee and blasted off a round from the shotgun locked at the side of her left thigh. She clearly wasn't ready because the simple blast threw her off balance. A silver gun snapped up to her wrist, and she fired off another shot. Then fear filled her eyes as the rogue moved in on her.

Roll now!

Josh rolled, and, for extra measure, snapped a blade out in front of him. The rogue now contended with Petruchio and Jasper, and Josh found only one creature of interest at the moment. The right half of Genre. The tall, black right arm swiped at Josh. Cadence kept her distance and her aim.

Again!

The Left Arm leapt over The Right Arm and drove his claws down for Josh's chest.

Roll.

But this time, Josh couldn't roll. The Left Arm had the paladin's foot and positioned Josh for the attack that even Neon hadn't predicted.

Josh raised his arms to protect his chest, a futile attempt to escape—but perhaps The Right Arm's assault wouldn't pierce his internals enough.

Suddenly, The Right Arm's chest burst. A silver bar broke through his ribs, and a loud, familiar clicking sang from inside it. Steel-spiked tips popped out of the side of The Right Arm's lower abdomen and through his clavicles. He gripped at the steel pole jutting from just above his sternum and appeared confused as to what had just happened to his use of gravity. He was suddenly torn off of his feet, high above Oliver, who held his stone-gripping staff like an elongated sledgehammer, and The Right Arm was its striking head. Oliver slammed The Right Arm back into the ground only inches from Josh.

Josh rolled once more, this time without Neon's encouragement. The Right Arm raised again to as high as the steel pole could reach and slammed back down into the ground.

"Bad doggy," Oliver reprimanded, slamming The Right Arm over and over, and, when The Left Arm was able to overcome his confusion himself, he flew at the giant. Oliver dodged, back handed, and smacked The Left Arm away with The Right Arm, who still clawed at his protrusions as though it would save him.

As The Left Arm charged again, Oliver plunged the opposing end of his staff through his shoulder, and the popping click announced that Oliver had indeed captured that monster as well on the opposite end of his steel rod.

The rogue, left his pursuit of Cadence and stormed after Oliver who instantly batted away one attack. Jasper and Bean, both trying not to show signs of fatigue, saw to it that the rogue was too occupied to land the next several attacks. Josh found his feet, and helped Cadence to hers as well. He didn't know how she was still alive after confronting the rogue. He was only glad that she was. She had saved him, again. Petruchio stationed himself between the rogue and the injured friends until they could attempt to regain their beings.

"Packages confirmed," the doorman's voice announced through the radio. "And you were right."

"Let's see if I can be right again," Josh said.

"Already en route," Thug's voice replied. "Just tell us when."

"Check in," Josh requested, as he watched Oliver turn about his heels, bashing away a general with the end of his staff that held The Left Arm. He fanned his staff and the impaled Genre over his head and battered down one more attacking monster, and then another, with such speed that other generals who now moved towards him were greeted only by the end of his spinning fury of steel and what appeared to be even more durable wolf flesh. The Right and Left Arms continued to attempt to pull themselves free as they, themselves, constantly took their own pounding against whatever foe Oliver threw their weight into.

The rogue continued to face Oliver and pivoted calmly on his feet as though trying to time the right step to approach his giant dance partner. Naturally, this wasn't as easy at it sounded either, because he, the rogue, was also contending with Bean and Jasper as well.

Then, a moment did open, not for the rogue, but for Oliver. The giant swung, surprising even Jasper and Bean in their own assaults. He struck the side of the rogue and sent the villain flying. It was the first successful strike upon the rogue. Bean and Jasper took a moment to realize what had just happened, but recovered well enough to race after the rogue once more.

Josh, however, hadn't lost sight of his nemesis, and had already begun chasing after him. He was only a few paces behind Bean and Jasper. The rogue's face screwed itself into a knot as he flew back on his feet. He leapt straight back for Oliver, bounding past his own pursuers. This time he danced rather meticulously on the balls and heels of his bare feet. Oliver spun his weapon, stabbed, swung, twirled some more. The rogue twisted himself along with Oliver's counter attacks as though he were one with Oliver's horrible weapon.

Then, as he finally maneuvered himself alongside Oliver, the rogue gripped the staff. He caused the grave keeper to first smack down Bean and then Jasper with such force that neither were quick to regain their footing.

Josh fell next. He wondered if Oliver had killed him, which he might have done had an ash child not appeared out of nowhere to take the brunt of the force of the attack.

Cadence was now there to help Josh regain his footing, Petruchio no longer accompanied her.

Meanwhile, the rogue and Oliver had taken to struggling head-on over the giant's staff.

"Stop pulling, dummy," Oliver shouted. "You break it!"

The rogue finally wrestled the weapon from the giant's hands, the staff clicked, and Genre immediately drew itself free of the ends of the impaling instrument. Then, as Oliver reached for his armament again, the rogue leapt up onto the giant's back and wrestled him into a choke hold, all while maintaining control of the giant's deadly weapon.

"Here lies the retard," the rogue said melodically into Oliver's ear before snapping his neck and riding the behemoth back to the floor of the desecrated cemetery. Oliver made no cry, and his killer turned towards Josh. The rogue stood atop Oliver and gripped his new staff as though proclaiming himself king of the mountain. Then he stabbed the implement into the earth and applauded his handiwork for a moment, perhaps to stir a misjudged reaction on the part of one of Oliver's allies.

Genre attacked Josh, but Bean and Jasper quickly fended his moves away.

The rogue grimaced, and Josh knew he was trying to figure out how Genre was being held at bay so effectively. Yet, for whatever reason—pride, learning, or noble laziness—the rogue had gone back to observing, analyzing perhaps. Josh knew, he'd enter the fight again at some point, and Josh wasn't eager to launch again at him just yet.

"Whatever plan you have, Bean," Josh said. "Do it now."

"We don't have everyone," Bean replied. "You want that distraction yet?"

"It won't do any good," Josh replied. "He's not even sweating yet."

"Agreed," Bean said.

Josh could hear the strain on his breath as he and Jasper had once more taken to facing Genre, whose own injuries didn't seem to hinder his ability to be killed.

Three generals, however, refused to let Josh go unnoticed. They attacked.

"Oliver is dead," Josh scowled between a dodge and a lunge. "We need some back up."

"Rogue," Thomas cried into the earpiece, but could be heard in the distance, where he currently bolstered a group of hunters attempting to keep more adversaries from encroaching upon Josh's own tasks. "I'm coming for you, Rogue!"

"Oh good," Bean responded coldly. "Abandoning your post for selfish purposes is much more beneficial to us right now!"

In that instant, Bean deflected a blow that would have severed Josh's spine had The Right Arm connected. Then the chainsaw blade of shark teeth, sheared open the chest of one of Josh's own general attackers, and Cadence sent two deadly diamonds through the new gash. One general down!

Still, the rogue simply watched.

Josh barely thought about what he was doing as he and Cadence took on the two immediate and remaining attackers. One general, alone, pushed him to his limits. The paladin now threw everything he had at two adversaries instead of three, knowing he couldn't sustain the energy for long. Quite frankly, he had no strategy, he was just a fury ball of blades, razor cloth and "don't touch me."

"We could use Natalie," Josh said.

"She's at her limits," Bean breathily replied.

"Something better happen fast," Cadence added. Her Glocks chirped, Josh's cloak sliced upwards.

The second attacking general bent sideways.

"I'm sorry," Josh said. "It's all hands on deck. We need her."

"Are you saying you want that distraction, afterall," Bean asked. "She's part of it?"

"She's already in more danger than you are," sputtered Bean.

The second general fell, and it didn't register until much later that it was one of Bricktain's shots from the Silver Bullet that had accomplished the feat.

"We need a new plan, son," Thug's voice gently crept into Josh's ear.

"We have this," Bean said. "We just have to hold on a little longer, I'm sure of it."

"Thomas," Josh asked, feeling an attack breeze past his neck, but not realizing how lucky he was that it missed striking him.

"Umm," a voice Josh couldn't place replied. "Thomas is a little busy going berserk right now. Would you care to leave a message."

Jasper shot out a quick laugh.

Josh did not laugh, and the last of his attackers finally fell.

Josh drew back to his stature and found the rogue glaring at him. He matched hate for hate with the paladin. Genre suddenly retreated from Bean and Jasper to rejoin his master.

Jasper and Bean took position on each side of Cadence rather than Josh, in case he should break out into his usual song and dance again. They all used their time to catch their breaths and prepare for another round.

Now, the rogue decided to approach casually.

"All right," Josh said. His limbs were hot and his chest heavy. He couldn't keep this pace. It was time to rest at least some, even if that meant giving the rogue something he desperately wanted. "Time to catch our breath then."

"Change the tempo, What," Jasper shouted. The demon, still standing in his same perch atop the mausoleum, quickly switched his tune, and his children stopped dancing around. Their ash fell to the earth, revealing wrapped ancient corpses strewn across the ground, one was no more than fifty feet from the rogue. It would only be a matter of time before the rogue found the ancients that had been rescued from the cave. Josh hoped not too soon, but he felt he had to give the rogue something at this point. The more of the rogue's resources spent on playing hide and seek meant fewer resources to spend on the hunters. Without the children, many of those generals were free to focus on Josh.

What blew a single powerful note, and his children turned into large spikes jutting from the ground, as though the earth itself was tearing open between the paladin and rogue. He let up on the note, and the spikes fell as dust. He blew again, and the jagged barrier erupted once more in a different formation. He repeated the note after each breath retreated him; each time a new family of spikes erected a somewhat effective barrier.

The rogue, however, had his fill of the horrible note and took aim on the piper. He hurled Oliver's staff through What's body. What's cage toppled from the mausoleum and landed near his flute, his body remained on the roof.

"Trouble for you, rogue," What cried. His cage began rolling towards the rogue. "Trouble for you. Eat you, become you. Eat you become you. Trouble becomes you. Then can have anyone What wants!" He erupted into his insane laughter.

The rogue seemed amused once more, and one of his wounded generals raced in to destroy the creature, but as the general made his attack, What's cage rolled onto its side. His jaw stretched through the bars and bit off the general's hand.

The rogue, still intrigued, continued to allow the general to deal with the matter of the head in the cage.

While the rogue turned his back on What, Neon drew her vacuum.

As Neon's actions went unnoticed, the rogue seemed more intent on reaching one of the wrapped bodies that now lay on the ground. The generals rallied to various places around the graveyard themselves, and the battle came to a near standstill.

"He's mine," Thomas said, suddenly standing alongside Josh. He drew his blades. The rogue focused a steady smirk towards Thomas.

"Oliver did what no one's ever done before," Josh said, realizing Thomas's gaze was one intent on straying from the established strategy. That gaze turned quickly on Josh with coldness and anger. Josh wondered how much hate was directed towards him more than the rogue. "He got to the rogue."

"Of course he did. He's my son," Thomas replied, and something shifted in his face that frightened Josh instantly. His weight shifted in the rogue's direction.

"You're smarter than that," Josh said and halted Thomas. "Don't screw the rest of us on this."

Thomas exhaled frustration and sheathed his sword without tearing his gaze from the taunting rogue.

"Since Thug's previous task has mostly been performed," Bricktain's voice emerged through a bit of static. "Might I suggest that he get back to the Bullet?"

Josh agreed.

The rogue and Loraine peacefully approached Josh again. Genre, though wounded, now carried an ancient's body and walked behind his master.

"Are we done with this game," Loraine asked. "How do you expect the master to keep his word, if you don't let him."

This time, Josh decided to remain silent and simply match glares with the rogue as he marched around Josh and his small group of allies in this part of the cemetery. He kept his distance as if an invisible barrier surrounded them. Josh was certain it was more of a barrier for the rogue. The sound of battle from other groups around the cemetery reminded him the rogue was not truly set on standing down for the moment, and Josh had to be mindful he was still amidst a warzone.

"No more guessing," Loraine said. "Which cart is it?"

Josh said nothing.

The rogue broke his gaze for a moment to look off towards the black carriage that sat parked beside Aggon's golden chariot some distance away. Genre began his way towards it. He didn't appear as quick in movement as before, perhaps from being wounded, or perhaps out of some profound respect for his cargo.

"It's not powered up," Josh said. "You know your test won't work, right?"

"Then we'll power it up," Loraine said. "Starting with your head."

Before the rogue could follow through on the threat, the whistles came.

The first panged out of the sky. The silver disk plunged into the dirt where the rogue had been standing, but side-stepped the surprise attack. The orbit raced back into the air as a second one shot downwards past it, acting like some strange fish hook. It wrapped around Loraine's neck and pulled her high off of the ground. The flickers from the violently burning tankers revealed the shadow of some person in the air whose fluid movements were not unlike Josh's. It appeared as though she were wearing another Wolf's Breath. The Josh-like shadow tore Loraine's dark outline into many smaller silhouettes.

Blood rained down on the cemetery, followed by Loraine's sundered limbs.

"Amber," Josh asked himself, but had no time to seek an answer as the rogue and his generals now moved. Tens of generals rallied to the rogue, bringing up his rear.

Again, Josh was staring off against the ancient.

"Guess it started with her head," Josh said and then drew his crossbows.

The rogue's lips drew tight, and then his eyes rolled white and closed at the same time. He crossed his arms over his chest and fell backwards. His generals enveloped him into their numbers. More generals rallied to and surrounded the rogue. Then they began dog-piling him.

Screams burst in the distance. Many screams, human screams, retched into the night. Josh had heard them before, but not like this, not in this unison, not this many. This must be what Hell would sound like, horror. Countless human voices, beyond the cemetery agonized, singing the song of turning into guardians and scouts.

"How," Josh asked.

"He must be exercising his full control over them," Thomas questioned rather than stated.

"Well, they are his," Jasper said.

"But the demand that control would take," Bean added.

"Might shut him down," Jasper finished.

"So if we kill him," Josh said. "The shock will kill everything under him."

"Works with generals," Jasper said. "Don't know about ancients."

"That means it's about to get even more crowded in here," Josh said. He evaluated what he knew was coming and tried to understand the growing mountain of generals that now encapsulated the rogue. It had currently reached a height of around twenty feet and continued to grow out and up as more generals came from the shadows and added their bodies to it.

"I assume they protect him because he's weak right now," Josh said. "So while he's weak, we power the hearse with everything we kill."

"Using us to kill his own to power the hearse," Thomas concurred.

"Then the more of those he's controlling that we kill, the less energy he has to exert and the more strength he has to focus on us personally," Josh suggested.

"I'll be out of ammo before we can get to him again," Cadence said.

"We'll all be too tired, to fight him," Josh added.

The screams from the distance began to howl, like waves crashing on the shores of a hundred beaches that Plattsville certainly did not have.

"What are we doing, Boss," Bricktain's voice called.

Josh answered immediately.

"Thomas, you and Petruchio have Genre," he ordered.

Thomas chose a strategy and ran off.

"That should be us," Bean objected. "We have a better chance."

"I need you to hurry your plan," Josh explained. "Whatever you've got up your sleeve, we're running out of time—and check on Natalie, would you?"

Bean and Jasper quickly disappeared off towards the mausoleum where Natalie struggled.

"Bricktain," Josh said. "No stray bullets, please."

"Right," Bricktain replied.

"And us," a voice that Josh recognized as one of the skaters asked into Josh's ear.

Josh pointed off across the cemetery towards the sea of green and red dots swarming into the field of tombstones, dots that shouldn't be out on this of all nights, eyes that should be human. "Hold your positions and keep those off of us. We're digging that rogue out."

As the sea of silvery-black guardians and their lesser powered scout cohorts flooded into the cemetery, Josh turned his attention upon the mound of generals and the rogue they hid.

35 ~ The Nutcracker

The miniature Schnauzer bit into her hands, tearing them away, mutilating one completely, and then bit at her throat.

The bombastic choir of Silver Bullet cannons sang loudest of every other sound in the graveyard. Even Bricktain cursed that he didn't think he could order the computer to reload fast enough. Bricktain urged they keep driving, but Thug suggested it wasn't safe. They wouldn't simply be plowing through wolves, they'd be running down hunters too, most of which were too inexperienced to keep up with the war machine's movements.

"Josh," Thug asked.

No answer, the paladin was too lost in thought.

Neon, Josh asked.

A little busy, thank you, she replied.

Do you need help?

I'm trying not to get eaten by this head in a cage, She said. *Go away!*

Josh further examined the pile on top of the rogue. The generals continued to crowd into one another. Their limbs interlocked each other into a tight structure, as if trying to set a world's record for the most bodies involved in a cheerleader dome.

The paladin wanted to rush the pile, but recognized that any general visible or not could move and unleash some jack-in-the-box trap from within, and the rogue was the clown.

The sounds of battle burst behind him. The cries of guardians, scouts and humans mingled the air into incoherent cursings against each other.

Josh turned at one particular grunt, that sounded a little too close for his own comfort, only to watch Nick in his SWAT gear destroy the beast with a pair of baseball bats that had several embedded axe heads. However, Cadence had already shot it down.

"Where'd you get those," Josh asked, nodding to the new bats.

"Not sure," Nick said, waving a bladed bat in the general direction of the front lines. "Over there somewhere?"

"Why haven't you turned back," Josh said.

Nick shrugged. "Too much man for him?"

"That'll be the day," Cadence said.

Josh returned to pondering how to tear the dogpile apart as safely as possible.

"Thug," Josh called, hoping he could be heard over the other noise in the headsets.

"You want me to come crack that shell, don't ya," Thug asked.

"Too much to ask?"

"Let's hope your shootist is as good as Speatsh must have thought he would be."

The Silver Bullet raced off to find a better position to help Josh. Bricktain swore from earpieces throughout the graveyard. Thug sped the diesel out a ways. The cab suddenly plunged downward, its nose digging into the earth and tossing debris before it. The massive machine suddenly stopped. The trailer swung wide, pivoting around the tractor, knocking down headstone and guardian alike that dared remain in its path. Josh counted three hunters dodge. How? Who knew any of them could be so fast? He doubted he could have reacted so readily.

Then the Bullet raced into the distance, again stopping, again swinging wide and clearing another area of ground of enemies and giving hunters room to take a fresh stance.

"Mind the hunters, please," Josh said.

"Thank you," Thug replied, with clear irritation in his voice.

As before, the bladed-nose plowed farther into the graveyard. Guardians and scouts suddenly swarmed upon it. The earth shook, and a deafening explosion erupted. The Bullet launched itself up and out of the swarm of attackers. After spinning one full barrel roll, it landed perhaps twenty-five feet from where it had first launched.

It lost little speed in the jump, but now it had claimed its path and drove its sharp nose straight for the pile of generals.

Josh joined Cadence and Nick in common sense as they watched the silver diesel rev straight towards them. The three quickly fled its path. Here, Josh caught the shadow of another hunter in the air racing high over his own footsteps. He still wasn't sure who it was, but he guessed it had to have been Amber—not his Amber, an Amber from a difficult future. He felt himself suddenly gain hope that she was still alive. When the Bullet hit the wolves and sent them flying into the air, this Amber could dispatch them as she had the rogue's blonde pet, Loraine. Josh, Cadence and Nick would deal with what remained.

That simple, huh?

You're not helping. Have you beaten that piper yet.

You wanna do this, Neon growled.

Josh readied himself as the Bullet raced forward and then saw the attack almost too late.

"Bullet, watch your right," Josh cried.

Left, Josh.

"Left," Josh corrected, but all too late.

"Geez," Bricktain said, through short breath over his fresh injection of gun blasts. "Stay out of my peripheral."

The wall of guardians rushed the side of the silver diesel. Bricktain dropped several rounds of bullets and swear words, many in fact, but the mob kept charging until it struck the silver diesel hard against the side, toppling it onto its opposite.

One side of the sharp blade dug down, lacerating dirt and lawn. A severed water line spewed a single, solid fountain perhaps fifteen feet into the air. The guardian assailants began attacking the vehicle in various ways.

White, small explosions burst from between the ground and the fallen side of the Bullet, and the percussive power of the cannons lifted the rig a small distance but then dropped back down.

"Did you really think that would work," Thug cried.

The side of the trailer fired again and rose a little more.

"Stop wasting the ammo," Thug yelled. "You'll blow us up."

The monsters began piling onto it.

"A little help," Thug calmly requested.

"Clear the Bullet," Josh yelled. For the time being, he abandoned his immediate plan to crack the rogue's shell of generals.

He ran.

"Stay with Cadence," Josh ordered when he realized Nick was following too closely at his heels.

The beasts swarmed Bricktain's chrome weapon until it was hardly visible, and still more monsters poured upon it. Meanwhile, more assailants continued to fill the cemetery. Too many slipped past those hunters that maintaining the front lines and sped for the Silver Bullet.

Even running had become difficult for Josh at this point, but he still pressed towards the quickly disappearing Silver Bullet. Too many bodies took up safe footing. Bean, was already returned from the mausoleum and to the fray, his chainsaws a flurry of hair and blood. He was in Josh's path.

"Paladin coming through," Josh announced in his earpiece. He watched Bean step back, already expecting Josh to unleash one of his deadly motions.

Gunshots burst from the topside of the trailer, as careless wolves would make the mistake of standing over various gun ports.

Josh reached the vicinity of the toppled vehicle and poised himself for another combination of moves, but his face was suddenly thrown against the underside of the trailer. He kicked backward, knowing he'd done enough to injure the fool who got to him. As he turned and launched another attack, he realized they were ready for it. He completely missed all around him, and before he could move again, he was in the air and slashed at several times by many sharp claws before he hit the ground.

They were everywhere.

"I think the paladin's down," the elemental queen cried into her earpiece.

"Then why don't you help him," Bricktain shrieked.

"Who do you think's keeping out the majority of wolves," she replied.

"Keeping out a few more might help," Josh replied.

"Oh," she said. "You're alive, then."

"Can you spare anything down here," Josh asked, once again all-a-frenzy.

A blast of wind shot across the cemetery rolling guardian and hunter alike away from the area.

"Are you out of your mind," Bean cried. "You'll kill us."

"I'm not firing bullets, here," the elemental queen said.

"Can you blow that pile of generals away for us," Josh requested, then was once more tumbling on the ground. When he finally stopped, he was on his back, then to his knees and thrusting away four guardian mouths at once. He could see two more trying to get to him as well.

Then, he felt it. The pain shot into his leg. Hot.

"I'm bit," Josh cried.

"I can't get to you," several of his allies cried in some form, one after the other. Josh continued to fight.

"Somebody get them off of me," Josh ordered.

"I don't see anyone who can," the elemental queen said. "You're all down—Oh, hold on. There's one, I'll bring him to you."

The wind suddenly picked up.

A glint of gold flashed past Josh one way, rather bounced out of the sky. Aggon cried, and the gold chariot shot back up Josh's other side. He swung back around, each sweep knocking attackers away from the paladin. Finally, it stopped beside Josh.

"Not no more friends," he cried. Josh crawled his way into the back of the chariot. "We go." The golden chariot sped into the fray, this time carrying Josh in the back.

"Do as old man did," Aggon demanded. His chariot began to circle the Bullet, tearing through bunches of guardians. Josh obeyed, throwing his cloak out to his sides and eventually in all directions, turning the chariot into the bloom of black, a deadly speeding rose. He raced past other monsters attacking his friends, he fell what he could. As he rode past Cadence, he ended a close attack that would have certainly finished her.

A sudden twister, two feet in diameter, touched down and threw guardians in all directions. Josh dodged one, another hit the side of the chariot.

"Stop that," Thomas cried.

Josh cursed under his breath.

"I heared that," Aggon said. "Dis be for orientated family rides only."

"Wind queen! Can you open the general's dog pile," Josh asked, getting back to his attacks once more.

"We can try," the elemental general said, but we're already neglecting too many guardians."

Another cyclone stretched from the sky and landed straight upon the pile of generals. It grew and drew its finger tip around various points on the heap of generals, searching for a weak spot. The funnel bent like an elephant trunk. When it had no affect, it dug into the earth, throwing debris into the generals' faces and then quickly attacked the pile again. The twister disappeared.

"No good," the elemenatal said. Then "Uh-oh, gotta go. We left a hole in our defenses, and a group of them are getting through. Not to worry. We'll seal it."

Josh acknowledged that she should continue to keep up the perimeter that allowed the hunters at the front lines to fight in various bottle necks around the cemetery.

Still, Josh attacked. He ordered Aggon to continue circling as closely as he could to the Bullet. They circled it twice more, freeing a few hunters who had come to help, only to have to free them again moments later.

The guardians continued to spill into the graveyard, called from all directions. Thousands at least.

"We should think about getting out of here," Thomas suggested.

"We can't do this again," Josh replied.

"I agree," Bean said, "But we're done. Our numbers are dwindling, I can't keep up."

"We is not done," Aggon threatened, and his chariot picked up speed, racing around the Bullet. "No more friends," he kept repeating.

Josh held onto the sides of the chariot, unable to throw any attacks and keep himself from falling out of his cart now. Aggon kept screaming until his words seemed to have no more meaning. At once, they raced away, spun quickly around and sped back towards the bullet and onslaught of countless guardians. Josh nearly fell out of the chariot. He saw, dogs and guardians alike—too many of them, even more than had attended to the junkyard. They should have been too many to drive through, yet Aggon and his determined steeds did just that, echoing their limbs and bodies against the golden walls.

The chariot suddenly leapt up and then landed square on the side of the toppled Silver Bullet.

"Dis for my cripple," Aggon regaled. Then he yelled an order to the horses in a language Josh hadn't heard Aggon speak before. "Hide in wind elemental doggies," he screeched. "Hide well!"

The horses stamped their forelegs in unison, Aggon stomped his own foot against the floor of his cart. Light grew. It emanated from beneath Josh's feet. It began to fill the area, radiating from the chariot itself, beaming from the engraved suns on each side, until Josh had to cover his eyes.

"You letted me drive," Aggon's voice said. "I don't ever forget you pallypally. Tell all hunters, cover eyes."

Could Josh's eyes have borne the radiance that had been building, he would have witnessed the power of pure daylight break from the chariot, flooding every inch of cemetery, blinding all, as the power of the sun itself. Josh issued Aggon's order, followed it in fact. Even with his eyes now shut, the light grew, warm, not like the normal sun, but something more personal, something familiar. A feeling of protection, of fondness, of love encompassed him. It powered Josh's own emotions until he felt his eyes swell. He fought to keep them closed. Somehow, he knew this was a sacrifice.

Then all was black. The light was gone, and the cries of wolves had changed.

Josh opened his eyes to an ocean of flames, where guardians once stood. Hunters, now took courage in reload of weapon and posture. However, just as many hunters did not find this privilege, for they had already fallen. Those hunters that were able take new hope quickly returned laying waste to the scouts that appeared confused at the sudden loss of guardian allies.

Josh stepped from the carriage, And stood atop the bullet's side amidst the flames fueled of guardians' remains. They crackled deeper than wood, but unlike wood.

The chariot, once gold, was now as obsidian.

"Aggon," Josh called. But no Aggon appeared.

A harsh breeze blew away flames that Josh had hardly seemed to care drew dangerously near to him.

Yet, still, more guardians continued to spill into the cemetery and replenish those numberst that had just fallen.

"Elemental queen lady," Josh said.

"You can call me Tandem," she replied. "I do have a name."

"All right, Tandem," Josh obliged to correct. "Can you do anything more to stop these things from getting in? We can't do that again."

"Means we can't help you on the perimeter," Tandem replied. "And we have our own little problems up here."

"What's going on up there," Josh asked.

"Think we're the only elementals in existence," Tandem asked. "Believe me, you don't want to know what we've kept from raining down on you."

"Can you give us anything," Josh asked.

Josh thought he heard a sigh. "I have a volunteer for you. She'll be down once she's open, but only because your girl in the air has had our backs up here too."

"Give 'em hell, Amber," Josh said mostly to himself.

Immediately, one of the burning tankers burst into a mushroom as it had done when it first exploded and a four-legged fireball shot out from it. It raced past the hunters and guardians alike, towards the front gates. A barely noticeable leap, quickly set it at the entrance drive. The fireball drew in, almost dark with only a hint of ember crackling in the distance. Even here, in this dim light and from this distance, Josh recognized the distinct shadow of a guardian within the fire itself.

Right then, a stream of flames appeared to blast out of the monster's mouth and flooded the entrance and its walls with red and orange heat. After a long eruption, it breathed the flames back over its own body, allowing itself to combust one more time. A moment later, it seemed to suck up the flames from its flesh and fur and spit fire again, ensuring that its long, exhaling scald had enough breath left to immolate itself once more.

"Sorry I can't do more," Tandem said. "Firemasters are a little rare in elementals though. Keep her safe, she's very important to me."

Josh thanked Tandem for her generosity and then moved on to his next objective. He ordered all hunters to thin what numbers they could. He climbed down from the trailer. He could have jumped it, but he figured this was an inopportune time to risk breaking a leg in pride. "Can we get the Bullet up? Or is it lost?"

"Hate to say it," Thug replied. "Think she's out of this game."

The Bullet's earth-side burst with gunfire once more, and Josh leapt out of the way as it leaned slightly his direction.

"Stop wasting the ammo," Thug yelled down the trailer to Bricktain.

"What would you like me to save it for? Rabid earthworms?" Bricktain cried. Again, cannons exploded into the earth, lifting the trailer and falling once more.

"It's not going to work, idiot," the doorman bellowed.

Again the cannons blasted, this time in different order. First the top row of cannons, then the bottom and then a continuous round of fire upon recoil. The blasting continued to fire with such force and alternating dispersion that the Bullet rose and fell back onto its wheels.

"No way," Thug complained. "No freaking way! In all my years, I've never seen anything so stupid. Josh, get him out of my truck."

"Settle down," Josh replied.

"I mean it," Thug continued.

"Uh, guys," Bricktain jumped in. "They're up to something."

"Where," Josh asked.

"I see it," Cadence said. "Other side of the Bullet. They're lining up."

Josh began to circle the back of the vehicle to get at the other side. Here, he caught a quick glance of a handful of hunters holding up against the advances of wolves at the fence-line of the graveyard. The guardians' numbers had grown again, but the rogue's army still received a well-deserved fight. Josh also felt immediately impressed with the twister of fire that had formed at the front gate. It turned down upon wolves and dogs that tried to sneak past. Some succeeded, some did not.

Farther down the fence line, two more slender twisters stood like sentinels as well. One of them suddenly turned into a tidal wave of water and washed a group of attackers off the cemetery fence. As this twister disappeared, a lone guardian ran to the broken water line spout and strangely began gathering up water into another vortex. No sooner had it built the watery weapon, than it returned to the wall with it. Josh watched one of the rogue's brave guardians try to jump through it only to fly into the air and flail back outside of the fence-line.

Just then, three more fireballs erupted from the burning tankers and they too ran off to other areas around the cemetery borders.

Josh thanked Tandem once more as he finally rounded to the other side of the diesel, ready to face whatever enemies awaited there. He was drenched now himself, from the geyser of water that rained down upon him as he continued to stand near the Silver Bullet. His feet had begun to slip against the grass, which worried him, but he still hustled to the side of the bullet to find Cadence, Nick and more guardians.

Here stood some of the creatures that had gotten through the defenses of elementals and hunters. They stood in lines, perhaps a half a dozen rows deep and twenty feet long. They marched revolutionary-style towards the silver bullet. Josh found Cadence and Nick already standing between the beasts and the trailer.

Cadence drew her automatic weapons. Nick took stance to brawl.

Yet, Josh saw what neither one of them did and before he could reveal it, the first row of guardians stopped only a few feet away.

"Get out of the way," Josh ordered. "Get out of the trailer, Brick!"

The small wisps of smoke that rose from the guardians jowls, trails that Nick should have seen first, were followed by the sounds of hacking. Josh could have tried to run for them, but he wouldn't have been fast enough. Yet, he ran towards them anyway. That's when Nick finally realized. He turned to Cadence, grabbed her about the waist and spun her around him like an ice dancer throwing his partner. He launched her towards Josh just as the choir of forced choking erupted into acidic spew. Cadence struck into Josh with such force that they both flew backwards, landing in a filthy pond created by the broken sprinkler line.

Josh climbed to his feet just as Nick began screaming. Cadence echoed the sound as she and Josh watched Nick's body armor burn. His SWAT face-shield melted. Nick dropped to roll beneath the trailer, and the second line of wolves took their turn exactly as the first line of wolves, which now smoldered from their own suicidal attack, had done.

Cadence ran for Nick and fell. Josh had kicked her feet out from beneath her and then tackled her to the ground.

"That won't help him," Josh yelled. Spitting sprinkler-line rained from his face.

"Uh. Guys," Bricktain cried. He fired off several shots towards the line of approaching dogs, but suddenly stopped. "Uh, my guns aren't working."

"I told you not to waste ammo," Thug replied.

"It's because your guns are gone on this side," Josh replied, catching glimpse of the melting wall of the Bullet, dripping with acid and rotting steel.

"Get me out of here," Bricktain pled, realizing his back wall had already begun melting away. He threw his guns into the cabinet to disengage his harness, but it didn't release.

"Someone else is going to die, right now," Josh yelled, breaking through Cadence's scream to get her to listen. "I need you to put on the mask, the whole mask."

Cadence did. She didn't want to, but she did. Josh summoned his own best to drench himself in the spray of the geyser sprinkler line.

He hoped Speatsh was telling the truth about Wolf's Breath, or this would be a short attack. He'd never practiced it before.

The second row of monsters fell from their acid attack and the third brigade overtook them, unleashing the next wave of acid at the side of the trailer.

Wolf's Breath was heavier now, which meant he had to apply more effort and strength to work it, which also meant getting tired faster. Josh started running under the added weight of water.

Whiny diamond bullets cried from behind him as he raced down the side of the chrome trailer and discovered two-thirds of it melted away. Bricktain hunkered over his metal boots and fought to release his restraints at the same time. The doorman and Thug argued nearby about why his quick release wasn't working, and both flinched as Josh leapt in through an annihilated hole in the side of the trailer. He instantly felt the laceration in his left thigh from jagged metal of a sleeping cot frame that either Thug or the doorman had thrown down to act as a shield against the acid after the trailer wall had disappeared. The cot too had also vanished. He'd worry about the injury later, but right now it took his mind off the burning bite mark lower down his other leg. Josh hurled his cloak over both himself and Bricktain. He ordered Thug and the doorman out of the vehicle, and they fled just as the next wave of acid struck.

He felt the wave end, and his cloak began to feel warm.

"Stay down," Josh demanded. He stood a moment and sliced through Bricktain's remaining tie-down straps. He returned to covering Bricktain in time for the next wave of attack.

Now that Bricktain was completely free of his safety straps, he dropped his harness and helped himself escape his boots before the next corrosive onslaught fell.

"Wait," he cried, pausing a moment as his diamond glasses flipped off of his face in the escaping commotion.

"We have to go," Josh said. "The acid's drying out the cloak. I need more water."

They fled through the back of the trailer. Then he and Bricktain ran down the opposite side of the vehicle where they stumbled across

Nick, who knelt over coughing up blood, but then Josh realized, he wasn't coughing up blood. His heart was pumping him dry through his disintegrated neck. Bricktain rushed to his side, but Nick had fallen flat before the robotic man could attempt to aid him. Nick was dead.

"We need help at the Bullet," Josh announced to anyone who could hear his wireless communication, mostly to keep himself in control of his emotion.

Josh left Bricktain cursing at Nick's side, the paladin quickly rushed back to the broken spout to wash off the venom.

Josh didn't have to tell Cadence about Nick. She saw it on the paladin's face. The two unholstered their hatred and ran back into the revolutionary-style fighting wolves. Before either could land a single blow, another figure suddenly blasted from the sky in a ball of flurry and fabric. They didn't get the best of looks at her, but she had white hair, wavy, half-way down her back. The orbits shot from both hands, cracking a moment to create the deafening sound, and, as her tactic caused the crowd of monsters to recoil their efforts, she spun and twisted her body, dispatching several guardians with her own Wolf's Breath.

Josh joined her in dispatching all he could, dodging the orbits, familiar with their sounds, and then when all but a few of the monsters had fallen, the white-haired stranger climbed away into the sky without so much as a nod to Josh, allowing him to finish them off. He completed his task and returned to the Silver Bullet, where he found Cadence screaming at her fallen comrade for being stupid until Bricktain convinced get her to redirect her hostility towards something that would help the fight, which Cadence didn't particularly take too much kindness to.

"Did we pull it off," Josh asked. He didn't have the luxury of mourning or Nick wouldn't be the last. "Did everyone get out?

"I think so," the doorman replied.

"Did we lose it," Josh asked. "Tell me we didn't lose the bullet!"

A vortex of water broke over the front of the of the Bullet.

"That should help wash off the acid," Tandem announced.

"I believe your package is ready," she added.

"Folks," Thomas's voice announced, slightly worn, perhaps frazzled. For while Josh had been sidetracked from breaking the rogue's protective shell, Thomas and Petruchio had taken on another challenge: Genre, who seemed to be healing every minute until his chest wounds were barely pink scars now. "Genre's got one of the ancients and he's making his move."

"What do you mean one," Josh asked. "He's supposed to have them all."

"He's got them all," Bean shouted. "He can't fit them all in at once, now can he?"

"Josh," Cadence said softly. "It's a good plan. Let everyone do their parts."

Josh scanned the area and eventually spotted Genre. The Left Arm hauled an ancient's body, wrapped in its white covering, over his shoulder and towards the black carriage, Thomas and Petruchio gave the right half of Genre fight. No other guardian appeared to give the vampiric duo a second thought, most likely because the rogue believed Genre capable of destroying Thomas on his own. Perhaps, the rogue found Thomas an adversary worthy of an honorable fight, unlike the other hunters. After all, Thomas was perhaps his oldest nemesis. Or maybe the guardians were just too scared to face him.

Thomas had been instructed to make it convincing. While the majority of Thomas's encounter with Genre was trading blows and blocking, Thomas's real objective was to keep Genre from introducing his cargo to the black carriage, but allowing it to collect the bodies from the museum once more.

While The Left Arm made his move towards the black carriage, The Right Arm contended with the vampire. During the encounter, blood had barely spilled. Although, Petruchio did time a flying roundhouse perfectly into the side of The Right Arm's head, stunning him enough that Thomas had to fake a fumble to keep up appearances that he was getting tired, which wasn't too far of a stretch to pretend when it happened. Perhaps this was also part of the reason The Left Arm seemed more intent on getting his corpse to the carriage rather than paying Thomas any attention.

"Don't overdo it," Josh said. "Let him have the moment."

"I don't imagine you would want to trade me places and decide whether that was humor or not," Thomas scowled

Again, Thomas had to fake yet another move, a dangerous move. He feinted right, just as The Left Arm half-heartedly slashed for Thomas's gut. The strike flew inside Thomas's coat and he played a stumble backwards, grabbing his side. He cursed, then he fled towards Petruchio, taking a moment to smack Genre's other half in pretense of fleeing from the two halves of the maniacal monster.

The Left Arm huffed after Thomas, his way of calling the fleeing vampire scum a coward. The Right Arm joined him, and both drew upon Thug's black hearse with its dark windows. The Right Arm pulled open the door and carefully set the corpse inside.

"I hope this isn't a repeat of last time," Thug said.

"It's about to hit the fan either way," Josh replied.

The carriage bounced, just a little at first. Then it swayed and rocked as if it might tip over. Something screamed from inside, moaned and screamed some more, no light, just angry noise. At once, it stopped. The Left Arm reached to the door and swung it open to examine its contents.

The Left Arm suddenly stumbled backwards, grabbing its face. A fury of gray vengeance attacked from within.

"You little bastards," Speatsh shrieked as he leapt from the black carriage, no longer a ghost, returned to human form. The hearse worked! He smashed something silver, his leg brace, against the side of The Right Arm's head. "You hairy Bobsy twins, I'ma beat your asses with your own cheeks!"

He was quick, fast enough to counter Genre on his own. The fight that Jasper and Bean had put to Genre seemed feeble, at best, compared to Speatsh's capacity. The steel brace that he had removed from his leg, and now wielded as a weapon, no longer inhibited him.

"I'll slap you to death with your own arms," Speatsh continued to yell.

Genre regrouped. One half lunged at Speatsh, but Speatsh ignored the distraction and flew at the other before it could perform a follow-up move.

Speatsh didn't even bother to draw his clawed gloves over his fingers, just punched the left half of Genre, slapped the other and pummeled his brace into whichever arm was closest to his next attack. He reached to his shoulder for Bear.

Not there.

He cussed his missing favorite weapon, then he butted his head into The Left Arm's and then used The Left Arm's skull to bash The Right Arm's face.

"That's for killing me, Tweedle Dee and Tweedle Dum," he screamed as the two halves quickly rallied to each other once again.

The Left Arm swung wildly at Speatsh, while The Right Arm dodged to Speatsh's back. Speatsh seemed to bend on rubber legs as he dodged the blow and then stood; punched The Right Arm in the throat; stabbed his fingers into the snout of The Left Arm; and kneed its jaw shut in a powerful backflip attack, launching and landing him in the same spot.

The Left Arm bellowed in Speatsh's face, and was interrupted with a sandwich punch against the sides of his head.

"No one wants to smell your poop breath, Poop Breath," Speatsh yelled. Then he quickly turned and uppercut The Right Arm who had attempted another back-stabbing attack.

"Shoryuken," Speatsh added for fun.

This half of Genre flew up and back until he landed hard on the ground. Before he could rebound, Speatsh stabbed the metal of his brace into the right half's chest. Speatsh's clawed glove appeared over his fingers now, and he quickly sawed at his opponent's right arm until he could pull it off entirely.

One disarmed! He spun back to The Left Arm who now wailed at Speatsh.

Speatsh yelled back, slapped The Left Arm with the Right's appendage and screamed again.

"Did you think I was lyin'," Speatsh asked, and he pounded the Right's arm into the Left's head over and over. "Did you think I was tryin' to be funny, you pathetic tick?"

The Left Arm bit at Speatsh and the rejuvenated Speatsh Cheatham blocked the attack by shoving The Right Arm's appendage into his jaw. In this distraction, Speatsh immediately amputated Genre's left arm as well. Speatsh gathered both arms and proceeded to beat The Left Arm in the head until the monster stumbled backwards from Speatsh's hate-driven power. Speatsh dropped both arms, reached into his fur pelts, drew his blunderbuss and fired a hole through the Left Arm's neck. A quick kick suddenly removed the head. Then Speatsh turned back to The Right Arm, who was trying to return to his feet despite having no arm to aid him. Speatsh kicked him back down and quickly destroyed the beast with another blast from his blunderbuss.

Speatsh gained his posture.

"Bashes to bashes, you two suck-its," he said, as he used one of Genre's appendages to cross himself. "May the devil neuter you every day with hammers!" For added eulogy, he kicked The Right Arm in the stomach. "Amen!"

He threw the arms to the side.

Josh ran to Speatsh, who realized none of the guardians currently had the courage to take him on.

"Where's my bear," Speatsh complained.

"He's running around here somewhere," Josh replied.

Speatsh quickly caught sight of Bear dragging a long draped body away from the black carriage. A blanket of black ash suddenly covered him and his cargo, and they all disappeared into the cemetery.

One general with a particularly bad limp tossed another body into the carriage.

"Good," Josh said. "Fill it up."

"Are you stupid, or do you just naturally take joy in giving me gas," Speatsh asked

Josh was afraid to respond.

Speatsh burst out laughing in Josh's face. "You should see the look on your face. You're still a pansy."

Josh suddenly thought of some appropriate responses.

"Relax," Speatsh complained. "It was a smart play, but I'm feeling a bit pent up," he turned his attention to a group of hunters and a batch of guardians giving each other plentiful beatings. "Let's play with some guardians."

"Actually," Josh said. "We need in there," he gestured towards the dogpile of generals. "The rogue's in there."

"Use the Bullet," Speatsh suggested.

"Were you not paying attention," Josh asked.

"Uh, no," Speatsh replied. "I was too busy not having an earpiece and waiting quietly to jump out and yell 'you little bastard' and stuff!'"

"The Bullet's not an option" Josh said. "Can you get us in that shell?"

"That's a lot of generals," Speatsh replied, examining the dogpile. "Maybe if I ate first."

"I thought you might need a little pick-me-up," Thomas said, riding up atop Petruchio. He leapt down and held out his arm to Speatsh.

"I need real blood, not your gross stuff."

"Believe Dracula; you want this," Thomas said. "A little concoction I stole from the rogue for such an occasion."

"You injected that into your system for him," Josh asked. "You knew!"

"I got a bit of a heads up, yes," Thomas replied. He held out his wrist, and Speatsh carefully grasped it.

"Forgive me, Mother," Speatsh said.

"Why would you care what she thinks," Thomas asked.

"Not her, Brit," Speatsh chided. "That nun from Chile."

"Oh."

"I promised her."

"You can always fight without it," Thomas said.

"Are you stupid," Speatsh asked, then bit hard into Thomas's flesh.

"Umm," Josh started to ask. "I lost my mind with that."

"You're not Speatsh Cheatham," Thomas replied. "You'd never been awake before. Still, please, stay in control, Mr. Cheatham."

"Think I can't hold my liquor," Speatsh asked, pulling away. Before he could return to his feast, his body tensed. "Yeah, that don't feel so good." He suddenly screamed to the heavens, his limbs stretching, his face cracking and every bone shifting. When he dropped on all fours to the ground, his quickly-growing white hair almost glowed gold in the night.

He looked like the white wolf Josh had seen drag off Natalie, only he was larger, and his legs resembled more of a parachute than a dog's.

"Wait," Josh said. It just occurred to him. "You told us that was your mother in the bunker!"

Josh thought he heard Jasper suddenly laugh.

Speatsh howled and leapt into the air. His arms filled out like that of a flying squirrel. He sailed towards the pile of generals and immediately began his task to crack the rogue out of it.

"All right, folks," Cadence announced over her earpiece as Josh suddenly stood stunned at his realization. "I think we're game on again."

36 ~ Drawing the Circle

Chirp!
Strange. Deafening.
The sound surprised Harvey as he released its cry. The Schnauzer's head popped and the dog fell on the woman's chest. Immediately it grew heavier on her. The gang rushed to help remove it and despised the odd event of it turning into a bald, naked teenager who should have been in high school.

Detective Harvey Bruce threw down a large bag with many stacks of decent bills falling out as it hit the ground.
"Now, who's buying me that drink?"

The hunters numbers had dwindled. Josh didn't recognize most. They fought as hunters though. They grouped as such—staying their fight, dealing their own personal vengeances against their foes. Their faces scarred with the hatred and pain of those who had lost and never forgotten. Josh flashed an observation of one such individual with roofing hammers contending with four guardians. Another hunter used flashes of light of some sort to blind his foes; what he finished them off with was uncertain, but he was effective, fast and still alive.

As a group of guardians broke through this line and raced towards the inner depth of the graveyard where the heart of Josh's plan had taken life, two hunters, sharing one strip of what appeared to be razor wire, caught and destroyed the insurgents. Another group of Josh's allies poised themselves with rifles and machetes. All around the boundaries of the battleground, those with skateboards grinded over headstones and ran when their boards could not roll. Using the narrowly-paved roads, they herded what enemies they could into areas where they could be contained or dispatched by other hunters.

Even then, by sheer number, the guardians continued to creep into the graveyard.

"We're tiring," Josh observed then asked, "Bean?"

"Still waiting," Bean replied. "They can only dig so fast."

"Get a move on," Josh demanded. "Geez! The rogue will be dead from old age before your idea pans out."

"Would that be so bad," Bean replied.

"If you're not ready by the time we crack him, we're moving forward without you," Josh said.

"Do you want your diversion now," Bean asked.

"No," Josh answered. "He's still in too much control."

Bean groaned. "Well, get a move on. Natalie might be the one in the most danger here."

Josh returned to evaluating where best he should strike the mound of generals.

Speatsh's attacks helped to some degree. He was a most vicious force against the rogue's shield, yet they still had the numbers on even him. Every so often, a few would leave the mound and pummel the resurrected ancient, but they returned to their shell, leaving Speatsh only angrier and fiercer than before. The rogue, it seemed, was just as tactful as Speatsh. Once the weaker monsters realized what he was doing, several guardians and scouts left their own melees with other hunters to attack Speatsh, who had become a demon of speed, but they had their advantages too. Whenever the revived ally lined a killing blow upon a single general, that's when the numbers swarmed him. Guardians and scouts alike came to defend the pile so that the generals could maintain their hold. They weren't strong, sure, but number, even weak ones can still be annoying and slow any creature down.

Despite his efforts, Speatsh had failed to end a single creature. Likewise, no general, guardian nor scout had accomplished no more over Speatsh than annoy him. Still, Speatsh countered, dodged and traded the best of blows and most timed of attacks Josh had seen in his friend yet. The numbers of generals were simply too great. Josh estimated the mound to be about thirty feet tall. Despite being a master of delivering death upon wolves as Speatsh's reputation preceded, most of his energy was getting spent on dodging the hundreds of attacks that all came at him at once from those who weren't in the mound.

So how did Josh assist? How could he help remove the rogue's protection? He wasn't stupid. He knew he'd be mobbed just as Speatsh was, only Josh would be destroyed before he even landed a single, wounding blow.

"What's the plan," Cadence asked.

"To get in there without that becoming us," Josh said, motioning to Speatsh who suddenly noogied one general a moment before unleashing a variance of attacks upon at least a score of weaker assailants all focused on bringing him down.

"Too bad we don't have a giant stun gun of sorts," Bean cried into Josh's ear.

"Good idea," Josh said. "Where is she?"

"Where do you think," Bean asked. "Like I said, too bad we don't have her here."

Still, Josh had to get through the barrier of generals, but even Thomas, who currently stood directly to Josh's left wasn't racing to get into this brawl.

"We can try wind again," Cadence said.

"No," Josh replied. "We're not holding the borders as it is."

Josh watched. He knew he needed to fight. He wanted to race in and take up arms with Speatsh. Perhaps, a week ago, he would have, but he was a little older now. "They're just so fast."

"What if we," Cadence started, then, "No. That wouldn't work."

"Thomas," Josh asked.

"I'm thinking," Thomas replied.

Neon?

Ask me later, Neon said.

What are you doing, Josh asked.

Running away from What, Neon replied. *Nothing to be concerned about, really. He just wants his flute back.*

Give it to him, Josh said. *He needs it to help us.*

But I need it, Neon complained. *Besides, I already stole it from him.*

Really?

Why would you think it was fantasy?

Josh groaned, and of course no one understood why.

"If we could just slow them down, at least," Josh said.

Suddenly a group of guardians were upon Josh and his group.

"We tried," one hunter yelled into his ear. "There's too many."

Josh, as well as his allies, moved quickly. They fell to their strengths, each raining carnage throughout the numbers upon them.

"We may need you, Tandem?" Josh spoke after a small moment of inhale, but not enough to really breathe.

"Trust me," Tandem said. "You need us here more."

Cadence roared in pain and a monster fell at her feet. A deep laceration cried blood from her arm. Thomas was quick to her side, wrapping a handkerchief around it, sealing it back together, all while managing a small fight of his own.

Josh's hands were full. He could offer no aid, and the number grew about him. The paladin stumbled. Two guardians pounced. Josh saw to it they didn't finish.

"I liked this a lot better when they couldn't all come out at the same time," Cadence said.

"Only one way to take the numbers down," Josh said. "We have to break the rogue's concentration."

Bricktain joined the group and made some remark that he thought was funny, but which Josh chose to ignore. Just for the record, it really was funny, and it upset Bricktain. He rarely had something funny to say, and no one appreciated it now that he did.

Jasper rolled towards the group atop his wooden barrel.

"Please tell me that's a nitroglycerin bomb," Josh said, amidst a thrust of his swords in two different directions.

Jasper laughed. "That's what you'd choose of all things to be in this barrel, something that just goes boom. Please, go back to college if we win this."

Jasper stood the barrel on end and pulled off the lid.

"These, my friend," Jasper explained, but was suddenly caught off by the roaring engines and bright lights that suddenly sped into the graveyard.

Motorcycles, rumbling Harleys, grinding garbles of Ducatis, screaming rare Yamahas and a choir of other behemoths—only the best—charged into the cemetery.

Cheers rose up from the groups of hunters throughout the sea of tombstones.

"What is this," Josh asked.

"Who cares," Bricktain said. "They're on our side."

"Ha, ha," Chandler's voice screamed. "He did it! Paladin, my friend brought you Nomads."

"You mean gypsies," Josh asked.

"Aren't they a biker gang," Cadence followed.

"They might not be hunters, but they love a good fight," Chandler replied.

"Put 'em to use," Josh said. "Reinforce those lines."

The bikes roared, speeding around groups of dogs, their drivers touching off firearms upon them, cutting off their escapes and smashing at their bodies with tire irons and pipes.

"Get nitro-bullets to the Nomads," Cadence ordered. "Can anyone do that?"

"I think I can help drop that off to them," Tandem replied.

Josh's group continued to end the numbers of wolves that had reached them.

"You were saying," Josh asked, turning to Jasper, who still stood at his barrel, and had hardly done much to enter the fight. Although, he did stab his sword a time or two as if to protect the barrel.

"What I've brought you may help you get into that shell," Jasper said. "These are leeches."

Josh laughed.

"Uh-huh," Jasper said, clearly taking offense of Josh's response. He tore off the lid. What looked like giant, black rain, burst into the air, and sprayed into the immediate enemies upon Josh's group. Guardians and scouts, suddenly fell away, smacking at the little, black leeches as they leapt from one creature to another.

Josh and his allies wasted no time taking advantage of the distraction and dispatched the confused monsters until all were gone.

"Leeches are good," Josh acknowledged.

Jasper nodded. Like bullets, the leeches then shot straight for the dog-piled generals and those guardians and scouts that were annoying Speatsh. The worms quickly disappeared into their skins, leaping back and forth among the monsters as they had done with the guardians. Just like the guardians, they too were prone to distraction as the little slugs began feeding off of them.

It was what Speatsh needed. He made his first kill at the dogpile, then another, then a third, drawing enough attention that it convinced an even greater number of generals to leave the shell and contend with him.

Other generals swatted at themselves, stomped at the ground, bit at Jasper's vicious breed of werewolf leech. The distraction was enough that Josh too found an angle of attack, and he ran into the vicinity of the rogue's shell. The first wolf he struck didn't even predict that the paladin's flimsy blades could end his life so suddenly. Josh raced around the base of the pile launching more attacks. To his left, Cadence and Bricktain traded off keeping pace with him, firing off shots from a distance at those beasts Josh couldn't always see try ing to take a swipe at him.

Now, Thomas and Petruchio ran past Josh. They circled the mound counter to Josh's approach, and they adopted Josh's strategy of attacking any opportunity that presented itself. Jasper now got involved but his cries came from the top of the pile, flailing his sword into several monsters, ending one of them only.

Josh thrust his swords forward at an attack he saw coming at him all too late.

*   *   *

Something seemed to be glowing in the grass. He wasn't sure what it was. He'd felt useless the entire night. The best he could manage was to leap out as a distraction. The problem was, sometimes his distractions startled the hunters as well. He did his best not to do that. He had been hovering around a group of hunters who eventually got used to the sight of him. They had taken courage when the Nomads appeared.

Now that this group was reinforced, he set out to find a smaller band that could use his help more. That's when he saw it, faintly glimmering. The fallout from the geyser tried to hide it. The earth and grass here were soppy with water, or would have been, just not to him.

He was drawn to its light like a dying luminescent bulb from a cheap, pastel, plastic flashlight that ran on two D batteries, but never worked.

It hummed. He didn't notice it at first, but it hummed, and grew louder as he drew closer. Its essence was like his. He could tell that now. In the distance he heard a whinny of what must have been Petruchio.

He reached for the light. It shook. He could feel the vibration. He hadn't felt anything except when he relived the sensation of when he had melted to death, but he felt this. It was warm. He had forgotten warmth. Suddenly, it leapt into his palm. It was larger now, brighter.

Again, he heard the whinny, not from the distance, not Petruchio.

The object was a handle of some sort, with thick fiber holding it into the earth. He pulled. It held to earth, like a stubborn root. He searched for leverage but found none. He circled the root, still no leverage. He continued to pull. Whatever this item was, he knew he had to have it. It wanted him to have it. It wouldn't let go of him.

Then he cursed at whatever the object was that he hadn't noticed was behind him. He bumped into it as he continued to search for leverage to draw out the glowing root. It shot a sensation from his elbow up his arm. How? Since when could he feel, especially pain? He reached for the object that he bumped into. It was hard, cold. How? Returning his gaze upon the object of light, he realized what he held. He knew this object. He understood now what it was that he was drawing from the ground. Gripping the black wall that he shouldn't have been able to feel, that had fallen from atop the Silver bullet, he used it to anchor himself and pulled against the object embedded in the earth.

Still nothing. The bright root didn't pull, per se, but there was much more of it showing now.

He moved around the black wall to where an opening allowed him access to step up behind the other side of it. The item of light stretched with him, but the earth still held it tightly, yet it didn't matter because he felt the sturdy floor beneath him, inches above a wet soppy ground that he couldn't feel. He coiled the glowing handle and its root shape around his wrist. He leveraged himself against the wall of the container that he now stood in.

This time he yanked with a control that he hadn't been able to find until now. He continued to pull upon the ropey item, slowly stretching it from within the earth. Finally, it broke free of the soil, long and white, limber and almost like a worm. It sprang up into the air and cracked a familiar and loud strike.

Suddenly, a whinny erupted from his side. He looked.

"Kate," Richard asked in surprise.

The spectral steed appeared in a white harness, her reins tied fast to the front the black chariot.

Richard looked off towards the dog pile. He quickly caught sight of his nephew aiming his crossbow and firing a shot. The paladin leapt, turning his body sideways. A set of swords shot into his pathway while his cloak slashed across the faces of two guardians that were close at his heels.

Richard raised and twisted his hand and suddenly snapped his arm down. The spectral whip panged once more. The black walls surrounding him, flushed gold. The suns on both of his sides recharged, and he felt everything. He took up the spectral reins.

"To Josh, Kate!" Once more, Richard cracked the whip, and the chariot that had once been Aggon's, with an army of horses, now lurched forward under the power of only, Kate.

*　　*　　*

The paladin's lips were dry. If he'd pursed them, he doubted they'd have the elasticity to peel themselves apart.

As Thomas ended a general only paces ahead of Josh, and after several thrusts, slashes and parries, Josh realized something was amiss as the foe fell dead.

"No screaming," Josh said over his earpiece. "His slaves aren't dying on the battlefield."

"Because the generals aren't the ones controlling the slaves," Jasper yelled from his high position.

"So kill the rogue and they all die from shock with him," Josh asked. "Is that what you're saying?"

"Good question," Jasper replied.

Suddenly, Josh was down. A general sliced at his face, another stomped on his gut and then kicked. Josh was back to his feet only because Thomas pulled him up, but he might as well have left him down as now Josh found the attacks from all directions, guardians, scouts and generals alike.

"I can't get to you," Jasper said.

Josh moved quickly—not even aiming or thinking, just throwing attacks wherever he could naturally toss them. He wasn't sure if his approach was working, but he wasn't getting kicked anymore.

Then a guardian pummeled Josh's head a moment before its own shoulder exploded after a burst from Cadence's Uzi. Now, Bricktain was beside Josh, contending with such speed and reflexes that Josh had never seen him bear. Bricktain fired a shot and wounded another guardian, in fact every shot Bricktain made created a wound of some sort or killed a guardian.

"We'll hold off the guardians," Bricktain said. "Do what you do."

"That easy, huh," Josh asked.

The gold chariot drew in front of Josh with its new horse and driver.

"Get in," Richard said.

The sight of Kate and Richard was almost enough to distract Thomas and Petruchio both, but then a sort of smile grew across Thomas's lips, and he suddenly seemed reinvigorated. He returned to his fight with greater frenzy and enthusiasm.

Josh started rounding the mound again, but now inside the back of the chariot. At once, Speatsh appeared in front of Josh, hesitated a moment as Jasper's swarm of leeches launched across his path. The blood-sucking worms seemed somewhat larger to Josh than they had before. Speatsh suddenly grabbed the chariot and tossed it, passenger and all, over his head and out of the hornet's nest that was Speatsh's own contention. The chariot landed, actually softer than Josh might have anticipated, but generals instantly surrounded him, already delivering some effective blows to both him and the chariot. The chariot began to race off again.

As Josh made his fight, he caught a glimpse of an opening in the mound.It wasn't large, but it was enough to reveal what appeared to be a human within the mound of beasts—and here, Josh unleashed his furious attacks at the mound as the chariot continued to race around it.

"There," Josh cried to Richard. "Get me there!"

Josh dropped one of their pursuers.

Richard pulled hard on the reins. Kate leapt to the side, planted her feet and twisted her body around. The chariot swung about, with her as its axis and whipped back into the surprised group of chasing generals.

Josh used the moment of their dismay to leap from the vehicle and run for the opening.

In the process, he discovered it wasn't a mound, it was a dome, and laying beneath it was the rogue as if asleep. No more running.

"I found him," Josh cried. "I can get to him."

"Well, don't take him alone," Thomas screeched into Josh's ear.

However, Josh wasn't stopping now. Every general that tried to confront Josh and seal his view received the full extent of Josh's stamina. Until Josh felt himself lifted from behind. He launched his attacks at whatever it was, and Speatsh roared at him for the wounds he'd suddenly received from the paladin. Speatsh placed himself at the crevice Josh had discovered. Josh ignored Speatsh's warning and bounded his way to the opening once more. Instead, he was promptly whisked away by many hands, all of which now beat Josh's body with paws that had retracted their claws, battering every inch of him. Their intent was to bruise him, not kill him, for they could easily do both. For some reason, they restrained themselves to simple torture.

Josh was to the ground, his arms wrenched wide, his cloak stretched beneath him and the generals pulling at its edges, as children who play with a parachute in gym class might do. Try as their hands might, they hadn't quite figured out how to tear Wolf's Breath. No matter what Josh attempted to break their hold over him, he found no leverage in his weaponry to fight back.

Voices rang through the earpiece, and a few of Josh's friends rushed to get at him, but the generals threatened back, pulling at his limbs, to tear them off if any approached.

Josh struggled, but the hands that bound him and his cloak were stronger and unafraid.

Suddenly, she was over him again, the white haired woman. This time she hovered only a foot above his body and madly flipped her own cloak in his defense. The orbits sank deep into one general, and he fell gasping, then dying. One-by-one she peeled away Josh's captors, freeing him to stand.

This allowed his other allies, Bricktain, Richard, Cadence and Speatsh to join in the defense.

Josh stood and saw her—Amber, but somehow not Amber. Her face was dark and hidden. She contended fiercely with the group of generals she had stolen from Josh. When she realized Josh was free to fight and also observing her, she fled back into the sky.

Josh returned to Speatsh's side, but his eyes fell upon the opening in the rogue's shell of generals. He could still see the fiend, as if asleep on the ground. He thought Speatsh should be the one to enter. He was the strongest. Then again, Speatsh wouldn't fit, so, accordingly, Josh did what he does best and took the stupider approach.

None of his allies were quick enough to stop him this time.

Get out of there, Neon yelled into Josh's brain.

Josh didn't care. The rogue was unresponsive, concentrating, too busy controlling the guardians. He lay on the ground beneath an open dome. The round walls and ceiling of generals watched him, but dared not break their structure to chase after the paladin. They might let in far more hunters if they did.

Josh threw out the front edges of Wolf's Breath, intent upon beheading the preoccupied villain. The rogue moved with speed as though he had already been standing, grabbed the edges of Josh's cloak and threw him into the inner wall of generals as one uses a sling to hurl a stone.

The shell burst. Josh's earpiece, as well as the air, filled with cries of surprise, cheers and jeers.

"Everyone to the rogue," Josh forced himself to groan and order after landing a harsh flop against a headstone. An instant later, he was compelled back into fighting with another general who chose to stand in the way of him and the rogue.

"You want us to leave the guardians," Tandem asked.

"They're still coming," Bean asked.

"Generals too," Tandem added. "They're our priority right now."

"Either his concentration's better than we thought," Josh said.

"Or he's showing off," Jasper added.

"Can't fight both, Josh," Thomas said.

"Stay there, Tandem," Josh relented and finished hacking his current opponent to death. "Someone at least get to the rogue then."

Josh caught a glimpse of Speatsh leaping to the rogue, the two tussled. Speatsh was fast, the rogue was faster, smarter too: wiser from his longer life, more skilled from his own experiences and knowledge of Speatsh.

Eventually Speatsh was apprehended by the numbers of generals who were near-impossible to destroy from their quantity alone. The majority of generals swarmed to the rogue's proximity to give battle to Josh and his allies. Unlike their last strategy to protect him in a shell, they stood alert. several created a small ring around the rogue as if protecting a presidential candidate. Josh raced for the rogue and his body guards and quickly found other generals upon him.

In fact, any time an ally drew upon the rogue and his protectors, other generals surrounded and gave fight so that the rogue went untouched. The rogue just stood his ground, entertained.

You're in danger, Neon cried. *Why didn't you say something?*

What do you think I've been doing, Josh replied.

Run to me, Neon ordered. *To your left.*

Josh abandoned his opponents and ran. His opponents gave chase.

Kicking you!

Josh flipped, landed on his feet and listened to the howling that erupted behind him because of an attack that had missed its mark.

"Where are you going," Cadence asked.

"Stay with the group," Josh replied and kept running. "And can you get these things off my back."

Three chirps sang.

"Done," Cadence replied. "Hey! where'd you go?"

From the shadows, Neon appeared. She moved fast and ran hard. In one hand, she carried her small rechargeable vacuum— in the other, something silver. Ahead of her, a tall general seemed to flee from her and towards Josh. Only, as it drew closer, it wasn't a general. Josh realized its body belonged to a general, but its head was a cage.

"Our deal is complete," What shrilled. "I claim the paladin."

Neon dropped to her knees and started vacuuming the ground.

What are you doing, Josh asked.

What's it look like, Neon fired back. *My vacuum is empty.*

Neon suddenly stood and ran off.

"Paladin," What cried as he charged towards Josh. "I helped as long as I could and now I seem to have lost my flute, which means, time to pay the piper!"

"Get out of there," Bean cried.

"I'll tear him apart," Josh retorted.

"Don't try it," Thomas's voice demanded over the earpiece.

He'll kill you.

That means a lot coming from someone vacuuming the lawn a moment ago, Josh replied.

She said nothing.

"You're the deal," Bean's voice stated through the earpiece. "Jasper promised you to him for his continued help. He's cashing in."

"Why would Jasper do that," Josh asked.

"He's a jerk," Bean replied.

"Hello paladin," What sang as he stepped before Josh and tipped his cage as a human might his hat in greeting. "I do apologize, but I'm here for your head."

Josh gripped his cloak, ready to tear What's cage off his body.

No, Neon cried into Josh's brain. *It won't stop him. You have to run.*

Where are you, Josh asked.

Run. She ordered.

Josh did and What's general form chased fast behind him.

General to your left and one coming straight at you, Neon instructed.

Josh snapped his blades to his left, and readied to shoot upon What should he overcome the paladin.

Just then, What's general body, gripped its cage off its shoulders, and hurled it straight into Josh's shoulder, knocking him onto his front instantly. Josh rolled to his back to sit up, and What's cage leapt upon his chest.

The head was heavy. Every time What's cage rocked back and forth, Josh felt more of his breath beaten out of him. He tried to breathe. What laughed and suddenly turned angry.

"My paladin," What scowled.

It took Josh a moment to realize What was actually addressing a stunned general which was now standing over Josh and ready to flatten his head with a mighty stomp.

The general strangely complied to What's complaint. The wolf looked about him as though he didn't know how to act.

"Mine," What screamed. "Or eat you first. Mine! Shoo! Flea-face! Butt-sniffer, go now!"

The general watched confused.

What's head rocked back and forth towards Josh's face. "My paladin! Mine!"

Josh drew a fang and fired into the cage.

What ate all three cylinders. His cage leapt up and down on Josh's chest. "Not do that, Paladin. Not do that."

What's teeth began stretching through the cage for Josh face.

"Get that cage off the paladin," Bean's voice cried.

"What cage," Bricktain's voice followed.

"If I miss and hit that cage, the bullet could go anywhere," Cadence complained. Instead, she took aim on the wolf near him, but had to withhold taking the shot and screeched, "What is she doing?"

I have you. Neon assured. Her figure leaped over Josh and What. She planted herself squarely in front of the confused general that still towered over the paladin and had been mesmerized by the behavior of the strange head in the cage. She looked up to the general, stabbed her cordless vacuum into its mouth and drew the piper's bone flute. She blew a note she had heard the piper command, a note that had ordered the ash children to turn into spikes.

What's head suddenly shrunk back into its cage, fear and anger controlling his face as he shouted his objection, but still Neon blew that one powerful note.

From within her rechargeable vacuum, a long, black spike burst its plastic barriers and stabbed into the general's brain, several sharp points burst through the top of his head, face as well as completely through one of his eyes.

The general fell dead; Neon stopped blowing and the spikes exploded to dust, leaving a destroyed rechargeable vacuum in Neon's hand.

What screamed, and the children of ash rose from the earth. The child closest to Josh gathered up What's cage. This girl handed off the cage to another child with a long French braid.

"Bad man," the children discussed among themselves in agreement as they gathered around Josh and throughout the graveyard.

"Bad man," they chanted as they walked away with What's screaming head. They carried him into the dark where his cries suddenly fell still under a metallic thud and a rupture of child laughter and applause.

At this, Neon snapped the bone flute. The children broke their bonds of the black ash and rose as white wisps—free, as they should have always been.

Neon hovered over the general she had just dispatched and covered her eye with her palm. It was a mirror of the eye she had just ruptured in the General's head. "Pirates only take a test like this once because they don't need two glasses."

Now you can talk to me, Neon said.

"What about What," Josh asked.

His innocent have shed blood, Neon replied. *He is destroyed. We must fight now.*

Josh and Neon returned swiftly to the battle. Neon perched herself once more on top of a mausoleum where her presence seemed only through the slight glow of her colorful hair.

Bricktain chided Josh for his sudden retreat, and he wasn't the only one.

"Where's the rogue," Josh asked, scanning the area. He found that the ring of bodyguard generals had enlarged to allow the rogue more room to conduct whatever he was now working on within it. On the outside, his strongest allies of Speatsh, Thomas, Bean and Jasper contended with a growing mob of wolves that contended to keep them from breaking through the wall.

"His sheep have rounded up the ancients," Thomas said.

"Does anyone know how many they've collected," Josh asked.

"All of them it looks like," Tandem replied from her high perspective over the cemetery.

"How many has he put in the carriage," Josh asked.

"All of them," Tandem replied.

"How many revived?"

"All but two."

All but two. The number of lives the hearse had taken was staggering. Josh had to remind himself not to get lost in the thought of trying to estimate how many tens of thousands of lives the ancient vehicle had absorbed.

"We're running out of time then, Bean," Josh said.

"They can only move so fast," Bean replied. "Stop rushing."

"We'll just have to do this without whatever you're working on."

"I don't think you can," Bean snapped. "And as long as he can't find the rest of the ancients, we still have the advantage."

Josh scanned the area. Was it time to call for that distraction? He found the carriage from Thug's easily enough. The ancients from the museum all stood on their own now, racked tightly together as if they might be expecting to be bowled through for the rogue's entertainment.

Strange. No generals attacked him as of now. Then, he noticed the other tall, white creatures now standing among the fight. Their hands appeared bound to their waists, and their legs bound at the ankles because they were alive. They lumbered among the headstones, as if purposely positioned. Four had been placed in what resembled a crescent line. The rogue appeared from a nearby mausoleum with a fifth ancient, and no hunter could reach him. The distraction would do no good now. It needed to happen when it could make him stumble, give a hunter an opportunity to make a killing blow, or, at least, a viciously crippling one.

"Well, he found our ancients," Josh said.

"Should have hidden them better," Cadence said.

"I doubt it would have mattered," Josh replied.

"If anyone should have an idea of how to slow this down," Thomas said. "I'm listening."

"Has to be the rogue. That's how we slow this down." Josh said, realizing if no one else could get to rogue, he had to try. He raced after the barefoot man once more.

Instantly, the generals were upon Josh, and he was forced to retreat. After he had fled some distance from the ring of bodyguards, the defending generals returned to the vicinity of the rogue, the ancients and Thug's black wagon.

"Will someone get to him, already," Josh asked in frustration as he started to run back for the rogue from a different angle.

"Trying," Thomas said. "He's just doing to us what just happened to you."

"Until he's built the circle."

"Looks like it."

You have three, Neon said.

That much I know, Josh replied as he was once more fleeing the rogue's vicinity.

Yes, but if you run and your friend shoots the slowest one, there will only be two. Can you kill two?

I'm having a hard time killing one, Josh answered while managing to keep the same three monsters on him.

Then your other friend can shoot the next slowest one.

The rogue placed his fifth ancient and expanded the crescent.

"Hate to be a broken record, but might be a good idea to think of a plan of retreat," Jasper suggested. "What was our way out before."

"No," Josh replied. "We finish here. Bricktain, can you free yourself and join Cadence?"

"What do you think," Bricktain replied.

"Run to Cadence," Josh ordered. "And if anyone sees Aggon." He caught himself on his mistake. "I need my uncle."

A short moment later, Bricktain appeared with four generals in pursuit. Josh broke towards him and drew his fangs, each crossbow taut with darts. He sprayed his ammunition from both, dropping one general, not dead, but not interested in running any farther from the rest of the rogue's immediate vicinity of protection. Bricktain, likewise fired upon the three that currently chased Josh. Josh ran between two of Bricktain's generals, snapping his cloak at each, beheading one, sending another into regroup. Meanwhile, Bricktain released a gunshot that tore into one of Josh's generals. Josh had two left now.

Bricktain's remaining assailants retreated back into the core of the fight where Speatsh, Thomas, Bean and Jasper persisted in trying to break through the mob of wolves to reach the rogue. Unable to be reached, the rogue moved about, ignoring any of his assailants and positioning his next restrained ancient, his wall of defenders moved about with him to magnify his workspace.

Josh continued to flee his own attackers.

"Shoot, please," Josh requested.

Bricktain fired. Cadence fired.

One left, Neon's thoughts said.

Josh dropped and spun his body tightly together, slicing the legs out from under the general that had remained in the chase.

The chariot halted beside Josh. "You summoned," Richard asked.

Josh climbed into the back of the chariot again and looked down to Cadence and Bricktain.

"Let's see if we can dwindle this down. We'll cast the line," Josh said calmly. "You two pick off whatever bites."

"Good thinking," Thomas said into Josh's ear.

Josh and Richard raced to the rogue and returned with two generals in pursuit. Cadence and Bricktain dropped one.

"Do it again," Josh said. This time, the chariot returned with another general at its heels. The general's life ended with a quick couple of Cadence and Bricktain's bullets to the head.

Upon Josh's next entry into the fray, he noticed the rogue had now set up nearly half the shape of a circle with nine ancients, all bound in cord, and spanning a hefty portion of cemetery.

After a dozen turns of Josh and the chariot diving in and retrieving generals, and after thirteen dead enemies, the rogue's defenses stopped taking the bait to chase Josh and maintained their huddle. They quit trying to attack him all together. Yet, the paladin still couldn't get through to the rogue without gaining more attention than he could safely draw into the line of fire.

"We could just shoot into the crowd," Bricktain said. "They're tightly huddled. We're bound to hit a wolf."

"Don't you dare," Bean replied. "We have enough to dodge in here."

"Hey, Josh! What if Richard just rode around the ring really fast and you just stuck your arm out and beheaded all the generals," Bricktain said.

"Why not," Josh said.

He and Richard set out to perform the maneuver, and somehow Josh found himself torn from the back of the chariot by the folds of

Wolf's breath. He might have ended right there, but Richard quickly retrieved him.

"Well, that was stupid," Josh said.

The chariot retreated, and Josh gathered his breath, he counted twelve ancients that now stood in a semi-circle, which continued to grow to surround Thug's black wagon. He took stock of his forces surrounding the rogue. Thomas, Bean, Jasper and Speatsh still contended with trying to make a hole in the ring of generals while simultaneously keeping enemy force attention on them instead of the paladin.

They were outnumbered, but still putting up a fight that the rogue's minions couldn't end themselves. They had all but disappeared into a mob of beasts that spanned the entire width of the ring surrounding the rogue.

The time was upon them. Soon Josh's plan could unfold entirely. He needed it to last just a little longer. He needed Bean to come through a little faster.

"Shoot the rogue," Josh replied, preparing his crossbows again.

"Yeah," Cadence said. "We tried that already. Watch what happens."

Cadence drew her rifle, found the rogue and fired, which would have hit him, but he slapped the air as if swatting a mosquito and continued building his circle of ancients around Thug's carriage.

"There is another option," Bricktain said. "Shoot the ancients."

"Yeah," Josh replied. "That's what we need, more pissed off ancients."

"That leaves us with go in and fight or try to pick off that mob," Cadence said.

"No," Thomas's voice yelled into Josh's earpiece from somewhere within the horde of monsters. "Do not shoot our way."

"The last thing we need to contend with right now is you three bumblers," Bean snapped clearly.

"I have the mask," Cadence said.

"Weren't you wearing that when you shot Speatsh," Thomas asked. "We don't need you shooting him again."

Cadence cursed. "I'm better now."

"Don't prove it here," Thomas replied after a moment of silence. "Speatsh is about the only thing keeping them from overtaking us."

"That leaves the other option then," Josh said, clenching the sidewall of the chariot. He studied the ring, then asked, "Richard. Think you can punch me and Brick through that ring?"

Bricktain's arm began to ratchet back into his close combat sword and joined Josh in the chariot.

"Let's find out," Richard said. "Might want to brace yourselves. I'm pretty new here."

With another crack of the whip, the chariot began speeding from the outskirt of one fight to the heart of an even fiercer battle. As the chariot approached, a group of generals locked arms and moved to counter the chariot.

"Red rover! Red Rover. Send Joshua right over," Josh could practically hear them taunting.

When the chariot struck the mob, the chain of wolves didn't break. The golden carriage quickly sped away, and no wolves were tempted to give chase and get picked off.

"If we can't get through, then let's focus on cheapshots," Josh said. He watched several fat leeches dive into the generals once more. "What about the leeches, can we use them against the rogue."

"Tried that," Bean replied. "He steps on them. They're content where they're at right now, helping us."

Josh and Richard made a second approach, the generals locked arms again and Josh waved off the attack. For an instant, he could see Speatsh as vicious as ever, aware of every angle and enemy at once. Thomas and Petruchio maintained their balance and coordination with each other. Only, Thomas had lost his steel and now wielded Reggie's sword pommel, lashing out one strike of ghostly blade after another. What his ghostly blade missed, his near invisible diamond or his loyal steed did not.

"Is that Amber," Bricktain asked, hearing the familiar whistles of the orbits. Josh looked quickly and caught sight of the familiar stranger as she climbed into the air. All at once, she stopped and dived back down into a mob of generals trying to bolster the rogue's immediate ranks. As she fell back to the earth, she flailed Wolf's Breath and her orbits into a flowering missile.

Josh would be impressed later, but had his mind on another matter. The rogue, began to close the circle of ancients around the black carriage.

"We're out of time," Josh said.

"This is going to get messy really fast if he tries to use that carriage," Bricktain said.

The usual voices returned their judgments and complaints.

"Oh, duh," Richard said and turned the chariot to race back for the ring of wolves once more. "Too simple I almost didn't think of it!"

Kate leapt into the air, the chariot followed. Bricktain cussed at the surprise. A wall of generals began to construct itself to deflect the aerial assault, and would have, but they could not inhibit the grip nor strength of Kate's ghostly hooves as Richard encouraged her to use them to keep pulling the golden chariot up and over the attempted blockade.

In the midst of the assault, Bricktain fell from the chariot and found himself haphazardly deflecting several guardian cheapshots on his way back to the earth. Upon hitting the ground and Bean's encouragement, Bricktain quickly fled the area to continue looking for pot shots. Cadence fired away at one general that seemed interested in chasing the robotic-armed man.

The chariot, however, soared towards the other side of the defensive barrier, but suddenly jerked downwards under numerous generals that had lunged upwards for it. The chariot was now falling into the very fray of beasts that currently held Speatsh, Bean, Thomas and Jasper's attention. Josh quickly climbed the chariot wall, even as it fell, and leapt in such a fashion that generals hadn't time to prevent themselves. He landed on the other side of the rogue's defenses and immediately climbed to his feet as he ran straight for the rogue. Five general's pounced at Josh's heels, missing. Astounded at the speed of the human still exhibiting his residual strength.

"I'm in," Josh announced.

"Mask is on," Cadence informed.

She raced towards a mausoleum that she believed would give her some higher ground to peer into the rogue's ring better. Bricktain had rejoined her; boosted her to the roof; and discovered a means to climb up to her. By the time Cadence spotted Josh, the paladin had already dropped one general and left another to bleed out of a severed pair of legs.

Both Cadence and Bricktain opened fire on his other pursuers. Between the three of them, Josh was able to resume his attack on the rogue.

"I have the rogue," Josh said.

"That stupid kid," Jasper's voice screeched.

"You're clear," Cadence replied staring down her scope.

"Take his head off, Boss," Bricktain added.

"Get to the paladin before he kills himself," Thomas ordered, but every general now within the area of Josh's strongest allies and within the circle of ancient dogs were now encompassed on all ends as if they had invaded a hornet's nest.

The rogue glanced to Josh, but continued his work. The body guard generals maintained their ring, unconcerned that the rogue couldn't handle the simple paladin.

No one's coming, Neon said.

I have Bricktain and Cadence, Josh replied.

They won't be able to touch him.

Well, that's all we have, so what do you suggest, Josh replied.

Good point, she conceded, then, *I have chosen a style of fighting.*

37 ~ Passing Judgment

The circle was complete. The rogue held the tongue of the black carriage and began to pull it behind him towards its more accurate center. He marched past Josh, hardly acknowledging the approaching and vengeful paladin.

Josh struck.

Or would have if the rogue was fat, slow and inexperienced, but he wasn't, and Josh was suddenly down and eating grass. The rogue continued positioning the carriage with a careful eye on Josh.

"We're in trouble, Paladin," Thug's voice informed from the battlefield. "We have too many down. Ammo's low."

Josh requested Bricktain and Cadence locate and get some bullets to the other hunters as he climbed to his feet. His friends objected, but Josh insisted.

"Let me remind you, I'm the protector," Cadence countered.

"That is protecting me," Josh explained.

"I guess this would be a bad time to inform you that the next wave is positioning itself," Tandem's voice echoed from behind a blustery background.

"They've been coming in waves," Josh asked.

"These are generals," she added. "They're going to spearhead openings for the weaker ones to get in. They'll overrun us."

Josh re-evaluated an attack he was planning and reached for his crossbows.

Just then, an explosion shrieked from the roof of the silver bullet's cab.

The black carriage wagon tongue exploded, shattering to pieces. The rogue remained untouched, but stunned. He regained his poise, switching glaring glances between Josh and the chrome diesel. How the rogue clearly hated that machine. Another round blasted from the diesel, and the rogue ducked, and a general in the protective ring fell dead instead. How close the rogue had come to being struck was impossible to tell, but when the third shot fired, he caught the projectile and threw it back at the silver diesel with such speed that his arm movement was hardly noticeable.

Ow, Neon said.

Josh lurched forward grabbing his stomach, even screamed in pain before he realized he was in pain. The rogue glanced quizzically upon Josh.

"Who's firing my guns," Bricktain demanded to know.

What was that, Josh asked.

Blood, she replied. *I think I'm dying.*

That was you in the Bullet?

Well, no one else was using it.

The rogue returned to the black carriage and began moving it again, despite its broken tongue. Josh noticed several generals break off their fight with Speatsh and Thomas's group, moving towards the rig.

"Bean, enough waiting," Josh ordered. "Give me something!"

"You want your distraction now, then," Bean asked.

"No," Josh snapped. "It's not time. I want whatever magic you've been concocting for us."

"I have nothing to give," Bean replied.

In that moment, Josh realized how futile his strength was. He was no match for the rogue, who was fast, more powerful than anything Josh had encountered. If that wasn't enough, Neon could be dying in the back of the Bullet right this very moment. If that should happen, Josh's design should fall, and the rogue would know everything.

"Group of guardians and generals headed for your diesel," Tandem announced.

As the generals approached the diesel, Josh felt a flood of despair and the anger from earlier filling him once more. No more thinking. No more planning. They'd wanted him to be a thinker, that wasn't him. Speatsh, Jasper or Thomas were the thinkers. That was his uncle Richard, even his friends, but Josh never was that thinker everyone wanted him to be. So, Josh decided to do what he did best, make what was most likely another mistake.

Josh ascended the black carriage quickly.

"Call them off the bullet, or I'll destroy it," Josh yelled. When the guardians didn't stop their pursuit across the battle-scarred graveyard for the Bullet, the paladin threw Wolf's Breath into the carriage roof and carved out two large pieces. "I said, call them off now," Josh ordered.

The attacking generals stopped, and Josh prepared himself to unleash a much more brutal attack. "If you think I can't do it before you kill me, you're not as smart as I thought."

Now, Thomas and Petruchio finally breached the rogue's ring, leaving three dying generals in their tracks. They raced past the rogue, fleeing their own current contest with the generals, Cadence and Bricktain picked off his followers. Thomas leapt from Petruchio's back and took stance in the carriage driver's seat between the rogue and Josh.

"What is wrong with you," Thomas said.

"Who do you think you're talking to," Josh snapped back. "The paladin doesn't justify himself to you." Josh watched the rogue, who now stood somewhere between amused and agitated. Even the rogue's slightest movement in the wrong direction, and Josh would destroy his treasure.

"Thomas de Soleil," Josh said. "You want generals, you show them why they should fear you. You want this filth, get in line."

The vampire suddenly stepped down and bowed deeply to Josh. His white hair fell smoothly down his back and he and Petruchio set to finding a new group of generals to entertain.

"Do what you do, Monsieur Revlon," Thomas said. "I will avenge you. I swear it."

"Neon's in the Bullet," Josh announced through his earpiece. "She needs help."

"I'm on it," Bean returned.

The rogue suddenly smirked.

"Don't think you've won," Josh said.

You should move quickly, Neon suggested. *I won't be able to block your thoughts for much longer I'm afraid.*

"I thought you were supposed to be smart," Josh said.

The rogue's smile grew.

"You've lived too long," Josh continued. "I figure you probably save your energy for the conversations you actually think are worthy of you opening your fat mouth for."

The rogue tipped his head.

"What I can't figure out, then," Josh said. "Is why you'd be so stupid as to kill the djinn."

The rogue's face became stone.

"You idiot," Bean cried.

"That's right," Josh gloated. "We found her—your only chance to winning this war—and you killed her."

What are you doing, Neon asked.

Something has to push his button, Josh replied.

But I am not dead yet.

He doesn't know that, Josh explained.

Ah, this is what you call a lie, she said. *I think I understand.*

"All your life's work is worthless. You spent all this time rallying your master plan, but I had two oracles and a djinn to tell me exactly what yours was, and now, in a few minutes, you'll be dead. You are where I want you to be," Josh continued to lie.

Now the rogue was visibly angry. He moved—and Josh was wrong, he couldn't strike fast enough to destroy the rogue's prize.

Josh tumbled from the top of the black carriage, landing squarely on his back, A moment later, the ledge of a flat tombstone toppled and smashed upon his rib cage. For this, the paladin couldn't even open his mouth to scream. Somehow, he rolled the stone off of his chest. He wanted to stand, but he couldn't find the strength through his own agony to even consider the task. He gasped at air but nothing came, his throat completely sealed from the internal debate of whether to cry, breathe, curse or call for help.

The rogue appeared above Josh, dropped to a knee and punched his chest, punched again. Josh reached to kill the rogue with his thoughts, but the rogue heard them not.

I am coming for you, Neon announced.

No, Josh rejected. *Don't!*

The white-haired woman was suddenly at the rogue. She unleashed her entire arsenal, whipping orbits, flailing Wolf's Breath. Silver shuriken flew, but seemed to fly right through his body as he twisted in avoidance. The rogue kicked at a headstone and struck the woman. She returned quickly to resume her attack.

The rogue grabbed Josh's leg and tossed him towards her.

She fled Josh's approach. The paladin smashed into a headstone, which had stood much taller earlier in that night. A spear of granite along its broken edge pierced into Josh's bicep. Before Josh could attempt to free himself, the rogue tore him off the stone; dropped him onto his chest; and kicked him onto his back.

Josh finally inhaled, not by choice, but because his body forced it upon him. Only, he wasn't certain how much healthier breathing was for him, for he could feel the wet in his lungs.

The rogue then lifted Josh and reset him against the impaling tombstone. He smacked away a feeble attempt on Josh's part to cut him with his cloak, and then punched him again. Josh fell, his only chance of dodging the blow, and the jagged tombstone cracked apart under the rogue's contact instead.

He snort-chuckled at Josh and raised him again, this time holding him while he drew back a fist intended for Josh's head.

Josh pulled a crossbow, but it wasn't his fang that caught his enemy. The rogue recoiled, leapt back, forgetting Josh and now focusing on the old man, Jasper, and his trusty cane sword.

Jasper parried, poked and parried some more. He was fast, faster than Josh, but the rogue was faster still. While Josh had tried to get close and start a fight with the rogue, Jasper had taken a tactic of using his speed to increase distance between the paladin and the rogue.

Bean too joined the fight, his chainsaws missing the rogue each time. He appeared to be defending more than attacking, using the spinning blades of shark teeth to guard his body. Surely the rogue could still be cut. Although the rogue was fast, Bean was still Jasper, still a general and still only needed to move quickly enough to block his vital parts.

When the rogue appeared to get a locked attack on Bean, Jasper reappeared and prevented it.

From here, Josh watched Thug lead a charge of several hunters towards Josh. They yelled; Josh didn't know what exactly, nor was he certain how they finally broke through the rogue's defensive ring. Behind his charging heroes, Josh watched Thomas, still in the battle with guardians, dispatching two or three in one blow. What the rogue had been to Josh in annihilation, Thomas was that and more to the onslaught of guardians and generals, so much that even his surrounding comrades had regained strength, enough to contend with fewer enemies of their own.

You have to breathe, Neon said.

Not really, Josh replied. *I can die. Apparently, I've done it before.*

You're not finished.

Thug got to Josh ahead of three other hunters: A biker with a green patch on his right breast that said "Nomads" in red letters, and two skaters. They poised to join the fight between the rogue and the two Jaspers, but Josh waved them off, knowing their fate if they tried.

"Can you stand, son," Thug asked.

"But this is such a lovely view," Josh thought he spoke, but he only groaned.

Ha. Ha, Neon chided.

I'm entitled, Josh replied.

"He'll be okay, I think," Thug, battered with blood and tired, told his companions. "We're going to get him out of here though. We should start thinking of retreating."

"No," Josh said, then finally began to force himself to his feet, even though he had to use one of the skaters for support. "No more running away. We have to finish this."

"You're done, Josh," Thug started to argue and suddenly fell silent. For, right then, Bean had aligned the perfect shot at the rogue's chest and discharged one of the oversized chainsaw blades. The blade ejected from Bean's arm with magnificent force and speed. The rogue, still too fast, dodged and the blade buried itself into Thug's back, breaking through his chest and almost into Josh's. The Nomad kept Thug from falling into the paladin.

A lone warcry shrieked from several yards away. A second joined it, and Josh soon sighted the doorman and Ty running towards the rogue.

Josh tried to warn them off, but realized that his earpiece was no more. He forced himself towards his fallen godfather, falling atop him, and tore his transmitter away from his limp head. By the time his fellow hunters helped him draw to his feet once again, he saw the doorman jump, leaping to the top of one of the many shattered headstones that now littered the cemetery. From here, he then launched himself even higher. His fist was cocked to punch and, just as the rogue started to parry what would have otherwise been a deadly strike to a lesser foe, Ty appeared from below the doorman and tossed up his shotgun. The doorman snapped the trigger without gripping the weapon.

The rogue dodged most of the shot, catching what he didn't in the shoulder and neck. At the same moment Ty buried a rapier-type blade, which had been surgically-taped to where his hand had once been, into the rogue's stomach.

Before he could repose, the rogue pulled out the blade, still attached to Ty. He snapped it out of Ty's make shift bracing and stabbed at the bartender, but Ty had allowed himself to fall and dodged the attack. Then the doorman struck. The rogue stepped off balance and Ty kicked his feet out from beneath him.

The rogue twisted back to his stance as though the attack never happened. The doorman and Ty now fled. The rogue flew at Ty first.

Again, it was Jasper who was fast to their defense. He deflected the blow with his own blade, parried another and thrust for the rogue.

Then his sword fell to the ground. Ty's foil was now buried in Jasper's chest. Jasper retreated some distance, falling over his own footsteps and nearly tripping Bean. As the rogue and Bean continued their duel, the doorman and Ty returned to Jasper's side and quickly began to pull him away. Bean continued his assault to buy time for his mistake.

The rogue gave no chase, but he appeared to take mental stock of which enemies he had left to attend.

The doorman retreated with Jasper a short distance and took cover beside a large, fat shade-tree. He propped Jasper against the trunk and then punched the tree. In that moment, Josh thought he could feel the reverb carry to where he, himself, stood next to Thug's body. Jasper's shadow remained still against the tree, but eventually fell to the side. The doorman didn't have to say anything, didn't have to signal with any information. Josh already knew.

Jasper was dead.

Josh pulled himself to his feet and immediately wished he hadn't.

"Guardians at your back," Tandem's voice screamed. "Sorry. I can't get to you."

"Then, I guess it's over." Josh said.

At that moment, to Josh's left, the mausoleum doors burst open. Another black wagon entered the graveyard, this one made with glass, the second one from the bunker. An iron plow pulled at the carriage until it had made its way out of the mausoleum. Winter sat in the driver's chair. Lisa stood atop the roof, donning the arsenal-cage that she'd swore she'd never wear again. As the carriage pulled into the cemetery, Lisa drew two automatic weapons and opened fire on a group of guardians. When the clips emptied, she set the Uzis on her back and drew two Glocks from atop her shoulders. The cage ratcheted its eagerness to intimidate. Then, from behind the chariot, an onslaught of generals rushed from the mausoleum and spilled out into the cemetery.

Lisa cut the rope holding the heavy plow, and it too tore its way into the fight.

"Watch out for the plow," Lisa's voice announced. "It goes after wolves, doesn't know good from bad, can only move forward, though. If that helps any."

"Any distraction's welcome," Josh said.

"Sorry to interrupt," Tandem announced. "The second wave of generals is through."

"So are ours," Bean replied.

"As many as can, get to the front lines," Josh struggled to say, though he wondered what fight he had left in him. "Thomas, they need you there."

Thomas said nothing, but he did obey the order.

"Well, we're here," Cadence called from her position, which was now next to Bricktain and Speatsh, the three of them working together as one unit against a handful of generals and guardians. "Now what."

"Bean," Josh asked. "Where'd you get the backup?"

Bean now kept distance between himself and the rogue. He had sliced off the mitt that had once carried the saw blade that was now in Thug and now took up Jasper's sword. Bean grunted, though he wanted to chastise Josh for interrupting his most difficult fight.

Josh ordered the doorman and the other hunters trying to babysit him away and back to the front lines.

Josh wanted into the fight, but, even maintaining to stand, he was shaking. He doubted he could perform a single spin, wondered if he could even make a fist and draw a weapon.

The sounds of guardians and hunters surrounded the cemetery edges, while the elementals kicked wind into the areas of the park of death where the hunter's strength was weakest. To one end of the cemetery, Speatsh and the white-haired Amber fought while Cadence and Bricktain continued to annoy the outer stragglers.

"You're not going to believe this," Tandem said. "A third wave is building."

Thomas's group now took on the brunt of the guardians and now many generals at the other end near the entrance.

The generals that had arrived with Lisa pressed farther into the cemetery. Hewing down guardian, scout and general as they could. Who were they? Josh wondered, and then pondered how his surroundings had become so empty. Why hadn't he been attacked yet by even one of the weaker dogs?

"Bean's down," Lisa yelled, and she raced into the immediate vicinity.

On cue, Bean groaned, his chainsaw silent, and he rolled quickly to avoid a stomp from the rogue.

Lisa dropped her firearms and immediately unleashed her electric lasso. It was silent, barely any sound of preparation. The rogue turned upon Lisa's footstep, but had arrogantly misjudged that her silent cable must have been a whip. He grabbed it, a hateful smile directed her way for being so foolish.

Lisa shot a gleeful snort and unleashed the charge. The rogue's body clenched and his face instantly tightened. It lasted only a brief moment, until her charge ran out, but it was enough that Bean was able to repair his concentration and stance towards the rogue.

"I won't start," Bean said smacking at his remaining chainsaw. "I'm unarmed."

"Get out of there," Josh ordered.

As the rogue regained himself, Richard's chariot smashed into his side.

Surprised, the rogue watched the gold chariot spit dirt as an apparitional Kate wheeled it around before charging once more. The rogue hunkered, bore his shoulder into the front of the chariot and screamed into Richard's face.

"That all you have," Richard mocked. "I'm taking you out, you piece of sh—"

The rogue suddenly punted the chariot, and it soared into the distant sound of battle near the front gates of the graveyard.

Cheers erupted around the cemetery.

"Don't kill the humans," Thomas's voice ordered. "Paladin, he's losing his concentration. The guardians and scouts are turning human."

Aggon's whip in Richard's hand cracked again, this time obeying Thomas's immediate command to join the battle at the front gates.

The rogue lurched as Lisa's lasso miraculously struck his back, just enough to shock him again.

At this, the rogue ran for Lisa: this step a man, the next step a man-beast. Finally, he charged in his full ancient power and form for Lisa and her cage until his wide shoulders smashed into her front.

Lisa rolled backwards. A loud pop from her limbs, as she toppled, announced something now bent in her lower body that was not to have bent. Yet, her cage kept her back from breaking against a jagged tombstone. Then, the rogue was back at Josh, and Josh was in the air, watching the distance grow between him and the rogue, until his back and head cracked against another hard surface.

Josh tried to keep his eyes open. He tried to focus.

It was a good fight, Neon said. *Can you see anything?*

The rogue was to Josh once more. He swatted his chest and made some strange noise as if to taunt the paladin.

A lot of voices cried in Josh's ear, but it was Bricktain's, "We can't get to him either," that settled in. Josh couldn't see them, but something must have happened that suddenly kept Speatsh, Thomas and any other, who would have been at his side, away from him.

"This isn't winning," Josh coughed out, and he himself chuckled as he took in one last view before the rogue put his life out.

Here, his friends would fight to the end. Here, they would spit their last breath against those that had destroyed so much. He hoped they could finish it right this time, but it would still be without him.

Josh watched for someone, anyone, to move on his behalf.

The only movement Josh could make out was the small shadow that crept out of Oliver's stone carving workshop.

His eyes fell to Winter who stepped down from her driver's seat and threw her silver revolvers away. She held the attention of the generals around her, some of those that had come to reinforce Josh's numbers. They appeared to gather to her as the rogue's guards had to him. Acotactac joined her and they all three marched towards the rogue as if to—of course!

Josh chuckled. It hurt, but he couldn't stop. What he had just realized was worth the laugh in the rogue's face. He forced it even. He felt the blood push its way over his lips as his laughter cleansed it from his lungs.

"And I thought you were supposed to be a genius," he said, turning his eyes to the rogue who, back in his human form was preparing his final punch through Josh's ribcage.

The rogue stopped, bit its teeth and drew a blank stare.

"You lost," Josh snapped. "And aren't even smart enough to see it."

He broke into an even louder painful laugh and then stopped to complain a moment about how much it hurt.

"The only reason you don't kill me is because you're actually intrigued," Josh cooed. "All these years, you've lived, planned and manipulated, and right now, at the end, you're intrigued."

"What are you doing," Bricktain asked. "Don't be stupid!"

Don't stop, Neon urged. *You're right. He doesn't see, but you do now.*

'Kill me, and you still lose," Josh said. He risked pretending a menacing step against the rogue despite the rogue's readiness to kill him, but he realized his confidence may well be his weapon in this war.

He shrieked in agony and grabbed at the rogue's arm to pull himself up. The rogue didn't back away. Of course, he didn't help neither.

The rogue maintained his poise to attack. Any movement, any attack would be fast enough that Josh couldn't stop it from claiming his life anyway.

"They said you were smart," Josh wheezed through shallow breath. "You spent so much time trying to be in my head and outsmart me, you didn't even realize who you were really fighting."

Now, Josh felt his face fall cold. He owned the rogue, and, for the first time, he watched the rogue flinch in thought, lost, trying to think of that one detail he overlooked.

"All that time you spent on predicting and outmaneuvering me, and somehow—maybe it was all those years behind you or all those voices in your head—but you overlooked one tiny detail," Josh hissed through his teeth. "One you probably found insignificant in a sea of details. One that probably came to hate you more than any has ever hated you."

The rogue held a look that Josh couldn't translate.

The paladin drew himself up, polished a smirk over the rogue and said, "My sister."

Suddenly, Acotactac, Winter and Cracey surrounded the rogue. As soon as the rogue noticed them, they all three moved upon him. All three changed into ancient forms and laid siege upon the him. The rogue himself turned back into his monstrous shape in a matter of a few maneuvers. Josh couldn't tell all of the ancients apart at first, except for the rogue. He was the one getting beaten. It took him another moment to decide the smallest one was Cracey. The other two were identical. He didn't know which was Winter and which was Acotactac.

They attacked fast, before the rogue had time to fully understand what Josh had just told him.

One ancient used the opening to charge into the rogue's left side, and before he could regain his footing or plan a counter attack, another had unleashed a bout of fury upon him at his right.

While one of the rogue's ancient opponents attacked, another mauled and the third found weak spots. Still, the rogue was powerful, and fended well. The new ancients were fast, subtle, smaller than the rogue. The rogue gave them all a feverish fight that Josh could hardly see, but it was clear the rogue was still the dominant one, dominant from years of never fasting, never turning his back on being a wolf. He was the ultimate demonstration of years of power filled from blood of prey that never ceased to flow through his veins. No creature was stronger in this way. He was the perfect demonstration of power in his kind. No general, no guardian, no other ancient had feasted and maintained their meditation as a beast as this rogue who still stood firmly against the three, merciless ancients who gave him battle.

Which is why Bean decided, in this very instant to execute the diversion that Josh had asked for.

You can stop now, Bean instructed Natalie.

The barrier she created fell and Jasper allowed the rogue to sense him once more. It was an older, wiser Jasper, back in his mind.

Boo, Bean simply said.

The rogue fumbled in this instant to keep his guard up. He knew that mind. He'd killed it! Where did it come from?

One of the three ancients fighting the rogue was more than the other two. Yet one was slowest of all of them, learning her abilities that would take centuries for her to fully begin to understand, and it was this inexperienced one who, driven by her wild new strengths, took advantage of the Rogue's sudden lapse of reason to pull him to the ground.

Genius, Josh thought.

That was her plan, Neon replied.

The rogue began cursing Winter, Acotactac and Cracey's ancient forms as they now wrestled him to the ground.

Josh began to lose his posture and slid back to the earth. He wanted to stand. He wanted to die. He had reason to die.

Yet, he had to stand. He stood. He had to walk. He tried to walk, but couldn't. At least he was, in fact standing, but he still needed to walk. He had to be over the rogue in his last moment.

Bean appeared at Josh's side. "You earned this," he said as he slipped something into Josh's hand.

Josh examined the object, the wooden puzzle knife that Bogi and then Thomas had given to Amber.

A few more steps, and Bricktain was aiding Josh's other side, and cursing.

The rogue was suddenly stretched over the ground, shrieking howls of failed desires. Generals throughout the cemetery now fled their fights and ran to aid their master, but they were met by the generals that had come from the mausoleum. Josh realized who they were. They were the Taichomée. It made the most sense, not that he was good at making heads nor tails of sense. Yet, who else could it be?

They fought viciously, not in their frail human form that Josh had grown to love, to trust, but in their forms as generals. They headed off the rogue's reinforcement at every angle, while Thomas and Speatsh maintained their fight upon those monsters already within their own striking distance. Neon herself, and the strange figure that Josh believed to be Amber engaged those who attempted to set their eyes upon Josh, both fighting with prejudice.

The rogue shrieked and howled in horror and prayer into the sky. He called any he could. The guardians and scouts, having fled the cemetery after returning to human form, now began to return once more to their servitude, but many were hurled away by wind or caught by hunters before they could change.

"He's playing his last card," Bean said.

Cracey, Winter, and Acotactac pulled at three of the rogue's limbs, drawing him into a helpless flat mat. Bean left Josh's side and leapt at the rogue's remaining leg, which had become more of annoyance than a weapon against the three imprisoning ancients.

"I think I have it figured out," Josh said, now peering over the rogue as he and Bricktain approached. "You see, you did win, but my father found the djinn, and my sister wished that we would send back reinforcements to help us win."

Josh dropped to his knees and spit blood in the rogue's face.

"I'm not sure how the whole wish thing works," Josh said. He brandished Amber's wooden puzzle dagger.

"But I now know that one of her wishes was to send herself back and find the help we needed to beat you, and she found it in the Taichomée: Bogi's pride, which she did as Acotactac." Josh had to laugh once more. "While my mother rampaged and became dormant all those years, Bogi's powers waned too. And my sister watched her mother and chose the right moment to wander into Bogi's camp of generals like an orphan girl, generals your sister, my mother, was saving as support for you, for this very fight, should it arise. Yet, my sister stole them away, one by one, and closed their minds to you and my mother. I imagine Bogi was quite surprised to find he had no ally waiting for him after he fled the bunker. How long do you suppose my sister waited to approach the Taichomée? Centuries? Millenia? To learn to steal them away?"

The rogue fell silent, lost in thought.

"Do you see," Josh asked. "The first time you won because you had Bogi's army, so my sister took it away from you. So the djinn sent her back to an appropriate time to be able to steal it. Then something happened, you still won. Her second wish was to keep me in the fight. So the djinn sent my friends back to keep me alive, but you won again and the third wish was to try it once more, but this time they brought a little extra firepower with them. Always, among those sent back again was the same sister who stole the Taichomée. In case you're wondering, this is why your little attempt to infect me failed, for the most part.

"That might have given you a chance right there, only you created a masterful tactician who tricked a fourth wish out of the djinn. Granted she played him, but that wish ensured you would never find her. A final wish was to free the djinn, which allowed her into right here," Josh tapped the side of his head with the wooden blade. "And you couldn't read my thoughts and plans anymore. Even now, she tells me the plan and she is the reason my mind is blocked from your own."

The rogue's lips curled, and tears swelled in his eyes.

Josh poised himself.

"I'd be embarrassed if I were you," Josh said. "You got played by a little girl and an old man."

Josh plunged the wooden puzzle blade at the rogue's chest, but it wouldn't drive in. He lacked the strength. He pressed, but it was his own chest that exploded with agony. The skin was tough. Josh cried, screamed at the rogue, and found that connection between his ribs and lungs demanding that he cut the angry death sentence short. He bore his weight over the blade. The rogue's flesh wouldn't tear. Josh cursed at his own frailty tearing him apart from inside. The paladin's flesh was not as strong as the rogue's. It wasn't fair. Even as the rogue lay helpless, he still inflicted more pain upon Josh.

Finally, he drew back in defeat. He cried. After all he'd overcome, he lacked the strength now to finish the job.

He held up the knife, too embarrassed to announce that someone else would have to finish what he could not.

Cadence's fingers appeared, held Josh's hand and helped press the dagger back against the rogue's chest, but nothing. Even Cadence grimaced strain.

Bricktain's steel hand suddenly struck down on the top of the blade's handle. The knife sank into the rogue's chest.

"Die dammit," Bricktain yelled into his face.

The rogue screamed, but when the clicking mechanism of the blade-puzzle burst, signifying that it had expanded inside the rogue's heart, he fell silent.

"Unbelievable," Speatsh cried hovering in human form above the group. "My entire life hunting this monster, and Brickface not only kills him, but he turned it a Hallmark moment too!"

The sounds of battle suddenly changed. The guardians and scouts fell, most dead, some unconscious. Others stood still, unmoving, while others fled along with their generals who disappeared into the dark.

Those that remained snarled.

"They didn't all die," Cadence said. "I thought they were supposed to die from shock."

"They weren't shocked," Bean replied. "We weakened him. The fight, the strain, the revelation. When he started losing, his slaves didn't all run to help. Many fled. That's not a demonstration of a master in control."

"That's not good enough," Josh said. He brought himself to his feet and took a stance that told his familiar allies to move. He unleashed the fury of his cloak. It pained him, but his anger, frustration, relief and what was still to come drove him. When he was done, the rogue lay in pieces and a puddle—the evidence of its creator sprayed across the paladin's face and uniform, which suddenly felt heavier on his shoulders.

"I am the paladin," Josh groaned, but then fell quiet quickly to the pain in his chest. "This wolf is dead."

Are you okay, Josh finally asked Neon.

I believe so. A big burly man found some painful water in the cab and said I was really lucky. He's gluing me back together and telling me I remind him of his daughter. Do you think his daughter was shot too?

Does this mean you can get out of my head now?

No. We are mates. I will always be there, and no one else ever will be again.

Bricktain suddenly laughed, cried just a little and screamed adulation at the sky as the reality of their victory set in.

Josh leaned on Bricktain once more to stand. "Not yet," he said. He began to make his way towards the black carriage. The others hadn't noticed it, but Josh had, even expected it was coming. "This isn't over yet."

Cadence now helped Bricktain trudge with Josh through the cemetery. She herself limped heavily on her right side. The three friends approached the circle of ancients left surrounding the carriage that had been retrieved from Thug's basement. Josh ordered the others to free the ancients' bindings. He opened the carriage that earlier this night released Speatsh against Genre. He painstakingly climbed in.

The ancient sat, her withered hands held her knees as if expecting some amusement ride to begin. Her eyes sharpened at Josh's intrusion, and her snout curled a set of black teeth from the insult.

Cadence drew in the opposite side of the carriage and seated herself besides Josh.

"Hello, again," Cadence said.

The ancient's eye's widened.

"I hear you two met," Josh told the ancient. "Cadence said you gave some pretty impressive clues to help her realize that my mother was really a traitor."

The ancient coiled back as if ashamed.

"Pretty slick play, there," Cadence said.

"I assume, you're angry," Josh added. "It's hard to tell with dogs."

The ancient's brow widened, and she sighed at Josh's feeble attempt to get under her skin.

Josh reached into one of Wolf's Breath pockets and withdrew the pictures that Thomas had torn from the ancient book in the museum.

"Did you know my uncle was an antiques dealer," Josh asked. He handed the pages to the ancient. "Well, of course you do. You know everything, don't you?"

The wolf said nothing. Her long fingers fumbled a little with unfolding the thin pages.

Josh offered to help, but in reaching wondered if he shouldn't have gotten some sort of medical treatment first. The ancient accepted the gesture, and Josh opened the parchment to her.

"He gathered weapons," Josh continued. "Weapons that made us stronger, but you knew that too, didn't you?"

The ancient said nothing.

"See, they told me that the rogue had this connection to my mind, and I had to ask myself, why would he have access to my mind?"

Still, the ancient returned no reaction.

"And what is the process of shunning a member of the circle," Josh asked. He pointed to the papers in the ancient's hand. "That record suggests the circle grants power. Now, if I were kicking someone out of my house, I wouldn't let them leave with the keys so they could get back in. I'd take them away. I imagine your little family must be able to take power if it can give power. So why did the rogue still have power to know my mind. I mean, I can understand still being a wolf and all, but being able to connect to the community's mind seems like, at least to me, something that would be denied as part of the excommunication from the community. After all, being kicked from the community, but still being in the community's thoughts isn't really an exile, is it?"

The ancient's eyes now looked to Josh, then floated back to the ancient text in his hands.

"So, if he was cast out from the circle," Josh started to explain again, "Why would he have the ability to connect with me? And how did you exile him if you were all bound, well most of you," Josh pulled out a small crossbow and began looking for cylinders to load into it.

He had none and somehow found it humorous.

"I wager, the only way, he could have known my mind after being cast out was if he had some help," Josh suggested. "I'll bet that when this energy draining ceremony took place, somebody in the circle didn't quite take back all the power they were supposed to, did you? Perhaps you let him hold just enough so you could talk to him. You were the one who was really in my head, weren't you? And you told him what I knew. Am I right?"

Now Josh had her full attention.

"Granted he'd always be a wolf, he'd always have that power. After all, a human can't stop being a human even when exiled. I'm sure it's the same for ancients." Josh said. "You have to fast the wolf out of an ancient's system, but you're still an ancient. You used your power to promise him a way back in, didn't you?"

The monster sat motionless, unblinking. Josh thought about taking the challenge and staring her down, but he knew he'd shutter first. "At first, I thought it could be my mother, but she was killed, wasn't she? So how did my mind-reading friend get into his head?" Josh pointed a shaky, gloved finger at the ancient. "You were the only one who wasn't bound when Cadence found you. I also find that interesting. We thought our own guardian had gotten into his head because you were all naturally linked, but that wasn't it, not fully, was it? His link to others was through you. You were his conduit, and you're the one that's linked to everything, aren't you?"

The ancient shifted in her seat and stared down at Josh. The paladin's height in the tall carriage must have appeared most unimpressive to the taller ancient. She could have swiped him and Cadence down in one blow, no doubt, but Josh assumed she was aware of the demise that his allies would bear upon her from outside the wagon. After all, her starving form, hidden beneath earth and calcium couldn't have exactly helped her fighting skills any.

"I know, these are silly questions, but I don't think I would have had them." Josh explained. "But then, I saw this picture," Josh helped her locate the ink drawing, the one with the lone wolf leading the others towards the hearse. He brought it to the top of the pile of papers in her hand. "At first, I thought this was instruction for how this hearse was supposed to work, but then it occurred to me, this figure was a collector, just like my uncle."

The ancient's head snapped from the papers back to Josh.

"You're the genius," Josh said. "All of this was about you, wasn't it?"

Her brow sharpened upon Josh's accusation.

"You're the true rogue," Josh said confidently.

The weakened monster loosened the grip on the paper in her hands. She flashed her teeth and hacked a dry breath.

"That probably should frighten me," Josh said. "Are you frightened, Cadence?"

Cadence agreed. It was frightening.

"But you respect life," Josh said. "That's the rule, right? You have to respect life, or you can't be part of the circle. Take life and you can't have any power other than being dog."

The ancient shifted in her seat again, this time inching towards the door.

Josh relaxed in his seat, even sprawled out to find comfort for his ribs. He coughed some.

"If you were a killer, you'd be the one laying dead out there, wouldn't you? So you needed someone to do it for you," Josh said. "Know what I think? I think you planned all of this. I think you were tired of your role. What were you? The janitor?" He waited a moment while he laughed at his own joke. Ow! But he needed to laugh, so he laughed some more.

"Doesn't matter, whatever it was. Someone told me it was something not important," Josh said. "I'll bet you thought you got the absolutely worst task that the circle could possibly give. While everyone was getting roles of queen and protector and royal taffy puller, you were called to be the royal vomit eater or something else just as worthless."

"Historian," Cadence said.

"That's right," Josh said. "There's an exciting job."

The ancient growled.

"So you convinced some of your friends, like the rogue and my mom to turn their backs on the circle, didn't you," Josh asked. "I don't know how, but you did, huh? You knew things that historians would know. You were the smart one so you convinced one of them to actually leave the circle and find someone who could build you a device to take the power that your own kind wouldn't give you. And you convinced the queen to entrap the others, or try to. That's why you had a war, isn't it? Am I off here?"

The ancient regained her elegant, pompous poise and looked forward, past Josh. She appeared to be waiting for something more important than Josh to happen.

"The rogue was your collector, wasn't he," Josh continued and touched his finger to the prominent figure that appeared on the page in the ancient's hands. "See, that picture shows one dog leading the others by a leash. He wasn't bringing them to life. He was collecting them for whoever was sitting here," Josh rifled up the ink picture of the hearse and tapped the drawing that portrayed light erupting from the hearse. "So I had to ask, if this figure was collecting the others, who was sitting inside the carriage? I knew it couldn't be my mother," Josh bit back the cocktail of emotion that now accompanied this word. "After all, she was already queen. She already had the power. So I knew it had to be somebody else, but whom?"

The ancient puffed up, sitting even more regal and inhaled a majestic breath. She smirked upon Josh in a way that made him fear that he may have misjudged her self-restraint from attacking him.

"And then I open the door and find you here," Josh said. "Who else would be sitting here other than the mastermind? You convinced the rogue to help you gain power. You convinced my mother too. Now, both are dead. If you wanted, you could probably bind them and bring them back, couldn't you?"

She remained still.

Josh felt himself getting annoyed that he wasn't getting a reaction.

"The only reason I don't kill you now is because that would be depriving the family you had wronged of their own well-deserved judgment," Josh said.

The ancient laughed, or seemed to laugh, but it came out as a dry cackle.

"I don't know why you're laughing," Josh said. "I'd be angry if I were you. I mean, I'll bet you had the rogue—excuse me, the one you wanted us to think was the rogue, commission someone powerful to create this wagon. I'll also bet that its maker had a change of heart and hid it, and you had to spend all those long, miserable years looking for it. Well, not you. You had to stay in the cave and listen to nonstop *drip, drip, drip,* didn't you?"

The historian huffed into the air in a way that Josh assumed was supposed to demonstrate her importance above his own.

"Know what's really funny, though," Josh said. "This isn't the hearse, and it's not giving you one ounce of power."

Now, the ancient looked down upon Josh, her brow beginning to quiver with trouble.

"Not a bad little misdirection, was it," Josh asked. He laughed, but stopped short when he gurgled up another throat full of blood. He apologized for coughing it up. He cleaned it away from his mouth and wiped it on the seat next to him. "We used the real carriage to bring them back to life, and then we had a little bear sneak them in here to make you think this was really it." Josh laughed a little more and stopped yet again to spit out the accompanying blood. "Those little ash children are really great decoys, aren't they. They have a real talent for hiding things on the ground so we can—say—sneak a dead ancient body into one magical carriage and then move that live body to this fake carriage. Of course, they did it right under your nose and made you think it all happened right inside here."

"That was a bit confusing, Josh," Cadence said.

"Oh, did I talk too fast," Josh asked.

"It was confusing," Cadence repeated.

"It sounded confusing out here," Bean's voice cried from outside the carriage.

Speatsh cursed. "Punch her in the throat with your sword already!"

"Quiet," Bean replied. "He's being all smart and stuff."

"Oh, God," Speatsh cried. "He's gonna get himself killed."

Josh flexed a sword then chanced leaning forward in his seat, his turn to intimidate.

Bad plan!

He changed his mind and tried not to let his pain show.

"The real hearse was kind of a surprise to me too." He pointed out the window of the carriage to the injured body of the Silver Bullet. "I thought it was crazy when I first thought of it myself, but we snuck your dead friends into it and it brought them back to life. Which you might have known, except, I have a feeling you were lost in your own anticipation of thinking you were going to finally rule the world and stuff," Josh shook his finger as a teacher scolding a day-dreaming student. "You weren't paying attention, were you?"

Now, the ancient looked stunned. Josh felt better.

"When your boys tossed one of your dead siblings in here, we changed it out for one we already revived in the bullet, and you were all too happy to see what you wanted to see, that you were going to be queen and that this was your long, lost hearse!"

Cadence laughed this time, startling the historian. "Any of you stupid wolves might have heard their hearts beating if you weren't so easy to egg into a fight out there."

"Especially the so-called rogue," Josh said.

"Especially him," Cadence agreed. "If he hadn't been so busy trying to control every mind of every slave he owned, he might have heard their thoughts through your own conduit, but—no—he just had to beat up Josh."

The ancient looked through the window towards the Silver Bullet and then down to the picture that Josh had been carving in the door with a tip of a sewing pin that he had found stuck to Wolf's Breath. The picture was a stick man fighting a stick monster. A conversation balloon appeared over the stick man's head saying, "You suck!"

The ancient let the pages in her hands fall to the floor. Here, Josh relished as he watched her realization that her hopes, and who knows how many years of planning and dreams, crumple at her feet.

"I know," Josh said also looking out to the Silver Bullet. "It doesn't look like a carriage, but I remembered what Thug said, that's my godfather who's lying dead outside right now because of you." With this, Josh somehow found the hate needed to ignore the pain of flexing his sword up to the historian's neck. "My godfather said the engine for the diesel came from a nuclear powered stagecoach in the eighteen hundreds. I mean, he really thought it was nuclear powered, but it wasn't, was it? It was powered by the dead that had been killed in its presence. Then that also made me wonder about how many times that carriage might have been rebuilt by hunters who didn't know what it really was and were only trying to make it more modern and helpful. And then, somehow, it still ended up right under your nose and you were too stupid to see it."

The historian's eyes fell softly upon Josh, and she slouched back into her seat, much as Josh had done to make his own pain more comfortable.

"How many lives do you think had been collected into its engine over the centuries by hunters? How many packs of dogs destroyed? Or dens? Tens of thousands? More than that? Enough to bring back your dead kin? Enough to bring my Godfather back," Josh asked and then scathed out, "How about my wife?"

The paladin might have tried to leap, press his sword into the historian's neck, but this time, he exercised the restraint, mostly because he doubted he could actually perform the task without tearing his lungs apart first, which he needed to swear while he was stabbing her.

"And then I saw those," Josh pointed to the pages that now rested on the floor. He'd thought about bending over, but he'd played stupid enough for one night. "They're really old. Now, my friends, they thought I was crazy, so I suggested we try it out on Speatsh first, and, you know, it worked. Can you believe that? Do you realize that if it hadn't worked on Speatsh, you might have been getting what you wanted right now?"

Josh straightened up.

"Well, anyways," he announced. "Thought you should know, this thing isn't stealing one drop of power for you." Josh turned and made his way out of the carriage, practically falling into the hands that suddenly reached to catch him as he did so.

"And I thought you were the stupid one," Bean said, assisting Josh safely to his feet. Bricktain watched at the door to ensure that Cadence had exited as well.

"I thought she looked like a constipated Chihuahua," Speatsh, in his human form once more, said as he assisted Cadence down. He purposely pronounced the hard Hs in *Chihuahua* like some ignorant school kid.

Speatsh was much quieter now that he didn't have his brace. He almost didn't seem like Speatsh without it, Josh thought. After

Cadence and Josh had exited. Old Cheatham approached the door to the carriage and leaned in.

"My turn," Speatsh greeted in disgust, then he yanked the long monster through the door by her ankles. The ancient fell flat on her back, and her head cracked loudly against the runner. "You wanted to rule it all," Speatsh announced dragging her out and a few feet away from the carriage, before dropping her at Thomas's feet. "Well come on! Rule us!"

Speatsh leaned down to force the historian to her feet, but the elder monster suddenly rose on her own, and lifted off the ground.

"No cheating," Speatsh cried in confusion.

He finally realized that the circle of dogs surrounding the area grew bright. Their eyes, radiated silver, but not blinding, The historian remained in the air, silent and unmoving in the center of their circle. The ancients making up the perimeter howled in sequence, first one, then another. Their calls were not strange. They weren't high-pitched, not monstrous. Nothing about them seemed out of place, they were of any average wolf or dog baying at the moon. Each ancient then took a turn howling a dry, long call until every member had made their say. Upon the last member's howl, the historian fell.

From the circle, one ancient stepped. Despite his mummified appearance, he moved in long smooth strides to the fallen historian. A set of long silver nails began to stretch from his fingers, and he suddenly buried them into the historian's chest. His claws shrank and the executioner returned to his place in the circle.

"Nicer than I would have been," Josh said. He suddenly felt eager to remove himself from among the ancients.

"Good idea," Bean agreed, then he suddenly rose into the air as well.

Speatsh moved quickly to catch Josh in his surprise and sudden theft of his crutch that had been the time-traveling biker. Bean rose as the historian had and floated steadily towards the center where the false hearse remained.

"I helped you," Bean yelled. "I helped!"

This time the ancients' eyes appeared gold. The entire circle appeared as fire emanating from their faces.

"We can't let them kill him, Josh," Cadence said.

"Leave him alone," Josh yelled, but wondered how he could possibly stop them.

Again, the ancients howled in sequence, followed by a unified high and long howl. Then Bean lowered back to the ground.

Bean continued to helplessly object.

A different ancient emerged from the circle and approached Bean. He touched his left index finger to the fallen historian's head and his left one to just above the bridge of Bean's nose. Bean's head drooped forward, and he became silent. The creature touching him breathed into his face, and Bean suddenly inhaled. The creature returned to the circle.

Now, Bean fell. His bones shifted as all wolves' bones shift, their loud crackling above the graveyard. Only, Bean didn't scream. In a moment, he was his golden-brown, werewolf form. He then began to grow white and tall until he had taken on the form of an ancient—not decrepit and devastated as those who were now free of the rogue's intention, but silvery white and fiersome, muscular stature.

Another ancient walked towards Bean. This one took his hand and escorted him back towards the outer circle to an empty spot where the historian should have been standing. Bean then turned inwards and stood silently and respectfully.

A fourth of the creatures, stepped towards Josh now and gripped his head, its snout folded into its face. Then it pressed its mouth over Josh's own and nose. Air flooded the paladin's lungs, but air unfamiliar, air fresh, sweet. It was easy to breathe now. Josh found himself taking in long deep drinks from within the ancient's lungs. Once Josh felt the pain drain from his body, something moved into his mouth and down his throat.

Eww! Tongue!

Josh's instinct was to pull back, but the ancient held him. The paladin's chest began to feel firmer, stronger. His ribs cracked, twisted as the ancient's healing knowledge repaired him. Finally, the creature drew away and returned to its own place.

Josh took a moment to realize that his strength had returned. He let go of Speatsh and maintained his own weight once more.

Another creature then turned and howled. "You," it seemed to say as it extended a long finger outwards of the circle. It yelled again. To any other being, it sounded like another dog growl, but, to the ancients, it said, "Oldest!" It took a moment for Josh to realize that the ancient's finger had settled upon the three Cracey's. In particular, it rested upon Winter, or the third and oldest Cracey.

Winter moved towards the circle, then into the circle, where she too raised up and went through a similar process as Bean had gone through. Then, after she lowered to the ground, each ancient, in turn, approached and pressed a finger to her chest. Last to approach her was Bean. Upon performing his duty, he returned silently to his position in the circle.

Presently, the circled bowed, dropped to a knee and genuflected even more deeply. Winter motioned to them and they stood. Then she approached Josh and kissed his cheek and then the other before embracing him. She smiled. How had he not seen it before, her eyes, his little sister's eyes? Tears streamed her face, and she exhaled.

Winter placed her hand on Josh's chest and took Cadence's hand.

"Protector," the wolves howled in unison, not in any humanly sound, but in choir of the creature's song that sings to the moon, hollow, soothing, high-pitched. "Protector." Strangely, Josh understood what they were saying.

Winter lifted Cadence's hand to her mouth, and her teeth grew long and straight, with far too many teeth than any mouth should have.

"No," Cadence replied and withdrew herself from Winter's grasp. "I'll protect you, but not that way."

Winter pointed to Josh. "Him," she said, her voice smooth and soft, but without tongue.

"Him," Cadence asked. "Protect Josh?" Cadence looked back

over the battlefield and paused upon the Silver Bullet, knowing her Nick would never stand.

She then perused the circle of creatures, looking for familiar faces or what might be two particular faces that she should know.

"Where are my parents," Cadence asked. She turned her head back with tears and twisting, sad lips. "Why not them? They're the protectors."

Winter's head bowed and then turned to Bean.

Bean shook his head.

"Why," Cadence asked. "Why not them?"

Bean stepped forward. The circle's gaze turned suddenly on Bean and he stepped back to his place within it.

The circle gazed next upon Speatsh and he raised into the air.

"Don't bring me into this," Speatsh spat. "I'll knock your whole kennel club out, right now."

Winter glared.

Speatsh glared back. "Do you like being alive," Speatsh asked. "All you all can thank me by leaving me the hell alone."

Winter nodded. She smiled a little, and Speatsh lowered to the ground. Winter turned to Acotactac instead. Acotactac turned from Winter to Bean.

"You bit Bean," Lisa suddenly announced. "It wasn't Barbara. It was you." She looked to Bean. "You a liar!"

Bean nodded. Winter quickly chastised him with a glare. When she turned back, Lisa was standing in front of Winter. She slapped Winter with such speed that it even surprised the powerful wolf.

"He is not your slave," Lisa's hatred oozed with each vowel. "That stops with you."

Winter stepped back in apology. Lisa charged past Winter and approached the newest member in the circle ancients. She hugged onto him. He waited for Winter's approval to hug her back.

"This isn't what you've earned," Lisa muffled into Bean's embrace as he pet her head. He pressed her back.

Cracey appeared at Lisa's side. "He chooses this," Cracey said. "Just like Speatsh didn't choose it. No more blood. No more shame. He wants to preserve us, to protect others."

Lisa pulled away. He continued to pet her head.

"I guess you didn't lose your humanity after all," Lisa said.

Bean nodded and looked strangely intent upon Cracey. Cracey was silent for some time then, "Okay," Cracey finally said in reply to Bean's look. "Your parents."

Cadence, once more, looked hopefully over the circle. Which were they?

"They didn't leave any bodies to recover," Cracey explained. "They destroyed themselves. We do not know why. They hid themselves. The circle never found them, but Jasper believes they did it to protect you, hoping they'd placed you where you needed to be." Cracey nodded towards Josh, who now clutched Neon's shoulder and his chest at the same time to keep standing. The flu-like symptoms of being healed had started to hit Josh.

"I promise," Cadence said. "I'll protect him."

That's my job, Neon's voice snapped into Josh's mind. *We are mates.*

The circle suddenly shifted in one motion. They left their places and began moving towards Oliver's studio.

"What are they doing," Bricktain asked.

"There is still one who needs judgement," Cracey answered.

"Mom," Josh asked. He hadn't forgotten about her. He'd even contemplated including her in his plan, but felt she served the cause better by staying unrevived.

"She won't come back either," Cracey said as she sat with the others, watching the circle disappear out of the graveyard and back into the mausoleum, which led into the bunker where Barbara's body still lay in the cavern where Jasper and Cadence had left it to be forgotten.

"To take back her power," Josh asked.

"No," Cracey replied. "Her power comes from blood. She was exiled, like her brother. They wish to ensure her body cannot be revived."

Josh's eyes fell upon Jasper's body. This had been his enemy, and he had fallen at an unjust hand.

"Wait," Josh called after the migrating group.

He approached Bean.

The gold dog turned to him, a familiar, mocking look peered down upon the paladin, even if he was a dog.

"Thank you," Josh said.

Bean smiled, but Josh didn't know it; it's difficult for humans to know a dog smile. When he realized Josh didn't understand, he licked the paladin's face until he did. It was a silly behavior, but humans comprehended so very little of anything else.

38 ~ The Littlest Host

Thomas and Speatsh stepped back from the garden wall, a hedge of ivy and a large door. Josh knew where they were. Everyone who grew up in Plattsville knew about the first grave in the oldest portions of the cemetery. Here, even the battle of the previous night had not touched it.

"This will stir stories," Bricktain had said the previous night, upon looking over the graveyard where shattered stone and fallen flesh littered every corner. The Silver Bullet stood as a junk heap. Bricktain couldn't even spot the bodies of his fallen allies.

"How do we clean this up before anyone sees," he asked.

"I have this," Neon said, holding up the handle to her broken vacuum.

Stop that, Josh thought.

Relax, Neon answered. *It was a joke.*

Now, in the morning light, the wall of ivy before Josh almost appeared blue and hedged like some maze from Alice's wonderland.

Josh startled his two friends. He said nothing. He didn't know what he could say.

"I see the elemental queen has finally left," Speatsh said.

"Yeah," Josh scanned the cemetery just to make sure Speatsh was right. Then he kept scanning because he'd forgotton Speatsh had said anything.

Though it appeared ragged, the cemetery seemed nothing more than the site of mass vandalism. Tandem, to her chagrin, seemed unchanged. Or maybe she needed to fast. Either way, she and her kind's final contribution was to whisk away the bodies and much of the ungravely debris. She left the bodies of those who had someone to claim them.

Before leaving, she suggested that Josh visit Dublin if he ever found himself in the vicinity.

Remaining hunters, mostly walking dead it seemed, roamed the cemetery repairing gouges and digging graves for the honorable fallen in hopes of restoring some respect to the garden of remembrance.

The Nomads volunteered to fix the waterline, fence and other items that could use some repairs.

"How is Miss Meade," Thomas asked. Then asked again. "Sir Josh?"

"Huh? Oh. She's not waking up," Josh replied and turned to Speatsh. "How do you do it? How do you, Jasper and my sister do it, but Natalie's not waking up?"

"Natalie did what no one should have expected from her, and learned it from a teacher no one could have expected any less from. Jasper may have been the best at blocking his mind," Speatsh said. "Pain hid Brickface's mind from what I understand. I can't say how our sister did it, but she had a long time to practice it. As for me, no one wants to be in the mind of an angry old man."

"How did you keep them from knowing you knew the truth about my," he snorted, then continued, "Our mom and Bogi."

"I lied," Speatsh replied. "I lied a lot, especially to myself. Flood the truth with enough lies, and it's easier to hide it in plain sight. I created too many false images. If you can't remember what is truth and what is a lie, the person reading your mind can't tell neither. I imagine my mind wasn't a favorite nor reliable hangout spot for the rogue or anyone else."

"So that's why all the different stories," Josh said. He quickly changed the topic. "And you both knew what was going on this entire time."

"Hey, don't look at me," Speatsh objected. "I was in the dark on a lot more than you realize. Everything I knew, I figured out on my own—Well, almost everything. The only thing that made it easier was convincing Barbara to disconnect herself from the link so we could accomplish a few tricks without her knowing, or anyone she was connected to for that matter. This would have ended differently if she hadn't believed me, and I imagine her pride to not get caught may have had some to do with it as well."

"You lobotomized her—"

"Hey," Speatsh scowled. "It wasn't a lobotomy."

"Whatever," Josh replied. "You did it to keep her from waking me up."

"It's not all about you, paladin," Speatsh said. "I did it to keep her, and Bogi for that matter, out of your dad's head, after you sister bit him."

"Cracey bit him," Josh asked. "But I thought—

"No, dummy! Your other sister. Barbara tried to kill your dad," Speatsh said. "She left him for dead. He was her emergency escape package, just like my father had been, only I didn't piece it together in time. Little sis saved him. I taught him how to use lies to confuse psychic intruders. He picked up on it better than Dustin's dad."

"And he turned Nick and Dustin," Josh added.

"Yes," Speatsh replied. "Under Acotactac's presence and protection. He was learning."

"And Natalie," Josh added.

"He would have turned Natalie, and all of you for that matter," Speatsh said.

"But mom got to Natalie first."

"No," Speatsh interrupted again. "Mom actually tried to eat Natalie, but your girlfriend put a pole through her head, which is pretty vicious for a human in my book. Acotactac bit Natalie to hide her, and to make sure no one would find her. Our Taichomée sister dropped her into the hands of the one person whose responsibility it was to discover encroaching generals in this territory, and the one person who had become so proficient in blocking and invading the minds of other wolves. Exposing Natalie to him, exposed her to his abilities."

"And somehow, mom didn't know about dad surviving," Josh asked.

"He's not my dad," Speatsh said. "But, yeah, she knew about him, but she thought she had done it after failing to kill him. That's how good Acotactac was. She bit Stan after your mother attacked him, then hid him so well that she convinced Barbara that Stan actually belonged to her. Then Stan stayed in limbo until I disconnected

Barbara and taught Stan to do what I do. That's also why the rogue couldn't get into Stan's head."

"Did Eric ever know anything," Josh asked.

"Some," Speatsh continued. "I believe Acotactac helped shroud them, probably the same way she hid that she stole the Taichomée from Bogi and Jasper from who we had all thought was the rogue. Eric just stayed in the dark, which wasn't easy for Stan, but Eric didn't quite take to the shroud. Most of Stan's recruiting in taverns were for misdirection than anything. Stan did a lot of work on his own. If Acotactac had more time, she might have been able to solve that, but it just didn't happen, and we needed Stan to get to work. Nick never fully went to Acotactac either. I mean, he could block, but his ability was spotty at best. From what I heard, he wasn't completely closed until Jasper and Natalie started training him after they had fled to the island. Even then, he was still unreliable at it. Unfortunately, we had to work with Nick's handicap or we might have seemed a little suspicious. So not only did I have to lie to myself, I had to lie to all of you—Nick mostly, but especially you."

"So why didn't my mom know about Cracey," Josh asked. "If Cracey was a dog—"

"That's the mystery. All I can think of is she hadn't awakened," Speatsh said. "She was weak enough that Jasper could turn her into his line. I mean, he actually turned an ancient by blood to his own line. You got bit last night and you didn't even get rabies. I think that's what hid her, camouflaged her. Worked to our advantage."

"I wasn't awake either," Josh said. "They read my mind."

"The historian can do that," Speatsh said. "The link is never broken for him from ancient blood."

"Except Cracey's," Josh said, almost laughing.

"Because she was camouflaged," Speatsh replied annoyed. "Personally, I think that was just a helpful twist of fate thanks to Jasper's ignorance. Plus, he really is amazing at it."

"And explain how Acotactac was able to make guardians," Josh said. "I thought ancients made generals."

"You saw it yourself when they turned a general into an ancient," Speatsh said. "They choose how much strength they can give someone."

"Why not make everyone generals," Josh asked. "For that matter, why not build an entire army of generals to fight for us? Why not just bite me and everyone else here and make us stronger? And for that matter, why didn't Acotactac tell us where the entrance to the cave was when she was in the bunker? Also, why did you need blood to become a wolf?"

"I am ancient, but I have never received any power from the circle," Speatsh said.

"What about the rest?"

"Do I look like someone who knows everything," Speatsh roared. "You sound like one of those lazy movie critics who has to have everything spelled out for them and confuses the invitation to use their imagination with a plot hole.

"I don't even know what's going on inside my head, you numb knob. Maybe she didn't do it because she has your resentment against human slaves. Maybe she didn't do it because it was a drain on her mind. You saw the rogue, he basically went catatonic and had to be protected when he used his own power. Maybe she didn't tell us because she didn't know. Or maybe she knew we'd all die if we discovered them. I don't know! But this I know—I don't know. You don't know, so why should I have to. We won, so get off my back. Whatever her plan was worked, didn't it?"

"Did it," Josh asked.

Speatsh opened his mouth to speak and must have realized Josh was referring to Amber. He stayed silent.

"You knew all this." Josh said.

"No," Speatsh replied.

"And you," Josh asked, flashing a glare at Thomas.

"I wasn't sure how much to believe," Thomas said. "And I wouldn't have believed except," he stopped himself. "It's complicated."

"So uncomplicate it," Josh said.

"I was warned," Thomas explained, "But I didn't much heed that warning until, I got an untimely visit from Bean. If Bean hadn't come to me, I probably wouldn't have given a second thought to it. I wouldn't have shaved Bogi and remembered a scar that I had given him. I knew there was truth to Bogi's betrayal when I discovered it.

"Then we went to the museum, and I noticed some graffiti before we went in, and we found the book. You seemed to have an idea about it, and that's when I realized the time of which I was warned about was upon us. I didn't rightly know how to plan for that, so I thought on the spot."

Josh voiced his disbelief.

"No," Thomas replied. "It's true. I knew two things: the warning was real, and, if there was a chance the hearse was real, you would want to bring someone back who could strengthen you most. Speatsh seemed the most likely candidate for whatever plan you might have concocted."

"Not my wife," Josh asked.

"She wasn't dead at the time of my deduction," Thomas explained. "I realized many would have died, myself included, if I didn't come up with an escape plan. The rogue provided it. I suspected that if we survived and did figure out where this hearse was, you would find a way to test it on Speatsh—well, most likely Speatsh. Should the test prove fruitful, I thought why stop there. I had planned on giving him one of my blood pouches when he arose, but then the rogue created his own concoction to turn you, and I thought, 'what a much more intriguing idea.'

"I knew having some of my food handy might give Speatsh an edge, having the concoction the rogue made—well—that would make him a menace. I doubted if I'd just taken the syringe and tried to run with it that we would not have survived the escape, so I stored it in the only place I know I could protect it, in my veins. That silly wolf thought I had tried to turn myself."

"But the other person," Josh said. "It was planned."

"Other person," Thomas asked.

"She helped you fight me all the way back to the bunker," Josh said.

"That wasn't planned," Thomas said. "Once she made the first attack on you, I—"

"She looked like Amber," Josh said.

"I realized she was trying to drain that poisonous blood from you," Thomas replied, ignoring Josh. "That's when I knew what to do."

Thomas recognized the pain that Josh kept hidden just now.

"I'm sorry we couldn't revive her," Thomas said.

"Why didn't it work," Josh asked, barely audible to even himself.

"I," Thomas started. "We—"

"We think the hearse was designed to only work on ancients," Speatsh said. "Or their bloodline. That's why it didn't work on Nick or Richard either."

"Or maybe the Bullet ran out of power," Thomas added. "We're not sure. I'm sorry, Mr Revlon."

"The other Amber," Josh said. "Where is she? She came back with the others. They told me she did."

Thomas fell silent. He excused Speatsh, who trumped off complaining that he was tired of the stupid conversation anyway.

"Did you know this used to be a schoolyard," Thomas asked, and gestured to the hedge wall and gate looming besides him and Josh. "Inside this hedge is a little piece of land where Oliver made a friend once."

"The dog attack," Josh said. "Every kid knows that story."

Thomas nodded. "The dog attack? Is that what they call it?"

"It's legend," Josh replied.

"I wasn't a good father," Thomas said. "Nor a good man. I heard little sense in mortals, so I ignored most, despised most. I've loved mortals, but when your life keeps moving forward, and the lives of those around you don't, you tend to belittle the short-lived, devalue what they can actually do for you. It's less painful not to get involved with mortals."

Josh waited for Thomas to make sense.

"I've only bit two human beings," Thomas said. "One was Oliver's mother, when she nearly died giving birth to Oliver. She lived a long time, but her body finally learned how to fight my disease, and it eventually killed her. I couldn't watch it. I left her. I left her care, left her Oliver. She loved him so much. She taught him to garden, and this was our backyard. This is—was my son's garden. It's his place."

Thomas drew a key from his pocket and turned to the gate within the hedge wall. He was unable to hide his own agony over his lost son.

"Until now, I had believed that only Oliver set foot in here, but I believe we're going to find that's not true," Thomas explained.

"You've never been in here," Josh asked.

"It wasn't my place."

"Because his wife is buried here," Josh said.

"Is that how the story goes now," Thomas asked.

"Just rumor mostly. Some people have said that they remember Oliver making friends with a small girl who went to school here."

"Yes," Thomas said. "That's true. She played ball with him right inside this place. Then she grew and came back as a teacher, and they continued to be great friends to each other. Then an old man returned to town with some ravenous dogs."

"Jasper?"

"Oh yes," Thomas replied. "He appeared, then he disappeared, became a hermit until people forgot him and then he emerged again like a new old man that no one remembered. He wasn't always so friendly, and his dogs weren't so nice."

Thomas unlocked the gate to Oliver's garden and invited Josh in. Josh followed.

"Josh. The little girl was Amber," Thomas said.

Josh suddenly stopped and tried to process this statement.

"When I met her she had grown up to become the teacher at the school," Thomas continued. "Oliver had saved her and called for me to help her. I wouldn't have, but my son was persuasive, threatening you might say.

"When I arrived, she had been injured some time. She was dying and delirious. She made no sense. I wouldn't have come to see her at all, but Oliver was adamant and he's—he was usually so well-behaved.

"She warned us. She tried. We didn't understand. You have to understand. She was delirious and made no sense. She said something about not letting her give him the needle. She kept saying, 'when you see the needle, don't let her give it to him.' For three weeks, that's all she babbled. We were sick of hearing it, but she made sure we heard it—screaming sometimes until I was ready to kill her myself, but Oliver took care of her. Only, she never got any better. Then we learned why. If I hadn't brushed off mortals as I had after my wife died, I might have recognized Amber the moment I first met all of you."

"What are you saying," Josh asked.

"It's not my place," Thomas said. He directed Josh's attention into the garden. "She should be the one." He grabbed Josh's shoulder. Josh withdrew and realized he wasn't wearing his devastating robe.

"The other person I bit, was unexpected," Thomas said. By now, he had led Josh inside the realm of Oliver's sacred hedge.

"Upset her, and you upset me," Thomas left Josh alone.

Shade painted the enclosed block of land, but the entire acre was more colorful even in the shade than perhaps his own backyard when the garden was in full bloom and harvest. Tall vines with blossoms of elementary colors drew curtains across trusses and decorative lamp posts. Secondary hues carpeted boxed beds and, all walkways were lawn. Ivy drew into a thick ceiling, allowing ribbons of sunlight inside. An overhead sprinkler system, painted in chocolate morning glory, spanned the entire garden, or at least as much of it as Josh could see. Above that, was a large glass roof that spanned the entire enclosure.

To the far end, a one-level house sat. It was trimmed in pink and green, while its skin was a heavy blue. Its roof was covered in a rainbow of irises. A black horse with a white stripe chewed at grass in the front lawn.

Perhaps the main attraction was the large, flat mausoleum built for one. It was mostly cold, free of ivy, but black daffodils with red stripes saluted the sun from its top. Beside it stood a small, white-picket box, which was crowned in Blue Hermosa. Were they red, the pickets would have looked like blood dripping from each pike down the slat.

A simple tombstone, barely knee-high and etched with the name *Lucy,* stood within its center. Small tufts of color blossomed around the edges of the stone. The rest of the area was lawn, a lush green and black grass, and Josh was certain that not one blade among it was too proud to stand higher than any other. Beyond this box and before the small front yard of the one-story house, a tree with fat green apples threw shade over grassy velvet. Within it, a small, stone, garden swing gently hovered a foot above the ground, and here she lounged. Her body spanned the entire length of the swing as she looked up and into a book that she held in one white hand. Her other hand brushed the carpet of lawn beneath her as she swayed here to there and back again.

Crumpled on the ground, near the foot of the swing, was her collection of black fabric that she had fought with the previous night. Josh instantly recognized it. He'd created that same pile himself many times. It was Wolf's Breath, but how? Did more than one cloak exist? Beside the clump were the coiled orbits. Josh could almost hear Bogi screaming at her for such a lack of care. On top of them sat a pair of short black slippers.

The girl in the swing hadn't noticed Josh. She was enthralled in the words upon the pages before her. Her hair, white as silver, but not as white as Thomas's, flowed past her shoulders and through the obsidian slats of the swing. A black band wrapped from behind her head and above her crown. In all other features and respect, she was Amber.

"You were the one who saved me," Josh said.

She stopped her reading and stared emptily at the pages of her book.

"More than once," Josh added.

She abruptly sat upon the sight of Josh, then she stood.

"Amber," Josh asked.

She quickly cleaned herself. That is, she straightened her green jeans and gray tank-top over a white t-shirt, as if she thought she wasn't presentable. She may have blushed, but the sun currently bleached her skin with too much radiance to tell.

"I kn—know you," she said. "I saw you f—f—fighting."

"Amber," Josh asked a second time. She appeared as Amber, young even. She sounded as her almost, but her reserved nature made her seem different. He would have smiled upon his fortune, if she didn't appear such a stranger to him.

Thomas excused himself from the scene without stirring too much commotion.

"Why didn't you say anything," Josh asked.

She shifted uncomfortably, and, as Josh stepped towards her, she stepped back. "I'm not Amber," she said, her tongue stammering only once on her words. "I would have said something, but I—I didn't know any—if—if—if you were real."

Josh didn't know how to respond. "Real?"

"You—you hear the stories. Well, actually, I s—saw them, m—memories m—mostly. But you don't know what to believe," she rambled.

Josh wanted to respond, but with what?

You know the feeling, don't you, Neon asked.

Not now, Josh replied.

Listen to her. Don't interrogate her.

"I've dreamt of this day, a long time," the white-haired Amber continued, and Josh ignored her stutter.

She fidgeted her hands behind her back and in front of her. "I've seen you," she said. "Well, images, but they weren't complete, shadows mostly. Some things made sense, but some things were just in pieces."

She stepped back again; bumped into the swing; and seemed to startle herself, perhaps because she had no escape behind her. She remained silent a moment and looked off to a spot in the hedge wall. The black horse now appeared intent on Josh's presence.

Josh still didn't know how to respond.

"Sometimes, I thought I could hear your voice," The girl said. "But it didn't sound like this."

"I don't understand," Josh finally said. "Amber came back. You came back. I don't get—"

Shhh. Listen. You're not dealing with wolves and hunters any more.

Josh fell silent.

"Amber was my mother," she said after several deep breaths. She looked cautiously back upon Josh. "My name's Olivia, after my dad—well, not my dad, because I already have a dad, but kind of like my dad b—b—because." She stopped, and tears stained her cheeks. She wiped them and guffawed nervously and wiped them again.

"My mom, Lucy's, real name was Amber." She composed herself and wrung her hands against her pants pockets with her thumbs clinging deep inside. "You're my dad," she stuttered only twice.

Again, Josh said nothing. He tried, but nothing came to his mind that made sense.

"Umm," Olivia said. "Surprise?"

"How," was all Josh could seem to get out.

Well, you see, when a mommy and a daddy kiss too much.

Stop it!

"Grandpa," Olivia started. "Uh, Thomas, do you remember that he bit my mom—uh, Amber?"

"Yeah," Josh replied. "Just a few days ago."

"Was it," she asked, and her eyes seemed to sparkle as if she had tracked down some long, lost detail of life. "Well, her virus, grandpa's virus, Mom didn't get it, but I absorbed it. I was never born because I stopped developing, and I'm immortal now."

"You've lost me," Josh admitted.

"My mother was attacked by dogs," Olivia explained. "And she didn't survive. And umm, Oliver, my kind of dad, he came and took her from the dogs and he tried to bury her in his garden, only—" She stopped. "Would you like to sit down?"

Josh really didn't, but he didn't know what he wanted. Yet, this person, this Olivia, was clearly uncomfortable, and he was too. So he sat, right there, on the lawn. He took a moment to be careful of where he set Wolf's Breath only to realize, once again, that he had already taken it off and remembered that it now sat draped with the rest of his gear in Oliver's stone-cutting studio.

"I remember things," Olivia said. "Like, mom was sick all the time. I remember that because she didn't know she was carrying me. There was a time she knew she carried me, but she eventually thought she had lost me. I learned what I was though, eventually, on my own. I also learned what language was and how she used it, but she was always sick, and I realized that was my fault too, well partly my fault. The virus makes you live a long time, and I developed differently, she had a kind of immortal morning sickness."

"But you look just like her," Josh said.

Olivia blushed, this time, Josh knew it despite that her white face didn't change color.

"I was aware when my mother was sent back to protect you, when we were sent back," she said. "I heard the plan. I heard her thoughts, and then she came back, and there was nothing for a long time. But then I heard her again. And I remembered some things and I got smarter."

"I'm sorry. I'm not getting smarter," Josh said. "What are you saying."

Josh's mind flooded with too many questions to clear his confusion.

Olivia stumbled beyond stutter for words and, upon realizing she didn't have any, she approached Josh and took his hand. She placed it on her stomach. "This is me," she said. "In here. I was never born. When Mom was bit, I stopped aging, like grandpa, only I didn't exactly get past the fetus stage.

"What you see here was Mom, and grandpa's virus through me. We came back a long time ago. Then she died, and I remembered her discussion with her friends before we came back to get you; and I remembered how I felt when she thought of you and how she felt when she remembered you. When she got injured she felt she'd failed. I knew some of her thoughts, and I wanted to do my part, because I remember how she and I felt when she thought of you. Only, as she got older, her memories were mostly emotions. They lacked clarity. She couldn't remember you, not all of you. Not all the time, but she remembered how you made her feel."

Josh felt himself starting to feel fidgety now.

"When the dogs killed Mom, I didn't die," Olivia said. "You think I'm a freak."

"No," Josh blurted, mostly just so he didn't hurt her feelings. "Okay, yes I'm freaked out, but look at it from my—Wait a minute," He suddenly realized. "She was pregnant even when she was sent back?"

Olivia shook her head.

"How did you," Josh started to ask.

"Before Mom died, she told Oliver to call his dad home," Olivia explained.

"Thomas mentioned that. He said she kept mentioning the needle," Josh said.

"When I realized mom was dying, and I would with her if I didn't do something, I tried to tell her not to die, but she didn't listen. We hadn't saved you. Eventually, I touched her mind and took over."

"What do you mean," Josh asked.

"When she died, I'd learned how use her brain. Mine wasn't strong, and the only thing I could do was touch hers. After I did though, Oliver, helped me learn."

"So you weren't married to Oliver," Josh asked.

"To Daddy, well sort of Daddy," Olivia scowled. "No, eww! Gross! Is that what people say now?"

She shuddered the thought away.

"No way," she said. "But he did love mom, and he realized I was here. I know he thought she was his wife, but no. He was the only one who believed Mom before she died, and I could take control of her body. He took care of me after she went catatonic, and I had to do something to survive. I couldn't function at first. I didn't know about organs or physiology, and, it turns out, those take a lot of work to keep working. He helped me learn to read. I had to learn most of it on my own. For bed time, he held books, and I read them first to myself, then out loud. When he realized I could make words, he got so excited. Eventually, I was able to speak and I asked him for bed time stories about the human anatomy. From there, I learned about organs, and I got them working again. My functions are entirely voluntary. I am aware of the command that makes my heart beat and my lungs breathe. By the time she died, I'd learned enough to take over. Well, Mostly. It got touch and go for a moment there, but I knew she had a job to do."

"Help me understand something," Josh asked. "These stories happened before I was born."

"Yes," Olivia said.

"You didn't grow out of being a fetus because of the virus," Josh said, mostly to help himself reiterate his own understanding.

"Grandpa's virus," Olivia said.

Josh decided to lay completely down, staring up into the canopy overhead, and absorb it all. He wiped his face. He had hardly noticed that he had been crying. Just then it struck him. "You're an immortal fetus inside what used to be Amber."

Olivia nodded. "Didn't I say that? I thought I did."

Josh nodded. He realized he wasn't thinking as quickly as he'd like to right now.

"You weren't supposed to know about me," Olivia said. "But when they were hurting you, I had to do something. The other night, when you went to the museum, I remembered something from mom's memories and I started to watch because when I saw mom's memories, I saw what happened to you. I didn't want you to see me. Normally, memories aren't vivid like that, but for some reason they were that night. I was afraid to have you know about me, but I had to help. At first, I thought you were just a story, but then Grandpa came and asked for my help, and then I tasted your blood when you were that monster, and there was something familiar."

Josh didn't know how to respond.

"You're disappointed," Olivia said.

Josh remained lost in thought for some time before realizing what she had said.

"No, just a lot to take in," he suddenly sat, stood and refuted. Then he truly allowed himself to sob. His Amber was gone. She'd saved him when he was gone, and he failed to save her, even more, he killed her, caused her death, twice. "Yesterday, I was fighting wolves. Today, all my friends are grown up. Heh. So is my daughter, it seems."

At once, it hit him. His fight was over.

He had finally recovered Cracey. He stood in the open now, without guard, without weapon, without fear of the rogue. All he'd known was loss for so long: Cracey, Dustin, Natalie, his mother, Nick, Speatsh, Oliver, Amber, even Jasper and people, allies, he never knew. He'd lost and lost again, but Amber was his gain. Amber was his hope and through her a second gain. A daughter? It wasn't loss. For once, something in all of this wasn't a loss.

But dang if it's not weird, he thought, standing again.

I know, Neon replied. *But she is still your daughter, and she has a fairly slow learning curve from the sounds of it. So, might want to tread well, Daddy-O.*

He embraced his newfound treasure. Even though he didn't fully understand all, she was a win. She was his, and she hugged him back.

Olivia too cried into Josh's shoulder, and they remained with each other while the two dwelt on their own torments until this moment.

Finally, Josh pulled away and laughed some. "You look like your mother."

Olivia started laughing, but not sure if she thought it was funny or because she was trying to be polite.

"You're the only one who came back who kept your looks," Josh said.

"The first step to shrinking a head," Neon said. "You have to remove the skull first."

Josh and Olivia both jumped at the intrusion.

"I know you," Olivia said. "You look the same, but different."

"I am same, but same," Neon said a bit confused. "Bean said I am only one."

"What are you doing," Josh asked. "Did I look like I wanted company?"

"We are mates," Neon said. "You always want company."

Olivia seemed suddenly angry.

"We are not mates," Josh snapped.

"Then why am I in your mind," Neon asked. *Why am I in your mind?*

"We need to teach you about privacy," Josh said.

"But you didn't know the answer," Neon said. "Why she looks like Amber. She does not understand her host."

I'm glad you survived, Josh thought. *But, this is kind of a daddy-daughter thing, if you don't mind.*

Kind of is, Neon retorted. *You're so bad at this.*

'I've offended you," Olivia said. "You seem upset."

Josh tried his best to assure her that he was not.

"We are umbilicaled," Neon explained.

Olivia was confused.

What is wrong with you, Josh asked.

Your vocabulary is ambiguous, Neon replied. *Tell her we are talking.*

'We're linked," Josh said. "She can talk to me inside my head."

"Like me and mom," Olivia replied.

"Umbilical," Neon said. "We are mates, like you and your host."

"What do you mean by host," Olivia asked.

"I'll ask," Josh replied and tapped his head. "Her language is better in here."

So, Josh asked.

I'll show you, Neon replied.

Images began flooding through his mind. People, not ones he recognized, not a time he recognized, old, many made wishes. He heard all the wishes, selfish wishes.

"Give me. Give me. Give me," they all cried.

He saw Neon, only different somehow, a slave. He watched her read her strands of hair. She saw time in all its extent, seeing, but not comprehending, searching and calculating variables that would form other images in her mind.

He saw people whisked through time, riding Neon's hair, becoming people they weren't and attempting to make a wish come true. Usually they were unsuccessful, often ending with them begging for their final wish to return them to where they had come from.

Josh tried to explain, not well, but Olivia listened, and the images continued to fill Josh's brain.

"You need a host when you wish on a djinn," Josh said. "Someone who died in the past so that the person coming back could take her place at just the right moment to fit into the world, and she, the djinn, has to guess which host will put the person making a wish in the right spot to help make the wish come true."

Images of hosts scattered through his thoughts. He heard them arguing with their new psyche. He saw convulsions, spasms, hosts dying instantly under their own accord and then filled with a new being. Josh was sick. He vomited. Too much headache.

I'm sorry, Neon said. *You're not ready for so much.* The images began to fade.

No, I want to know what happened to her, Josh replied.

The images raced back, and he saw the hosts reawakening, same but not the same.

He saw a biker, shot in the chest at a drug deal gone bad. He watched the attackers leave the biker for dead and then saw Jasper fill him and become Bean.

He watched Cracey reawaken in a lost child's body in the woods, her clothing predating any European influence. He saw that body grow over centuries into Acotactac. He watched an RV roll off a road, Bean's bike skidding beneath it. He saw the rodeo queens, Lisa and Winter, wake with Cadence and Acotactac within their shells.

He watched Nick's mind, saw what Nick saw, knew what Nick knew as he woke up screaming after his host, an old ally, bled to death on a table from the loss of an arm.

Kind of like Bricktain, Josh thought. His spine ran cold. *You've got to be kidding! I don't know which is worse: thinking Bricktain married my baby sister or thinking Nick did.*

Your baby sister is older than you, Neon said.

Josh yelled.

Olivia startled.

I'm just saying, you shouldn't call her a baby when she trumps you in age technically by, well, a lot, Neon explained.

"My host," Olivia asked, confused at the strange event before her.

Then, Josh saw her, Amber, older. Sick, vomiting, never bearing a child. Yet he saw life within her. He watched an angry and scornful Amber grow cold, blaming Thomas for killing her unborn child.

She accepted her illness for Thomas's virus, a virus that never did more than make her ill. Amber grabbed a strand of Neon's hair, and suddenly she fell into darkness, and the immortal life within her went too.

Then he saw a fetus, not Amber's, but Amber's host. A woman screamed in pain and through what sounded like water. Then he saw the woman bending over the arm of a chair, only a moment, before she brushed the miscarriage off as a cramp. Then the screaming stopped and the fetus grew, Amber had given it life once more.

He watched the fetus grow. The woman screamed again some time later. He heard voices, encouraging, loving, but one not so much, as it responded to the woman's cries with forceful commands.

Then light, blinding, hurt Josh's brain. Someone hit him. It was an ill-mannered doctor with a half-smoked cigar sticking out of his mouth. He assured the woman that her baby was fine.

Josh watched the baby grow now, grow into Amber, a young Amber who met Oliver. Josh saw her insides grow, develop into Amber's, her blood filling her veins, changing to Amber from the inside out and bringing with her Olivia's unborn fetus. She was still pregnant. Olivia had come back with her mother but was waiting for Amber to grow so she could develop into her original form herself.

He saw an Amber who never realized she was pregnant in this new host with an immortal child. He witnessed her body's health turn on her. He watched Amber grow up sick as Olivia remained within her.

While Josh's sister and other friends kept the image of their hosts, changing on the inside only, Amber's host hadn't developed its image, so it grew into Amber's form. He watched Amber endure the illness, and doctors who treated her for minor maladies out of the rampant ignorance of their time. He witnessed Amber begin to remember Josh while she was a child. He sat by and observed her reside in depression with only one purpose, to save Josh, and she could tell no one.

Josh relayed all Neon had shown him to Olivia.

"Her host was incomplete," Josh said. "That's why she kept her look, she finished the development with her own image, not just what was inside."

Suddenly Josh was confused. He fell silent a moment.

"Wait a minute," Josh cried. "Did Amber develop with Wolf's Breath in the womb too?"

Neon had to stop and think. "If you don't guess all the letters in hangman, you lose oxygen."

"Where did the second cloak come from," Josh asked.

"I made it," Olivia replied. "Oliver snuck the original out for me when I asked to see it. I'd seen it in my mom's memory." She stopped when she realized Josh appeared confused. "It was my dad's. I wanted to see it, and when I saw it, I tried to copy it. It wasn't easy. It's not as good as yours, but it still works. Finding the material wasn't easy, but Oliver helped."

"Did you make the windriders too," Josh asked.

"I cut mom's down and made a second pair out of them. The boots used to be taller. I'd been goofing around with them for years."

"You're spooky," Josh said.

"I also took the orbits when you weren't looking earlier," Olivia shouted in boast. "I'd never used them before, but mom's brain showed me how she used them and it was fun!" Olivia suddenly shied away. "I'm sorry. I just wanted to help," she said, quietly now. "You're the only real family I've ever met."

Josh watched her. She was pale, her hair silver, Amber, but not Amber. She appeared ashamed. It was good to see Amber's face whole once more, but he knew it wasn't her. Her eyes were Amber's but they were someone else's now and they smiled upon Josh, admired him, not like Amber had done. Amber had known too many of Josh's mistakes to have been dumb enough to admire him as Olivia seemed to do now.

What did a dad do? What would his have done?

What would you have done with Cracey, Neon asked.

Thank you, Josh replied.

"Want to go for a walk," Josh suggested, and he held his hand out.

Olivia hesitated. "You mean outside? Why?"

"Why," Josh asked. "To meet some of your mom's other memories."

A Word on Heroes

(Now What?)

Today, Josh stared at his lunch. It cost more than it should have and it looked like a dry mess of weeds shriveling on his plate. He looked down to his book, tapped his pencil, crossed out a word and drew a picture of a butt under some staunch man's nose. He remembered when that was actually funny, but had forgotten why. He was trying to remember a lot lately.

He tried to care, but he just couldn't.

Across the cafeteria, a man ate alone, his face intent on whatever appeared on his electronic screen. Two tables down, another guy pounded on the keys to his laptop. A woman who had been sitting behind him a moment ago, stood and accidentally spilled her drink across the man's work space.

He raised his hands in insult and stared from the table to his lap. He shot out of his bench, his front stained from wet. The woman apologized. Apologies weren't enough for him. Apologies had no place on university campuses, only bent ego.

Josh told the man to simmer down. The girl left. Josh stayed to read. The man sat and tapped away at his phone. Josh finished ignoring his sandwich and continued trying to study. Two friends joined the computer user, and Josh tried not to pay attention to the fact they kept looking over to him.

His tablet buzzed; his break had ended, and his next class started in ten minutes. Josh packed up his book, threw his bag over his shoulder and tossed his lunch in the trash. Then he exited. The three friends followed him, taunted him. He ignored them, his pursuers acting more like high school twits than adults. They had a couple years youth on him. They outnumbered him, but he was pretty certain he could take them nonetheless.

Don't, Neon said. *Just don't. They'll go away.*

Then, on cue, a campus cop appeared on a bike and took interest in the situation of taunting intimidators. The officer inquired a moment as to the activity, the three friends stormed on about how Josh had something to say.

Josh refuted, tried to explain their stupidity.

"Hey," the campus Rambo finally yelled into Josh's face. "I don't need your help to know what's going on. It's something new with you every day. So who do I believe? Them? Or some constantly annoying pr—"

Perhaps if the cop had stopped there, it might have been okay, and Josh could have continued on to class, but the cop had to clout his authority and spout off idiocy.

"Hey," he yelled. "Get back here."

Walk away, Neon said.

Josh did, and the cop foolishly chose to abandon all good and legal sense and chose to grab his wrist and try to fold it in a way meant to make Josh more submissive. Which, of course, worked brilliantly for the officer.

Josh reacted suddenly, punched the cop in the throat, then turned to the group of bullies. He broke four fingers on the first, knocked the wind out of the chest of the second and bloodied the nose of the third. Well, wait. Yep! Broken.

I tried, Josh said.

Yeah, Neon sighed. *You did. I'll let Bricktain know.*

* * *

Josh sat at a plain, brown table, steel, but painted to look welcoming. People talk in environments they feel comfortable in, maybe. His hands lay in his lap, the silver cuffs pinched much more tightly into his wrists than they should have been allowed.

A fat officer glared at Josh. He clearly thought he had some sort of authority that would frighten the paladin.

He overly-grilled Josh about the attack on campus, tried to convince him that he was certain to be expelled.

"No," Josh said. "It's not unlawful to walk to class. Your officer had no reason to stop me, and he had no reason to lay his hands on me."

"Oh," the fatman gloated, "are you a lawer?"

There it was. The magic question that Josh had learned every officer seemed to fall back on any time someone seemed to know something legal, thinking that question would discredit any person in their purview: are you a lawyer? Josh couldn't help but snicker at the faulty logic.

"That funny," fatty asked.

"No, I'm not a lawyer," Josh replied. "And neither are you."

The man disregarded Josh's comment as well as his claim that he was simply walking to class, and that the campus cop had overstepped his authority. Instead, he tried the approach of riling up the person in custody so he could add some more charges and say Josh wasn't cooperative with the judge. He called Josh worthless—*humorous*—said he was scum—*laughable*—said he didn't appreciate his clear disrespect to his community.

K, that's crossing the line, Neon fumed.

Let him have it, Josh replied. *He just wants me to retaliate, give him a chance to hit back for injuring one of his own.*

"Mom, not raise you right," Officer Fatty asked.

Josh smirked at the cliché cheapshot, but it wasn't entirely ineffective.

"Trying to make yourself a better person," Officer Fatty said. "Prove you're a man? Get away from your delinquent friends? Go to college and finally make your parents proud?" He drew too close to gloat in Josh's face. "How's that working for you?"

The fat man pulled back with a jaw that ran with blood. Two teeth now fell and ticked against the table. Josh pulled back a forehead with a cut from the interrogator's teeth.

Several officers filed into the room, some got their hits in on Josh. Some drew back their own injuries. One stomped on one of Josh's handcuffs. Another drilled a Taser into Josh. As he laid on the cold floor spasming, the entire room fell silent.

He was finally aroused by the adulations of officers who now stood over him. They got in a few more taunts and fell silent again as Josh heard the steel door bang open and strike a wall.

"Stand down," a familiar voice shrilled.

Police chief Bricktain Morris entered the room, and, at the sight of Josh, screamed orders for his subordinates, "Don't even breathe!"

The officer's faces turned white as they retreated against walls and into corners, forbidden from fleeing the room. Chandler helped release his friend from his unjust cuffs. He barely contained the pain and anger it gave him to see Plattsville's hero beaten this way. He wanted to speak. He wanted to say what he felt everyone should know.

Bricktain put on a show of explaining how he'd just watched the whole thing, how they'd just attacked an unarmed man, and it looked that way on tape. Of course, there was no tape. Josh was impressed with how quickly Bricktain convinced the officers they'd be lucky if their perp didn't own them all before the end of the day.

"This is done," Bricktain scowled.

"You're out of your jurisdiction here," one officer suggested.

Bricktain laughed in disbelief. "You are an ignorant half-wit, aren't you."

"He assaulted me," the fat officer cried through pain, blood and missing pieces from his mouth.

"I'm about to too," Bricktain retorted and then added, "you assaulted my friend?"

Bricktain drew himself intimidatingly close to the fat officer's face. "Delinquent friends. I believe that's what you called me. Isn't that what he called us Assistant Chief?"

"Who am I to argue with what the recording shows," Chandler replied.

Bricktain smacked the loose teeth off the table and hoped they couldn't be found. "You need a doctor." Bricktain pointed to the door and waited for the injured officer to take the hint to leave.

"With due respect," one officer said. "He assaulted a cop."

Bricktain smashed his steel fist, hidden beneath a black glove and long brown suit jacket, into the table, denting it and frightening the officers. Josh wondered if Bricktain's weapon was public knowledge among any on the new forces. Bricktain shook his head sharply at the officer.

Upon Bricktain's orders, Chandler began helping Josh to the door.

"With due respect," the man who Tasered Josh started.

"Don't you 'with due respect' me," Bricktain said coolly.

"You want to protect your own," Chandler said, stopping a moment before exiting with Josh hanging on his shoulder. "But you don't even know your own."

"We'll be seeing you, Revlon," one officer suddenly shouted.

Bricktain flew. He gripped the officer's uniform about his chest and drew a fist. In an instant, the glove and his sleeve could tear apart. Surely his hand unfolding into a sword would finally demand silent tongues.

"Brick," Josh said, knowing his friend's thoughts as he exited with Chandler out of the room. "They haven't earned it."

* * *

Josh stroked the heavy metal brush over the broken headstone. With each sweep, dust, like the profane confusion in his head, bloomed in a powdery tuft.

He cleaned several pieces of stone; mixed his stone polymer and fit the headstone back together as completely as possible. Here, in what was once Oliver's stone-cutting studio, no one interrupted him. Even Neon gave him this privacy. They had a deal.

It would take some time for the patchwork and compound to dry. This one was finished. He decided it was too late to start trying to locate the pieces to another of the demolished tombstones. He'd fixed up quite a bit of grave markers since the death of the rogue, but many more awaited their own repair. Mostly, he spent the time cataloging, locating which graves were now missing identification. Now he was gluing.

He cleaned himself and swept the shop, then made his way out to an SUV, a little trophy he decided to take with him from the compound. About ten minutes later, he stood before a steel door at the end of a familiar alley.

The small window slid open, and the door granted entrance without a word being said. Josh and the doorman non-verbally greeted each other. The paladin took a seat at the rebuilt counter, now made of polished railroad ties and steel bands.

A man sat at the far end, his face perched on his fist while he played with his potatoes.

"Hungry, honey," Neon asked cheerfully with a Texan accent. She stood with a server's attention from behind the bar. Her hair had been fluffed into a ball of 70s server stereotype. She had a pencil behind one ear and a pen behind another. He really wished Cadence hadn't introduced her to *Alice*.

"Whiskey," Josh replied.

"Bad day," Neon asked, setting down water instead.

Josh laughed a moment.

"Hey," the hunter perched on his fist grouched. "Keep it down."

"Hey, now," the doorman called from behind his eyelids as he leaned back on his stool besides his arsenal of weapons.

"I thought this was supposed to be a place for hunters, not preppies" the hunter cried.

"If I let you in, I have to let him in," the doorman said. He huffed in exasperation.

"Food," Ty announced, dropping a plate overflowing its edges. Neon picked it up and set it before Josh. She winked at him in a way that drew an uncomfortable Flo-like side smile out of her lips. She snapped her gum, tried a bubble, but spit it on the counter instead. Suddenly stunned, she might have been preparing to cry.

"We can get you more," Josh said.

"No," the hunter ordered and stood from his stool. "No," he continued to shout and marched his way down the counter to where he threw Josh's plate to the side, and it toppled to the floor. "There's a Denny's down the street for you."

"And there it is," the doorman said, dropping his stool to the floor. He then sauntered over to Josh who was now beating the side of the rude hunter's head between the bar and his fist.

Josh's blades suddenly *ka-shooked* from beneath his brown jacket.

"Come on," the doorman said, friendly enough to catch Josh's attention, wise enough not to touch him. He nodded towards Neon, who was intent on watching Josh's actions. "You know how she gets with blood."

"Let's get this straight," Josh said twisting the hunter's face to meet his own. "This table is mine!"

"Well, kiss my grits," Neon replied.

"This how you run your haven, Cookie," the hunter asked, pulling away from Josh, only after he was finally released. Josh allowed his blades to retreat into his ruined coat sleeve.

"Ask the boss," Ty said. He nodded towards Josh and dropped another plate of food for his employer on the counter.

"I see how it is," the hunter said. "We'll see you around pal." He pointed two fingers at Josh and pulled a pretend trigger.

"Everyone wants to see me later," Josh said. "Sure you want to?"

"Now, now. Stop agitating the paladin," the doorman said as he forced the ignorant hunter back into his stool.

The hunter's face paled.

Josh thanked Ty for the meal, but had already stood to leave. He allowed the doorman to hold the exit open for him.

Josh returned to the cemetery by way of the 24-hour liquor store. He stopped near Olivia's garden, where a previously untouched piece of land now donned sod that was only now beginning to blend into the rest of the lawn. Young, thorny shrubs encircled several headstones and would some year soon enclose this entire section.

Josh saluted the fallen hunters and thanked them for their help. He cursed Jasper for ignorantly starting this whole mess and then just as rudely dying. He then thanked him for his help. He apologized to Nick and shared a joke with Dustin at Nick's expense. He reported the day's business at the haven to Thug.

"Pray for Natalie," he said. "Tell her to keep fighting if you see her wandering around the gates or something. Tell her to wake up. She just lays there, you know. Tell her she needs to wake up."

He stopped at a new gate, a short and black ornamental decoration. Someday, it would have a wall of hedge.

"Goodnight folks," Josh said. "As always, rest in peace." He rang the silver bell that had once hung at Thug's haven for hunters, now hanging from an aluminum archway over the ornamental gating. "May the beasts burn."

Several paces later, and Olivia's garden opened up to him. The houselights were off now. He approached a new headstone outside of the picket-fence area and near the apple tree.

Josh leaned against Amber's stone; cracked open his bottle of whiskey; and took a drink as easily as he took a deep breath. Eventually, he fell asleep to the sobs of a small copper bell they had recovered from Oliver's belongings.

"Please wake up," he pleaded, with each ring, until he faded into surreality of false dreams and nightmares.

He dreamed. He always dreamed, mostly nonsense anymore, memories now. No dream helped, no dream brought anyone back. No dream made his anguish go away. Once, every so often, he would turn in his sleep, and he imagine he could see Amber, his Amber, laying beside him, watching him.

He awoke to the familiar sound of Olivia reading from her book to the headstone within the picket-fenced area.

"I'm sorry, Dad," she said. "I was trying to read softly."

Dad? He still wasn't used to it.

He shrugged off her crime and sat up, realizing that one of his empty bottles was stabbing into his side.

"Mom would be mad," she said.

Josh pulled a shot-bottle from his jacket pocket and popped the seal.

Olivia glared.

"You wanna try some?"

"Really," she asked sternly.

"Oh," Josh said. "Right. Sorry."

The ornamental gating swore at its surprise opening. It clanged against it's own hinges.

"You," Cadence shrieked as Josh was about to let the contents of his tiny bottle dribble down his throat. She charged into the garden. "I should have checked here first!"

"I told him mom would be mad," Olivia tattled.

Behind Cadence stumbled Neon. "Yoo-hoo!"

Cadence marched upon Josh and slapped the bottle out of his hands, but only after he had quickly drained it, fully knowing what she would do if he didn't hurry and swallow it. "Your brain buddy spent the whole night singing to the toilet bowl," Cadence screamed.

"What's wrong with that," Josh asked.

"She can't sing!"

That's a fun drink, Neon said.

"What are you thinking," Cadence asked.

Josh waved her to stop yelling.

"I'm pretty certain this isn't how your daughter envisioned her hero father," Cadence scowled.

Josh waved at her to lower her voice then leaned forward and threw up behind Amber's headstone.

"So we're back to this," Cadence said.

"Get off my back," Josh retorted.

"And you're still the only person who's lost here," Cadence cried. Then she started slapping him. "What is wrong with you."

Neon started laughing and used the picket-fence to hold herself up from stumbling over.

Josh fell back against Amber's headstone and gave up the fight. Cadence read him and stopped hitting him. He wanted to cry, but he didn't. She could see that. She'd delivered her message and he'd heard it.

"What am I doing here," Josh asked.

"Making a fool of yourself," Cadence snapped.

"No," Josh replied. "I mean why. Why am I this? We saved all these people, and, at most, we're a conspiracy myth on the Internet now. I can't do something nice for a stranger; can't even walk into my own café."

"We talked about this," Cadence said. "You really want anyone knowing the truth."

"No, but I don't deserve this," Josh yelled, smacking Amber's headstone. "We deserve something! A medal or something, or a free dinner."

"You think I don't know that," Cadence screamed back, her face turning deep red.

"Oh," Josh realized. "A free vacation. We should get one of those, and an amusement park—and Canada, they should give us

Canada." He wrinkled his nose. "No, not Canada. Japan, somewhere people want to go."

"I don't need this," Cadence said trying to calm down. "I have my problems too."

Josh consented that she was right and used Amber's headstone as a chair, sinking into implied apology.

"What am I supposed to do now," Josh asked. "Thomas and Speatsh took the ancients into hiding, wherever his little island diamond mine is. Bricktain's city sherriff and married to my little sister—oh wait—my older sister."

"Believe me," Cadence said. "I'm not happy about that one neither, but he's not my Nick anymore. Mine's buried over there."

"Yeah," Josh said. "And how long are you going to stick around?"

"You're the only family I have now, Josh," Cadence said, stung.

"Didn't seem to stop, mine," Josh replied.

"Your dad didn't leave you," Cadence replied. "Stan just needed to get away from the town, not you. You know that."

Josh reluctantly nodded. "And, here I stay," Josh asked.

"This is home," she said. "You fought the most for it."

Josh found the idea laughable.

"I'm not going anywhere," Cadence replied. "I made a promise to protect you."

"As if I didn't need to feel responsible for anyone else's life sucking," Josh said. "You promised to protect the heir, and that turned out to be my sister."

"I promised to take care of you, stupid," Cadence said more gently. She set herself beside Josh on the headstone.

Neon fell over laughing and suddenly passed out on the lawn.

"You really are a bad influence on her, and I mean that in the liberal sense," she took a moment to look about. "Where's Cracey? Shouldn't you be with her."

"She's fine. I'm sure she's at home," Josh said. "She's not exactly a little girl anymore. You know she's smarter than I am now? I used to know everything she wanted to know, and now she doesn't need that."

"Yes she does," Cadence said.

"Nah. She pretends she needs my help just to feel like she hasn't outgrown me," Josh said. "She's trying to be my little sister, but she's not. You know what she did last week because she was bored? She created a new online first-person shooter and launched it, all last week. She has four-hundred-thousand subscribers already. I'm the child she watches over now."

"I hadn't thought of that."

"I did," Neon's voice blurted in her sleep from the ground. She belched. "so much smarter than you."

Josh was silent.

"Have you been to see Nata lately," Cadence asked.

Josh shook his head. "I would have stopped her if I had known what she was doing."

"Nata wouldn't have done anything if it wouldn't have saved you," Cadence said.

"There it is again," Josh said. "Just something else on my plate to gnaw on. I fought for a town and what have we all gotten out of it?"

"You've still got school," Cadence said. "I'm liking going back actually."

"I can't even walk down campus."

"Yeah," she replied, unable to convince even herself. "So, three fights yesterday, huh?"

Josh clammed up. "Bricktain has a big mouth."

"He only knew about two."

Josh glared at Neon, who was now hooting and hollering about how she was the one who told about the brawl at Thug's. She fell into a snore.

"I can't live like this," Josh said.

Cadence and Josh spoke well into the day. Neon awoke as Josh sobered. Olivia retrieved some old aspirin from the house, unsure it was any good. It wasn't.

Finally, Josh said he needed to get back to work. On top of repairing the broken cemetery, he was trying to clean up the bunker and seal off the cavern.

"That's not a bad idea, you know," Cadence said

"You want to help," Josh asked.

"No," Cadence replied. "I mean. Let's get out of here. Go to work."

"What are you talking about?"

"Let's do what your uncle did."

"He was a hunter," Josh said.

"Yeah, that and an antique dealer," Cadence replied. "Who's gathering the weapons to hunt the survivng wolves that are out there now? Who's finding revenue for this little hunting operation with Richard gone? Someone's got to start adding the funds back."

"For what," Josh asked. "The wolves are no longer enslaved. I don't even know why I reopened the haven."

"Yes you do. It's because they're still out there," Cadence said. "And they're not all happy with what we did. The elementals didn't change. If any still intend harm, we could do something about that. What if the rogue didn't find all the ancients, the live ones? Isn't it worth investigating at least?"

"An antique dealer, huh," Josh contemplated.

"And a hunter," Cadence replied. "We could repair the Bullet. Then we could go."

"We'll need a gunner," Josh said.

"I think we could find one of those," Cadence replied. "He hasn't exactly liked getting back to his life either."

A cell phone rang just then, and it took Josh a moment to realize it was his.

"How many blenders did you just drink your brains from," Speatsh's voice yelled from within the small speaker. "Antique dealing? Looking for wolves? More ancients?"

"How do you even know about—," Josh started to say and then realized the small phone in Olivia's hands, texting. "Really? You're tattling on your dad?"

Epilogue

I should, at least, apologize for my failure in upholding the highest of integrity upon relating this tale. As one would expect, many details and explanations have been left out of this story. Many have been omitted because they do not matter to this immediate telling without destroying the integrity of another, and I am not one to destroy another story.

Some details have been abandoned to protect the living. Likewise, I duly apologize to those individuals who took part in these events. As you may have noticed, I was forced to compile many of your characters into one. You know who you are, and you know the character.

I realize I have not answered many of your questions, but you should know by now that's just the way I am. I will answer your questions in due time—that is, my due time. Or, to be more precise, when I feel like it. As for my silence, I've earned that right.

What I share, I do as an observer. As we have no storyteller, I was the next logical choice to present this history of my family. Any faults to the truths presented are really no one's fault, but I suppose if you have nothing better to do than to play your MMOs and scratch yourselves, all while spewing ignorant veracities on the topic which I have just related, I'd just like to say: what do you know?

I've seen many the mighty hunter, many deaths and many who would pretend to be a hunter because they would wish to be like a werewolf. Maybe they simply find the lycan cute and cuddly. When you know them as I do, then perhaps you may enter the scholarship where you can stand argument about what is and isn't possible in this sacred realm of monsters—they that come out when the moon is full, and those enslaved when it is not.

I rarely get the opportunity to speak or share my observations as my role is to remain silent and observe. My role is to ensure the circle is not forgotten. My role is monotonous, but it is my role, and no other is entrusted with the memories of the past historians.

Many served with pride. Many served to their dying breaths, and one sought for more power, seeing all, knowing all, and betraying all. It remains unfortunate that her wisdom was in her knowledge—and she was most powerful concerning knowledge—for no other holds this power, except for the historian.

For those who have nothing better to do than find fault with my presentation or language of the story, you morons who throw the word grammar around without truly understanding its linguistic relation. To those who say, "that explains a lot," with your heads stuffed so far into places that trying to properly withdraw them would only induce hernia, again I ask: what do you know? Moreover who cares? I merely tell the story as an observer is required to do. I suppose if you have a problem with that you can take it up with my boss. Good luck finding her. She likes me better, and she has no use for someone who thinks they're smart because they minored in English truancy.

However, should you decide that you are in possession of that knowledge and information that I, the wisest of observers, who holds memories handed down since the beginning of the circle, am not in possession of myself—by all means, bring it to the circle and ask for the historian.

For I am the historian, who, unlike my predecessor, hears all, including the voices of broken, ash children. To the circle, I am preservation—to my fellow hunters, I am Jasper Zheegan, and you no doubtedly know by now that I epitomize the very essence of open and comforting conversation.

Which is why it pains me so deeply to have to tell you that I now know what I had missed. It came to me in a scream from Natalie's well-funded hospital bed, and she wasn't alone. Another binds Natalie to her coma, and her message was clear.

Paladin. England. Now, or she dies.

What I had missed, was that the rogue, rather the rogue's pawn, had a daughter.

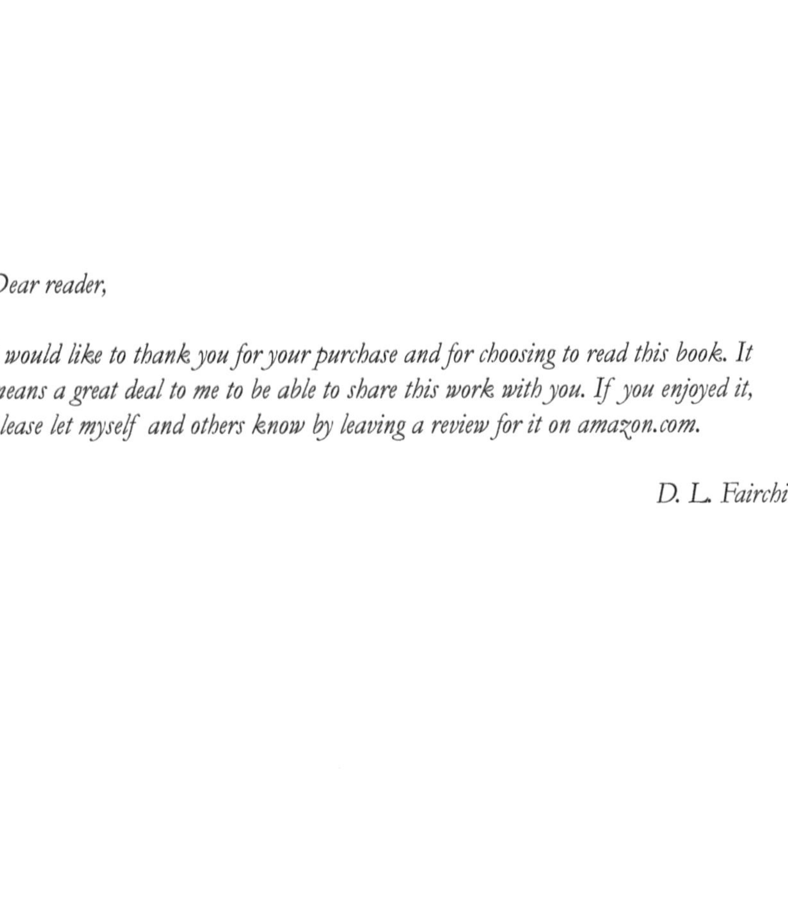

Dear reader,

I would like to thank you for your purchase and for choosing to read this book. It means a great deal to me to be able to share this work with you. If you enjoyed it, please let myself and others know by leaving a review for it on amazon.com.

D. L. Fairchild

Visit davidfairchild.com to learn more about the author, his other works and news regarding his forthcoming books.

www.ingramcontent.com/pod-product-compliance
Lightning Source LLC
Chambersburg PA
CBHW020743020826
48980CB00019B/774/J
9780982635575